MEDUSA'S HEART

JOEY W. HILL

SUMMARY

Special operator John "JP" Pierce has an embarrassing obsession. He's in love with a myth—Medusa.

"Mad Merlin" Maddock doesn't think he's crazy. He believes in powers stronger than men or gods, a connecting energy like the oceans. Healing a broken heart could create a ripple effect in the universe impacting all, even if that heart lives in the alternate dimension of folklore and myth. JP is the first Maddock plans to send across those lines to bond with the woman he's always wanted.

JP agrees to be his guinea pig for two reasons. One, Maddock is so damn convincing, and two, the need for her has tripled since he met him. If Maddock can send JP into Medusa's world, he'll do whatever is needed to become the Master, lover and protector she needs, offering her the love she's always deserved.

He just has to avoid being turned into a lawn ornament first.

ACKNOWLEDGMENTS

Part of the pleasure of writing this particular book was not only learning the many different versions of Medusa's tale, but how her story connected to the mythology of other cultures. It was also uplifting to find out how, in some circles, this legendary character has evolved from the monster originally portrayed, into a symbol of female empowerment. I thank the readers who offered me leads to explore those different paths. Many of those references ended up in this book!

Thanks as always to my team of critique partners, a dedicated group of both readers and authors. This book in particular was a complex and lengthy challenge, so I deeply appreciated your help. Any mistakes left are entirely my fault. I hope there won't be too many, because I was editing and polishing right up to the final wire, thanks to the book being quite a bit longer than originally intended! But whatever dings are present, I hope they don't interfere with anyone's enjoyment of John Pierce and Medusa's journey together.

Finally, many thanks to Lady D, for her very important distinction between the therapeutic value of BDSM (good) and using BDSM as therapy (not always good).

PROLOGUE

The familiar dream always started simply. She knelt at Athena's feet, and rapture filled her, the joy of pure service, of living to praise the Goddess and carry out Her wishes. She was young, so sometimes she felt a passion about it that was almost physical. She wanted to stroke the Goddess's feet and press her lips to them. Something deep inside her was stirred by doing that.

And that was when the dream would change.

She was with the unicorn. The creature's mane felt like mist against her face, the coat smooth as rippling silk beneath her legs. But she'd sensed someone else, and slipped from the unicorn's back to see who it was.

The man was on a beach, walking. The weight of his gaze made her tremble. When she laid her hand on the unicorn's shoulder, she whickered and somehow started to feel less substantial.

Medusa stroked her, a mutual reassurance, but moved away to walk toward the man, drawn by his compelling gray eyes. As she walked, she felt her body grow...and change. What should have startled her, the snakes twining over her shoulders, didn't. Because this was a dream and she could walk between childhood and adulthood, between happiness and loss. Through a curtain of tragedy, she emerged into a darker yet sharper world, more in focus.

When she reached him, her knees quivered and she wanted to kneel, to press her lips along the top of his foot, glistening with the surf. Yet her reasons for it were different than with the Goddess. Something was awakening low in her belly, a fire that made her feel restless.

"You want to kneel to me, don't you, snake-girl?"

She nodded. "Why?"

"Because of a gift you have to give. One that I thank God you want to give."

He put his hand on her shoulder and spoke in a voice that stroked her throat and breasts, the sensation tingling down over the rest of her like a light rain. "Get on your knees."

When she did, she turned her face toward his hand and rubbed her cheek against his knuckles. Her snakes twined around his forearm, accepting him, holding him to her. He chuckled.

"Trying to bind me, hmm? I think you might like it better if I do that to you. Make you helpless to give you pleasure. Say please, and I will."

"Please," she whispered.

"Head to the floor, hips in the air. Arms behind your back."

She was no longer on the beach, but in a room with black strips of cloth fluttering and concealing the walls. Gemstones hung from the ceiling, sparkling in a soft light like the moon. She was naked, and felt self-conscious about putting her hips in the air, but he had commanded it. When she hesitated, he slapped her backside with his open palm, a stinging blow that awoke nerve endings she didn't know she had. She wanted to please him. She put her forehead to the ground and her haunches in the air, and swallowed a moan when his thick fingers probed her slick flesh, teasing her.

"Already wet for me. That's the way I want you."

His approval warmed her and took away her embarrassment. When she adjusted her head so she could see his face, she memorized every feature. The serious gray eyes held memories he could not escape. The set of his mouth told her he preferred to be kind, yet the lines around it and his eyes said he had to be cruel and unyielding far more often, and it had taken its toll. His face was a story she needed to read and understand.

He moved around her and bound her wrists at the small of her back, which awakened even more mysterious feelings. She felt like she did when she spent hours in the surf and her body was still moving with the force of the waves, even though she was on dry land.

This shouldn't be right. She was no longer the child on the unicorn. She was a woman grown. She shouldn't want him to bind her. Being helpless was bad.

No, not like this. This was the way she'd dreamed of being helpless...before the bad thing happened. The thought awoke an ominous foreboding. Behind the strips of cloth, shadows moved, and she saw glittering eyes that stirred fear.

"Master..."

When she looked up at the man with the piercing gaze and hands that stroked her flesh, heightening her desires, another's image overlapped his. One that awoke dread in her body. Pain, terror...

She would never call him Master. Not that one. She would tear apart the whole world, turn every living thing to stone, before he would lay hands on her again.

She was at Athena's feet once more, only it was not the Goddess. It was a statue, inanimate, uncaring. She was being pummeled, destroyed, torn apart. She cried for mercy, for help, and nothing and no one came. Nobody stopped it.

Yet when she lay there, broken and bleeding, the man on the beach came back. He lifted her in his arms, held her, and carried her to the bathing chamber. He cared for her, making all the blood slip away, all the pain.

She didn't accuse him, didn't blame him, for not being there to stop the pain. Somehow she understood he would have burned down his own world to do that if he could. But he was here now. That mattered.

He laid her out on a mattress that was like a cloud, and bound her wrists and ankles with ribbons. Though he didn't tie them tightly, once they were tied, she couldn't free herself.

"No," she whimpered. "When you do that, he comes."

"Not if you let go of your fear and trust me. We have to trust one another."

He began to kiss her, starting at her feet. It made her heart hurt and yet grow inside her, to see his mouth on her foot, so reverent and loving. As if he was worshipping her, even while he had her bound. Fear of someone else gave way to fear of herself, of what she wanted.

"Oh Goddess..." She arched as his mouth teased and played up her calves, her thighs, and then between them, his tongue stroking her.

"You're mine," he murmured, raising his head. His gaze dominated her vision. "You want a Master. A flesh and blood one, who will demand your surrender and give you pleasure, help you find yourself again. And you're my light, snake-girl. You don't know it yet, but you're the flame that can't be quenched, even in the middle of the storm. I need for you to be real."

She was bound, yet his words gave her a power that, through her surrender to him, could never be taken away.

The images of the two men overlapped again, and she saw those glittering eyes once more. The other was there, just beyond her decision. If she chose wrong...

I will be waiting. And this time you will be mine forever.

Medusa woke, her heart pounding, her snakes moving restlessly over her shoulders and neck. She felt like two people, because her heart was stuttering in terror from that last whispered threat, while the swollen flesh between her legs begged for the man who'd tied her with ribbons.

She put her hand down there and moaned at the reaction that seized her, triggered by a single touch. While her body's instinct was to curl into a ball, containing that powerful sensation, instead she spread her legs wide, so that it rippled over her and tore a cry from her throat. If he were there, he would command her to spread her legs, because he would want to see her release, the moisture bathing her hand and making her knuckles wet. He would let her keep nothing from him. She wanted to keep nothing from him.

Only when the climax ebbed did she turn on her side and draw her legs up to her stomach. She folded her arms and tucked her face into their shelter, hiding even from her snakes. The dreams held so many things beyond her understanding. Innocence and fantasy, nightmares and pain, surrender and pleasure. And pain somehow was a part of the surrender and pleasure, as much as it was part of the nightmare. But a different kind of pain.

Would darkness and light forever war within her? She wanted to embrace the dark part of her soul that craved one man's mastery. But how could that not be more of the same sickness that had gripped her ever since she'd come here? She was a force of destruction, only she seemed to be destroying herself from the inside out.

Yet despite that knowledge, she soothed herself to sleep not with unicorns, the Goddess, or trying to forget what could never be forgotten, but by imagining him holding her, whispering all the things he would do to her and for her. He parted her legs and entered her, stretching her body, demanding everything from her. Heart, body and soul.

It was the only way to be free.

Or lost forever.

CHAPTER ONE

*J*ohn Pierce Zeus laid the branding iron in the fire and stepped back, contemplating the shore. Sunset would come in a matter of moments, and he wanted to see it, since it would be the last he'd view in this lifetime.

There were other ways he could have done this. Ensorcelled contacts that Maddock was 99.9% certain would work. Eye drops that could temporarily take away sight.

"Science and magic can eliminate the need for noble sacrifices. Make them pointless. Idiotic—in case my sarcasm isn't getting through your thick head."

Maddock—"Mad Merlin" as they'd dubbed him—had delivered that scrap of wisdom in a tone as dry as coffee beans. But he'd also told JP that intuition was the key to finding his path on all of this. Stronger than science and magic combined, intuition was the closest kin to love, devotion, loyalty...need and yearning.

He had to do this the right way, the way she would understand. Not a happily-ever-after, but a battlefield, where blood and honor meant more than victory. He understood that path, too.

His chest expanded on a deep, painful breath as the sun approached the horizon, its movement accelerating as it always did, the decline of the day rolling the golden sphere toward the pocket of night. His throat ached, but he wouldn't shed tears. It wasn't his way.

His buddy Lot Lakeney called him Triple-D, the "Dungeons & Dragons Duke." Lot said JP stayed fortressed in his head like a mother's-basement-dwelling geek, yet he was built like John Wayne on steroids, and possessed the Duke's cinematic stoicism in the face of any threat. He also had the best grasp of all the things Maddock had taught and told them. It was as if the information had always been inside JP.

But that was why he was here, wasn't it? Every person Maddock had brought to his unlikely cause had been identified based on a specific criterion. Namely, that each one dreamed of someone who was the stuff of legend or mythology, someone whose story had been marked by tragedy. "Dreamed" was probably too kind a word. Haunted by, obsessed with, driven to...what? Fix it. Fix something the world believed was fiction, a legend or myth. And by doing that, the world would be a better place.

No, the drive was less altruistic than that. Each one of them believed that fixing it on the back end would balance something inside, fill an emptiness.

So he was here not just to save her, but to save himself.

He'd been recruited barely out of his teens into a world that was as opposite to Maddock's world of magic and unicorns as Bubble Yum was to napalm. Maddock had had a hell of a time convincing him that he wasn't fucking with him. But in the end, it was one point that brought JP to the table.

"The number of people who've done what you've done, for as long as you've done it, probably wouldn't count up to a full set of fingers. If anyone deserves to get lost in a legend, it's you, JP. I can get you there. I promise."

The word "deserves" wasn't a word that any covert ops agent wore comfortably. But Maddock had talked him into this, and here JP was. Because he needed to be near where she was, even if it was a fucking fantasy Maddock was creating in JP's head, and he was really in a padded cell somewhere, thinking he was on a Mediterranean island.

It didn't matter. He'd take that reality, because on the back end of twenty years of pretending to be part of the darkest underbelly of society, she'd become far more real to him than anything else.

He knew she'd been watching him ever since he'd arrived this morning. The portal was supposed to open up on the beach, but apparently there'd been a tide miscalculation, so he'd been dumped ignominiously in the water. *Way to make a cool entrance, JP.* Dripping and feeling foolish, he'd trudged onto the beach. Seeing the number of rotted boats and pillars of crumbled stone littered along it, useless pride had given way to sober realization of the challenge he faced. Some of the boats were beached on the sand, while others rocked in the shallows with a hollow creaking.

The view facing away from the beach was less ominous. The island had lush forests and plenty of fresh water sources, but the greenery and meandering streams decorated a variety of rocky peaks, the stone providing gray and earth-toned contrasts where they jutted up through the forest. In his world and time, centuries in the future, the island was a coveted vacation destination for advanced rock climbers. At the end of their day, they enjoyed the poolside bars, restaurants and exclusive resorts.

As he'd put down his pack and set up his camp above the high tide line, he'd sensed an attentive presence. Not close, but he expected she had a clear view from an elevated vantage point. Her home wasn't readily visible, but he was trained to look for the hidden.

Based on the wreckage on the beach, he'd deduced she'd set her abode where she had a scout's view of the best approach from the nearby populated land masses, several of which could be seen in hazy silhouette from shore. After some intent study of the island topography, he'd found it. A small stone and wood structure, carefully embedded in the surrounding rock formations and screening forest. It was at an elevation almost impossible to reach...unless one could fly.

He approved of her tactical skills, though it would present him some unique challenges if this went how he hoped it would.

After he'd figured out her location, and before he'd set up camp, he wrote his message to her in the dry sand, using a bucket of water to darken the letters. He'd made it large enough a plane would see it, like an SOS.

Returning to the present and the dying daylight, he smiled, thinking of it. What would she think of a plane?

I'm here to serve you, my lady. That's what he'd written on the sand. Time to start proving it.

He'd find beauty and color through his other senses.

But gods above, he was truly going to miss sunsets. Not that he owed any loyalty to the gods. They'd pissed him off the first time he'd read her story, and he owed them nothing. His loyalty was to her.

Which was why in about a minute's time he was going to blind himself.

As he knelt by the fire, he pushed all other thoughts away but what tasks needed to be done. He had the necessary aftercare items, including antibiotics, a stack of clean dressings, and several bottles of fresh water. He'd taken careful note of where he'd placed all of them, but he wasn't worried about being blind in unfamiliar surroundings.

JP had spent months blindfolded, training himself to not rely on his eyes as his primary sense. Him and Luke Skywalker, using the Force. Or rather, JP's covert ops discipline and Maddock's magic mojo.

He could have had Maddock take his sight before he left his world, in far more optimal and less painful conditions, but JP knew it had to be done here, where she would see him do it.

Or maybe his motives weren't that noble. Maybe he'd hoped to have a chance to see her before losing the opportunity altogether. He'd brought a shield whose convex back offered blurred reflections, because Maddock had said an actual mirror wouldn't work. The reflection would be too clear and JP would end up a lawn ornament. He'd take that blurred reflection, though. Any glimpse at all of her.

JP didn't need to see her to confirm his decision. That was a decision of the heart, not the eyes, and he'd made that choice some time ago. No, he'd merely wanted to absorb her with every sense he'd ever possessed or ever would.

Taking a steadying breath, he laid his hand on the handle of the branding iron.

"What is this you do?"

He froze. His sword was staked in the sand next to the shield. A miscalculation on his part, since he couldn't reach for the shield, no matter how carefully, without her thinking he was going for the sword. Not only was she supposedly in possession of a headful of snakes, but every scrap of information he could find about her had convinced him she could move as fast as one. She'd whip around an opponent and have him staring into her deadly eyes before his brain had a chance to tell him to shut his own.

"How will you serve me if you cannot see?" she asked, telling him she'd already figured out what he was about to do.

He wanted to answer her promptly, but he was caught up in

hearing her voice for the first time. It sounded younger than he'd expected. He could deduce her age based on historic information about priestesses in Athena's temple, though sources on that were often dubious. In truth, everything he'd researched was somewhere between educated guesswork and pure speculation. But thanks to Maddock, suddenly he was getting a whole lot of firsthand detail.

In the same way he'd been loaded up with vaccinations before he went on overseas assignments, Maddock had loaded him up with spell work to prep for this one. One of the things had been a trans-lation spell, so he would hear her and respond in a common language, and they'd both be a little less lost by colloquialisms rele-vant to their respective worlds. The second was augmentation of his additional senses, to compensate for the loss of his eyes. Hearing, smell and taste, as well as proximity awareness, were enhanced threefold.

She had a melodious voice, as female as a dew-kissed flower with silken petals so delicate they'd bruise at a touch. He paid close atten-tion to all the information a person's voice could offer, but Maddock's craft took him further, so he could hear even deeper nuances.

Her syllables were strained and flat, filled with suspicion. The former told him she wasn't used to raising her voice, and the latter said she was prepared for him to attack. He didn't hear fear. He was glad she wasn't afraid of him, though that was far more likely due to her confidence in her own skills, not the belief he meant her no harm. She would have stopped trusting that sense a long time ago.

"I have taught myself how to do many things using my other sens-es," he said, realizing he hadn't answered her question. "I do not need my eyes to serve you, my lady."

"A trick, to get close enough to take my head. With this." The rasp of his blade being drawn from the sand made battle-ready muscles tense. He forced himself to remain still as metal heated by the after-noon sun notched against his throat. He could imagine her standing behind him, silent and imperious. There was no tremor in the weapon. She was more than capable of using it. His best play was to stay still and talk them away from that.

But sometimes you had to take the stupidest risks to prove your-self. Or to impress a girl. He could hear Lot's tongue-in-cheek obser-vation without him being here to make it. It didn't matter. JP had spent so much time around the guy, it was as if their brains had been mashed together like two handfuls of ground beef.

Shutting his eyes tight, he ducked, spun. Her lightning-quick back step and shift of weight impressed him, but he was pretty damn good at this himself. He came up under her guard, clamped down on her wrist and wrested the blade from her hand. A hiss, and he jerked to the right. A snake scored his ear as it shot past his head, narrowly missing the likely target of his face or eyes. In the same unbroken motion, he released her wrist, pivoted and went down on one knee, the blade planted firmly and harmlessly beside it, his hand clasped on the hilt and his head bowed.

Eyes cracking to a slit, he saw he'd landed where he'd intended, at her feet. The skirt of her tunic fluttered against his shoulder. It was short, like a Greek soldier's would be, revealing long slim legs, golden-hued from the sun. Inked drawings on her flesh showed serpents twining around flowers. The work was detailed and deft, perhaps a way to pass the time in her solitude. She had a silver toe ring on her right foot.

He'd smelled several different fragrances on her skin as she moved. Flowers, fresh fruit, earth and the sea, and a woman's warm flesh. Despite its advantages, Maddock's augmentation spell could also be a tempting distraction.

"I can hardly be of service to you if I'm missing my head, my lady," he said, proud that his voice was steady, since his stomach had done a serious half gainer with a twist during their short scuffle. So much could have gone wrong there, causing this to be over before it started. But if he second-guessed himself like that, he'd fail.

"Indeed." Her voice cracked. He'd startled her with a fight that was over before it could begin. Then her tone steadied. She had a warrior's temperament, finding her center again quickly. "You have skill with a blade, but I wonder to what purpose, if you intend me no harm. There is nothing to fight here, except me."

She paused. He wondered what she was thinking, seeing. At best, a nuisance; at worst, an enemy. "There is gardening and harvest, and minor repairs to maintain my home," she continued. "Beyond that, there is the watching of tides, and the rise and set of the sun."

Did she realize she spoke like a poet, measured and rhythmic like the rise and fall of waves? He could almost feel the caress of the syllables against his skin.

Focus. This isn't like being undercover in a cartel, but she'll still chop you up for hamburger if you keep daydreaming about her rather than talking.

He was channeling Lot again, obviously.

"So you need a gardener, a cook and an occasional carpenter," he said mildly. "I can be or do any of those things. I'm not without those skills. My fighting ability is just what's always been most in demand from those who need me."

Another silence, as if the straightforward answer had surprised her, and he expected it had. When was the last time she'd had an actual conversation with anyone? "I did not say I need any of those things," she responded at last. "I take care of myself sufficiently without help."

"No doubt, my lady. But I am here to serve you, and can take some of those burdens off your hands."

She made a dismissive noise and moved on from that. "You have fought in wars."

"In a sense. I worked on special missions to secure peace, aid in ongoing conflicts, catch criminals. Seems I've always been in that kind of work, even in past lives."

That was according to Maddock. *Your soul was born to protect and destroy, JP. The guardian angel or the boogeyman in the closet, whichever one's most in demand.*

The ancient Greeks knew the theory of reincarnation, even if it wasn't a common part of their spiritual philosophy. She proved it now by not inquiring what he meant. Or perhaps she just had bigger priorities.

"I see no boat. You walked onto my shore at dawn. Where are your reinforcements?"

"I came to you through a portal in time and space. Not by sea."

Additional silence. She was probably wondering if she should put this poor crazy bastard out of his misery with a one-shot from her lethal gaze. Or, more likely, she'd assume he was telling her a wild tale to cover the reinforcements coming from a different invasion point.

Part of the prep he'd done for this had included extensive think tank sessions with the other team members. They'd postulated what her life must be like, based on the data they had, so that he might be better able to anticipate her needs and help her lower her defenses with him. It had been strange for JP at first, working with a team on ideas that normally he had only himself to develop and hope he was on the right track.

Since Lot was the one in the group with the heavy military background, it wasn't surprising that he'd looked at her life from that perspective.

"For however many years she's been on the island, she's had to stay aware of any threat and meet it. She's going to mistrust everything you say, and frame everything in terms of threat assessment. If, as we suspect, there have been repeated attempts to take her out, she'll be hypervigilant."

JP thought of the wrecked boats and the crumbled stone. It angered him that she'd had to deal with any kind of threat, let alone so often. She might think he was crazy, talking about portals and past lives, but he was going to stick with bald honesty. If she mistrusted everything he said, the truth was the only way he'd get a leg up, if he was going to get one at all.

He opened his eyes to stare at her feet and the silver toe ring. While her soles had to be callused to go shoeless all the time, the shape of her feet and toes was pleasing and delicate, her nails neat and surprisingly clean. The only nod to her rustic environment was that the deep blue ink she'd used to draw the serpent coiled around her ankle was smudged over the joint bone. Perhaps she'd scraped her leg against a rock or tree, for the skin around it looked abraded.

She might be alone on her island, but she cared for herself as if she were in more civilized surroundings. She hadn't lost herself to the animal-like instincts that could take over in extended isolation and from perpetual threats of violence. Which was probably another reason he was still alive.

"I can swear a hundred oaths that I intend you no harm," he said. "That I'm here to do what I wrote on the sand, but words are meaningless when you know nothing of me. I ask for an opportunity to change that. If it is your pleasure I keep my eyes, I will stay blindfolded in your presence, and unarmed unless a threat comes against you. You need only to pull the blindfold away to gain the advantage over me."

Something like braided rope worn smooth slid over his knuckles where he clasped the sword. Realizing it was a snake, he stayed still as the creature coiled around his wrist and the hilt, a loose figure eight that effectively hampered his use of the weapon. Clever and intriguing, the evidence of a communication link between her and her snakes.

He mentally thanked Delia, another of their team, for her suggestion that he volunteer at a serpentarium as part of his training. The typical kneejerk reaction to treat a snake as a threat had been overcome with a far deeper understanding of the reptiles' nature and behavior.

While there was no doubt that the snakes physically attached to her had some differences from their counterparts in the natural world, he'd proceed on the assumption that they would have some qualities in common.

Medusa shifted, and something sharp and hard touched his knuckles. A claw? Was it part of her, or had she donned an ancient Greek version of a bear claw brass knuckle? The snake drew back, so perhaps the touch was a wordless command to bring the creature to her. Regardless, that small strip of skin where she'd made contact tingled with awareness. Skin was the largest sensory organ there was, and Maddock had augmented that, too. Again with the blessing and curse.

"What you call my advantage is more deception," she said. "You've proven your quickness and prowess with a blade. More time here gives you more opportunities to achieve harmful intent." She sighed.

"I'm too weary for this. Begone, however you came. If you are not off my island when I seek you again, I will carry you out to sea and drop you. It will not matter to me if you are close enough to land to reach it before you tire and drown. If you swim at all."

She'd just confirmed what her choice of home site had told him. She had wings. She could fly. There were so many accounts of what she looked like, only meeting her would allow him to verify anything. Once again, he longed for that one quick glimpse, to verify wings and claws, to see how she matched what he'd seen in his dreams of her.

Yet his interest in that was overtaken by the emotions he was picking up from her. She was being as honest with him as he was with her. He could hear the truth of her fatigue. She had no energy set aside to play games with an enigmatic stranger. Any natural urges for companionship were buried beneath a dump truck load of necessary defenses. He had to figure out how to remove some of them. Fortunately, he was experienced in winning the first vital scrap of trust from criminals, warlords and dictators who trusted no one. The only difference was that he had to win their trust with lies or modified truths. For it to work at all here, he had to be completely honest with her.

"My lady, you say you have no need for a warrior," he said slowly. "I've no doubt you're formidable. But maintaining a constant defense alone takes its toll. If you did have one other person here that you could trust, that burden could be shared."

"I will not debate the improbable with you. Whatever your motives, I want you gone." That strained quality in her voice had increased.

"Could you give me a day to prove myself?" he persisted. "I could familiarize myself with your living arrangements and show you the things another pair of hands might do. I don't think you'll kill me without cause, my lady, and I pose you no readily identifiable threat."

"Why do you think I want any company?" she said coldly. "Let alone yours, a strange man who tells wild tales. I do not fear solitude. It has been the best of company since I came here."

"Solitude is as necessary to the mind and soul as company," he agreed. "I won't impose on your solitude when you truly desire it. But when you don't, I can be company."

"No." Her feet moved out of the range of his vision. She was walking away from him. "Heed my words. Leave before I look for you again."

"I'm not leaving, my lady." He set his jaw. "I'm going to do as I said. So if you're determined to be rid of me, you'll have to do it now."

His pack was close enough he could snag it with one long arm. Removing the black lined eye mask from the side pocket, he began to lace it securely about his head. As he did so, it molded to his forehead, his eyes, the bridge of his nose and cheekbones. Hearing the friction of sand, and no further footsteps or wingbeats, he suspected she'd pivoted to watch him. Good.

He'd moved away from the sword to make it clear he didn't intend to use it, even though he did intend to defend himself if necessary. Balancing on the balls of his feet, he adjusted to a crouch, flexed his hands and cocked his head. "Do your worst, my lady, or give me permission to learn how to be a help to you."

"You are not listening," she ground out. "I did not ask for your help. I do not want your help."

He ducked and rolled, but not fast enough. He'd hit a nerve, a deeper one this time. He might consider that progress, except he was airborne. Those hard claws clamped on his legs, pinching cruelly, and he was tossed into the air, landing on his back in the water with a resounding splash. He should count himself lucky she hadn't carried him out to sea. Instead she'd dropped him in water shallow enough he thumped uncomfortably on the sandy bottom. He rolled, sloshed back out. "Impressive, my lady. But—"

She used the cloaking sounds of his movements to seize him again, this time by the biceps, claws digging into his arm pit. Yanking him in the air by that hold could have dislocated his shoulder, except she released him quickly. Into deeper water this time, a warning.

One he ignored. He came out of the water, and was tossed back into it once more. He cursed his slowness, albeit there wasn't much he could do about an air attack. Especially blindfolded and when he refused to do her any actual harm.

When she dunked him the fifth time, he detected an odd noise from her as she released him over the water. Replaying it in his mind, he realized what it was.

A chuckle.

It startled him to the core, and moved him. Of course. He'd detected the youthfulness in her voice, but as she'd continued to speak and he'd heard more womanly inflections, he'd realized it wasn't so much a reflection of her physical age as her state of mind. She'd been young when she'd come here, and they'd estimated she'd been here at least five to ten years on her own. Someone to play with was another need, wasn't it? One that could get buried but might not go away, not if other factors kept the desire for it alive.

He didn't come out this time. Once he was where he could touch bottom, he stopped at waist height and listened. She was hovering above him at a...ten o'clock angle. He sent a sheet of water splashing up and out in that direction, and grinned at a gasp. He swallowed a laughing oath, as well as some seawater, when she retaliated with a veritable punch of ocean in the face. Had she used her wing to scoop up and fire the shot? If so, her wingspan was considerable. She followed it up with what felt like a wet hunk of seaweed, splatted in the middle of his chest.

A giggle and a flutter of wind told him she'd changed positions again.

Wow. He'd expected a lot of things in his first few moments with her, but this one beat all. He was grinning like a loon, but reminded himself not to get too swept away in it. They were a long way from being BFFs. She might be entertaining herself with a hapless victim, or toying with a viable threat, trying to ferret out his true intentions.

Yet that giggle charmed him, probably in a dangerous way.

Slogging back onto the beach, he flopped down on the warm sand, relieved when he wasn't immediately picked back up and dropped again. A temporary truce. His lips curved as a couple drops of water and rhythmic flow of wind told him she was poised in the air above him. "All wet, my lady?"

"You're far wetter."

That was true. His tunic, a belted mid-thigh deal that likely came close to the soldier's garb she was wearing, was plastered to his body with no underwear under the damn thing. Greeks weren't modest. He didn't worry much about that either, but he missed his jeans or even a proper wetsuit. He'd tried not to imagine what was wandering around in the water, looking to pinch off dangling appendages.

"We could go for a swim together and be equally wet. Do you swim?" he asked.

"Quite often. You seem familiar with it."

"Yeah. I've had to do some amphibious missions, ones that involve approaching a target by diving gear or boat. Not as much as my buddy Lot, because he's a SEAL, a type of special ops soldier where water's kind of their specialty. Gotta say, though, this is far more fun." He paused, letting the word *fun* sink in. Maybe it would give him another toenail sliver of access through a cracked door.

"You mentioned watching sunrises and sunsets, my lady," he added. "I've been known to enjoy those myself. Might be nice to share them with someone else."

"I do not need that." Her voice went taut again. But it was the tension of rope, holding something back stronger than her words.

"You've never wished for company? Someone to share the burdens of life? To laugh with? Cry with? Go to sleep at night knowing another human was breathing nearby? Someone you can depend upon? Trust?"

Stillness. He curled his fingers into the sand, trying to appear relaxed when everything within him was coiled in anticipation of her next move. He'd heard a hitch in her breathing. Trying to interpret what it meant, what feelings he'd invoked, he hoped he hadn't hurt her.

But it might be necessary, because piercing through heavy defenses sometimes required using some sharp weapons. That was something he knew quite a lot about, thanks to the primary way he spent his leisure time. Another reason he'd been considered the best fit for this mission. The only fit, because he wouldn't have tolerated any other man taking it.

"You have given me nothing to trust you," she said woodenly. "Not even your name."

"John Pierce Zeus. People call me JP."

"Zeus? You are a son of Zeus?" He sensed she'd hopped back a few more feet and was in the air. Before she could take off, he propped himself up on his elbows and spoke quickly.

"No. Not hardly. Where I'm from, it doesn't mean that. It's just a name. One that my very fanciful mother tacked onto me when she left my dad. She said he was like a cheating, faithless god who didn't care what devastation he left in his wake."

His mother had never considered what legally changing his last name might tell her son about how she felt about him, the offspring of that painful relationship. But Mom had been on and off different meds for years. She'd been sane enough to pass herself off as fit for parenting; crazy enough that her kid knew differently.

Rubbing the water off his face, JP sobered. "My lady, in your position, I would feel no different. You've no reason to trust me, but I sense you'd like to. You were maybe enjoying yourself there for a moment. Right? Can we use that as a starting point? You can easily avoid me as I look around and figure out how to be a help to you. Whenever you wish to seek out my company, just give me a heads up and I'll put on the blindfold."

He set his jaw as she said nothing. "If you're worried about my intentions, I will do as I first said, and strike myself blind for you. Then there will be no doubt of your advantage over me. You just proved it well enough by throwing me in the water. I couldn't stop you."

Well, true and false. If he'd had the sword and had been willing to use it to slice off limbs as she grabbed for him, he might have had a chance, but that wasn't his purpose here.

"What's the harm of giving me a couple days to see if my company is bearable?" he asked. "Yes, you risk that I'm lying, and I'm just a scout stalling until reinforcements get here, but you know this island in and out. You can spend the time making sure I'm telling the truth."

"You could have others coming through that portal. I have no ability to prevent that."

"Yes. That is true," he admitted. "You have to trust someone you have no reason to trust. But I'm asking you to do so."

"Why should I?"

"Because I'm different." He said it staunchly. "Has anyone ever approached you the way I have?"

"Not exactly." He detected a subtle distress in the response, but she didn't give him a chance to question it. "Why do you wish to serve me?" she asked. "If I could understand why you were here, it might help."

He flashed on his mother, bedtime stories, and dreams too haunting to ignore. None of that would work right now. The simple truth was too simple. Too unbelievable.

"That's a tough one to explain up front," he said, "and you already think I'm crazy, talking about portals and time travel and crap like that. I'll talk about it now if you want, but I was hoping we could get to know more about each other first."

"I think you must talk about it some, because none of this makes sense to me. What I do not understand, I cannot trust. How could you think of me, if you came from another time and place? I know you come from far away because your accent is unknown to me. You speak my language, but your word choices and mannerisms are strange. Foreign."

She'd drawn closer. Still prudently out of reach, but he could feel her nearness. He'd practiced reading people when he was blindfolded —including in some very intimate ways, thanks to an idea Lot had had —but JP hadn't considered the emotional toll of not being able to look at her and meet her gaze. Get a sense of what she was feeling as she looked at him, if she found him pleasing or intriguing. Or a menace.

In the presence of the woman he most wanted to look upon, desire was also interfering with that training. If he couldn't look, he wanted to touch, and that was so not happening right now. She was giving him a slim-to-none margin of error to prove himself to her, a generosity he hadn't anticipated having this quickly, so he better pull it together.

"Stories of you have come down through the centuries, my lady," he said, closing his fingers in loose fists to resist the destructive urge. "Greek mythology permeates our popular culture." He flashed on the Nashville, Tennessee Parthenon replica with the forty-foot-tall statue of Athena inside it, but decided to hold off on explaining that. That was even trickier ground than he was treading. He needed to distract her before she asked—

"How do these stories portray me? What do they say or know of my life?"

Too late. "They are myths, my lady," he said carefully. "A lot of dramatic embellishment for storytelling purposes. Plays, books." He wasn't going to give her a rundown of *Clash of the Titans*, either version.

Solitude could impose a dulling melancholy on a prisoner of extreme circumstances. But she'd sustained herself with the resources of the island and figured out how to protect herself from invaders, so isolation could also hone the mind willing to put in the hours to sharpen it. She'd already proven she had that kind of discipline, and she underscored it now by demonstrating she was no fool.

"A monster. A bedtime story to scare children." She paused. "If you truly are not here as a foe, you have bought into the beginning of the story. The young, virginal priestess, raped by Poseidon and cursed by Athena, the Goddess she'd committed her life to serve. So you come to be brave and manly, defy the gods to rescue me from...what? If you come through time, John Pierce, you've arrived too late. A story is a story, as you said. Distorted past recognition."

"So it didn't happen that way?"

"Humans embellish," she said, with barely concealed bitterness, fragile and sharp.

"I am here to do you no harm, my lady. I'd fall on my sword before I'd make that an untrue statement. Nor will I let anyone else bring you harm, not while I have breath to prevent it. What I said about company—"

"I seek no one's company," she reminded him edgily. "It is why I'm here."

"With respect, lady, I think you have fled the kind of company no one would want. One that offers no kindness, mercy or forgiveness, no warmth or love, no laughter or friendship. You chose isolation, as anyone would. But that really isn't a choice, is it? You can choose my company."

"I can also not choose it. Or are you refusing to heed my wishes? If so, it makes you a poor servant."

"I said I came to serve, my lady. Not be a servant. There is a difference." When he purposefully injected an edge into his tone, her sudden startled quiet, that little catch in her breath again, sent a promising signal. Unfortunately, that included a stirring in his cock. He quelled it. Way too soon to focus on that.

"How about we set a deadline? Give me three days. If you don't want me here in three days, I'm gone, back through my portal, poof. Like I was never here."

"You said one day."

"Three is a luckier number, better for balance."

"We'll see." Though she sounded suspicious. "I reserve the right to change my mind."

"I've never known a woman who didn't."

She touched him. Even with his enhanced senses, he hadn't heard her approach. She must have crossed the ground on silent feet, for when she used her wings, he could hear their movement. Every muscle stilled as she explored the blindfold, the way it molded over his face. He felt her fingertips, but he also felt the press of the sharp claws along his forehead. She moved her examination to the lacings on the back.

"How curious. Take it off and give it to me. I will return it to you."

If I don't decide to turn you to stone first, was implied. Either she wanted a closer look at it, or she was testing how willing he was to trust her. He could answer that easily enough. "Very well, my lady. As I'm exploring, I assume you'll announce your presence so we don't find ourselves eye-to-eye. Unless that's your intent."

He wanted her to understand that he wouldn't be trying to hide his gaze from the possibility of her popping up in front of him. He was going to trust his fate to her hands.

Removing the blindfold in the subsequent silence, he kept his eyes closed as he extended it. She plucked it from his grasp without making contact with him. The beat of her wings heralded a spray of water, what had collected on her wings during their splashing. Then she was gone.

Christ, what did it say that the loss of her presence, even after this one brief encounter, was like a blow to the chest? The reminder of their water play made him smile, though. He was sure she was feeling far less pleased, likely plagued with doubts and suspicions. He wished he could alleviate those in some instant magical way, like with a wave of the wand they were all sure Maddock was hiding somewhere with his pointy hat and blue robes.

Maddock had once told him human emotions could be manipulated with magic, but not ethically, even if the intent was for good. "People have to work their own shit out," he said often, and bluntly.

JP had no assurances that she might not still drop him far out to sea as she'd threatened. Or save herself the trip and turn him to stone. As he opened his eyes and dropped to his heels, he noted the evidence of her presence. Footprints in the damp sand and a series of marks that suggested where her wings had touched. So they were long enough to reach the ground.

While feathered wings would leave a brushlike stroke, these marks were short, decisive crescents, like what would be made by a finger. Or a claw, he surmised, recalling the contact along his knuckles and face. Were the tips of her wings barbed like a dragon's? Would it surprise her to know he'd seen a real life dragon? Pissing-oneself close, too.

He squatted to place his fingers in the foot print. Small. Perhaps a size five or six. When he'd grappled with her for the sword, he'd determined she was a small woman, but one who was extremely strong and flexible, like a sleek mongoose. As he traced the outline of the sole, he imagined the shape of her arches, the way her ankle would feel in his grasp, the smooth muscled curves of her calves...

He shut his eyes again to increase the potency of the imagining. Through his lids, he could tell the sky was still lit by twilight, something he hadn't been able to surmise with the blindfold. The eye mask did an excellent job of putting the wearer in total darkness. Not only could he not see any details around him, he couldn't determine the time of day except from the degree of sunlight on his face. Once laced in place, it didn't shift and it couldn't be quickly removed.

Being an experienced sexual Dominant with access to lots of dungeon paraphernalia had its perks. And that was another reason why Maddock had been sure JP was the perfect guy for this job.

JP had dreamed of her for too long to believe anything different. He prayed to any gods worth a damn that he wasn't wrong.

Medusa was strong and dangerous, with an underlying fragility that called to him. She was a well-shielded, high-powered and damaged submissive soul, the ultimate test for a Dom who craved that challenge. Who craved her. Go big or go home.

He wasn't going home.

CHAPTER TWO

*T*hough he was too revved up to be tired, he decided not to explore the island in the dark. She'd be suspicious if he did, and he might be interfering with her sleep. Birds did tend to roost after sundown.

As he stretched out with a smile on the sand to study the million stars in the sky, he reviewed the day's events. He'd started the day sitting in a quiet corner of Central Park with a Starbuck's coffee and a paper talking about a bunch of stuff he didn't give a shit about. He'd scanned articles without reading them, his mind brimming with anticipation about this. Now here he was, on her island.

He'd met the woman behind the legend, something that interested him far more than the myth. He'd touched her, inhaled her scent and spoken to her. She'd spoken to him. He thought of her tripping his Dom radar with that little erratic breath. He could say he was making too much of it, but he didn't embellish what his senses fed him. In the jobs he'd had, there was a vital distinction between reasoned deduction and fatal wishful thinking.

One little breath wasn't irrefutable evidence, but he had other things to support his theory. He hadn't talked about that part of things with the think tank, but he had with Maddock and Lot, both Dominants themselves. They thought he was right. Probably.

"If you're wrong, she'll likely castrate you," Lot had said cheerfully. "Then you won't have to worry about it anyway."

JP thought of the blindfold he'd brought. He'd laced it on plenty of willing female subs at the BDSM club he frequented back in Tennessee. Sometimes he'd done it in the small dungeon room he'd set up in his home, on those few occasions he'd had an ongoing relationship with a sub. One who wasn't interested in getting too serious and setting up house with him.

By donning the mask himself to practice being sightless, he'd been learning how to serve her. It might sound twisted around thinking for a sexual Dominant, but not one who knew exactly what his goal was. He'd had several of those seasoned, lovely submissives help him conduct sessions while he wore it, so he could be certain he knew how to pick up their cues with touch, hearing and intuition.

Initially, he hadn't been sure it was a good idea. Despite his gut feeling about her nature and his own, too many variables were unknown, and he always ruthlessly evaluated his mindset as a potential flaw. Even though Dominant and submissive cravings had existed since the beginning of time, Medusa had been a virgin in Athena's temple, delivered there when she was little more than a child. His experience with subs, for the most part, was with those who had already embraced what they were and what they wanted.

It was Lot who challenged his doubts, and suggested he practice topping with the blindfold. "You're already a hell of an intuitive Master with your sight," he'd said. "This will build your confidence and prove to you how little you rely on your eyes to determine the state of your submissive—or just how much of a submissive she is. You use your heart and gut more than any Dom I've seen. Which is why you always get the best pussy."

John had lifted a brow. "Your respect for women is a role model for young men everywhere."

"There's nothing I respect more than a woman and her cunt," Lot said gravely. "I will willingly worship at that altar. And show her my devotion by tying her to it and giving her a dozen orgasms."

Maddock had tested the same theory from a different angle, asking him if he'd be able to set it aside if it wasn't in her nature. "Or let me put it this way. Yes, she might have a submissive nature, because she did commit her life to a goddess's service. But there's a submissive nature and a kink nature. What if she has one and not the other?"

"Then that's fine. I don't care what she is, Maddock. She's just mine to care for and protect. That's all. It's the one thing I know."

He meant it. But he'd also turned Maddock's own words on him, the ones he'd used to recruit John for his insane theories. "I've dreamed of her all my life, Maddock. Felt this connection. Every time I tried a long term relationship with a woman, Medusa's image, her presence, has imposed itself between us. The only time I've ever felt that dumbass dizzy 'falling off a cliff into a vat of rose petals' feeling you get toward a woman is when I was thinking of her. Until you came along and wanted me to join your little psych ward, I thought I was nuts."

He'd ignored Lot's smirk and kept his eyes on Maddock. "I've been a sexual Dominant since I sprouted my first chest hair," he said. "After I left covert ops, you know I started doing therapeutic sessions with women who identified as submissives before they became abuse or assault victims. The ones who needed a Dom who could help them reclaim their submission without the dark shit closing in on them."

He'd fallen into it by accident, when Monica had approached him for help. She wanted to re-embrace her submissive side, but couldn't get past a plethora of fear-driven hard limits, all related to the sexual assault she'd endured at the hands of a random client at the bank where she worked. After she and he worked through that, she'd spread the word. Next thing he knew, people in the lifestyle were referring other female subs to him that needed his intuitive brand of Dominance to find their way back to themselves.

It had helped him as much as them, since he was still decompressing from a life in covert ops. He'd liked the challenge. He'd loved helping a woman put herself back together again, a woman some violent asshole thought he'd broken. He'd taken some counseling courses to ensure he didn't mistakenly offer his skills to a woman who clearly needed professional counseling first. The Mistress who'd recommended that to him had summed it up nicely: *"People shouldn't use BDSM as therapy, but it can be therapeutic."*

He returned to his memory of the discussion with Maddock. "That path, my interest in that, wasn't chance. I've spent my life thinking about what she went through, and how much I wish I could have stopped it, or been there to take care of her afterward. Everything we've learned about her says she went above and beyond the call in committing herself to Athena. She might have been given to Athena by her father, but she embraced a life of submission and service. If the connection between us is true and fated, why wouldn't that part of ourselves be relevant and useful to bringing us together?"

Lot was right about the castration thing, though. She'd been trained to fight, because Athena was a warrior goddess. Plus, she'd been cursed with a gaze that could turn people to stone, wings that increased her speed and maneuverability well beyond mortal boundaries, and a head full of snakes willing to fight for her when she was threatened. No matter his skill set, she could likely take him out whenever she wished.

At dawn, he collected his backpack and headed away from the beach, finding the best route into the thick interior forest. Since he'd figured out where her home was, that was where he was going. It was a beautiful day to scale a death-defying cliff.

JP approved of how she'd put her nest at the most defensible part of the island. She might have acquired her initial fighting skills from the temple, but her tactical skills had evolved from necessity.

Yet even when life demanded it, not everyone had the intelligence, will and sheer luck to live long enough to develop those skills. After their initial encounter, he had no doubt she had plenty of the first two qualities. The gods who owed her so much had given her enough of a dose of the last to survive inevitable missteps.

He remembered his earliest assignments, the moments of sheer luck when he'd done stupid things that might have gotten his ass put in a trash compactor. Like her, he'd had little to nothing in the way of backup, and had had to figure out how to take care of himself.

How lonely she must have been, Johnny. Don't you feel sorry for her? Don't you want to fix it?

Okay, not channeling the crazy mom monologue. He shoved that away firmly.

As he continued his winding hike through the forest, he sensed when she was watching him again. That might be Maddock's enhancement of his senses, or his gut connection to her, but either way it was useful. He didn't look for her, knowing the peril to them both in that, though he kept his ears tuned for any rustlings that might suggest a creature of her size in the trees nearby. Since she was staying at a careful distance, she hadn't changed her mind and decided she wanted to turn him into a concrete doorstop.

When the forest at last thinned, he found himself looking up a perilous vertical expanse of jagged rock. Sparse vegetation dotted the upward terrain. This was the starting point for the "best" ascent to her home. Studying cracks, finger pockets and edges, access points for his climb, he noted that about halfway to the top was a very narrow ledge. It could provide a resting spot before continuing along the even more sheer face above it. Fuck, she'd chosen well. It would be a slow and difficult climb to reach her dwelling place, well nested at the top of that craggy mount. He ultimately might not be able to reach it without a pair of wings. Only one way to find out.

"The only easy day was yesterday," he murmured to himself, Lot's SEAL mantra. Crazy bastard. Though, if he was being honest, the unofficial covert ops mantra was even more twisted. *Yesterday, today, tomorrow; it doesn't matter. You're always fucked.*

He wasn't hiding what he was trying to do, and she could tell him if she didn't want him climbing up there. Her silence made him deduce she wanted to see if he could do it. Testing him. A challenge.

He bared his teeth in a smile, entertaining himself with visions of tying her up with her own snakes, tumbling her over his knee and giving her a good spanking for putting him through this. With how pretty and sculpted her calves were, he expected she'd have a nice, toned butt.

The humor helped, but the vision made him hard, not a good decision for a difficult climb.

"Okay, put the freak flag at half mast, JP," he muttered. "Euphemistically and otherwise."

He'd had to betray the trust of so many who didn't know who he was, and yeah, while some of them were bad guys, a lot of them weren't. Just family members, people caught in that world because that was where they were born and lived, what they'd always known. By taking command of a sub's pleasure, bringing her emotional and physical release, plus sometimes healing hurts inside of her, it balanced something for him. Might not be more than a grain of sand in the karmic scale, but that wasn't why he did it.

He did it because he needed it. Topping could be just as therapeutic as bottoming. And, though it all came back to Medusa, he wasn't here just because she was another damaged sub.

He had climbing gear he could use, but he saw enough decent access points to reach that halfway point ledge. Yeah, he was still in the gotta-impress-the-girl mode. Even so, he'd free solo climbed in far more dire circumstances, where his need to scale up or down had been cloaked by darkness and his window of opportunity was measured in minutes. Far different from climbing at a relaxed pace while enjoying a mild Mediterranean sun. Lot would scoff and say this was recreational climbing.

"My grandmother with a bad hip could make this climb."

Asshole.

He did take advantage of the climbing gloves and shoes he had in his pack. After donning those, he tightened the straps on the backpack to hold it more securely against him. He'd left the shield concealed in the foliage along the beach but had brought the sword, just because he felt better having a weapon with him, in case she had need of his defense. Some of those abandoned boats looked as if they'd been more recent arrivals, and she and he hadn't yet had a chance to discuss how often she had to repel unwelcome guests.

He scabbarded the blade in the lacings down the spine of the pack, and took his first grip. He made steady progress upward, bracing his feet, tensing his thigh, arm and back muscles where needed to hold position and then reach up for the next handhold. Balance was the biggest issue. Plus a whole lot of strength from core, grip and legs.

He reached the first ledge without being out of breath. Maybe he was still riding an adrenaline rush. He'd walked through a portal into the freaking world of Greek mythology, and was with the woman of his dreams. Heady stuff.

Stretching out on the ledge, he folded his arm over his face as he took a break before the next far harder ascent. He was glad he'd traded out the tunic for a pair of cut-off denim shorts, because the rock would have shredded the thin cloth. His skin was tougher, though he had a few scrapes from the effort.

"Why are you really here? Tell me the truth."

She was behind and below him, where he couldn't easily twist his head to see her. Was she hovering in the air? From the pleasant swirl of air over his face, he thought she was, because he also hadn't heard her latch onto the vertical rock surface.

Second time she'd asked, and the answer was still as complicated as a ten-page long math equation, and simple as taking a breath. "Just like a woman," he observed. "Wait until a guy's hanging off the edge of a cliff and ask him to talk about his feelings."

"You are trying to be amusing, but I do not understand your humor."

"Yeah, maybe." Bits of the truth might work, he reflected, even if they offered only the tip of the iceberg. They might also get him tossed off the cliff.

"I'm here to seduce you, my lady. Among other things."

He closed his eyes, feeling the heat of the sun on his face. Would she come hover over him, shade him with her wings? He expected she wouldn't, but he could hear her hovering nearby still. The pause was pregnant with her unspoken thoughts. Why not push it a little farther, see where it went?

"I want you in my bed, begging for my kisses," he continued.

"You have no bed here. And I would not beg you for kisses," she said stiffly.

"I'd do things that would make you feel wave after wave of pleasure, until it's unbearable, in the best kind of way. But I would command you to bear it, and wouldn't let you reach release until you begged for a kiss."

If the comment frightened her, he'd know she had no understanding of sex without the company of violence. Instead she scoffed, making his lips curve.

"You speak foolishness. Earlier you said you were here to protect me. Serve me. So you are lying."

"I don't lie. Not to you. Not ever."

The surge of feeling was strong enough to knock an elephant off his feet and banished the playfulness he'd been trying to initiate with her. How many times had he been called a liar, by those few who'd found out who he was and why he was among them? And liar was the nicest word they'd used. He knew his triggers, damn it, and knew how to keep them under control. But being around her, he wanted to be a truer version of himself, in every way.

He took a breath and added a gentler explanation. "Both things can be true, my lady. I'm here to protect you, seduce you, and bring you companionship. Let you belong again."

"To you?"

"If that is your desire."

"Is it yours?"

"I've always thought you were mine."

Another pause. "You are mad," she said shortly. "What if I find you repulsive? Your company irritating and unbearable?"

"Then you can turn me to stone, dump me in the sea, or tell me to go home."

"I already told you to do that. And threatened the other two."

"Yes, but you didn't mean it."

An exasperated huff, and she was gone again, the swirl of air dissipating back into the steady, one-directional breeze from the ocean. Though John grinned at her response, yearning twisted in his gut at her proximity, so sparingly given and just as quickly taken away. She had no idea how long or how far he'd come to be with her.

And yet, in the end, as she said, she might not want him. If that was the case, he would honor her preferences. There was a fine line between a man deciding a woman was his ultimate fate and becoming her stalker. But even if it turned out that she didn't want him, he'd honor his first and primary reason for being here. He wondered what she would think when he revealed the full truth to her.

Serious thoughts for a later time, if they became necessary. It was all chess right now, and he was glad she was showing an interest in playing. John cracked open an eye and considered the upward path. Limbs jutting out from the rock in a couple places might or might not hold his weight. If not, he might be able to manage a controlled fall if needed, rather than bashing against the rocks between here and the ground like a pinball.

He started again. Muscles and limbs quickly exceeded their maximum capacity and reach this time. The backpack was probably a bad idea, light though it was, because this was a ballbuster of a climb, but he'd learned to carry essential supplies with him in unfamiliar terrain. If he had to traverse this climb regularly, he'd work out something to help him get up and down more easily, something made of natural materials that he could pull up and conceal so no enemy of hers could find and use it. He wasn't going to weaken one of her best defenses.

As always seemed to be the case, the final fifteen feet were the most precarious. He was drenched in sweat, moving carefully from hold to hold, some of them barely fingerprints in the rock. Only a testosterone-driven moron would have chosen not to use the gear for this part. He should climb back down to the ledge and start over.

He didn't, being the testosterone-driven moron he was. He wasn't immortal. If he fell, he'd break like a wooden toy and she'd watch him die. If not from the fall, from the resulting shock, sepsis, infection or another horrific thing. He didn't want to do that to her. He'd end himself first. He was pretty sure she had a kinder heart than she wanted anyone to know about. Him being alive was dubious proof of it.

Just a little farther. His body screamed for relief and it was waiting for him in another few feet. Toes found crevices, hands gripped, and he thanked the athletic companies that made quality climbing shoes and gloves.

Unfortunately, Mother Nature had no respect for high priced climbing gear. The pull of his weight against the small spike of rock proved to be too much. Before he could do more than register the slight pop and hairline fissure, the rock broke away in his hand. He flung himself toward the next hold, but couldn't latch on. He slipped with a grunt and a curse, the rock taking a layer of skin off his forearm as his feet sought purchase and found none.

Son of a fucking bitch. As he fell, he flipped through possibilities at the speed of a Vegas card dealer. What was below, how he could twist himself to grab something, could he land on that pencil-thin ledge too many feet below.

A smear of blood marked the rock face as he slid down it, too fast. If he could stay hugged up against the rock, he'd land on that ledge. He...dammit, he was not going to tumble... fuck he was falling, the angle of the cliff face and gravity working together to pull him away from the solid surface.

He grunted as he was stopped in mid-air and slammed face forward against the rock face. There were no handholds available, but Medusa was holding him, her claws locked under his arms. The shoulder she'd strained when she threw him in the sea yesterday sang with pain as it bore the brunt of all his weight once again.

He and she needed to do some Schoolhouse Rock together. A rope master he'd met had had all those mentoring with him sing the old leg-bone-connected-to-the-so-n-so-bone song, part of their training on how to properly suspend their subs without damaging joints.

"Close your eyes." Her voice was urgent, and he obeyed as she shifted her grip from under his arms to fully around his chest. Now he did regret wearing the backpack, because the move pressed her body against it. He could have had a nice last-moment-before-I-die impression of firm breasts and soft nipples. A lesson for his next life.

She pulled him clear of the wall before he could protest. Her petite frame shouldn't be capable of holding his weight for a prolonged period, but he was dangling more or less securely in her grip, and she was ascending. Up and up. And up.

This was it. He'd annoyed her past repair and she was going to drop him from such a height over the sea that the water would feel as hard as the ground he'd been about to encounter.

Though her careful but not overly laborious movements told him she had more than a normal woman's strength, her arms didn't feel overly bulked with muscle, though the biceps flexing against him were firm enough. Up until now, he'd had the impression of a slim, delicate creature, but a bird was delicate—and some species could carry something multiple times their weight.

He bit back an oath as he was dropped, but it was only a few feet, and he hit a flat, tiled surface, not the ocean.

"It is hard to prove you can protect me if I am the one rescuing you from your own foolishness," she said. "I will return at sundown. Be aware of that."

Just like that, she was gone, as if she'd had a pressing doctor's appointment or something. Since, up until his mishap, she'd been watching him, he had to assume it was her way of saying she wasn't interested in chitchat.

She also hadn't returned the eye mask to him, a further warning that the jury was still out about him. Nevertheless, as he lay there, getting his breath, he pumped a victorious if shaky fist in the air. He'd made it, and she was too curious about him to let him die outright.

He remembered a scene he'd done with Olivia, a lush, redheaded sub he'd trained for another Master. He'd instructed her to make his dinner, lay it out according to his specifications, and then blindfold herself and kneel by the door at sundown to prepare for his arrival.

Maybe he could figure out what to make Medusa for dinner. What would she think of finding him naked, kneeling and eyes closed, waiting for her? He managed a half chuckle at the image. Well, not only did he not have the blindfold, that would be way too much, too soon—*you think?* It sure gave him a nice and needed spike of adrenaline to reverse the roles and picture her in the same position, though.

With a groan of relief, he stripped off the backpack, rose and rolled his shoulders, and took a look around.

"Fuck me."

He'd expected something rudimentary, like a hut or lean-to. He stood on a clay tile patio attached to a sturdy stone, wood-framed home. The patio offered a stunning three-sided view of the ocean, blue-green waters sparkling with sunlight. The forest spread out below the patio and gradually descended toward the beach, a set of rolling green hills made up of tree tops. Glancing over the edge of the patio, he could see just how steep the cliff face was he'd mostly traversed.

Yeah, she'd had to save his ass the last few feet, but she damn well should be impressed he'd made it as far as he had.

Pivoting, he looked into the rest of her home. She'd kept it three-walled, open to the patio, no enclosed box for her. It wasn't opulent, but it was far better built than he would have expected from one small woman building it on her own. A clay tiled roof protected a clean and inviting living space decorated with flowers, shells and draped pieces of cloth he expected she'd salvaged from the boats. There were a couple chairs and a table she might have made herself.

The table had a chaotic pattern of grooves along the surface, a maze of circling and straight lines that looked almost like a piece of sheet music where the parallel lines had been freed to rise, fall and loop like the musical notes normally written upon them. A rope cot with a mattress and pillow of stuffed grasses was nestled in the back corner.

A creek passed through the western side of her home, and she'd dug out a shallow water basin in it, providing a sink of sorts. When he followed the creek out of her home and around to the rear, non-cliff side, he saw a half-wild, half-landscaped garden. Large rocks had been hollowed on top to form semi-comfortable places to sit for contemplation. She'd created arbors with sticks and rope, training vines laden with colorful flowers along them. A path traversed the garden area, disappearing back into forest.

He returned to the indoor living space to study the small handful of personal items she'd collected from a world she no longer inhabited. Two books, a broken plate with gold edging. A bracelet with silver beads and black stones. She'd strung some of the pieces of salvaged cloth over the cot to form a canopy.

What drew his interest most of all was the stack of papers carefully placed in an alcove cut into the back wall. Some of the paper was rough, natural-colored pulp, perhaps parchment she'd made herself. Some of it was water-stained pages torn from ruined books. From the ink on her legs, he knew she'd figured out how to create ink from the vegetation. Here she'd done more artwork, the colors a pleasing and unexpected variety of hues painted over the words of the books or blending with the colors of the pulp paper.

She wasn't an artist, but her drawings had a rough charm, like that of a budding naturalist alone on a deserted island. He saw animals and flowers, the sea. She wrote expressive lines to go with the pictures, words that spoke of her life here. As he read them, he revised his opinion. Not a naturalist after all, but instead a poignant poet.

Looking out at the sea, sunlight glittering off my face.
Soft rabbit, heart pounding, no need to fear my touch.
How wild and free a prison of the mind can be.

He was glad Maddock's translation spell worked on the written word. But as he paged to the bottom of the stack, his mood shifted from pleasure to darkness.

Monica had worked at a battered women's shelter. One day the women and their children were on a field trip and he'd volunteered to do some handyman work. Monica had shown him some of the residents' therapy art, which chillingly reminded him of this.

Medusa had drawn a female demon with forked tongue, demonic eyes, a twisted body and wings lined with spikes. Snakes wrapped around her, fangs sunk into her flesh while she clawed at them with talons as long as her fingers. This was how she saw herself.

As he paged onward, he realized, with some relief, that the

pictures likely had been stacked in the order in which she'd done them. The ones closer to the top were more recent. While they had some bittersweet images, they did not possess the angry darkness of those closer to the bottom.

He noted a common theme in all of them. Spirals. In multiple colors, styles and patterns, she incorporated the shape into the bodies of animals, twisted the trunks of trees, and made the clouds and sun reminiscent of a Van Gogh. Every picture had coils. Like snakes.

And speaking of which... As the day was moving into mid-afternoon, the sun getting warmer, he realized the whisper of the wind through the branches framing her patio was no longer only the wind. Lifting his head slowly, he noticed a flash of sunlight against scales and felt the weight of slit pupils upon him. When he straightened and stepped back to gain a better perspective, he realized the tree branches interlaced over the patio had become populated with snakes. He was looking at a couple dozen of them in a variety of species, lengths and thicknesses. They seemed curious, not threatening, which was good. Since he had no doubt they were somehow connected to her, he didn't want to have to fend off an attack.

They didn't appear to be doing anything but watching him, so he moved back to her cot. Curious, he lifted her pillow and smelled it. The worn fabric, probably salvaged from one of those ominously empty ships, was filled with grasses that bore the scent of the sea and the forest, and her.

It reminded him of when she'd grabbed him. That scent had been elusive and sharp, like mist with the edge of a lightning storm. There'd also been an underlying odor of female sweat, not an unpleasant musk. She kept herself clean, probably in one of the many water sources, but she didn't overlay her natural smell with the many products of the women of his own time.

Studying the cot, he surmised this was a lounging area, not a place to sleep, unless it was for the occasional nap. He couldn't see how it would be comfortable for her wings. As he'd thought last night, birds usually preferred to roost.

Returning to the patio, he stayed mindful of any aggression from the snakes. They didn't seem to care, continuing to make sibilant noises and pursue their own interests with flickering tongues and twining bodies. Stepping out to the edge of the tile, he looked up into the thick web of branches that provided the patio shade. It took several moments, but he found what he expected. A spot where a thick woven mat of branches was denser than they would have accomplished on their own. She did have a nest.

He'd wondered why she had so little concern about him being in her home unsupervised. A moment later he discovered it wasn't only because her bed was at a higher elevation.

As soon as he put his hand on the lowest branch, intending to climb up and check out the nest, a full half dozen heads reared up in strike position. Jerking his hand off the branch, he stepped back. The snakes reinforced the point by slithering down closer to where he was, overlapping one another on the branch he'd been intending to use as the first rung of the ladder.

"Okay, got it. Off limits."

When he went back outside to her small, half-wild garden, he found a similar situation. He tried to follow the path into the forest, but the snakes once again barred his way just before that threshold.

They weren't trying to keep him from leaving her home, however. When he chose another route out of the garden, they didn't block his way. So she was only giving him access to certain areas. There was something specific down the garden path she wasn't going to let him see. And she didn't want him to see the place where she chose to sleep most of the time.

The nest made sense to him, but the blocked path was puzzling. As he mulled the why of it, he arrived at a more functional garden area, an open sunny spot where she raised a variety of vegetables and herbs. The priestesses at the Athenian temple weren't much different from the nunneries and monasteries from his own time, where everyone learned and helped with food preparation and storage. He wondered if she kept multiple gardens at different points of the island, wherever soil content and sunlight was best for the foods in question.

The island didn't lack for water, but he was impressed to see she had minimized her labor by rigging an irrigation system from the nearby creek. Following the creek to its source, he found treasure. Passing through a thick growth of trees and foliage, he discovered a deep pool. The rush of noise told him what was there before he could see it, but when he did, he was glad to have his eyes. The waterfall was about ten feet high. Rocks clustered around the pool, perfect for sunning after a dip. The trees permitted an almost perfect circle of sky above the pool. It reminded him of a cathedral ceiling with its drifting clouds.

When he circled around to the top of the waterfall, he discovered another panoramic view, this one of the interior of the island. The valley was like an excavated volcano or a crater from a long ago meteor, a deep basin that had become repopulated with verdant vegetation over the centuries.

He stepped carefully over a black snake coiled up on a flat rock, the creature enjoying the mist off the crest of the waterfall. During his exploration, he'd seen plenty more snakes that he suspected were monitoring his progress. Could she see through their eyes?

There was plenty of other wildlife, too. He glimpsed deer and shy rabbits he was surprised managed to exist here at all with the snake population.

Numerous birds dotted the landscape with wondrous colors, shapes and sizes. When she flew, did they join her? Did they dip and soar against the blue sky together, or did they avoid her, likening her to a hawk, something that meant danger to them? Her poetic line about the rabbit suggested if she took from the wildlife on the island, she did so sparingly. Based on what he knew of ancient Greek life, he suspected her protein of choice came from the sea. Fish, crabs.

He'd stood before the ruins of Athena's temple. Inspired and awed to stand where he'd hoped Medusa's feet had walked, he'd closed his eyes and tried to imagine it for her there. Had she loved it? Hated it? Had she had other dreams than being dedicated to a goddess's service for her whole life?

He had much to learn of her life here, to ensure he complemented it. The garden was well-tended, but weeds were a problem for every gardener. He pulled those that he saw, but there weren't many. Regardless, perhaps she'd notice his small effort and know he'd help out without having to be nagged. He grinned at the thought. Several of the fruits were ripe and ready to be picked, so he removed those and carried them back to her home, stacking them in a wooden bowl on the table. She might be hungry later. Or her snakes might be.

Make friends with the pet, win the heart of the pet parent. Yeah, right. He expected her relationship with the snakes was a bit more complicated than that. He remembered that close strike when he'd taken the sword from her, the snake fast as a cracking whip. Talk about surviving a serious injury out of sheer luck. If he'd been a hair slower, he might have been half blinded anyway.

Scaling a wall and nearly plunging to his death could take it out of a guy. Stretching out on the floor next to her cot, he crossed his ankles and stacked his hands behind his head. Putting himself in a light sleep mode was easy as flipping a switch, thanks to the necessity of grabbing shut-eye in less than optimal surroundings. In a heartbeat, he could come awake with full awareness. It was the best kind of sleep for riding the edge between rest and survival.

That said, a snake dropping on his chest like a long, scaly brick was still a shock.

"Son of a..." He woke with a startled oath, sitting up and backpedaling as the three-foot brown spotted snake rolled away and slithered off, coiling in a corner and gazing at him in baleful challenge. Glancing up, John noticed the rafters above him now held a vanguard of snakes. Since the snake seemed as startled as he'd been, he figured it out.

"You were dozing and fell off, didn't you?" Despite his racing heart, he chuckled. At the sound, the snake raised its head and then lowered it, tucking itself into a more comfortable knot. In the face of JP's peaceful response, the snake's aggression disappeared. JP recalled how they'd all gone on the offense when he tried to climb the tree, though. Curious.

If Medusa was a sorceress as some of the mythology suggested, the snake was obviously her totem animal to call.

Settling back, he shut his eyes once more. After careful thought, he crossed his ankles so the openings to his cut-off shorts were not so gapingly inviting, at least for a snake.

Yeah, it might be typically male and irrational, but he'd much rather have a pissed-off snake strike at his eye than a friendly one exploring his testicles. And he didn't think there was a man in the world who would disagree with him.

CHAPTER THREE

*I*t was a peaceful place to sleep, with the sea breeze moving through the trees punctuated by the distant whisper of the ocean. Her scent was all around him, that appealing mix of elemental fragrances and woman. He dropped off without difficulty.

About an hour later, that internal trigger woke him once more. This time he kept his eyes shut, because what had woken him wasn't an incursion of curious snakes. It was the rustle of wings and the light tread of feet landing on the patio.

His lady had returned.

She moved almost noiselessly, and through cracked lids kept carefully lowered, he saw her feet once again. Since last he'd seen her, she'd added anklets woven from tiny white flowers. The inked patterns on her legs were gone, so she must have washed those away. She still wore the toe ring, which he found incredibly sexy.

He closed his eyes fully as she drew closer. He sensed when she was standing over him, probably trying to decide what to make of him. From the quick snap of sound, he surmised she'd picked up one of the fruits and taken a bite.

She hadn't alerted him to her presence as he'd requested. Did she hope he'd "accidentally" meet her gaze and no longer be a problem she had to solve? It was a discomfiting thought, suggesting a more precarious morality than he'd initially assumed for her. Well, there was a reason for the saying: "To assume is to make an ass of you and a statue of me." Or something like that.

"If you have reinforcements here, they're cleverly hidden," she said, confirming her awareness he wasn't asleep.

"I expect you've been here long enough to know all the hiding places, my lady. You would not have missed one."

"You've been doing your own explorations."

"Within the limits you have set. Your able guard kept me from your sleeping quarters and a section of your gardens."

"A man should wait to be invited to a woman's bed."

"No argument there. How about a woman being invited to a man's?"

"I've never known a man to set any obstacle between a woman and his bed." The dry observation gave her voice an intriguing edge. That was helpful, since the usual melodic rise and fall could make him hard. It had when he slept last night on the beach, his subconscious remembering it like an erotic lullaby twined with the sound of the surf.

He chuckled. "We're simple when it comes to that. At least when we're young. Eventually some of us grow beyond our hormones and learn to be more selective."

"Oh? How many have you selected?"

"That's a complicated question. Not many, technically."

He could hear her chewing, quiet, neat. He imagined the juice of the fruit glossing her lips. "You did not harm my snakes." It was a statement, not a question. "Many people consider them enemies. But they are allowed in our temples, because they are favored by the gods."

"Even the venomous ones?"

"The most venomous creature ever created walks on two legs, not on its belly."

He thought of the biblical bad relationship between humans and snakes. He expected human mistrust of the slithering creatures had been around far earlier than that and the Bible had merely capitalized on it, giving people a familiar enemy to understand.

However, he was far more interested in pursuing the dark edge in her voice than a theological discussion, but she had her own questions.

"This word...technically. It is confusing."

"It means that a yes or no answer isn't really the right one."

"So it is a complicated answer, how many women you have had."

The woman wasn't much on small talk, that was for damn sure. "That's probably a conversation for another day," JP suggested. "When we know one another better."

She made a derisive noise. "Aren't such conversations how people get to know one another better?"

"Yes, but it's like...a poem or song that tells a story. You don't dive into the middle without context."

"Charming words. You are worried what you tell me will make me dislike you."

He thought it through. "Yes. Because it would be easy to misunderstand, before you know me better."

He suspected the honesty had surprised her, because her tone was less antagonistic when she spoke again. "How will you know it's time to tell me, when you won't be misunderstood?"

"Instinct. Like how you know the proper moment to launch into the sky."

"That is no more a decision for me than walking is for you."

"Good thing for me, because you knew the right moment to catch me before I was turned into matchsticks at the bottom of that cliff."

She made a dubious noise, as if she were doubting the wisdom of her decision to help him. But he was pleased. She wanted to converse with him. She didn't seem hesitant or stumble over her words as someone would who had spent so much time alone, so he expected she spoke a great deal to her snakes or even to herself.

"If you did come through a portal, what is your world like?" she asked, confirming it. "How far in the future is it?"

"You believe me, then?"

"No. But I want to hear the story you've created to support it."

Fair enough. He'd pretty much said the same thing to Maddock when he'd brought his story to JP.

A creak suggested she'd taken a seat in the chair on the far side of the table. It kept several items of furniture between them. He admired her vigilance even as he wished they could just jump ahead to when she would trust him. But as he well knew, the journey of winning someone's trust gave the relationship—wherever it ultimately ended up—its richness and value.

"Okay, then. We're about twenty-five hundred years ahead of you. There are a lot of people. Over seven billion, and growing."

"That is impossible. How do they survive, with so many? There would not be enough to eat."

He attempted to explain industrialization to her, comparing it to how they worked together in the fields and came up with streamlined processes to make that easier. While not being able to gauge her reaction from her face or body language was somewhat dissatisfying, her attention was a dense heat that never wavered. Plus, her alluring combination of scents, imprinting itself on his consciousness like a permanent memory trigger, compensated for the lack of ability to see her.

He could imagine immersing himself in that scent with her in his bed, beneath him, her arms and legs around him. Her breath sighed along his cheek, her silken muscles gripping him in the aftermath of a climax that sent them drifting through a world for just the two of them, where there were no barriers or misunderstandings left between them.

Remember, she will kill you if you forget yourself, you romantic idiot.

"Those things you describe," she was saying. "The ideas are clever. You are an accomplished storyteller."

"I'd like to take the credit, but those things really exist in my time. There's a drawback to all of it. Most of the people in my world would be lost in yours. They don't know how to take care of themselves out of range of the nearest Walmart, ATM machine or Starbuck's. Those are stores that provide us money, food, and basic necessities like what you've created from scratch here."

"The first season was the hardest. It takes time for things to grow, and I had to learn what wild plants were edible and how to hunt when necessary. I did not do much of that at the temple. Others were responsible for that. But I... It was difficult for me to kill other living beings. Then."

The one word was laden with a bitter darkness he sensed was best not to pursue right now. As much as he wanted to delve into everything about her, he understood what she'd faced on that. He didn't have to think about who his first kill had been. The faces were always there. He smoothly changed the subject, for both of them.

"I like your home. Can you describe how you're sitting, my lady? Your voice sounds higher than it would be if you were sitting."

"Your sense of hearing is exceptional. I'm perched on the chair. Perching is easier than sitting with wings."

"Do you ever wear shoes?"

A sudden silence. "You looked."

"Only at your feet. I figured the lack of shoes is how you move so quietly. The snakes you drew on your legs earlier—do you do that often? From your papers here, you seem to like to draw."

A slight weight landed on his thigh and draped. The eye mask.

"Put it back on," she said tersely.

He could have argued, pointing out he'd purposefully kept his gaze on her feet to prove there was no risk that he'd foolishly attempt to look at her face. But he also had to prove he would not oppose her needlessly. As he sat up and laced the mask in place, he continued the conversation as if there'd been no sudden injection of tension between them.

"Can you tell me about your snakes, my lady? The ones attached to you."

She was probably interpreting all of his questions as an attempt by an enemy to gather intel, so there was no point in trying to pick innocuous questions. If she was reacting the way he would in a similar situation, she was probably analyzing each one to determine if a truthful answer would lose her an advantage. Perhaps she would give him an untruthful one to throw him off, but it would still be conversation.

"There are five. Sometimes they weave together to form a crown on my head. Other times, they hang loose, like my hair, and twist together for their amusement."

"How do they eat?"

"They get their nourishment from what I eat. Though sometimes, despite my wish otherwise, they exercise their hunting instincts on a bug or tiny lizard." He was amused to hear the grimace in her voice. "I perceive the taste and texture of what they are eating."

"Complete with still wiggling legs?"

He surprised a chuckle out of her, one she muffled. He marveled again at how girlish she could sound when she laughed. "Yes. But I have tried to adapt to their preferences as they have done to mine.

Fortunately, most the time they are happy to steal bits from my plate when they want to ingest food in the normal way."

"If I pull on one of the snakes, does it feel like someone tugging on your hair?"

This time the mirth in her voice was even more obvious. He'd hoped such whimsical questions would help her relax, and it seemed to be working. "I've never had anyone suggest such a thing. Or attempt it, but I expect yes, since they are attached to me, it would feel like having my hair pulled."

"Are they separate beings?" He wasn't sure if she'd understand the question, but she did.

"Yes. We share dreams when we sleep, and I know which are theirs and which are mine. I hear their thoughts. Different from mine, much simpler in some ways, yet far more intuitive. They live close to the rhythms of the earth. It is hard to describe, more like feelings than language, but it comes through just as clearly." She paused. "They told me their names and, though their language is beyond my tongue, they consented to me calling them by the meaning of the name I understand in my language."

"Would you share those with me?" he asked, intrigued. Maddock would be having kittens. This was the type of data the scientist-wizard snorted up like crack.

"Earthson, Treebark, Waterlight, Tunneltrap and Ratqueen."

From the warmth in her tone, he had the feeling she was touching each as she spoke their names. "Earthson and Tunneltrap are males. Ratqueen is the leader, in a sense. The strongest personality, though there are times they speak in one voice, or two will speak as one mind. Tunneltrap and Waterlight are siblings. The others are not related, and they are four different species. Treebark and Ratqueen are not of any species I have ever seen before... Ratqueen is all white with pink eyes, an albino, and far larger than the others. Treebark looks like his name, as if he is covered with the rough bark of a tree."

"Is his head kind of like a fat diamond shape, almost a square?"

"Yes, somewhat."

"I'd guess he's a bush viper. Ratqueen I'm not sure about. Albinos are usually a gene mutation, but if she's bigger, she may be some kind of python."

"Oh. How do you know of this?"

"I worked in a place that had lots of different snakes. Studied them both to help the species and to educate people so they wouldn't always treat them as enemies."

"Oh." The suspicion that entered that syllable suggested she thought he was playing on her obvious attachment to the serpents, so he didn't linger on that.

"You said they are attached to you 'in a way.' Why did you qualify it? You don't have to answer anything you do not wish to answer, my lady, but I ask not only for myself. Maddock—he's the man who figured out how to use the portals and helped me come here—speculates on scientific and magical phenomena. It's his passion. If he were here, he'd ask you far more questions. You'd want to turn him to stone to shut him up. Depending on how I feel about him that day, I might support your decision. He can be even more irritating than me."

"I find that hard to believe."

But he heard a touch of precious humor in the wary statement. She was revealing a sincere desire to enjoy another human's company if she could, all while she was keeping her distance, obviously ready for it to turn into a confrontation. Though he was glad for her curiosity, deducing what she'd faced while here, he was amazed she was still reaching for that connection. Perhaps after being here so long on her own without human company, it was a compulsion that couldn't be denied, bursting free and insisting on seeking as much pleasure from the connection as could be found before it ended. Or had to be ended.

He pushed that dark thought aside as she answered him. "It is deeper than just a physical attachment of their body to my head. It is as if the rest of them is...inside me. All through me. They became part of me..."

"After the curse" was implied in the trailing sentence. It reminded him that the challenges she'd faced on the island, as difficult and dangerous as they'd been, probably couldn't hold a candle to what had happened to bring her here. But he heard the warning in her tone. She was prepared to draw away if he crossed the line into painful, intimate areas he didn't have the right to know. Yet.

"Sounds like they keep you from feeling too alone."

She swallowed, a subtle noise that betrayed emotion. Her voice drew farther away, as if she'd moved up to the rafters to perch. But she didn't leave.

"When I dance, there are times I feel like a snake myself, the way my arms and legs, my whole body, moves. And the snakes move with me, as if they are as influenced by my rhythm as I am by theirs."

"You dance?"

"Sometimes. I enjoy it. Particularly when the moon is full and all the creatures of the island sing. Sometimes I lay down on the earth so the snakes can stretch out on a rock or the warm earth as they would do if they were free of me. I know they wish for that sometimes. What creature doesn't wish for freedom? But they are tolerant of me, and we only have the occasional argument anymore."

He thought of the demonic picture where the snakes were sinking their fangs into her flesh. "Was it bad, in the beginning? Getting along with them," he added quickly, so she knew he wasn't asking about other things, probably much harder to discuss.

"In the beginning, when we understood one another far less, we fought. They bit me, and I would seek to pull them from my head." Her voice held regret. "I severed one from me with a sharp knife, when I didn't understand. The pain of it struck me unconscious. I was feverish and unable to rise for several days. Another snake grew back during that time. Only when he was fully mature did the agony cease. That snake was Earthson. I never knew the name of the one I killed."

She took a breath. "But I understood then that they are part of me, and offered gifts to the Snake Goddess and Asclepius to ask their forgiveness and that of the snake spirit. It took quite a while for the others to learn to trust me again, but not as long as it might have taken were they not in my head and able to understand my ignorance, as well as my true contrition."

She'd come closer again, returning to the chair. From a rhythmic sound, he realized she was likely stroking one of the snakes as she spoke. "When they bit me, it caused them a proportionate amount of pain also. So it only happens now if they get frightened or startled, when it's unthinking instinct. We've learned to live within our limits and discover other strengths together."

"Like your wings. I'm grateful for your wings. I would have had a nasty fall without those."

She returned to eating her fruit. He wondered if she was offering pieces to the snakes. The silence wasn't uncomfortable. He didn't sense she'd stopped because he'd said something offensive. While she seemed to enjoy talking, she wouldn't be used to doing it for prolonged periods, at least not to humans. But maybe she was worried she was becoming too friendly, sending him the wrong message. Perhaps...

"Do you like it when I talk, my lady? Do you enjoy that?"

Another thoughtful silence, the kind that seemed to precede almost every question he asked. "Yes. So far. You ask things no one else has."

"You can ask me to be silent when you tire of talk. I'm fine with being quiet." Most of his life he'd preferred it, because when he spoke, it was usually to lie, whether he was covering for his mother with the guidance counselor or social services, or convincing a small time drug dealer why he could trust JP with more info about his network. "But I'd love to hear your voice, talking about any topic you choose."

Chewing. Swallowing. "At the temple, there was a senior priestess who wanted us to be silent unless commanded to speak. When she was not around, the younger girls, we would whisper and laugh. The priestess in charge of us, Klotho, she didn't mind. She told us we must be demure at festivals and perform the rituals properly, but when not performing our duties, it was acceptable to laugh. She told us Athena would enjoy hearing our laughter."

A rasping sound suggested Medusa was running her claws over the table, hard enough to betray some deeper emotions. Now he knew the patterned grooves were not merely decoration, but a tapestry of contemplation or agitation, like now.

"What do you have in this odd carrying bag?" she said abruptly. "The weight of it is likely what toppled you off the cliff."

"I've had to climb with it before. It's usually better to have it with me than not." He found the pack by feel and pulled it over to her chair. When he unzipped it, her hands brushed his away and she took it from him. He heard it land on the table with a thump and then the sound of the zipper moving forward and back.

"How remarkable. Like tiny teeth."

As he imagined her peering at it curiously, he bit back a smile. "There are many pockets," he said.

More zippers were opened and snaps popped free. A different kind of noise told him she was loosening the shoe string style lacing along the back spine, the ties he'd used to sheathe the sword. He'd leaned the weapon in a corner of her abode.

Olivia's daughter had a doll with plenty of zippers, ties and buttons, a teaching aid to increase finger dexterity and help her ultimately learn how to dress herself. Within a week, she'd torn the dress and lost the laces to the doll's shoes so the toy was permanently barefoot.

His lady proved she could be an equal force for chaos and destruction. A rattling and a shift of the canvas across the table surface, followed by an erratic thump-thump-thump noise, told him she'd upended the opened pack and was shaking out the contents. As items fell, clattered, clinked and rolled away, he masked a wince, thinking of his careful packing job to ensure he made the most of every inch of space. He heard a couple of hisses, as if the snakes had been startled by the emergence of so many items. Or something had bounced off of one or more of their heads.

"Odd garments," she remarked.

He'd brought one pair of jeans and a couple T-shirts with the shorts, in case he hopped back through a portal and needed to blend. More for his comfort than anything else, since a man in a Grecian tunic in the middle of Times Square would barely elicit a blink from jaded New Yorkers.

"If you hand me what you're looking at, I can explain more about it. If you wish."

A lot of debate had happened over the modern items that went into the pack. Maddock had agreed John should bring some things to intrigue her. He'd seen no danger to the space-time continuum from a pair of jeans or Nikes. On the flip side, they'd agreed that firearms were a no-go.

She was a myth, yes, but she was also part of a historical time period. Whether this place was real or a legend in a dimension slightly off kilter with theirs, an advanced weapon could change the course of human history, since war ironically carved much of the shape of civilization.

The jeans landed in his lap, a mute request for him to explain as he'd offered. "These are called jeans. A form of pants, trousers. And that, yeah, that's underwear, to go, well, under them."

She took them back from him. He imagined she was testing the elastic of his boxers like a kid playing with the stretchiness of a rubber band, or fingering the holes of the fly. He contained another chuckle because he didn't want her to think he was laughing at her, but he was charmed by her innocent and uncontained interest.

He heard a rushing noise, like a small rain stick. "You've found the seed packets."

"Seeds?"

"Yeah. Don't open them until we can plant them, because some of them are pretty small. We thought some plants from my time and place might grow pretty well here. Figured you raised a lot of your own food and might appreciate some new stuff."

"That is very...thoughtful." Then her tone changed from guarded pleasure to borderline threat. "This knife is not for food preparation."

She didn't hand it to him. As he heard the military grade weapon leaving the scabbard, he quelled his instinct to reach for it, a protective gesture she might misinterpret as an aggressive one. The blade was honed to a lethal sharpness.

"It would be handy for cutting up an overcooked steak, but you're right. It's a pretty good throwing knife, but its best use is close quarters fighting. The sword and knife were intended to prove my ability to protect you if needed."

"I trained in the warrior arts at the temple," she said stiffly, not mollified. "All of us did. I have continued my training here. As I have told you, I am quite competent."

"Then it would be my honor to fight at your side or back if the need comes, my lady. You can never have too many hands in a fight. Easier to call up a reserve when you need him than to find yourself outnumbered. Right?"

"Hmm." She moved on. "A book of scribblings."

"A notebook. Those are portal calculations. Tells me where on the island to find them and how to open them. Portals can exist in a lot of unlikely places."

"Portals to go back to your world. Or to let others through." She surged up and away, prowling around the room with agitated movements. "So you can outnumber me."

"If that was the case, my lady," he said steadily, "Why would I tell you about them? You're holding my knife and my eyes are blindfolded.

Why would I reveal all my options while you have such advantages over me?"

He was thankful for his battle-honed instincts, because she moved so swiftly and silently he never heard her, even with the augmented senses. He caught her wrist as the knife plunged down. Twisting it to make her drop it, he couldn't maintain the hold, both because he had no interest in hurting her and because she left him no choice. She wrested free and leaped back from him with a swirl of movement he would have liked to see.

The grace and effectiveness of the defensive move underlined her abilities, yet he noted her movements had been as deliberately controlled as his own.

"That is why you would tell me," she spat. "Because removing an advantage does not make you less dangerous. You seek to win my confidence with trinkets." A thump and clattering told him she'd swept a pile of the pack items from the table. "That is half the battle in overcoming a foe."

"Perhaps," he said quietly. "Has anyone attempted it before?"

"It was only a matter of time, since so many other strategies have failed. No one comes to this island without a strategy to kill or capture me. I ask nothing but to be left alone. Why will you all not leave me be?"

The sudden harsh despair was meant for her enemies, not for him. She didn't yet know the difference. He told himself that as he swallowed the shards of glass her words made him feel. He could only answer for himself, not the others whose purpose in tormenting her he despised, and regretted not being able to prevent.

"I've traveled a long way to meet and be with you, my lady. During my months of preparation, I was far more worried about how to make my company bearable to you than in planning how to overcome you. At least not that way."

"What way do you mean?" she demanded.

"I told you," he said patiently. "I'm here to claim you for my own."

"Ridiculous," she scoffed. "And I am no one's slave."

"I think you know that's not what I mean. Else you would have already turned me into rock. And I would deserve it."

Something else was puzzling him. She could have tried and likely succeeded in damaging him during their scuffle, but she hadn't. He knew when his opponent had every intention of doing violence. That heat had pumped off of her, yet she'd called it back. He'd felt the same thing when she first dropped him in the ocean, before it had morphed into something cautiously playful.

There was rage and darkness there, a violence pretty close to the surface, but she kept reining it back. He didn't want to use up whatever meager bit of luck that afforded him, but as the stillness between them became more weighted, he wanted to reach out and close his hand on hers. Shift that grip to her delicate wrist and let her feel how he could hold her, touch her. She hadn't rejected his words outright, after all.

Or he was deluding himself. His reasons for being here might seem mad and suspicious, but an insane diversion was better than no diversion at all.

"You might still deserve to be turned into a rock."

He grinned. "That may be true. Will you come back and sit with me? Tell me what else about my pack interests you? I tried to bring what would amuse or intrigue you. I don't want any of it to cause you worry. Any item you think is a threat you can take and hide as you wish."

He'd prefer her not to destroy the notebook, but he'd memorized several of the calculations in the event he lost it. He could still open a portal. For both of them, if the need arose. He'd done an inventory of the boats on the beach and concluded several things from their rate of decay and size. The attempts to harm her happened far too frequently, and they'd been sending greater numbers each time.

He put the sobering thoughts aside for now, because she returned to the chair, evidenced by the closeness of her scent, the brush of her bare soles on the floor, and a creak of movement from the chair. Further sounds told him she was pushing around the remaining items on the table. "Why do you have these?"

He reached out and found the satiny strips dangling near his face. After he touched them, she took them away. The whisper of fabric suggested she was sliding them between her knuckles, testing the silken feel. "Those are for your hair, my lady. Or to adorn your clothes, or wrists or throat. However you wish to use them. You can also tie your hair back with—"

"I know what ribbons are, John Pierce," she said with a touch of impatience. "These are lovely. I meant, what are their practical purpose?"

"Their purpose is to please you. Same reason I brought the two—"

"Books." He heard the riffle of the pages. "Soft, thin books with pictures."

"They're what we call magazines. They can show you more about my world."

One was a women's magazine, the kind filled with fashion, beauty and home decorating tips, as well as a handful of recipes and celebrity news. He and Lot had picked it up in the grocery store.

"This one," Lot said. "The home decorating tips are focused on outdoor living spaces. She'll find that useful."

The female shoppers who'd seen him and Lot standing shoulder to shoulder, trying to figure out the right one, had been helpful and amused. Lara, a divorcee with a yoga-toned body, had told them the magazine they chose was her favorite escape treat. "I learn a little bit about everything without being too serious about any of it," she'd said.

Lot had charmed her into dinner, and probably afterward into revealing the sculpted body under her designer jeans and trendy tunic top.

The other magazine was a thick Time-Life edition, *The Century in Pictures*. The issue had been created at the end of the millennium. Maddock had thought magazines the perfect conglomeration of info that would initiate discussion about JP's world, prove he came from a different time and, most importantly, increase the chance she'd expect different things from him.

"Those are yours," he added.

"Another gift."

"Yes. I can read the text for you whenever you're curious about what the pictures mean." Maddock had said he could give her the words to the translation spell to help her read them—if she knew how to read her own language—but JP liked the idea of the more intimate interaction.

She paused. "There is more in your...notebook. Not just scribblings. What is the rest?"

"Quotes I want to remember. Pictures of my family. My parents. They died some years ago, but I like to have their picture with me. Another is of my dog, Ferdinand. He was a German shepherd. Went everywhere with me and died last year. I miss him, and my parents. I think about them every day."

He could hear her paging through the notebook, stopping as she perhaps saw the things he was mentioning.

"These pictures...they are not like paintings."

He took a few minutes to explain photographs. After that she examined his toothbrush and toothpaste and asked about them. In return, he learned she used a finger wrapped in cloth and herbs like laurel or mastic gum, a sap from the mastic tree, to keep her teeth clean. He suspected that was one of those fragrances clinging pleasantly to her he hadn't been able to identify. Thinking of it lingering around her mouth drew his mind to the idea of tasting it firsthand.

He had no idea what was in his toothpaste, something she found peculiar.

"How do you know it will not harm you?"

"Well, the company that sells it has to guarantee that it won't."

"And you trust them?"

He chuckled. "Well, more or less. It's one of those things you don't think about too much."

She had him explain a handful of other things in the pack, including a straight razor and sharpening strap. While not exactly what her people used for shaving, it was close enough his explanation of it seemed to satisfy her.

"What is this?" She dropped the thin wrapped bar in his lap.

His lips curved. "I brought this to test a theory. To see if a woman of your time would like it as much as the women of mine."

The eye branding, the decision to devote himself to her on her home turf, had been based on his belief that her heart had to be won in her reality, not his. But he'd seen no harm in bringing a few things that could increase his chances. Feeling her attention on him, he opened the wrapper on the chocolate bar. He was glad for the mild temperatures of the island and the insulated liner in his backpack that had kept it from melting too much. Though as he thought what he could do with melted chocolate and her fair skin, he was besieged by some very distracting images.

Sight wasn't necessary to experience color and wonder, after all.

When he offered it, she managed to take the candy without touching his hand. He'd noted she'd avoided most incidental touch, except for their initial meeting when she'd scraped the claw down his hand. He knew all about sensory deprivation, how it could heighten the desire to have the senses fed. He was usually the one doing the depriving, rather than the other way around, but he was understanding better how his subs could reach a level of hunger for touch that had them straining against the bindings he'd put upon them, their bodies quivering with eagerness. He'd pretty much be willing to break someone's arm for the chance to lay his hand upon her arm, her face, her slim throat.

He counseled himself to patience as he heard the faint rattle of paper and smelled the aroma as she took a nibble. It had melted enough she'd either have to use a finger to scoop it off the paper or lick it directly.

Imagining her tongue sliding through the chocolate, or her sucking on a coated finger, added to that hunger exponentially.

"The snakes do not care for this," she said.

"How about you?"

A pause. "I'm glad they do not care for it."

She rose. "You will stay the night here so I will know your whereabouts. I will stay elsewhere."

"I won't drive a lady from her home." He shook his head. "I meant what I wrote in the sand. I'm here to serve you. I'll climb back down and stay on the beach where you can see me. If you want, you can fly me there and drop me on the beach so I get there all the sooner. Though I would take it as a kindness if you didn't interpret that literally. I'd prefer to *land* there instead of falling."

She said nothing, so he stood. "Just give me a second to repack my bag, minus any items you prefer to keep yourself. Including the magazines and ribbons."

Her answer was a long time in coming. "Very well. I will return you to the beach. I will keep the knife and your notebook. And the chocolate."

CHAPTER FOUR

*S*he did land him on the beach, but she didn't stay for further conversation. After making him take off and hand over the blindfold once again, she left him with a curt, "Stay in this area, where I can see you throughout the night. Else I will find you and show my displeasure."

He didn't doubt she was ready to dispatch him as a threat the second he proved himself one. What was curious was her almost palpable wish that he not be one, so she didn't have to do so.

Lore had painted her as cynical, bitter and guarded at the best; bloodthirsty, cruel and savage at the worst. So far, he'd seen nothing but a woman who'd learned to protect herself and was slow to trust anyone, but who was curious enough about someone new and different not to kill him outright. Her guarded nature hadn't surprised him, but many other things had. Despite an abundance of justifiable caution, she had those delightful quick moments where she lowered her defenses enough to laugh, to play, and to investigate things that intrigued her.

Was it a unique response to him? Could the bond he'd felt with her for so long be two-way? She hadn't argued with him when he'd told her she knew what he meant about coming to claim her.

But lack of dissent didn't mean agreement. She could think him insane. His theory sounded like a romance novel, grounded more in wishful thinking than reality. However well things seemed to be going at certain moments, the thread of her trust was tenuous. Her parting words made that clear. And he couldn't forget the message of those boats and crumbling piles of stone.

It was far more likely her reasons for tolerating him had to do with missing pieces of the full story. There were too many things unsaid, things that he didn't yet understand.

"Remember," Maddock had admonished him, like a hundred times. "Every single thing we've gleaned about her has come from poetry, myth and crackpot speculation. You won't know the full truth until you're there."

"And by then it will be too late," Lot had said. "Just like getting married."

JP shook his head, though he was glad for the lift in his spirits the recalled banter brought him. He wouldn't trade anything for finally being here with her, but he did miss his two closest friends. And he hurt for the darkness and despair he'd felt from his lady too many times today. Unrolling his mat on the sand, he laid down and considered the puzzle of her and the wonder of a sky full of so many stars. Most of his last ops and the time he'd spent with Maddock had been in more urban settings. He actually fucking loved the quiet here. The tranquility.

When at last he fell asleep, she came back to him in dreams. He was still on the beach, stretched out on his mat. As she knelt by him, she woke him by resting her palm on his face, hiding his eyes until he woke and clasped her wrist, telling her he was awake enough to remember to keep his eyes shut around her.

"It's difficult," he told her. "I want to look upon you more than I've ever wanted to look at any woman." Her wrist was so slim, her skin soft, the pulse beneath beating against his hold like a tiny heart.

"The dream is better than the reality," she breathed, so close to his mouth. He imagined the fullness of her lips giving way beneath the firmer press of his. He tightened his grip on her wrist, wanting to draw her closer, to prove her wrong, but she slipped away, back into the fog of his dreams.

"You cannot stay, John Pierce. You will turn my heart to stone."

At sunrise, he was alone, with only that disturbing comment drifting through his mind. Pushing up on his elbows, he ran a hand over his face and then felt a jolt. She had been here. Maybe not to touch him as she had in his dream, but she'd left several fresh fruits and a small bowl of seeds and nuts mixed with bits of dried bread, like a type of trail mix. There was also the surprise of a covered pitcher of goat's milk.

He'd brought some dried rations, one of the things in the pack he'd explained to her. She'd found them fascinating, in a different way from the pure curiosity invoked by the magazines or chocolate. Ways to preserve and store food were understandably a more practical priority. He set aside powdered eggs in favor of her offering, though, and enjoyed a sense of optimism about the day ahead. While his welcome wasn't on a guaranteed footing, she was treating him somewhat as a guest.

That is, when she wasn't thinking she might have to kill him.

After his breakfast, he decided to go in search of the goats. He found a dozen of them on the northern side of the island, all of them friendly. One or two kept him company for a while as he discovered their paths that took him to further fresh water sources and grazing areas. He saw more deer. While they were shier than the goats, he noticed a brief hesitation when they saw him, as if they expected him to be someone else and only bounded away when they realized he wasn't. It made sense. There was only one human inhabitant they were accustomed to seeing regularly. But it confirmed his theory that she wasn't hunting game on the island, for the animals would be more fearful if she was.

He also found several more of her garden sites. She was growing grapes, vegetables, and fruit and nut trees, the source of his breakfast. Legume vines were staked out in neat rows. A rough lean-to served as a garden shed, with a few tools and one bucket. She didn't have a wheelbarrow or cart.

As he started to consider the materials he had on hand for that, like what the forest could provide and other items salvageable from the beach wrecks, he thought of another project to pursue.

He didn't want to have easy access to her home until she felt comfortable with that, but when it happened—when, not if—he wanted a quicker, less perilous way to get there that wouldn't impose on her. The spikes and clips for rock climbing would make it easier, but not less arduous or fast.

Since he envisioned a stirrup-ladder system of sorts, on his way back to the beach, he stripped a few vines, plucked some grasses and tested tangles of tough, whip like branches for suitability. He had an overabundance of survivalist training, though he'd never actually created such a thing. He might end up cracking his head open testing it, but that was a concern for another day.

He realized he kept thinking of this as a long term op, but was that the right word for spending the rest of his life in seclusion on an island with a fascinating woman? If so, it was the best job he'd ever had. Even if she did end up turning him to stone.

Once back on the beach, he foraged in the wreckage of the boats for things to create a wheelbarrow or cart. He'd brought a small group of tools in his pack to help him build things. Surprisingly, she hadn't kept those, but, except for the knife, she hadn't kept things that would help him with his own needs, even though she could have made good use of them. Another clue to the kind of person she was.

As he started to pull apart one boat where the wood was the least rotted, he saw she'd done a good job stripping the interior. Since most of the wrecks were open skiffs that had come from nearby islands, they'd traveled light. But he did note markings, faded paint that told him the owner had decorated the vessel and made it his own. If the boat was still here, the owner had not returned home.

When she turned someone to stone, did they crumble over time and become part of the sand? His gaze slid to some of the piles of rock in disturbingly uniform sizes, scattered near the boats. Was the beach a garden of bone dust?

He didn't flinch from the thought. He knew firsthand what a person under siege would do to survive. Based on the story he knew, she had no reason to retain even a scrap of compassion for her fellow humans. Yet she had. It was evident in her behavior toward him. Or had he arrived when her isolation had become too much, enough she'd been willing to for once give someone a chance to stay awhile?

Perhaps she toyed with all her visitors this way, obtaining the latest news and some conversation from them before she dispatched them. He might be on a countdown clock and not realize it. She didn't seem that duplicitous, but he couldn't ignore the subtle signs he'd seen, the violence and hints of darkness, evidence of a person who'd been alone too long without her own kind, driven here by trauma. Her moral compass might no longer fit a predictable pattern.

Where was she? Having had only a taste of her company, he wanted much more. But it was possible he'd have to dig in for quite a while. It might be days before she approached him again. The thought frustrated him, but that was why he was doing what he was doing now, to head off that unpleasant outcome. He'd keep coming up with things like the wheelbarrow to interest her, draw her closer again. He could use her curiosity to both their advantages.

By the time the day started to wane, he'd worn himself out, but he was pleased with the fruits of his labors. He'd created a rudimentary wheelbarrow and cart, both useful for transporting foodstuffs and other things she gathered. He'd repaired a couple buckets he'd found on the boats.

He'd also created a necklace of wildflowers, just for the pleasure of giving it to her and thinking about her putting it around her neck. Maybe the reason she didn't let him get too close to her wasn't all because of mistrust. When she moved, he occasionally heard the snakes hiss or slide across her skin. The peculiar rasping sound had taken him a while to identify, but a day spent wishing for a woman to appear gave a man plenty of time to think about her. Maybe she didn't want them to take a piece out of him if he got too close. Until she wanted them to do that, that is.

One of the things he'd also done today was plucked up enough rocks to section off a portion of the beach into a sparring ring. He'd use that court to practice his own fighting skills. Eventually he might be able to talk her into trying it out with him. He'd enjoyed their little wrangle in the ocean, but it had whetted his appetite to match skills.

As he rinsed off in the ocean, he considered trying to climb back up to her home and initiate another conversation, but that was his frustration talking. After the day's exertions, he didn't have enough energy for that kind of climb. Plus, intuition said to let her come to him. She needed to feel comfortable around him in her own time and way. But it was fucking hard, when he'd had such a tempting taste of her the night before.

After he ate dinner from his rations and the remainder of her morning gift, he worked under the stars, testing the strength of the vines and branches, playing with different options for his ladder system, until he tired enough to lay down and go to sleep. He wished he'd at least felt her proximity today as he'd done before. He expected she'd kept a watch on him from her distant perch, but it wasn't nearly close enough.

"Good night, my lady," he said to the empty sky and whispering surf. "I hope you'll seek my company tomorrow."

She was in his dreams again, and this time she was not in shadows. She stood naked by the shore, her back to him, her golden skin bathed by moonlight. When he came up behind her, he saw a slithering movement within her dark, silken locks, a pair of gleaming eyes, but he would never hesitate to touch her. He never wanted her to think anything could keep him from it. As he wound his arms around her body and pressed himself against her, he was also naked.

He cupped her breast and molded his other palm over her hip as the snakes slid over his shoulders, down under his arms and to her front, winding around his wrists, binding the two of them together again. Did they do this in dreams to remind him of what he believed so strongly, to reassure him? It would be nice to think so.

She made a sound of quiet pleasure, and turned her head toward his, as if for a kiss. He met her gaze. It was green like the ocean...for a blink. Suddenly he was gazing into a snake's eyes, slit-pupiled and focused on prey. Her lips curled back, baring fangs and a forked tongue. The hissing was as loud as a hundred tea kettles in his head, and pain exploded in his chest.

He wasn't with her any more. He was back on a road outside Kabul, and the Jeep ahead was immersed in flame. He tried to lift his weapon, to help defend the soldiers against the crowd of insurgents leaping out of the ditches on either side of the road, but he couldn't. Looking down, he realized he was turned to stone and could do nothing. He was helpless, screaming inside a sarcophagus of rock as they shot the soldiers, as Medusa stood in their midst, eyes frightened, her hands reaching out to him...

And of course the kid had to be there. The kid was always there, even though that wasn't the op where JP had met him. His dark eyes stared at John as the life died out of them and blood trickled from his slack mouth. But his hands were still reaching for John, grabbing and holding on, getting tighter and tighter...

He surged out of the dream to find it was dawn, the sun emerging from the horizon. He was breathing hard, sweat making his slick back gritty with sand. Christ. Damn flashback dreams. He hated his own head mind-fucking him, and it pissed him off worse that it had drawn Medusa into it.

Shucking off the shorts, he plunged into the water, ducking beneath the surface of wave after wave to wash off the grit, sweat and dream. For good measure, he swam against the current a mile and back to prove he was stronger than those memories. Strong enough for her, for himself. For his friends. All two of them.

When he'd proven himself an exceptional asset to the DEA at such a young age, eventually that had led to South America, the CIA, and him going deep cover on a drug cartel lord. He'd become one of his fucking personal bodyguards for months. Being built like a tank had its uses, and trusted bodyguards were around to hear pretty much everything.

But then came the day his op crossed with the mission of a Navy SEAL team. Everybody on the ground was fucked that day, because, as too often happened, the top brass didn't communicate with each other.

When the gunfire had started and explosions rocked the compound, he'd snatched up Manuel, a four-year-old kid playing freaking Legos on the carpet. He'd headed for the nearest and safest escape route, but the SEAL team breached the compound a breath later.

The kid was what had saved JP's life. Lot had pulled his gun muzzle up when he and JP came face to face.

"DEA," JP had said shortly, to save a lengthy explanation of his shared status between DEA, CIA and other special teams that had no clear reporting connection. Plus, since he identified Lot as a SEAL, he figured saying CIA might get him shot anyway.

Lot's eyes had widened a fraction and then the drug cartel's rein-forcements arrived. He and JP, still holding the screaming kid, dove for cover. A firestorm escalated into a fucking tsunami. Lot covered his six as they crawled and fought their way out of there. During the retreat, one of the SEALs was knocked out by the explosion. JP hefted him onto his shoulder while keeping the clinging Manuel under his arm. It wasn't until they all got out of there that he realized he'd taken three bullets.

Unfortunately, a fourth had caught the kid. It turned his tiny gut into a swamp of internal bleeding and ruptured organs. Nothing they could do.

Sloshing out onto shore, JP dropped to his hands and knees, breathing hard. The speed and exertion of his swim had left his arms and legs shaking, but better to be shaking from that than from that fucking dream. The only thing worse than that kid's empty eyes and slack face were the moments before he'd died. Ever since Bambi, the unanswered cry of a kid for his dead mother was the most heart-shredding sound in the universe.

It was as he was staring at the ground he saw the shadow. Medusa was above him. One wing was only half articulated, but the silhouette of the other revealed barbed hooks on the top and bottom joints, as he suspected. Her body was a graceful, elongated shape printed against the sand, her trailing feet crossing and uncrossing like cloth fluttering in the wind as her hovering shifted her up and down.

His gaze moved up the wet packed ground to the silhouette of her head. Long locks of hair flowed in the wind. Several things weren't hair, but snakes. They bobbed and weaved in upraised positions around her, reminding him of a picture Olivia's daughter had drawn of the sun, with squiggles of bright yellow representing the sunbeams.

His lady as the sun. He liked that idea.

The shadow disappeared from his view as she dropped down behind him, so close her feet straddled his calves. It was the closest she'd been to him for more than a blink, and he stayed where he was, heart in his throat as he rested on his elbows. A claw trailed over his shoulder blade, along his spine, to the rise of his buttock. Her touch shifted, pulling the claw away so he felt the brush of fingertips instead against his lower back.

"You are acting..." The word she used didn't translate, which Maddock had warned him might happen on occasion if the derivation or meaning was vastly different in their two languages.

"Sorry. I didn't get that. I'm acting what?"

She found another word that matched, one that hit him in the solar plexus. "Haunted," she said. "You are...well?"

"Yeah. Just a bad dream. I get them sometimes."

"So do I. It is hard to wake alone when they happen. You have a fine form, John Pierce. It is a pleasure to look upon. I've left you some breakfast."

After that remarkable amalgamation of sentences, she was aloft, winging away. He took the foolish chance, lifting his gaze to watch her wings pump and carry her up over the trees, back toward her home or other places on the island currently beyond his reach. She was gone so fast he couldn't internalize many details beyond the fluttering of her short tunic over tantalizing curves of flesh, and one outstretched arm, a snake coiling around it from biceps to elbow.

"A fine form." If he'd been looking for a way to dispel the lingering effects of the dream, that had helped. He was half-hard merely from the light stroke of her fingertips. He sighed, dropping his face into his hands.

"You know, the Greeks found a small penis aesthetically pleasing," Lot had said, a couple weeks before he came here.

"Probably the Greek men, who had to take them up the ass, so they preferred them smaller," JP retorted. "They weren't known for being that interested in their women, except for dowries and heirs."

"A misconception, like much of history, which gets rewritten with every new political perspective," Maddock tossed in absently. "Pederasty was an accepted practice, but sex between adult males was more problematic. I'm sure there were just as many men who loved their wives as we see now."

"Well, all that aside, if the women liked small penises, JP's going to be out of luck." Lot scoffed. "She'll run screaming at the sight of that beast."

Apparently not. He managed a grin. While she had flown off pretty quick, he didn't think that was the reason. Maybe she'd liked touching him as much as he'd liked her touch. Regardless, it was better than coffee to kick him in the ass and get him going.

After eating a quick breakfast of her goat cheese and a tasty crusty bread, he went back at the ladder idea full force. By midday, he had two sizeable lengths of rope made out of natural materials. He'd fashioned stirrup loops every two feet. Figuring it was sound enough to test it, he followed one of the goat paths to a cliff face similar to the one that held her home to try out his invention.

It took some tweaking, a series of curses, a couple of short falls and a lot of sweat, but once he got it working, he then worked out how he'd draw it up and down like a blind to conceal it, whether he was at the bottom or top of the ladder.

Pleased with the day's work, he took a swig of water from his canteen while he sat on the top edge of the cliff, his feet dangling. When a black snake slithered up to him, he glanced down, canteen frozen at his lips as the creature unconcernedly did its smooth zigzag movement across his thighs and continued on its way, as if he was no more an impediment than the rock itself. It was the eighth snake he'd encountered while working along the vertical or horizontal surfaces of these rocks, so apparently it was a favored sunning area for them.

One had bitten his shoe, but only when he'd inadvertently stepped on it. Otherwise, they were uniformly nonaggressive. Some were more curious about him than others, but for the most part, he was ignored. Maybe they were channeling their mistress.

He suppressed the wry thought, the mild irritation. She'd been watching him for the past hour now. Ever since he'd sensed her arrival, he'd been talking about what he was doing as he did it, a one-sided conversation. Now, though, he stretched out on his back, his feet still dangling, and closed his eyes to enjoy the sun and quiet.

As a place to end up for the rest of one's life, this one didn't suck.

Something small bounced off his head, and he opened his eyes as it hit his lap. Straightening, he saw a small crimson berry. It was followed by a small shower of them, too targeted to be caused by a stray wind loosening fruit from a tree or an animal randomly doing the same. He caught the suppressed laugh he was beginning to anticipate.

"You are teasing me, snake-girl," he declared. "I've spoken to you for the past hour, and not a word in return. Now, you're pelting me with fruit."

A long silence, as if the nickname had given her pause. She didn't comment on it, but he thought he detected a rattled quality to her tone, despite her casual words. "Not at all. I am merely offering you a snack. Taste."

He estimated she was about twenty feet up, screened in the forest behind him.

He put one of the berries in his mouth and sampled. It was tart, juicy. Good.

"Sure you're not trying poison to get rid of me?" he asked.

"It has crossed my mind. You are my most persistent visitor. In a few hours, you will have been here the longest of any of my visitors. Or rather, the one who lived the longest while here." She went silent, as if she hadn't meant to take it in that dark direction. Not wanting her to talk herself into flying away, he changed it.

"Did you find the wheelbarrow I left near your garden?"

"Yes. It moves fairly well. The back left wheel is somewhat stiff. I adjusted it and it is fine now. A useful thing."

It had been on the tip of his tongue to say he'd fix it, but she'd anticipated him. "You've had to figure out how to do a lot of things yourself here."

"We had to know how to repair many things at the temple, though there were men who came in and did some of the things it was considered more appropriate for men to do. Things they thought we weren't strong or clever enough to be taught to do for ourselves."

"If only they could see you now. You'd teach them a thing or two."

"I had no quarrel with men doing certain things and women doing certain things, if both sides respected those skills. It is being treated as if...I was not capable, that is now annoying, when I think back on it."

"It wasn't then?"

"I was different then. A child who saw the world a different way and did not see the offense in others' assumptions. Did not see the harm it could do until it was...harmful. I do not understand why you are here, John Pierce."

They kept coming back to that. It was obviously the puzzle that troubled her the most. And he couldn't blame her. He'd said she was shrewd. He was telling her portions of the truth and she was seeing the holes, not the whole.

He frowned, because he'd promised her honesty. But he couldn't give her an answer he couldn't quite explain to himself. Right?

"You did tell me your stated purpose," she continued, before he had to repeat it. "But if you seduce me and leave after that, you meant only to seduce, not to claim."

"That is not my intent, my lady, and to imply it insults me as much as it does you. While lying with you would be a wondrous experience, it's a long way to come just for that."

"Indeed," she said dryly. "But if you truly meant the second part of your goal, to claim my heart, to what end? You are a capable man, a soldier. You wish to languish on an island for the rest of your life in the company of one other human being? I am here because my options are limited. Yours are not."

"If this is where you desire to stay for the rest of your life, my lady, yes, this is where I wish to be. If you don't, I'll follow you where you want to go, and pledge my life to protect and serve you. Perhaps, in time, you'd want to follow me through a portal, to a different world, where things are different."

"So that is your end goal," she said, with a note of grim triumph. "To take me somewhere unfamiliar, where I do not have the advantages of known terrain and resources."

"My lady," he said patiently. "You can keep trying to discover plots against you behind every word I speak. I understand why you're doing it and, in your position, I would do exactly the same. But I will make you a promise. Should I ever break it, I will stand in one spot and willingly meet your gaze so you may end me."

He'd injected the resolve in his voice and hoped she heard it loud and clear. "I will never speak an untruth to you. I may not tell you certain things until our relationship advances, because in my judgment they would be misinterpreted because of our level of trust. But I'll never lie to you. I can tell you now, tomorrow, the next day and forever, that neither I nor anyone involved in sending me here have plans to harm, kill or capture you, or compel you to do anything against your will."

"No one commits their life to another without ever having met them."

"Had you ever met Athena before you committed to be her priestess?"

Silence. Then, "That is different. Service to a Goddess, to a divine purpose, is different than committing one's life to another person."

"I committed my life to an ideal that I found out wasn't what I thought it was, but I valued its underlying truth enough that I stuck with it for twenty years."

"Underlying truth? What do you mean?" A trio of leaves floated past him and over the edge, caught on the wind. She'd dropped out of the trees and was perched on a jutting rock behind him, about five feet away. Progress.

"The underlying truth that I was protecting something worth defending, doing something worth doing. Something right. That wasn't always true, but by having people committed to that ideal, they can keep it pointed toward that truth way more often than it would if they weren't there."

It still had been knocked off true north more times than he wanted to think about.

A scraping sound against the stone. Maybe she was running her talons along it like she had the table in her home. "You are interesting, John Pierce. You speak to me in a way no one ever has. Even...before, but I was young, then. Silly. I'm not sure I would have been as interested in these subjects then as I am now."

"Well, when I was nineteen I was recruited by the DEA as an informant, which eventually turned into me training to be an agent and working undercover to get a foothold in a drug cartel. Eventually that morphed into me working for a special operations branch that worked in the shadow of the CIA." He waved a hand, anticipating her snagging on the terms. "Basically, our government has different divisions to enforce local laws, protect us from foreign enemies, et cetera. That's what the DEA and CIA are. Which sounds great in theory and, in my deluded brain during those early days, I imagined myself single-handedly saving everyone in the world."

That thought stirred the unpleasant memories, but he'd learned to accept those spikes and move on without letting them bog him down. Mostly. Lot and Maddock had helped him with that, helped him find the part of himself buried deep inside that could open up to her now, be the man who could smile, laugh and enjoy this island with her. Forever.

"When we grow up—if we grow up—we start finding things other than ourselves way more fascinating. Thank God."

"Which one?"

He chuckled. "Well, I only have the one. That's not to say I'm denying you or anyone else your own gods. It's just simpler for me to have one deity to bitch at when things don't go my way. Or to thank for saving my stupid ass so many times."

She'd shifted closer. When he leaned back, bracing his arms, she stopped. There was maybe a foot between them. He had to remind himself to breathe.

"It's okay," he said. "I'm not going to turn around. Would you touch me, my lady? I liked the feel of your hands on the beach."

"All of it?"

He wasn't sure what she meant, and then he thought of the scrape of the claws. The carefully guarded tone and the question revealed the truth to him, which he realized should have been obvious. She wasn't wearing a weapon like bear claw knuckles. The claws were hers. She had talons extending over her still human fingers. Like Wolverine, only curved. He'd have to tell her about that. Not right now, though.

"Yeah. All of it." At the weighted pause, he spoke again. "Touch me, Medusa. However you want. I won't change position. I promise. How long has it been since you touched another human being? One not trying to kill you?"

He tipped his head back to the sun, conveying that he was relaxing and not going to be a threat. "Touch me one place that you want to touch. For a few seconds. If that's something you desire, give yourself that."

"You think too much of yourself." She sniffed. "How do you know I desire you at all?"

"On the beach, you said I had a fine form." He put the hint of a smile in his voice, but spoke seriously. "I can't see you looking at me, but I feel your eyes like your hands. That's not vanity. My body's in good shape, pleasing to women, but it's scarred and seen some mileage. My hope is your desire comes from the same place mine does. I feel a bond with you that has nothing to do with my sight."

The birds chirped in the trees, the sea whispered in the distance. Letting the breeze move over his face and lips, he imagined her fingers there, learning him. The wind blessed him with a lock of her hair, brushing against his shoulder. He said nothing more, though, letting her choose. He wouldn't show disappointment if she didn't respond to the gentle command, but he'd have to make an effort. *C'mon, sweetheart. Trust us both. Touch me. I'm dying here.*

One fingertip. Two. Then three and four. She passed them lightly over the expanse of his back between his shoulder blades. There was a tattoo there which he was sure had drawn her curiosity the first time she'd seen it, but she'd yet to ask about it. Her touching it now told him it wasn't because it didn't interest her. Since other things, like the items in his pack, had incited a rapid fire list of questions, he assumed the tattoo concerned her in some way she didn't yet want to address.

"How old are you?" she asked.

"Forty-five. I served twenty years with the government, then spent the last five years figuring out what else I was going to do with my life. Maddock found me about two years into that problem and helped me solve it. Can I ask you how old you are?"

"I don't know," she said, puzzlement flavoring her melodious voice. "Age does not seem to apply to me. When I was...changed, I was perhaps seventeen years? Years pass oddly for me. Like time on this island is slow and the rest of the world is fast. From things I've overheard from those who came here with ill intent, I deduced fifteen years had passed in my homeland. Yet here, I keep track of the days, and it has been five. So I could be twenty-three, or I could be thirty-one, depending on your perspective. When I look in a reflection, I cannot tell. The form I carry now seems to stay the same, my face..."

She stopped, obviously not wanting to go there. While she spoke, she'd stopped stroking his skin, but she'd left her hand in place, until now. He missed her touch, but he considered her words. So the curse carried some kind of time warp magic with it that slowed things down, while the world outside her island moved at its regular far-too-fast clip.

He knew she'd been appallingly young when her transformation had occurred, but now her combination of youth and maturity made sense. Her mannerisms suggested a woman in her thirties, though the sudden flashes of whimsy or curiosity were that of a younger version of herself. She was a woman whose youth had been cut too short, but a strong thread still attached her to it.

"You seem a good man, John Pierce," she said abruptly, interrupting his thoughts. "If you have come to serve me, your loyalty is misplaced. You should go home."

He opened his mouth to object, but the rush of her wings, the rustling overhead, said she'd taken flight. She must have had more berries in her lap and not realized it, because they pinged down on his head and shoulders.

"Medusa, don't—" But she was already gone.

Damn it. He wished he could keep her from taking off like that in mid-conversation. He had a sudden lovely thought about falcons, tethers and jesses, the damn Dom side raising its irrepressible head. And wasn't that a sexual entendre impossible to miss?

His brow furrowed. What had gone through her mind to upset her? When she told him to go home, he'd heard the despair he'd detected earlier. It was the kind of darkness that came from a person looking too closely at their own soul. He'd come out of assignments with that desolation in his heart, sure as shit. Why would she be so different?

The capacity to kill wasn't in everyone, but being brutalized yourself helped overcome the civilized veneer. Even if other parts weren't true, the rape was the consistent part of her story, as was the transformation into what most would consider a monster. He'd come out of ops where he'd felt on the inside like she might be perceived on the outside. Something dangerous and twisted, something unnatural. Or perhaps closer to nature than was comfortable. Elemental, savage. Besides defend herself, what had she done that ate at her? Because the poison of guilt and jagged-edge regret was what he recognized in her voice.

He went back down the rope ladder, still thinking. Twenty-three and forty-five. Christ, she could be his daughter. Yet time didn't move that way here, right? He didn't think of her in a fatherly way at all. He wasn't the Daddy Dom type, for sure.

He grimaced. His sexual orientation definitely fell into the category of things he would tell her as trust built between them. She'd discovered sex through an act of brutal violence. Helping her find out if her natural submissive orientation could not only add to her pleasure, but possibly help heal any scars on her soul from that violence, would not be a straightforward task. As an experienced Dom, he already knew he'd have to let her lead on that, in the way that a horse led while a rider kept gentle but firm guidance on the reins.

As he'd told Maddock, he'd be whatever she needed. As well as not be what she didn't need. He was here for a larger purpose, at least in Maddock's view, but that didn't mean that JP's personal reasons weren't relevant to accomplishing it. He knew what he knew, and the scent of her submissive nature was strong in his nose, particularly after that light touch on his back. The Dom part of him was already on the hunt. If it worked the way it should, it would open up a whole lot deeper shit between them, and bring to full light their bond with one another. A bond he found it impossible to believe didn't exist, because he was becoming more and more certain she'd never given anyone else the chance and time she was giving him to win her trust.

Whatever her reasons for it, he'd take them as a gift.

CHAPTER FIVE

*A*nother meal on his own. After that he decided to do a little weapons practice. Carrying the sword, he moved to the court he'd made with rocks. He'd donned a T-shirt for his meal, but he didn't like putting cloth over where she'd touched, so he stripped it off again along with his shoes, leaving him only in the shorts.

He went through the movements he'd learned relatively recently, compared to his other training. Prior to the fencing and sword lessons he'd been a hand-to-hand, knife, gun or explosive guy. But regardless of the weapon, there was a similar way of thinking underlying every fighting style. The primary keys always seemed to lots of footwork, and keeping your balance, inside and out. He worked himself into a glistening sweat, using the exertion to purge tension and keep his skills sharp. It bugged him, that recurring anguish in her voice. He wanted to find her, get her to talk more about that. He didn't want her unhappy, and he'd made her think about things that caused unhappiness.

In a dungeon environment, a sub put herself in a position that let him help her purge demons, if that was part of what she needed in the sessions. There might be a necessary fight, a struggle of wills, but because they were within four walls, the sub knew when she tried to retreat, he'd back her against a wall, hold her to a corner, and let stuff come out. It gave her a safe way to fight and yet surrender.

When Medusa was in his presence, and that frustrated pain came to the surface, he sensed her desire for a wall, a way to keep herself from retreating. But they didn't have that. She was being forced to shoulder the bulk of that fight, because she wouldn't stay around long enough to give him some of the responsibility. If he thought a lasso and hog tying would do the trick, he'd give it a shot, but it was probably a little early for that.

When he finished, he stripped the shorts and bathed in the ocean as before. He enjoyed surfing the waves, turning and twisting his body with their movements, then floating along in peaceful harmony. It did almost as much as the sword practice to calm his mind. The Zen of island living.

He headed back out and sat on the towel naked until the wind dried him enough to don the shorts. This time he did retrieve the T-shirt, a navy blue solid that would absorb the late afternoon sun rays to keep him warmer as the evening cooled.

As he closed his eyes and listened to the waves, he felt that peculiar tingle that told him she'd come back. His whole body rippled with anticipation, his cock stirring.

At ease, soldier. I doubt she's here because she's suddenly decided she wants to be ravished.

But he didn't need that possibility to be deeply pleased she was here. They'd talked a lot earlier. He'd let her decide if she wanted to talk more, or preferred silent company. Stretching out on his mat, he laced his hands behind his head. As time passed and she didn't make herself known in a more direct way, he figured she intended to keep her distance. He was tired and he'd worked hard, so he turned on his side, pillowing his head on his bent arm, and let himself drift.

That propensity for light sleeping came in handy. He roused fully at her approach, nearly silent though it was. It took a few minutes of patient waiting, of keeping his breath the same steady rise and fall, before she drew even closer. He inhaled her earthy floral scent and nearly interrupted his smooth breathing routine, thanks to the slight give of his cushioned mat which told him she'd knelt directly behind him.

He'd told her he wouldn't lie to her. Not telling her he was awake wouldn't fall in that category, would it?

For someone as wary as her, yes, it would.

"I'm glad you came back to see me," he said without moving or opening his eyes. From a ripple of air along his back, barely discernible without heightened senses, he wondered if she'd been reaching out to touch him, and cursed his overdeveloped conscience as he sensed her drawing the hand back.

"You don't have to talk," he said. "I'll just keep dozing if you want me to."

"Yes. I prefer that."

He grunted, settling his body further. By some miracle, he did talk himself into dozing, probably because drifting back and forth into an awareness of her was a pleasant surprise every time. Then she touched him.

It brought him instantly awake, but this time, conscience be damned, he kept his breathing and body the same as if he'd been in the world of dreams. Because this was like a dream.

He felt the pads of her fingers and the claws together this time. The curved tips grazed his skin a couple inches above her fingertips. She moved her touch along his shoulder, his back.

"I prayed to Athena for strength. And she sent you. I don't know what that means. I know what I want it to mean, but my wants... I stopped wanting things. I thought I'd stopped wanting things."

We never stop wanting things, my lady. We just sometimes stop asking because it hurts too much to not have them. He'd felt that way plenty of times, until Maddock had ferreted him out. But he stayed silent, because she wasn't talking to the conscious him.

She slid her touch down to his waist and fingered the waistband, the back pocket of his shorts, the front pocket. She was obviously intrigued by the way they fit. When that talon slid along the inside of his waistband in back, inadvertently stroking over the crease between his buttocks, he bit back his natural desire to turn and take over.

Had she ever touched a man by choice? Without fear? He didn't know, and didn't want to stop her. He remembered her chiding of him for thinking she didn't know how to fix a wheelbarrow, or what a ribbon was. Reminders that he didn't know much more of her life and world than she did of his, no matter how much reconnaissance his team had tried to do.

"You are awake."

"Yes, my lady. I didn't want you to stop." That was honest, for certain. "I thought if I spoke, you would."

"You are wrong about your body. The scars only make it more interesting. Many women must have enjoyed looking at you."

"How about you?"

She poked him with a talon, and he jumped, not expecting it. "You seek compliments."

"I seek to know if I please you, my lady. You're the only woman I want to pleasure. Stab me again with those claws, I'll pinch you in a soft spot."

He kept his tone mild, slightly teasing, but with the underlying threat still in place. He couldn't see her face to determine her reaction, but he detected that coveted slight catch of breath, and savored it for the intrigued response he knew it was.

"You have no soft spots I can find to pinch back," she mused, moving to his biceps. "I like this drawing, between your shoulders."

Then, as if she realized she was becoming too familiar, she left the mat and moved away. "Good night."

"My lady?"

But the rush of his wings said she was gone again. He bit back a frustrated breath. Patience. He was good at patience, normally. Yet while he'd played with a lot of women in the dungeon scene, dated some, he'd never truly wanted one. Yeah, he wanted sex, like any guy did, but he was hard-wired to want only one woman. And now he was with her, finally. *Finally*.

He had to get out of an operation mindset. An op always had a timeline, milestones, and he didn't have that here. He could savor every step forward, take the time to analyze and troubleshoot every step back, without the worry that delay would result in a blown cover, an operation falling apart, or him having to take out someone in the wrong place at the wrong time. Falling in love wasn't a mission. Not that way.

As he moved to his back, the shorts strained over his inevitable erection. He rubbed the heel of his hand over it, but he didn't want to give himself relief. Yeah, he was hard, but he wasn't in the mood for that. Or desperate enough to relieve the pressure. Yet.

As he adjusted, his back slid along the mat, making him think of her touch there, and her comment. The tattoo between his shoulder blades was a tangle of stylized snakes, artfully arranged around the words *Medusa's Heart*. He'd first had it done when he was a teenager, a simpler, less expensive design. He'd had it re-inked by a top rated tattoo artist within the past couple years, but even when the original design was faded, its message had never dimmed. The heart that beat in his chest was all hers.

While she couldn't read the words, she'd said she liked it. That could mean so many things, none of which were conducive to sleep. Eventually, he managed it, because he knew he had to be awake for whatever the coming day would bring, but his slumber was fitful enough he heard her return one more time.

It was during the gray light that came before dawn. Fruit and other appetizing smells said she'd brought him breakfast. Since it was close enough to sunrise, he was about to speak and suggest she stay to eat with him, but he sensed her behind him again and fell silent.

When she knelt on the mat again, his heartbeat felt as if it were thudding against his throat. Because this time she stretched out behind him on her side. *Christ, don't let me screw this up.*

With so little space between them, she'd start like a flock of pigeons if he moved at all. So he didn't, absorbing the coveted reality that she was lying next to him, staring at his back.

When something slid along his ankle, he realized she had her wing folded over her shoulder and hip so that the barbed tip was grazing his calf. She hooked her clawed fingers in the waistband of his shorts, a clever way to anticipate any sudden movements from him. Her breath evened out. She wasn't sleeping, he was sure, but she was in repose, like a roosting bird watching out for predators that might invade her nest.

In time, he shifted as he might when sleeping. She tensed, but then settled again. He did it a couple times over the next fifteen minutes, until she became more accustomed to it. Each movement brought him a little closer to her. At length, he felt her breath between his shoulder blades. If she was in hypervigilant mode, she would have moved, but he was banking on the interest he felt from her, innocently sensual. The temptation was too great for him to resist, so he hoped he was following instinct instead of his burning desire to touch her. It would be nice if the two were in accord for once.

When her fingers hooked in his waistband twitched, giving him a tentative stroke, he made his decision. Reaching back, slowly, so slowly, and bracing himself not to react to a full retreat on her part, he closed his hand around her wrist. He stayed that way another minute, caressing her pulse, the soft skin and delicate bones.

"What are the words inside your drawing?" Her voice was like the song of the ocean breeze, curling around his heart and cock.

"Medusa's Heart."

A long silence. Her other hand brushed over it. "It is permanent."

"Yes. It's tattooed. I had it first done when I was in my teens, then added to it a few years back."

Whether she believed him or not, he wanted her to know it hadn't been done recently, another ploy to gain her confidence.

He drew her hand forward from his waistband so she could rest it on his side. Her talons curved over the muscles and flesh and pressed against his abdomen. If he was gauging the sharpness of those claws correctly, she could excise his internal organs in one swipe. But she didn't. And though she'd tensed again, she didn't draw back.

A few more moments of silence. A thick blanket of energy vibrated around her.

"You will not move, John Pierce."

It was phrased as a command, but it wasn't. What he heard behind the words made his heart hurt. *Don't lie to me. Don't make me hurt you. Don't be like everyone else.*

"I promise, snake-girl."

He heard that same odd note to her voice when he spoke the nickname, but this time she gave him a clue about her reaction.

"I have dreamed of a man calling me this. For many years."

He froze. In two sentences, she'd taken his breath, and made him want to tighten his grip on her to permanent lock. Yeah, he'd dreamed of her for years, but there was still a part of him that thought he was half bat-shit crazy. To hear that maybe she might have dreamed of him, that made it even more real. Things started hurting he didn't want to hurt right now, but the pain somehow mixed with the importance of this moment, increasing the significance.

When she inched closer, he realized she was spooning around him, drawing her knees up under his ass, her breasts coming in contact with his back. She wore a top that was laced in the front, perhaps some kind of modified halter style that would work for her wings. The fabric was thin enough that he could feel the give of her curves.

She slid her arm farther around him, fingers spreading out on his chest and upper abdomen, the claws still pressed into his flesh. It could be a reminder that the position was a vulnerable one for him and he should be on his best behavior. Or she was like a cat and, when experiencing something pleasing, she liked to dig in a bit. He hoped for the latter reason.

That smooth worn rope feeling heralded a snake sliding against his upper arm and down to his hip, then it retreated. The other snakes seemed to be keeping their distance and staying still, for he didn't hear or feel any others.

Medusa sighed, a puff of breath on his neck that told him her face had to be within an inch of it. Her other arm was bent to pillow her head, since he felt the point of her elbow against his shoulder.

Wondering if she would allow it, he lowered his hand and rested it on hers again, stroking her knuckles, the veins leading to her hand and wrist. He didn't grip, didn't impede her movement in any way, though he would have liked to intertwine fingers. He wanted to hold her hand firmly against him, keep her tethered to him throughout the night, though he'd also prefer their position to be reversed, where he could be curled around her. Everything in time.

"Do not make too much of this," she said abruptly. "I have not had human company in some time, as you said. If you take advantage, I will be quick to retaliate."

"Good night, Wesley. Good job, and I'll most likely kill you in the morning."

"What?"

He smiled, though the emotions still swirling around in his chest made it a tight gesture. Her hands were a working woman's, the knuckles rough and the palms callused, but the fingers were slim and elegant to go with the clean nails. He already knew he could circle her wrist with his thumb and forefinger with room to spare, but he liked doing it, seeing the contrast of their skin. She was golden where he was tan.

"It's a movie...a story." He'd heard somewhere the film came from a book, but he gave her the salient points of the movie *The Princess Bride* to explain the relationship between Wesley and the Dread Pirate Roberts.

"Do you know the whole story?" she asked.

"Yeah, pretty much." Almost word for word. He'd stayed with Olivia after she'd had to have surgery while pregnant with her second child. The baby daddy was in the wind, and she was coming off an addiction to prescription pain meds. The movie had been a remarkably effective sedative for her. "I've probably seen it fourteen times." All in the same three-day crisis recovery period.

"Will you tell it to me?"

"It'd take a while in one sitting. How about we do it in serial?" It would also be a great way to keep her seeking out his company, at least once a day. If he did a good job with it, that is, but his subs said he did great and very realistic role playing. Monica had said she couldn't decide which was her favorite—or which one she found scariest, in the best kind of way. Cop, teacher, vampire, slave owner...

He launched into the tale, starting with the "As you wish," part between Wesley and Buttercup.

As he took her through that chapter, her talons started to do a press, release thing that did remind him of a cat kneading. Her fingertips were also moving over the muscles of his abdomen, a distracting tease, all the more potent because of its shy execution. He managed to do a credible job with the first chapter, stopping when Buttercup received the news that Wesley had been lost to her by an attack at sea by the Dread Pirate Roberts.

"But she didn't," she pointed out. "You said he and Wesley spoke nightly."

She'd been fully focused on the story even while touching him. Women and their ability to multi-task. He'd like to take her beyond that, to a state of mind where she could think of only one thing. Begging him for a release.

"Yeah. But that's getting ahead of the story. I want to leave it on a cliffhanger. You'll have to come back tomorrow night for more."

"You could tell me tomorrow, during the day."

"So you're going to spend some time with me tomorrow? Not ignore me or stay far away?"

"I wasn't ignoring you. I was watching at a safe distance so you didn't have to wear the blindfold while you were doing things where you might get hurt if you couldn't see. If you get hurt, I have to tend to you."

"I'm glad you added that. Else I'd think you were concerned about me. Though I guess you are, aren't you? Otherwise, you wouldn't bother tending to my wounds."

"Be quiet. I am sleeping."

He highly doubted she would sleep so close to him, but he was heartened by her spirited responses.

"So you will tell me more of the story tomorrow?" she prodded.

"I'll tell you a chapter at daylight and a chapter at bedtime. That way you have to see me both times to get more of it."

"I will likely tire of it soon. I cannot be so easily manipulated."

"It's one of the best stories ever. You won't get tired of it. I've been told I do great voices."

"You did sound very much like a princess named Buttercup."

Her teasing, with a biting edge, delighted him. Reaching back, he swatted her backside, a light, glancing blow, easily accomplished since she had her legs drawn up under his. He'd done it on playful instinct, no thought to it, and smoothly returned his hand to overlapping hers on his chest.

For her part, she'd stiffened instantly. He thought she might be about to bolt, but he spoke casually, as if nothing alarming had happened. "Rude, snake-girl. Just rude."

Her stillness was hard to interpret. Shock, yes. But after that passed, he wondered if she was thinking about how it felt. He knew he sure as hell was. His palm was tingling, he was fully aroused, and he wanted to do far more than what he'd just done. He'd gotten as much hip as bottom.

What he really wanted was to make full contact in that sweet spot between thighs and buttocks, see those lovely cheeks wobble upon impact. He wanted to hold her fast on his lap so he could enjoy the kicking of feet, the rub of her naked breasts against his thigh, her struggles against his strength as he made the swats sting.

"Just can't turn it off, JP, can you?"

Maddock's amused voice emerged loud and clear in his memory. Catching JP studying the swaying, full backside of one of his handful of lab techs, the scientist-wizard had read him like a book. "And yeah, that one loves a hell of a spanking. She's also an exhibitionist. Occasionally screws up something minor just so I'll take my belt to her in front of the other techs."

"I'm so relieved you aren't allowing yourself distractions while working out detailed equations that will scramble our atoms through the time-space continuum."

"Certain distractions keep us loose. Make some bolts too tight, there's no room for the machinery to work the way it should," Maddock had responded. "And what are you worried about? If we can't put your atoms back together, you'll never feel a thing anyway."

JP expected that advice on staying loose was why he'd done what he'd just done. If he calculated every move he made, she would sense that calculation. Acting naturally, on impulse, in limited ways, hopefully would encourage her to do the same. Which might be why she was here on the beach with him tonight.

"Not rude," she sniffed at last, easing his tension. "I was admiring your drama skills."

"Sarcasm gets the same treatment as rudeness." He lifted his hand in mock threat. "There's more where that came from."

Her silence, neither encouraging nor refusing, said enough to make his palm itch. The sensation had intrigued her; he'd bet money on it. But if so, she backed away from her response.

"Do not threaten me or I will pull your insides out." She said it mildly, though.

"You could do it," he said, stroking her knuckles, following the lengths of her fingers down to her talons. Her hand flattened as if she wasn't sure she wanted him touching that part of her, but he made the stroke a continual, circular motion, not backing off but not lingering, either. "These are a pretty good weapon to have literally right at hand. How'd you figure out a fighting style with them?"

He hadn't yet seen it, but due to her success with any interlopers to her island, he was pretty certain she had.

"We have some small wildcats on the island. Not many, and they are shy, but I have watched them play at the waterfalls or capture prey. It seemed more intelligent to study their methods for using claws that are already attached to their body, rather than treating the claws like a knife."

"Yeah. Good thinking." He wasn't a sexist bastard, at least not in the wrong kind of way. He admired a woman who wanted to be able to take care of herself. Only a fool thought he could handle everything and always be exactly where he needed to be for his woman. And she'd had to fight a lot of foes without him.

But not anymore. He thought of what she'd said, about praying to Athena for strength. As he'd told her, no matter how tough the fighter, eventually everyone needed reinforcements. He would keep proving his usefulness in that regard whenever and however he could until she knew she could count upon it.

She'd fallen silent. Hoping he could encourage her to do the same, he let himself doze some more. While they weren't on any set schedule here, so they could stay up all night and sleep the day away, it seemed a shame to pass up the tranquil chance to sleep under a vista of stars with a warm body pressed against him. He'd been in far worse circumstances.

"You do not fear me," she whispered, as if she thought she might be talking to his sleeping self. "I do not know whether that is arrogance or something else."

"What would the something else be?" he asked. His voice was genuinely groggy, which perhaps helped her be more forthcoming.

"You do not fear me because you intend me no harm. And you trust that I will not hurt you as long as I believe that is true."

"I've been accused of arrogance. Goes with what I did as a job for so long, and the alpha male stuff. Sorry, no help for it. But yeah, you nailed it. I trust you won't if I don't."

"Then you are a fool," she said, even more quietly.

An attack without any kind of warning wasn't easy to pull off around him, so he gave her major points for that. On his next indrawn breath, she slashed her claws down his front, opening him up from pecs to lower abdomen, a vicious swipe that took skin and fountained blood.

And then she was gone.

CHAPTER SIX

"Son of a bitch." No way he could have prepared for that, except by being far warier around her, and therefore keeping her equally wary around him. Sacrifices had to be made to gain trust, and apparently giving her a pound of flesh was one of those sacrifices. Damn it, two of the snakes had bit him as well. He had some medicine, and a very helpful incantation from Maddock to expel snake venom if he caught it fast enough, but when no evidence of it came from the recitation, he surmised he'd only need the antibiotic for the bites.

As he fumbled out his first aid kit, he mitigated the pain by indulging in a nice dark fantasy where he took a switch to her while she was spread-eagled on his bed. He'd fuck her into oblivion while she was still smarting from the pattern of pretty welts he'd left on her fair skin. He bet she'd have a sweet, feminine little squeal.

He supposed he should be glad she hadn't poisoned the tips of those lethal claws. Well, as far as he knew. However, after about ten minutes had passed without any effects other than raw agony from the open wounds, he figured he was fine. If she had developed a poison, he expected it would be a quick killer. Or she would have just used the snakes who were packing venom already.

He pawed through the first aid kit, hissed through the burn of the alcohol. Four deep gouges, six to seven inches long. While they initially bled like he'd been gored by a boar, she hadn't gone so deep as to hit any organs. But she'd gone through enough layers that staples or sutures would be advisable. He'd brought both, but he went with staples, grumbling curses as he clicked them in and bandaged his midsection to keep the wound clean.

This was going to knock him out of any hard labor for the next few days while the skin mended. He wouldn't be able to climb up to her place unless he wanted to tear the staples. Was that part of her intent, to ensure that as she became friendlier with him, she wasn't making herself more vulnerable?

Probably part of it, but he suspected the impulse had been deeper and less strategic.

When he was all done stapling the wound, his hands were shaking, but he paid no attention to that. It would pass. His mind was clear enough. Detaching from pain was part of the job, and he had more important things to think about. Time to analyze exactly the whys of what had just happened.

As he considered the question, he pulled out a flask. Lot had tucked it into his pack with a grin. *"For medicinal purposes,"* he'd said. *"Or for when she's about to drive you so bat shit you want to wring her neck. With a woman, that'll take about a day."*

He didn't want to wring her neck, but he did take a bolstering shot from the flask, choking on the contents as the liquid scalded a path to his gut. What the fuck *was* that? Some kind of moonshine, probably cooked up in Lot's backyard. But as it settled, the warmth it spread through his lower abdomen did help. JP screwed the top back on and put it away. With a sigh, he lay back down on his mat, wincing at the stretch to his abdomen. He turned on his side, which brought back the memory of her body so close behind his. Why had she done it?

The move had been deliberate. It wasn't a sudden act of panic, the response of a cornered wild animal.

It was clear she was warming to the idea of having him around, and maybe the realization had spooked her. So maybe she wanted to drive him away. Or see what it would take to drive him away.

He thought of the note of despair in her voice earlier. Maybe driving him away helped her avoid whatever that feeling was about. Having him here was stirring up bad stuff for her, and she was using pain to break something loose. It just happened to be his pain.

Ironically that kind of bad stuff got worked out when a person wasn't always having to deal with it alone. Though he knew how hard that was, too. He and guys like him reacted to PTSD shrinks like peasants did to plague boils. For a long time, he'd joked that he'd cut out the middle man and leapfrogged right past PTSD into being a psychopath. *"Just a little benefit of my training."*

The last time he'd made that smart-assed comment, he'd been sprawled out on the crappy rooftop of Lot's crappy apartment building. JP had his feet in a hot pink kiddie pool bright enough to be used for target practice by the pilots at the nearby Jacksonville military base.

Lot was in a lounger, his mirrored sunglasses hiding his eyes, his body deceptively relaxed in nothing but a pair of Hawaiian swim shorts.

"What we do isn't okay," he'd said, a more serious response than JP had expected. "Not in the slightest. Doesn't mean it doesn't have to be done, because humans are the most fucked up idea for a species any god has every created."

JP returned to the present. Medusa injuring him as a way to determine what would drive him away felt like the right track, but not quite there. Maybe she was testing him. Gauging how much of her shit he would take before he would retaliate, and how he would retaliate.

He considered that one carefully. As pleasurable as he'd found his fantasy of giving her a good switching, he knew it wasn't solely his own desires that had brought it to mind. To some people, it was unfathomable that a victim of sexual abuse might crave not only submission, but sometimes hardcore levels of pain and punishment.

Monica had been his first. She'd approached him, as if she'd sensed what he could give her even before he did. Though she was in professional therapy, she made her first, significant step toward healing when he'd switched her ass while she repeated, "It wasn't my fault" until they were both satisfied she meant it. Probably because she went from issuing it as a plea, to screaming it in a rage. And then the tears had come. He'd held her until she'd cried herself into exhaustion.

But that was Monica. He didn't try to make a woman fit what he wanted from her to the point he ignored her true motives or interests. However, the more he thought about it, the more he believed that was a component of why Medusa had done this. One he couldn't overlook, unless he wanted to set a dangerous precedent. He believed he was willing to sacrifice pretty much everything for her; else he wouldn't be here. But he wasn't going to let her kick him around anytime the mood struck her.

While confronting it head-on might get him even more seriously injured, when had self-preservation ever stopped him? He bared his teeth in a grim smile and started thinking of how to put in motion a retaliation that would benefit them both.

Even after taking some ibuprofen, he slept fitfully, and when he woke well after sunrise, his upper torso had the flexibility of sheetrock. Today was not going to be the day to enact his plan, so he'd put it on account.

She'd taken away the breakfast she'd brought him. Was it a message to go away? Or maybe she thought he'd leave as a result of her actions and she saw no reason to waste the provisions. Shading his eyes, he looked up at the section of forest where her home was nestled. At this distance, he didn't think there was any chance they could meet one another's eyes. Even if so, he didn't expect she had that kind of range. Otherwise she could take care of intruders without ever leaving her nest.

The wind was up, concealing the balcony, though he could see hints of the stone and wooden framework as the trees blew back and forth.

Fine, then. He'd spent the first few days closer to the shoreline to be sure she could see his whereabouts at night, but it was time to make himself more of a shelter where he could leave his pack items secured. He liked the beach, so he investigated the tree line and found a tightly clustered grouping of foliage where he could carve out a lean-to. While he had to move slowly, he made decent progress through the morning, using more of the boat wreckage to form the frame and then lacing branches over and around it, creating a shallow cave.

Making a box was easy, for he had some nails with him. Maddock had said the pack could be re-supplied when needed with any essentials that could fit inside it. JP would write out his list in a small notebook Maddock had supplied him—with the dark admonition *not* to crease any pages, suggesting it wasn't merely just a fifty-cent notebook he'd acquired at a dollar store. Then JP would put it in the correct pocket, and press the snap closed. Which would activate things on

Maddock's side and send the contents of that note like an email message, though it could take a little more time to get there.

Using the same portal technology he used to transport a live human being, Maddock would dump those supplies back into the pack. Very Harry Potter, to his way of thinking. However, since John was pretty resourceful, the plan was to do that as little as possible. Mindful of the liberties they were already taking with timelines, they didn't want to bring too many items from the future to her island.

The small notebook hadn't raised any questions with Medusa and she hadn't retained it, however, so there was no barrier from that side of things if JP thought of other things from his world she might enjoy.

JP unpacked his belongings into the finished wooden box, arranging them for easy access. Lifting a small container, he considered the contents, rocking in their saline solution. Maybe it was time to use the contacts Maddock had devised. The wizard believed they would shield JP from the effects of her eyes, while still allowing him to look upon her and retain his sight. He could have been wearing them all along, but he'd wanted her to know for sure she had the advantage for their first couple days. Now he expected she was more worried about unexpectedly catching him in an unfortunate glance.

He put them on, blinked and set the case back in the box. Maddock was 99.9% sure they worked. Well, if the opportunity presented itself, JP would seal up that last little gap. Or widen it to 100%, in entirely the opposite direction.

When his stomach started growling, he finished up his nesting and went fishing. Fish were plentiful in the ocean and the freshwater sites. After frying up a couple over a small fire, he ate them and followed it up with a dessert of some small melons he found in the forest. He was pretty certain they weren't poisonous, thanks to his survival training, and they had a sweet, cantaloupe-like taste.

Now that he'd set aside the problem for a couple hours, he looked at it again to ensure he wasn't making the wrong assumptions. He could be arrogant, but he wasn't clueless. As a special ops guy, he wasn't wired to think of failure. At least not in those terms. If a mission failed, it was only after every other option had been exhausted, and he'd retreat merely to figure out a better way to achieve the objective.

A woman's heart wasn't the same as a mission—though winning it might take even more effort than penetrating the Taliban—so he had to set aside some of that thinking and examine her reactions thus far as objectively as possible. But he trusted his gut. As he kept thinking about her and everything that had occurred over the past day, he became more certain that she wanted him here. She was just afraid of it going sour.

"That's the risk of any relationship, sweetheart," he muttered. "They can always tank. But you don't strike me as a coward. Just tired of the bullshit and of being hurt. I hate that you've had to deal with that, but I don't think you've given up trying. Hell, you've never been given the chance *to* try, not really."

He didn't beat a point to death when there wasn't any further intel to change the current analysis. That resolved, he finished his meal, cleaned up and went exploring. When he crossed paths with the goat herd, he discovered one had birthed a kid since he'd seen them last. Watching the new baby cavort around his mother and figure out his world was a balm to the parts of his mind that remained agitated about Medusa's actions and unhappy about her absence. The mom didn't seem to mind when the babe settled in his lap and let him stroke the floppy oblong ears.

After that, he visited Medusa's garden sites, and harvested off some of the vegetables and fruits that were ripe, using the new buckets. He left them tucked into the garden shed so she could retrieve and take them up to her home.

Mid-afternoon, he found another smaller waterfall and pool area combination at a lower elevation. He was sitting by the fall with his eyes closed, letting the mist cool him, when he sensed her near. As she landed behind him, he didn't move. Didn't flinch as she traced the cloth wrapped around his torso, across his back. "This is twisted," she said quietly. "I'll fix it."

"Knock yourself out." When she draped the blindfold on his shoulder, he reached up and set it aside. "No. I'll keep my eyes closed. Or you close yours."

Her fingertips rested on his shoulder. "All right," she said at last. "Keep yours closed."

He could explain the contacts to her, but he had a feeling until he proved they could work, she'd be too afraid of them not working to permit him to use them. A chicken or egg dilemma.

But if she learned by accident he had a way of neutralizing the danger of her gaze, that wouldn't go well, either. Which meant he needed to tell her. But before he did, he decided to try a small test of his own. When she bent over his front and unwrapped the bandage, he cracked his eyes to look.

He wondered if she heard his heart skip a beat, or his breath catch in his throat. It wasn't her looks that caused that reaction as much as his first chance to gaze upon her face.

She was beautiful.

Maddock believed it took her direct stare to turn someone to stone. Since JP was wearing the contacts, he couldn't test that. Her eyes, what he could see of them peripherally, were so crimson red they seemed to glow like jewels. Her features matched her wrists. Her delicate chin and sloping cheekbones were as finely formed as dainty blown glass figurines. Her lips, pursed with her concentration on his bandage, were full and soft-looking. Her glossy black hair that tumbled down her back had hundreds of silky ringlets marked by threads of copper, bronze and gold.

The magic had to have done that, because no woman's hair had that many colors without the help of a bottle, and he was pretty sure there was no drugstore around here. He realized the hues matched some of her snakes, giving them further camouflage.

Two black ones were coiled on one shoulder, twined together and draped down over her biceps, heads resting on the inside of her elbow. They had to be Tunneltrap and Waterlight. Her arm had a toned muscularity that confirmed her training. Without her magic, she wouldn't be stronger than him, but, depending on her fight training and how well she used advantages like her wings, she could be faster and more agile. They'd be well matched. That would be useful for his future plan to address the four stripes on his torso.

Two more snakes curled around her head, forming a living circlet that kept her hair out of her eyes. Ratqueen was as she'd been described, bone-white with reddish eyes, an albino. She was twice the thickness of the black ones, whereas the one nestled in her coils was slim as a pencil, with brown, black and gold markings. He was twined around the white snake like the color on a candy cane. Medusa had said Earthson was the smallest, so JP deduced that was him.

The fifth nestled in a curtain of hair against her neck, his squat diamond head resting on her collar bone. JP had been right. Treebark, so named because of his spiky skin, was a bush viper. Deadly poisonous.

Earthson looked like some kind of asp, a breed of snake which was also poisonous, but the two black snakes weren't, and he still thought Ratqueen was probably a constrictor, though apparently not a danger to her mistress. From what he could see in his brief glance, the snakes had enough length to give them an advantageous range as weapons in her defense. He could confirm that himself, remembering those first few moments on the beach, when one had struck at his face.

He hadn't expected the snakes to be different species, since most Medusa artwork suggested a homogenous group, but he doubted she sat for many portraits. What was curious was that the bush viper and black snakes weren't native to her part of the world. The vagaries of magic.

At last he could see her claws. The talons grew out of her knuckles as he'd deduced and created a close arch over her fingers. They were ivory-colored, with symbols scratched into them. Had she done that, or was it part of the curse upon her?

When she'd first been transformed, he expected she'd had a lot of mishaps, learning how to coordinate their fixed position with the movements of her fingers, but she wasn't having any difficulties now. Fascinated, he saw she employed them like a backup set of fixed fingers, lifting and adjusting the bandage as her actual fingers beneath the claws' curved arch smoothed the skin around the stapled wounds. His muscles flexed under her touch, an involuntary reaction. She had a dusting of freckles on her forearms.

His gaze moved to her clothes. Her short skirt was a natural linen color, belted with an embroidered sash. The laced shirt was like a short halter top, pretty much what he'd deduced she was wearing. Very Gabrielle from *Xena: Warrior Princess.* It worked well on her. Gabrielle had been more his type, with her fiery spirit and submissive personality. He could certainly conjure some creative visions of team-topping Medusa with the tough and beautiful Lucy Lawless.

Her clothing were practical choices, likely made in consideration of the warm climate, her altered form, and the labor she did here to care for herself. He doubted she gave much thought to the dictates anymore on modesty imposed on ancient Athens women. Those requirements would have had her wearing a far longer and more concealing garment in front of a man not of her family.

He didn't sense she thought of her outfit as provocative, though. Which was intriguing, since his lady exuded Xena's overwhelming sensual nature, in a temptingly innocent way. Was it part of the curse, to lure her enemies to her? She didn't have the sexual experience to have that aura emanating around her, but it sure as hell was distracting. When she walked, he expected her body moved and swayed in just the right ways. His palms itched to cradle her curves.

The bandage wasn't twisted enough to need to be unwrapped, but he realized she'd wanted to see how he'd tended to himself. She'd caused the wounds, so that might seem confusing, to alternate harm with care, but not to him. It made him even more certain it was a test, on two levels. She was issuing a challenge to what it was about him making her antsy at a subconscious level. She'd also tested him because it was a necessary step toward one you weren't sure was ally or enemy.

She looked as if she wanted to touch the staples but, perhaps thinking the wounds were sensitive, she stopped short and put the bandage back in place. Then her eyes lifted and met his directly.

They were a snake's eyes, with the slit pupil that gave them a dangerous, flat look, unless one looked closer and saw so much more, the swirl of emotions trapped under that predator's unwavering stare.

Less than a blink of impression, and it hit him like a bolt in the chest. He'd been so caught up in looking at her that he hadn't shut his eyes fast enough, and now there was no turning back.

She hissed in alarm, revealing fangs and a forked tongue. He grunted in pain. In her panic, she'd slapped her palms against his four stapled wounds to shove away from him and launch herself into the air.

"Medusa, stop." He felt like he'd been stabbed four times in the chest. "Don't go. Wait. I'm wearing contacts...a magic covering over my eyes, of sorts. I'm fine. You looked at me and I was fine."

She'd already disappeared back in the trees. "Put on the blindfold. Right now. Do it. Or into the sea you go."

He could chide her that that threat was getting a little old, but right now might not be the time to test his Dread Pirate Roberts theory.

"Okay. It's on." He managed the lacings, though his torso grumbled when the movement pulled at his abused and torn flesh. "Look. See?"

"You should not have done that. Why did you do that? You could have... Damn you."

The raw words spiked through his heart. She was furious, freaked out. Afraid. He regretted that, even if he couldn't regret the one stolen glance.

"It takes a second for my curse to take effect," she said. "If you'd looked at me longer..."

"The contacts would still work."

"I don't care. You don't...you should have asked first."

He would have banked money on her taking off, but she hadn't yet, so he went with bald honesty. "Yes. I should have. I'm sorry. I wanted to see you. I was impatient."

"I wasn't prepared for you...to see me. To know what I look like."

That stopped him in his tracks. He'd assumed her only worry was turning him to stone, causing harm to another. He hadn't thought about that side of things. While it was good to know it mattered to her, what he thought when he looked upon her, he could reassure her on that issue.

"You're a beautiful woman."

The noise that came from her was ugly, harsh. "You mock me."

"Why would I do that, my lady? You are beautiful."

"Then you are one of those wrong-minded individuals with unnatural desires for deformity."

"No, I'm not." He set his jaw. "You can trash yourself all you want, but you're not going to put those words in my mouth. I saw a woman who's beautiful, desirable and fascinating. But that doesn't make me any less pissed off at you."

"What?" She'd paused to digest the colloquialism, but she picked up on the meaning quickly enough. "What right do you have to be angry with me?"

"Hello?" He gestured to his chest. "What the hell did I do to deserve that?"

"Oh." He'd derailed her from the sight issue, at least for now, which was his intent, but his demanding question was sincere.

"I wanted to... I don't know. You made me feel...comfortable, and I was reminding myself that I shouldn't ever feel comfortable."

His brow creased and he took a step in her direction. She was up in the trees, but it didn't matter. What he heard behind the words made him want to be closer. "You weren't going to say comfortable. What were you going to say?"

"My thoughts are not yours to demand."

Not yet, but we're getting there, he thought, with a surge of satisfaction. Because he heard the truth.

She'd wanted to say *safe*. He'd made her feel safe, and she couldn't trust that feeling. Because she hadn't felt safe in a long time. She'd both rejected it and tested him, a dual purpose she might not even have recognized in her own mind. Okay, he wasn't a hundred percent sure, but close enough.

"Fine," he said evenly. "But there'll be a reckoning."

"A...what?"

"You owe me an apology. In trade."

"I'm not going to let you—"

"I would never break your skin like that, my lady. No matter what you do to me, I'd never strike you with the intent to do harm."

Those silences of hers were always filled with so much, he could almost feel the thoughts whirling around him. "Then I am sorry," she said stiffly. "I should not have—"

"In your place, I might have done the same," he said. "Until you build up enough evidence to the contrary, you have no reason to trust me. And I didn't do a good job of helping with that, just now. But to make it square between us, there needs to be a reckoning. Because I didn't do anything to deserve these marks, did I?"

Another pause. "No."

This time when she spoke, he finally felt the age difference between them, in an intriguing way. He'd purposefully made his tone stern, and he could hear her discomfiture. She had a conscience, he knew it, warring with deeper, more difficult and darker things.

"Well then," he said lightly. "After I heal up, we spar. First one to put the other on the ground three times wins. And we'll state the stakes right now, up front. Once agreed, no reneging."

"Why would I do this?"

"Because you're feeling guilty about it. Not only did you wound me, you left me all alone to deal with it. You know how hard it is to tend your own wounds?"

"Yes. I do."

He cursed his clumsiness there. "Yeah, I guess you do. Be nice to have someone around to help, right?"

"Men are babies." Her tone was droll, telling him she'd picked up his exaggerated wistfulness.

"Sometimes. I appreciate you straightening that wrap for me. So if you win, what do you want?"

A rustling told him she'd come down out of the trees. She was standing on the rocks about ten feet away. Her proximity was a relief to him, and he realized he wanted to take this to the next level. Enough of this standing outside of range shit.

Taking another couple of steps toward her, he dropped to one knee, a nonthreatening pose. He held out a hand. "Will you come here, my lady?"

"Why?"

"Because I like it when you're closer. I like the way you smell. I like the warmth of your flesh. I like to hear the movement of your clothing against your body. Tell me what you want, if you win."

Her soles slid over the rock as if she was shifting from one to the other, debating. She didn't come to him, but she answered his question. "If I win, you leave the island."

"The stakes have to be something you want. You don't want that, Medusa. You're just worried what will happen the longer I stay around."

"You seem sure of your appeal."

"Am I wrong? Can you tell me you don't want me around at all, for any length of time? I think that was part of what upset you about me looking at you. You've found someone's company you can tolerate, who might not be here to kill you. I risked that without consulting you first. Again, I'm sorry."

Another shift of feet. "Very well. When I win, you will leave the island when I desire you to do so. Whenever that might be. No arguing."

He imagined himself standing in the surf for a few hours and then returning to shore, confirming he had "left" the island. "Okay, but when it's not because of fear or anger or whatever. When you genuinely don't want me around anymore. That's fine, but it's really subjective."

"From your perspective," she responded tartly, and he grinned.

"Even so, I'd advise different stakes."

"Like what? What more could I want from you?"

Oh, baby, that's a loaded question. He'd love to demo the a la carte menu for her, but now was hardly the time. "You could have me repair or build you something. I can also requisition new supplies from Maddock. Maybe you'd like him to send a crate of that chocolate."

She paused. "No. I'd like you to tell me more stories like *The Princess Bride*. Two chapters. In the morning and evening. Every day."

He'd give her that anyway. He'd give her pretty much anything she wanted. He just wouldn't leave. "That I can do."

"More chocolate would be nice. Though a crate would be too much."

He could point out that was two things, but he'd leave that alone.

"Plus a dress like one I saw in the...magazine. Can you...requisition that?"

He was pleased she'd been looking through it. "You're pushing the whole prize-winning thing."

"Well, if I put you on the ground three times, three prizes seem reasonable."

Actually, that kind of did, and it worked for his own purposes, if he won. "Okay. Leave the picture of the dress at my camp. If I can't get that exact one, I'll find one as close to it as possible." *And please God, let it not be some five-figure designer thing worn by an Oscar recipient, else I'll be indentured to Maddock's craziness for the rest of my life.* "You'll have to let me figure out your size, though."

"Oh." She hadn't thought of that. Female clothing for her people, at least within the privacy of the home, was pretty much a piece of draped fabric belted at the waist and open on the sides. Thinking of her in that gave him a nice surge of lust.

He'd already had enough glimpses of her petite frame to guess she was size small and fighting weight lean, but whatever dress she chose might need to be more specific than that. And with the wings, it might need to be tailored. But he'd deal with that after he had all the necessary information.

"Do you approve my requests for winnings?" she asked, an impe-rious note to her voice.

"I do," he said, just as formally.

"What about you? In the unlikely event you win, what do you want?"

He flashed his teeth. "Pretty confident there, snake-girl. Four strikes on my chest, I want four times four strikes of my own. Open palm, on your pretty backside. I want to spank you."

He would have given a great deal to see the look on her face, because he bet it was priceless.

"Your price for me tearing open your flesh is to swat my bottom a few times." Her tone was affronted. "I am not a child, unaware of the consequences of my actions."

"I'm aware of that. I promise you'll feel very much like a grown woman while I'm doing it."

"If you win," she said suspiciously.

"When I win."

She sniffed. "If I were you, I'd be finding my dress and chocolate."

He'd get those for her, regardless. "Yes, my lady. I was going to go back down to the beach for a swim. Want to come with me and sit on the beach for a while? Make sandcastles?"

"Maybe in a while." She sounded pensive, as if she had more on her mind than she wanted to reveal.

He deduced that being on the beach so soon after last night would remind her not only of what she'd done to him, but what they'd been doing right before then. The intimacy she'd allowed herself with someone she shouldn't yet fully trust.

"Okay. But we're square. We've set terms for a reckoning, and that's all that needs to be said about it. I don't hold any hard feelings. I'd like for you to come join me and hang out when you're ready. I like your company."

"Hang...out."

"Yeah. It means spend time together in a friendly sort of way."

"You have a strange way of speaking. And we are not friends."

"Not yet. Maybe soon. Did you have friends before, at the temple?"

"Yes. Before." That one word was loaded with lots of things. He'd lowered his hand when she refused to take it, so now he rose and took several deliberate steps in her direction. When he stopped, he'd gauged right. He was standing in front of her and close, her short skirt fluttering against the bare part of his thigh below the shorts.

"Maybe this is a chance for you to have one again," he suggested.

Her touch slid over the bandage she'd rewrapped, fortunately before she'd noticed him looking at her. His chest, aching though it was, welcomed that testing caress. He lifted his hand and brushed his fingertips over the back of hers. "Medusa."

She drew away. "We shall see."

Her footsteps told him she was preparing to leave him again. She paused, though. "If I tried to kill you, I would want you to fight back, John Pierce."

"Then I suggest you never try to kill me, my lady. I said I'm here to serve you, and I meant it."

"I suspect you staying alive is of better service to us both."

As she took flight, he nodded in satisfaction. "On that, I'd say we're in agreement." *More progress.*

CHAPTER SEVEN

*S*he joined him on the beach after dinner. He'd left the blindfold on for most of the past few hours in the hopes that she would, and was glad his patience was rewarded.

He didn't say anything as she took a seat on the sand beside him, but he offered her some of the fruit juice he'd made, since he didn't care much for plain water.

"This is good," she said, after a sip. "I have a punch I've put together with this same fruit. Additional herbs give it a pleasing flavor. I will show you which ones I use next time you make more."

"Sounds good." He rose and went to the shoreline, intending to rinse the stickiness of the fruit off his hands. As he straightened, he felt her behind him. "Mind if I remove the blindfold a moment, my lady?" he asked casually. "I'd like to watch the sunset with you."

"As long as you promise not to turn around. I do not care that you wear the…contacts. I don't wish you to look upon me until I permit it. You must promise."

"You trust my word?"

"I do not know. I expect you will prove that to me in time."

"True enough. What I will promise is it will be a hardship not to look upon your loveliness."

His enhanced senses somewhat detected mood changes, if those changes were strong enough. It was curious, how certain things he said turned her tenuous accord with him into a tight, closed coolness.

"Please do not say such things to me. You claim they are not a mockery, but I cannot accept that. Your words hurt."

Her words hurt him, because he heard the genuine pain the sincere compliment provoked. Removing the blindfold, he stuffed it in his shorts pocket. The sun's descent was a glorious painting, as it often was. A miracle offered to everyone, rich or poor, sick or well, good or evil. Or morally compromised beyond repair.

The poignancy of sunset could always do this to him. *Stop it, John. You're past that. You made sure of it, before you came here. You didn't want to be some wounded thing she had to save.* Yet there were things about her own struggles that took him back to the darker days of his own.

"So animals can look at you, can't they?" he asked.

"Yes. The spell...curse, was only directed toward humans, to keep me...isolated from them. How did you know?"

"I haven't seen any statues of animals, and you can't tell an animal not to meet your gaze. Plus, the deer look like they're always expecting someone else when they see me."

"Yes." A smile crept into her voice, adding a sensuous tag to the melody of her words. "I do as little harm as possible to the beasts who share the island with me. They are friends and company. It is nice to have their trust and contact."

"They'll let you touch them?"

"Yes. The male deer have taken the longest. There is one with magnificent antlers who allows me to stroke his flanks and scratch around the antlers and ears. It seems all furred animals like that."

"It makes sense. Even our scant amount of fur can cause itching."

She chuckled, a pretty sound. "Yes, that is so."

Her hand slid under his arm, her fingers settling lightly on his bandaged chest. "You took this off when you swam earlier. Didn't the salt burn?"

"It did." Like a fucking son of a bitch. "But it's good for the wounds. Part of why I did it."

"What you used to close the wounds, those slim pieces of metal? I haven't seen that before."

"Medical staples. I probably should have used sutures, because it's hard to align the skin with staples if you don't have a second pair of hands to help, but staples are faster and I don't care much about scarring. I have my share, so I don't worry about that anymore."

Plus, a part of him had wanted the scars. In case this didn't work out, he wanted something permanent to carry from her. He didn't share that, since he didn't want her to entertain any thoughts about making him leave again. He also wasn't sure if she'd interpret that as more evidence that he was some kind of twisted individual who liked "deformed" women and wanted to be wounded by them, literally. Christ.

"Yes, you do have many scars." Her other hand traced several of them on his back. "You must be a fierce warrior."

"Or a pretty bad one. One that doesn't know how to get out of the way."

"No." That smile was back in her voice, tempered with something more serious. "You have implied you chose a dangerous profession, and you were in it for many years. If you were not skilled, you would not be alive."

"Anyone who's had to go into a fight to the death will tell you that's as much luck as skill. Right?"

"Yes." One syllable conveyed a wealth of understanding. Kinship.

He closed his hand around hers carefully, giving her time to pull away. She didn't. As he turned it over, he saw calluses on her palms. "You work hard to provide for your own needs here."

"No harder than at the temple."

That couldn't be true, since at the temple there'd been far more people to share the load. But also far more people to feed.

"Gifts were always brought," she said. "But we grew our own food, toted water, washed our linen. Each priestess cared for her own needs and communally supported those of all. There was a simple pleasure to it. A flower, herb or vegetable grows and flourishes if I care for it properly. It responds to my love. Honest labor can bring much joy."

"Do you get bored? There doesn't seem to be much to do here except deal with your necessities, and you seem to have those well under control."

"Idleness is only unwelcome for the thoughts it can bring."

"Yeah. A-fucking-men to that. But the white noise of other people can be as bad sometimes. Make it worse."

"Hmm. That I would not know, but I do enjoy my solitude. I don't want to be back in the world."

He wasn't sure he believed her. She didn't want to be back in the world she'd left. But there was a lot more world out there than that. He'd found that out himself these past few years, on his way back to a version of himself that he could accept, that could see the beauty of the world again.

Thinking of what he'd told her about how young he'd been when he got involved with the shit that had turned into a dark and dangerous career path, he figured that was another thing he and Medusa had in common. His nineteen-year-old self hadn't had a chance to be young. He'd been young for a blink before he'd been old.

He made himself ask the question he might not want answered, since more than once he'd heard the darkness in her voice that hinted of it. "Do you wish for death?"

"Of course not." Her quick and indignant answer was a relief. "There is plenty to experience in solitude."

She spread her hands out before him. She'd threaded the other under his arm so they were like two elegant fans held before him with their ivory sharp tips. "My hands look the same to me as they did when I first came here. If I die of 'old age,' I suspect I will merely cease to exist in the form I have now." She paused. "When you... looked at my face, how old did I appear?"

"Early twenties. The curse may be preserving your age, as you suspect."

"Yes. The curse."

How she said it, with a flat tone, made him curious. "My lady?"

"Things are not always what they seem, John Pierce. Just as I suspect your nature, and your reasons for being here, have still not been fully revealed to me."

One of her hands settled back on his chest and the other withdrew, so there was still space between their bodies. He stroked her knuckles, following them to the points of her wrist, her forearm. Despite her impassive words, she didn't draw away, or tell him to stop. She touched his back again, tracing old scars, exploring. The surf frothed around his feet, as it would be doing to hers, standing so close behind him.

A slight bump against his back made him realize one of the snakes had come down to investigate the movement of her hand over his skin. As the sea breeze picked up, her hair teased his flesh as well. If she'd permit it, he'd turn around, put his mouth on hers and draw her fully against his body. The snakes could wind around their torsos and bind them together, just like he'd dreamed.

"Will you tell me a small part of it?" he said. "Would that make it easier, to do it in pieces?"

"Perhaps. If you will do the same. And you must go first."

Fair enough, right? But every time she asked, *why are you here*, it felt like he'd shoveled down another layer to a grave he didn't want uncovered. But this was why he'd finally turned himself in for some professional therapy, after he'd spent enough time helping subs that he'd seen the mirror reflecting back on him. The poor bastard who'd drawn the short straw at the counseling center JP had chosen had probably checked himself in for patient-induced PTSD after he helped JP, but thanks to him, John was better at opening up. Plus— the deciding vote—Lot had pointed out if he was too fucked up, he'd be no good for her. He wanted to be good for her.

"Maddock told me I'd spent most of my life on the nightmare side of a fantasy, making up roles for myself, living in worlds that weren't mine, always split between who I was and who I had to be. Why not give myself the chance to enjoy the other end of it?" He sighed. "It was my mother who started it. She was...she was never right in the head. My dad left her because he wanted other women. Lots of other women. Because she was messed up in the head already, that sort of became a catalyst that twisted her up further. She was the first one to read me your story, when I was five. That was right after my dad left."

He closed his eyes, seeing himself at bedtime, her curled up around him, but not the way a mother spooned protectively around her child. More as if she wanted him to protect her, tell her it was going to be okay. And maybe he'd been looking for a way to make the world safer for everyone ever since, as if that was his mission.

"When she got to the part about you coming to live in exile on an island, she whispered in my ear, 'Imagine how lonely she must have been, Johnny. Abandoned by everyone, because of something she couldn't change or be.

"Mom was talking about herself, because she was always caught in this narcissistic haze where everything came back to her, but..."

He realized he'd tightened his hand on hers, a little too hard. He eased his grip, but her fingers turned, the talons scraping him a little as she stroked over his knuckles. She was comforting him.

"I think it spoke to something in you," Medusa said quietly. "Because you were isolated, a child with a mother who could not be one."

"Yeah." She'd picked up on it instantly, which didn't surprise him much. Not since he'd come here and started learning just how many threads beyond the crazy inexplicable fate stuff connected them.

"But if the story had just connected to my fucked up home life, it wouldn't have stuck with me the way it did, the way you did. I think I was meant to be here, but maybe as much for myself as for you. There's a lot of shit dumped on the path I walked to get here, Medusa. I don't intend to dump it on you; I dealt with it, but it drives me and connects me to you. I just hope you don't end up thinking it's the only thing that does."

He left it at that, waiting her out. He wanted to give her the option of speaking along the same lines or changing the subject, but he couldn't help giving her a small nudge.

"Would you tell me something of your own story now? What really happened?"

The air filled with a portentous feeling, a return of that darkness. It meant she was going to grant his request. For a second, he wanted to suggest they do it another time, so he didn't pull her into bad memories, but he bit it back. He wished he could know all of it through legend and secondhand fact so he wouldn't have to distress her, ever, but knowing the truth—both of their truths—was obviously critical to getting past her barriers. That was a no-brainer he'd know even if his sharp intuition wasn't right on top of it. Even if he'd rather cut open his own demons with a rusty knife blade than have her face even one of hers.

"You were told I was...forced by a god and cursed by Athena for the transgression, were you not?" She spoke at last. "I have been told that is the story. Did you believe that nonsense?"

"I'm open to all possibilities, my lady. Otherwise I wouldn't have believed you existed. You're a myth in my world, and myths come with a lot of assumptions. For instance, that gods and goddesses can do such things."

"As if they would care enough to consort with mortals, or protect them from their own folly." The bitterness in her tone was unmistakable. Since she'd moved her hand back to his chest, he was careful not to hold her, tangle with her fingers or clasp her wrist as would be his normal preference. But he did keep the contact between them, stroking the top of her hand slowly, from forearm to wrist and knuckles and back again.

"Athena did not curse me," she said in a hard voice. "Nor Poseidon, though He was involved, inadvertently. There was a powerful man, Ukrit, who visited our temple. The senior priestess who did not like us to laugh, Berenike, pursued political alliances with him against other factions in the city. Klotho explained that to me later...for I did not understand any of that. Not then."

Her talons curved in, pressing against his chest. Now he did move his hand to her wrist, a light clasp, a reassurance that he was here. "When he visited," she said, "sometimes he would corner me in apparent jest, flirting. I always slipped away laughing, but he made me feel nervous in ways I could not explain. I told no one but my friend Callidora, who was as innocent as I.

"Late one night, when all my other sisters slept, Berenike woke me. She took me to the part of the temple I liked best, the pediment where Athena is fighting the giants. She has a snake shield." She paused, and he heard a wistful note in her voice. "I liked Her face in that sculpture the best. She is in battle, yet She still looks so wise and kind. Berenike told me to kneel in front of Athena and submit to Her Will, however that Will presented itself."

He had enough elements of the story to know what was coming. Yet he felt the burning rage he always felt, no matter how often he'd heard this kind of tragedy.

"Ukrit came to me there. He was...there was magic clinging to him, a dizzying power. He told me Poseidon had sanctioned the sacrifice of my virginity to his desires. Despite what Berenike had said to me, and despite that magic, I was a frightened girl and I denied him. But this time...he wouldn't be denied."

A man taking what was not given willingly, destroying the beauty of a woman's soul with his cruelty or lust. JP wanted badly to turn and put his arms around her, but instead she stood behind him like a rigid statue, her voice painting terrible pictures in his mind.

"I fought as hard as I could, but his power rolled over me. It was as if I were drowning. I smelled the deepest, darkest part of Poseidon's sea and it choked me. He beat my head against the stone until I was insensible. He took my body several times, in shameful ways, telling me there was no part of me that was not his."

Fucking, goddamn bastard who should rot in hell forever. Why it was worse, hearing it was a man and not a god, JP didn't know. Maybe because the god story made it more like a fairy tale. A horrible one, yes, but still somehow detached from the grim realities he knew of rape, of violation, of violence and death. Of the horrors men visited upon one another.

She was right to question how he could have believed it was a god who had done such a thing, since only humans tormented one another in such a way. Her hand was shaking, but when he tried to hold onto her, she slipped away and stepped back.

"Medusa, let me turn around. I'll keep my eyes closed. Let me hold you, offer you comfort."

"No. There is no comfort you can give me for this. I am simply telling you, and you promised to keep facing the sea."

"Okay." He set his jaw, accepting the unacceptable. "Did he take off like the coward he was after that?"

"No. In his mind, he'd done no wrong. Since he'd stolen power from Poseidon to commit the act, he believed it was a sanction from the god himself. And Berenike...whatever it was between them, I was the price she'd promised." Her tone became dull. "It is ironic that harming a priestess of Athena was an insult to the whole city, even an act of war, if committed by a foreigner. Yet no one knew of this crime, for it was done with the sanction of one of our senior priestesses and covered up by her lies.

"Berenike came after he finished, as if he had some black magic way of summoning her. While I lay there, he told her he would return in several days to take me home as his slave, after they tended to me. He did not wish to be burdened by my care."

He heard her swallow. "After he departed, Berenike summoned Klotho. She told her as I was no longer a virgin, pure for the temple. I was out of favor to perform her rituals. She made it sound as if I..."

As if Medusa was some kind of base whore who'd taken a lover at the very foot of the Goddess. For some crimes there was no punishment great enough. But he'd met people like Berenike on his own assignments. Medusa had been just a pawn to her. Like Ukrit, she likely hadn't lost a moment of sleep over what they'd done to the young girl.

Medusa's voice had broken, but now it steadied again. "She told Klotho a wealthy man was to take me into his home, and he intended to offer a generous donation to the head priestess. Nothing more would be said of it, and there would be no shame placed upon the temple."

"Humans do evil and blame it on the gods," Medusa added abruptly. "Athena's only crime was Her apathy, and yet I cannot blame Her even for that. It was my assumption that She would care. I begged for help while he was attacking me, and Her statue loomed over me, inanimate, unresponsive. The wisdom and kindness I saw in Her face...it became a mockery. That was when I knew the gods were far beyond concerns with us. We are here to serve them, not the other way around."

She fell silent, her bitter words adding an edge to the air around them.

"I did say you could tell it in pieces," he said carefully. "Don't keep going if it's causing you too much pain."

"This part is one piece, and no different today than it will be tomorrow. Berenike left me with Klotho after that. She did not wish to be burdened with my care, either."

"Klotho tended to you."

"Yes. She held me for a little while." Medusa cleared a thick throat. "I was too insensible to realize it then, but Klotho's anger and frustration on my behalf was deep, down to her soul. She was a true priestess of Athena and knew what a terrible crime had had been perpetuated within the sacred walls of Her temple. She was also frustrated by the political realities that would make it impossible for her to override Berenike or prevent Ukrit from taking me. So she chose another way."

Medusa took a breath. "When I calmed enough to listen, she told me she had a plan to keep him away from me forever. It would involve witchcraft, twisting the residue of Poseidon's magic he'd left upon me and combining it with what lay within my own heart. Then she summoned the other priestesses. They were told not to clean me or tend my wounds. That was the hardest part."

Her voice wavered, then firmed again. "I am ashamed to say I begged for at least a little water and a cloth. Klotho put a kind hand upon me and counseled patience. She told me it would all make sense soon. Mercifully, she allowed them to give me a tonic to make me sleep for a few hours while they prepared. When I woke, she told me more of her plan, and let me know it was my choice. I could take my chances with him, or I could do what she had devised."

His mind hitched over that. Hearing that a man, not a god, had raped her could be digested without too much of a paradigm shift. Knowing she'd made a conscious choice to embrace the form she currently held pulled him off the track of what he'd always believed.

Choices made under duress could be rightfully considered no choice at all, but after his momentary surprise, it fit with the strength she'd demonstrated to him ever since he'd arrived. She hadn't capitulated to being a victim. She'd made a choice and had given herself a chance at saving her own soul, rather than losing it to the darkness that swallowed so many victims of violence.

"The stumbling point was Klotho did not know the exact form the spell would take, what it would do to me. She knew only that if we did it, I would forever be free of his desire. I agreed. Begged for it. Will you turn toward this side without looking at me?"

She'd touched his right arm. When he adjusted in that direction, she moved behind him, farther into the water. He heard her bending down, the water splashing. He suspected she was cupping handfuls and letting it run down her arms and legs, anointing herself in the cleansing blue surf.

"She took everything I felt inside and twisted it into the magic. My rage and pain, my sense of betrayal and confusion. I blacked out during the ritual..." She hesitated, and he heard uncertainty in her voice. "I woke...as this. One of the priestesses told me to take what I needed from the stores and make my way to an uninhabited place. I... So much of that time is unclear. I don't want to remember... Perhaps I shouldn't have told you at all."

"Hey, it's okay." As her voice broke, revealing even deeper distress, he cursed the inability to touch her once again. Instead, he put everything good about the wish in his voice, hoping it would help. "You tell me only what you want to tell me."

He wished the priestess had chosen a different way. Just put Medusa on a boat and get her the hell out of there. But a man who could pay for magic that could twist Poseidon's power and pit it against a priestess of Athena in the temple itself would have had a long reach. And he had the support of a senior priestess who JP hoped was currently rotting in Tartarus.

At different times in his life, he'd had the same thoughts as Medusa about the apathy of the gods. Yet he wondered if she believed it all the time, or only in more despairing moments. He'd been to the Old Temple, the Archaic temple to Athena in Athens. Standing at the base of the old ruins, he'd felt a residual power, and it had been tranquil, enduring. A Goddess still alive in the stones.

"I think the gods care," Maddock had told him once. "They just see a far fucking bigger picture than we do. And they know we're tougher than we think we are. The things we do with adversity? You put all of it into a gallery, you'd have a series of masterpieces."

No argument there. He found her a work of art, in every way. He wished she believed that, and saw the beauty he felt from her, inside and out.

"I am tired," Medusa said in a small voice. "I will see you tomorrow."

"Do not go, my lady. Such retellings bring on bad dreams. Please stay with me and I will keep them at bay. Sleep next to me like you did the other night. If you think you can keep your claws to yourself, that is."

He added the dose of humor even though her story left him feeling anything but. He channeled the anger into a genuine desire to care for her, keep her close so the demons in her story could not have her.

"Maybe."

He'd been expecting more deliberation, or an outright no, so he suppressed the grim surge of victory.

"You do me honor with your trust, my lady. I made a dessert out of coconut and some sugar I brought. Why don't we take a little walk, and then we can try it together?"

CHAPTER EIGHT

*H*e put the blindfold back on and walked along the shoreline. At first, she walked with him in a silence weighted with what they shared. However, as often happened, the beauty of the world around them, and the chance to walk with someone who understood, made things ease.

She stopped. "Look at this. Oh, I mean..."

Her little stumble warmed him. He extended his hand, and she placed a shell in it.

"It has a pretty color. Purple and pink."

"It feels as smooth as your skin." He ran his thumb inside the curve. "When I was young, before they broke up, my parents took a beach trip every year. My mother liked to walk on the beach in the mornings. I'd go with her, swim and look at the shells she picked up. My dad wasn't a morning person, so he'd come join us later. I'd make sand sculptures while they were talking."

Which usually turned into arguing and tears when his dad couldn't keep his eyes off the other women on the beach.

"I made a long, long snake one time. It was this wide..." She grasped his wrists and spread out his arms to encompass several feet. "It would have taken ten minutes to walk from the head to the tail," she said triumphantly.

He was getting accustomed to feeling her snakes sliding over his arms when she moved inside his personal space, like now. She hadn't commented upon their movements, and he wondered if that was because they'd been part of her for so long she didn't see their touching him as anything separate from her putting her hands upon him. He was also getting very fond of her increasing willingness to do that.

She walked onward, picking up more shells and putting them in his hands so he could feel their shape. She described their colors to him. Easy conversations about nothing while strolling along a beach. Had she missed doing that? Did she find it surprising that she could fall so easily into doing it now, especially after what she'd shared?

Maybe because of what she shared. When he didn't ask any follow up questions, but made it clear with his attentive silence she could say more if she wished, she seemed to get even more relaxed. He felt the same. Tit for tat.

At one point they sat side by side on a rock, so close that with a slight adjustment they'd brush hips and shoulders. Perhaps her wing would curve behind him and he'd feel it.

"Was it hard to get used to the wings?" he asked. "To learn how to fly?"

"In the beginning, yes." She shrugged, because her shoulder did move against him. Then she shifted away, as if she hadn't realized she was sitting so close. "I was like a fledgling fallen out of the nest without a parent to show her anything. At first, I didn't use them much at all, but I realized I was not using one of the best weapons I have. Most enemies don't look for an attack from above. They aren't prepared to counter it."

"Aside from that, there's the plain old awesome factor."

"The awesome factor?"

"Being able to fly like that has to be incredible, exhilarating. Swooping like a bird all by yourself."

"Yes." He heard the smile in her voice. "At first I was terrified, because I'd get a few feet in the air and would turn or twist the wrong way and send myself plummeting. I broke some bones, but found they healed in a matter of several days, some less. So I realized the spell had given me greater healing ability, which in turn made me more confident about learning to fly. I did most of my experimenting once I was here, where I had time to figure it out on my own. Before that, most my energy went toward hiding from

people who were far too close to the places where I found temporary refuge."

He expected those first days had been difficult beyond description.
Especially as the follow-up to what had caused the curse initially. Get
raped, then immediately transformed into something else. Wake up
and go on the run to find a safe place. She'd had to deal with so much
on her own. Hell, instead of feeling dismayed by her reluctance to
trust him, he should be focusing on what a miracle it was she was
talking to him at all.

He echoed the promise he'd made to her to himself. He wouldn't
do anything to lose her trust. He wanted her to feel like she could let
her shields down enough to "hang out" together like this, try out his
company. Learn that he could be a friend, as well as lover. And maybe
Master.

He had all the time in the world. He could walk along the beach
and "look" at shells with her for a full day without tiring of it. Since
she hadn't found an excuse to leave his company, citing the need to
wash her snakes or something like that, his company was still being
rated better than nothing. Good thing they were on an unpopulated
island, because he'd never been known for his charming social skills.

Women liked him because of his looks and the John Wayne thing
that made them feel safe. Then there was the Dom thing. It was close
enough to the surface that a woman with even the slightest touch of
submissive orientation or spice-it-up fantasies would feel its pull. That
combo had caused him occasional trouble in ops. Drug dealers got
touchy when their girlfriends or wives gravitated toward another man.

But now there was only one woman whose response mattered.

Leaving the rock, he knelt in the sand close enough to the shoreline that it was damp and easily packable.

"I'm taking off the blindfold, but keeping my back to you, my
lady."

She said nothing, but she didn't object, so he did that and began to
build his sculpture, feeling her attention as she remained sitting on
the rock. He started with hips, torso and breasts, and spread out to
wings, flying hair and twining snakes. He was no artist, but he showed
her as closely as possible how he saw her, adding shells to her wings
for decoration. However, instead of legs, he created a serpentine
curved tail that began at the swell of the hips.

"What is that?" She slid off the rock and came up behind him.

"There's a story that describes you without wings, but with a snake's tail."

"That would have made it very difficult to be upright."

"Well, Hollywood makes anything possible." When he explained what that meant before she needed to ask, he incited initial disbelief and a barrage of fascinated questions that drew her away from her contemplation of her troubled past.

"Moving pictures," she said thoughtfully. "Like a play."

"Well, yes, but they're not where you can touch them. They're on a screen." He held up his hands and formed a box with them, through which she could look at the sky. "Like that. They're also able to film all sorts of special effects that you couldn't do on a stage. Like big explosions and creatures of myth and fantasy. Women with snake tails who can move upright without effort."

"Learning to balance with the wings was difficult enough," she said. "Having a human body and wings is not as graceful as having a bird shape and wings."

"Well, much as I like birds, I'm glad you have a woman's shape." He was still squatting next to the sculpture and he swept his gaze meaningfully over it, the swell of hip and breast.

"Men think of little else."

"No, we think of lots else. We just keep that thought firmly pinned in the front at all times, because it motivates most of the foolish things we do."

"That I believe. My breasts are not that large."

"Sorry about that." He made a show of sculpting them down while enjoying a full caress of the curves. Then he framed them with both hands. "Better?"

"Miscreant." She snorted at him, punctuating it with a yawn. It reminded him it was getting late, the moon high in the sky. Living without electricity meant she likely woke and went to bed with the sun. Plus he had no idea how much she'd exerted herself today, keeping track of him and tending to her own needs.

"Why don't we head back up the beach? Time to get some sleep, right?"

"All right."

He donned the mask again. As they walked back toward his camp, they were close enough he brushed against her. She eased away, but it wasn't a startled jerk. One of the snakes slithered over his shoulder, making a sibilant noise as it passed close to his ear.

"You have a lot of snakes. More than these, I mean."

"Yes. They seem to be called to me. Wherever I have stayed, within a few days, the population becomes far more evident. But they never seem to be too many, thankfully. Else they'd overwhelm the other animals on the island."

"Can you talk to them the same way? Is that how you manage to get them to guard your garden and your nest?"

"Somewhat. I don't really have the same communication with them I have with my five snakes, but they seem to understand what I need and act upon it for my wellbeing. They will take fruit from my garden, but never too much. They will alert me if they see an arrival on the island they don't think I've seen. I've never been sure if they are sending me those impressions through my snakes or directly to me."

"Hmm." Testing a theory, he put out his hand, palm up. A second later an oblong head rested in it briefly, explored his fingers and then disappeared. He smiled. "They're not unfriendly."

"Only to those whom I deem a threat. You have large hands."

"Paws, my friends call them," he agreed. "I noticed markings on your claws. What's that about?"

"The spell. The words reinforce the magic upon me."

"One day, if you'll allow it, you should let Maddock take a look at them. He knows a lot about magic and science, and where the two overlap."

"Why?" She stopped. "So he can steal the magic I have? Or use my curse for his own purpose?"

"To help you, my lady." He kept walking and speaking in a casual tone. "If you wish the magic to be reversed. If you don't want to turn someone into stone merely by looking at them."

"It is the way I protect myself." She'd quickened her pace to rejoin him. Her tone was still suspicious, but less so than when she'd made similar accusations the day before.

"People can protect themselves a lot of ways. I meant no harm by suggesting it."

"You speak of things about which you know very little."

"True. But anytime you want to share, I'm happy to listen. And I'm not asking for information to use against you."

"There is no way to prove that to me."

"Sure there is. By you giving me more information and me not using it against you."

She made a strangled noise that he suspected was somewhere between a snort and a huff of exasperation. "You think this is a game, John Pierce."

"No." Now he did stop and face her. He couldn't look her in the eye, but he could show her how serious he was with his tone of voice and the rock hard set of his jaw. "I know it's not. What you told me earlier? I'm glad you told me, but it fills me with an anger I can't describe, that someone would do that to you. If I could have appeared to you before it happened and stop it, I would have. Even if that left you with no need or desire for me in your life."

Though the idea left him with a hollow feeling, he meant it. While thankfully fate had had its own plan, he never would have wished such a fate upon her.

"So you think I have allowed you to remain here because I have need of you."

"Or you feel sorry for me and think I have need of you. Poor crazy bastard who lost his mind to his job and is now chasing myths through time portals. You're kind-hearted that way."

She chuckled. "You are a foolish man, John Pierce." Then she sighed. "I wish there was a way to trust you. If I could..."

"Hey. I get it." He reached out, accurately gauging where he might find a curl of that abundant hair alongside her delicate face. He stroked it back and took his hand away before she could get antsy. "But that's what I want you to understand. I'm not going anywhere, and I'm not going to betray your trust. We've got nothing but time." He extended his palm. "How about you trust me enough to hold your hand the few hundred yards we have left to get to camp?"

This time the pause wasn't as long. When she laid her hand in his, he closed his fingers over hers. She lifted their linked hands, apparently considering them, and how her claws curved over his knuckles.

She didn't speak further, but they walked the rest of the way like that, his elbow brushing her arm and her wing, which she had folded along her back. He had so many questions about her wings, snakes and life, but he was trying hard to pay attention to what was going on in those emotional energy readings around her. As Maddock would say: "Why do I give you tools if you won't use them?"

JP's reading was that she had all she could handle right now. She'd offered him a glimpse of her truths, trusting him with that much. It was enough. Telling her about his mother and some of the decisions he'd made because of his childhood hadn't been a cakewalk. They could both use a break.

When they reached his lean-to, she didn't leave, another victory. He offered her some of the coconut sugar pudding he'd made. After they ate that, he stretched out on his mat. She stayed on the other side of his shelter, not coming closer. He didn't encourage her to do so, instead bringing up more topics of casual conversation in the hopes she'd continue to stay. Sleep here with him under the stars.

She told him how the Greeks spent a day swimming at the beach, and he learned that body surfing and love of the ocean had been around since ancient times. No big surprise there, but she painted a pretty picture of it, all the priestesses in the water, splashing and laughing. He told her about surf boarding, and a field of brightly colored umbrellas at a crowded Daytona Beach.

As he spoke, she moved closer. She stretched out next to him on the mat where he was lying on his back, looking up at the stars. Her head was close enough she could almost put her head on his biceps, since he had his hands stacked behind his head, elbows bent. When he pointed out a constellation he knew, she shifted and closed that distance.

The snakes were still. Sometimes he could feel their life signs when they lay against his chest or biceps. Even though he'd worked with snakes, he hadn't thought about feeling their heartbeat or breath until now.

"So as you said, I am a story," she said slowly. "In your world, I am not real. I am a tale. A...myth?"

"Yes. Myth, fairy tale, folklore. It's Maddock who realized you exist, that the most enduring stories pull from alternative dimensions. They're part of a flow of energy deep in the subconscious, no less real than our own day-to-day lives. When a person like me feels a particularly strong pull toward a story, it's because we're somehow connected to it. We sense that reality more vividly than most."

It wasn't a serious break from reality caused by PTSD or being undercover so long he'd lost his marbles. That had been his initial, pretty traumatizing belief. Maddock had convinced him otherwise, pointing out facts that supported it. Like how he'd always felt that Medusa was real, ever since his mother read him the story.

"So if I am very certain a beast never seen before exists, it does?"

"I don't see why not. What beast have you imagined?"

"It was a creature like a horse, but different. So full of light, she glows even at night, like moonlight. She bears a single spiral horn, which looks like a seashell, and her eyes are the blue of the sea. Her coat is the white of clouds, and her golden mane is softer than any silk I ever felt. I would dream of her sometimes, before...I left the temple. Then the dreams stopped coming."

Miracle of miracles, she laid her hand on his chest, considerately above the stapled wounds. She propped her head on her hand as he casually curved his arm around her shoulders, above the joining point of her wings.

"There was a scholar who visited Klotho who spoke of wild asses in India who had a horn like this creature, but his drawings did not look like her, and in my dream she calls herself a unicorn, not an ass." She paused. "I miss dreaming of her."

He wouldn't tell her why the dream had stopped. He couldn't bear to tell her a unicorn was only drawn to a maid's purity. But he couldn't tell her about a unicorn without getting into those sticky waters. So he diverted the subject into similar but less painful areas.

"I've heard tales of another amazing creature. A woman with thick ropes of hair the color of sand down her back, all the way to her ankles. She has skin like the copper of your small snake, and she, too, has a bond with them. She carries them in a pouch on her waist and is known for her fierceness, her wisdom, her protective nature and generosity to her people. She has a mask she dons to scare away any who threaten them. She is revered."

"Who is she?"

"She's you. Another story of you, from another culture and people. We have lots of scholars who analyze our history and try to parse fact from fiction, where they've meshed, overlapped or been rewritten by conquering peoples. It's believed the Greek story of your existence was a derivation of her story, when the Greeks invaded the African tribes and tried to stamp out their view with their own. That's one theory."

"You don't believe it?"

He traced the curve of her shoulder. Skin that begged to be touched, lean muscle, elegant bones. "Not sure. Hindsight is usually skewed vision, where we imagine the author had a purpose other than writing an interesting story. Ovid, the one who wrote your story for the Greeks, may have taken pieces of the Libyan story and created something he thought his audience would like better. Or he tapped into your true story in his creative consciousness."

She shifted so her lips innocently brushed his T-shirt. He felt the impact in his all-too-aware flesh beneath the cloth. He knew she was looking at him, and her fingertips proved it, gliding over his cheek, his lips. They firmed with the need to move, to kiss her fingertips, to kiss her everywhere.

"Do you know the ancient Romans invented names for different kisses?" He closed his fingers around her wrist and touched his lips to her knuckles. "There was an *osculum*, a publicly appropriate kiss."

She got very still. He adjusted to his hip, moving slow but deliberately. He wasn't backing away from this. Touching her chin to find her face, he slid his fingertips along her cheek. "I'm going to lean in and just touch my lips to the corner of your mouth, less than a blink."

He tipped her head up to mark that spot, putting his mouth against it. God, when he felt the quiver go through her body, he wanted to taste her with teeth and tongue, but he kept it casual. A brief and yet lingering contact, a delicate balance. "That's a *basium*," he said, clearing his voice. "A lip-to-lip kiss, but still light. Perhaps not chaste, but not so passionate as to incur disapproval from anyone watching."

That slight tension through her body remained, but her fingers and talons curled against his chest spoke a different message. He eased back. "They had names for other kisses as well," he said.

"Oh, really?"

He heard the wry humor, her acknowledgment of his cleverness. The other quality he heard—intrigue—invoked a tempting anticipation.

"Really." Humming a little under his breath, he distracted himself by thinking about the night sky wheeling above him. He'd like to take off his blindfold and see it. While he could promise her he wouldn't forget and look at her, he doubted she'd go for it. What was gratifying about her vehemence was the proof—he hoped—that she liked having him around. She didn't want to risk the contacts not working. Or she didn't like losing the tactical advantage, a more morose thought.

"Well? Tell me another," she said at last, with impatience.

"Tell you, or show you, my lady?"

Her grip pricked his chest, telling him her tension had increased.

"Only what you wish," he reminded her. "Nothing more."

Her wings rustled, one brushing him as she sat up. She flattened her palm on his chest, so he expected she was gazing down at him. Part of why he'd like to remove the blindfold was to gaze at the night sky at the same time she did, a sharing of vision. But a deeper connection of spirit surpassed sight, a melding of all the senses at the source, in the mind itself. He felt some of that between them through her touch.

"Tell me," she said at last. "And I will show *you*."

She'd managed to surprise him, in a very satisfying way.

"It's a *saviolum*. A passionate kiss, placed on the lips. A taking of the lips, if you will."

The world stopped on the head of a pin for him as she bent toward him. Her abdomen brushed his, her breasts sliding along his chest. Her breath was on his face. Sweet, like clove honey flavored with mint.

Her mouth was so close to his own he could inhale her breath and he did, his lips parted when she touched them. When an involuntary quiver ran through his muscles, she startled like a cat, twitching away from him. He stopped himself from reaching for her and kept his hands laced behind his head, waiting her out. Seeing if she'd dare to take more.

She did. Her mouth returned, moving on his, her lips a pleasing cushion, her breath a little irregular. Nerves, but maybe something else. With the blissful ignorance of the sexually innocent, she followed her curiosity, parting her lips to taste his bottom one. She was killing him. He felt a glancing brush of her tongue, but she was shy about that. Yet her body, responding to primal instinct, was resting fully on him. His stapled wounds complained, but he told them to shut the hell up. Her hand rested against the base of his throat, fingertips against his crashing pulse. If she shifted over him, she'd come in full contact with the involuntary reaction of his body, his cock starting to pulse right along in time with his carotid.

One of her tiny fangs pinked his lip, unintentional, but when she kissed away the drop of blood, he bit back a groan.

I'd like to touch you. Need to touch you. Just in time, he came up with better phrasing. "Would you like me to touch you?"

"As you did before. My face...my neck and shoulders." She paused, hovering over his mouth. "The more I do this, the more I want to feel your hands, so many places. As long as it can feel as it does while on my face. Good. Necessary. Not like necessary as in required. It is the wrong word."

"Desired, my lady. You desire me to touch you. Will you say it for me?"

"Will you stop if—"

"I will stop the second you tell me," he said instantly. "And if you tell me you want me to touch you again a blink after, or whenever it feels right again, I will. Just as I will stop if you say so right after that. All I desire is to give you pleasure."

"Has it been like that for you and other women?" Her touch was on his face still, her lips brushing the corner of his mouth, but she paused there, her forehead resting against his blindfold. One of the snakes stirred, tunneling through his short hair and resting its body against the side of his head while it explored the sand. They were getting used to him. Or they knew their mistress was.

"A constant stop, start, stop, start," she clarified when his brows raised in question at her comment.

"For some. When they needed that." He wasn't going to get into the therapeutic scenes he did with submissives right now. Definitely the wrong timing. "But for others, I read their consent from their physical responses to me, and the way they touched me. Their eagerness and desire were the paths I followed, rather than the spoken word."

"And they trusted you to go no farther than they desired." She drew back, but her hand remained on his chest, an encouraging sign, though he missed her mouth intensely.

"They did. When desire becomes passion, and you're in it

together, the fear goes away, because demand is created by the passion. It's a form of violence, the right kind."

"The right kind." She mused on that. "Is that why one part of me doesn't want you to...be so courteous?"

For someone with her past, it was an incredibly brave question to ask, and he treated it with the respect and reverence it demanded. "It is very normal, when you desire someone. And when you trust them not to hurt you."

He unlaced his hands and laid one on hers, but she took it away. "How would you like to touch me?" she demanded. Her voice was worried, but he couldn't tell the source of her tension.

'There's no way I wouldn't like to touch you. But for right now, if you permitted me, I would touch and stroke your face, your throat and shoulders, slide my hands down your arms. I'd trace the lines of your palms, caress the pulse in your wrists. I'd clasp my hands around your wrists, feel that beat."

"You like holding my wrists."

"I do," he said carefully. "Do you like it, my lady?"

She didn't answer that, merely saying, "Keep telling me how you would touch me."

"I'd trail my fingers from your throat, down between your breasts. I'd like to cradle them, feel your nipples get hard against my palms. They do that when a woman is aroused."

"I know that," she said defensively, as if it bothered her that he thought her so unschooled.

"Do you?" He was intrigued. "How?"

"At the temple, in the baths, the women would sometimes please one another with their hands, their mouths. I never... I was too young, but I would watch, hidden. It was not spoken of, because maidens of Athena were to be chaste, like her, but Klotho said Athena was strong, a warrior woman. She had no doubt she indulged in self-pleasuring, since the desires of the body are a sacred gift from the gods. After what happened with Ukrit, I thought she was mistaken. I forgot what I felt when I watched those women."

He could feel her scrutinizing his face closely. "What are you thinking?" she asked.

"I've just figured out where I want to go after I die," he said.

When she understood, he heard her chuckle.

"You are right, John Pierce. Men are very simple to please."

Christ, he'd love to see her laugh or smile. Just hearing it in her voice made the whole world shine, even in the darkness behind his blindfold. Maddock had never doubted that when JP met Medusa, her reality would only enhance his feelings, rather than diminish them. Maybe because JP had never doubted it himself. But the confirmation was still a miracle.

"If I was one of those women, where would you have me touch you?" he asked.

She cupped one of his large hands in hers, turning it over to play with his fingers and stroke his knuckles. "These are not the hands of a woman, John Pierce. And I can't imagine you as one of my sisters. Except maybe Phyllidos. She was six feet tall and strong like a man. Yet your shoulders are far broader than hers, your thighs so muscular." Her fingertips trailed along his body there, the shorts making it a skin-to-skin contact.

If she wasn't so innocent of sensuality and caught up in the worries of her past, he'd accuse her of being a terrible tease. Arousal was starting to get painful. Fortunately, the hold of the denim and the night shadows concealed it.

"My lady, you have the makings of a delightful Dominatrix."

She didn't respond to that, telling him her attention was firmly caught by priorities other than asking him to clarify a term she wouldn't have heard before. He had no objection, since her next move was to place his hand on her side. Her laced top was short enough his hand was on her bare waist.

She was thin. Not a surprise, because a bird had to have a rapid metabolism to fly and he expected a winged humanoid would be the same. Plus she kept herself battle-ready. It pained him, knowing she'd been taught to defend herself from an early age, but she hadn't been taught what kind of enemy she should be prepared to face. It didn't matter how much training anyone had; the element of surprise could overcome it if it came at one the right way. Like from a man who'd stolen magic from a god.

He suspected she'd adapted her training since then, and far surpassed whatever was taught at the temple. The mantra of "never again" had likely powered every drop of sweat.

He imagined the pleasure of matching skills with her in that promised sparring bout. While the bet was putting the other on the ground three times, he indulged the fantasy of pinning her there, having her at his mercy, feeling her body tremble for all the right reasons at that kind of play.

Optimistic thought, John. She could just as easily kick your ass and you end up at her mercy.

Well, that could be fun, too.

Yet this give and take was the ultimate sensual strategy game he desired. He picked up clues from how her breath held and caught, the minute tremor through her limbs. The way she softened under his touch as he did the exact opposite.

He slid his hand up her side, his thumb following the outside of her breast. He didn't linger but he didn't rush, giving them both the full measure of sensation. The curve lifted, as if she'd drawn in a breath, and he continued up over her shoulder and to her collar bone, thumb sliding in the pocket between the two, down the sternum, only halfway, then across, over the tops of her breasts. The halter-style top was blissfully low cut, laced at a deep point in her cleavage. He sensed her lifting into his touch again, and he reversed course, now curling his hand to let his knuckles glide up to her throat.

Her chin became part of the vertical track, telling him she'd dropped her head back on her shoulders. He wanted to ask if she'd closed her eyes, relaxing her defenses that much, but he didn't want to raise them again with the question.

His knuckles glided along her windpipe and the area around it. When one of her silken curls of hair looped around his finger, a snake's head brushed his knuckles. He felt its forked tongue feather him before it retreated, as if the creature knew it shouldn't interfere with his mistress's absorption.

JP made his way up over the slim point of her chin to find her lips. As he caressed them and they parted, male satisfaction surged through him, especially as the tip of her tongue touched him, tasted, but again quickly withdrew before he had a full sense of it. He moved his fingers over her cheekbones and the bridge of her nose, eyebrows and forehead, and then he did what he hadn't done before. He tunneled his fingers through her hair.

The snakes weren't woven into a crown on her head right now. Instead they seemed to be uncoiled and moving over her shoulders and arms. As he passed his fingers through the thick strands, the contrasting braided-skin texture of the snakes alternated with the silky feel of her locks. He stroked the snakes, too, not avoiding them, giving them the same message of ease and nothing-to-fear. Descending to caress her nape, he glided around to the sensitive skin beneath her ears. The movements of her head were following his touch now, increasing the pleasure of the attention for both of them.

"Your snakes are sleek. I bet their scales shine in the sun just like all this gorgeous hair."

"They sometimes look like they are dipped in oil," she agreed. She hesitated over the syllables, as if struggling with arousal. Just the thought of that being true was enough to get him harder.

"I only feel four."

"Treebark is avoiding your touch. He is more cautious than the others."

He slipped his hands back over her face, spreading his fingers out. It was a fine boned oval his palm and fingers could easily cover. "What color were your eyes, before?"

"Green. Like the sea on an overcast day, Klotho used to say. Now..." She drew a painful breath. "The pupils, all of it...are like snake eyes."

"The irises reminded me of rose petals." Yeah, he wasn't a poet, but that deep rich color had only one comparison in his mind, the perfection of the crimson flower.

Though she stiffened at the reminder of his stolen glance, he didn't interrupt the rhythm of his touch. He wanted to keep reminding her he could look at her without her worrying that a glance could turn him to stone. He also wanted her to remember that when he'd looked upon her, nothing about her had repelled him.

"You have a snake's grace and quickness as well, my lady. In addition to the rose petal eyes and forked tongue."

Stillness again. Maybe she was debating whether or not to take off. He could feel that something was happening, some kind of mental struggle. Hoping to help her resolve that in a way that kept her right here, he slid his hand back over her shoulder and returned to his track down her sternum, over the rise of her breasts.

Her hand closed over his wrist and he stopped. He didn't withdraw, but he didn't press forward. Waiting to see what she wanted to do.

One heartbeat. Two heartbeats. Three... Clasping his other wrist, she brought both his hands up, guiding them to cup her breasts as he'd described his desires. Her hands were shaking.

Firm and round, two lovely words. She wasn't overly large, perhaps a B size in his world, perfect for her warrior-slim frame. As he already knew, her top wasn't thick enough to conceal the tightening of her nipples as they responded to his touch, but he resisted the temptation of focusing on them. Instead, he savored the incidental pleasure of having them press into his palms as he caressed her curves. He wanted those taut peaks aching for an isolated touch, a gentle pinching that could become less gentle. He let his thumbs play in the laced valley between her breasts, cleavage he deepened when he constricted his grip, letting her feel a taste of male demand at what he hoped was just the right timing.

It was. A moan caught in her throat, fueling his own response. When he allowed his thumbs to pass over her nipples, the lightest of brushes, she reacted as if jolted by electricity. Her hand dropped and inadvertently brushed his erection.

Shit.

Direct contact revealed what shadows and denim had done a halfway decent job of hiding. Her response was immediate and volatile.

She jerked away and was gone, the blast of air from her wings mixed with a chorus of surprised hissing.

He sat up. "My lady? You do not need to run away. You need only say stop if you are uncomfortable."

"You were going to take me against my will. You were...hard."

That was an understatement. In its current state, his cock could knock a ball out of a major league baseball park. Her response told him she hadn't left, thankfully, but she was perhaps twenty feet down the beach, a distance safe enough to allow her to take flight before he could reach her.

"Yes. I am. You felt desire at my touch. Didn't you, my lady? Your body was responding. That's what arouses me, your pleasure. I would find no pleasure in taking you against your will. Do you think the husbands of married women force them?"

"I do not know. I was not exposed to married women enough to talk to them about such things."

But she'd heard stories. He could hear the fib in her voice. She was just uncertain of her own reaction and his.

"Did you get afraid? Is that why you ran away? I don't want you to be afraid of me." He communicated it in the rough earnestness of his voice and was glad when she responded as if she believed his sincerity.

"I was not running away." She drew a few steps closer.

John laid back and laced his fingers behind his head again, figuring the relaxed pose would help. "So why'd you go over there, instead of saying stop? I won't act on my desire, my lady. Never without your consent or invitation."

"Never. I will never consent to what he did to me."

"That's good. Because I'd chop off that part of my anatomy before I'd do that to you." He let her hear that in his voice, too. "You enjoyed touching me, being with me, yes?"

"Yes. I wasn't afraid exactly. How I reacted when you touched me...it took me by surprise."

"Did you like it?"

Silence. "Yes. It is still nice when I do it to myself, but I like it better when you do it."

He bit back a groan at the vision of her pleasuring herself, exploring her breasts and nipples with intrigued fingers.

"Then come back here."

Did she react the way he'd often seen a new sub respond to a clear command? Desire would war with wonderment at the body's instant answer to a display of dominance. Damn, he missed his sight when he thought of things like that, but it was icing on the cake. He knew she'd reacted like that, because he could *feel* it. It might startle her as much as her arousal at his touch, so it was disappointing but no surprise when she didn't come back.

When she left him entirely.

Hearing the rush of wings, JP imagined her flying to a tree at the forest line behind him and perching there to watch him. Perhaps she'd stretch out on a branch while the snakes wound around it. Had she ever been stuck until she could coax them to unwind and let her rise?

In his aroused state, he couldn't help an idle fantasy of being a snake charmer who could command the snakes to do just that. Bind her to a branch so her head was restrained, perhaps one winding around her throat and across her shoulders to keep her that way as he charmed not only the snakes but aroused her body past all fear. He'd take her mind beyond every worry.

Rein it back, John, he warned himself. Yet he wondered if he was being too careful. What was the charming way she'd put it? Being too courteous.

Because he no longer felt her near, he could remove the blindfold, but he kept his eyes closed, absorbing the lingering impressions of her flesh and voice, her breath, and all the things that could fill both silence and darkness.

He remembered the surprised hissing when she'd taken off. Were the snakes lulled by her desire? An interesting idea. Did arousal act as a sleep tonic for them, so she could focus fully on her pleasures? He could ask, perhaps when she was less agitated, but she might not know the answer to the question. He'd love to help her find out, if she ever let him touch her again.

Never. I will never consent to what he did to me

She thought that meant she didn't want sex ever again, but he knew better. Her body, her pounding pulse and that sexy little catch when she tried to talk to him while he was touching her said differently.

When he drifted off to sleep, his dreams were punctuated by erotic images that had him waking up several times with an unabated hard-on. If this kept up, no pun intended, tomorrow morning he'd head for the waterfall at the lower elevation. Based on the current state of his knitting skin, he knew he'd be able to take out the staples first thing, so the cold water would help soothe the irritated area at the same time it calmed his libido. If it didn't work, he'd just take his troublesome dick in hand and deal with it that way. He wasn't going to have it interfering with his judgment.

Patience. He could be patient. He had all the time in the world for her. He wanted to know everything about her, but more than that, he was content to spend a lifetime doing so.

From his experience, that was what love was all about.

CHAPTER NINE

*M*edusa flew low over the treetops touched by the morning light. Ratqueen didn't care for flying and usually ducked her head under her thick mane of hair as it streamed behind her and down her back. The others were indifferent to it, draping themselves on her shoulders. Well, except Waterlight. She loved flight, usually positioning herself in an upraised position above Medusa's brow, like a figurehead on the prow of a ship. Her tongue would flicker wildly, like a flag, as the snake scented everything brought to her in the wind.

Spiraling up, Medusa landed on an outcropping of rock at the highest point of the island. From here she could see miles of ocean, white clouds and endless sky. Between the distant land formations, the occasional ship appeared, headed out to destinations she could guess but never know. Unless they had nefarious purposes toward her, they gave her island a wide berth. Except for the infrequent curiosity seekers, usually young men daring themselves to be brave.

Mostly.

She didn't want to think about that memory, but it flashed through her mind anyway. That particular boat of young people had been as youthful as she'd been when all this had befallen her.

She'd stayed hidden when they made shore. As John Pierce had discovered, finding her camouflaged home was not an easy task, and reaching it required an arduous, slow climb or wings. She hadn't driven off this group right away as she should have, because she'd longed to hear human voices. Laughter. Flying down close enough to eavesdrop, she'd learned they had snuck away from home, daring one another to stay overnight on "Medusa's Island."

They stayed on the beach, except for a brief exploration that revealed one of the waterfalls to them. They'd swam and played in the deep pool until dinner, and returned to the beach to make a fire.

The young men sought to impress their lady friends with their daring, but they had no desire to hunt anything on the island but what lay beneath the girls' clothing. She could tell from their dress and mannerisms the males were from the aristocracy, whereas the girls were from the serving class or poorer families. The girls had flirted and occasional kisses had been exchanged. It was a display of youthful innocence and first love, things she'd once understood better.

She overstayed her welcome. As darkness fell, they started telling scary stories to tease one another. Stories about her. Her monstrous features, her bloodthirsty cruelty. When she'd had enough, she left them, flying silently back to her home and spending the night watching them well out of hearing range. She would have done better to watch them like the moving pictures John Pierce had described. The early ones, with no sound.

The next morning, right before sunrise, she noticed one girl leave the campsite while the others still slept. Medusa tracked her to the waterfall. The girl was not there for another bath, though. Taking out three pretty colored stones, she put them on a flat rock. Kneeling, she spoke in a clear, earnest voice.

"Great Athena, blessings upon you and upon your faithful servant, Medusa. I pray she has found peace and release from your curse here, for she only wished to serve you. I believe she serves and loves you still. It was not her crime, so I pray she is punished no more."

"Glykeria, what are you doing?"

The girl looked up and smiled at a young man who'd followed her to the clearing. "Praying to Athena and leaving a gift for Medusa. See, I painted a blessing on each stone."

He frowned. "Your devotion to Athena is good, but your first responsibility under her law is to me, your intended husband."

Glykeria rose to her feet, her expression open and kind. "You are a desirable man, Kev. Many women wish to be with you. I wish to serve Athena, as one of her temple priestesses."

"You have to be a virgin to do that."

"I am." She lifted her chin proudly. "Your touch is pleasant, and I enjoy our kisses, but if you respect my devotion to the Goddess, you will honor that."

"If you were truly devoted to her, you would honor my rule as your husband and your father's command that we marry. Your family is poor but your name is good. A good marriage will honor your family." Drawing her away from the rock with a firm hand, he gestured to an expanse of lush grass. "Take off your clothes. You will be no virgin when you leave this island. It is my right."

"It is not your right." She pulled away, then bit back a cry as he seized her arm and slapped her face. She put her hand to the red print, her eyes widening. "Kev. What is the matter with you?"

"I did not hit you hard. It was merely a chastising. But I can make it worse."

When she tried to bolt around him, he caught her again. This time he tore her tunic down to her waist and pushed her to her hands and knees on the rock. Glykeria fought, but she was no match for him.

"Stop...struggling," he said between gritted teeth. "You'll understand eventually. Don't make me hurt you worse than necessary. It's for the best."

"Yes, it is."

He spun, and his wide-eyed, choked-on-his-own-surprise look was his final, fixed expression.

Medusa watched the effect take place with a countenance that reflected the stone he became. His obvious excitement from forcing the girl was captured as well, but she'd strike that part off and grind it to dust. She would do the same to the rest of him or drop the pieces into the sea. She did not want any part of him to remain on her island.

She knew she shouldn't have done it. She should have driven them away last night. But the girl's cries were an echo of her own. No matter the passage of the years, that terrible, life-altering memory could be brought back to life in a hateful heartbeat. This time it had taken nothing more than one girl's forlorn plea to *Stop*.

This was why she destroyed anyone who breached her shore. Just like the memory, the rage was always there waiting, and never seemed to lessen in its intensity.

A distressed wail snapped her out of her head. Quickly she averted her face, lifting her gaze to the trees as the girl scrambled to her feet, pulling the pieces of her dress back over her breasts. "Kev...oh no. My lady, no. I beg you."

Glykeria was against her legs, her hands on Medusa's thighs. It was the first time in many years she'd felt the touch of another who intended her no harm.

"He was wrong, but please, turn him back."

"His choice was made." As hers had been. "Return to your home."

"But his family is powerful, and mine is not. He...oh no." The girl pressed her forehead against Medusa's knee. "I'm so sorry. You saved me for Athena, but I didn't want... I never want to hurt anyone."

"No one with a pure heart ever does." She'd been this girl, so long ago. This girl would never be that girl again, after today.

"Go home, but go immediately to Athena's temple. Tell the head priestess Medusa has sent you to her care. Tell her what was done here and why. Leave nothing out. Tell her if there are any repercussions against you or your family, my wings will bring justice to those responsible, as swiftly as my eyes can turn them to stone."

She did not care to subject the girl to the care of one like Berenike, but she knew the temple had far more priestesses like Klotho. It was the best she could do for her, regardless.

"Go. Leave my island now." She could bear the girl's touch no longer, even as she wanted it to continue forever.

Glykeria fled, crying. That was the end of it, her and her friends departing the island within minutes.

Soon after that, from later marauders, she heard the rumor that a new talisman was sometimes being carried by women. It was a replica of her monstrous face, intended to protect them from harm, because she was seen as a champion of women. Another twist to the legend that made it even harder to separate truth from fiction. She was an avenging angel for the innocent, who would bathe herself in blood and surround herself with pillars of stone to handle the burning pain of her own rage.

That last part might be true, at least. Coming back to the present, Medusa remembered the blessed stones the girl had brought. For all she knew, they remained at the waterfall still. She would go look. Wind and rain had probably moved them off the flat rock, and dropped them into the pool. Or birds had seen the sparkle and pecked at them, accomplishing the same end. But they had been placed in a shallow depression of a larger rock when the girl prayed, so it was possible they were still there.

Anything to dissuade her from what she really wanted to do today, and that was to go find John Pierce and pursue the confusing feelings he roused in her. With his large hands and strong body. Those very distracting shorts with the fabric that indecently molded the part of his body that had been so...aroused.

But it wasn't his physical appeal that disturbed her the most. As she flew toward the falls, she thought of the way he'd spoken to her. *"Then come back here."* He'd delivered the command with unsettling authority. It had brought her a strong longing to do as he said.

Yet why would she feel that way, when Kev commanding Glykeria to remove her clothes with similar imperiousness brought her mindless rage?

If she could believe John Pierce, his command was intended to draw her closer to her own desires and will, muddled as they might be. Kev's command had served only his own, and intended to destroy Glykeria's will at the same time.

As Medusa glided in for a landing at the waterfall spot, she realized it was inhabited. In the next breath, her desire to look for the stones was derailed by a much stronger emotion.

Dropping into the trees, she crept forward, folding her wings tightly against her back and shoulders so they didn't disturb the undergrowth.

His senses were noticeably sharp about her proximity, but she thought he wouldn't notice her this time. Not right away. First, he was standing under the waterfall, where his hearing would be occluded by the rushing noise. Second, he had one strong arm braced against a jutting finger of rock while his other hand was wrapped around his cock. He was stroking, pleasuring himself. Water sluiced over his muscles, the hair on his chest and legs gleaming. Muscles in his buttocks and limbs flexed as he pushed himself into his grip.

A quick dart of her glance showed he'd removed the blindfold for his bathing, but he had his eyes closed. She wouldn't look at his face

again, though. She would take no unnecessary chances. She kept her
eyes lowered, though she would love to continue gazing upon his face,
absorbing the tautness of his jaw muscles, showing his concentration
on the building response of his body. Was that why sex and violence so
often crossed lines into one another's realms? The passion that drove
both was so easily connected, as he'd suggested.

She remembered the expressions on the faces of the priestesses as
they pleasured one another, and she saw the same in his face. Crossing
the rocks on nimble feet, she drew closer, her body low to the ground.
Obeying a compulsion she didn't care to examine, she sank to her
knees a foot away from him on the slick rock, her gaze transfixed on
his body from the chest downward. The spray of the waterfall misted
her, droplets that bounced off his shoulders pattering on her.

She liked his powerful, broad upper torso, the way his wide chest
matched his shoulders. Her people valued elegance, not the rough,
bulky forms of barbarian races, but she'd been away from them too
long to be influenced by anything but her own mind. She wanted to
mold her fingers over his shoulders and biceps and feel the strength in
the hills and valleys. His fingers would curve when she reached his
wrists to tangle and stroke with hers. He didn't seem to mind her
talons. He didn't mind her wings or snakes. She'd forgotten herself
somewhat when kissing him, but he hadn't seemed to mind her
tongue, if he'd noticed its split form.

She'd accused him of having unnatural preferences, but she didn't
believe that. She didn't want to believe it.

Her gaze returned to his abdomen, the constriction of the layers
of muscle in response to his quickened breath, the movement of his
hand, and his full body reaction to the stimulation.

His cock was thick and rigid. When his thumb passed over the slit
she saw a glimpse of pearlescent response before the water took it
away. She wondered if he was thinking of her, of how he growled at
her to come back down to him, and somehow she knew he was. As
she'd noticed, he liked restraining her wrists with his hands, subtle and
not-so-subtle hints of that desire to claim her. Yet he seemed equally
determined to draw a matching desire from her to be claimed before
acting on it.

Such thoughts were dangerous to her sanity.

Was he imagining how she would have touched him last night? It was all she'd thought about before falling into a fitful sleep, and she was thinking of it vividly now. She wanted to know how he was imagining her, how he was seeing her in his mind, which at present was the only way he could see her. Did he see all her aberrations when he imagined that, or did he make them disappear so he could fantasize about touching her without those things? Could she blame him if he did, since she'd imagined it herself, coming to him as she'd once been.

But another part of her didn't feel that way. Because he didn't make her feel like a monster. He thought she was beautiful.

His movements and breath quickened. Her gaze stayed latched on the movements of his hand, the increased rigor of his body. The ripples of muscle reminded her of water coming into shore, fluidly smooth, irresistible, able to knock her off her feet.

She stretched out her hand to touch his thigh without thought of consequence. Before she could recall herself and draw back, he shifted. Her hand brushed his leg.

As he started, she knew his involuntary reflex would be to open his eyes. Ducking her head, she scrambled backwards, averting her face in a panic. As she did, she inadvertently kicked out, pushing against him. With an oath, he overbalanced and lost his footing. She gasped, worried he might hit his head on rock on his tumble, but he made a clean and hefty *kerploosh* as he landed in the pool. He toppled with the grace and impact of a solid tree.

She dashed back into the tree line above him.

"Son of a bitch."

When he surfaced, he looked disgruntled but uninjured, and she couldn't help herself. She stifled a giggle. The absurdity of the whole incident, his surprise and grumpy curse, amused her.

His head swiveled around, but she saw he'd closed his eyes while pinpointing her location with his other senses. For some reason, the gesture pained her, despite knowing he showed such caution out of necessity and to ease the bite of her worries. His lips curved ruefully, his irritation disappearing in the expression. It was genuine, not a mask for annoyance. He was good-natured, not one to get his ego easily bruised. She liked that.

"Snuck up on me there, snake-girl."

"I merely came here to look for something. I didn't expect to have company." And certainly not doing what he'd been doing.

"Did you find it?"

"I…I have not yet had a chance to look."

His expression broadened into a knowing grin, making her fingers tighten against the tree's branches to balance her.

"Something distract you?" he asked with deceptive casualness.

She managed a sniff that could be heard over the falls. "You once again overestimate your appeal, John Pierce."

"I'm just imagining how close you were and what you were think-ing." He floated lazily, using his arms to butterfly through the water. "Want to know what I was thinking about while I was doing that?"

Yes. But she shouldn't say that. "Yes," she said.

The smile disappeared. "Would you mind bringing me the blind-fold? I'm turned around here and don't want to spook you if I open my eyes."

She hadn't seen him disoriented yet, but she was willing to go along with the small deception. She landed on the rock, her wing tips scraping it as he stroked in that direction. Picking up the blindfold where he'd left it on top of his small pile of clothing, she dropped to her haunches at the rock's edge. He folded his arms on it, resting his chin on them.

"You know," he said, "If *you* put on the blindfold or just closed your eyes, I could look at you. See what I was imagining in my head."

The idea was so startling, it almost sent her fleeing the rock, but she held her ground. Daring herself, she reached out and stroked his wet hair from his temple. It was like silk between her fingertips. Her talon slid along his skull, his jaw. When he lifted his head, trusting her enough to let the wicked edge glide along his throat, the pumping artery, a strange thickness almost took away her voice.

"Your imaginings would bring you more pleasure than the reality," she said. "That is always the way of it."

"You said that to me in a dream, my lady. I didn't believe it then, and I don't believe it now."

He'd said things to her in her dreams, too. Far more than she'd told him, since she kept resisting the idea it was the same man. Too disconcerting.

She tied the blindfold around his eyes securely. As she figured out the intriguing lacing in the back that molded the mask to his face, she smoothed her fingers over it, following those planes. He didn't try to stop her, though she could feel his dissatisfaction. But not impatience. He'd not yet been impatient with her.

Lifting his hand, he closed it around her wrist. "Come in the water with me."

She drew back. "Or you could come dry out in the sun on the rocks. And...finish what you started. While telling me...your imaginings."

The words charged the air between them, dissipating his dissatisfaction and replacing it with an anticipatory heat.

"You liked watching that?" he said, low.

"I did." It served no purpose to deny it, for the truth might bring her the pleasure of watching his release.

"Would you like to be the one to finish me?" He'd let her go the second she'd drawn back, but now he found her hand again, meeting palm to palm. "Wrap your pretty fingers around me, control when and how I release?"

Yes and no. She couldn't explain her mixed feelings on it. She wanted to touch him while he was in the throes of such self-inflicted passion, no matter what fictional Medusa he might be imagining. No matter the twinge beneath her breastbone at the disparaging thought.

"If you show me how. Maybe. Maybe not."

Her experience of a man's passion had been in taking. Her pleas to stop had only excited Ukrit, as Glykeria's had Kev's. The thought brought the fear back.

"Medusa." John was not touching her, and she realized why. She had her hands clasped in tight fists at her sides and she'd backed away to take a defensive stance. How he sensed that, she didn't know, but his voice was calm, tender. There was also a hard note beneath it, the kind of hardness associated with the walls of a gate, meant to stand between her and her fear. How she wished that was true, but fear was a parasite that latched on and burrowed into the mind, blood and body, with no way to purge it.

"I suggested it because it might give you pleasure," he said gently. "The choice is yours. If you do not desire it, I can finish with you watching at a safe distance."

"It was easier when you didn't know I was here," she admitted. "Though it's the first time that has happened. Except for the day on the beach, you always seem to know I am here."

"Well, in this case, it was because you were already here. At least in my head." Tapping his temple, he gave her an appealing twist of his lips and flex of cheekbone and jaw. If she could see his eyes, she expected they would have glinted with an intriguingly intent look. "I think that's why you startled me so much. I was imagining you on your knees, looking up at me. Your hand rested on my thigh and your lips were parted as if you wanted to taste me, put me in your mouth."

He paused, as if he thought that might be too much, but when she said nothing, he continued. "I was going to spill my release on your beautiful breasts. Then I'd clean you with my mouth, work my way to your nipples. I'd love to suck on your nipples. Hear you moan, sigh with pleasure, and get slippery between your legs because of the things I was doing to you. For you."

He stopped. "So when you touched me, it was like my fantasy became instant reality."

"It made you fall in the water."

"In all fairness, you pushed me."

"I did not. I—" She stopped, thought it through. "Well, maybe. But not on purpose."

"And you laughed at me," he added in an aggrieved tone. "Just deflated my ego entirely. Among other things."

"Did talking about it...help fix that?"

"I think it did, yeah." The growling purr came back into his voice, sending a shiver down her spine. "I'm going to get out of the water now and finish what I started. You can come as close as you want, touch me however you want. I won't touch you unless you ask me to do so. That's a promise. The one thing you're always going to be with me is safe. Okay? And if you're not sure of that, remember, all you have to do to kick my ass is take off this blindfold."

"I don't want to turn you to stone. Even if I had to...kick your ass, I wouldn't want to do that."

He smiled. "Good to know. I can't wait to spar with you, woman. I think it will be fun as hell for both of us. Okay, getting out now."

He hefted himself up onto the rock ledge in a shower of water. She watched as he stretched his long, powerful body out on the heated rock. When he put one hand behind his head and reached for himself, she spoke, stopping him.

"You said I could do it, if I liked."

"Yeah. I did say that."

She moistened her lips. "Can you show me how? I'm afraid of hurting you with....my nails." *Claws* came to mind, but she didn't want a verbal reminder of their differences right now.

He was still partially erect. As he took her hand, guiding it to him, the organ jerked at her touch. She stayed on her knees, eyes trained on the fascinating evidence of his arousal. While it was impressive and intimidating, her fear was absent for a blissful moment. Perhaps because of the distracting pulse between her legs as he curled her fingers around him.

"Not too tight. Loose enough you can move the skin under your palm as you stroke up to the head and back. Ah, Christ, that feels... Fuck..."

"Tell me what you imagine," she said, her voice barely a breath of sound, her eyes fastened on the slit, where more of that pearl-like fluid gathered and gleamed. She leaned forward and tasted it with a flick of her tongue. Her gaze shot up as he groaned.

"You're killing me, darling," he muttered in a husky voice she liked, his other hand dropping to her shoulder to stroke and fondle her hair, grip it. Earthson slithered through his fingers and away.

"Tell me," she asked again. "Why would I be on my knees in your imaginings? Is it to put you in my mouth as you described?" He seemed to like it, very much, when she took just that one taste.

"That's part of it, yeah. The other reason I'll explain another day. Just answer me one thing. Why did you kneel in front of me when I didn't know you were watching? Was it only for the best view, or to give you the best escape route?"

"Both."

"Any other reason than that? Just a feeling like maybe that's where you felt most comfortable?"

Comfortable wasn't the right word, but she wasn't sure which one fit. She slid her grip along his length, her body aching. Her core felt so empty and throbbing. She wanted him inside her, and nothing about her desire for that connected to the pain and fear of the past.

It startled her, but not so much as it once would. She'd been that girl too long ago. Even in isolation, as she matured, she'd been able to look on the past with a woman's greater understanding. Although that same isolation left many gaps in her knowledge.

Despite being a virgin, Glykeria probably had more sexual experience than her.

He was thrusting into her hand, his words deserting him except for her name and some reverent expletives. He gripped the rock close to her thigh and hip. She wanted him to hold her like that. She did. It was on the tip of her tongue to ask.

Then his cock convulsed beneath her grip and his release fountained over her fingers. It startled her so that she almost stopped, but his hand curled around hers, holding it in firm fingers, so they both worked his shaft. She watched, fascinated, heart pounding as he came, his body a thunderstorm of energy, pouring a crackling heat over her skin to match the heat of his seed. His lips were drawn back from his teeth like a baring of fangs, and she wanted to touch his mouth, graze the sharpness of his teeth with her own.

She bent as he was coming down, as his chest was rising and falling so rapidly, and brushed her lips over his mouth. She jumped when he cupped her neck to hold her. Lifting his head from the rock, he sealed his lips over hers, every contact point demanding and strong. He shifted, rising to a sitting position to put his other arm at her waist, holding her as he kissed her so thoroughly.

She expected the snakes to react adversely to his demanding motion, but they did not. They continued to move upon her shoulders and head, curious but not intrusive, allowing her to experience all he was making her feel.

Curling his tongue around hers, he stroked it, and nipped her with his teeth. He acted as if he wanted to devour her, his passion that living, demanding thing he'd described.

Her head swam with visions of the past, present and future. He was making her think of possibilities she'd buried. It was too much.

She wrested away and shot into the air. Her wings didn't coordinate, a problem she hadn't had in years. The snakes hissed in alarm as she nearly dashed herself against the rocks and pitched herself into the pool as he'd done. Fortunately, she regained her balance, moving away from him and all the confusion. Her body didn't agree with her decision. Its flushed heat and tingling nerves wanted only one thing. Him. The throbbing between her legs, and what she'd seen the priestesses do, told her she might be capable of a release somewhat like his own. She wanted to know what it felt like.

She'd stroked herself between the legs as she'd told him. She'd even started to climb toward that pinnacle, but the memories always interfered, making her stop before she reached it. Only when she'd dreamed of him had it worked, and usually she climaxed in the dream, or from a single touch as she came out of it, her body already falling over that edge.

If she was dreaming of him, she reminded herself. But it was weak, her attempt to imagine otherwise failing miserably. Of course it was him. Not just because of him calling her snake-girl, but because of his touch, his scent, his voice. His presence. It was all him.

When she landed on the patio outside her home, she was as aroused as she was in those dreams. Putting her hand against her sex, she was shocked by how strongly her body reacted. It demanded that she stroke, rub, pinch. She braced her other hand against the wall, to help her fight the dizziness that this overflow of need brought.

Her mind seemed magnetized to the vision of John Pierce stretched out on the rocks, muscles rippling, his face tense as he focused internally on his body's desires. He'd experienced a near violent passion, but had not done violence. He'd promised her never without her consent, never against her will.

She didn't believe promises, but she wanted to believe his. He'd come to her from another world, another time, from some place altogether different. Could she believe he was different, or was she giving in to something that would only bring her tragedy?

She forced herself to pull her hand from between her legs. Collapsing to the stone, she curled up on her side and held her legs tightly together to kill the desire, the feeling. The wanting.

Of all the things she knew were a danger to her, the wanting was the worst. Wishing could kill her far more quickly than any other threat.

She needed to make him leave. But she couldn't, could she? She was lonely. So lonely, so eager for his company. Would anyone have sufficed? Or was there something special about him? Even as she scoffed at the idea, she knew it had planted herself in her mind. And like a seed, it would take root and only keep growing.

Unless she made him leave. Which she already knew she wouldn't.

CHAPTER TEN

"I'm not seeing how this is going to be fair, with you blindfolded," she said stiffly.

"Good point. You should let me take it off."

"Or we shouldn't do it."

"Reneging already. So sure of your defeat?"

She sighed. "Annoying man."

"Stubborn woman. All right, so we're doing this with me blindfolded. You're not going to hold back."

Lot sure hadn't, when he was testing JP's fighting skills with the advantage of enhanced senses and the disadvantage of the blindfold.

"Why do you persist about removing the blindfold?" The querulous tone was covering another issue. JP could tell something was bothering her today. He hoped physical exertion would bring it to the top, because so far she wasn't in a sharing mood. Best to get to it before she changed her mind about the sparring match altogether, though he did answer her question.

"I will obey your will, my lady," he said, though he let her hear the regret in his tone. "But if ever you give me that one act of trust, you will see my heart through my gaze, and you won't be worried about how I see you."

"I am protecting you. I care naught for how you see me."

Well, there was a big, fat lie. Since he expected she was telling it to herself as much as him, he'd let it ride.

"And you say such honeyed words to confuse, mock or annoy me," she added.

Okay, that one he wouldn't let go. "No," he said evenly. "I don't."

He'd been gauging her position from her scent, the direction of her voice, and took the advantage of surprise. He was holding one of the sticks he'd picked out for them to use for their match, and swung it now to give her a smart slap on the flank. "And I wouldn't advise maligning my motives again, unless you want more of the same."

"You..." He almost grinned at the splutter of reaction, and danced back as she came at him with her own stick.

Since he'd arrived, he'd been putting together a profile of the girl she'd been before her transformation. What he'd deduced up until now was that she'd been down-to-earth, playful, inquisitive, and spirited. As a testament to her strength of will, those things had not gone away. She just hadn't had anyone to exercise them upon in so long, they were rusty. They were also sometimes hampered by the darker traits she'd acquired since then. While she now had more of the advantages that wisdom and experience could bring, they'd stolen some of her joy.

He wished he could give it all back to her, but he'd do whatever he could. Because over the past couple days, whether she realized it or not, she'd been giving him the same. Before he came here, he'd found his way back from darkness and made a tentative truce with his demons, but he hadn't remembered that a guy could actually enjoy life like this. He could not only immerse himself in worthy goals, like coaxing a woman to smile or laugh, but he could take as much pleasure in that as she could, no strings attached, no end goal other than to be with her because he wanted to get to know her. Because he was attracted to her, because she fascinated him, and because he hoped and thought she might need him as much as he needed her.

Stuff a high school kid pursued without thinking about it twice, and it had taken him all his life and a couple years of hellish therapy to get there.

He'd entered into so many covert operations where the seven deadly sins were daily fare. As bad as that had been, what was worse was the disconnect of seeing a guy who'd dismembered and tortured a competitor on Saturday night play with his son Sunday morning. As the drug lord had pushed Manuel on a swing, JP couldn't deny the true paternal love in his eyes. Another guy, a dictator destined for hell for all the mass graves he'd created, had asked JP to figure out what his wife's favorite flower was so he could surprise her with a whole roomful of them in her bedroom, a sorry-for-being-a-prick gesture when he'd snapped at her earlier in the week due to "job stress."

It was the things that didn't make sense that sometimes cut the worst.

He'd had to be the man behind the mask throughout all of that. It was ironic that he was wearing an actual mask here, but he was pursuing a goal wholly as himself. Not for the first time, he thanked Lot for the wisdom that had convinced JP to do the dreaded counseling. So trapped behind the façade when he came out of covert ops, he'd had no chance of giving a woman the true parts of himself this freely. He'd been too locked into all the disguises he'd had to don, layer after endless layer.

The readiness to do violence when needed had been so close to the surface, people had unconsciously given him a wide berth when he was out in public and hadn't been paying enough attention to keep on his fake "normal" face. Deception had been second nature, a lie easier to tell than the truth, because he'd lost the truth, when it came to who he was.

But when he'd figured it out, he'd been able to use his true self to help women like Monica. Being a Dom was the first thing the counselor had helped him realize was all him, and he'd built back the facets of his real self on that foundation.

So no matter what else happened here, he wouldn't let her believe for a minute that anything he told her was less than the real truth. Even if he hadn't gotten a glimpse of her, he'd know she was beautiful, because that was what his heart knew. He'd been so good at covert ops because he could be anyone he needed to be, but he never lost sight of the truth of who the people around him were, no matter how much that knowledge could tear the soul to shreds.

All that passed through his mind in a flash as he fended her off, using the tells of air currents and the slide of her feet through the sand, combining that with his honed fighting instincts. "Hey, we're not even inside the practice court yet," he protested.

"You struck first." But she did stop and allowed him to lead the way to the court he'd marked out on the beach. "So are there any rules, beyond putting you on the ground?" she asked.

"Since sometimes one of us might drop and roll to get away from a blow, and that doesn't really count as being off your feet, let's make a three second rule. If you're on the ground three seconds, it counts. That's one Mississippi, two Mississippi, three Mississippi. And no hitting above the neck. This is all wrestling and strategic body blows to bring the opponent to the ground. By whatever method you prefer."

"Mississ..."

"Mississippi," he repeated. "It's a way to make sure the count is uniform. Rather than 1-2-3," he spoke rapidly. "Or 1...2...3."

"Ah. I understand."

They stepped into the area he'd marked out with stones. "I'm surprised you didn't eliminate the use of my wings," she said. "They give me a decided advantage over you."

"If you and I grapple, my strength and size give me the advantage. Seems a good way to level the playing field." Facing her, he took a relaxed but ready stance. "Are you bringing it up to head off any of my whining if I lose?"

"Perhaps."

He grinned. "You won't have to worry about that, sweetheart. Because I'm going to kick your gorgeous ass."

It was all the starting bell needed. She made the first strike, coming in low, which was unexpected. Son of a bitch, she'd thrown out the mention of the wings as a decoy. When he fended off the blow with the stick, she used the shift of his balance to sweep his leg. He rolled before the three second count and was back on his feet, but she was a blitzer, continuing her assault with barely a pause between tactics. A good idea with her speed and agility which, as he'd anticipated, were impressive and deadly.

While she used her wings to give her some height and maneuverability, he thought she wasn't making as much use of them as she normally would have. She had a spirit of fair play. Time to help her remember what he'd said about not holding back.

He seized her mid-body when she was a couple feet off the ground and wrestled her to the ground. Her wings slapped him smartly alongside the head, making his ear ring, but he told himself that was reflex, not a breaking of the rules about head shots. She wriggled and bent her legs beneath him to shove him back and roll free.

When he captured her ankle and dragged her back, she twisted, broke his grip and spun behind him. Rapping him in the balls between his open legs with the stick, she shoved him face forward into the sand with the tip. She straddled his back in a blink, grabbing both arms and twisting the wrists up to hold him in a very effective pin.

"One Mississippi, two Mississippi, three Mississippi," she chanted. She sprang back, releasing him. "That's one. Do you wish to capitulate now and salvage your pride?"

"Even if you beat me, you're going to have to earn that dress and chocolate," he said ominously. His balls were aching, but he could hear the smugness in her voice. He hid his satisfaction about that, able to quite sincerely cover it as he maneuvered carefully back to his feet, fighting pain. While that might have been a dirty shot, the rest of it had been pretty damn effective hand-to-hand. He was learning her skills and tactics, though, and that patience would pay off. He hoped.

"You sound pretty cocky," he said, circling her. "But you have two more to go before you get to do a victory dance."

She was hopping along the ground like a bird would. Hop, then up in the air, then down again, looking for an advantage.

"This is usually the trash talk part of a fight," he mentioned. "Insulting one another's manhood, mothers, favorite sports teams, that kind of thing."

She interpreted his casual conversation as a good opening. He ducked her frontal attack, caught her leg and hip and flipped her, taking her to the ground on her back and using sheer strength and weight to put his body perpendicular over hers to hold her down for the three count. "One Mississ—"

He grunted as she hit a radial nerve in his upper arm with two combined fists. When his hold loosened, she propelled herself back up with wings and legs. He brought her down again, and this time put her on her stomach with an arm behind her back, and his knee pressed against her delectable ass. He counted it out and let her go.

"That's one and one, my lady. Breathing down your neck."

"Not for long."

In their next round of grappling, he managed to drop his arms around her from behind and band them over her chest and waist. He lifted her off her feet, holding her wings trapped between their bodies while she kicked. But as she squirmed and he tried to figure out how to put her on the ground, another appealing idea came to mind.

For one brief, blissful second, she stilled, the only movement the quick rise and fall of her breath against his hold. He realized his mouth was close to her neck, and he turned his face into the thick mass of her dark hair. He grazed her crashing pulse with his lips as one of the snakes—Ratqueen by the size and feel of her—slid along the side of his face and tunneled under the neck of his T-shirt.

She grew even more still. One clawed hand had latched over his forearm, probably with the intent of trying to wrest loose, but the grip tightened and held. Feeling her body so motionless against him, but with so much energy pulsing beneath the skin, he let his mouth stay on her throat, and gave her the slight edge of his teeth.

"All mine," he murmured. "My lady."

He could feel the desire for surrender, so close to the surface, the eagerness of her soul, needing that capitulation. It all happened in a blink, and then it was gone. She twisted against his hold and broke free, and he let her go, knowing it was best to let the moment pass, though the impression of her body against his felt like a brand.

"I was not on the ground and you did not say the Mississippi three times," she said. "It did not count."

He grinned at her, a dangerous baring of teeth. "It counted as something far better, my lady. But yeah, I'll concede that, so I guess I better get down to the business of winning."

She scoffed and made a comment which didn't translate, but he suspected was the Greek version of insulting his manhood. They circled one another again. While he knew he'd take that moment out later and look at it from a lot of pleasurable angles, he set it aside for now. He wanted this win.

They each scored one more point. After that, they abandoned the boundaries of the court, wrestling and sparring back and forth over the sand, down into the water, getting drenched in the process. No more chatter now. They were pushing one another hard. He knew he had her on experience, because though she obviously trained extensively, she didn't have the close quarter fighting skills he did, except for dive and attack maneuvers, quick, vicious strikes intended to be decisive and immediate. But he expected she was 100% lethal with that effective strategy, so he couldn't fault her for focusing her training more on it than toe-to-toe fighting she likely hadn't had to employ as much.

She almost had him down for the third, but, risking a break to his wrist, he threw the pin and reversed it. She struggled magnificently so he adjusted his hold and straddled her, pinning her hips with his and her wrists down on either side of her body.

"One Mississ—"

"Off. *Off.* Please, get off—"

Her abrupt shift to mindless panic and the plea were as effective as being propelled off her by a cannon blast. That, and the sudden aggressive punching of the snakes against his torso, the warning graze of a fang. He immediately released her and jumped back, cursing himself. He'd been so involved in the sparring and impressed by her skills, he'd forgotten. Past traumas had fucking nothing to do with present abilities. Triggers could make someone helpless as a baby in a blink.

"It's okay, Medusa. It's all right. I didn't—"

"Goddess, I'm sorry." Her voice told him she was upset with herself, not him. He'd rather her be mad at him. "I didn't mean... No, don't come near. Please, don't. Not right now."

She was breathing too rapidly, because they'd exerted themselves hard and the panic attack had rushed in on top of that, stealing her oxygen. "Okay," he said, dropping to his heels in a squat, a non-threatening pose that kept him close. "Just breathe. Try to slow it down. Just breathe."

He thought she'd rolled from her back to her knees and might be trying to rise. "Don't get up yet," he advised. "When you're having trouble breathing, you could pass out."

"Y-yes. Of course. I'm sorry."

"Nothing to apologize for. You just about kicked my ass, my lady. You're a hell of a fighter."

"Oh." The praise distracted her, as he'd intended. "I meant..."

"I know what you meant," he said quietly. "And I meant what I said. That's nothing to be sorry about. Pinning you was a bad plan."

"No, it wasn't." Her voice became cynical, unpleasant, though he expected the negative reaction was still self-directed. "How else could you gauge my fighting skills if you are truly here to overpower me?"

He bit back an impatient retort. She'd switched into full defensive mode. He wouldn't fuel it. "If you truly thought that," he said, "why'd you consent to the match?"

"So I could do the same. But I showed you a weakness you could exploit." Her voice was dull.

Maybe anger had its place. "Damn it, that wasn't the point of this. Yeah, I was interested in your skills, but you have to stay in fighting shape here, and so do I. I figured it's more entertaining and useful to do that with a partner than by yourself, and it improves your skills to be exposed to other combat styles. Right?"

The twisted, difficult tangle of emotions that emanated from her drained his anger. She only had herself and her snakes, he reminded himself. How would anyone handle years of isolation where every visitor was a risk to assess and handle?

"You don't have to do it, especially if you think I have ulterior motives for asking," he said in a kinder tone, "but I'd like to see how you got behind me that fast without using your wings. That could come in pretty handy against an enemy in the future."

"Yes, it would." The wet sound told him she'd lowered herself to the sand.

"I'm going to come and sit beside you, my lady."

She didn't say yes or no, so he eased closer to her. A brief touch of her head and shoulder found that she was sitting with her forehead pressed into her bent knees, arms linked over them. She'd taken refuge, both physically and mentally.

"It's all right." Sitting down next to her, he ran a light hand down her back, then did it again. She didn't draw away. "Once, on an amphibious mission, my tank, what I used to breathe underwater, caught on some wreckage. I got disoriented and couldn't figure out how to get it loose. For the longest minute of my life, I faced the very real possibility I was going to die down there under thousands of pounds of water, where no one could find me. I had a few other amphibious missions after that, so I figured I'd taken care of it, gotten back up on the horse, over and done.

"Then I took a ride on a coaster with a friend's daughter." Sierra, another of his subs, or harem, as Lot liked to teasingly call them, got sick on pretty much every kind of ride, so JP had gone with her and her eight-year-old son to the local amusement park. "Wasn't even a huge coaster, but it took us below ground through this narrow-assed tunnel. A mechanical malfunction happened and the coaster stopped on the rails in the dark down there. Nothing to be uptight about, but I was clammy and pale as an oyster when they got it started back up a few minutes later."

He knew she had no context for half of what he'd just said, so he boiled it down. "Memories can come back and grab you at unexpected times. There's no shame in it. All I had was a bad scare. I didn't actually have something awful happen to me, like you did."

She lifted her head under his hand. "What is...a roller coaster?"

When he explained it to her, she had questions, and he ended up not only detailing roller coasters, but the concept of amusement parks and the existence of Disneyland.

"Some of the things you describe are so outlandish I know you are making them up," she said. He was glad to hear she sounded more like herself again.

"Some things have to be seen to be believed. Not only has the world become far bigger centuries in the future, but the things in it as well."

She sighed. "You're kind, John Pierce. I don't trust you. But you do and say things that make me want to do so."

"Glad to hear it, because I can't think of a better gift from you than your trust. It's the gateway to a whole lot of other great things."

"Yes. But also very bad things when it's misplaced."

"True." He'd shifted close enough they were hip to hip. When she dipped her head so it almost brushed his chest, he cupped his hand over it, briefly holding her. The snakes were at ease again, and one coiled on his shoulder. "Which one is that? The little one, right?"

"Yes. Earthson. He has a particular liking for you. He finds you fascinating."

"How about you?"

"I suppose he finds me interesting enough, though he's been exposed to me for far longer."

He grimaced, but her tiny chuckle warmed him. "Wiseass. Serves me right, fishing for compliments when you're getting your composure back."

"I anticipated you thinking I might have a weak moment and admit to liking you."

He snorted. "You have no weak moments, lady. I'm wet to the skin and coated with sand. You aren't afraid to get dirty in a fight. I like that in a woman. Want to swim, get some of it off?"

"You go ahead. I might go inland. The snakes prefer the fresh water."

"I could meet you there if you want company. I know you're sad and unsettled right now. Don't go off by yourself. That won't make it better."

Her fingertips slid against his chest, her breath touching the base of his neck. "Sometimes it does. I draw strength from the solitude."

"Is this one of those times?"

She sighed again and straightened. "Perhaps not. But maybe... come join me in a little while. Give me some time."

"Anything you need."

JP gave her a half hour, taking a swim in the ocean while he waited and hunting up a snack of berries and nuts. He retrieved the rest of his chocolate stash from a sealed plastic bag he'd put in his makeshift cooler, a hole in the ground with cool earth walls. He'd give her the dress later. Maddock had found one credibly close to the one in the magazine, and it had showed up in his pack this morning, right on time.

Since the sparring hadn't ended on the note he'd hoped, he'd have been willing to let it drop with no clear winner declared if that was in her best interest, to not push her too soon. But she'd told him otherwise when he'd held her off her feet, her body flush against him, her pulse rabbiting under his lips. She could have broken free. She'd proven she'd had the skills to throw a hold like that, but she hadn't. Something in her had wanted to experience what it was like to have him holding and restraining her like that, the illusion of being helpless in a way that wasn't frightening because it was her choice. It was like a drug to a Dom, feeling a sub try out those waters.

He suspected she wouldn't go for him passing on the win, anyway. She had her pride. But he was still bringing her the chocolate. He wanted to give her things. It made him feel good, because gifts seemed to please her. Pretty simple logic, but there it was.

He headed into the forest and made his way toward the smaller waterfall, figuring that was where she'd headed. As he drew closer, he put on the eye mask again, finding his way to the water's edge using his other senses. She didn't speak, but he knew where she was. She was sitting on the rock ledge beside the waterfall, the same place he'd stretched out and let her touch him before.

He imagined her bare feet dangling over the edge, her hands bracing her, talons carving thin white lines in the rock as she gazed pensively into the water. Sitting down next to her, he dangled his own feet. Hers brushed his, confirming his guess on her relative position. He proffered the chocolate.

"Consolation prize," he said. "For a fight well fought."

"Oh." He heard the surprised pleasure in her tone and was doubly glad he'd brought it. "That is...not necessary."

"Oh. Well, okay. I'll just eat it myself then."

He grinned as she caught his arm with one set of claws and plucked the chocolate out of his grasp. The paper crinkled, and her shoulder rose against his biceps as she drew in the smell.

"This makes me believe some of the stories you tell."

"If you only knew. Medical breakthroughs, architecture, technology...nothing comes close to all the things we've learned to do with food, now that hunting and gathering isn't an all-consuming task for everyone."

"I'm surprised you are not three times your size, if it's all like this."

"Well, moderation in all things, right? There are plenty of things I enjoy doing. If I was overstuffed with food, I couldn't do those things."

"Like what?"

"Rock climbing, training, working out. Travel, seeing new things, new places." He told her about some of the out-of-the-way places he'd hiked, a pursuit his counselor had advised to help him get back in touch with his own inner voices again. She listened so attentively, it reminded him of what she'd wanted most of all, if she'd won. He touched her thigh above the knee.

"Whether you won or lost, I planned to tell you a story every morning and evening anyway. You know that, right?"

"No, I did not know. But I would like that, very much."

"All right. Let's get in the water."

"I'll watch you."

It was the second time she'd passed up on a swim around him, and he was pretty sure she liked swimming. Thinking through why she might be avoiding it, he plucked at the hem of her tunic. "Take your clothes off so they won't get wet. I can't see you, so no reason to be shy."

He'd ignored her comment and made the direction to take off her clothes a calm command. Now he'd wait to see how she handled it. Stripping off his T-shirt and leaving it behind, he pushed off the rock and slid into the water. He'd left on his shorts, thinking that and his blindfold might help her feel more secure.

JP would commit to a hundred years of agonizing celibacy if he could take away her fears and worries. He wanted her willing and at ease about it, at least in the right ways. That was the difference between a Master and a monster.

He heard her rise, and the waterfall covered the sound, but he was pretty certain she'd removed her clothes. She'd be standing on the ledge naked, her hair and snakes twisting and falling down around her shoulders and waist. Her long limbs, small breasts and the juncture between her slim thighs would be visible. Yeah, "wanting her badly" didn't even pass the starting line of how he felt.

She went into the water with a ripple. As they both drifted and treaded water, he encouraged her to talk about her life in Greece, the day-to-day stuff, the other temple priestesses.

"Was one of them your best friend? Favorite friend?"

"Yes. Callidora. She and I tended the garden and handled kitchen duties on the same assigned schedule. When we had free time, we would read together, or sit along the top wall of the temple, watching the townspeople go about their business. She could imitate senators or Klotho in such a funny way. She always made me laugh."

"Is she still there?"

A long pause, filled with a puzzling confusion and no small amount of sadness. "I don't know. I assume so. I miss her. When you make me laugh, you bring back memories of her. It pleased her, making me laugh."

"Did she think you were too serious?"

"No. She said my laughter was the kind people never tired of hearing, that my joy made others feel better. So she said making me laugh was a selfish act on her part, to make her and those around me happier."

"I can see that. The few times you've laughed, it's had that effect on me."

"I do not laugh as I once did. It still feels good, but not as light."

"Yeah, that happens. The shit we see can weigh it down. But that means when we do laugh at something, it's an even bigger gift, if that makes sense. Like hey, though the world is hell sometimes, I can still laugh. Something in this world is still good enough to make me do that."

"Yes." She was closer now, a few feet away. He held out his hand.

"Will you come and let me hold you, and know that I'll do nothing you don't want me to do?"

It was intriguing how her hesitations created a different weight in the air than her pauses. He hoped the sense augmentation Maddock had given him was permanent, because he was discovering far more nuances of body language than he ever knew existed.

"Would you like to come closer? Touch me?" he asked in a steady, firm voice.

"Yes."

"Then come here." He kept his hand out, and when he heard the movement of the water and felt her wet fingers in his, talons curving over them, a surge of satisfaction and contentment filled him.

"You like that command. 'Come here.' 'Come to me.'"

"Yeah, I do. I like how you respond to it." He drew her closer. Her arm was tense, but she wasn't actively resisting him. He brought her into his arms, his lips and nose twitching as her wings fluttered, like a falcon brought off her roost. They showered droplets on them both.

"Easy," he murmured. "Put your arms around my neck. Let me carry you through the water."

She slid her fingers up his chest, through his chest hair, onto his shoulders. Her other hand clasped his biceps as he closed his arms over her back and hips. So much smooth skin, the curves coaxing his fingers into places he knew she wasn't yet ready for him to go. "You can coil your legs around me if it's easier to hold on that way. You're safe with me."

"I'm not sure of that." But she did it. As she put her legs over his hips and adjusted her arms around his shoulders, it took an effort beyond description not to hold her so close against him they would seem like they were breathing together. His light hold caused another torture, though. The tips of her breasts brushed his chest, disappeared and brushed him again, a pleasant repetitive friction while they floated together. Using his one free arm and legs, he turned them in slow, wide circles to get the full benefit of the cool water's flow.

"Now tell me why you're not sure you're safe with me," he said.

"If I tell you, I'm not sure I'll be safe with you anymore."

Way to make his blood heat. Thank God for cold water. When he idly tangled his fingers in her hair, he was amused to feel that all the snakes except one were piled on top of her head like a wedding cake, avoiding the water as much as possible. He followed the line of the other snake's body and discovered it was in the water, the serpentine form moving sinuously around Medusa's side. "Let me guess. That's Waterlight."

"Yes. She alone enjoys the water, though Earthson does on rare occasions."

"How do you wash your hair, when four of them are so averse to water?" Because her hair was definitely clean and regularly cared for. Either she took pains with that shining mass of ringlets, or the Xena-like sexual allure she had was a magical defense as he'd speculated, and her hair was part of that. He knew a lot of women who'd claim to take the curse she bore in a heartbeat, in exchange for hair that could be so thick and shining without effort.

"When I immerse myself in water where they can't avoid it, they've learned to tolerate it, but if they have the ability to avoid it, they do."

"Like a dog having to take a bath." He trailed his fingers over her shoulder and earned a shiver of reaction. Her nipples pressed against his chest more firmly and he realized he'd tightened his grip. She hadn't resisted.

"Medusa." He stopped their rotation and touched her face. "You remember what you said about me not being so courteous?"

"Yes." She sounded wary.

"On that same note, do you *want* to be entirely safe with me?"

A weighted pause. "I'm not sure. Sometimes not."

"Okay." He hoped his reaction to that came off as a reassuring warmth, rather than a blast of lustful heat. "I'm glad to hear it. I'm going to kiss you, but that's all I'm going to do. No matter what you beg me to do, kissing is all you're getting. Got it?"

She stiffened. "I will not beg you to do anything. And—"

His lips were so close that when she formed the *And*, her mouth brushed his. Whatever else she was going to say died away, and he took that as his cue, closing the distance. He constricted his arm around her like one of her snakes, coiling it around her waist and dropping the hand so it cradled her buttock while the other stayed high on her back. He bit back a male animal noise of pleasure that might have scared her. Christ, her ass was such a nice handful, soft and firm at once, a pleasing curve he could explore for days, rousing all sorts of erogenous areas she probably didn't know existed.

Her arms, wrapped around his back, shifted so her hands framed his neck. Her fingers slid into his hair behind his ears, the talons digging in. She'd essentially put a set of knife blades against vulnerable tendons and his spine, but he didn't sense she'd done it to threaten him. She was getting into the sensations, trying to figure out how she liked them. *Keep trusting me, sweetheart, and I'll help you with that.*

He deepened the kiss, coaxing her lips apart, playing his tongue over her sharp teeth, then tangling with her tongue. He felt her sudden tension, but he merely increased his grip on her head. He intended to make this a slow, long, wet, kiss that would alleviate any concerns she had about him being put off by a forked tongue.

If she knew some of the fantasies he had about how that tongue would feel on certain parts of his anatomy, she might be both reassured and more anxious. But her words, about not always wanting to be safe with him, told him that anxiety was starting to take some key steps away from fear and into a far more pleasing direction for both of them.

He loved kissing the way most men loved fucking. While he found the latter pretty damn pleasurable, kissing a woman thoroughly had rewards that men who rushed past it to get to the fucking part missed.

Focusing on the kiss and doing it right affected a woman's whole body. Teasing her teeth and lips with the tip of his tongue had her arching her body into him. Thrusting deep with it while pressing harder against her lips, making things more demanding, elicited a little whimper. One hand dropped from his hair to his shoulder and the claws bit into his flesh. Her thighs quivered as he eased up the pressure of his mouth to play along her lips, nip with his teeth, make her chase him for more.

In short, every bit of foreplay could happen between their two mouths. If he did it right, a woman was so wet and wild by the time he was done, she might come the moment he thrust his cock home inside her willing, writhing body. He loved to see that happen, that total loss of control from nothing more than a full, merciless seduction of her mouth.

He'd never been gladder of his pursuit of that skill than now. Before this, he'd noted a constant level of tension when his hands were moving below her neck. As she grew more lost in the kiss, that tension was ebbing away. He stroked her spine, her hips, and clasped her waist. She was unconsciously climbing up his body as she pressed more insistently against it. One of her arms was tight around him, the other hand braced on his shoulder as he cupped one side of her face and neck with his large palm and kept her kissing him and being kissed.

The sounds coming from her were perilously close to the begging at which she'd scoffed, but he wasn't going to tease her about that. Not when the heat rushing through his veins was making his cock so hard and thick he might do some begging himself. He was thankful he was wearing the constricting wet jean shorts, because he didn't want his reaction to startle her as he'd done the other night. But it seemed they'd made progress there as well.

Her mons was pushed against his abs, creating friction against his sectioned stomach muscles. As she rose and fell, the base of her ass was rubbing against the steel cock caught behind the zipper. He growled into her mouth but eased back, wishing he could see the look on her face. Swollen lips, moist from his mouth, dazed eyes.

"I will take my prize now, my lady," he said.

Her fingers convulsed on his shoulders, her body shuddering from arousal. "Wh-what?"

"It's time to collect my prize." He brushed his knuckles over her face. Her lips *were* swollen. He moved her back toward the ledge. "I think you're in the best mood for it now."

"That was all...to prepare me?"

"Oh, hell no." The quick flash of amusement helped his own sexual frustration. "I wanted to kiss you and hold you while you were naked. The two don't necessarily have to be related." Though they were, enough that he probably was going to be nursing a painful hard-on for the next hour.

"But...I wanted..."

She wanted him to keep kissing her. He knew just how she felt, but he'd stopped at the right time, since she couldn't verbalize it. She was on the verge of spooking herself again. He guaranteed she was marshalling her defenses, trying to backtrack. She cleared her throat.

"Perhaps I am not ready to grant you your prize right now."

Lifting her onto the ledge, he pulled himself out of the pool, water splashing onto the rocks from his body. "I've won, my lady. So I can demand my prize at *my* leisure. You're a woman of honor."

"If I had won, you could have produced my dress right away?"

"Yes, I could have."

"You have no way of proving this." She had that snooty edge to her voice that was a goad and a defense both. He was sensitive to the latter, even as the other added fuel to his desire to redden her ass right here and now.

"You're arguing an irrelevant point, my lady. It's a spanking. You've seen it done to children. Surely it doesn't scare you."

"No." *Yes.* The unspoken word was hovering on her lips, because some part of her knew how her body and mind would respond to it, even if she didn't consciously acknowledge that. "But I will dress first. You made no demand that I be...unclothed."

He put out a hand. "True, but that's the way I prefer you. Come to me, my lady. I hope you're learning you won't come to harm from me. At least enough to trust me for this."

"I don't understand why you wanted this as your prize."

"When I'm done, you will."

He could hear her feet shifting as she rose, a ripple of nervous movement going through her wings. Then she came to him, and put her hand in his. While he'd kept his tone steady and unrelenting, which could have a compelling impact on a sub, her compliance humbled him enough that he lifted her hand and pressed his lips above her knuckles. "You awe me with your courage and trust, my lady."

"You are a strange man."

"No argument there. And you're a miracle, putting up with me the way you do."

The dubious sound that came from her lips made him smile. He guided her closer to the falls, sitting down on the flat rock near it, where the spray would mist their skin. He wanted her bottom glistening wet, so she'd feel the sting acutely, but not so wet it would interfere with other plans he had in mind.

"Come down here, over my knees."

He imagined her lips pressing together nervously, betraying some self-consciousness, and he helped her this time, drawing her down to him, easing her over his lap. As he smoothed his hand over her buttocks, he bit back a groan again. Christ, she felt like heaven. And he wanted to see her.

"I'm taking off the blindfold, my lady. You need to keep your head down so we won't make eye contact, unless you're going to trust the contacts."

"No, I don't..."

"I assume turning me to stone isn't an issue when looking at your backside." Well, except for one key part of him, but that had nothing to do with her lethal gaze.

"No. But I don't like you not wearing the blindfold."

"Tough. My prize, my rules. I want to see you."

He removed the blindfold before she could say anything further. It said a great deal about how far they'd come already that she didn't put up an argument fast enough to stop him.

Yep, he was right. Heaven. Curves of golden skin, with a faint blush of color, and still damp from their swim. Since she was stretched over his thighs, her bottom was canted up enough to hint at what was between her closed thighs. Her long dark hair was falling forward, but he could see the curve of her breast under her arm, below where her elbow was braced on the rock. Waterlight was resting on her shoulder, facing him as if interested in what he was planning to do.

Hopefully she and the other snakes wouldn't interpret this as an attack on their mistress. He wondered if they knew the difference between agitation from fear versus arousal. He supposed if they didn't bite him, he'd have his answer to that. He got a closer look at Treebark, the spiny, venomous snake peering at him through a parted curtain of hair at her nape. Tunneltrap and Ratqueen were still coiled around the top of her head and seemed unconcerned.

"Will your snakes be okay with this?"

"Yes. I can tell them it is what I wish."

Her voice was quiet, and he coiled his hand in her hair, giving it a tug that lifted her head several inches from where she had her face tucked down between her flattened palms on the rocks. Her breath drew in at the firm hold. He knew it had caught on words of warning not to look upon her face, but his grip conveyed a different kind of warning.

"Is it what you wish, Medusa?"

"I don't know. I don't understand your desire to do this but, as you said, it makes me feel... I want you to do it, and I don't."

"Then let's do it and see what happens."

CHAPTER ELEVEN

*W*hen he'd held out his hand to her, Medusa had stared at it for a few heartbeats. After what had happened at the beach, she'd told herself she was going to be sensible about granting him his prize. She wasn't going to let that despised panic take over again. Her inability to control it had made her furious with herself. Up until then, she'd not only made a good accounting of herself in the match, she'd earned John Pierce's unprompted praise.

It should have built her confidence, not only about her trusting him more, but trusting her own strength to protect herself. Instead, when his body had covered hers in what wasn't even the most secure pin of their match, the memories had surged up instantly. It had been like a surprise attack by a powerful predator, paralyzing her.

Time had helped her regain some perspective, as well as pride about holding her own against him. Though, based on his skills, holding her own in a fair fight against John Pierce Zeus, meaning him not blindfolded or holding back, might not have had such an equal result.

She knew he had held back. Oh, not on the wrestling part, which was why she was proud of herself there, for pinning a far stronger opponent twice. But whereas she'd utilized kicks and blows with fists in addition to wrestling maneuvers, he'd limited himself to the wrestling. He would not strike her.

Well, until this moment, and she had a feeling this was a far different kind of blow.

He was a formidable warrior, one who seemed determined to convince her he was not here to harm, but to protect and serve her. If it was a ruse, he was being remarkably consistent about it.

Seduction or rape. If the end goal of the male was the same, to take, what was the difference? She'd felt a decided difference when he was kissing her, however. Perhaps that was what had her hesitating when he'd reached out a hand to her, a tacit gesture to confirm her consent to his prize. He had an undeniably seductive effect upon her, and she was drawing ever closer to surrendering whatever it was he wanted to take.

He'd stopped instantly when her fear had taken over on the beach, and he'd seemed genuinely concerned about her. She was starting to believe him, when he said she merely had to say stop, and he would. Well, yes, he was being insistent about this spanking idea, but in a way that didn't feel so much like he was ignoring her protests as tapping into something inside her that wanted him to insist. To take charge.

No, not that. She wouldn't agree with that assessment. This had to do with honor, because he was right about that. He'd won fairly, and she'd agreed to the terms. She ignored the sly voice inside that said it was convenient for her to capitulate to something she might want just as much as he did.

She put her hand in his.

As his large fingers closed over it, he ran his thumb over her knuckles and drew her close to the falls, where the spray misted the skin. Since he was blindfolded, she watched carefully to make sure he did not come too close to the edge, but he seemed to know his footing. His wet shorts clung to his body like a snake's skin. They were no longer than a man's short tunic, but the fit drew her eyes to his groin, to the size of his muscular thighs, to the way the fabric clung to his backside.

Then he brought her down over his lap, and insisted on removing the blindfold. She would have protested, but the other things he was doing had shortened her breath and increased her heart rate. She made herself press her palms into the rock, but when he gripped her hair like that, refusing to let her put her head down, more unusual feelings coiled in her lower belly.

She wanted to see what this was about. Why it intrigued her, the description of it, without her having any experience of it.

He rubbed his hand over her bottom, slow, as if to reassure her, but it awoke nerve endings. Maybe they were anticipating the pain, but it wasn't that which had butterflies whirling in her stomach. He was looking at her. At her back, bottom, legs, at the snakes in her hair and her wings, her claws scraping against the rock. She stiffened at the thought but then—

Whap!

She jumped at the sting and, just in time, remembered to reassure the snakes. *Play, no fear. No attack.* They took anything she said at face value, but more than that, they read her emotions. She was pretty sure they would not pick up fear from her right now. Not the kind that would put them on the defensive.

Her adrenaline spiked, her body tensed, and her claws dug deeper into the rock. John went back to rubbing.

"You have a gorgeous bottom. All drum tight but round and soft, like that pretty pale green melon that grows here."

Another strike. This time she felt more of the sting, and warmth washed over the pain. The tightness in her lower belly was a different kind of trepidation. He trailed his fingertips along the crease between buttocks and thighs, a quick impression, but one that sent a surprising shudder through her. Another blow fell, making her jump again.

They started falling in regular intervals, mixed with caresses, and strokes. Some of them stung more than others. She struggled, yet let out a strange sound when his bare palm smacked the widest part of her buttock, hard enough it wobbled and sensation speared through her core. Her wings fluttered out from her back and then folded down tightly again at his husky admonishment.

"Stay still, snake-girl. You have to stay still for your punishment. You feel it more intensely that way. If you keep moving, I'll add to the count."

That was no part of the prize agreement, yet words to argue the point dried up as his fingertips slid down again. It gave her a needed break from the punishment, but she went even more still than he'd ordered as he teased the lips of her sex, stroking her as easily there as she might one of the newborn kids in the goatherd.

It felt as it had the other night, when she'd wanted to touch herself between the legs, only it was him touching her.

"You're wet, all nice, slick and warm. Fuck, you're killing me." He followed that crease between thigh and buttock again, and it made her clench, which caused a hum of male pleasure.

"Lift your bottom up for me some. Lift into the blows."

She did it without thought, only following her desire to feel more of this and ignore the alarm at her uncontrolled reaction to it. She wasn't even counting. Shouldn't she be counting, to make sure he didn't take more than he'd won?

She flinched, because the next one hurt. "These last four," he said in a voice of sensual menace, "are the ones that are the real punishment for wounding me without cause. They'll hurt. But I'll follow them up with something nice, if you ask me nicely."

She bit back a weak retort and instead yelped as he smacked her with punishing intent, as promised. He held her down, hand in the middle of her back, pinning her wings as he gave her a healthy spanking that had her ass throbbing and her flinching at each blow, wanting to beg him to stop...somehow without stopping.

"Please...John. It...it hurts."

"Yeah, it does. But it feels good, too, doesn't it?"

She couldn't answer that, because the answer was yes and that made no sense.

"Tell me to keep doing it. Ask nicely."

She should shake her head, but her body was throbbing. It was like he'd woken something up in her with his kiss. For some reason, this was making that reaction even stronger, making her feel like she needed something he knew how to give her.

"Medusa." She heard that growl in his voice, the tone of command that made her tremble. He was ordering her to say the words, yet it was what she wanted, too.

"Yes. Please. Please, John Pierce."

More blows, and the stinging became true pain. On the last slap, she yelped and tried to get away, but his hand dropped, and he was stroking between her legs again.

"Open your legs farther."

They slid apart, giving him more room, and she turned her face against her arm, mouth opening as her hips lifted into his touch and the spiraling feeling got tighter and tighter in her lower belly.

"Say 'please' again. I love to hear that word on your lips."

"Please. Oh...Goddess, please..."

It flashed through her like lightning, white and strong and electric, her body almost levitating off his lap except for that one anchor point where he was rubbing and stroking, pinching, scraping her with his nails. He pressed his palm against her core at the height of the wave, moving, massaging, as she cried out, as the sensation concentrated there exploded outward, making her legs and arms go rigid, her lips part. The snakes wound tight around her head and upper arms, their constriction mirroring what was happening throughout her body. Something else inside her whipped loose and lashed every nerve ending.

As the sensation ebbed away, it kept changing its mind, returning in small spurts, seemingly called back by the slow massage he continued against her with his rough palm.

"John. John Pierce." She spoke his name, because she knew not what else to say. A vague alarm tried to marshal itself in the aftermath of that feeling. This was what she'd seen when the priestesses had pleasured one another. What Ukrit had experienced when he took her...

Goddess, she'd never made that connection, never thought of it as the same, but a physical reaction was a physical reaction. *Seduction or rape, what was the difference if the purpose was to take...* But John Pierce had just given to her, not taken. Right? Yes and no.

"Hey, no. Don't get lost in your head. Not after that. You stay right here or I'll give you another spanking, this time with a switch that'll drive anything else out of your mind."

He turned her over. She would have panicked about him looking at her, but one, she had her eyes tightly closed, and two, he cradled her in his arms and tucked her against him so her head was beneath his chin, face buried in his neck. She was trembling, breathing like she'd been running.

"But that was what he...that feeling...he experienced that."

"Yeah. When people have sex, they can climax. Release, orgasm, whatever you want to call it. But there's the right way and the wrong way. He did it the wrong way. The fucking totally wrong way. What you just experienced, there was nothing wrong about that. That was pure and clean as this waterfall."

She wanted to believe that. But she still had questions. Uncomfortable questions, particularly about the arousal she could feel beneath her.

"He...was able to do that because hurting me, taking from me... excited him. I think that was the main reason he...climaxed."

"It's like that for a sick bastard like him."

"But..." No, she wasn't going to ask it, because John Pierce was nothing like him. Right?

"I got excited from spanking you, from making it hurt some, feeling you struggle. Yeah, I did."

Anxiety bloomed in her chest, and she would have moved away, but he held her. Not in an imprisoning sort of way; he just stroked her and made a soothing noise.

"Here's the key, sweetheart. You enjoyed the spanking. You got aroused by me spanking you, taking over like that. I wasn't taking anything you weren't wanting to give. That's the difference. If you'd been frightened, there would have been nothing arousing at all about that to me. I would have stopped, and held you the way I'm holding you now, making sure you knew you have a say in this. There's nothing I'll do to you that's one-sided in the pleasure department. Got it?"

She was confused, and overwhelmed. As if he sensed it, he pressed a kiss to her crown, his arms loosening but still holding her, giving her the option of moving away. "Don't worry about it right now. Just relax."

She didn't move away. She wanted to be in his lap, held like this. She didn't want to question it, because she knew if she did, she'd move away. They stayed that way for a while, her breathing settling as she recovered from her explosive reaction. He was still firm beneath her, but not quite as hard. She found that reassuring, though she also wondered about giving him a release the way she had before. She wanted to. She was pretty sure she did.

It was too much to digest. At length, she sat up and moved to the rock next to him. She was close enough he stroked her hair, the snakes giving way for him. She clasped her arms around her bent knees, laying her head on them again as she'd done on the beach. She kept her eyes closed, but she wanted to open them. She wanted to look upon him, trust those "contacts" he'd mentioned. But once again, her desires were only frightening her, making her want to withdraw as much as she wanted to experience more. So she sat silently, averted her face and opened her eyes so she could gaze away from him, at the water.

JP wished she would look at him and trust the contacts. But he'd pushed her all he would for now. He let his fingertips drift over the back of her neck, between her shoulder blades, over the curve of a wing, and he felt the tension. He could imagine the troubled look in her gaze, those darker things he'd felt from her earlier finally close to the top.

"Will you tell me what was bothering you, my lady? Before we started sparring."

She stiffened even more, her arms flexing in their hold on her knees. "How did you know that?"

She sounded so suspicious, as if she thought he could pull thoughts out of her head. He could, but not in the way she worried about.

"I'm good at figuring people out. What they're thinking. And I was worried about you. Still am."

She made a hard-to-interpret noise, but relented. "Do you remember what I said to you the other day?"

"I remember every single thing you've said to me, my lady. I hang onto your every word. You'll have to give me more of a clue."

She snuffled like she'd bit back a chuckle. "What was the word you used? Wiseass?"

He smiled. "That's the one." When her shoulders rose and lifted in a hard sigh, he sobered and molded his hand over one. "Please, my lady. What did you say to me?"

"That if you have come to serve me, your loyalty is misplaced. And you should go home. You said if I would let you look at me, I would see your true feelings, which is why I do not wish you to do so."

"They are nothing to fear, my lady. Wasn't I right about the spanking?"

"Yes. And no. It is something to fear. The way you make me feel terrifies me. You are a step ahead of me, seeing the way you wish this to go, and I am following blindly."

"No, my lady. Not blindly. When you put your hand in mine, some part of you knew how it would feel, and you desired it. You have a formidable spirit and I have no wish to destroy it."

"Yet I am an agent of destruction, am I not?"

His brow creased. "I don't understand."

She sighed and straightened, shifting away from him. She clasped the edge of the rock as she dangled her feet over it and stared into the depths. "Having a man force himself upon me was a betrayal beyond anything I could conceive," she murmured. "Yet each time I've seen the horror when someone looked upon my face, it was a betrayal, too. A denial that I am one of them anymore, pushing me outside the boundaries of their lives...I know that sounds foolish."

"No, my lady. I can see how it would feel that way. You were a young woman who enjoyed her friends and her life. You were inside a world, and suddenly you were shoved outside of it."

"Yes. But that excuses nothing." She swallowed. "Perhaps being harmed as I was can magnify other betrayals beyond their import. But I can think of nothing that would hurt me more than knowing you looked upon me and saw the evil that was summoned from my soul to garb me forever."

"I would see no such thing. You possess no evil."

"How am I to take such a naïve comment? You are so persistent; you are a man who is like a boy with a crush." She startled him with her sudden vehemence. "You have said it yourself, John Pierce. Every soul has darkness, and the gods may pull it from us on a whim, no matter how noble we think ourselves. You think all that rubble on the beach was something I was helpless to stop?"

Her tone went flat. "For many of them, perhaps most, I could have tried to stay hidden in the cliffs, until they tired of their hunt and left. But I grew angry and let them see the monster they expected to see. You asked me about how little there is to do here. In the beginning, I felt that way, too. And the rage became flavored by boredom, so sometimes when they came, I made it a sport, letting them think they had the upper hand for several days before tricking them into my gaze."

"You were just—"

"No." She sighed. He was looking at her in his peripheral vision, so he registered the pale shape of her body. She was hunched over, her claws clutching the rock ledge as if she wanted to spear it with her grip. "You are a warrior," she said. "You know that there are things that happen when violence takes you, bloodlust that can't be undone, that opens dark places inside that sometimes grow so strong, they release urges you fear can never be called back. Yes?"

He swallowed. "Yeah." There were no hidden corners in the dark side of human nature for someone who'd done the things he had. The problem was how that darkness could expand and hide the light. Every guy he knew who had served in some form of military or covert capacity had grappled with that in his own way. Some better than others.

"Please put the blindfold back on, John Pierce."

He didn't want to do so, but up until now she'd been keeping her lids lowered, her eyes on the rippling waters around her slowly moving legs, so he could gaze upon her profile. It was an important step forward, and he didn't want to take any steps back by refusing her.

After he'd complied, he felt her shift. Her fingertips brushed his face before she rose and moved away. It sounded as if she'd perched on an outcropping of stone a few feet above him. He wondered if, for the first time, she'd used the blindfold not as a safety precaution, but as another way to shield herself.

"One day, not too long before you arrived, an old woman and her grandson came to the island. I had given myself fully to that dark place, because of something that had happened with a group of young people who'd preceded them by a hand span of weeks. I would no longer seek the best in myself. Instead, I was determined to destroy anyone who landed on my beach, whether their purpose was to hunt me or cruel, ignorant curiosity."

"My lady..."

"You bring me pleasure, John Pierce. You see me as someone worthy of your protection. You will hear me out to find out differently."

He set his jaw. "There is nothing you could tell me that would do that, my lady, but continue. I will not interrupt again."

"I descended on their small boat, swooping down like a bird of prey. I landed before the grandson when he was pulling the boat out on the sand, and he looked up and met my eyes. It is an instinct, something we think nothing about.

"The grandmother cried out in horror. She told me they'd brought food for me, and gestured to the basket that proved it. She said it was an offering. She told me her grandson had felt pity for me, in addition to the usual curiosity. Only his curiosity was the true kind, not the fascinated disgust the others brought."

If JP wasn't already blindfolded, he would have closed his eyes against the ugliness he heard in her voice. But she wasn't done.

She drew a painful breath. "She kept calling his name, hoping he would answer. They live in the stone a short time, I think. I could almost feel him trying to answer her, pleading with me to help and release him. I could not, and I was angry with her, with him, for their pity and foolishness. For being undeserving of my rage that anticipated only enemies coming to my shore."

"My lady..." He wanted to close his hand over hers, but she stayed out of reach, refusing comfort. He could almost imagine her, sitting straight and tall above him like an eagle, her face a brittle mask, hiding the agony he heard beneath the incriminating words.

"When she realized I could not undo it, she asked me to turn her to stone, for he was her heart and soul, and she had no desire to live beyond him. I could have shown her mercy, and I did not. I had killed him without a second thought, yet her, pleading for her life to be taken, an old woman a step from the grave, I could not do it. I left her crying on the beach, close to where you camp now."

She stayed silent another few moments and this time he left it unfilled. "In the morning," she said at last, "I found her at his feet, barely alive, overcome by the stress, refusing to take food or drink. I knew she would not move from that spot. I put my hand under her chin to lift her face to look at me. She curled her fingers around my wrist right before she raised her gaze. Her last words were 'thank you.'"

Her harsh laugh was brimming with self-hatred, a sound that bit into his own memories. "Thank you for taking my only family from me. Thank you for killing me when all I brought you was kindness. That is what you have come to serve, John Pierce. If I were still the maiden I once was, unfairly despoiled by a selfish, violent man, I would feel the pleasure and confusion you give me without weight on my soul. But I am no longer that girl, and I will never be her again. Here, alone, in a comforting numbness of day to day chores, breathing in and out, nothing more expected of me than that, I could bear it. You wake me up and make me face that darkness. I deserve nothing you are giving me, even as I want it so much it hurts. It is unbearable."

"Don't. Goddamn it..."

He actually tried to grab her, anticipating her retreat. It was in the broken sound of her voice. The foolish move was propelled by his reaction to her pain, his desire that she not leave with it. His attempt failed. A flap of wings and she was gone.

Damn it. JP removed the blindfold and rubbed a hand over his face. His heart and gut ached with a desolation he understood far too well. For some things, there was no comfort to offer. There was only living with it.

At last he had an answer to why she'd seemed more amenable to his incursion on her island, more willing to give him a chance. Guilt was eating her alive. As she'd just said, he'd brought a double-edged sword.

The more he wanted to offer her, the more those gifts cut her to ribbons.

CHAPTER TWELVE

*S*he'd left him a problem that had no easy answer. He spent the rest of the afternoon mulling on it, thinking about the path he himself had walked to grapple with the things he'd done. He'd helped bring down drug rings, undermined dictators, and done a bunch of things, small and large, for which the stated purpose was making the world a better place. A few of the things he'd done had accomplished that. Maybe. But he'd begun to wonder if, in the cosmic scheme of things, the ultimate judgement wasn't on those end results, but the shape of the soul once the goal was reached.

Wasn't that Maddock's whole point, about why they were doing this? The underlying philosophy he hadn't yet shared with her, the track that had set up the train that had brought him here?

Whether she knew it or not, she was on far surer footing than he was with his past. Yeah, the grandson and grandmother thing was pretty awful, but one person, alone and pretty constantly under attack, never having had the resources, beyond the voices in her own head, to grapple with being raped, mutated and exiled? A trauma counselor would barely blink over the incident, identifying it as the inevitable result of hypervigilance, overstressed survival instincts and unresolved rage that blurred lines of morality. As he'd already deduced for himself, the amazing thing was how much of herself she had held onto, not how much she'd lost.

She'd acted to protect herself from the others who'd come to harm her. Though she claimed she "could have hidden," her offensive tactics had been the better strategy. Her reputation as a force to be feared had likely reduced the number of incursions she'd had to face. And if more had come, the chances that one of them would have succeeded where the others failed would have increased exponentially. Selfish or not, he was glad she'd become so good at scaring the shit out of the local populace.

He went to find her, which meant he went to do things that might draw her to him. Hanging out with the goats, planting some of those new seeds in one of her gardens. He twisted a branch into a clothes hanger and left her new dress in her little garden shed, the sheer blue fabric fluttering in the breeze before he latched the door. It was a halter-backed sheath thing with sparkles he thought would look incredible on her. He hoped she would see it sooner rather than later so it would help her smile.

After that, he used his ladder to climb back up the smaller cliff where he'd first tested it. Then he lay back to watch the clouds scudding across the sky.

He wasn't sure if she'd come to him or not, but eventually she did. He heard her land behind him, but she didn't come closer, so he suspected she'd taken a seat back there, out of view but not out of range.

They didn't say anything for a while. She was drawing something from his company. Solace or comfort, he hoped. He remembered a day Lot had taken him out fishing on a boat. They really didn't do much fishing. JP eventually just laid down in the rocking boat and stared up at the sky while Lot fished and said...nothing. Asked for nothing, but gave a lot in the silence. Acceptance, understanding.

He did that, but in time, he found the words came. Just as they had that day. He'd spoken to Lot about things he'd done that would be far beyond the counselor's understanding or capabilities to answer. But Lot could. So maybe he could do the same for her.

"Time is going to help you manage it better," JP told her. "But it will never go away. Something like that, it's not supposed to."

He took a breath and sat up, locking his hands around his knees as he stared out at the ocean through the trees. "I told you I did covert ops work. Everything I promised you that I'd never do to you—betray you, lie to you, harm you—that was part of my job description. I never did to any woman what Ukrit did, but the things I did...there isn't a jury in the world that wouldn't claim some of what I did was just as bad.

"It was considered 'okay' because it was sanctioned, but I think that was because they really didn't want to think about what went into the results they wanted. They didn't even want me to lay it out in reports. If I got too detailed, my handler would tear it up and tell me to do it again. Or write it up as a summary with all that dropped out of it. 'It's a report, not a confessional, JP. You did the job, let it go. Go get laid.'"

He shook his head. "He was right, but it was also wrong. Those of us who face violent situations, there's this moment. It's not always the first kill. It's something you do to someone else that's so different from how you ever imagined yourself being or doing, it changes your view of yourself forever. You know you'll never get that other version back."

He cleared his throat. "I told you I got into it because I thought I was going to be a big hero, save the world. Well, even if I had saved the world, there's no way I'd ever look into a mirror and think of myself as a hero, no matter how many other people tried to tell me otherwise.

"So yeah, you're right. I can't tell you that it's all okay, what you've done or become. I can only tell you that I look at you and I see someone that makes me feel okay. You're someone I want to be around, who I think is an incredibly strong person who's had to deal with a lot of shit no one should, especially not by herself. Some of us never figure out how to recreate ourselves, take what we are and what we've become and make it into something we can live with."

He shifted so she could see his profile, the closest he could get to looking toward her. "You did, my lady. You could have turned me to stone the same way. You could have let that darkness take you completely. You didn't. You've learned the consequences of giving yourself over to it in one of the hardest ways possible. And that's the difference between someone who's evil and someone who isn't. If you bury regret, if you don't use guilt to find a better version of yourself, you don't deserve or get anything but pain. But you didn't do that."

"I cannot make amends to the dead," she said uncertainly. She wanted to believe him. In her voice, he heard the poignant plea of a teenager who'd never thought she'd be facing such a dilemma, who wished things could be different. He also heard the mature woman who knew she had to carry on, grapple with it the best way she could.

"If one believes that the dead are beyond cares, are in a world where all is forgiven and they hold onto no fear or anger, then one expects their wish would be that the person who took their lives finds redemption, makes amends and finds their way out of darkness. We think we have to flagellate ourselves with our crimes forever, but I believe a truly penitent soul must do even worse than that.

"We have to live our lives, embrace every gift fully, specifically because we've deprived someone else of the chance to do so. That's why every laugh you experience will carry weight, and moments of joy will come with bittersweet sorrow. But it's life, and we must live it, because otherwise nothing changes and the darkness wins. It's punishment and reward both."

Seeing if she was ready to be touched, he closed his eyes and turned around, reaching out toward her. During the conversation she'd come close enough he could stroke a lock of her hair back from her face. She didn't move away, though she didn't lean into his touch either.

"Thank you for the dress," she said. "It is very pretty. I did not win our match, though."

"Doesn't matter. It's a gift."

She paused for another of those protracted silences. "I must show you something," she said at length. "If I am truly to believe why you are here and what you want to give me, I need to know you see every dark corner, John Pierce."

"I'm good at bringing light, my lady. I don't fear your darkness."

She flew him back up to her tower, as he thought of it in his mind. She carried him under the arms, uncomfortable but the most practical way to do it. He could tell picking up his two hundred plus pounds of muscle took some effort, but she managed it impressively, and the flight was much shorter than the climb he'd attempted. She deposited him on level ground and they walked from there. She'd had him don the mask. The one advantage to it was she held his hand to help him navigate the unfamiliar terrain past the boundary of her garden she'd allowed him to see.

At length, she moved behind him. "You can take off the blindfold now, but do not face me. I will walk behind you and explain what you are seeing."

"All right." When he removed it, he saw they were on that twisting path that led away from the landscaped area he'd already seen. Whereas the snakes had guarded the passage before, there were none there now, apparently heeding their mistress's bidding to allow him to pass.

She'd created a long, cool arbor, a thick lacing of branches that screened out the sun as the forest did at lower elevations. Rocks and broken logs placed along it created places to sit in the shade. He wondered if she sat here often, as there was a peacefulness to it, a sense of sanctuary. As he emerged from the tunnel, a tangle of exotic plants, trees and flowers spread out before him, but not as random as they appeared at first glance. It reminded him of coming upon ruins in South America where the foliage had taken over the broken rock, enhancing the haunting beauty of the odd shapes.

There was stone here, but all of it wasn't rubble. He was looking at a garden full of people. For a moment, he could imagine he was at a sculpture garden, like he'd seen in New Orleans or Litchfield, South Carolina, thanks to one of his subs who was an art enthusiast.

But these weren't the creations of an artist up to his or her elbows in sculpting medium. The reason these sculptures looked so lifelike, possessing expressions so poignant their eyes were difficult to meet, was because their life had died captured inside the stone.

These were her creations. Her victims, to her way of thinking. Most of them he knew had come against her, but he was mindful of her words. She would be aware to the exact number how many she believed could have been spared or driven away.

"They look different than I expected them to look." He'd assumed they'd all have that frozen look of horror she'd described. Instead, it was as if a divine hand had passed over a group of people ambling about a garden and captured them forever in the tranquil poses he saw.

"Yes. The temple of Athena...it is closely guarded knowledge, but part of what priestesses are taught there is spell craft. It was why

Klotho's suggestion to help me in the way she did didn't come as a surprise. My abilities are far more limited, compared to Klotho. She had true magical ability, whereas I was what she called a kitchen witch, able to follow a recipe." She made a self-deprecating noise. "But she said I had a special aptitude for that, for figuring out even more about a 'recipe' than I was taught."

Hmm. That was a bit of knowledge that hadn't made it into anything they'd found out about the temple of Athena. A pretty damn closely guarded secret, indeed.

"So there came a time I experimented with the stone, to see if I could reverse the process. I thought if I could figure it out, I could reverse it quickly enough to save a life..." She paused, and he knew she was thinking of the grandson. "Unfortunately, I never found a way to do that. But I did find I could soften the stone and make it malleable, but not like flesh. More like clay, and the softening was temporary. However, it helped me carry them up here and change how they looked when they died. I tried to make some of them appear...at peace, as if by doing it to their outside I could make it true. Though I suspect it was only to ease my own guilt."

"It was not a bad thought, my lady. Many people believe how you treat the body in death eases the passage to the afterlife."

He wandered through them. It was both a sobering and wondrous sight. He saw many young men, likely challenged to come to the island to try and slay "the Gorgon" as a test of manhood. To become a hero. There were also older, seasoned warriors, evidence of organized campaigns against her, possibly financed by a warlord or king hoping to give himself additional political clout.

He paused by two of the young men who appeared to be wrestling, or...he bent closer. It looked like one was lifting the back of the tunic of the other as he started to go down on his knees. She shifted behind him.

"The night before they came after me, these two slipped off into the trees to enjoy one another. I'd never seen two men together like that. So when I brought them up here, I thought they would like remembering that moment."

"Hmm." They moved onward. There was only one woman, the elderly grandmother she'd told him about. Medusa had put her and her grandson in a circle of feathery plants and bright flowers. The grandmother was sitting on a rock while her grandson sat at her feet, leaning against her leg, his arm raised and a remarkably animated look upon his face.

"I imagine him telling her about his day, or a girl he favors."

"That's nice," he said sincerely. "So their clothes turn to stone with them?"

"Yes. I'm not sure why. I think it's because anything in direct contact with them turns to stone, for a certain range. For instance, the ground beneath their feet turns, but the effect stops less than a hand span from them. This soldier over here, you see he was holding a spear, but only part of the shaft turned."

A foot above and below the soldier's grip remained polished wood, though it was showing signs of weathering. JP's gaze slid up to the steel tip. "Have they ever been able to wound you, my lady?"

"Once or twice. That soldier there"—she nodded toward one who looked like a veteran warrior—"flung his spear with strength and accuracy. It went through my waist."

John reached back. "Show me where."

She drew close, took his hand and tucked it beneath her belt, fastened loosely enough his fingertips could slide over a scar above her hip bone. "It gave me a fever, but I know herbs to draw out infection. I was very weak for several days, then it healed."

He shifted his grip to hold onto a handful of the skirt and belt and bring her closer, so her thigh brushed the back of his. "I'm not sorry he's dead," he said, his gaze on the soldier's face.

"I expect they are told the stories you had heard," she said neutrally. "I was an enemy to be eliminated before I caused unimaginable harm. And when the time came, I was attacking his fellow soldiers. In such situations, the motives become less important than protecting your comrades in arms. Right?"

He couldn't argue with that, understanding it all too well. Sometimes protecting the person at your side or back became all that made sense anymore.

He remembered when he and Lot had come face-to-face in that firefight. Lot had had no proof that JP was telling the truth about being with the DEA, but he knew JP wanted to protect the kid, and that was all that was needed to make getting him out of there the most important thing to both men.

She sighed. "I walk through this garden and I study their faces. I see fathers and sons, brothers and friends. Husbands. They were more than this; it is sad to me that they ended their lives, ended all that they were to others, doing this.

"Those who were transformed when they were sweating look like slick wet rock, so smooth and glistening." Her arm extended past his elbow to stroke the forearm of one of the soldiers, then withdrew again.

"As the rock wears down, the expressions change, becoming more muted and mysterious. Eventually they all dissolve and return to dust. Some are taking less time, while others last and last."

"Have you ever broken one apart? To see what was inside?" He didn't intend to be macabre or disrespectful, but he was curious, since she'd done her own explorations of the nature of what she'd created.

Her voice moved to his right, lower, as if she'd sunk down on a bench. "Yes, I have broken them apart, but not to do that. I did it to remove them from my island and drop them into the sea. I try not to look too closely when I do it, because the insides are...different colors. Like blood and flesh. It is better if I can hold onto the belief that they are like any other statue, more stone on the inside, instead of anything...else."

"Why did you bring these here? Instead of leaving them all on the beach like the ships or dropping them in the ocean."

She was silent long enough he wasn't certain she'd answer. He would have apologized for prying, but he sensed it was best for him to keep pushing, to help her feel that he'd earned the right to ask, whether or not that was true.

"I don't know," she said. "For the grandmother and her grandson, it was remorse. I couldn't disrespect them by putting them into the sea like that. For the others...maybe I was trying to understand them better. Maybe it was a pathetic desire for human company, no matter how inanimate. That likely sounds insane."

"We're social creatures. You may have strong bonds with your snakes and other creatures here, but you grew up interacting with people. You miss their company. It's normal."

"I wish I didn't. I wish I never wanted to be around another human being again. It would be easier."

"Life isn't generally designed to be easy. And I'm glad you still have the desire, my lady." He reached out. "Will you come back over here?"

"For what purpose?" But she came, and when she allowed him to capture her wrist, he drew her hand forward under his arm and banded it around his waist and chest. She was easier about it this time and leaned against him, propping her hip against his buttock. She laid her cheek on his bare back. Two of the snakes slid over his shoulder, one curling around his biceps while the other nuzzled his nape. He quelled his reaction to the ticklish sensation, focusing instead on the feel of her fingers beneath his grip as he stroked them, tracing the claws.

"Some sins feel like they will never be forgiven, my lady. And while we know deep in our souls some sins never should be forgiven, forgiveness is something that cleans not only one heart, but many." He'd seen that first hand with the subs he'd helped, when he'd given himself enough breathing room to focus on their needs instead of his past garbage.

"Good or bad, everybody's just trying to figure out what life's about and how to take care of what matters most to them." He'd realized the size of that never changed, and that had become a fixed point in his universe. "It boils down to what's right in front of you and what's inside you."

Pressing her forehead against his shoulder blades, she lifted and let it drop against him in a little bump of contact. "You are right in front of me, John Pierce."

"I was hoping you'd notice that. Will you show me more? Tell me what you know about the people here?"

He deliberately changed the subject before the intimacy became too unnerving for her. She moved back from him without comment, though he hoped he wasn't imagining her reluctance to break the contact. As she directed him forward through the garden, she explained each statue to him. How that person had come to the island, what she'd been able to glean of their purpose and background from eavesdropping on their position, studying their actions covertly and exploring the vessels on which they'd come. She'd acquired decent deductive reasoning and intel skills from such exercises.

He learned many of the items she'd secured for her comforts here had come from the larger boats, the ones who'd come from longer distances.

"Those were the ones after glory for their names. But there have not been too many of those. I think I am not quite the achievement that a war or the random hydra can be."

"I'm not sorry they're dead, either."

"I felt that way at one time, but now there is no one in this garden I am sure deserved their fate." A cold note came into her voice. "Except one."

They'd reached the back of the garden. As he came to a halt, her arm extended past his, one sharp-tipped finger pointing. JP saw a tangle of briars that formed a thicket. An access path cut into it, so narrow the thorns scraped his skin and caught on his shorts as he passed through it sideways.

The briars formed the illusion of a cage for this last statue. The man had been broad-shouldered and tall, uncomfortably similar in stature to John. His intimidating size was evident despite him being on his knees, his hands forever frozen in a helpless flailing motion. Unlike the others, she hadn't changed anything about his final position in death.

He'd had a silken, thick mane of hair. There were long gouges on his chest and arms, his clothes appearing to have been torn front and back before they were petrified. But even with that and the evidence of his pre-mortem wounds, he was handsome as a god. JP saw a combination of arrogance, hate, fear and pain in his face. His anguish was such stark evidence of self-awareness during her fatal transformation process it was disturbing to look upon it.

But he looked, because JP knew who this had to be. Not only from his placement and her unwillingness to empathize his features in any way, but from the turbulent waves of energy she was emitting against his back. They were a dark complement to the negative aura pulsing from the statue.

"I do not know what compelled him to come and find me," she said. "But his intent was to destroy me. Perhaps others started to blame him for the perceived danger of my existence and he was determined to rid himself of that blight on his name. Or he refused to let me go, and the only way to completely possess me was to kill me."

Her tone transformed to a flat deadness. "He thought I'd be as weak as when he first took me. He didn't realize how the spell had enhanced my strength and quickness. He had no chance against me, even less than the veteran soldiers who took nothing for granted. His helplessness gave me such visceral pleasure I have nightmares about it."

"My lady, you don't have to—"

"Yes. I do. If you think I am worth serving, I have to be certain your conviction is based on truth. I tore open his flesh. Not just one or two times. I dove down on him again and again, like a vulture tearing pieces from a carcass. I disarmed him, drove him to his knee and made him beg."

JP swallowed. "Did it help?"

"It only fueled the rage in me," she said. "Because his begging was goaded by fear, not remorse. In the end, his true nature came forth. He despaired and all of the ugliness within him could not be contained. He called me names. He said fucking me was the best thing that ever happened to me. That if I could do it over, to avoid this fate, I would have gotten on my knees to him every day and..."

JP's hands closed into fists and she stopped, telling him how closely she was watching him.

"Despite the beauty of life here, I have faced despair many times," she said. "Because of what I've become, there are times I wished he'd killed me that day. Or that I had accepted my fate and become his slave, with the hope of finding a way out of it someday. There is no way out of what I am now."

"No." He unlaced the mask and set it aside. Her snakes hissed, a warning, but he didn't care. He turned to face her. She moved faster than he could follow, a flash of cloth and hair in his peripheral vision, and she was behind him, her hands cupped over his eyes. He put his fingers over hers. "I want to see you. I will look upon you, my lady. I've had enough of denying myself your face, the beauty of your eyes and all the truths they can tell me."

"No. Not right now. Cease, or I will leave your company."

He ground his teeth but subsided. "You don't know that there's no way out of what you are now. Maddock thinks..."

"It does not matter. Because what I am outside is now what I am inside. No one can change that. I do not wish to speak of it. It was when he said that, about serving him every day on my knees, I turned him to stone. He is the only one I've ever hoped is still alive inside it." The weight of it was in her voice, on her heart.

"It's why I've never destroyed him." She pressed her face once again against JP's back. Her arms looped around his waist. He would have been heartened from the contact, but it felt more like a desperate attempt not to face him, rather than a desire for contact between them. "I will leave you here to think on that, John Pierce. What it says about the woman you think I am. You are welcome to stay up here and enjoy my home as my guest. But if you wish to leave...I will take you to the beach whenever you are ready. I will be within calling distance."

A rush of wing noise and, once again, he was deprived of her company.

CHAPTER THIRTEEN

*H*e'd put the blindfold back on for her comfort when she returned, but it had been awhile before that happened. And when she did, she hadn't come into the house. She'd taken up residence in her nest above the patio, not encouraging further contact or dialogue. He sat below her, thinking about the incomparable view he couldn't see and everything she'd shared with him.

She'd told him the story of everyone in that garden, and yes, many of them had come with the intent of doing her harm. But she'd given herself no quarter. "This one was barely out of boyhood. I could have disarmed him, snatched him up and dropped him in the sea, and it would have been enough to send him scampering home." Or "This group was merely cruel, here on a bet to prove that they could spend the night with the monster."

He couldn't deny that it did change his view of her. No matter how idealistic it was or how competent he knew she had to be to survive this long on her own, he'd seen her as a damsel in distress when he arrived on her beach. His image of her had been wholly painted by stories and his own hopes and desires. The past couple of hours had sculpted off those shiny edges, but he didn't regret that. How he felt for her might have a different, leaner, shape, but it was more real, while the core remained the same. Unshakable.

That reassured as well as grounded him, no matter that it had no basis in experience, only in the way he'd always felt about her, even before knowing her. Now he knew more about her, and the feeling was only stronger. That had to mean something. Fate sometimes dictated who you loved more than any other factor. That was the whole basis of Maddock's theory, after all.

"When did it happen?"

"My lady?"

Her voice was hard like asphalt, baking in the sun. She perched on the chair next to him, a puff of wind telling him she'd settled her wings. "That moment when you had to reconcile who you were with who you'd become."

He chided himself for the cowardice that had him hesitating to share it with her. He could fear that she'd see him differently, but he couldn't shy from it, not when she'd opened all of herself to him. He wasn't going to deny her the same dubious gift.

"I had to kill a family sympathetic to a terrorist faction. It was critical that no one blew my cover. The intel I'd gathered and was still gathering...a lot of lives depended on it. And the fucking hell of it was that it was just bad luck. The son-in-law figured out who I really was and confronted me in front of his family, because he figured that would protect him, that his father-in-law would know how to handle the situation."

It was as vivid to him now as it had been then. "I killed all of them. The son-in-law, his father-in-law. The eldest daughter and her mother. The daughter was pregnant, pretty far along." He stopped. She didn't touch him, and he was glad for it. He'd never been able to handle the comfort of another when relaying it, and he'd told damn few people.

"I imagined that baby dying inside her, not knowing what was happening..."

"Entirely innocent."

"Yeah. My grandmother, who died before I was born, left my mom this framed quote, done in needlepoint. It was something about hoping her children would know only times of peace and happiness throughout their whole lives."

"She would have been sad that you went through that."

"At least it was my choice, being in covert ops and traveling outside of the country to do most of the things I did. Not sure how much a choice that family had, being born in the middle of all that shit with limited options to get away from it." He paused. "Kind of like you and the soldiers that came here to attack you. They had far more of a choice than you did."

"I think in your case it is not so simple. You have never mentioned doing what you did for glory, as they did. For the trophy of a Gorgon's head."

"No. But when you get into something like I did when you're young, there's a certain amount of adrenaline and heroic stupidity."

"Yes. I saw that in some of them." She paused. "How did you... come back? From killing the family."

"You don't come back. You just go forward." Now he wanted to touch. He found her hand and was glad when her fingers curled around his, held tight. "There was no other way I could have done it without more loss of life. I understood that. But it told me what a fucked-up world it could be, when killing a pregnant woman and her unborn baby was a necessity to save other lives."

"Yes. That makes sense. But I guess I meant, how did you..." He heard her draw an unsteady breath. "Do you have nightmares about it? Like on the beach, when you seemed so...haunted?"

"Yeah, sometimes. The same scene, over and over, though sometimes she's holding the kid in her arms, already born. How about you?"

"I see the stone come to life, only their faces are horrid, distorted. They are laughing at me, pointing, still cruel and violent. But this time I can do nothing. I am bound up in a net, and the more I scream and rage, the more they laugh, and they pick up sticks and start hitting me, like I'm some type of...game."

His fingers tightened on her, but she continued. "I want the nightmare to be something different, I want to see their faces as kind, or laughing, or something that tells me I killed them unfairly. Somehow that would be better and make more sense. But they are as horrible in my dreams as I imagined them in life, and yet I still wake with the guilt."

"Hey. Come here." He tugged her hand. "Come over here and sit with me."

"I am sitting with you." But she shifted and then made a surprised noise as he guided her into his lap with a little thump as he tugged her off her feet.

He wound his arms around her. When she might have stiffened, wondering at his intent, he let out a sigh and laid his head on her breast. She went still, and then her arms crept around his shoulders to hold him as well. Her chin touched his hair, and she rested her head on top of his.

Though the touch brought her comfort, her distress was palpable in her silence. Their time by the falls had been marked by pleasure and discovery, a breakthrough of sorts. While he understood why she'd wanted him to see the garden as a natural result, it had brought back her melancholy.

John had had enough of not being able to register all levels of her distress, and address them however was needed. "Medusa, I know you said no in the garden, but let's really talk about me taking off the mask, once and for all."

"No." She spoke sharply.

"I'm done arguing about this," he said firmly.

"So am I."

He tried to hold onto her, but she wormed out of his lap. "No more of this...intimacy between us. It leads to bad things."

Intimacy? "You mean what happened at the waterfall?"

"Yes. It made me speak of things I should not have. Encouraging you to be closer to me than you should be."

She was out on the open air patio. If he pushed it, she'd just fly off, but so be it. He wasn't backing down this time. "What things?"

"I do not need to explain. If you wish to stay, there will be no more discussion of this."

"Medusa."

"Do not say my name. It means monster to the world now. I..."

He moved toward her, kept moving purposefully even as she dodged him again. It was a calculated risk, but as she seized his arm with a startled oath before he could walk off the edge and tumble over, he turned and slid an arm around her, bringing her close. Her wings beat at him, and the snakes hissed, but didn't bite. She didn't straight arm him, but she did go rigid, her fists closed against his chest. He pressed his face against her hair, the snakes bumping his jaw and neck, one coiling against his nape.

"I don't want to frighten and upset you," he said. "But I can't bear not to look at you anymore. Not when I know it will be okay and that it will be better for both of us."

Her fingers crept up his chest and joined the snake at his neck. It slithered away so she could curl her fingers against his flesh.

"If I had to add you to my garden, *my* heart could not bear it. You have said you have no magic to overpower me, but you do. I need to banish you from my island. To protect you. To protect myself. I cannot risk being this...weak."

The surge of victory came with a tearing pain in his chest, because of the anguish in her voice. "If I do possess such a magic, my lady, it is only because you have the same magic hold over me," he said roughly. "That's the way love works."

"Love." She said it as if it was an unfamiliar word and perhaps it was, in this context. She'd loved a Goddess who'd ultimately seemed apathetic to her. She'd had no family but priestesses who pointed their devotion and loyalty in mostly one direction, upward. Though he reminded himself they'd cared for one another in their own way, because they'd given Medusa the dubious escape method from her attacker.

"I will not speak of love," she said. "How can you be sure the contacts work?"

"Because I've never known Maddock to screw that kind of stuff up." Yeah, there was a first time for everything, but he wasn't going to point that out.

She was still as stiff as a board, so he made a soothing sound. "Easy. And you're not a monster, my lady. Did you know your name means protector, guardian? I think it's a beautiful name. Listen to how I say it. Medusa."

He purred it, bending to find her throat with his lips. For the first time he did it without calculation of her reaction, and instead followed desire and instinct. He gave it full effort, using the heat and moisture of mouth and tongue to stroke her pulse, taste and nip her tender flesh. He paid close attention to the pocket of her collar bone, the slender line of her throat up to the sensitive spot below her ear, and then made his way back down to tease her carotid again.

When her hands clutched him, he knew he'd made the right call. Her lips parted on a sigh, and her sweet nipples he'd kill to suckle peaked against his chest, her body moving restlessly against him. He could detect the heady musk of arousal gathering between her thighs.

"I want to taste you again," he said against her pounding pulse. He was testing the edges of the passion they discussed, seeing if she would panic or respond in kind to his demand. "I would willingly stay between your thighs for hours, bringing you to climax over and over."

Her nails dug into him, summoning a growl from his chest. What would have sent her startling like a flock of birds not too long ago only had her drawing away from him now. Not too far. Not far enough to let him go.

"It was unexpected, what happened at the falls," she said slowly. "The pleasure, the desire to give myself to you completely. I felt like I was surrendering to the Goddess's power, riding that bliss one cannot describe to those not in a spiritual ecstasy."

He knew she spoke of things in the framework of her experience, but he couldn't help teasing her. "I'm going to have you write that 'surrendering to a God's power' thing down and sign it. I want to show it off to my buddy Lot Lakeney, who thinks he's God's gift to womankind and always giving me shit."

"I said a Goddess's power."

"Yeah, I edited it to impress him more. He's kind of a sexist old school bastard."

She made a little huffing noise he took to be a chuckle. "He dislikes you? Or you dislike him?"

"No. He's one of my best friends. Insulting one another is kind of the way men bond."

"Oh." The puzzlement vanished from her voice. "When we were permitted to attend the festival competitions, I witnessed this among the male competitors."

"Yeah, I expect male razzing has been around since ancient times. We don't change much."

"I may consider letting you use the contacts," she relented. "But let us not test them this moment. Please."

"All right." He agreed reluctantly, but cupped her face with both hands so she knew he was looking into her face, even with the blindfold in the way. "You know, if you ever give me permission to look upon you, I'm not going to be disappointed or repelled. I know it makes you uncomfortable for me to say these things, but I'm going to think you're the most beautiful woman I've ever seen. There's nothing you can show me of yourself that would make me think otherwise."

"You have not seen the look of horror on their faces at the end. All of them."

"Well, let's think about that. Maybe that's not because of what they see in front of them, but what's happening inside. I was gut shot once. When the pain and reality hits, everything you're reacting to is inside, wrapped up with this sudden realization you might be about to die. The whole world narrows to that. I barely registered who the shooter was."

"I'm not sure I understand."

He shrugged. "Lot was the guy bent over me right after it happened. He probably saw that same look on my face you've seen, but it wasn't for him. What happens when you look at someone is fatal, right? There's going to be a pretty fast and terrifying chain of reactions through their whole body and brain."

Perhaps her ability to kill with her gaze made her a monster, intent aside, but intent was the difference between saving a soul and losing one, right? Yeah, acts against those like the old woman and her grandson couldn't be ignored. He'd killed and had regrets, and those regrets were sharp, piercing him to the core and waking him in the middle of the night. He wouldn't be the idiot asshole who trivialized her crimes, but he'd damn well stand at her side to balance that scale with other viewpoints.

Yet he also knew how much helping the damaged submissives had helped him with that scale. It would never be level again, no, but somehow being able to throw pebbles into the plate opposite the boulder of his past had given him room to breathe again. She'd been trapped on this island, no chance to do that, and it was clear the result was guilt and bitterness that could eat her alive in the darker moments. And if more enemies kept coming, men with wrongheaded thinking but not necessarily all with wrong hearts...

A problem for another day. Dropping to one knee, holding her hand, his other at her waist, he lifted his face to her. "If you could simply want, without worrying about any of the rest, what would you want from me, my lady? What could I give you?"

"I have continued to ask you why you are here. I think, the last time, when you told me of your life before, that was a great deal of it for you."

He nodded, and she shifted under his touch. "But I feel like there is still a piece missing. Like why is this important to Maddock? Why did he do this, help you get here? I must have your honesty, John Pierce. You seem to want me to give all that I am to you. My trust, my soul, my heart. But I must know you better. You understand?"

"Yeah. I do." The first time he and Maddock had sat down and JP gave him a real shot at convincing him of his lunacy, the scientist-wizard had put it in words he could understand. He would give them to her now. He wouldn't hold back this time, no matter how crazy it probably would sound.

"There isn't a grand purpose to it, not really. We tend to judge progress through battles and territory, wealth and prosperity. Some judge it based on what they can take—like the body of a virgin priest-ess, no matter her own feelings about it."

Tension strummed through her fingers and increased his hold on them. "But Maddock believes in powers deeper and stronger than men or what men call gods. A connecting energy, like all the drops of water in the oceans. To those powers, the point isn't to win a war that's already been lost, or to stop a death that turned bones to dust long ago. It's to heal a broken heart. Because that can cause a ripple effect in the universe impacting everyone.

"Maddock believes the key to all of it isn't saving the world, but one soul at a time. That's how he talked me into this. Because I wasn't interested in saving the world. I've been down that road and know how pointless that is. I came here to save you. And Maddock believes, when those souls start adding up, the selfishness of a selfless love might just save us all."

He shifted. "But that just makes me sound like the hero, and the truth is it's two way. What I said about my mom, pointing out how lonely you must have been? I heard it as an answer to what was inside of me. Always lonely. Always feeling alone, even in a crowd."

Feeling her gaze on him and trapped in the darkness of the blindfold, he couldn't seem to stop himself from giving her more than he'd intended. "Probably the second worse thing I remember about my job was this kid. Four years old. He died, shot in my arms while we were trying to get him out. He was crying for his mommy until his last breath.

Then he was gone. Ten years before that, there was a woman, another undercover agent in the DEA. She and I worked close together on a job, but she got strung out...addicted to the drugs we were trying to stop. She switched sides so she could pay for her habit. When I confronted her, she blew her brains out in front of me rather than face prison as a cop."

He wasn't explaining the terms that might be unfamiliar, but her hand fell onto his wrist, gripping, and he knew he didn't need to explain.

"Lot was the one who took me to Maddock. Before the two of them, I'd always been kind of on my own, had never had what I considered family. I was in pretty bad shape after that op with the kid, physically and emotionally. Being so badly shot, all of it piled up on me. Lot helped me...figure it out. When I got out of all that, I was helping women who had been through things like you had been. For the first time in a long time, I felt clean and real. And then he introduced me to Maddock."

"Oh." Her hand drew away. "So I am a mission of sorts, like the others. Which is as you said at the beginning."

"Yes, and no." He cocked his head. "You're kind of getting mad at me, aren't you, thinking that I see you as another woman in need of rescuing?"

When she said nothing, he felt a tightness in his chest that wasn't unpleasant. "That actually makes me feel good, thinking that it matters to you, that I see you as special. You are, Medusa. I said the women were like you, but I never took one for myself. No one ever belonged to me, and I couldn't figure out why I had no interest. I thought I'd broken something inside myself, like I was dead."

He shook his head. "But I kept dreaming about you. When Maddock told me his theory and that how I felt about you was something not only special, but real, it's like I woke up. To the world I came from, it would sound like the biggest pile of crap, and maybe it does to you, too. No one believes in a fantasy love you've dreamed about since you were a kid. One that, when you finally get the chance to meet her, you feel this miraculous moment of 'Fuck, it was real.' I don't expect anything of you. I just—"

"It is a very romantic notion," she said cautiously, before he could continue the line of thought. "Yet it feels...true."

"Yeah, doesn't it?" He was relieved she thought so.

"I suppose it makes sense, to send a man who believes in a bedtime story, to heal the heroine's heart."

There was no mockery in her voice. She was speaking sincerely. With belief. His throat went dry. Understanding it himself was one thing; hearing her understand it, the mythical character herself, was nothing short of a miracle.

"So that's what it's about, my lady," he said at last. "That's all of it. Promise."

She drew away and paced in front of him. He held his tongue, not sure what she was considering. Then she stopped and put her hands on his face, stroking her thumbs over his cheeks, his eyes. He sensed she was looking hard at him, so hard he could feel the heat of her stare, a peculiar tingling over his skin.

"My lady..."

"Please, be silent another moment."

So he did. And then she began to unlace the blindfold. His heart thudded to a halt. Her hands were trembling.

"You ask me what I want from you. Yes?"

"Yes," he said roughly, reaching up to close his hand around one quivering wrist.

"I would lay down my fear and my anger. Lay it at your feet and trust you, John Pierce." Her voice was as female and vulnerable as he'd yet heard it. "Trust you to care for me. I would have no fear of betrayal and believe there is one moment, one person in my life, who I can trust to lay my head on his heart and know I am safe with him. Whole with him, with no need to be on guard. It is a simple wish, but it is everything to me."

The blindfold fell away and she was looking at him, and him at her. He saw her shudder, hard, as his gaze rested upon her face. Her body was rigid and her eyes teared with the effort it took to not close them, to risk this. He could tell her heart stopped in that first fateful moment, too, when she fully expected he might be wrong and he would turn to stone right before her eyes.

He caught both her hands, holding them tight until she could breathe again, until it sank in that Maddock had been right about the contacts. Thank God. He wouldn't like to be stone, but the true agony for him would have been leaving this life knowing he'd hurt her exactly as she'd feared he would.

Having all the time in the world to gaze upon her now took his breath away. Her eyes like deep garnet gemstones, the riotous mane of black silky hair curling around her fine features and falling to her hips. Her snakes poised at various places on her crown, shoulders or breast. Her slim, athletic body, clad in the sleeveless short top and skirt. Her wings, at half spread behind her, the claw at the joints marked the way her own claws were, with the spell craft that made her this way. This fantastical, noble female.

"I would have you touch me and there be nothing between us but those feelings and sensation," she said abruptly, reaching up to touch his face. "I want you to take over all of me. Chase away every demon, bring light to every dark corner, and make it clear to me in every way that there is no room in my mind for bad memories or fear. That as you serve me this way, protect me, so I serve you, as I believed I served the Goddess. With room for nothing in my heart, mind and soul but love."

Her moist lips parted to reveal one small sharp fang worrying her bottom lip. She was thin and small. Christ, too thin, the bones of her shoulders sharp and her face possessing an angularity he expected would disappear with more nourishment. But there was a tough resilience to her features that matched all he'd learned of her since he'd come. Her chin was tilted up and her slim jaw set in a determined line that held back so much emotion, especially in this overwhelming moment. His was the first human face she'd gazed upon without worry in how many years?

Every word she'd spoken to him, every hint of body language he'd picked up, suddenly found this missing piece. In a blink, he knew even more about her, which also came with a whole world of new things to discover.

He smiled at the pleasure of it. Her features eased, as well as showed a flash of gratitude and relief so strong it gripped her like pain. When he reached out and traced her temple, cheek and jaw, she closed her eyes, pressing her face into his hand. Her ringlets of dark silken hair curled over his knuckles, her snakes moving restlessly over her shoulders and his forearm. She'd described them well. Ratqueen looked like the ghost of a large snake, curled at the crown of her head. Tunneltrap and Waterlight were sleek and black. Treebark had the spiky texture and color of a peeling birch tree. Little Earthson had the hue of copper pennies streaked with red. He was a tiny curlicue on her collar bone, watching JP.

Her wings were at half fold, as if she'd considered taking off in that first second. JP hooked his fingers in the shoulder strap of her laced top, his thumb making a slow, sensual pass over the jumping pulse at the base of her throat.

"Thinking of flying away from me, snake-girl?"

She swallowed beneath his touch. As he increased the range of his stroke, he was fiercely delighted at her response. When he glided the rough pad of his thumb up and down that small section of her throat, her chin lifted to give him more access.

"You don't look like you would allow that."

Her choice of words was a shot straight to his groin, making him harden more. "Damn straight. You said you want me to lie with you. I'm not going to let you back out of that."

The memories of the past warred with the present in her face, and he constricted his grip. "You know the difference between us, Medusa. Don't let your head fuck with that."

She shook her head. "No. I won't. I won't let it spoil it."

"Nothing could spoil it. Nothing could spoil a single moment I get to spend with you. How about you let me take things from here, so you don't have to worry about anything but the way I'm making you feel?"

It was intuitive for him, knowing when he needed to let that part of himself take the upper hand. Though with her speaking those trigger words, he wasn't sure if he'd summoned his Dom side or she had. Or some combination of both.

A slight nod told him she'd agreed. Moving slow so as to savor the moment as well as not to startle her, he unlaced the short top in front. As he released it, he pushed it away so he could cup and frame her breasts in his large hands. Her eyes half closed again as she leaned into his touch. Stepping closer, he unbelted the tunic, holding onto the braided cord as he let the fabric flutter to her feet. No underwear, so she stood before him naked, a wild creature of myth and legend whose garnet eyes lifted to his and lowered again, her breathing shallow. He bent, holding her chin with two fingers as he pressed a kiss to the corner of her mouth.

"Hold your lips open but very still," he commanded. "I want you to stay as still as one of your stone statues, until I tell you otherwise."

He would kiss and tease her until her body was quivering so hard that, if had been encased in stone, it would crack and fall away. He played with that sensitive corner of her mouth with tongue and lips, loving the little puffs of her aroused breath on his face, which strengthened as he moved fully over her lips, slipping in to dance with her tongue, trace the fork. She stilled at that, but he didn't pause, moving on to caress her teeth, then out to the other corner of her lips, to her cheek. Slipping his fingers under her hair, he put his mouth beneath her ear. Her hands were at her sides, the fingers curled.

"Open your hands. Let them stay loose. You'll stay open to me in all ways, Medusa. No fear, nothing but trust that I'll take you where you wish to go."

"Deep inside you," she whispered.

He lifted his head as her eyes opened. She hadn't realized she'd spoken, he could tell. "Tell me what you mean," he said.

"Deep inside you, where there is no thought, nothing but..."

"Surrender." He supplied her the word she'd used earlier, when she was less vulnerable than she was now. Here she was a babe, shivering and exposed, but he was going to bring her warmth, be her blanket, her refuge. "Surrender and service."

"Surrender and service," she repeated, her face paling a little as she probably realized how deep down this road they might go.

"Joy and pleasure," he added, to help with that. "The way it's supposed to be."

"The way it's supposed to be."

Repeating his words seemed to be steadying her. He resumed his tasting of her flesh, working over the point of her delicate shoulder. He lifted her hands to his shoulders. "Hold on to me," he ordered, and picked her up under her arms, bracing her against the wall so he could cup her breasts again. Meeting her gaze briefly, he lowered his and took one sweet peak into his mouth.

She gasped, her head falling back as her claws dug into his shoulders and her legs coiled around him, bringing her core tight against his abdomen. He kneaded her small curves and pushed them together, letting her feel the strength and heat in his hands. His cock strained for contact, but he was going to deny it until he had her truly mindless. He'd told her he'd draw her deep into himself, where she'd be safe from fear or memory, able to experience this fully and purely.

He suckled her breasts, licked the curves, nuzzled and nipped until she was writhing against him, rubbing her cunt unconsciously against his stomach, making it slick with her arousal. He'd love to keep going until she came that way, but he'd save that for another time. Curving his arms around her body, he took her away from the wall and to the bed.

"How are your wings most comfortable when you're on your back?" he asked in a husky murmur.

"Fully stretched out."

"Do that."

She did it as he lowered her, so that she looked like an exotic Goth butterfly unfurling against the pale cloth. The slim arms he told her to put above her head became the graceful antenna. He removed his shorts, adjusting himself as he did so to avoid injury against the zipper, thanks to his engorged size.

Her eyes focused on his loins and briefly widened. He saw a trace of fear as memories that had no place here tried to get a foothold.

"Hey." He brought her gaze up with the one stern word, spoken in a low voice. "Right here. You look in my eyes, because they tell you the truth. What did I tell you, over and over?"

"That...I'm safe with you."

"Yeah." Leaning down, he pressed his mouth to her thigh, worked his way over her hipbone and to her navel, teasing her with his tongue there until she was squirming and giggling, despite herself. He looked up at her, grinning with lustful pleasure. When she met his gaze, he saw her surprise that he'd made her laugh, that he'd chosen to be playful. But it had had the desired effect.

"My buddy Lot said that the Greek women prefer men with smaller equipment. That you'd run screaming from me out of disgust, not fear."

"He is your friend, so I will not insult him, but I will say he does not know as much as he thinks he does."

John smiled, then his gaze heated anew. "Spread your legs for me. I want to taste your desire."

She did, with a lovely little tremble he savored. He dragged moist kisses up along the inside of either thigh, passing so close to her core that his nose brushed her smooth mound. He wondered if the spell craft had made her hairless there or if she kept herself that way, like the neatly trimmed and clean toenails. He wasn't complaining, because it would make her all the more sensitive to friction. Her clit was swollen, the labia glistening with her juices.

He made a couple more passes, watching the way her hips lifted in little involuntary jerks, her body knowing what it craved even if her mind didn't. When he put his lips over her labia and clit to indulge a nice, probing taste, she nearly came up off the bed, pressing her cunt to his mouth. He slid his hands beneath her buttocks, gripping tight to hold her still as he licked and got her moaning, her fists grabbing the edge of the bed.

When he finally moved up her body, her eyes were glazed, fangs fully visible, claws caught in rips in the sheets. But no matter how he'd prepared her, as he began to cover her with his body, he saw that old terror trying to pierce through. He had an answer for that.

With an effortless lift, he turned them so she straddled his body. He'd angled her so the head of his cock was lodged at her opening. Her gaze caught his and he gripped her hips, holding her fast.

"Feel me, sweetheart. All that desire is for you. I want to be deep inside you, too. Let me in."

Her hands were on his biceps, clinging like she was at the edge of a cliff. Her jaw was quivering as if her nerves were making her teeth chatter, but he wasn't having any of that.

"You're a warrior of Athena," he reminded her. "No man takes what you're not willing to give. Are you willing to give me your body, Medusa?"

"Yes." Her eyes were glistening with unshed tears. "But I also...I also want you to take it. I don't know why, but..."

"It's okay. I do. And those are the sweetest words I've ever heard. Wanting a lover to take is different from a man forcing himself on you. Come down here and kiss me. I'll prove it."

He drew her down to his chest to help her comply. As she did, he wound both arms around her, putting one hand on her buttock to guide himself into her, adjusting their bodies so he knew he had the angle he needed. When he started pushing her down on him, he took it slow. If her only experience with sex was that one terrible incident, years ago, she was going to be tight. And she was. The sensation was an excruciating pleasure that had him growling in her mouth. She answered with a similar noise, a whimpering plea he loved, part savage animal need, part womanly desire, all Medusa.

Her fang cut him, but that didn't matter. He relished the pain, her loss of control. Lifting and lowering her, he let her feel the way of it, the pleasure that could build and build. She started working with him, her fingers clutching and releasing in the same rhythm on his shoulders and biceps.

But she'd wanted as much take as give, hadn't she? He could handle that, and the time was now. As she was gasping, her body rising toward climax, he rolled and put himself on top of her. He saw the flash of fear amid desire, and he gripped her face to make her stare into his eyes.

"I'm not him, am I?"

"No," she whispered.

"Say it."

"You're not him." Tears trickled down her face and he thrust into her, not breaking the rhythm, making the emotional pain tangle with the physical pleasure to drive her higher, to break down more walls for him. He could be ruthless when he knew it was where they both needed to go. Her tears tore into him, but being cosseted and coaxed wasn't what she needed now.

"Keep saying it," he commanded.

"You're not him...you're not...him..." She was sobbing, but amid that response, something else was shoving forward, something that had her clawing at him. "Oh, Goddess..."

He lay down upon her fully, though holding his weight mostly on one arm. His other was wrapped around her back, hand still palming her ass to make his thrusts deeper and more potent. The position put his body in full contact with hers, from breast to knee, and allowed her to shift her grip around his back. When she pierced skin with her claws, she felt the shudder that ran through him.

Her vision cleared somewhat. "I'm sorry, I--"

"Don't be. Mark me as yours, Medusa. Your Master. The one you can cut to the bone, and I'll still protect you with every breath I've got."

She stared at him, and then her fangs bared, the climax surging up and claiming her. Her cry vibrated through him, gripping his heart, soul and balls, calling forth his own release. As she tore into his back with her talons, a mindless response to the power of the climax he gave her, a savage, primal possessiveness grabbed him as well. She marked him without; he marked her within, jetting his seed into her.

Her body continued to convulse. She sobbed against his ear, called his name and begged for mercy she didn't really want. He kept going until they were both spent, until she was shuddering in his arms, limp and quiet. He pressed kisses along her brow, her lips, and lifted his head enough to gaze into her lovely eyes once more. "I'll never blindfold myself again," he swore. "I'm not depriving myself of the sight of you."

She was dazed at every level, he could tell. Pale and trembling still, she lifted her hand to his face, but flinched and stopped short of touching him. She had blood on the claws. He caught her wrist and cleaned it off with lips and tongue. Moving down to caress her palm with the same, he suckled on her wrist and gave her a gentle nip.

"No words," he said quietly. "Just let me care for you."

Her gaze said she thought he needed care, and he probably did, but right now he wanted it to be all about her. Lifting her off the bed, he carried her back to the patio and looked up the fifteen feet to her nest. He wished he could carry her there, but he didn't think either of them were up to that exertion yet. So he sat down on a patio chair, because she seemed to enjoy that view the best of all places in her home. For a while he held her cradled in his arms like a babe, murmuring to her, rubbing her as she quivered and occasionally let out a small sob.

Sometimes she lifted her head to look at him and meet his eyes. It was so new to her, to be able to do that without fear. She was transitioning from avoidance to craving it, confirming for herself she had the ability and the right to do it. He'd had subs he'd made do the lowering of eyes thing, a submissive protocol they needed. He'd never require it of her. Being able to look in her face, and have her look back at him, had such meaning and importance, he'd never take that away from either of them.

Though he needed to clean up, he didn't feel comfortable enough with her emotional state to leave her for even a few minutes. So he carried her to the large waterfall area and placed her on the bank before wading into the pool to rinse his back. It was deep enough he could dunk his head underneath by dropping to his knees, so he did.

When he surfaced, she was in the water behind him. Her hands slid down his back, around the scratches. She pressed her lips against one, and everything inside him broke open. When she used her own palms and ribbons of her hair to clean away the rest of the blood around the now coagulated wounds, he was moved in a way he couldn't explain. She kissed each gash and looped her arms around his waist, standing that way until he turned in her arm span and cradled her face. Full darkness had fallen, so he used moonlight and shadows to find her lips once more for a lingering, no need to move ever again, kind of kiss.

He'd worried about idealizing her, yet today she'd told him what he was sure were the worst things about herself. She was as fragile, fallible and sometimes ugly as anyone else, including himself. It was impossible to love an ideal. But a real woman...that was someone he could love forever. He had the reality in his arms, and would let the myth go without regret.

Lifting his head, he stared her in the eyes and said what he was now more certain than ever was the truth, as miraculous and unlikely as it should have been. "I love you."

CHAPTER FOURTEEN

"What exactly is this for?" JP looked down at the rope Medusa was tying around him in a harness, and thought of how pleasant she'd look in the same rig, for entirely different reasons.

She stood on her tiptoes to adjust it over his shoulders. With a grin, he put his hands to her waist and lifted her to make it easier for her to do what she was wanting to do.

"I do have wings for that," she said primly, though her cheeks tinged with color at his touch. She'd been doing that ever since they'd made love, as if his merest contact made her think of embarrassing things he'd love to be in her mind to see. Though if he was, they might be back in the bed in a blink.

He'd woken her earlier this morning by teasing her with the friction of his five o'clock shadow. Holding her loosely pinned against the mattress, he aroused her once more and slid into her body, taking them both to an easy morning climax. He'd given her sweet, simple pleasure, proving to her that intimacy could be enjoyed in a wide variety of mindsets. Laughter and curiosity could be as much a part of it as shattering one's hold on reality and giving them a glimpse of eternity. Like last night.

At least that's the way he'd felt about it. She hadn't said she loved him back, but he wasn't expecting her to do that. He'd probably jumped the gun, saying it to her, and was lucky she hadn't either decked him or taken off as a result of the impulse share.

She'd been quiet this morning. Respecting that she had a lot to digest, he'd kept things light. During breakfast, she'd told him about the view from the top pinnacle of the island, all the surrounding lands she could see. He'd asked her if there was a way to hike there. There wasn't. She was going to fly him there.

"I'm too heavy," he told her again. "Carrying me up here from the base of the cliff was a much shorter trip."

"I can carry you longer and farther, with the help of the rope. Can you do a harness like I just did on you?"

She blinked at him with guileless crimson eyes. She was going to kill him. Rope bondage wasn't his main focus, but he'd played with it enough to enjoy the art form.

"Sure." He picked up another length of rope, measuring out about eight meters. She was a smart girl, always salvaging things like rope from the boats. She knew how to maintain them, for what he was handling was sound and well-conditioned.

He modified and combined a Shibari breast harness design with his rope climbing skills and came up with a pleasing solution that would frame her breasts and provide carrying support. He paid close attention to her reaction as he ran the rope around her upper torso. When he cinched it a little tighter beneath her breasts than he ultimately intended to leave it, he suppressed a pleased reverence at the flush climbing higher in her cheeks. Her hand resting on his forearm clenched in a sexually anxious curl. Bending, he put his lips to her shoulder. As she tipped her head, giving him more access, he twisted his fingers in the rope, which constricted the hold around her breasts. She let out a little gasp.

"I can do a lot of things with this you might like," he murmured, brushing her ear with his mouth. "Keep that in mind."

"Um, you mean...tying my hands and feet?" She was struggling to maintain her boundaries and protect herself, for pretty obvious reasons. He wanted her to not worry about those reasons, but he knew that was going to take time.

"Sometimes. But sometimes it can be just like this. Your arms and legs free, but your torso bound, similar to how you let yourself be held in my arms." He did a knot and ran the remaining rope between her legs, catching it up in back and cinching it between her buttocks in a quick jerk that had an outright moan breaking from between her lips as the knot rubbed against her clit.

"Goddess. You're a sorcerer. You must stop....just stop."

It was the faint note of alarm that told him he was pushing it. He'd told himself to take it slow. Not to act like a drug addict who'd just gotten his first taste in months. But it felt like that.

Letting the rope drop free, he ran his hands up and down her arms in a soothing way before finishing the harness in a purely practical manner. He did stroke her face, neck and shoulders when he was done, meeting her gaze once more. "Sorry, sweetheart. I'm just a little worked up after last night. I could steep myself in you for days without leaving that bed."

Her cheeks went a deeper rose color, telling him her thoughts weren't too far off from his. But she made a commendable and amusing attempt to get back onto their practical topic.

"I'm going to attach us to one another so if for any reason I lose my grip, you will not fall."

He drew the knife she'd returned to him last night. "I'll have this to cut myself free so I don't drag you down with me."

She put her hand over his. "No. You won't do that."

"It's good to prepare for any contingencies," he reminded her. "If I don't take the knife, we don't go."

"Then we don't go. For isn't that what love is supposed to be?" she questioned. "Being in things together?"

"Dragging one another down into oblivion and death?"

"If necessary. Better than living alone afterward with the idea that you didn't do everything to protect your love."

"But what if you did?"

"Not possible," she said. "If one did, the other wouldn't be dead."

"I don't think that's always the case."

"You would feel that way if it were you," she pointed out. "You're just a protective male who thinks you must give your life to protect me, regardless of how futile the scenario. What if I tumbled off a cliff when you were not around? Would you dash yourself on the rocks?"

"Women," he grumbled. "Want to be so damn pragmatic when we're trying to be noble and self-sacrificing."

She smiled and stepped out on the ledge, looking up. "It's a ten-

minute flight," she said. "The harness and these metal hooks you have
to connect us will make it easier. We will be fine, regardless. I have
greater upper body strength than most human women."

"Even though you have bird bones," he pointed out. "I want you to
eat more."

She shrugged. "I am rarely hungry."

"For anything?" He bumped her with his hip and leaned down,
stopping just short of her mouth. Her gaze riveted on his. "Because
I'm finding myself pretty damn hungry all the time right now," he said.
"We'll have to eat soon."

"We just ate breakfast an hour ago," she said, though how she delicately touched her tongue to her lips said his meaning wasn't lost on
her. She was just feeling shy about things, too shy to tease. Another
warning for him to ease back.

Brushing his mouth against her cheek and lips, he straightened.
"All right, then. Let's go see the best view on the island, according to
you. From my viewpoint, it looks like it's standing right in front
of me."

She shook her head at him, but gave him a little smile. Pulling a
short stool up behind him, she stepped onto it and used the position
to secure his harness to hers with the screw lock carabiner clips he'd
showed her how to use. Though she'd mostly figured out a tandem
jump rig all by herself. Based on that and the other things he'd seen
her invent to care for herself, he thought she was a pretty good
common sense engineer, with more than the usual mechanical skills
for someone untrained.

She thought problems through, unhampered by anyone telling her
she didn't know enough to try something. Courage and intelligence
filled in where training wasn't available. Like her harrowing story of
trying out her wings until she could get them to work. She didn't seem
to have an Achilles' heel when it came to figuring things out.

He wondered if they had that Achilles' heel saying yet. After all, it
had taken about five years past *Happy Days* for "jump the shark" to
catch on as the catch phrase for a TV show that was about to be
cancelled.

They could spend a lifetime catching up on common cultural
references. Not to mention all the other things they could talk about
or do together. They never had to leave here.

A twinge in his gut told him the problem with that theory, but he wasn't going to get into that now. She was speaking to him.

"Ready?" she asked.

He pulled her down for a warm kiss, holding her as it deepened. Her hand curled into his shoulder. He was wearing a T-shirt today so the ropes wouldn't chafe, but he liked the heat of her touch through it. He could still feel the gouges she'd left on his back, and he relished their discomfort. They'd been pretty good slashes, like he'd been attacked by a bird of prey, which wasn't too far from the truth.

Some might say he had a masochistic side, but he knew better. He loved carrying the evidence of the pleasure he'd given her. They framed the Medusa's Heart tattoo in a pretty significant way he liked a lot.

He'd have scars from her front and back, each set a permanent reminder of a very critical step in their relationship.

"Okay. Ready." He pulled back to let them both breathe, glad to see he'd accelerated the pulse in her slim neck. "And if I get too heavy, promise you'll touch down. There's some interim places you can break on the way to the top, right? I might be able to climb from those spots, if you need me to do so."

"I promise. I have no desire to plummet either of us to our deaths today."

"Good. Because I'd hate to pick a day where you were in that kind of mood."

That little feminine chuckle shook her, followed by a ripple through her body as her wings spread and she prepared herself for the leap. They'd already talked about the best way to do it, but he wondered if she'd really expected him to have the balls to do it the most effective way.

Which was running forward with her piggy backing, and taking a horizontal leap off the ledge without hesitation. Just like a bird would do it, his arms spread out to help balance her.

She might not have expected him to do it so decisively and swiftly, no hesitation, but jumping out of a plane with a chute wasn't a drag-your-feet kind of thing, either. As a result, the takeoff went better than probably either of them anticipated. There was a brief jerk as she had to summon more strength from her wings to accommodate his added weight, but then they were gliding, her leveling out before she maneuvered into a turn and began spiraling up toward the top peak. Her command of flying skills impressed him, and not just because he didn't end up dashed on the rocks below.

He'd initially suggested climbing to the top of another nearby peak, like the one he'd used to test his ladder theory, where less of a vertical lift would be needed. She'd assured him she could do this, no problem.

Now that the decision was made, the best way he could help her was by flowing with her energy. It was a pretty amazing spectacle, the island spread out beneath them, her lifting him from above, her body pressed against the back of his. He saw the goats, the sparkle of the sun on the numerous streams that etched out the hills and valleys of the island. Far out on the water, a boat was passing between other land masses, its sails tiny triangles that blended and reappeared against the watery background.

He wondered if she realized how strange it was, her isolation here when human civilization moved forward so close by. Knowing the human propensity to multiply and spread out, he had an uneasy thought about what would happen when they finally had great enough numbers she could be overwhelmed. The only reason some enterprising governing authority hadn't claimed the island from her yet was that so far they had sufficient resources for their needs. When that was no longer true, she would be even less safe here than she was already.

A problem for another day. He was here, and he could help her with those decisions if she'd accept his help. While Maddock hadn't advised transporting her through the portals to JP's time, it was one option, if it came to it. Especially if she was immortal and he wasn't. He pushed that thought away. He wasn't going to envision a world where he was eighty years old and she remained young and strong as she was now.

Despite that strength, she was starting to show signs of strain. She'd warned him of it, that when they drew closer to their destination, the flight pattern would become steeper.

"Okay?" he called out. She didn't answer, likely saving her breath. He was an idiot. He'd known this was a bad idea. He shouldn't have asked her to do it.

She came in for a bumpy landing, tumbling them into spongy turf.

When she released the clips holding them together, he turned over and scrambled to her side. She was lying on her back, gasping for breath while smiling. The snakes looked a little like he did, just on this side of *oh shit* mode, but they were regaining their composure, taking advantage of her position to slither through the thick green grass.

"That was fun," she said. "I knew we could make it."

He sat back and shot her a reproachful glance. She laughed. "You underestimate a woman's strength and determination, John Pierce," she said reprovingly. "I'm quite aware of my capabilities."

"I was afraid I was asking too much."

"No." Her tone softened and she touched his jaw. "You have asked much, but not too much. Not yet."

Before he could respond to that, she rose, offering him a hand up. He took it, and stood at her side. "Look," she said. "All the wonder of the world is here."

He had to agree with her. There was no cover from rain, but the patches of thick grass were large enough he wondered if she slept up here some nights. Why limit herself to just one bedroom?

The pinnacle offered a full diameter view that covered her island, the surrounding shorelines, the expanse of ocean, and the lands in the distance. He estimated she was about five miles from the nearest one, which didn't ease his worries. From here he could see other beach accesses on the island than where he'd arrived. Many had matching fleets of abandoned boats, small weathered heaps that darkened the pale sands.

Christ. She'd said she'd regularly repelled invaders, but he'd reacted to that based on the boats on his beach alone. While he still wouldn't mourn those who'd come with murder or capture as their intent, he knew that those deaths and disappearances would weigh heavily enough on the minds of relatives or governing authorities that the attempts would continue, even if at more infrequent intervals. It was a miracle she'd let him come off the beach. He owed that grandmother and grandson a debt.

"You did well, jumping with me," she said, pulling him out of his thoughts. She helped him out of the harness and he did the same for her, though he once again noticed how still she got as he was handling those ropes against her skin.

Easy, JP. Just enjoy her.

After he set the harnesses aside, she took a seat on the grass. Drawing her knees up, she linked her fingers under them, catching the short skirt against her lower body. Greek women were modest in public, but nudity wasn't considered the taboo it was in his world. He expected her attempt to not blatantly reveal that underwear wasn't part of the Greek wardrobe was because of how intimate they'd become in the past day or so. His snake-girl was being a little shy. He found it appealing and perversely arousing. He set that aside in favor of conversation, so she wouldn't think he was insatiable.

Though he was.

"When I took off, the way you pushed off with me, spread your arms and managed your balance with mine, it was as if you knew what it is to have wings," she said.

"I've done jumps before." He briefly explained planes and parachuting. "Sometimes I was flown into territory where planes couldn't land. Lot did HALO jumps, but I never got that opportunity. HALO means high-altitude, low-opening jumping." His lips curved. "He says it's like being so close to the heavens when you jump, you're flying with the angels. You can see the curve of our earth. It looks like a beautiful white and reddish glow against a curved dark shadow. Eerie but totally kickass at the same time."

At her blank look, he offered a full smile. "It's so astounding, there are no words to describe it."

"The world is so much bigger than I imagined," she said, looking back at the view, her gaze pensive. "I thought about that when I first came here, to this highest spot. This was the first place I found ease since...I changed. I looked around me and realized that the world was so much bigger than what had happened to me, than my life at the temple. Your words tell me no matter what I imagine, the world will always be bigger than that. It is bigger than my mind or existence, and there is comfort in that. As well as some despair, if that makes sense."

He sat down next to her, bracing his arm behind her so she could lean against his shoulder and chest. She did, gratifying him. He nuzzled her hair, closing his eyes as Ratqueen bumped his brow and slithered onto his shoulder, coiling under his arm and resting her head on his biceps. She held him tethered to Medusa, and he wondered if the snake was responding to her mistress's needs, or if it was that they were getting so used to him that he was another convenient perching place. Some of both, he suspected.

"They accept you," she said, as if reading his thoughts. "It is an additional reassurance to me, John Pierce. And you show no aggression toward them, which is how men usually react to snakes. That pleases me. I was not kind to them in the beginning, but they have become a part of me, my family, if you will not laugh at me for saying so."

"And if I did?"

Her eyes sparked with humor. "Then I will tell Ratqueen to bite you."

"She can try." Studying the snake, he rested his fingers on her tubular body and stroked. The snake shifted, but didn't seem to mind the contact. The way Medusa's eyes half closed, he wondered if she felt the caress in some secondary way. He settled in, enjoying the feel of her leaning against him. "What you said, about the size of the world making you feel good and bad at the same time? That makes sense to me. There's this thought, 'if the world is this big, why the hell do I matter? I'm just another ant scurrying along.'"

He paused, considering the view. "But Maddock would look at it this way. Say there is some big Cosmic God or Goddess who tossed us out here like seeds on the ground, waiting to see what would happen, how we grow. Maybe the way we do that, embrace who we are, is by reaching out to one another, forming connections. That net gives us shape and weight, and makes us part of something bigger, an energy we draw upon from each other."

"I am not connected to anyone, John Pierce," she said. Her gaze was on the boat moving in the distance, and he expected she was gauging its course. She had to stay on guard about things like that, for exactly the reason she'd stated. He touched her face, drawing her gaze to him.

"You're connected to me."

She studied him, wisps of her black hair drifting across her golden cheekbone. "You think I belong to you."

"And me to you."

She lifted a shoulder and looked back at the ocean, her red eyes catching the sunlight like glowing rubies. "Yes and no. The first has a particular significance to you. I think the other is more what you hope

I will feel for you. Do you remember when I asked you how other women acted with you? You said the 'few' you've been with, you read their consent from their responses, how they touched you."

"Yeah." He warily wondered where she was going with this, and found his wariness confirmed with her next unsettling observation, which reminded him just how clever she was, even when she didn't have context for what she was sensing.

"You have an odd way about you with a woman, John Pierce. Some of the things you say, how you tie me in that rope"—she glanced at it, moistening her lips—"the spanking...it excites me, in ways that I find confusing, for I have not seen these desires among my own people. I had too little exposure to them. My reaction says these two parts of us mesh, but it is still beyond my comprehension. In the beginning, I asked you if you were reluctant to speak to me of your nature because it might be misunderstood. Is this what you meant?"

"Yeah, for the most part. You already have the rest."

"Will you speak of what might be misunderstood, now that you trust my responses more?"

"If I don't, will you refuse to carry me back down?"

A slight smile touched her lips. "Of course not. But I might find a faster way to get you to the ground if you prove stubborn."

"Lady, I'm all over stubborn. Just ask anyone who knows me."

She shifted away from him to lean back on her elbows, stretching her legs out in the grass, her wings folded along her back. Ratqueen uncoiled from him as she moved. That happened often, as if the snakes were connected to her brain waves so they coordinated effortlessly, not tangling her up when she was moving. Maddock would be keenly interested in their mental connection. And JP was procrastinating.

"I'm still concerned you won't understand," he admitted. "That you'll misinterpret it and become afraid."

"It's possible. But we have nothing but time on this island to resolve those things. Right?"

Good point. He was beginning to appreciate her practical side more and more. He stretched out on his side and decided to go with a tactile approach. Closing his hand on her wrist, he lifted it between them.

"Do you like it when I touch you here?"

She nodded. He leaned forward, drawing her arm behind her, holding her wrist against the small of her back and the rise of her buttock, which arched her body into his as he paused. "How about now?"

Her lips had parted. "Yes," she breathed.

"It feels different, doesn't it? A little scary, edgy, but exciting, too. You know about men who prefer other men? Or women who prefer women? Not just for sex. They prefer relationships with the same gender."

"Yes."

"In my world, we call that homosexual. Those who prefer the opposite sex are heterosexual, and those who prefer either are bisexual. Those are sexual orientations, but they're not the only type. There are Dominant and submissive orientations. People who prefer clear lines of power in sex. Sometimes in other parts of their lives as well..."

He continued, giving her examples and anecdotes. He had to separate it from historical context, because in her world, men held control of pretty much everything, and this wasn't about political or societal inequity. Since that was something people in his own time and world had trouble understanding about BDSM practices and Dominant/submissive personalities, he expected she'd have even more difficulty grasping the concepts. But he was wrong.

Many women from societies where women were subjugated couldn't fathom why a woman would willingly embrace submission, but she was not one of them. He figured the reason was two-fold. In the temple, she'd seen a different side of service and submission, and she had a naturally submissive nature and soul. Two, she had been forced to change every paradigm of her life in a short time. Ever since then, she'd had to adapt fast to survive, which meant continually re-examining preconceived notions.

As he worked his way through his answer to her question, her eyes would widen at certain parts, her lips pressing against one another nervously. Yet the strum of tension he felt when he released her to stroke her body from arm to upper thigh and back again, slowly, repetitively, wasn't fear. Which made it an effort to stay on topic.

He told her about dungeons, play parties, scenes, and the basic give and take between Dom and sub. But he'd left something impor-tant out, and she caught it.

"You speak of all these things as an observer, John Pierce. But you are telling me of yourself, are you not? You think I will not want you if I know how you express this side of yourself? Or you wish to convince me it is something you can set aside if it is not something I desire."

"I can."

She lay back on the grass, gazing up at him. "Perhaps that would be true, if you did not sense something in me that responds to that side of you. But when you sense that, you are unable to ignore that part of yourself." Her gaze drifted down. "The way I am reacting...has made you react. The way I respond to you feeds it, which makes you believe I am...a submissive?"

He didn't believe it. He knew it, but that was irrelevant. There were plenty of people with a submissive craving who never acted on it, or who channeled it other ways.

"I thought of the Goddess as mother, sister, friend," she said unex-pectedly. "I was brought to the temple at an early age, for my mother had died and my father knew not how to handle a girl child. My sisters were already grown, and they were not like me. So the priestesses encouraged me to think of Athena as my mother, as well as to serve her. I'd bring flowers and pretty stones to lay at her feet when I was younger. As I grew up, I would sing, or dance for her, even read to her. Serving her, making her happy, became my passion. It filled me, made me content far more quickly than other acolytes who took a far longer time to adjust to leaving the outside world behind."

She sat up as he continued to lay on his hip, and trailed her fingers over his side, curling her talons in the hem of his T-shirt.

"When I was transformed into this, for a long, long time, and perhaps in my heart, I still thought myself to blame for incurring Ukrit's attention. It is what we are taught to believe, is it not? That a man's lust makes him strong as a brute but weak in the mind, and women must bear the burden of being chaste and not indulge passions. Else we will incur that lust and deserve their brutishness. Yet I was in those walls, where I was innocent, and I always thought myself safe. I didn't even think he meant any harm, not at first. He spoke to me, and I'd never spoken with a man before. Not to that length. He paid me attention, and I was flattered, warmed in strange ways."

JP expected she'd been like many girl children, first learning their flirting skills on their fathers, an innocent, growing up thing. None of the priestesses had seemed to imply her unconscious charm and joy had made Ukrit's behavior her fault. Was that guilt therefore something buried in women's subconscious? Because fuck it all, it always seemed to rise when they were sexually assaulted, yet another crime against their soul.

"Medusa..."

She shook her head. "He was...authoritative. On the previous times when he'd visit, he would command me to bring him a drink, or say things to me in such a way that I felt fluttery in my stomach. It wasn't him, for I felt no desire toward him, but how he said those things...I liked it. I would serve him, I would serve the Goddess...it was about the service, wasn't it? Is this more evidence of what you are saying about me?"

"Some of it, yeah. But that didn't give him the right to do the things he did. Submission is a gift beyond measure, Medusa. It's your gift to give to a Master or Mistress, never to be taken. I'm big and strong. I could take whatever I wanted from a woman weaker than myself, but the idea of doing that against her will sickens me, horrifies me. However, a woman kneeling at my feet, with the need for submission shining in her eyes, looking to me to make it okay for her to be swept away by those cravings? Fuck, there's nothing better.

"When I top her, I feel like I'm worshipping her as much as I'm Mastering her, if that makes any sense. I came here to serve you, my lady, as I said from the beginning. And that too is a form of service, if it's what you desire."

Her gaze had stayed fastened on his face throughout his explanation, her claws curved into his hip, but now she let out a relieved breath. "So it is different. What I felt...didn't encourage him. No matter what he said...while it was happening."

He was more than willing to help her there. "Fuck, no. I'd rip out his spleen for even implying it, for causing you to doubt what's inside yourself." He'd gripped her wrist again where her hand rested on him. "Some assholes will use any rationalization to justify their acts. She 'acted' willing, she 'wanted' it..." He stopped, knowing he was letting the anger creep up on him too hard and fast, but she'd already seen it.

"You said you helped those...like me."

"Yeah. I have. Submissives who had things like that happen to them, I was good at helping them find their way back again by doing sessions with them, opening up the pain inside and cleaning it out. It's a pay it forward kind of thing, because Lot and some other people helped me find my way back as well."

"Were there...other ways you helped these women?"

He thought she might be fishing to see just how intimate he'd gotten with them, but she added to the question. "With your other skills, John Pierce."

The edge to her voice, the brief hard flash in her eyes as she met his gaze, told him what she meant. It surprised him, but as he thought of her warrior-like mentality, it made sense she'd think of it.

"For most of the women, justice was served on their attackers in one way or another. For others, even it if wasn't, that wasn't their biggest issue. But there was one...yeah. I helped her with my particular skillset."

"Tell me. Please."

He glanced at her. She'd added the please, an interesting amendment, as if she'd thought she sounded too demanding. She couldn't turn it off any more than he could. Though he couldn't get hot and bothered by that at the moment, not with the question hanging in the air between them.

"She was at a party, got a little drunk, and danced on a table in a short skirt. These three guys, they flirted with her, pulled her into a backroom and then took turns on her. Strangled her to near unconsciousness when she tried to scream for help, used her underwear as a gag. Tossed her into a dumpster out back when they were done. She was nearly unconscious then."

They'd written "slut" across her breasts in permanent marker.

He glanced up as his hand was lifted, Medusa now gripping it with both of her own, her expression compassionate. "I'm very sorry. It is clear how much you cared about her. You avenged her, I am certain. Yes?"

He knew there were laws and a trial system in the Athenian society of her time, but due to her circumstances, as well as how long she'd been living outside of that society, he wasn't surprised by her pointed question or the dark urgency behind it.

"Yeah. I did." There was as much chance of those bodies being found as those she'd crumbled and dropped into the sea. Maybe that was another reason they understood one another so well.

"Good. You told her?"

"Yeah." Dru had tried to kill herself several months after the rape, and that was when he'd made the decision to go after them. He'd come to her, held her hand, limp and pale in the padded hospital restraints. He'd leaned forward, spoken in her ear. Tears had rolled from her eyes. It hadn't been enough to heal the emotional scars, but it had been one less thing to prey on her mind. They were gone. They were abolished from her world.

"Is she well now?"

He liked that she'd asked, that she seemed genuinely interested in the wellbeing of a woman she'd never met.

"She lives in this little town in Colorado with a friend of hers. The kind of place where everyone knows everyone else. She teaches kindergarten...young children. She hasn't had a relationship since, but it's only been a few years, so I hope eventually she'll get there. Meet some nice local townie who will love her, treat her well, and help her find her way back to herself when it comes to love, if that makes sense. The way you have, all on your own."

She looked at him, surprised, and he inclined his head. "Except for that one time when we were sparring—and we both know that was just an unusual combination of factors—your reaction to a threat is to fight. And if you retreat, it's strategic, not mindless flight. You found this place, made it a home for yourself and staked your claim. Everyone on those nearby islands knows you're here and, though they try to come for you far too often, goddamn them, they come in numbers now because they know you won't go down easy."

"Is that not contrary to how you described me? Submissive?"

He chuckled. "Some of the scariest women I know are submissives. It takes a lot of guts to maintain a service personality in the real world, to care about and take care of others while not backing down in front of the shit this world can dish out. When they get the chance to submit, part of it is their way of letting go of all that for a little while, recharging the batteries to fight the fight another day."

He noted the little lift to her chin as she looked away from him. There was a light in her eyes he liked. Tilting her head, she looked at him from beneath her lashes.

"Will you show me more of...that side of yourself?"

"I sure will. Right now." He leaned in, bringing his lips close, but when she turned more toward him, he met her gaze instead of closing the distance. "Lie on your back. I'm in the mood to taste your cunt, out here under the bright sky, in front of any gods who care to watch and be envious of *my* view."

That uncertain moistening of lips he loved came, and she eased back. He glanced at her hands, folded tensely on her leg. "Take a guess at where I want those. After you use them to pull your skirt up. Serve me my meal."

Her fingers curled in the fabric and slowly inched it up to her waist, exposing her bare mons and the treasure between her loosely closed legs. Lifting her arms, she rested them on the grass on either side of her head, arching her body in a beautiful way.

"Legs open. Shoulder width." Christ, he could barely breathe himself. He hadn't expected her to get it so soon, or to get it at all, yet here she was, actively seeking it. But why should he be surprised? As Maddock said, she'd taken to service in the Goddess's temple so strongly because of her nature, and this was a need that hadn't been met in so long. He'd predicted it himself, but before something became real, there was a fine line between hope and prediction.

Thank the gods and goddesses, she'd gravitated toward it as soon as she could halfway trust him. But he reminded himself of that trust factor, how fragile and new it was, and used that caution to guide his next actions.

She'd worn his ribbons in her hair today. They'd rippled in the wind as they sat together, and they drew his attention. Untying them, he slid them from around her tresses and the snakes. He put a couple in his pocket so the sometimes gusty breezes wouldn't take them away. Using the one he had in both hands, he looped it around her neck. He didn't tie it; merely threaded the silken strap around her throat, watching as her eyes reflected her arousal and her chin lifted to experience more of the pressure. Her snakes had coiled around her there before, but he doubted she'd had the same reaction to their hold.

Loosening the ribbon, he trailed it down her bare midriff, over the gathered fabric of her short skirt. He tucked that more securely under the belt so it would stay clear of his playing field, and let the ribbon drift over her hip bones, her mound, the cleft between, her sweet clit. She shuddered at the sensation.

He tied the ribbon high on her right thigh, working it in the crease between it and her outer labia, and extended his hand. "Give me your left hand."

He used the remainder of the ribbon around her thigh to tie another loose cuff around her wrist, testing the knot to make sure it wouldn't slip with pressure. He did the left thigh and right wrist the same way. Guiding her knees up into a bent position, he used the final two ribbons to secure her ankles to the thigh straps, so her knees would stay bent and legs open.

They were ribbons. She was strong enough to break them if she pulled hard enough, but he'd kept a close eye on her reaction. She looked unsettled, but other reactions were helping to balance that. He leaned over her.

"If you get uncomfortable, you just say so. All right, snake-girl?"

"And if I am?"

His gaze gleamed. "I'll figure out if it's the right kind of discomfort and act accordingly."

She swallowed. "John..."

He touched her face. "It's me," he said. "It doesn't ever stop being me and you, you understand? No matter where this takes us or how it feels."

She held his gaze a long moment. Nodded. He slid back, running his palms along her straight shins. She had a new drawing on the right leg today; a soot-colored tree, the branches winding around her leg and marked with blue inked blooms. He brushed his mouth over her artwork, then adjusted so he was kneeling and resting on his heels. It put him in a better position to cup his hands underneath her buttocks, and lift her lower body to his mouth.

At his first touch, she made a strangled cry. He licked slow circles over her, tasting, suckling, playing his tongue over her clit. She shuddered in her bonds, jerked, and he kept his eye on the slack he'd left, making sure he was right and the knots he'd tied would keep the bonds from slipping. He had his knife if he needed to get her out of them quickly, but he hoped that wouldn't be the case since she liked the ribbons.

He could get her more, yeah, but he'd given her these first. She was wearing them today, a pointed decision that made him want to claim her for his own all the more. Hell, he already had in a way, hadn't he? When he decided to come here. When he took her body. When he took the wounds she inflicted upon him, twice now. She'd acknowledged his claim. Even if she hadn't fully acquiesced to it yet, she hadn't shut him down, either.

He ran his thumb through her slick folds, and dropped his touch lower, massaging her rim as he returned to oral pleasuring. That sent another jolt through her, her body rocking up more eagerly against him. Stretching out, he settled down to do some serious pussy eating. Her first climax sent a convulsion through his cock, and he pressed it harder into the ground. Later. It would be even better later.

He blew on her ruffled folds, suckling the dew off of them. He did lazy swirls around her clit as she jerked from aftershocks. He worked a slick finger into her rear entry, playing there as he teased her pussy with his tongue, relishing the tightness of the post-climactic tissues. Tried not to think about how that would feel on his cock.

It was time to take this another way. He released her from the ribbons, uncrossing her arms but lifting them over her head again. "Knees bent, feet flat," he ordered.

She was staring up at him, eyes glistening, face flushed, lips swollen as if she'd been biting on them. He leaned down and kissed her, a deep, all-encompassing kiss. When she started to twine her arms around his neck, he made a noise close to a growl. She immediately dropped them back over her head, which sent lightning through his cock. Did a sub ever really understand how she could turn the Master into a slave? Probably not, because that was part of the sweetness, how she'd get so lost in her own responses she wouldn't calculate his.

He unlaced her top, spreading it on the ground to see her breasts, the tight pink nipples. He ran his tongue over them, nipped and squeezed, and she moaned his name.

"If you lift your feet, or take your knuckles from the ground, I stop," he said. "As long as you stay open to me, I keep going. Understand?"

She nodded, her gaze fixed on him. Some part of her was so still, though, he paused and touched her face. "With me, sweetheart? Speak to me."

She shook her head, but one hand trembled. He took it, placed it on his face, his throat, against his chest. She latched onto the T-shirt, pulling on it, and he took it off. Her fingers splayed over his chest, her gaze coming back to him. She still hadn't spoken, but something had settled.

"You need me inside you?"

Another hard nod, her lips pressed tight together. She was a non-verbal sub, so caught up in her head, she couldn't find words. That was okay.

"All right. But I want to make you come one more time with my mouth. I love taking you up that way."

She let out a breathy sound that was part protest, part anticipation. He slid down her body again, kissing the lengths of her beautiful thighs, her quivering midriff, and buried his face between her legs once more. It took time to build her up again, because the tissues were more sensitive, but he was a patient Dom. He also relished her squirming attempts not to move her feet or hands as he'd commanded. He looked up her body more than once, watching the way her breasts quivered and lifted, the arch of her throat. As he'd suspected, the snakes were somehow charmed by sexual arousal into a kind of languorous state, so they were spread out like her hair, barely moving as her hands and arms twitched over them across the ground.

"Goddess...John..."

Yeah, there she was. She was starting that climb again, and he put a hundred percent effort into it. When she went over, that was when he was going to replace his mouth with his cock and tumble over that cliff himself.

He savored her scent, her taste, the way her thighs brushed his ears as she tried so hard not to lift her feet. It intensified the sensation, so when she came this time, her screams were in danger of leaving her hoarse. She was nonverbal in words, but in climax, not in the least. He loved it.

He stood up over her, opening the shorts, dropping them and kicking them away. Her needy gaze was upon him, covering every inch of him looming over her. A quick flash of fear, but then it was gone as something switched in her brain. He knew what it was when she mouthed the words he'd given her, safe words that meant safety, not stop.

Me and you. Just me and you.

"That's right." Kneeling between her legs, he guided them onto his hips, giving her tactile permission to raise them. He stayed on his knees as he lifted her onto him and pushed into her body. She was a wonder to look upon, her arms over her head, the snakes and black hair spread out around her in a fantastical halo. He brought himself down on her and her legs coiled around his back as he braced himself with an arm and began to thrust, his gaze within inches of hers.

She kept her arms where they were, though her hands turned, those lethal claws digging furrows in the earth as he brought her to another release. He wanted to feel her muscles clench and ripple around him, pulling his release from him in one hard, convulsive stream that would have him calling out to her.

"Put your arms around me, Medusa."

Gratitude suffused her features. The expression made him want to give her the world, even more than he already did with every breath. Her arms wrapped around him. She didn't mark him as she had before, for she was on the downward side of her climax, but he still savored how tightly she held him, the way she buried her face in his throat and chest as he came, as he gave himself to her as she'd given herself to him.

"Perfect," he whispered against her. "You're perfect in every way."

Always before, she'd avoided the compliment, dismissed it, or asked him not to say such words, for they bounced against her history, her inner torment, and came out as a mockery, not praise. This time he felt the words break through the walls inside her, past the indomitable fighter who'd been so strong through everything she'd endured. His words found the woman with hopes and dreams and, beyond that, the wounded soul who'd yearned to reclaim what she'd lost.

She wept again, but he kissed away every tear.

CHAPTER FIFTEEN

They took a nap at the top of the world, her nestled in his arms, her snakes sunning in loose coils on his shoulders and her head. He chided himself for not bringing any food, because he could have stayed here the whole day. Even with the building sun, the breezes off the water kept the temperature pleasant.

But when her stomach growled in response to his, he knew there was no help for it. And there was no reason they couldn't come back. There was nothing but time for them. He'd spent his life going from one operation to another, and the last several years had been spent preparing for this. It was odd to realize he might have days, months and possibly even years of nothing but enjoying each day with her. Some might consider such an existence boring, but he wasn't one of them. He knew first hand why "may you lead an interesting life" was a Chinese curse.

She landed them on the patio more smoothly, since they were dealing with lighter winds and headed downward. During their untethering, he took his time freeing her from the rope harness, running his fingers over the light red marks upon her. She'd returned the ribbons to her hair, and he trailed his touch over the satin.

"I'm glad you wore them," he said. "So what sounds good for lunch?"

"I have some bread and goat cheese. And fruit. If you look over there, under the flat rock, you'll find the cheese. But I can get it."

"Much as I love having a beautiful woman serve me, let me do it. I want to learn where things are around here, so I can pull my weight."

He moved past her bed to the small area she used for food preparation, and discovered she'd created a cooler area much as he had, digging into the ground and lining it with boards to protect the cheese. The crusty bread was on her small table, covered by cloth, with the fruit neatly arranged next to it.

"I usually only gather what I need for a day or two, so it's as fresh as possible. But—"

John's head shot up as she strangled on the last word. He bolted into motion even before he fully digested what he was seeing, since her immediate peril was obvious. She was stumbling backwards toward the edge of the patio, with what looked like a rope looped over her throat. The rope ends disappeared into the air above either shoulder, but the tension on it made it clear someone was on the other side of a portal, pulling. But there wasn't supposed to be a fucking portal here, in this spot.

The snakes were striking at her assailant. Their bodies partially disappeared, then reappeared when they drew back to strike again.

As JP charged toward her, Medusa's eyes locked with his, bright with fear and the pain of betrayal. Her lips caught on a one-word cry. "Why..."

Christ, she thought he was behind this? He yelled in alarm and fury as her heel caught on the ledge and she went over, flailing, her wings no help to her with that rope holding her. He expected to see her disappear through whatever rift her attacker was using to strangle or capture her. But something didn't work.

He felt the snap of the energy as the portal fizzled out and closed, severing the rope. Her screams, the sickening, repetitive thuds of her falling body, the clatter of loose rock bouncing down the cliff side, were sounds he never wanted to hear again. Seizing the coils of rope they'd left over a chair, he secured one of them to the load bearing post in the middle of her home and rushed to the patio edge. He leaned out with his heart in his throat.

She was there, thank God. The broken rope had fallen upon her, an end trailing over the ledge where she'd landed. The flat rock was so narrow, it was a miracle she'd remained there instead of continuing her violent descent. She was unconscious, and he saw blood.

"Son of a bitch. I'm coming, Medusa. Just hold on." He forced himself to verify the rope could bear both their weights coming back, and made the fastest harness he'd ever tied. It wouldn't do her any good if he fell to his death.

But after that, he moved as swiftly as he'd ever moved. He kept replaying it in his head. What the fuck had happened? What was Maddock playing at? He was going to rip the wizard's head off.

No, this wasn't Maddock. He trusted the guy with his life. Something worse was happening. Someone had hacked the portal and found another opening that Maddock hadn't mapped. He'd said he hadn't had time to research them all yet, but as long as they had a good selection of them for exit and entry, finding all of them wasn't necessary. No one else knew how to traverse them.

Well, that theory was shot to shit, wasn't it? How long before they'd try again? Suddenly JP was in an active operation again, and his instincts kicked in accordingly, gauging what damage control he needed to do and how to prevent the next fuck up.

He braced himself on the wall above the finger of rock that held her, not trusting the ledge with their combined weights. He felt for a pulse. She'd implied she had exceptional healing powers, so he had to hope that she was right and she was just banged up some.

If he needed to do so, fuck the rules, he'd take her through a damn portal to modern medical care. No matter how many cans of worms that would open, and he was sure it was enough to supply a fishing trip for the entire membership of Boy Scouts of America.

Her eyes fluttered open. "John. *John.*" She was suddenly, drunkenly trying to get away from him, slashing at him with her sharp claws, not realizing where they were or how dangerous her disorientation was to them both. The snakes, fuck it all, jumped right on board, rearing up to hiss at him, preparing to strike.

It shot an arrow in his heart, knowing she thought he'd somehow been responsible for this. But hadn't he reminded himself her trust was fragile and new? What would he have thought in her place?

"Hey, stop it. *Stop.* Medusa, it wasn't me. It wasn't me."

He gave her a little shake when it was clear from her movements she didn't have a spine injury. She focused on him, her talons curling onto his shoulders. The snakes wavered in their resolve, giving him hope some of his words were getting through to her.

"There are a hundred ways I could have taken you through the portals against your will," he said evenly. "Why wouldn't I have done it before now? Somebody else found a way in. Let's get you taken care of and then we'll see what happened."

If he'd brought additional danger to her, he might let her cut his throat with one of those vicious claws. But he'd deal with that guilt later. A cursory examination showed she had a nasty gash on the back of her shoulder and on her head, though a probe of the area reasonably assured him the skull hadn't been compromised.

"Thank God you're hard-headed, sweetheart," he muttered.

He took a cursory look at the broken rope, but it was just rope, no clues to be had there. What worried him the most was her right wing. She'd landed on it, and it drooped at an odd angle from her body. Blissfully, she seemed to have lost consciousness again, because getting her back up this cliff wasn't going to feel good. He wasn't sure how much pain even adrenaline would mask.

Securing her to his back with the other rope he'd brought down, he began a much less pleasurable ascent than they'd experienced together earlier. Taking her down wasn't an option, because he'd brought his pack with the first aid kit up here.

When he reached the patio, he was drenched in sweat, but they'd made it. He lowered her onto her side on the tiles, hefted himself up onto them, and divested them of the rope. He carried her to the large grass mat she'd woven and placed in the area she used somewhat like a living room. After he placed her carefully there, he dipped a bucket into the creek running through her home and brought it, a cloth and his first aid kit back to her side.

He cleaned the wound in her head first, to verify it wasn't critical. Ratqueen and Tunneltrap were still wound up, weaving in and out of her hair around him, but they let him do what needed to be done. The wound could use a few stitches, but he would attend to that after he looked at the wing. He wanted to examine it while she was still out of it.

As he eased her to her stomach, he drew in a hissing breath. She'd fallen on the wing for sure, and a probing examination showed she'd broken it. It was like a leg bone, he realized, the way the two long bones connected. The lower one had snapped like a twig when she landed on it. He'd never wished for a Wi-Fi connection and Internet so much in his life, but he decided the right course for now was to set the bone best as possible and bind the wing close to her body with torn strips of cloth to restrict movement.

He'd had to set bones before, and he hoped to God it was the same for a bird. Or a woman with wings.

The snakes had grouped around her in a defensive circle. They kept weaving, refusing to settle, so tangled he could barely tell one from the other. Ratqueen kept circling back to bump his hand.

He supposed Medusa had been able to communicate to them that they should let him help her. Or maybe she hadn't, and they were learning to trust him on their own account.

He was relieved when she didn't wake as he bound the wing. The only painkiller he had was the ibuprofen, and he didn't think he could bear to hear her cries of pain, especially at his hands. Wryly, he thought if she knew that, she'd never again worry that he harbored some diabolical plan to hurt her.

He had to keep pushing Ratqueen aside as he stitched Medusa's head, but when he was done and tucking her into bed, the reason for the snake's distress finally penetrated. Fucking hell.

Bastard that he was, he hadn't given them a thought beyond what threat they might pose to him helping their mistress, and they'd been such a tangled mess, he hadn't taken a head count. Ratqueen was obviously okay, as were Earthson, Waterlight, Tunneltrap...but Treebark was missing.

He found him coiled under her hair, against her nape. The crusty, half dried mass of blood gave him a jolt, and if Medusa was awake, she would take no comfort in his relief that it wasn't hers. The bush viper had a deep cut close to where his head met the rest of his body, and he seemed disoriented, almost limp.

Christ, he hadn't the foggiest idea how to treat an injured snake, but he'd proceed just as he had on the wound to her wing. He cleaned out the gash, and slathered antibiotic on it. He wasn't sure if it was deep enough to have cut some nerve function, and the rhythmic twitch Treebark was doing was a discomfiting tic. But when he was done, JP laid the snake out on the pillow next to her and hoped for the best. He'd done all he could do for the moment.

He moved out onto the patio, getting a breath of needed fresh air and stretching cramped muscles. He'd tended to himself and others in far more dangerous surroundings, but his hands had never shook afterward, not like this. Her pain tore something loose inside of him. He hadn't felt such a strong urge to kill in a very long time, long enough he thought he might have forgotten what it felt like.

He hadn't.

The piercing cry of a bird of prey pulled him out of murderous thoughts and gave him a surge of relief. He knew that voice. Lifting his arm, he caught the attention of the pretty merlin winging through the sky. Wart was the way Maddock sent communications that couldn't wait for pack supply transfers. She was fearless, passing through the portal process as matter-of-factly as she winged through the forest around Maddock's compound. They called her Merlin's familiar, and she was so attached to the scientist, it probably wasn't far off the mark.

When Wart landed on his arm, JP gave her a quick stroke and unrolled the message from her leg. He cursed as he read it, though the note confirmed his suspicions. Fortunately, it also told him things were under control.

Portal system hacked. MyTech. Got it locked back down, so they can't get thru that way again. But stay on guard. She's on their radar. Send you more soon.

MyTech. A consortium of assholes fascinated by the magical-science combo stuff that Maddock did, only their interests were how to use what they found for weapons and profit, not to make the world a better place. Though the founder likely claimed it *would* make the world a better place. Meredith Molen, CEO, reminded JP of the Gary Oldman character in *The Fifth Element*. Destruction justified by production.

He offered Wart some fish Medusa had left over from last night and penned a return note. *Attack repelled, but need instructions on care for broken wing (hers) and deep cut neck injury to snake (one of hers). STAT.*

Once the bird took flight and disappeared into the sky, headed for God-knows-what portal Maddock used for her transmissions, John stared out at the beauty and peace of Medusa's island. It was so far away from the industrial chaos nearly a couple millennia in the future. He didn't want to take her there. He'd rather stay here with her, forever. Hadn't he had that thought just a short time earlier, that he'd be happy to remain in this peace and tranquility—relatively speaking —forever?

But the same niggling thought hit him now that had hit him then. Was that fair to her? She'd come here out of necessity and was living in isolation. She'd obviously enjoyed her friends and her life, before it had been disrupted. Yes, this was wonderful. But wouldn't it be more wonderful if it was a choice, rather than a necessary refuge she had to defend, over and over?

The merlin had returned. Fast, but time worked differently through the portal, which was why Maddock had sent a message less than a half hour after the attack happened. It had likely been several hours or even a full day there.

JP opened up the thicker wad of paper. He was relieved to find he'd done pretty much everything that was supposed to be done. The message contained some important follow up care, though, as well as a vital tube of pain killers and oral antibiotics that would dissolve and be absorbed through the soft tissue of the mouth. The note suggested once he gave them to Medusa, they would help Treebark, too.

He performed that task, and shortly thereafter, maybe because the pill had a bitter taste, he heard Medusa shift, then let out a moan. Getting her a cup of water, he shifted to her other side, dissuading Ratqueen from sticking her head into the water cup as Medusa's eyes fluttered open. In her dazed state, the bright red irises were paler somehow, like diluted blood.

"John." Her gaze slid around her, digesting the familiar surroundings. He saw the fleeting waves of panic as she likely did a checklist. Where am I? What happened? Is he responsible? Do I need to be on guard? Why am I bound?

"You're not bound," he reassured her as he saw her start to fight the restraint. "It's a bandage. You broke your wing. I bound it to your side and arm to keep you from moving it."

She settled back, though now there was a different reason for the alarm in her face. "The good news is that it's a clean break," he added quickly. "I set it and, if those healing powers of yours work, you should be okay." He hoped. He didn't know how long it would take her to be able to fly again. But he was going to think of that as when, not if.

He saw her pallor whiten as she moved the wrong way. "I gave you a painkiller," he said, gesturing with the pills, trying not to let the way her pain affected him make him sound brusque. "It should kick in soon and ease the discomfort. It will also make you sleepy, but that's not a bad thing. For the next little bit, you probably don't want to feel much."

"My snakes..." Her focus seemed to turn inward, and he knew she was doing that internal communication thing she did with them. Her head turned immediately toward the other side of the pillow. She couldn't reach across herself toward Treebark, though she tried, and winced again.

"Stop," he ordered. "I'll help you reach him." Easing her back down and then supporting Treebark under his injured area, he brought the snake over to the other side of her body so she could touch his head, give it a stroke. The snake's tongue flickered.

"Does he say anything?" JP asked.

"They never really speak to me, not that way. I can just feel him. He knows he's hurt but he's not afraid. He thinks I'm heavy and he doesn't want me to fall on him like that again, not when sharp rocks are beneath us." A tight smile touched her lips. "You tended him well. Does he seem...does your knowledge of healing tell you if he'll be okay?"

"I don't know. I hope so, though."

"Good. Ratqueen plans to eat him if he dies, so hopefully that will inspire him to heal quickly."

"Huh. Women." JP curled his hand around the one on her unbound arm. She studied him.

"I thought it was you."

"Still do, a little bit. I can see the questions in your eyes." He stroked a hand down the side of her face. "I don't blame you for having a hard time trusting. We haven't known each other for long. For all I know, I may very well be to blame, opening a portal and drawing attention to your island."

Briefly, he explained MyTech in terms he hoped she could under-stand. She seemed to follow it, but then, corporate competition had probably been around ever since two bakers had set up carts next to one another.

"What would they want with me?" When he hesitated, her tone

sharpened. "It is harder to protect myself if I do not have all information, John Pierce."

Yeah, she had him there. "They'd want to use you as a weapon, is my guess. They probably have some crazy idea that they can study the properties of your gaze and learn how to turn things into stone themselves. Or put some kind of directed goggles on you and make you do it for them. Turn you into their assassin."

"How would they make me do this?"

"People come up with all sorts of twisted terrible ways to bend others to their will. I'd rather not find out."

She swallowed, shadows passing through her gaze. "You are right, of course."

"I'm sorry," he said. "I know you came here to be safe."

"I have never been safe," she said bluntly. "The longest time that has passed between people coming to my island to cause me harm has been the space before you arrived. The grandmother and her grandson were my last visitors. Since then, I have seen two full moons." A softer emotion passed through her gaze, easing some of the hard feeling in his gut. "Perhaps that is why I didn't turn you to stone right away. I had become complacent with the unprecedented peace, and tired of the quiet. I determined I could at least enjoy your conversation before you did something that would require me to kill you."

"Well, thank the stars I wasn't a boring conversationalist."

"Being boring isn't a killing offense. Not usually. When you haven't held an actual conversation with another human for a long time, it would be hard to find you boring."

"I see." He pursed his lips. "So I could be boring; you just haven't filled up your need for human contact enough to know."

"Exactly." The weak humor died out of her face and she closed her eyes, which made her look weary and young. "It is helping, your medicine."

"Good. Just rest. I'll keep an eye on Treebark."

Her fingers curled around his again, the tip of one claw hooking the sheet. He freed it before it could poke a hole in the fabric. He thought of how he'd helped Olivia trim her cat's claws with fingernail clippers so the barbed tips wouldn't catch on the upholstery. He'd hold that helpful suggestion for later.

"Why do humans insist on harming one another?" Her words were slurred. "Some do more than others, some don't realize they're doing harm, but we all do it. We all do harm. Why? Why must it be that way?"

The pain in her voice wrenched him, touching the same question he carried in his own soul.

"Don't know, my lady. A lot of people come up with ideas about that, tests of faith, purgatory, whatever you want to call it, but maybe it's nothing so complicated. We're just flawed. And we each have to figure out how to overcome that flawed nature in whatever way we can throughout our lives, if we think that's important. Most people we consider good do."

Her eyes opened, the slit pupils considering him. "I hope you are good, John Pierce. You seem to be. I'm so afraid of being hurt by you. I'm afraid, not only of having to kill you as I have the others, but of my heart breaking past repair. I'm so tired of all of it. I might not survive having to do that."

"My lady." He touched her face and came closer so she was gazing straight into his eyes. "What did I write on the sand when I arrived?"

Her muddled mind searched through memory and found it. "I am here to serve you."

"Right. That's the beginning and end of it."

"It is the beginning. Some things never end. It would be nice if, for once, it was something I didn't want to end."

She slipped off, leaving him holding her hand and with a hollowness in his lower belly. He wished he had Meredith Molen of MyTech in front of him right now. If she was forced to see Medusa's pain, her sadness, would it change her? John would like to think it would. Maybe that's how people stayed sane, thinking only choices could be irreparably evil, not the people who made them. That there was always a chance the person could change, even if they couldn't change their past choices.

He'd stopped debating questions like that a long time ago. He expected Medusa had as well, except in vulnerable moments like these, when the hope that people could be better than they ever seemed to be managed to raise its weary head once more.

The next couple days were nerve-wracking. John stayed on guard, his senses honed razor-sharp for any evidence of a portal opening that might herald another invasion by MyTech, no matter Maddock's reassurance that he'd closed down the access. JP also kept his eyes on the shoreline. If two full moons was the longest time that had ever passed since she'd had someone coming to her island looking to cause trouble, they were long overdue.

His beach, the view from her home, was the most likely landing spot for approaching boats, because the visible, populated land masses were on that side, but it was always possible they'd try a different beach. Or MyTech would open another uncharted portal and arrive unseen, launching a land attack. Maddock did send a follow up communication indicating, first, that he didn't believe the hackers had the actual knowledge to open a portal, and second, that he'd done some spell craft that shut down all the known or suspected portals, except a one-way exit on the beach. The information relaxed John a certain amount, but he had other things to fray his calm.

Her screams woke him on the second night. Her bed was small and she was too uncomfortable to have him on it with her, so he'd taken the floor. The nightmare brought him fully awake in an instant. Unfortunately, it didn't bring her out of her nightmares.

"Stop. Stop. Please..."

She was back there, in that memory of her rape, and the way she was struggling against the bandages holding her wing and arm said they were contributing to the dream. *Fucking bastard.*

"Easy, easy." JP coaxed more painkillers into her as he soothed both of them, along with the snakes moving restlessly about her head. Treebark was still groggy and mostly unresponsive, stretched out on the pillow next to her. Hopefully because his body had all it could do to concentrate on healing.

JP held Medusa as closely as he could without causing her more discomfort or fear. She was crying. When she spoke to him, her voice was so much younger and more vulnerable, it raised the hair on his neck.

"Please don't let him hurt me, John. Help me...keep him away."

"I won't. I'm right here. You killed him, Medusa. He'll never hurt you or anyone else again."

"But he's here. He's come again. He's here."

"No, he's not. I'm here. Not him. He won't come again."

Her other arm was folded up against her front almost as tightly as her bound wing. She pressed her face into his chest, her tears wetting the tunic he was wearing. "Never again," she whispered.

"No. Never again." That hollowness returned. He'd die to protect her, but he knew that didn't mean he could protect her from everything. No matter the amount of training and prep, luck could turn sour. Which was why there was prayer, hope and the psychological games they all played. Like telling her he'd never let anything hurt her again.

She wasn't an idealistic girl. She knew he couldn't protect her from everything. But if she knew he wanted it to be true more than he'd ever wanted anything else, it helped. He had to believe that.

Medusa dropped her head back, her wet eyes trained on his face. Lifting her fingers to his mouth, she traced his lips. "Please be inside me, John Pierce. I know I am not strong right now, but I need your closeness to feel strong. Can you... Would you mind terribly? Can you be very gentle?"

He couldn't think of an answer to that which would sufficiently convey how very *not* terrible he found that idea. And how very gentle he could be. He answered her with action, closing the distance between them to kiss her lips, stroke her hair and throat.

He slid his hands up her legs. Because of her wing's binding, she'd preferred wearing no clothes at all and lying beneath a light sheet, so as he drew that from her, he encountered only smooth skin. Her eyes fell half-shut as he caressed her inner thighs, coaxing them to open to him. Biting her lip as he brushed his knuckles over her clit, she opened her eyes fully again to meet his and hold.

He kept stroking, a slow, rhythmic massage, watching every change in her face, the beautiful transition as it became suffused with arousal, banishing any pain or discomfort she was feeling. The beauty of endorphins. As she said and he knew, she had limited mobility and she was in a fragile state, so he slid his erect cock into her with utter gentleness but implacable demand. The combination worked for both of them, if the tightening of her hand on his arm and the latch of one of her legs over the back of his was any indication.

He kept himself braced as he thrust slowly, watching her lips part, her forked tongue touch them, her eyes go to a red glow in the darkness, as if the fire he was building inside was coming forth in that direct gaze.

He realized she didn't have the strength to climax, but she'd conveyed that wasn't her primary reason for this, and he understood that. She wouldn't let him deny himself, though.

"This is all I need," she whispered. "But I would love to hear you release, feel your seed inside me. Will you please..."

"I will. But for every climax you get from me, you'll owe me two of your own when you're all better."

A glimmer of a smile touched her lips. "It will be...arduous, but I will pay the price."

"Yeah, you will." He shot her a look that brought forth that tiny flush, and then he had to concentrate on reining in the strength of his body's response. He managed the release in a shuddering, near-motionless way that didn't jostle her or give in to his urge to rut on her like a beast. There'd be time for that later. All he wanted to do now was care for her, and he was humbly grateful for the gift of her trust that was allowing him to do just that, in this and myriad other ways.

～

She'd been right about her healing. Within three days of the break, he was able to remove the bandage and she could stretch out the wing, exercise and test it. To their joined relief, her healing powers and the medicines finally worked on Treebark too, the wound knitting far more quickly than John would have expected. Her stitches were also ready to be removed, the gash in her head sealed beneath their hold.

When he unwrapped the bandage from her arm and wing for the last time, he had her sitting on a stool he'd constructed from green branches and woven grass during his idle time spent watching over her. While he'd created it, he told her more stories. She'd listen and doze. Sometimes it looked like the other snakes were listening too, lulled by the rise and fall of his voice.

Now she sat down on the stool tentatively, making him grin at her probably justified lack of faith in his furniture-making skills, but once there, she seemed pleased with it. She watched him closely as he began to unwrap the bandage. "You look tired," she said. "You need to sleep. I am recovered enough to keep watch."

He lifted a shoulder. "I'm good. I've been catching some shut-eye here and there."

"You will take a much longer rest this afternoon. I will sit on the patio and keep watch on the shoreline while I re-tell your stories in my head."

He wasn't sure he was ready for her to be anywhere near the patio because of what had happened to her last time, but she shook her head at him impatiently, reading it in his face. "Your Maddock told you that he has sealed all the portals they know about. And you said he is never wrong."

"I just don't want to see the day he is, especially not with you in the crossfire." But he knew she was right. He was dragging his ass, and he was no good to her that way. At the height of his career, he'd been able to function capably at high levels of sleep deprivation, but he'd gotten out of the habit. He needed to recharge. He finished unwrapping the bandage and set it aside, caressing her shoulder. Ratqueen had been following the unwinding of the bandage from the top of Medusa's head, spiraling around with his movements until she'd almost tied herself in knots and toppled. "Idiot," he told the snake. "Sometimes I think you do things to purposefully entertain us."

"They do," Medusa said fondly. "Snakes have a very good sense of humor." She tested the wing and John watched her face closely to be sure she didn't overdo, but he needn't have worried. She'd been on her own for quite a while and understood the limitations of the healing process. She knew taking two steps back to take one step forward wasn't a smart plan, which was probably why his practical girl had admonished him about his sleep.

He was relieved to see the wing looked pretty much the same as the healthy one when she stretched the latter out. So the bone setting might have worked okay. He'd know for sure when she could fly again.

"So how does it feel?"

"It is tender, but I will try a test flight in another several days." She gestured to the bed. "You take my place. I will sing you to sleep."

"Oh?"

"I am an accomplished singer. The songs I know are mostly praises to the Goddess, but I also know a few others that can help you rest."

"I really am fine."

"You are saying that because you are male and you think it is against your rules to admit you are less than a god. But I could 'kick your ass' right now, even with this one injured wing."

His brows raised at the charming mischief in her face, the twinkle in her eyes. "Yeah, yeah, big talk, snake-girl. Keep it up and I'll squash that sassy attitude like a bug."

She merely pointed to the bed. Truth, nothing had ever looked so good except maybe the same thing with her in it, her arms raised in eager invitation for him to go into them. He managed not to groan in relief as he collapsed on the mattress. She dragged his stool closer to take a seat by the bed, leaning forward to stroke his hair. Despite their teasing, he saw the concern in her face.

"I'm okay," he said. "Just tired."

"You cared for me well," she said. "Now let me care for you this little while."

As she began to sing, his eyes drooped like pulled down window shades. "Wake me if you're worried about anything."

"No," she said, bending down to touch his brow with her lips. "Because you're the only thing that is worrying me. Trust me, John Pierce. Trust me to watch over you as you have done for me. You are part of my family now."

In his entire adult life, he'd never had anyone express that to him... not with the potent weight of simple truth behind it.

He'd tied this female up and brought her submission to glorious life. He'd tended her wounds and vowed to protect her. He'd always thought it a man's job, to care for a woman, and he still thought that. He'd just forgotten that women could feel the same responsibility, and do a hell of a job with it besides.

She'd pulled him off a cliff before he could do himself grave injury. She'd also trusted him enough to help him achieve a lifelong dream, to find a woman whose heart and soul he wanted to serve forever. Now, in this blessed moment, she would watch over his sleep.

He might have longed for this dream, but thinking about it and having it were different. He had a lot to learn. He looked forward to it.

She sang of Athena in her guise as an owl, soaring on strong winds above the forests, dipping wing tips into a sparkling stream. Perching above her city and seeing where justice and wisdom were needed. He took Medusa's voice into dreams with him as he drifted off to sleep.

Medusa listened to his breath evening out. Treebark rested on her shoulder, and she stroked him in reassurance. All the snakes had been quiet during her recuperation, as they were when the soldier had wounded her side. At such times it seemed her body's need for healing energy pulled from all reserves, including theirs. She hoped Treebark was getting the benefit of that, too. He did seem like he was healing.

John was sleeping deeply now, something she'd not yet seen him do, since he typically came awake at the slightest sound. She could take the knife he'd left on the side table and cut his throat.

She thought of the day on the beach when he'd trusted her enough to curl up behind him. She'd rewarded his trust with four wounds on his chest that had become permanent scars.

It alarmed her some, to realize her hand was on the knife, fingers curled around the hilt. When she'd felt the pull of the rope around her throat, that horrible vortex of energy at her back like boiling water too close to the skin, the rage had broken open inside her.

That terrible rage that always lived within her had howled at the betrayal, at John's betrayal. Animal response had taken over, so no matter how illogical it was, she'd been absolutely certain he'd engineered this. He'd won her trust, her body, just to get close to her and take her off guard. If he'd been close enough to her, she would have killed him without hesitation. She'd been heedless of her own fate; just determined that he would not survive to see it.

She lifted the blade as the snakes moved restlessly over her, picking up her mood. So sharp. It would cut into flesh so easily. He kept his weapons well honed. He was a fighter. He was foolish to sleep around her simply because she reassured him. Just as she'd been foolish to trust him for the same reasons. Why could she never learn?

Because he has done nothing to betray you. Nothing. That darkness inside her was a worse vortex than what had opened behind her before she fell off the ledge. It was the gloom she'd expended on those who'd come to her shore before him. She often thought that the ritual the priestesses had performed had taken her soul when it turned her outer body into a monster's. Perhaps that was why she could remember so little of that night.

She'd implied she'd let some of the others leave the island. That was a lie. Except for that young girl and her friends, she'd let none of them go. They'd all died here. She remembered how unexpected it had been, that first time interlopers had come to her island. An abyss had opened up inside her when she saw their intent was to harm her, mock her, treat her as a monster. In those early days, she didn't even really remember killing them, not until she came to shore later and saw the motionless statues. But eventually she did, and she acted with full knowledge of her actions. Ironically becoming exactly what they accused her of being.

Why had she lied to him? Because she didn't want him to believe her a monster, to know that when she was threatened, the darkness was as much a part of the spell that had been placed upon her as anything else. Or so she told herself.

It was better for him to think she was like a wounded predator, striking out in fear. Not because she wanted to kill and harm, to assuage this rage inside her.

He was alive because of the grandmother and grandson. That was why he'd made it this far. They'd reached inside her and found her humanity, at a terrible cost. But the darkness was so close. Too close. She'd given herself to it far too many times. John was the exception. Whoever came after him would meet the same fate as those who had come before.

"Goddess, help me," she whispered to herself, bowing her head. The pain inside was too much. She closed her hand over the blade, intending to cut into her flesh, move the pain from within to without. She gasped as his hand clamped down on hers, and she looked up to see John Pierce's eyes open, his mouth set in a thin line as he pushed up on an elbow and took it from her.

"No," he said.

"I killed all of them," she blurted out. "I lied. I was not afraid. I wanted them dead. Had it not been for the grandson, you would have been dead, too. This evil, it comes upon me. I look at you asleep, vulnerable, and I think of killing you, merely so I won't have to have this endless ache inside me, waiting for your true side to show. I can't let down my guard around you, and it's exhausting."

"Yeah, I get that." He spoke slowly, his steel-gray eyes measuring whatever he saw in her face. His fingers had eased on her wrist, but she still felt their hold. He wasn't letting her go. "But you did trust me. You've been sleeping for the past few days."

"It suited your objective to return me to health. I could find an explanation for your behavior that allowed me to sleep. Plus, I had no choice, injured as I was." She tried to remove herself from his grip, and felt a surge of anger when he wouldn't let go. "Do not excuse my actions. I am not some helpless damsel, broken in mind."

"You're not helpless at all, my lady. But yeah, you are broken. You just told me so. Being around anyone is exhausting for you, Medusa. You're not used to it. And you're always waiting for them to hurt you, which makes it doubly strenuous. Just because I get that doesn't mean I'm making excuses for you. I just won't give up on you."

Her fingers curled into tight knots over his. "I do not know how to do this with you."

"You don't have to know. We can just feel our way." He paused, and his fingertips stroked her pulse. "What happens if you say fuck it, I'm going to trust the crazy guy from the portal? I'm going to stop worrying about it and, if he betrays me, the hell with it. I'll tear out his liver when the time comes. If it never happens, well…maybe over time, that feeling, that worry, will lessen. You just have to weather through it until repetition, waking up each day and going to bed each night trusting me, starts to make it true."

She blinked, and he took the knife from her hand, putting it on the opposite side of the bed, behind him. "Is that what you have done?" she asked slowly. "You will trust me, even if I one day end you?"

"I expect you *will* be what ends me," he said mildly. "One way or another. But it's the end I've chosen. I've chosen you, on every level." He squeezed the hand she'd intended to cut, lifted it to his mouth and kissed her palm. "Don't let me catch you doing that shit again or I'll wear your ass out." He flopped back down on the bed and turned his back—*turned his back*—to her. A few minutes later, he was snoring.

She didn't know whether she should be insulted or laugh with despair. She didn't know if he was really asleep or if he did actually snore, but she sat there, fists clenched, mind whirling. She fought the darkness, beat it back, and focused on the man on her bed. The man who'd held her, taught her to trust her body's responses again, who coaxed things from her she never expected. Who had no fear of her, yet acknowledged her strength and power as a fighter.

I expect you will be what ends me.

She wondered if the same was true for her, but wondered if he meant it as she felt it now. Not an ending of her life, but ending of parts of her life she wanted to end, so she could embrace a different beginning.

With a sigh, she slid onto the bed, stretching out behind him on her hip. There really wasn't room for both of them, but it worked out, because her wing beneath was clear of the bed, trailing along the floor. Her injured wing was on the upper side of her body and, while not completely comfortable in this position, it was comfortable enough. She slid her arm under John's, and felt a spurt of confusing pleasure and relief when he shifted, pressing his muscular backside into the cradle of her thighs and abdomen. He wrapped his fingers around her hand and held it close to his chest, her talons ironically resting on the scars she'd already given him.

"Let them come if they're going to come, sweetheart," he muttered. "MyTech, your people, your darkness, my darkness. We'll knock all those bowling pins down together."

As she puzzled over that, his shoulder quivered. She realized he'd emitted a sleepy chuckle.

"I'll explain bowling later."

CHAPTER SIXTEEN

*J*P was told the next day, quite haughtily, that the ancient Greeks knew what bowling was. During her recuperation, they set up an alley on hard-packed beach sand and played a modified form with bowling balls and pins created from scrounged materials, grass, mud and rock.

A week after her fall, she'd taken her first tentative flights and could handle flights of short distances. The relief JP experienced when he saw she was going to fully recover her ability to fly was indescribable. They'd spent the past few days setting a comfortable domestic schedule, checking the garden sites, milking goats, making cheese. Trading skill sets so they could work together on building or crafting more things to make living on the island even easier.

He told her stories, she sang him songs, and promised to dance for him on the full moon night. She tried on her dress, allowing him to help her guide the straps of the halter-style top over her wings and work the garment down over her lissome body so her claws wouldn't snag the thin fabric. The fit was good, and he treasured her female delight with it, though he noticed she preferred to look down at her body in the dress or note his reaction to it, rather than viewing her full reflection in a body of water like the pool.

It was easy to imagine this could be their life for an indeterminate length of time, and he didn't see any signs she was discontent with the idea. He still had his concerns that, once she was used to having company again, she'd long for her world to broaden. However, while her wing was healing and they had no other identifiable options, he set aside that worry.

Yet he hadn't forgotten that day where she'd picked up the knife. The survival instinct embedded in him deep as blood and bone was what had brought him out of a sound sleep. When he'd first looked into her face, it had taken all he had to remain impassive. He'd had no doubt she was a breath or two from plunging that knife into him. Her crimson eyes had been unrecognizable, caught in a feral haze, her lips stretched back and teeth bared. Whatever thoughts had been going through her head, she'd been firmly caught in their net.

Was the darkness from something she'd revealed, or something yet hidden? The shape of it seemed almost like an enemy attacking her from within. He wondered if she knew what the face of that enemy truly was. It was a wound as grievous and distressing to her as one to her physical body, and he knew about that, for sure. Yet what she'd missed in her self-castigation was that she'd chosen to try and hurt herself instead of him.

He'd set her wing with so little knowledge and a lot of luck, and she was flying again. Could he help her heal an even deeper injury, one to her soul? She thought it was part of the spell, but he wasn't so sure. Not exactly. The spell had drawn not only from Ukrit's magic but from what was inside her. He had to believe the parts from inside her had to be somewhat under her control, if she found the right way to address them.

He mulled on that for those few days. The truth that started to face him was one he couldn't deny. One that opened ugly things inside of him, but that would do neither of them any good if he heeded them, rather than doing what he'd promised. To serve her.

To love her.

"We're doing something different today," he said that morning.

"What is that?" she asked.

"I'll explain when it's time."

She attempted to coax the answer out of him with a few more leading questions, but he wouldn't be budged. After breakfast, he took her hand and led her out into her garden. Along the winding path through the arbor, into the garden of posed people.

He'd left what he wanted here yesterday when she'd been napping, so he had both hands available to hold her, and was using one to pull her along, the other to nudge her at waist and hip when she dragged her feet.

She'd been pensive this morning, that weird moodiness and melancholy that descended on her at unexpected times. It had further fueled his belief this was the way to go on this, but her balking now had him entertaining some doubts. Well, he'd figure it out.

"What are we doing?"

"Tell you when we get there."

She'd said she hadn't kept all those she'd turned to stone, but there were still so many here. They moved through people standing, sitting, running footraces, chatting, eating. She'd re-created scenes from her life before she came here, he was sure. Except for the one. When they reached his intended destination, he saw her realize what had changed.

While she'd been down at the falls yesterday, taking a thorough bath, he'd hacked down the cage thicket she'd put around Ukrit. This would be a great place for a circle of those orange and red flowers or other landscape features she'd so artfully planted around the others. Enough of the sea breeze reached them here they'd nod against the green background, be a useful meditative or napping focus if he put one of those rock benches in the center.

Just one thing had to be removed for that to happen. Her nemesis, frozen on his knees in the middle of the currently barren patch of ground. A crude but sturdy sledgehammer JP had fashioned of wood and stone rested against Ukrit's shoulder.

Medusa looked up at JP. "Let him go, my lady," he said. "Fly free of one another. You owe him that. You owe yourself that."

"I don't understand." Her shoulders had stiffened at the idea she owed Ukrit anything, but JP faced her, blocking the statue as he placed his hands on her shoulders. "You discovered a strength within yourself that can never be taken away. You fear the darkness it brings forth in you, but you ignore what else comes with it. You are a one-woman army, fueled by nothing but your own determination that no one will take anything from you not freely given. I believe the darkness you carry within you can be released and something else can take its place, something no less fierce."

He paused. The pleasant buzz of insects, the chirp of birdsong, the heat of the sun on his shoulders, the blessed fucking quiet of this place...even if people tried to come get them every few weeks, it was still more peaceful than any other place he'd been in years. He didn't want to leave here. He didn't want her to leave here.

Because here he was her only choice. And that wasn't love. He shoved down the ugly spike of fear, loss and anger that summoned, and focused on her. Because he did love her.

"You remember that story you told me the other day, of the girl whose fiancé attempted to force himself upon her? You championed her innocence. There are stories that Athena eventually put an image of your face on her shield to dishearten her enemies."

Shock coursed over her features. "That cannot be true. Someone made that up."

"Someone made up a lot of stories about you. When there's a common thread through them, there's usually a grain of truth at the root."

"If I am on anyone's shield, it is because I am a weapon, a fearsome monster to her enemies."

"Maybe. Or maybe because She respected the hell out of what you made of yourself and she wanted to say to her opponents, you can't defeat this symbol." He gave her a hard squeeze. "You can try to turn it into something ugly, but guess what? She'll take what you think is ugly and make it something strong and beautiful, something a Goddess will carry as a symbol of pride on her shield."

"I helped just the one girl. There are no others like that who have been here. I can help no one like that." She stared at him, but he could see the wheels turning under the stress he was causing her.

"No. Not here." As he held her gaze steadily, she took a step back.

"I can't leave."

"Why not?"

She shot him an incredulous look. "Look at me."

"I am. There are ways to help you blend. Or stand squarely in the light exactly as you are, even if others believe it's a costume or body modifications. Such things exist in my world."

"You promised to keep me safe." She sounded plaintive, and he had to steel his resolve against the anguish he heard in the words.

"I did," he said evenly. "And I will. If you wish to stay here for the remainder of our lives, it is what I will do as well. But if you wish to see more of the world, I am telling you that is possible. There will be risk, but certainly no more than you've experienced staying here. The only difference will be a new playing field. And maybe a chance to live your life without always having to fight for it."

Going to the statue, he picked up the sledgehammer. "But first things first. You have to make sure the reasons you are staying here are the right ones. We don't have to talk any more about it, until you're ready. But I think you should take this step, my lady. Let him go."

He brought the sledgehammer to her and moved behind her. He put his hands on her shoulders again as her nerveless fingers closed on it. "You can think of what he took from you. How he hurt you. How he made you afraid and helpless. Those are the thoughts that drag you down, imprison you to that darkness. But you can also think of how you survived him. How you've reached out to me and are exploring how a man can love you, the way love is supposed to be. Whether or not you one day agree that you belong to me, you are no man's slave, my lady. And definitely not the slave of a man you turned to stone, punishing him for his crimes."

John Pierce withdrew. Surprised, Medusa twisted around to see him striding away, back up the garden path. He wasn't staying, which told her this decision was hers. She could put aside the hammer and abandon this nonsense. Why should she do this?

Why had he chosen to bring all this up today? Everything was going so well. She'd put away any dreams of ever leaving here long ago, and she resented him resurrecting them, making her think about impossible things.

Yet there'd been a weight to his words, as if they'd been a struggle for him to say. He hadn't wanted to have this conversation. She wondered why he had, why he couldn't let them both simply be.

He said Athena carried her image on Her shield. The idea unsettled things at her core. She told herself it was a foolish tale, but he'd told her such symbolism, of her as a protector of the innocent, wasn't an isolated incident. It was a view of herself she'd never had. Had she?

She did remember, as hollow as taking Kev's life had left her, she'd returned again and again to how she'd felt when she'd made sure he couldn't hurt Glykeria. And liked the feeling, wanting more of it. Wanting to make sure no one else was made to feel the way the young woman had felt.

Her gaze returned to Ukrit's frozen face. His eyes seemed to stare back at her. She remembered their feral excitement, the moisture at the corners of his sensual lips, as if he were a wolf salivating over his kill. Whenever she looked at this statue, she didn't feel the way that thinking of Glykeria made her feel. He took her back to that place, to that moment. To a woman she was no longer, but a portion of it still resided in her, connected to that frightening darkness, to all the rage. Was JP right, that she could learn how to control it, turn it to something else, something that hurt far less?

She remembered Klotho bending over her as Medusa curled on the flagstones, bleeding and weeping. Berenike had left, leaving Klotho to handle her instructions. Instead, Klotho had stroked her hair, murmuring to her about the spell craft she could do. "It will transform you into something he will not want," she said. "But it will also weave itself into who you are. What you will see forever after when you look in a mirror will be a mix of those things."

There was a bird bath Medusa had made from a clay basin and she moved to it now. She rarely looked at an image of herself, because all she saw was the monster. But today she looked with different eyes.

A delicate face, the face she'd been born with. Eyes so red even the water's reflection captured a hint of their color. Rose petal eyes, John called them. He'd told her it was a coveted and romantic flower in his world. Her rose petal eyes had turned her enemies to stone, but they turned everyone to stone, so she had to turn her face from the world or destroy it. All except John Pierce, and his special, magical eye coverings.

She parted her lips. The forked tongue had frightened her at first, and been the feature she'd found most repellent. But she'd learned how her snakes used their tongues as a sensitive and vital sensory organ and, over time, she learned to look at it differently. Hers didn't have the same useful properties theirs did, but it did have its uses. She flushed, thinking of John's reaction to it on his cock.

Then there were her snakes. They were so much a part of her, she couldn't imagine the callous cruelty of the previous version of herself that had hacked one off to see if she could rid herself of them that way. She'd felt Treebark's pain from his injury just as he'd felt hers. As if he knew how much she'd worried for him, he rode close to her neck these days, often coiled all the way around it like a spiky gray neck-lace, his head resting on her collarbone.

When she'd finally accepted that they were part of her, their consciousness had fully merged with hers and she'd been able to communicate with them far better. She counted them as her comrades-in-arms as well as family.

She straightened, spreading out her wings. The healing one could fully extend with minimal discomfort now. Her exceptional healing and the wings had been true and obvious gifts of her transformation. They'd enhanced her ability to defend herself and, beyond that, given her a freedom that she'd never have experienced without them.

Closing her eyes, she remembered the first time she'd soared, finally comfortable with her flying skills. How she'd learned to maxi-mize those skills, so she could move through the air the way her snakes did on the ground. Lightning fast, flexible maneuverings. Coils and loops. She smiled a little, thinking of the times she'd practiced over the ocean and toppled into the waves, until she figured out there were some limitations to her wings.

She straightened to her full height, staring down at herself in the basin. At a confident, winged warrior who'd become far more than a victim of someone else's barbarism. Someone a storyteller thought might be honored on a Goddess's battle shield.

She pivoted and looked at Ukrit, and saw only a man. When she put him next to John Pierce, he was so reduced in size and power, she couldn't remember why she'd wanted to keep him frozen here.

Because she wanted to think he was suffering in the stone, because she was still suffering. But she didn't have to suffer any more. John had made that clear. She could love. She could live.

She could leave.

That thought scared her, but that was because it was the unknown. John Pierce would be with her, wherever she went. He'd said so. If he meant it, she had nothing to fear. Or nothing she feared so much she couldn't face it, with him at her side. He was her friend.

He was more than that, even though he thought her heart wasn't fully committed. And he was doing his best not to make her feel trapped by his declared love for her.

He was an honorable man. The exact opposite of this one.

Picking up the sledgehammer again, she walked toward the stone man who had changed the course of her life irrevocably, but who had no power to do that anymore. Her life, her destiny, was hers and the Fates to decide. She could choose to love and trust John, to say "fuck it," as he said, and risk him hurting her. She was strong enough to do that. She was strong enough to survive anything, because at the end of the day, she had herself. And she knew who she was.

"I am Medusa," she said. "I believe in protecting the innocent. I believe laughter and love is greater than hate and fear. And while I cannot find it in my heart to forgive you, I do release you."

She swung the sledgehammer toward his torso. The stone crumbled beneath the blow, leaving a concave wound in Ukrit's side. She swung again, and the torso buckled, the stone starting to crack.

She had to guard her wing side some, which hampered some of her strikes, but she had time. Sweat trickled down her brow as need overcame discomfort and she started putting more emotion into it. Hammer, hammer, hammer. She'd hammer stone into a dust the winds would lift and carry away. The chunks of remaining rock would scatter through the garden, their source forgotten. Especially if she was no longer here.

People would come. It was a beautiful island, and eventually people would settle here. With clean white stone homes, and kitchen gardens, and children laughing, running on the beach. They would build a pathway to the peak and watch the sunsets from there.

She swung and swung and swung. All the possibilities were on the other side of this one task, all the beginnings. All the endings.

She started out of a feverish haze as hands closed over her trembling forearms, a welcome large body pressed against her back. She was bent over, breathing heavily. She was crying, she realized, opening her eyes to see the splashes of the tears on the stones. Her knees quivered, but John didn't let her buckle there. She wouldn't yet let go of her tight grip on the sledgehammer, so he lifted it with her, carrying her away and out of the garden.

He took her to the waterfall, placing her on a flat rock by it. Her grip on the weapon loosened then, and he set it aside. Sitting down next to her, shoulder to shoulder, he put his arm around her as she caught her breath.

"Okay?" he said at last.

"Yes." Her voice was hoarse, making her wonder if she'd been shouting out her thoughts to the sky and the pulverized Ukrit.

John glanced over his shoulder. "I'm going to hide that sledgehammer. If that's what you can do to a tower of stone, I don't want it close when I piss you off."

"Piss...make me angry?"

"Yeah." He smiled and she traced his lips.

"How would you do that?"

"I'm a man, you're a woman. It's what we do."

"Hmm. I've heard this said. When I would draw water at the communal well, the women would be speaking of how their husbands...pissed them off. But there was a fondness to it that told me they wouldn't beat them to death with a sledgehammer."

"Fortunately for them."

"I cannot imagine you would be more irritating than one of them."

"Ah, a challenge." He nudged her, then stroked a lock of hair from her brow.

"They had to live with them every day. And they were married, bound forever." She paused, realizing she'd stepped into a topic that might be uncomfortable to them both.

"I promised you forever, didn't I?" John said lightly, but she caught shadows in his eyes. "Until you don't want me. I plan on putting a lot of effort into that not happening. Want to go swimming before we hunt up some dinner?"

Rising, he offered his hand to help her up. She put hers in it, liking as always the strength and gentleness in his grasp, the way her hand looked in his keeping.

She knew what marriage was like in Athenian society. Sometimes there was love, but often it started with no more motivation than money or political connections, and the most basic courtesy between the couple. She and John had far more than that, yet she had an idea that marriage meant something different in his world than it did in hers, with far deeper expectations. Perhaps that was what had her hesitating to proclaim her feelings as strongly as he'd proclaimed his.

But what would happen if something terrible occurred before he knew what feelings she thought—she hoped—she was harboring for him? "John—"

A piercing cry interrupted her. Looking up, she spotted a bird of prey with a brown and white speckled breast angling toward them. John Pierce glanced up with her, but Medusa looked down first, and it saved his life.

Grabbing his arm, she jerked him out of the way as the arrow sliced past him, narrowly missing his arm.

No mortal could reach her home on foot, at least not without an arduous climb supplemented by ropes and hooks like John had. Yet here they were. Five of them, coming from different directions. John ran the two steps to the sledgehammer and picked it up as she went aloft.

"Don't depend on your eyes working," he bellowed at her. "And Medusa?"

When she met his gaze, she saw a fire in his that matched the rage being triggered inside herself. "Don't hold back on that anger this time, sweetheart."

"I want to love you," she said. "More than anything."

He grinned. Then they turned their attention to what was closing in on them.

The first thing she noticed was they all wore uniforms of a peculiar mix of browns and greens, as if they intended to blend into a forest. They also wore ovals of red-colored glass over their eyes, encased in dark rubber frames that clung to their faces.

"Wart, no!"

She tore her gaze away to see the merlin dive, screaming, its claws extended to attack.

In a blink, she understood John's alarm. The men bore crossbows with modifications she didn't understand but knew could end the bird far too easily. She dove sharply, swooping down on the man angling his cross bow upward. He spun in her direction, away from the bird, but she was faster. She slashed his face with one set of talons, the other swiping upward and hitting an exposed part of his throat. The fountain of blood told her she'd hit the vital artery, but her motion had dislodged the eyewear. As his dying gaze met hers, she saw his fate sealed.

"Without the red mask they cannot protect themselves from my gaze," she shouted to John, doing a somersault to avoid the next arrow shot. She dove down upon another assailant, Tunneltrap and Waterlight startling the male by striking at his face and giving her the chance to tear into flesh.

John had grunted his acknowledgment. She saw him swing the sledgehammer and take out the knee of another opponent. The leg folded in half like a broken stick, a sight she wished to never see again. The male he'd just crippled howled in agony, but his suffering was short-lived. As he pulled out something she did not recognize but which he obviously intended to use as a weapon, John followed up with a killing blow to the skull. The weapon spun out of the man's hand, but it made a loud noise, like a clap of thunder, with a brief flash of fire.

The noise startled her such that she propelled herself backwards, a flight instinct, and two arrows whizzed past where she would have been. She wheeled. They'd fought their way out of the falls area and closer to the side garden by her house. She saw more men coming over the edge of the precarious ascent with various weapons. Too many men, still coming from too many directions.

She soared into the air, dropped below the ledge and saw even more coming. Well, until she plucked them away from the rock, slashed their ropes and let them drop, screaming, down into the gorge. The snakes helped, though she kept them clear of two males who'd come prepared, swiping out at them one-handed with machetes in her grip.

She flew upwards to the top again, all-too-cognizant of the numbers who had made it to where John Pierce was fighting alone.

He'd taken down three, but the others were closing in and one had another cross bow. He spoke to John in a harsh language. John sneered, his bloody lip curled, body braced to continue the fight. Her battle instincts, roused by the attack upon them, took visceral pleasure in John's bravery, his obvious strength and skill that was making them hesitate. One man saw her coming and yelled a warning. As they spun toward her distraction, John charged.

He knocked two to their backsides and scattered the others, but his intent wasn't combat. He was headed for the cliff edge. As he met her gaze, she understood.

She twirled in the air, reversing course and leveling back out. As

John launched himself out into the open air, no hesitation, his faith in her absolute, she caught him under the arms. Her injured wing protested, but she had enough survival energy pumping through her to compensate, and she strained to stay aloft with as much will as strength.

"The beach," he called to her. "Maddock left us an exit portal there."

She counted no less than twenty armed men converging on her home. They must have landed on the back side of the island, a far more dangerous approach with few good beach options, but screened from her view.

The beach was clear, but she made a pass over it to be sure, and gave John the chance to scope it as closely. When she descended, she dropped him a foot above the sand and landed next to him, her wing screaming in relief. His hands were on her immediately, his eyes roving over her. Checking that she wasn't hurt, she realized. She was doing the same. He had a wound in his shoulder, an arrow he'd likely broken off and pulled out. It wasn't causing him problems right now, but she knew one didn't often feel that kind of pain in battle. There was only the surge of energy, anxiety and readiness for the fight, until the fight was done.

He took her hand. "We have to leave," he said.

JP hated doing this to her, but there was no time to prepare her for what lay on the other side of this portal. They just had to get her off the island now. Obviously, MyTech had overcome the portal blocks Maddock had set. Bastards.

Maddock had taught him how to open an exit portal. The path he'd left open for JP was the easiest, but the end destination was not. Not for her. He ran to his lean-to, and retrieved the earpiece that would give him a direct communication with Maddock once they were back in the same world. Maddock could remotely retrieve everything else in the pack, and the contents were all practical items, nothing compromising. JP had sent back the notebook with portal entry info the day after MyTech's first attack, for the purposes of security. As he switched on the earpiece, he registered the double beeps that told him it had retained its charge in the no-power state.

Returning to her side, John took Medusa's hands in both of his. Her beautiful eyes were wide with apprehension.

"I'm going to need all your trust for the next few moments," he said. "Where we land, it's going to seem strange and scary, loud and chaotic, but it will be okay. Trust me, it's a world I know and, as scary as it seems, it isn't. Can you do it, trust me for just a few minutes?"

Her hands on his forearms were cold. "Why can we not face them? Fight them?"

"They came with a magic greater than yours, with a number greater than I can overcome. They'll take you. I don't know if they want you dead or alive, but either way, they can't have you."

He could hear the men approaching, crashing through the forest. "When we get through the portal, your eyes have to stay shut until we see Maddock." He pulled the eye mask he'd worn for her out of the pack. "Will you let me blindfold you, my lady, and allow me to care for you?"

She met his gaze. She was trembling, but he could tell she was thinking. She wasn't making a rash or impulsive decision, which made her conclusion all the more humbling to him. "I will trust you, John." Her voice held that strained plea that he be worthy of such a gift. He'd burn down the world to make it so.

Putting the blindfold on her, he secured it and gathered her close. "Hold onto me," he ordered. "Keep your face against my chest and don't let go. If we get separated, we won't be far apart, I promise. It feels like falling off the same cliff. A jarring impact, but we won't land far away from one another. I'm going to do my very best to hold on."

Her arms tightened around him. "Me, too."

He pressed his lips to her forehead. "Don't let anything scare you, my lady. I won't leave you. I promise."

Not letting either of them have another moment to think about it, he recited the words, released the magic. A phalanx of armed men broke through the bushes and began to run across the beach to them. There was a snarl on the lips of the leader, a big red-headed bastard probably as well-trained as John was. Well-trained enough to know they were going to be too late. John sneered at him when he was still thirty yards away.

Yeah, you lose, you prick.

Then the vortex sucked them in and her world disappeared.

Maddock's cosmic vacuum always felt like it could tear atoms apart, but for the first time the destination was worse than the ride itself.

JP was going to kill the scientist-wizard, never mind it wasn't his fault. The blaring horns, the heated exhaust, the wall of noise, told him they were just where he'd expected, but anticipating Medusa's reaction, it all seemed magnified. Times Square was intimidating to plenty of modern-day NY visitors, not merely those who came from ancient Greece. And something in the portal was off, probably because he'd mispronounced a single syllable. They weren't on the sidewalk.

They were in the middle of the fucking street.

He had a breath to do what instinct told him was needed. He threw his body over hers, covering her in some futile attempt to keep a cab or bus from crushing her.

Traffic was in gridlock, thank God, but the muted roar of honking cabs, cars, buses and whatever the hell else made up the cacophony of New York City was smothering them. He understood why the NYC portal was the best, because the most crowded and public ones were. There was no chance anyone would think they'd appeared out of nowhere. But fucking Christ...

Nothing he'd said was going to help an initial fight-or-flight response. He couldn't blame her. She was freaking out. Which meant the snakes were, too. They were the advance warning and sometimes reflection of her state of mind, and they were in full aggressive panic mode. They were thrashing, striking, darting. In this state they would bite indiscriminately, even each other, and he gritted his teeth as their fangs sank in, tore, struck again, against his biceps, forearms, neck, ears.

He grimaced and bore the pain, both arms banded over her, protecting her face and keeping her arms locked to her sides so she couldn't take off the blindfold. Thankfully, he'd pressed his own face against her head to protect it, for however long that would do any good, but it gave him time to bark into the communicator of the ear piece.

"Open the Circus portal."

"Christ, John, what the hell..." Maddock's voice was crackling with static interference.

"We're in Times Square. We need to get her to the Circus."

"I need to clear that. You know how pissy Reese gets—"

"Damn it, Maddock."

Medusa was flailing, shoving at him. Even in this state she was a formidable opponent. He would have let her go, but he didn't sense anything but mindless panic and pain from her. If he hadn't decided the blindfold was necessary, she might have been able to handle all this—maybe—but she was on overload.

He somehow maneuvered them to the curb and used all his strength to move her to the relative shelter against a building, but there was no alleyway to be found. He heard a stream of curses following him, one of the million different dialects of cabbies that flavored the streets of NYC.

He couldn't take her into the Starbuck's, Christ Jesus. It looked like midmorning coffee rush in there, as big a crowd as what was on the street, only packed in even more densely.

"Hey, dude. Let her go. No means no."

Hands were on him, pulling, some idiot good Samaritan thinking Medusa was fighting to get away from him. And she was, but not for the reasons they thought. As he fought back, he took her down to her knees, molding her body inside the shelter of his own with sheer strength and will. He roared into the communicator.

"Now. Maddock. Goddamn it."

Somebody went by with a blaring boom box pounding *"Jenny, Jenny, Tommy Tutone 867-5309."* Really? Who the hell carried a boom box anymore?

She snarled and this time her thrust was powered by a warrior's skill and strength and augmented by the pull of several sets of hands, separating them. A shriek, high pitched and girlish, came from the deep voice that had called him dude.

"Snakes! Bitch has got snakes in her hair!"

Don't remove the blindfold, don't remove the blindfold. He chanted the prayer. He had to hope her awareness of the destruction her eyes could wreak would overcome even her panic. For a moment his vision was obscured by a crowd of bodies, but at the shriek they parted so he could see a straight path to her.

They'd knocked him back on his ass, but the hands holding him were uncertain, distracted, and their owners' attention was captured by the arresting sight before them.

She'd gone to a defensive half-crouch, her sharp teeth bared, wings half spread, the tips scraping the concrete, sharp enough to leave marks. Every muscle was taut and prepared to spring. She wore the belted short skirt with its embroidered sash and the sleeveless top that showed off the lean beauty and strength of her body. Truth, if he wasn't distracted by the utter peril in which they found themselves, he would have considered her awe-inspiring. Something of legend and myth, so obviously magical and filled with an "other" quality that was captivating and completely unforgettable.

The blindfold had slipped, he saw with a trip of his heart. He was afraid she'd lost all sense of him entirely, but he noticed she had her head ducked low, her eyes down.

The snakes were keeping everyone at bay, all in dodge and weave strike positions, a clear warning to stay back. With them swarming around her head, she looked like every dramatic emblem of Medusa he'd seen.

"John." She spoke in a hard, high voice, but he was glad to hear her acknowledgment of him.

"I'm here. Tell them it's okay. They think I'm trying to hurt you."

"He is mine. Let him go."

Only he heard the tiny tremor, because otherwise she sounded as commanding as a queen. The hands on him loosened, uncertainly at first, and then she straightened to her feet, reaching out in his direction, keeping her eyes tightly closed. Her hand was shaking but she held her ground.

Behind her, he saw the milling crowds shifting, parting for a pair of mounted police and one on foot, come to see what was happening. One had already unholstered his Taser.

"Okay, you're going to get my ass in a sling, but the portal's opening." Maddock's voice, welcome as a mother's. "Get out of there now. Fifteen seconds."

It was the longest and shortest fifteen seconds in his life. John lunged forward and seized her hand. "I'm sorry, sweetheart, but we have to go back into the street for just a second. Trust me one more minute. Next stop will be much better."

She wrapped her wings tight around her body and put her arms around his neck, which let him scoop her up in his arms in the same motion. Gridlock had eased up but he darted out, praying that NY cabbies were as quick in reflexes as they usually were. The blaring horns and screeching tires stopped his heart, but when only heated exhaust collided with his pumping limbs, he sent a silent prayer of thanks toward them. No matter that they were raining another hailstorm of colorful invective upon him and his precious burden in twelve different languages.

He could see and feel the wavy energy of the portal. He heard the deep-voiced Samaritan with the girlish scream pronounce, "That's some kickass street theater, yo," followed by a barrage of "Fuck mes" as the portal closed over him and Medusa and he knew they were sucked through and out of sight.

That wasn't going to be an unnoticed exit, but hell with it. It was done. The tabloids would have some new alien visitor fodder for their next issue. Maddock kept the security cameras at that entry point always on the fritz, so no chance of someone doing an instant replay. Cell phones were a different matter, but not his problem. Maddock would probably inflict a magical EMP throughout the block and fry everyone's smart phone.

Her arms were still around him, and things had gotten blissfully quiet. The swirling, dryer-on-tumble heat and chaos of the portal transport was gone, as was the matching chaos of the New York street.

Yet they didn't seem like they'd arrived anywhere. Everything around them was gray and peaceful, but there was nothing else. They weren't standing on anything. It was as if they were in the center of a box with no windows or doors, only without the sense of claustrophobia, for this felt open, endless.

"John."

If he could be sure of their next stop, what awaited them there, he would remove the blindfold so they could look upon one another. After the fright of the past few moments, he wanted her to have some sense of orientation and personal control. But they needed to take precautions, so he re-secured it. She allowed it, though her lips were pressed together, her fingers locked on his arms. Her snakes wove restlessly through her hair, but they were no longer in full attack mode. Just uneasy.

"Where are we?"

"Not sure." He'd never heard of a malfunction to the portal system that landed someone in a gray, endless fugue where they'd slowly starve to death or dehydrate, so he wasn't going to bring up the thought. He thought it far more likely that the Queen of the Damned —Maddock's personal pseudonym for Lady Yvette Reese, owner of the Circus—had them standing on her doorstep while she and Maddock argued over terms of entry. She and Maddock had a love-hate thing, so maybe Maddock would have to offer sexual favors she'd take out of his tight ass.

That worked for John, no offense to Maddock. It would be the right place for Medusa. He wished he'd thought of it several days ago when MyTech's first attack had happened. Then they could have programmed the portal to take them straight there in the event of an emergency like what had just happened.

He'd visited the Circus only once, with Maddock. They'd been performing a show the night they caught up with them. JP had had a couple days after that to hang out with the troupe in the day-to-day routine while Maddock and Yvette hashed out some stuff. What JP remembered of that whole experience was indescribable, which made him wonder again why he hadn't realized it was the obvious place for Medusa to seek refuge. She might even like it.

Her safety, and her happiness, the two most important things in his world, might be possible there. More so than locked up in Maddock's lab in New York. Or under attack on the island he was going to miss so badly, probably for the wrong reasons. But some right ones, too.

"We're okay," he reassured her. "I think Maddock's just negotiating our change of direction. I'm sorry about that."

"My snakes hurt you." Her hands were on him, sliding over the wounds, the smears of blood. "Oh, John Pierce. I'm so sorry."

"They were scared."

"Because I showed fear. I was a coward."

"Nothing of the kind. You just needed a couple minutes to pull your shit together, then you held your ground, got your feet under you and reached out to me. All without being able to see a damn thing. Pretty ballsy, to my way of thinking."

"Ballsy?" she ventured.

"Um, yeah. It kind of refers to a man's testicles. Testosterone, what's in them, sort of connected to aggression and probably very unscientifically connected to the idea of bravery."

"Oh." A faint smile touched her tense lips, inspiring him to trace her mouth.

"How are you doing?"

"Okay." It was a lie. She was still deeply rattled, but he could tell she was trying to keep it together. Her fingertips were making little strokes of his forearms, his biceps, trying to avoid the wounds but maintain contact with him at the same time. He was gratified that she wanted to reassure herself of his presence, but he didn't want her distressed about his physical state. She moved one hand to his shoulder and found more holes in the fabric near his arrow wound. Ratqueen had some seriously sharp fangs.

"It's all right." He clasped her wrist. "Don't worry about that right now. Let's think about something else."

She pressed her lips together in a visible effort to do just that. "Can you describe what was around us?" she asked. "You told me some of it, back on the island. Cars...those were the loud things going by us, like chariots. Many chariots."

"Yeah, that's a good comparison. Also buses, which are really large versions of cars. They can carry more people. There were a lot of tall buildings around us that trap in the noise."

"I smelled so many things, I cannot parse them out. Food...I think. Good food."

He tried to remember. "Yeah. We were outside a Starbuck's, and there was also a bakery nearby."

"Many bodies. With perfumes, and soaps, and..." She shrugged. "I can't list all of it. It was a great deal at once. I perhaps would not have minded seeing or experiencing it again, at a greater distance. The way you described it was interesting. I just didn't expect it to be a wall of noise and movement."

He heard how she was trying to pull it together, and matched her tone. "Did you ever attend any really big events in Greece? Like one where the whole city came out to celebrate? New York City is crowded with people like that pretty much all the time, especially where we were. People come from all over the world to see Times Square."

"There was so much... It was overwhelming."

"It's been a really long time since you've been around more than a couple people, let alone hundreds, and with machines that make bunches of noise and spit exhaust."

"I'm not sure I like this," she said in a small voice, her control slipping. "Will you be able to return me to my home when the danger passes?"

"If we can figure out when that is, yeah. But there are better places in this world, I promise."

If everything didn't turn out the way Maddock hoped, there was that private island in the Caribbean where John had bought a little house with the help of Maddock's connections and over two decades of barely touched income. It was populated by a colony of artists, less than half a dozen, most of who were there rarely and kept to themselves. It wouldn't be exactly the same, but if she couldn't have back what she had...

She shifted one hand to his forearm, and he winced. Her fingers found the bite mark again and wiped at the still wet blood before curling over it. "You protected me."

"That's my job." The snakes had finally started to settle, and Waterlight brushed his forehead, perhaps a tacit apology or reacquainting herself with him in that way animals did after a fright. Settling down himself, John finally had the free brain cells to notice something other than immediate threats or a need for action. Looking down at her hands, his own convulsed on her arms in shock.

"What?" she asked, alarmed.

"Your hands."

She curled her fingers and gave a start herself. The curved talons were gone, leaving just her slim fingers with the short nails. She pushed at the blindfold. "I want to see."

He unlaced it for her, to hell with it. As soon as he did, he expected her gaze to go immediately to her hands, but instead, her crimson gaze latched onto the blood on his shirt and arms where the arrow had gone through and the snakes had bitten him.

"Oh Goddess. John Pierce..." Now that she could see the damage, she touched his biceps around the bite marks again, only far more lightly, her face filled with consternation. "My snakes..."

"They didn't mean to do it. They don't hurt." They would eventually, especially the arrow wound, but for now he had the benefit of adrenaline pumping through him. "Look at your hands."

He closed his own over one again, feeling hesitation in her return clasp as she complied. It was the first time she'd been able to curl her fingers around his without worry that too tight a hold could do damage.

When she put her hand up to touch her mouth, he realized she was confirming the fangs and forked tongue were still there. "Are my eyes still red?"

"They are. Like the sunset."

"Not rose petals?"

"Well, I've used that a couple times. I don't want to throw you the same tired lines."

He caught a fleeting glimpse of wary gratitude, followed by puzzlement. "Where did my claws go? And why?"

"I don't know. But maybe Maddock will have some thoughts."

"Okay." She put her forehead against his chest. Then she put her newly changed hands into a pair of small fists under her chin, tucking herself against him. The strangely vulnerable movement made his brow crease. He slid his arms around her, keeping her close as they drifted in a gray world like dust motes. It was like they were inside a cocoon where gravity didn't exist. "Should I be scared of where we are now, John Pierce? Are you scared?"

"I'm not sure what's going on, but I think we're okay. I think Maddock is figuring out how to get us where we need to be."

"That is not exactly an answer to the question."

"Covert ops guys don't admit to being scared. Not ever. It's kind of a rule. Admitting it can be like letting a rabid bear out of his cave, so you can't think straight."

"Oh." A small smile in her voice. "Then I refuse to admit it, either."

"Okay." He was proud of her, and pleased when her leg curved around the back of his. "Did you know we call Maddock 'Mad Merlin' sometimes?"

She shook her head. "Why?"

"It's a nickname. There's a character, another legend, about a sword in a stone, a king named Arthur…"

She loved a story, and this was a good one. He told her the highlights, about the wizard who lived backwards in time, and discovered a boy who became one of the greatest kings of legend.

As he spoke, he could feel some of her tension abate. He should have been far more worried about where they were, too, or how they were going to get out of this stasis and into a final destination where he could control the variables around her better, to keep her safe. However, after the chaos and panic on the island and the first disastrous minutes in the portal, there was an alluring tranquility here. They had no distractions, no worries, nothing they could control but no threat either. He realized it might be the last moment he truly had her all to himself. She seemed okay with it, too, so it wasn't just him feeling it.

Even the snakes seemed to be doing pretty well, testing the lack of gravity by extending themselves out from her head to float along like spaghetti noodles in space.

The thought so amused him, he shared it and won her smile.

"I wonder if this is what it is like, before you are placed in a womb," she said. "There is no fear here, no urgency."

It was an echo of his own thoughts. He buried his nose in her hair, enjoying its texture as Earthson indulgently gave way and readjusted.

"If it's permanent, my fingers, you need not fear me scratching you again."

Her cheeks tinged with a faint embarrassment he treasured. Lifting her hand to his mouth, he caressed her palm with lips and tongue. "I treasure those scars, my lady. They are proof that I can bring you pleasure that takes you far beyond control." He adjusted so she was pressed more fully against him. The movement caused a shift of her hips that brought them core to core. Her eyes darkened to blood and he dropped his hand to cup her buttock. "But if it really bothers you, I could put some marks on your backside to even the score."

Her startled gaze lifted to his face. Then surprise turned to speculation, a slight moistening of her lips, a curl of her fingers into his biceps. He moved down to her ear. As she dropped her head back, he took a nice nip of female flesh, savoring her indrawn breath.

Nail tips bit in and he smiled. "Talons or no, I believe you'll still leave scratches on me."

She lifted her face. "It sometimes still troubles me, why your threats of pain do not sound like threats at all."

He felt an unsettling shift in their world, different from the one he'd just caused, and realized they were on the move again, so to speak. He brushed a kiss over her mouth.

"Later," he said quietly. "We'll talk about this later, my lady."

"No, I—"

He planted a hard kiss on her mouth, commanding enough to give her that half-aroused, half-confused look he loved and which stimulated him as much. "No reason it should trouble you," he said firmly. "We should probably put the blindfold back on in case—"

And then she was ripped from his arms.

PART TWO

CHAPTER SEVENTEEN

*A*nother whirling vortex, a fit of nausea so strong Medusa was afraid she was going to lose her latest meal, but then it was done. They were there. And *there* was much quieter this time than that place he'd called Times Square. Though she didn't sense John, which scared her, she forced herself to keep her eyes shut. Maddock was trying to transport them to allies, she assumed. It wouldn't do for her to turn them to rock before exchanging even a greeting.

The distressing idea and trepidation for the unknown were broken by music. A flute, playing a drifting, haunting melody, like mist over a lake at dawn. Her snakes, at the end of their patience with all of this jumping through time and space, were extended into strike pose, in an array around her head like sun beams. However, as she absorbed the song, it seemed to help calm them, too. They swayed, uncertain.

"There you are." A female voice, young. Perhaps mid-twenties. She touched Medusa's knee, where she was coiled up on what felt like a rough wooden floor that smelled strongly of sawdust. "Had to take a detour and got caught in traffic, didn't you? It happens, but you're here now. It's safe. There you are, sibilant spirits. Easy now."

The young woman was humming with the flute. Ratqueen slid along Medusa's neck.

"Aren't you something?" the girl mused, and Medusa had the impression she was touching the snake. "So smooth and strong, so protective of your mistress. No harm will come to her here. And to make sure of it, here comes her human champion."

The blast of energy was followed by a thump and a male curse, the most welcome thing she'd ever heard. Medusa pushed herself up on her knees, her hands outstretched. "*John.*"

"Ah, thank Christ. There you are. I'm here, my lady." The girl withdrew and John had his arms around her, no matter that last time he'd tried that after a portal jump, her snakes had gone after him, channeling her panic. She had those emotions under control now, but it still touched something deep inside her, that a threat from them would not stop him from holding her, would not even cause him pause.

"Having you pulled from me took about twenty years off my life," he muttered. "Remind me to punch Maddock in the face next time I see him."

"That would be something to see," a male voice said, faintly amused. "Think he'd set aside his magic scepter long enough to make it a fair fight?"

"If he did, we could take odds and make a killing," a deeper voice answered. "My money's on JP."

"If anyone is kicking that wizard's ass, it will be me."

John Pierce seemed to be paying little attention to the banter, but that comment, issued in a tone anyone with common sense would heed, had him lifting his head from Medusa's. He tensed enough to let her know the voice belonged to someone who could influence their fate in negative ways. Trying to regain her composure, she let him help her to her feet. Standing straight and tall at his side, she wished she could see, no matter that she was sure that would not be a good idea.

She did notice that he didn't put her behind him, his natural male instinct when he thought her in danger. So the woman who belonged to that chilling voice wasn't posing a physical threat. At least not right now.

"Lady Yvette, he would have given you more warning if he could. We couldn't stay at the Times Square portal. The police were about to get involved."

"Maddock's poor planning ends up being my responsibility. What a shock."

"We were attacked on my island and had to leave it suddenly,"

Medusa said. "If there was any way he could have observed the proper protocols, I am certain he would have, my lady. John is very respectful of such things."

A silence ensued, as if no one had expected Medusa to be capable of coherent sentences, let alone recognizing and acknowledging the authority of the speaker. John slid his arm around her back, his grip on her hip conveying his approval of her courtesy. Or perhaps he did it to be able to swing her quickly out of the way if needed.

Yvette laughed, a sharp sound like hanging knife blades striking one another in the wind. "Yes, he is. Unlike Maddock, who calls me Queen of the Damned and thinks his Anne Rice jokes are amusing."

The woman stepped closer. A dense energy pressed against Medusa, pushing her back against John's bracing arm. His muscles tightened further. Yvette had a heady fragrance about her, like the concentration of perfume from dying flowers.

"Be still now." Lady Yvette's hand fell upon Medusa's brow. Her snakes stirred but didn't seem alarmed, a mystery like the energy that began to coat Medusa from that contact point, enclosing her in a warm cocoon. "I am making it possible for you to open your eyes. This spell will cloak you and neutralize the effect of your gaze."

She said it so matter-of-factly, as if overriding the spell Medusa had carried upon her so long was as easy as a child's wish. Answering that unspoken thought, Yvette added, "Our little world here has many magical layers upon which I can draw. Including the universal trans-lator that allows so many of us human-like folk from different places to understand one another. This particular spell I'm drawing upon now will not work outside the boundaries of the Circus, so bear that in mind and learn where those lines are. If you step one foot outside of them, you will once again be petrifying anyone who meets your gaze. I'd rather you not turn the house—our audience—into pet rock gardens."

"Especially before they have a chance to buy their novelties," the first male said. He had a gravelly voice, but friendly.

"Hush, Gundar." The woman addressed Medusa again. "You arrived in unfamiliar circumstances, afraid and disoriented, but you did not open your eyes, a natural instinct to protect yourself. You protected my people instead, until you could ascertain if they were a threat, even without JP here to reassure you. I told Maddock to bring you in first so I could determine whether or not you could be trusted on your own merits. You passed the first test. I'm glad. Putting you in guarded isolation for the duration of your stay, with our blind dressmaker bringing you food, would have been time and labor consuming."

"We would have courteously taken leave of your hospitality before such extreme measures were needed," John said stiffly.

"Yes, because there are so many other places for you to go. The local Holiday Inn Express, the Bahamas Hilton. She would be a hit out on their beaches. There. You may open your eyes, young one. Your gaze will not cause harm to anyone in my Circus."

Medusa was unsure, so she turned toward John and opened her eyes. He was still wearing the contacts, after all, so if Yvette was wrong, he should still be protected. And she wanted to see his face before any other.

They'd gone from battle to two portal jumps, all three uncertain situations, and he still had that warrior's alertness in his steely gaze, the set of his jaw. That, as well as his stiff movements and the blood on him, reminded her. "He is hurt. He needs attention. An arrow went through his shoulder. And my snakes..."

She knew neither Earthson nor Treebark had used venom, but the bites still needed care. There were so many things to deal with at the moment, and maybe that was part of why she wanted to focus on only one thing, the thing that felt the most important to her. Caring for him.

"I'm all right, snake-girl," he said quietly. "Let's finish introducing you to Lady Yvette."

His tone held an undercurrent of warning she reluctantly heeded. When she hesitated to look away from him, he touched her face. "Trust Lady Yvette. She's very powerful. If she says your eyes are safe, they are."

Medusa could feel the solid barrier of energy Yvette had placed around her, a faint hum along her nerves. Placing faith in John's opinion, she turned to meet the gaze of their hostess and see the others in the room.

Lady Yvette Reese was as intimidating as everyone had implied. She also wasn't human. Medusa knew it as soon as she met her eyes, a swirling gold and gray, like the sun behind wisps of storm clouds. She was a black woman whose skin had the color and luster of bronze. Her nails, painted deep gold, were curved sharp points, reminding Medusa of her own claws—the ones she no longer had—only these were merely the woman's nails, grown out and filed that way. Her hair was plaited into numerous slim golden braids, piled in waves around her face in a manner that made the resemblance to a lion's mane striking.

Yvette's gaze slid from Medusa to John. When her gaze fell upon the blood on his clothes, she touched a delicate tongue to her full lips, exposing fangs. As well as an expression of undeniable hunger.

Lamia, daughter of Hecate and demonic blood drinker, had feet as bronze as Lady Yvette's skin, and was a seducer of men. The older priestesses had told the wide-eyed acolytes stories of Lamia's children. As Medusa had grown up, she'd realized they were just stories—until she'd become one of those nightmares herself and realized many unsettling things in the world were real, not merely figments of human fears. And Yvette was obviously not human.

She shifted in front of John in an instant. He gripped her arm as if to ease her back, but she set her feet and met the woman's gaze in challenge. They wouldn't stay here if John was in danger. Klotho had dramatically described men being drained in their beds, leaving only piles of bone with skin stretched over them. John wasn't going to become like that.

Yvette smiled, a glittering full baring of her sharp teeth. "She knows I am a vampire, John. She's worried I won't be able to resist my dietary impulses."

She cocked her head, the fall of locks below the pinned curves brushing her shoulder like silken ropes. "John's blood would be sweet, young one, but here at the Circus, we do not take what is not freely given. Though from what is freely given, I might demand much."

Humor sparkled through her gold eyes. "Introduce yourself to me."

"I am Medusa," Medusa responded.

"The Gorgon. The terror of Greece. I expect you've heard similar stories of vampires. They are often true. Looking at you, I'm not so sure your stories are. You are brave, you have killed, but you are no predator. Though you do fight the darkness, don't you? The one that steals into the soul when too many lives are taken. He has that as well, your John. It makes him a good fit for you, and for our merry band of misfits."

"Lady Yvette," John murmured. "Don't."

Medusa wondered if he was asking for mercy from her observations about him, or about Medusa. She couldn't seem to look away from Yvette's gaze. It felt like a cold shaft of steel was probing her heart. Yvette's gaze shifted back to John, easing the feeling.

"Do not attempt to command me, John Pierce Zeus. Your need to protect her makes you mindlessly foolish."

"It is a request, my lady. A heartfelt one. She's been through a lot today."

"Hmm." Yvette's still gaze returned to Medusa. "As I said, the blood I want is not his. I've already had his, a sample sent to me by Maddock in case JP ever had to enter our world outside the boundaries of the 'real world.' The price of entry into the Circus is that I take a taste of your blood to understand who you are, and to determine if it is appropriate for you to be here. If I should allow you to stay, send you back the way you came, or kill you so you can't be a menace to anyone else."

John's tension made a lot more sense now, but it had been his idea to come here, so Medusa couldn't believe they would come to true harm at Yvette's hands. Though as Yvette had pointed out, they hadn't had much choice, had they? She recoiled at the idea of letting a blood drinker feed from her, but Yvette had said a taste. She knew nothing of the species but what stories had been told, and she knew how inaccurate those stories could be. She needed to form her own impressions.

They appeared to be inside a large canvas tent. Chairs were piled up in one corner. Against them leaned a broad-shouldered man with dark hair shorn to the scalp, emphasizing a sharp widow's peak. His face was strong and sculpted, dark eyes like a piece of night. Another vampire, she suspected. At his side was a wolf larger than any she'd ever seen. His head was the size of a bear's. Even in a seated position, the wolf was level with the tall man's elbow, the pricked ears up to his shoulder.

Wolves had been a special terror to sheep herders when she was growing up, so seeing the creature gave her a start. However, he was sitting quietly, albeit with an alarmingly fixed predatory gaze.

On the other side of the tent, she saw a winged creature, but not like herself. This male had a mane of hair that reminded her of the glossy dark brown stones under the waterfall on her island. It fell to his shoulders and framed penetrating eyes that...had no whites. They were entirely dark from corner to corner. That should have disturbed her, but when she met his gaze, she felt emotions like the ones John inspired in her. Not those related to desire and need, but shelter, warmth. Everything about this male said one would be safe with him. His wings were feathered with glossy dark green plumage. While she had wings herself, she wanted to go bury her face in those abundant feathers, hold on as the wings closed over her and kept the harsher things of the world forever at bay.

Now she found the source of the young woman's voice. She stood at the winged man's side. She wore many rings and slim metal bracelets that jangled as she shifted. Intricate brown dye tattoos embellished her arms. Her dress was a gypsy style skirt and flowing sleeveless top. Straight red hair fell down her back. Medusa noted the young woman was with the winged male, for she stood in front of him and was braced intimately against his crooked knee, watching the proceedings with bright, inquisitive eyes. She winked at Medusa and dimpled, as if to say, "They have to act scary, but it's all okay."

To the right of Yvette was a dwarf, with a disarmingly sexy smile on his strong face and in his glittering coal-colored eyes. He had thick, sandy hair and wore nothing but a pair of black pants in a shiny material that clung to his impressive leg muscles and...

She pulled her gaze away before getting caught ogling the impressive bulge at his groin area. Dwarves had come into town during the festival events, yet they'd been dressed and presented as comical figures, like strange children that entertained and fascinated the populace. Gundar—for she'd realized from his placement near Yvette he must be the one with the gravelly voice—emanated as much masculinity as the much taller John, and not just from the evidence of his virility. When her gaze slid past his, there was a self-confident authority there that gave her the same messages that John's gaze did.

But the one behind Gundar unsettled her. Another winged male. His feathers were black and silver, the silver forming a jagged light-ning shaped pattern amid the darker plumage. His hair was even darker, but of a similar length. While his eyes appeared to be gray, like John Pierce's, she didn't linger on them.

She sensed this male had a similar power to the one with the dark green wings, but the blatant sexuality pulsing off of him, and the nature of that energy, didn't suggest safety or comfort. It made her step back so she was pressed against John's front. She needed sudden, tactile reassurance that he was there. His arm coiled around her. Glancing up, she saw he had his eyes fastened on the male, and the expression on John's face wasn't friendly.

All of Medusa's impressions had occurred in a blink, and now Yvette extended a hand. "Young one? I am waiting. As soon as we get this out of the way, we can show you to your quarters and tend to JP."

Medusa looked up at John. "She tastes all who stay here," he confirmed. "It's her way of protecting her people. The Circus belongs to her, and all its performers are under her protection. Which they need."

"Where are we?" she asked, because that was another thing she couldn't determine. She didn't understand what Yvette had said about being outside the boundaries of the "real world," but there was an odd feel to this place, like it wasn't entirely grounded in reality, hers or John's. He confirmed it.

"The Circus exists in the fringe area between worlds. They use the portal network, specifically those entries and exits that run along magical fault lines, to travel from place to place. It's an actual circus, so they emerge to do shows in select venues and then disappear again. Staying in the in-between places when they're not doing shows protects them. And us, because it will make you impossible to track. It's best not to make her wait. I can explain more later."

Clasping her wrist in his hand and keeping his eyes on hers to make sure she was okay with that, John Pierce extended her arm, offering it to Yvette. "Probably best to go with the arm, my lady," he said courteously to the vampire. "As sweet as her throat is, the snakes aren't used to you yet. They're more likely to keep their distance if you use the wrist."

"And you don't particularly care to see anyone tasting her throat except yourself." Yvette's amusement without rancor eased some of Medusa's concerns, but she still wasn't sure how she felt about letting anyone drink her blood. But John had expressed it was necessary to find refuge here. She would trust him once again. Up until now, she'd never trusted anyone with such monumental decisions about her life. Except for that fateful night with her fellow priestesses.

When she looked into Yvette's penetrating gaze, shadows moved within Medusa, trying to reveal nightmares she didn't want to think about. So much blood that night, and fear...

"Easy, young one." Yvette took her wrist with an unexpectedly delicate touch, sending shivers up Medusa's arm as she stroked her flesh with knowledgeable fingers. When she drew closer, Medusa realized she wasn't as physically imposing as she seemed. She was perhaps an inch taller than Medusa. "She's only been recently introduced to pleasure," the vampire mused. "At your hands, JP. You have done well at awakening her body and her intoxicating submission. Continue to attend to it and you will bring the rose to full bloom."

"Yes, my lady." But glancing back at him, Medusa saw John's jaw flex as if he'd like to tell the vampire to mind her own business and get on with it. Medusa suspected Yvette saw it, because there was a hint of laughter behind her forbidding expression as she dipped her head and bit.

She'd struck as quickly as one of the snakes. Medusa caught a cry in her throat, steadied by John's hands on her shoulders. The initial pain faded, however. As Yvette sipped at her blood, her golden eyes rose and locked with Medusa's.

Something rippled through Medusa's blood. Desire, hot and rich. She bit back a gasp as Yvette pulled on the wound, a sucking that thrummed through her arm, made her breasts tingle and her loins tighten.

She was suddenly, acutely aware of just how virile an assembly of males was around her. There wasn't one in the room that wouldn't attract a woman's eyes or desires. She found her gaze lingering on the impressive curve of biceps the man with dark green wings possessed, the silken mat of hair on the dwarf's broad chest. The slightly cruel, sensual curve of the other vampire's mouth as he stood next to his wolf. Even the wolf's gaze, sharpening on her, seemed to contain an unsettling sexual awareness. She didn't look toward the other winged man, because she could feel his disturbing presence like a blast of heat pressing against her.

The snakes started doing that languorous winding they did when she became aroused, the precursor to a torpor that would have them going limp on her shoulders the closer she came to climax.

She was in a tent, in front of strangers. Yet she was pressing her backside against John's groin, dropping her head on his shoulder and reaching back to grip his hip, a better anchor to rub against him. He didn't seem surprised or try to quell her reaction. Instead, he slid a tight arm around her waist and put his mouth to her throat, suddenly suckling on it in a hard, demanding way that had her gasping, arching up against him and against the hold Lady Yvette had on her wrist. When he bit her, a shudder went through her body, so close to a climax she had to quell a moan.

"Very nice." Yvette's touch whispered away from her and Medusa was held in John's arms alone. "A rose half opened is at its most beautiful potential. JP, if you aren't too possessive, you might allow Charlie to give her a massage. Our head costume designer and coordinator," she added for Medusa's benefit. "Though she prefers to be called a dressmaker. She has magical hands, and an insatiable desire to pleasure female flesh."

The Circus owner continued as if arousing someone with a mere bite was as ordinary as Klotho discussing the day's schedule at the temple. "You have passed the second test. Your blood is...intriguing, but I am satisfied you are no more dangerous than anyone else here. There were tales you know, about your blood being poison. And that a few drops on the ground brought a Pegasus to life. There are so many things people imagine, yet the truth is often far more fascinating."

Yvette pursed her glossy burgundy lips. "You are welcome, the both of you, though while you stay with us I will expect you to offer to help where help is needed. There is always work to be done, and we have a performance this week. You are also welcome to join the Promenade, our aftershow spectacle, if you care to interact with the children."

"Children?" Medusa blinked, surprised because of the very adult nature of this gathering, and the predatory species that surrounded her. "You don't...harm them?"

Yvette looked so offended, she was immediately reassured and shamed. "My apologies, my lady," she said hastily, before John had to do it. "I am not familiar with you as yet. And this has been very unsettling."

Yvette's expression eased. "While I might take offense at your assumption we would do harm to human young, I do not take offense at your protective instincts. Gundar, if you'll make introductions and get them to their quarters, come join me afterward."

"Sure thing, Mistress." Gundar nodded respectfully. Yvette disappeared, literally, leaving behind a stray breeze ruffling Medusa's hair. Medusa drew in a breath.

"She didn't poof into thin air," the dwarf said. "She just moves that fast. You should consider the Promenade," he added, drawing closer and studying Medusa's snakes with lively fascination. "The kids would love you, and they're the best part of every gig. I'm Gundar, which you've probably already figured out. That's Cai over there with Rand."

He gestured to the one she thought was a vampire, standing with the wolf, then pointed to the young woman and male with dark green wings. "Marcellus and Clara. And the miscreant leaning against the chairs who was unwisely trying to get something started with JP is Merc."

Medusa tensed a little each time one met her gaze, then relaxing when all she received were cautious looks of welcome. Or, in the case of Clara, a warm smile. The girl moved to stand next to Gundar and took her hand so easily Medusa didn't find the familiarity strange. Clara reminded her so much of Callidora. Those shadows stirred again. Medusa remembered Callidora laughing during prayer time, Klotho giving them a quelling look, but the priestess's face betraying her affection under the sternness.

Stop thinking about them. Why am I thinking about them? Because she was around more than one person, something that hadn't happened since the temple, not without her needing to kill. As John had reminded her.

To kill, to turn to stone...

She forcibly ripped herself out of her head, causing her hand to convulse under Clara's grip. The girl looked surprised, but merely released her as if she thought she was making Medusa uncomfortable with the prolonged contact. But it didn't dim her kind enthusiasm.

"I have wanted to meet you *forever*," Clara said. "I saw you were coming, but that was weeks ago. I couldn't tell exactly when it would happen, and the suspense was killing me. Gundar, I'll show them to their quarters if you want, so you can get to Yvette all the sooner. She needs your skills."

"Um, is it all right if I ask, what you each are?" She hoped the question didn't sound rude. Fortunately, Clara's beaming response suggested it wasn't.

"Well, I know you already figured out Lady Yvette is a vampire. So is Cai, and Rand is his wolf-shifter servant. Merc is…" She sighed and looked toward the winged man, who was giving her nothing but an indolent look. "Mostly, he's a pain in everyone's ass, but I don't think that's a species classification. He's part angel, part human, and part incubus." She glanced over her other shoulder at the male with dark green wings, and her voice softened.

"That's Marcellus. He's my guardian angel."

At Medusa's puzzled look, Clara dimpled. "No, it's not a metaphor. He's actually my guardian angel, assigned to keep me out of trouble and everything."

"A full time and exhausting task," Marcellus noted. His voice was impassive, but the rich timbre conveyed the same impressions of safety and wellbeing to the soul that emanated from him even in silence.

Clara rolled her eyes, but looked at John. "Maddock is going to bring you glasses for her, in case you all need or want to leave the boundaries of the Circus for any reason, like when we go through the portal for the performance. It's in this great little town with a fabulous ice cream shop. She'd probably love it. He said he'd also bring contacts like yours, but since some people can't stand touching their own eyes or having anything else touch them, they may not work. So the glasses are the backup."

The young woman's gaze shifted back to Medusa. "You're so beautiful, just like the stories say. I hope we'll become friends while you're here. Come with me. We'll get you to your quarters so you can rest and be tended."

Medusa was overflowing with questions, but caring for John took precedence and kept her silent for now. Plus, she'd rather wait for some of the answers when they were alone. She hadn't received the impression from him that she needed to censor herself, which further reassured her about their surroundings, but some questions just worked better privately.

She realized she was still somewhat avoiding all their faces. It was going to take time to get used to the idea she could look at them without causing tragedy, and that came with the worry that if she got out of the habit, she might make a fatal mistake when her eyes weren't cloaked by Yvette or Maddock's magic.

But it was too much to resist, being able to look at people, see how their expressions changed when they were talking to *her*. She'd met Clara's gaze, a couple times now, and she was still chatting and moving around just fine. If Marcellus was truly her guardian angel, he wouldn't seem as comfortable with her around Medusa as he seemed to be. Despite the secure feeling she received from him, his powerful appearance and those impassive eyes that seemed to perceive everything told her he knew how to back up those feelings of safety. She'd no doubt he could inspire terror in anyone who tried to harm what he deemed under his protection.

When they stepped out of the large tent, her hand securely in John's grasp, she immediately shrank back as the number of people tripled. It wasn't like Times Square, where they were all pressing in upon her, but there was a lot of movement. People busy at tasks, carrying buckets, a pole, an armful of sparkling garments. She jumped when, a few feet away, a cluster of men and women counted off and began practicing a musical number on brass horns and stringed instruments. She saw several with flutes and wondered if that was the source of the earlier solo piece.

"It's all good." John spoke in her ear. She understood, but was glad he didn't let go of her hand or stop being so close to her.

Another trumpeting sound occurred, only this one wasn't from a musical instrument. It was a giant gray beast with wide flapping ears and a nose that looked like one of her snakes. The creature was wandering without any obvious restraint, and no alarm, from any of the people who saw the beast. The animal stopped near the musicians and punctuated their tune with another blast, causing them to grin and make the tune even more spirited.

"That's Greygirl," Clara explained. "Yvette doesn't use any animals in the circus other than pets, like dogs, cats or horses, but we rescued Greygirl. She was part of a typical circus, where her life was constant travel and being penned up. Sometimes we let the kids on the back-stage tour ride her, if she's in the mood. Peanuts typically get her in the mood, if you want to ask her for a ride at some point. Have you seen an elephant before?"

Elephant. Now she remembered why the fantastical creature seemed familiar. "Yes. But only in pictures. A scholar who came to the temple to talk to Klotho, one of our senior priestesses, had traveled widely. He had a stack of drawings that included pictures of her kind." She squinted. "Are those...birds on her back?"

"Dragons," Clara supplied helpfully. "Babies. Mom and Dad are around here somewhere, probably taking a nap, since they're pretty nocturnal. Probably where Yvette was off to as well. Even though sunlight is different inside the portals and can't hurt her, she's pretty rigid about her bedtime. Part of why she was a little grumpy with Maddock," she whispered with a wink. "Cai is more of a day owl, at least inside the portals."

Medusa blinked, a little lost, but Clara returned to the previous topic. "Greygirl likes to babysit during the daylight hours. I'll tell you the story of how she won their trust one day. It's incredible, because dragon parents usually incinerate anyone who gets near their young."

She wanted to hear all about it, but it was too much. She was making a conscious effort not to put her back to John's and move through the area in a defensive circle.

"I think we need to get to our quarters, and give Medusa a chance to check things out more gradually," John suggested.

"Of course," Clara said. "This can be overwhelming to anyone. But I think you'll love it once you feel more comfortable."

All the others except Marcellus had dispersed, so with the angel following at a deceptively casual amble, Clara circled around the tents, leading them to a nearby field populated with several dozen colorful wagons in various sizes and shapes. The wagons were enclosed, large wooden boxes mounted atop gaily painted wheels. The conveyances were surprisingly similar to the type peddlers and traveling players had used in Medusa's time.

"It's funny how often one group will move on just as we have another arriving," Clara said. "More proof that there's a Wheel always turning, and it knows exactly where it's going." She gestured to the wagon. "We cleaned this pretty thoroughly, because Pigboy lived up to his name. I think it will be a nice space for you. It has a little kitch-enette and an outdoor shower. An indoor one for cold days."

She gave John a once-over with a twinkle in her eyes. "But when that happens, you may want to take advantage of the communal shower area, because it will be a tight fit for a big man. Though the cook house serves three meals a day, you can also place any grocery requests with them so you can have the option of occasionally preparing your own meals or snacks in the privacy of your own place."

Medusa noted Marcellus listening quietly. While he didn't speak and Clara didn't address him, there was a strong thread of connection between them impossible to miss. She thought of how Clara had leaned against him. She couldn't determine if they had an intimacy between them the way she and John did, but if they didn't, the potential was definitely there. Yet Clara was human and Marcellus...was he really an angel?

John reached out to touch the gaily painted side of the wagon. Purple, gold and green swirls surrounded letters proclaiming The Circus. An elephant and a dragon were worked into the design. Wooden scrollwork decorated the corners of the mobile living quarters, and the wheels, which appeared to be wooden, were painted purple on the outside and gold on the inside.

"Looks like something you'd see a couple hundred years ago, right?" Clara said. "More portal in-between magic. As JP said, we travel along the magical fault lines, and they're real resistant to certain types of technology, like engines. Wait until you see what happens when we exit the portal to do a show. That wooden wagon of yours turns into your standard RV camper unit. Soon as we pass back into the portal, it goes retro again. The first time the kitchen staff tried to bring in Coke Zero, it turned to classic, early 1900s Coca Cola, complete with the old fashioned thick glass bottles. You never know exactly what it's going to do, but it's always cool. I love magic."

While Medusa wasn't sure what most of that meant, John appeared intrigued and amused. "This is very kind of Lady Yvette, and all of you." He looked toward Clara. "You weren't here last time I visited."

"No, we're relatively new. There's some misguided souls trying to hunt me down, because of some things I saw in my visions." She shrugged. "This was a good place to hang out until the other angels resolve it."

"So you're a seer?"

"Yeah." A shadow crossed her gaze. "It has its perks, but other parts of it can kind of suck. And if you don't mind, don't—"

"I won't. We won't." John took Medusa's hand. "I expect that's part of the appeal here. When it's not show time, no one is called upon to perform."

"Yeah. It's more than that for me, though. I really don't want to know when you're going to die, or that you're going to end up facing some tragic loss, because I can't do a damn thing to change it, you know? Even if I told you, there's nothing you can do to avoid that fate. So all I am is a window. Sometimes it's best just to leave the blinds down."

John Pierce glanced at Marcellus. Whereas he seemed to take Clara's declaration in stride, something about the winged male kept drawing his attention. "So you're really an angel?" he said, echoing Medusa's thoughts.

Marcellus lifted a silent, questioning brow.

"Yes. The kind that live in the seven levels of Heaven." Clara supplied the info, giving the angel a narrow look as he continued to say nothing. "He's part of the Prime Legion—"

"Was part of the Prime Legion," he corrected her. His tone wasn't brusque or unkind, but it was clearly a raw point for him.

"That would be news to Jonah," Clara said, setting her jaw. "He still thinks of you as part of them."

"That must be why I'm here instead of leading a battalion."

Hurt flashed across her face. His gaze flickered as if he might have regretted the edge to his tone, but she turned back to John and Medusa, visibly shrugging it off. "Okay, then. We'll just leave you to get settled. Charlie is on her way. She'll care for John's wounds, and do whatever you need to see to your comfort. I'd really recommend one of her massages. I mean she does regular ones, not just...like Yvette said."

A tinge of red came to Clara's cheeks, which seemed to amuse John Pierce. Medusa noted a brief glint in Marcellus's gaze that might have been humor as well. "How long have you been here?" John asked, with a kind, teasing note.

Clara heaved an exaggerated sigh. "I thought I was pretty adventurous and open before I got here," she admitted. "I might as well have been Dorothy straight out of black and white, vanilla Kansas. I'm still getting adjusted."

She turned her attention back to Medusa. "But seriously, her massages make you feel better about everything. She knows how to relax the muscles all around the wings. Marcellus has let her give him one, so I've seen her do it."

Clara stroked a hand down one of Medusa's wings. Again it was so unselfconscious and smooth a gesture Medusa had no time to think it was inappropriate. Clara might not be as comfortable with the blatant sexuality here, but her sensual nature was as appealing as honey. Seeing the way Marcellus watched her hand move along Medusa's skin, she thought she wasn't the only one who thought so.

John opened the latch of the door to the wagon and put his hands to Medusa's waist, lifting her onto the first step since it was a considerable way off the ground. He paused, looking toward Marcellus again.

"Is there a problem, human?" the angel asked. Not unfriendly, but that neutral tone didn't encourage a lot of familiarity. Medusa realized except when he looked toward Clara, or she felt that surge of safety from him, he was pretty intimidating. Maybe more than Yvette when he chose to let that aspect of his personality come fully to the forefront.

"No." John recalled himself and nodded to them both. "Thank you for everything."

"You're so welcome. Just holler if you need anything."

Clara took her leave, the angel in step with her. As they moved away, Medusa noticed she reached out and took Marcellus's hand. He didn't pull away, though he gave the contact a bemused look.

CHAPTER EIGHTEEN

*A*s she went up the several stairs and John followed her into the wagon, shutting the door, Medusa let out a relieved sigh. Now that things were settling, no crisis to face, she was in need of what he'd described—a quiet space in which to become accustomed to her surroundings at her own pace.

The wagon had several windows, curtained from the inside. Being able to crack them and watch the activity of the Circus with open fascination and no immediate scrutiny had great appeal.

She saw a cozy living area with facing couches, one normal width and the other quite a bit wider. She deduced the wider one converted into a table or sleeping arrangement, since polished wood was beneath the wide cushion and the cushion was broad enough for two people to lay down upon it. Toward the back, she saw what she assumed was the kitchenette and shower areas. While the whole area was smaller than her bedroom on the island, it was clean, and there were fresh flowers on a side table. It had a nest-like ambiance she found pleasing. But now her mind turned to her companion.

"Sit down." Her eyes had already lighted on a box with the same red cross emblem his box of healing supplies on the island had. "I can go ahead and clean the wound so when this Charlie arrives, we've already done that much."

Mainly she wanted him to sit down, because though he'd been stoic throughout their transition, she was certain he had to be ready to sit. Since he complied without argument, it confirmed it. However, she was curious to see it was more than physical strain. He usually shrugged off attempts to cosset him as long as he was still standing under his own power. His mind was preoccupied.

She found a bowl for water, a washcloth and a bar of soap. It smelled different from what she was used to making for herself, but it was undeniably soap, in a bright gold color.

When she knelt on the cushions next to him, she helped him take off the shirt, working the torn fabric away from the dried blood as moderately as she could. He didn't seem to mind the pull, however. As she set it aside and dipped the washcloth in the water, she studied him surreptitiously through her lashes.

"What is it, John Pierce?"

He shook his head. "Something stupid. Do you spend a lot of time thinking about what happens after death?"

"The afterlife? Some." She rubbed the washcloth and soap gently over the arrow wound, removing the blood. His jaw tightened as the soap burned, so she cleaned and rinsed it as quickly as she could, not wanting to cause him additional pain. "I had reconciled myself to the gray netherworld where spirits who are forgotten by the living wander."

She shrugged at his sudden shift of attention to her. "If I am not aging as quickly as my brethren, it stands to reason that, unless someone killed me before my time, there would be no one left to remember me when I died. So there was no chance I could go to Elysium. Sometimes, during bad moments, when my darkness felt as if it would swallow me whole, and the blood of those who invaded my shores was still on my hands, I believed I'd end up in Tartarus as a damned soul."

John gripped her fingers. "That won't happen. You're not a damned soul. And I think even if someone dies before you, if they're where they can remember you, they will, and you'll be in Elysium with them. Do you...did your people believe in angels?"

"You are kind." She considered his question. "Yes. Messengers, couriers for the gods, or charged with other tasks. Sometimes we think of our gods and goddesses as angels themselves, though since Clara said Marcellus is a guardian, a warrior, I assume he is the type of angel charged with tasks."

A faint smile touched John's face. "So matter-of-fact. Death and afterlife aren't the big cosmic questions for you and your people that they are for us."

"You have a much bigger world," she said. "With your cars, planes and magic technology. Far more things to diminish the gods in your life and cause you to question, yes?"

He blinked at her, and that faint smile became stronger. "Yeah, I guess that's true. I think you also just proved yourself smarter than pretty much all our modern day theologians and philosophers."

She harrumphed. "I'm sure that's not true." Cleaning the snake wounds, she could tell by the spacing and size of the punctures who had done what. Her touch lingered on them as she felt dismay anew. "John Pierce would never hurt you," she chided her snakes. "He would never hurt us."

"So you believe that now, deep down inside?" He touched her face and she lifted it to him, meeting his gray eyes.

"I hope so. I have committed myself to your care in a world I do not know, have I not?"

He caressed her cheek. "What you said, right before the fight, about wanting to love me? If you meant that, I'd like to hear it again from your beautiful lips, right here and now. It made me fight like ten men then. And it would give me strength now."

He could take her breath. She wondered if he knew that. "I want to love you, John Pierce. It's the first thing I've allowed myself to want this much, in many years."

A muscle flexed in his jaw. "In Times Square, when I told you they thought I was hurting you, you said 'He is mine.'" His gaze burned into hers. "I liked the sound of that. Though that inner Dominatrix was coming out, I think, getting all possessive."

She sniffed. "I do not think wanting someone to call your own is limited only to those who wish to command, John Pierce."

"You sounded pretty commanding right then."

She clasped his wrist and brushed a kiss along his callused palm before setting his hand back on his thigh. "You must let me finish cleaning these wounds," she reproved.

His eyes twinkled. "Bossy snake-girl."

But he subsided and let her continue. She thought of his words, though, and they embedded themselves inside her, a permanent mark like the tattoo on his broad back. *Medusa's Heart*.

"You are an interesting mix, John Pierce. Scholar and warrior. You have the rough edges of the soldier that are...appealing." She smiled at the gleam of interest in his eye, which told her his wounds weren't too grievous. "But I think you have been alone much of your life, even when you were among others. You have the kind of wisdom that speaks to my heart and answers some painful questions for me in ways that help."

Despite her chiding to him to be still, he stroked his large fingertips down the side of her face. "I haven't felt alone lately," he said. "I hope you've felt the same."

She pressed her lips to his hand again in answer. The gesture seemed to please him. She returned to cleaning the wounds. Since she could tell from his stiffening that the soap burned with particular intensity on the arrow injury, she offered the distraction of another question.

"Will you tell me why Marcellus disturbs you?"

He seemed surprised she'd noticed, but shrugged. "His existence. You're right; in my world, there's a lot of debate about there being an afterlife, God, heaven, angels, all of it. I've always believed there's Something there, but in that nebulous way a lot of us do, not really sure, just...hoping. Hoping with all our heart and soul, especially when we brush with death or as we get older. And yet, there he is. An angel, just as real and immediate as this couch, as you and me. Proof of something that millions of us worry and ponder—poof—all right there. It's kind of a lot to take in."

"So fighting an enemy who suddenly appeared on my island, and then passing through a magic portal into two vastly different worlds, that's not unusual. But seeing an angel is life-changing?"

He grinned. "Yeah, smartass. It is. I'm used to the other stuff."

"I'm glad one of us was." She set aside the red-tinged water, but seeing that hue unsettled her anew. She took it back to the sink and dumped it. As she turned on the left spigot this time, she jumped back as heated water splashed onto her hand.

"The water is hot," she marveled, putting her hand back beneath it.

"Yeah. The trailer has a solar water heater hook up outside. These units are pretty good about taking care of basic needs. They're not opulent, partially for the reasons Clara mentioned about the technology transitions, but they're comfortable. Since Lady Yvette could have done exactly what she threatened, put us in a couple cages stuck in a leaky tent, this is the interdimensional Marriott as far as I'm concerned."

She digested the unfamiliar term, and filed it away as a question for a later time. Returning to sit cross-legged next to him, she touched his chest below the arrow wound and stroked him, concerned. She wanted to do more for him. In the shadowed confines of the wagon, with no immediate threat to either of them, he looked tired. "There are clean clothes back there." She gestured to a closet she'd peered into while dumping the water. "They do appear to be in your size."

There were some that seemed to fit her own dimensions, unfamiliar garments she was keenly interested to explore, but their appeal was not enough to draw her from his side. Threading her fingers through the light fur over his pectorals, she made her way down to rest her hand on the layers of muscle over his abdomen. She wasn't trying to be enticing, not exactly, but seeing her fingers, without claws, touching his skin, not having to worry about scratching him... she suddenly couldn't get enough of being able to do that.

"I'll wait until after Charlie gets here. I'd love nothing better than to stretch out on the bed and get a few hours of sleep, but I'm not going to do it until we're all squared away. Keep me awake until she gets here."

Though he'd laid his hand on hers and was clasping her wrist as her fingers moved upon him, he did look like he was having trouble staying conscious, which worried her further. The arrow wound had been so close to his heart, though he'd said it had passed through the meat of his shoulder. He had so many scars. Too many. Those she'd put on him, those round, shiny scars he said were bullets. Multiple wounds from scrapes and tears to his flesh in the dangerous work he'd done before he'd come to her. She was pretty sure he didn't want to answer questions about that right now, though.

"Can you tell me how the Circus came about?"

"I'm not really sure. Not even Maddock knows, I don't think. He stumbled upon it when he was first testing the portal system. In those early days, when he could open one, he'd just step through and see what was on the other side. Crazy bastard. Walked out right between a brontosaurus's feet one time. Those are giant beasts that walked the earth thousands of years before any humans did. Another time, he stepped into a full scale battle that happened several hundred years before my time. Once he emerged into an empty part of space that didn't even seem like it was part of our world at all."

"Amazing," she murmured.

"The first time he encountered the Circus," John continued, "he walked through a portal straight into Yvette's quarters. I think she was just stepping out of her bathtub. He's lucky he survived that. Apparently the fireworks shook the foundation of the universe. As you've likely guessed, she's as much sorceress as vampire. The complex charms and protections on this place are her work, though rumor has it she had the help of a Dark Guardian to set it up, which is similar to an angel, only he works for the Underworld side of things."

"She is hard to classify," Medusa said, thinking of the woman's arousing touch, her cool eyes. "Frightening, but..."

"Fascinating. Like looking into a snake's eyes. Can't look away even as it's about to eat you." John was teasing her, but he touched Earthson's head where the small snake was weaving through the locks of hair tangled over her shoulder. "He seems pretty excited about things."

"It was the dragons. Earthson has always wanted to be a dragon," she said, caressing the snake. "He wants to spit streams of flame. I see it in his dreams."

"He'd catch your hair on fire."

"That is what Ratqueen thinks. But there's no reason not to dream."

"True enough." John's lips quirked. "Yvette herself is pretty closed-mouth about how the Circus came about, but Maddock's found evidence of its existence as far back as the 1700s. They enter into the mundane world, do a few shows, and then disappear again into this pocket between worlds. There are quite a few of those, and she knows all of them, a secret map in her head for those who need to stay out of reach of the 'real world.'"

"Like me."

"Like you." He threaded his hand through her hair. "In our world, we've had what we call 'freak shows' for a long time in carnival environments. People who exaggerate features or create illusions to dupe people into thinking they're seeing fantastic things not seen anywhere else. The Circus is the real deal."

"Like the dragons."

"Yeah. Among other things. Once you feel comfortable, I think you'll love exploring this place. We'll figure out the boundary thing Yvette mentioned so you won't have to worry about the spell leaving you. How do you like being able to look at everyone?"

"It is...I can't really wrap my mind around it yet." She lifted her gaze to meet his. "But I do know the ability to look at you again makes things seem far more balanced. I am not so afraid to be away from my home as I thought I would be. I think that is because you are with me."

His gaze stilled on her face. The significance of all that had occurred in such a short time abruptly swamped her, and he must have felt it himself, for he clasped both her upper arms and drew her out of her kneeling position to tumble her in his lap.

"Your shoulder."

"Don't give a damn about it," he said, claiming her for a deep kiss. She melted into his hold, making a noise in her throat at the demand of his mouth and tongue, far more insistent than she would have expected, given his physical state.

When he lifted his head, keeping her close, his eyes on her were the kind of sharp that pierced her to the core. "That balance thing? Same goes. When she touched you, I felt your desire."

"I couldn't—"

"There's no shame in it. She can do it to anyone she chooses. Hell, if she'd wanted to get us hot enough to fuck each other right there in front of everyone, she would have. And she came damn near close. Before she toned it down, I would have bled out while wanting to eat you alive."

She felt it in his grip, the heat of his eyes, and trembled. "It is wrong of her, to manipulate people that way."

"She only pulls on what's there. You think I haven't desired you like that before, without a vampire's help? After all we've been through, I have this primal urge just to take you right now, reassure myself we're both alive, and that you're with me, all of you."

"I am," she said, unnerved by the sudden harshness of his voice.

She put both hands on his face. "If that is what you desire, John Pierce, my body is yours to take, even in this moment. Whatever I can do to give you ease."

She'd told him that there was often something in the way he made demands of her that took her back to those early, fervent days where she was swamped with nothing but pure desire to serve the Goddess. Only this was also wrapped up with her own womanly desires, and she hadn't hesitated to tell him what she wished now.

That glint returned to his eye. "Something else I noticed. It seems there are now way too many males around that have caught your attention."

Her gaze slid over him. "I have seen nothing yet I like more than what is beneath my touch now."

The resulting intensity in his gaze made her think he might take her offer, and her body responded eagerly to the idea, no matter the wisdom of pushing him toward sex when his wound was still not fully dressed. But then they heard footsteps circling the wagon, and a light rap on the door.

"Hello? It's Charlie."

Catching her nape, John gave her one more kiss, still so brutally demanding she made a surprised noise in the back of her throat, her heart leaping. He eased her back. "On account," he promised.

He started to rise, but she shook her head. Pressing him against the cushion, she went to open the door he'd latched.

Charlie was shorter than Medusa by almost half a foot. She wasn't a dwarf like Gundar, but she was definitely very small, her body possessing a willowy thinness under a dark blue dress of a soft-looking fabric that clung to what curves she had. She had long reddish gold hair, straight and tied back in a tail, and a sprinkling of freckles on her fair skinned arms and face.

She remembered Yvette saying the woman was blind when she tilted her face but didn't meet Medusa's eyes. Her gaze was unfocused and cloudy blue. When Medusa looked into her eyes, a wave of dizziness made her grab the wall of the wagon next to the steps to steady herself.

"Hold on." The woman's hands were on her, startlingly strong, guiding her back into the wagon to ease her onto the couch next to

John. "You've had an abundance of time and dimension shifts today. That's catching up to you."

Her voice was the flow of water, carrying along the listener, taking away the need to do anything but drift. A sensual undercurrent kept the waters flowing in a pleasant swirl over the senses and exposed skin. "First things first."

The woman set a box of medical supplies on a side table and curled up on the opposite side of John Pierce, her knees folded beneath her. She bent her head in a gesture of respect. "May I touch you, sir? Treat your wounds?"

"You may," he said, studying her with a perceptive look Medusa couldn't decipher. Another question for later.

Charlie probed the arrow wound. "You did a good job cleaning all of these," she said absently. "I'll just sterilize this one a little more."

She used a sharp smelling fluid and a gauze pad. The application made John stiffen again, his fingers curling into his knee, but otherwise he issued no complaint. Still, Medusa put her hand on his and held on. When he sent her a relaxed smile, she felt better, though it seemed like the contact also helped him.

"No infection, no splinters. You were fortunate." Charlie had her palms flat on both sides of the wound, one on his chest, one against his back, and Medusa saw a cool blue and white light shimmering below the touch on either side. "I'll put some salve on it and the snake bites and give you an antibiotic. A couple days of rest will handle the bulk of the healing. I don't recommend you participate in any strenuous work for the next forty-eight hours. I'll let Yvette know."

"You don't have to do that."

"Respectfully, sir"—she bobbed her head, a deferential movement —"I do. Else you'll be doing a lot of hard lifting that will make that wound become a lot more serious. Then you won't be able to help anyone. You can take your ease for two days, under my say-so, and no one will think the worse of you for it. Your presence here has already been accepted. You don't need to prove anything."

"I am more than capable of helping out so we won't be a burden," Medusa said quickly. "She's right. It's best for you to heal properly, rather than make yourself worse."

"Great. Three bossy women all in the same place." But John's expression said he understood the wisdom of Charlie's advice; he just didn't like to be inactive when others were working. He had always pitched in or pursued his own labors when she was doing chores on the island for her maintenance. But she would make sure he would care for himself, no matter who she had to snarl at, including John Pierce himself. If Charlie had Yvette's support for the care of her patients, then Medusa would have no concerns about upholding her tenets, particularly where John was involved.

"Now, let's care for you." Charlie turned her attention to Medusa.

"Oh, I wasn't wounded."

"Not a physical wound, but it has been a stressful day for you. As I said, interdimensional travel takes its toll, especially on someone who has never done it before. My understanding is you went through multiple portals today?"

"Well, yes. But—"

"And you're still healing from that recent wing break. That takes its toll, too. If you will let me give you ease, I think it will relax you, and help integrate into the current here with less stress and fear. Would that be useful?"

It would. Clara had said that she should take advantage of the healing properties in Charlie's massages. But the other things...

"Only a massage?"

Amusement touched Charlie's lips, sensual and moist in their curve. "If that is all my lady desires, yes. If that is all your Sir desires as well."

It was an odd way to reference him, but John didn't seem uncomfortable with the address. That intriguing flicker merely went through his gaze again.

"Will you stretch out on the bed, my lady?" Charlie gestured to the wider couch, her words confirming Medusa's thoughts on its dual purpose. When it was time to sleep, she hoped it was long enough for John Pierce's tall frame. She didn't want him cramped in their living space, though if this was a safe spot, she expected they could just as easily sleep under the stars, as they might have done on her island.

"It works better if you are unclothed," Charlie said. "May I help you remove them? I will start by giving you an energy cleansing, and then we'll move to the massage."

Charlie's voice lulled her like the flute music had charmed her snakes, but it was the look in John's eyes that decided her. And what he said next.

"Lie down for her, sweetheart. You deserve some care under the hands of a woman."

It triggered a wealth of memory. While she'd never been pleasured like the priestesses in the bathing chamber, she remembered being hugged often, her hair stroked or braided by the others as they listened to music, or Klotho read to them at bedtime. Once lights were doused, they'd curl up two or three to a mattress. She'd been so used to female contact. Getting accustomed to being without it had probably been one of the most difficult adjustments for her, though she'd pushed it into the back of her memory with those other painful things she didn't like to think about.

Sometimes they'd squabbled if someone took more covers or more space than they each felt was their share, but when she'd had to sleep alone, and faced the prospect of doing so for the rest of her life, she would have given anything to take back any unkind words the girl she'd been might have said.

Charlie's fingertips glided over her, figuring out the nature of her clothing before removing it. As she was undressed in the small wagon, she was standing so close to John she almost stood between his knees. His eyes did a leisurely appraisal of her. He'd seen her naked before, but she hadn't had the opportunity to see him look at her like this, while someone was undressing her. Ostensibly for her care, but suddenly it felt like it was for him.

She noted the unique possessiveness in his expression, his gaze leaving heat in its wake. She felt suddenly like a concubine being undressed before her Master, knowing he would take her body at his pleasure.

Charlie paused and tilted her head. "Have you looked your fill, sir? May I take her to the bed?"

"I'd like her to turn around first." John's gaze lifted to meet Medusa's eyes. "Turn for me, snake-girl."

She wet her lips and complied, pivoting on her foot and presenting her back to him. His hands touched her backside, sliding over the curves to squeeze her buttocks. As her knees trembled, he pressed a kiss to her spine just above the rise of her bottom.

"Now you may lay her down."

Charlie spread a sheet over the cushions and guided Medusa down onto her stomach on it. Her capable fingers trailed along Medusa's back, backside and thighs to confirm her position. Medusa noticed her snakes had not discomfited the healer, even when Earthson and Tunneltrap brushed her shoulders or jaw, or slid along her upper arm.

"How long have you been here?" she asked Charlie.

"For a very long time, it seems. Or just yesterday." Charlie had a non-intrusive laugh, barely more than a warm sigh that slid over exposed skin. It reminded Medusa not only of the quiet rush of surf along the shore, but the muted way she heard it far above the earth, in her nest above the patio. "Like many of us, my gifts, who I am, made me a prisoner of an ignorant and unspiritual world. Yvette discovered me and offered her invitation for me to be here. I've never yet had cause to leave."

At the rustle of cloth, Medusa realized the woman was also undressing. She turned her head, pressing her cheek to the cushion as she gazed up at the woman. When Charlie swept the dress over her head, she showed she wore nothing under it. The dark blue embroidery over the bodice had disguised the points of her nipples.

Her unnatural thinness was evident in her nudity, but it wasn't starvation. She had small, well-shaped breasts, and her ribs were layered with a healthy cushion of toned skin and muscle.

The flare of her hip under the tiny waist was embellished with an intricate tattoo that started above the right hip bone and coiled around her leg to her knee. It was a spiraling, twisting tapestry of images. Roses, a dragon, an elephant. Yvette, her body arched and arms raised as if she were embracing or the center piece of the puzzle for all the images. Her fangs were bared and head dropped back, her body in a dramatic arch like a crescent moon. *Property of the Circus* was worked along the right edge of the full design.

Charlie's smooth mound revealed the lips of her sex. She had a ring in the ruffled petals of those intimate folds. Medusa had never seen anything like that. She also had rings in her nipples, connected by a short, glittering gold chain strung with a tiny ruby. The ruby looked like a rose. Medusa recalled that Yvette had worn a necklace with beads exactly like that one. Gundar had one sewn into the belt he'd been wearing with the snug, sleek pants whose material reminded her of her snakes' skin. Was the bead something Yvette gave to permanent residents of her domain? Or those whom she considered uniquely hers?

"Lady Yvette was wearing a necklace of those. They're beautiful," she said, hoping Charlie would be forthcoming. She needed her to tell her a story. John's intent gaze was giving her thoughts that were surely inappropriate with Charlie here.

"Yes. She gives one to all of her second mark servants. That's those among us she has marked twice, so that we may speak inside her mind and she in ours, no matter where we are. We also regularly provide her blood for her nourishment. She has no full servant yet. That's a person she'll give all three marks and bind to her soul for all eternity. Yet it is an honor to serve her with two marks. I would ask for nothing more."

Charlie slid onto the sheet next to Medusa. She set out three bottles of oil, with silver, gold and bronze tones. "I need to put up your hair. Your snakes may be in the oil without harm to them, but if you communicate with them, you might alert them to what is about to be done so the choice will be theirs."

While Charlie started to gather up her hair, braid and twist it into a loose tuck on her head, Medusa relayed that to her five companions. The variety of intrigued impressions told her they might inadvertently decide to help spread the oil. She hoped Charlie wouldn't find them a nuisance, because there was really no way to dissuade them, short of putting them in that somnolent state that heavy arousal seemed to incur.

As she looked toward John, that seemed far more likely than she would have anticipated only a few minutes before. The salve and dressing Charlie had put upon him seemed to have brought him ease and the ability to focus on other physical needs. They should be exhausted, the both of them, and they were, yet the need that came from a near death experience and rapid change, a need to reassure themselves of the stability of their bond, was what she was sure was driving this sudden desire that was becoming more overwhelming by the moment.

Charlie poured out some of the silver oil and rubbed it between her hands, positioning them over Medusa's back, so the first drips fell against her skin and slithered down.

"Oh." It was warm, like John's tongue sliding down her spine.

"I usually tell those I am treating to close your eyes, to feel all the nuances of what I am doing to you. But I leave that to your preference. You have had to keep your eyes closed for far too long."

"At least I have had a choice. I am sorry...you cannot see."

"It is not a choice when your gaze takes life. You've been very brave to handle such a burden without it stealing your soul. And I'm not blind. Well, perhaps in the traditional way people think of sight. But I can see you, Medusa. I see everything through the veils of aura, of star, moon and sunlight. I see areas of health and sickness. I see spiritual ecstasy, and the hurt of lost souls. If it is blindness, I would never wish to see as other people see. Instead, I would wish they could see as I do."

"Indeed," Medusa whispered. She'd thought herself the most remarkable of oddities she'd encountered in her life, yet here, she was one of many. She was...normal. It was an amazing concept, one that made her understand why Charlie had never left.

She lifted her eyes back to John. He'd shifted so he had his legs stretched out across the short aisle where Charlie was working. She was stepping over his feet as if she did indeed see them and found them welcome in her field. When Medusa let her hand drop, she could rest her fingertips on his foot. He was still wearing what he'd been wearing on their island, except for the shirt, so all he had on was the one garment, his shorts. Nothing under that but his body, and his tempting sex, which was almost as evident as Gundar's in his much tighter garment.

He had his arms crossed over his broad chest, his head resting on the cushion behind him as he watched her through half-closed eyes. He might be tired, but his erection seemed unaffected by any of that. She knew how he felt, as she could feel the heat pumping through her in the same manner.

"The first oil is to help you relax the physical body. Ease sore muscles. The second oil goes deeper, soothing sore thoughts and fears, worries. The final oil will bring you nothing but pleasure, since the first two remove any cares. We will see what your Sir desires when we reach the third stage."

"Will you do this for John? He probably needs it more than I do." She didn't move, but she knew she should, because it was only the truth.

"What I do to you will benefit you both." Charlie pressed her palm into her back, holding her still with the light touch.

"Just relax, sweetheart," John spoke. "You aren't responsible for anything but enjoying."

Charlie was right, that the portal experience had been frightening and draining. Taking all of this in, absorbing the weight of Yvette's spell, had challenged her physical and emotional reserves.

John had bid her lie still and let Charlie care for her. Medusa wanted to listen, wanted to do as he said, to please him. To please herself with that acquiescence. She wondered if she'd stumbled on what Charlie meant about this benefitting them both. More of that curious thing she and John had talked about. Dominance and submission.

"Why do you call him that? Sir?"

"It is what I call all the Masters and Mistresses," Charlie said.

"You have met John Pierce before?"

"Yes, but it is there, in the light around him."

"Oh. Is it...in my light?"

"A Mistress? No. You are the submissive warrior, the servant who will submit to him as long as he is strong and good enough to match your own formidable strength. He has had to take a journey out of dark-ness, a darkness that almost claimed him, which is why you respond to him in the way you do. You are not fully in tune with it yet..." Charlie paused. "You still have things to face, things you have buried that still live. You have been removing weights upon them, facing truth after truth, so they are getting closer to the surface. But when you face that, your choices with him will expand, if you decide to embrace them."

An uncomfortableness gripped her, those shadows stirring. She wasn't sure what Charlie was talking about, but a part of her was. A part she didn't want to think about. Ever. "And if I don't? Will I... will he..."

"Love is love, my lady. It cares not what one is or isn't. He will stand for you even if it costs him his life. He will find happiness merely in your pleasure. He is a Master, but he is a service-oriented one, so strong that he can protect and care for you as your Master without you ever committing your full submission to him. He does not question what is in his heart. It is rare."

"Or idiotic. That's what Lot says," John murmured. His beautiful gray eyes were sharp under his half-closed lids.

Charlie made a noncommittal noise. "I have told Lady Yvette that the greater wisdom is usually bestowed upon the submissive, in order to keep a Mistress or Master out of the trouble that can come from overconfidence in one's own opinion."

John chuckled. "I don't expect she'd ever agree with that where you could hear her, even if she thinks it in her head."

"Another trait of your kind," Charlie said fondly. "Now, Sir, if you don't mind, I will focus entirely on your lady. You may interject your will at any time, but I want to help her reach a point of satisfaction for you both. My silence best allows me to do that."

John grunted assent, and Charlie began to apply the oil even more thoroughly, palms sliding over Medusa's neck and shoulders, around her wings and along her arms, which Charlie positioned to either side of her head, elbows bent. After Charlie was done with the arms, Tree-bark coiled around one forearm, Earthson around the other, the snakes flattening as if they were absorbing the soothing, healing properties of the oils.

Charlie massaged her throat, working her fingers along the column, under her ears and chin, down to her collar bone in front, and point of her spine in back. A wave of sensation, both tranquil and arousing, slid through Medusa. Out to her shoulders, down her back, as Ratqueen coiled around her neck in Charlie's wake. Charlie paid particular attention to the tight muscles around the base of the wings, making Medusa want to moan as knots of tension released.

When Charlie was done with that area, Tunneltrap and Waterlight rested there.

Now along her sides, over the curves of her breasts, to her rib cage, flare of waist and hip, then over her buttocks to her upper thighs. Charlie adjusted Medusa's legs to allow her to thoroughly massage both inner and outer thigh muscles, moving onward to calves and feet. When she did her feet, Medusa entered bliss. She hadn't been aware of the ache of her arches from the violence of their fight or the subsequent travel, when she'd been traversing all of that terrain barefoot. Her muscles were so relaxed her body felt as if it were sinking into the cushion and sheet, melting.

Charlie worked her way back up, just as thoroughly. She matter-of-factly slid the snakes—in an equally blissful state—from her path. As she finished an area, she replaced them courteously in their preferred spots.

"Now, let's turn you over on your back," she said at last. "The second oil is administered to the front of the body."

Easing into that position, the snakes adjusting with her, Medusa stretched out her wings to either side of her. This time Charlie started with her face, her thumbs coated with the gold oil pressed into her forehead, working outward. She didn't tell Medusa to close her eyes. The oil, when it seeped into her eyes, didn't burn. It felt the way tears did. She massaged her face, her ears, her throat, and Medusa raised her chin, letting out another little sigh that made Charlie's lips curve as if she was nursing a lovely secret.

She worked down to breasts, shoulders, arms. As she passed over Medusa's heart, Medusa became aware of a different sensation. Emotions were drawn to the surface by this oil, just as Charlie had promised. The fear from the fight, her panic in Times Square, tension about John's feelings for her, hers for him, what their future would be, whether she'd ever see her island home again. If the island was her home, or the place she'd had to make her home; an important difference.

But those feelings didn't cling to her and disturb her repose. She let them go. Her fears and worries slipped away. The guilt and regrets were still there, part of the fabric of her being, but quiet, at rest. It all drifted away, not lost, but stepping out of her subconscious for a time, giving her an oasis of peaceful, sensual feeling. She had a light smile on her face, and she was feeling...delicious. She stretched her arms out, arching into Charlie's touch, a purr on her lips.

Her gaze lighted on John Pierce as he shifted and rose, his fine form flexing in the ways that pleased her to watch. Bending over her, he slid a fingertip along the oil at her throat, over the top of a breast and then back again. When she lifted her chin at his intimate touch on her throat, his eyes darkened. Slowly, he put his hand over her neck above Ratqueen's loose hold, tightening his grip like a collar. A noise of pleasure and need broke from her lips as she stayed locked in his gaze.

"I'm giving her permission to pleasure you, Medusa," he said. "I'm going to watch."

There were so many wonderful feelings spiraling through her, and that part of her that Charlie said she was still trying to figure out came forth. She didn't know if it suited her all the time, but in this moment, it did. She liked what Charlie had called him.

"Yes, Sir," she whispered. At the look that swept his features, a contraction happened between her legs, damp arousal slipping from between the lips of her sex. Charlie was right. This was what he was at his core. When he reacted to it, she knew something in her longed to fulfill that need. To be his wisdom when he needed it, his sanctuary of mind and body. To be his in every way that meant anything in the universe, and let the rest go, everything that meant nothing.

His fingers tightened briefly and he returned to the couch, only this time his eyes remained wide open.

"Back over on your stomach now," Charlie encouraged. "It's the best position for this last part. You will feel his regard, never fear."

The oil made her so slick. Her skin was tingling in a million places and she was fully aroused, so her snakes were in their languorous state, staying loosely twined around her arms and neck.

Charlie picked up the last bottle. Medusa couldn't imagine how that bronze bottle could take her anywhere more pleasurable than where she was flying now, but she was soon to find out. Charlie started at her shoulders, and worked down. Medusa's arms were once again above her head, and this time when Charlie's palms slid along her sides, they tucked under and cupped Medusa's breasts, fingering the nipples and massaging them with the bronze oil. Medusa moaned, her hips lifting and pushing into Charlie's body, for the woman was straddling her thighs. She adjusted so she was between Medusa's spread legs, working the oil down over back and buttocks, and upper thighs.

She was catching on fire, her nipples and skin aching for touch. Charlie stretched out along her back, rubbing her naked body along the full length of Medusa's, her mound against the seam of Medusa's buttocks. When she coiled her fingers in Medusa's hair and lifted her head to meet her lips, Medusa was hungry for her mouth. Charlie only lightly brushed her lips, though, a tiny delicate tongue playing along the seam before she pushed her back down.

"Your Master prefers to keep your kisses for himself," she purred. "But he does not mind watching a woman pleasure you in other ways."

Medusa realized she hadn't been self-conscious about her forked tongue during that brief contact. Hearing Charlie's observation of John Pierce's desires and demands further swept away such concerns.

With that surprising strength, Charlie turned Medusa to her back and lay fully upon her again. She rubbed her slick clit against Medusa's, making a hard shudder run through Medusa's body from neck to knees. Charlie's hands were still massaging and stroking, so Medusa writhed and bucked beneath her, lips parted and moist, gasping for air.

Turning her head, her arousal was further spurred by John. His eyes were fiery with desire, and he had opened his shorts to stretch out his cock, fist and rub it, pleasuring himself with the sight of her. It sent another jolt of arousal rocketing through her.

Charlie put her hand between them, dipping down to Medusa's sex to knead. "Say when, Sir," she said in a throaty voice. "I will not allow her to go over until then."

"She can go when I go," John said in a growl Medusa loved, even as she latched onto him with a pleading gaze. She was dying, Charlie's fingers and magical oil taking her over wave after wave, but never allowing that wave to crest, until she thought she was about to go mad. Her sex was throbbing under Charlie's deft touch, her nipples hard, strands of arousal pulled so tight through her upper torso and thighs she thought she might snap at any second.

John seemed to be stroking himself in an almost leisurely way, though she noticed a tremor through his thighs and he was pushing into his grip, his fine backside leaving the couch cushion to add to the thrust. He wasn't as detached as he might appear. But she still wanted that release. She wanted to do it with his eyes upon her like this, devouring her as he'd said.

I want to eat you alive.

She had a brief flash of memory, Klotho holding another priestess's head between her legs, but her face had been turned, her eyes distant as if focusing on someone else. Had she been fantasizing about a lover she couldn't have, one she'd given up to be a priestess? One who'd never known her desire?

Medusa didn't have to stare into the empty ether of a fantasy that couldn't stare back. Hers was staring at her now, flesh and blood, and she knew even if she released, she wouldn't feel fulfilled until he had his cock inside her. She didn't want him to come outside her body, but she understood what was required of her here. She need only obey his desires to have her own answered. And it happened sooner than she expected.

"Move," he said, and it took a second for her brain to process he wasn't talking to her. Charlie slid away from her instantly and he rose, removing the shorts and coming to the bed to loom over her, overwhelmingly virile, his cock jutting up thick between his thighs. Putting his hands on her hips, he turned her back over onto her stomach and lifted her hips from the mattress. He sheathed himself inside her like an animal taking his mate, no preamble, no hesitation.

A feral sound tore from her throat, her fingernails cutting into the sheets. He hadn't taken her this way yet, and she wondered and reveled at the primal pleasure of it. He'd done it so deliberately, with her in such an aroused state, there was no time for fears or images of the past to intrude upon her. He clutched her hips, thrust, pounded, as she moaned at every impact.

She didn't know how he'd signaled Charlie, but she wasn't out of the picture. The woman knelt by the bed, her fingertips grazing Medusa's side as she oriented herself to her body and slipped a hand beneath, finding Medusa's engorged clit to stroke and pinch, rub in a way that had her spiraling toward that release, particularly as John continued to send reverberations through all her slick tissues with every thrust.

"Please..."

"Now. Go now."

She toppled over that edge, still trying to hold onto something, but what she wanted to hold was holding her, and that was what she needed. He jetted into her, making a noise between a snarl and a groan, his grip on her so secure she was sure she'd have bruises shaped like his fingers. She didn't mind.

Charlie kept pace with them throughout, ensuring that Medusa felt the full pleasure of the climax from beginning to end. When Medusa was coming down, and her body was becoming too sensitive for intimate touch, Charlie picked up on that, changing her strokes to feather-light movements that increased Medusa's tiny jerks and aftershock spasms. She was murmuring, a soothing kind of singsong that helped Medusa level out her breathing as she rested her forehead against her hands. John curled his strong arm around her waist, his palm cupping her breast as he pressed a kiss to her bared neck.

"Beautiful," he murmured. "You're overwhelming."

When he turned them so that they could spoon together on the bed, she noticed Charlie and her oils had disappeared. She hadn't even felt the rock of the trailer as the woman slipped away. "Should we have..."

She wasn't sure how to finish that sentence, but John picked up on her meaning and answered it. "No. She serves Yvette. Her pleasure is the vampire's to command. Don't worry. Yvette will reward her for caring for her guests so well. I'll make sure she knows how pleased we were."

She accepted that. "Is it like this...in your world? For this isn't your world, is it?"

"No. Yvette's world, the world of the Circus, is kind of a dark Disneyworld. The amusement park I described. You remember?"

"I do." Now that she was so close to his world, she might get to see it. Mightn't she? Then she reminded herself she might have lost her claws, but outside the Circus she would never pass as a normal human.

"Easy. Don't let go of what Charlie gave you." He'd sensed her tension, and pressed his lips to her neck again. "You can sleep here, Medusa."

He'd also apparently felt that, her struggle against it, wondering how much on her guard she needed to stay. "We're safer here than anywhere else. Yvette is scary as hell, and she lives up to that reputation, but once you're her guest, you're under her protection unless you break one of the big rules. MyTech won't find us here. If they did, I wouldn't want to be the one facing her if they so much as try to jiggle the locks she puts around this place."

He held her closer. "Sleep," he said again. "Tomorrow we can explore."

CHAPTER NINETEEN

They slept for hours. One of the times they surfaced, John explained in a groggy voice that multiple portal jumps exacted a cost, and sleep was payment. When Medusa awoke at last, it was mid-morning, and they'd been under since the afternoon light of the previous day.

She was famished, but there was no need to hunt up food, since someone had left an ample amount of it on a covered tray just inside the wagon's door. She wondered if it had been Charlie. The smell of freshly baked bread and coffee was likely what had woken her. That or Ratqueen flickering her tongue against her ear, telegraphing hunger, since the snakes obtained their primary sustenance from her eating.

As Medusa began to slither out of the bed, John's arm slid back around her, a place it had rarely left in the past dozen hours. He buried his face into her neck and nipped her, sending a pleasurable reaction sliding through her vitals. "Can't leave."

"There's food."

He lifted his arm immediately, making her giggle as she squirmed free and retrieved the tray. Propping himself on an elbow, he was a pleasurable sight with his broad chest and tousled hair, the sheet low on his hips. It brought back a vivid memory of him taking her from behind on the bed, or the look in his eyes as Charlie had massaged her.

She shivered. They hadn't been asleep all those hours. A few hours before dawn, he'd woken to take her again, easing her to her back and pushing into her willing body. As her arms twined around him, he brought them to a sweet, spiraling conclusion before dropping back into dreams.

"You keep looking at me like that, we'll barricade ourselves in this wagon," he said.

She wouldn't mind that, but she was eager to explore. Despite the nice spark of lust in his gaze, she suspected he wouldn't mind getting out of the wagon too. He'd managed well enough last night, but he couldn't completely stretch out on the bed without hitting the dividing wall between the sleeping area and the kitchenette sink.

She discovered a new world of food and drink while she ate. John Pierce introduced her to coffee, showing her how to use sugar and milk to mitigate the taste she found too bitter, though she liked the smell of the beverage. There were tiny powdered round cakes he called mini-donuts, fresh fruit, scrambled chicken eggs, and strips of salty meat called bacon. After having the company of her island animals for so long, she didn't care much for eating meat, but the other food was good. Her snakes and John had no compunction about such things, attacking the bacon whole-heartedly. She was amused to see John sharing pieces with Earthson. The snake was particularly fond of him, resting on his bare knee.

Entering and exploring the closet, she retrieved clothes for both of them. John wanted a pair of long pants he called jeans and a blue T-shirt printed with a white dragon. He explained screen printing to her before she returned to the closet and decided on a pair of jeans for herself and a short-sleeved shirt with the Circus logo on it, similar to what was scrolled on their accommodations. He called it a baby doll tee and approved. She was delighted to see whoever had left the wardrobe had been aware of her wings, for the shirt had a pair of slits in the back for that purpose.

There were other garments in there, too, and he crowded into the small space to help her identify them.

"Panties and bra," John supplied. "Undergarments. The bra is a different version of the *strophion*."

She'd worn the twisted rope *strophion* above and below her breasts over her tunic at the temple to provide support to her small curves, but this idea was new and intriguing. She figured it out easily enough, though John helped her hook it. After she stepped into the panties and slid them up over her backside, she smoothed them and twisted around, trying to see herself.

"Snake-girl." He was chuckling. He drew her toward their small bathroom and pointed to a mirror. "There you are."

She considered herself from all angles, pleased with the results. When she turned from the mirror, she saw John watching her with a peculiar look on his face. "What?" She looked down at herself quickly. "Have I put them on incorrectly?"

"Not at all." He stooped to avoid hitting his head on the top of the bathroom door, and then bent down farther to kiss her, bringing her up against his body. He hadn't yet dressed, mostly. He had undergarments as well, a pair of very clingy shorts that did nothing to conceal the size of his genitals, pressed temptingly against her lower abdomen. "It's the first time I've seen you look at yourself in a mirror."

"There were no mirrors on the island."

"No, but even when standing beside a reflective surface, like the waterfall pool, you tended to not look at yourself."

She was surprised he had noticed. But then, he noticed so much about her. Like now. He slid his arms around her. "You okay?"

Words caught in her suddenly thick throat. "You make me feel... beautiful. I feel beautiful."

He put his lips on the crown of her head and looked with her into the mirror. She'd pleased him, she could tell, but his arms tightened upon her, responding to her uncertain emotions.

"I may have helped you open your eyes to it," he said. "But you've always been beautiful. Look at yourself. The most magnificent woman I've ever had the pleasure of knowing. Those last few moments on the island...I knew you could fight, but holy God, girl. You're tough as nails. You were a sight to see."

"You were very impressive yourself." The compliments were flustering her, so she nudged him with an elbow. "You should get dressed so we can go see everything."

An odd shadow crossed his eyes, but it was gone in a blink as he gave her a casual smile. "I'll be happy to do that, but I want you to know...you'll be free to come and go around here without me. You're safe at the Circus, inside the portal."

"Oh. Well, yes, I guess I will when..." She didn't want to seem helpless, but as always, he seemed to pick up on her thoughts.

"When you're familiar with the environment." He touched her chin, making her look up at him. "That's smart thinking, Medusa. I'm saying it as much to remind me as to tell you. I want to give you the room to explore things on your own. Your world's had to be very controlled, even on the island. It's been awhile since you've been able to stroll through a marketplace or go to places the rest of us take for granted."

"I did not have that before," she admitted. "Women in my society are not like Lady Yvette and Clara. I was born in the noble class. Women stayed at home. Slaves went out and did the shopping. If I went out, I was escorted by a male relative. As a priestess, I saw more of the world going to events to sing or lead rituals with my sisters than I ever did in my father's home. When I heard stories of the Spartan women, how much more freedom they were given, sometimes I wondered, and dreamed about living that kind of life."

She paused, thinking of John Pierce's compliments of her fighting skills, and the independent life she'd lived on the island. Perhaps she *had* lived that kind of life. "I think Yvette would have liked the Spartan women," she added.

"Since I don't know how old she is, she could have been one of them," John said. Then he sobered. "If the spell was reversed, would you want to go back to the life you had as a priestess? Or as your father's daughter?"

"I was little more than a child when the head priestess accepted me as an acolyte. I found far more of a family at the temple than at the one in which I was born." She pressed her lips together, shifting her gaze back to the mirror. "As far as returning to the temple, I do not know. I don't think it is an option any longer, regardless. But it is always nice to have the choice to go back home."

She didn't want to think about that. The one option he hadn't stated, returning to her island, was more home to her than any other place. Yet now she could not imagine being there without him, so perhaps it was possible to make a home wherever they could be together. Would he think her fanciful for that?

He'd said he considered her his, but he had not asked her to be his wife. Each time issues arose related to their being together, she sensed a reserve from him.

She had not yet made it clear she wanted only him. Was that it? She'd been about to tell him, before they'd had to flee the island. But now, there was a whole new world for her to explore, people she could talk to, whose eyes she could meet without fear, and the words stayed in her heart.

How could she explain to him it wasn't because he wasn't her choice, but because having the freedom, the time to have choices, was so new to her? Her opinion on a husband would not have been consulted in Greece. Her father would have made the decision.

"John Pierce..."

"Let's save the heavy questions for another day." He didn't let her go there, his expression hooded but voice firm enough to dissuade her from it. Now he distracted her by stripping off the clingy underwear and wrapping a towel around himself. The quarters in here were so very close, he brushed against her at many pleasing angles as he managed the switch. With merely a shift of her body or lift of her hand, she was able to trail fingertips along his hip, the strong line of his back. The Medusa tattoo.

When he turned to face her, his broad chest was right before her eyes. She'd left her hand on his back so as he turned, it naturally settled against the rough curling hair over his pectoral, tempting another stroke. He was a large man, but inside this small space, it was enhanced. He made her feel so female, and her worrisome thoughts were encompassed by a cushion of other wants and needs.

His eyes rested on her face, and he clasped a hand over her hip. He put the other hand on her shoulder, his thumb sliding beneath the strap of the bra, an intriguingly intimate gesture she felt tingle all the way to her nipple. In the small area, they were almost pressed against one another, which only heightened her awareness of the sliver of space left between them.

"There's an outside shower built up against the wagon," he said, a huskiness to his voice. "Want to join me before we take off? I need to make myself presentable as the plus-one of the hottest woman here."

Her brow furrowed. "It is warm in here, but not overly so."

He grinned. "Hot means a desirable woman, because she has

sizzle, like fire. Fire's brilliant, mesmerizing and burns at the touch, but the heat of it keeps us close to it anyway, right?"

As she flushed like Clara, he cupped his palms over her warm cheeks. "See? Already getting hotter. 'Plus-one' means the guy lucky enough to be with you. C'mon."

As he drew her to the door, he wrapped a towel around her, fondling her hair and neck and collecting some of the powdered sugar from the corner of her mouth by licking it off. As she pressed against him just as eagerly, she wondered at how the need between them didn't seem to abate. They'd only recently done...what they obviously both wanted to do again.

He groaned against her mouth, his arms banding her against his full length as he lifted her off her feet. "Christ, I'm being an animal," he grumbled. "We better get out of this trailer."

"Should I take off these undergarments, as you did?"

"Once you get to the shower. You take them off here, we're not getting any farther for the next hour."

She giggled again when he shoved open the door to the wagon with his foot and carried her down the steps. He set her on the grass and pointed. "Look."

In the bright sunlight, she saw the Circus was camped next to a lake, the water so clear that it reflected the mountains behind it. Clusters of trees with large canopies shaded the various tents and transport vehicles. She heard the piercing cry of a bird and saw a hawk gliding over. The warning cries of smaller birds in the trees became chirping song as the hawk went on his way. A trio of dogs ran by, one of them playing keep away from the others with a stick.

An inquisitive *mrr* drew her attention to the top of their wagon. "Oh."

A pair of cats were curled there sunning, though at their appearance one got up, bowing his back in a strenuous stretch. He hopped down to wind around her legs. When she bent to pet the feline, John caught her arm. "Let me."

He nodded meaningfully to her snakes. She realized Earthson and Treebark had both caught the cat's eye, their movements a tempting target for a feline's predatory instincts. The snakes were ratcheting up their own aggressive posturing, Treebark hissing.

"We might need Yvette's magical help convincing the cats around here not to see your snakes as tempting toys. Avoiding injury on either side," John advised.

"Yes." She soothed her snakes, convincing Treebark not to execute a venomous strike as John petted the cat and shooed him away. Drawing Medusa around the side of the wagon, he opened the door of the roomy stall that had been built alongside it. She saw a silver spigot and a moment later her towel was tugged away and she was drawn in for her first shower. She found both the concept and company enchanting, as well as the experience of having every crevice of her body cleaned by John's clever fingers.

Though she was eager to explore her surroundings, when he lifted her up against the wall of the stall and took her again, she didn't object. She abandoned herself to his demands and returned the favor in full measure.

It was a glorious way to start the day.

Much of what she and John saw as they wandered the grounds was practice for the upcoming "gig," as Gundar had called it. Clowns juggled and executed comically clumsy maneuvers with a variety of props. Acrobats performed astounding stunts with bodies as flexible as her snakes. The trapeze artists made her heart leap in her throat as they worked on new routines, and she was glad to see there was a net stretched beneath them.

She saw ongoing repairs to equipment and new props being built. John paid keen attention to those activities, but apparently the word had been passed about Charlie's mandate. When he offered to help, he was waved away and told to come back tomorrow.

"We'll have plenty to do then," Gundar told him. The dwarf was covered with sweat, his muscles gleaming. They had a working smithy, and he seemed to be in charge of it, currently hammering and shaping a metal shield. She noticed a lineup of swords cooling and, at his encouraging gesture, she picked up one that interested her.

"We sell craft goods as well as perform," he explained. Opening a case, he showed her a row of finished daggers. The intricate hilts were decorated with crystals. "You'll want to check out Charlie's goods too. She makes dresses, skirts, scarves, all the things that enchant the ladies. Clara does jewelry and beadwork. I and two of my fellows also do armor, because we like to hit the Cosplay scene on occasion. The Circus takes one month off every three, to keep us fresh and give us lives away from it. Those of us who can move around in the modern world, that is. Those who can't enjoy the respite in places like this."

"Medusa."

She turned at the welcome sound of Clara's pleased voice. The young woman linked arms with her with relaxed familiarity and beamed over her head at John. "Good morning."

"Morning." John glanced around her. "Where's your shadow?"

"Oh, Marcellus had some security stuff to do. We're all safe here, or at least I've convinced him we're safe enough he doesn't have to be right on top of me."

Satisfied, John turned to answer a question Gundar had asked. "Much as that would be a lovely thing to contemplate," Clara muttered to Medusa.

Medusa gave her a curious look. Clara changed the subject though, dipping her head closer to Medusa's in girl-to-girl conspiracy. Not at all put off by her snakes, the young woman blew a playful puff of air at the bemused Waterlight.

"Already shopping I see. Another fabulous thing about being part of the Circus is you can earmark the stuff you like. First choice goes to ticket holders, but if you really like something, we'll make up another one for you during the off times, and charge the family price, which is basically cost of the materials. I came to find you because Charlie wants you. She has an outfit she says will look beautiful on you for the Promenade, if you decide to do it. No charge. Just part of the costuming she does for all of our acts. You give it back afterward."

Clara lifted her head again to draw John's attention. "Can I borrow her for just a little while and show her around? Marcellus is going to use you on the security detail, so if you go find him he'll show you some things. Nothing physically exerting; just explanatory stuff." She dimpled. "Yvette figured that would help you not go so crazy, seeing all this work going on around you and not being able to help out until tomorrow."

John looked a little sheepish and manfully tried to cover. "I'm okay. I can handle a day of relaxing, especially in the company of a beautiful woman."

"Even on the island, you preferred to spend time with me while we were doing something," Medusa pointed out. Then warmed from head to toe at his significant look. "Like gardening or repairing things."

"Among other things." He grinned. "But I guess we can't do those things all the time. Well, maybe here you can."

"Truer words. Some of the people here are capable of it. Yvette, Merc..." Clara stopped herself. "But it sounds like Medusa knows you pretty well."

"She does at that." John gave Medusa a more serious look. "I promised we'd spend the day together."

"Yes. But as she said, it is only for a little while."

She actually wasn't comfortable with the idea of being away from him, but her caution was based on long habit, not on any evidence she was in danger. If John Pierce had any doubts on that at all, he wouldn't be willing to leave her side. As much as she'd anticipated having a full day together, she realized now was as good as any other time to prove to both of them she could be away from him in a new environment without falling apart. She straightened her shoulders. "Go see Marcellus. I'll be fine."

"You are that." He stepped closer and tipped up her chin, brushing her lips with his own. His steel gray eyes held hers. He didn't seem to mind that Clara stood only an arm's length away. "I won't be far. If you need me for anything, you have someone find me. Say it."

"I will come find you." She whispered the words, because her voice had deserted her under that intense look.

It was on the tip of her tongue to say she couldn't imagine not needing him every moment of the day. That was such a girlishly romantic notion she held it back for fear of embarrassing them both. Though it didn't feel girlish at all. The words came straight from her woman's heart.

They'd established their connection on her island, but amid all these new people and experiences, it was as if was deliberately choosing behavior and words that increased the energy in that bond. She wasn't sure how he was working such magic, but when she made herself pivot and let Clara take her away without looking back, she realized her knees were a bit shaky.

"Wow," Clara murmured to her. "He can just...wow. Marcellus can do that, too. He just gets this look, and he steps into my space, and takes up all the air, and I don't care, I'd let him breathe for me and..."

She startled Medusa when she gave herself a quick slap in the face with her own hand. "Snap out of it," Clara said, seemingly to herself. She linked arms with Medusa.

"You're doing great," Clara said encouragingly. "He probably knows you're nervous about it, but I think he gets that you want to prove you can be independent in a not-so-familiar place. He might like it if you looked over your shoulder at him just once, though. For all the tough, sexy Dom vibes, he's a little nervous about leaving you on your own, too."

Relieved to have an excuse to do exactly what her heart wanted to do, Medusa glanced back. John Pierce was watching her, but at her expression, his own eased into a warm smile and he answered her wave with one of his own.

"There we go. Now you're both happier," Clara said.

Feeling somewhat foolish, Medusa sought something else to talk about. "I could help with security."

"Unfortunately, no." Clara nudged her. "You look more than capable of taking someone down, but the security detail has to blend. If people are crowding around you, wanting to see your snakes, it'd be hard for you to keep an eye on things. Marcellus has a way of disguising his wings so people just see a scary-looking guy doing security, and most of the rest of our security people are like that. You should see Caleb. He's built like a mountain. We've used him in strongman acts, but when we don't need him for that, he does security."

"What about Merc?"

Clara grimaced. "Merc can't tone down the incubus thing. Or won't. So Yvette keeps him as a performer."

"Is he...safe?" Medusa didn't want to offend, but Clara didn't seem taken aback by the question.

"Yes and no. Most of the women here avoid situations where we're alone with him. Just good common sense. Temptation is hard for someone with his nature to resist, and once you're caught in that net, it ramps up considerably. That part is kind of out of his control, but there's a twisted meanness to him that adds to it. That meanness came from the paths he's chosen. Though it may not seem like it, what with the sarcastic asshole routine, he is sincerely trying a different path here, which is why Yvette is tolerating him, for the time being. We all get that it's a rough road."

Clara shrugged. "Most Circus people have stories and pasts, some with bad triggers. He's probably the one of us with the worst. Yvette and the others keep a really close eye on him. Marcellus in particular, partly because of the angel blood and partly because, well, he's Marcellus. Protecting is what he does, even if it's protecting Merc from himself."

"What... I do not want to ask too many questions."

"That's not possible." Clara squeezed her arm. "I had so many when I came, it took days to answer them all. What else do you want to know? Fire away."

"Can you explain more about the Promenade?" She'd told herself she wouldn't even contemplate it. She had more than enough adjustments to make, but she'd woken thinking about Gundar's words, and wondering...

"Oh." Clara brightened. "It's the most wonderful part of every show. At the end of the performance, we parade past the audience, and then go up in the stands with them, or invite them down into the rings, depending on what kind of fun we're offering. Eventually everyone ends up milling around together like one big party, natives and performers."

She laughed at herself. "Natives being the local people who buy tickets. I'm falling into circus lingo more and more. Anyway, the Promenade post-show is where you see a better side of Merc. He'll give the kids rides and he's really, shockingly great with them. Something about children drops his defenses. It does everyone, doesn't it? If the security is covered, Marcellus will do the ride thing as well."

"So they touch you, talk to you?"

"Yes." Clara's gaze slid over her snakes. "They would adore you. You'd be a hit faster than a sneeze. Will the snakes let kids touch them?"

"I do not know. They pick up on my emotions. If I am comfortable and relaxed, usually they are the same."

"Cool. We have some kids here. We can see how they react. A mini-testing ground."

"I am not sure if I want to do the Promenade," Medusa said uneasily. Perhaps Clara would assume her questions meant she was going to do it.

Clara touched her arm. "There's no pressure at all, but go ahead and try out the snakes with the kids here. That way, on performance day, if it looks too fun to pass up, you'll already know how your snakes will do with the little people. But whether you participate or not, you should definitely still wear the outfit Charlie's recommending for you. It's kind of standard anyhow. Any of the players or staff wandering around where guests might see them are required to have a 'uniform' of sorts that says you're part of the show. We get to choose what that is, but it can't be what we'd wear for day-to-day."

She ran an appraising gaze over Medusa in her new clothes. "Though the jeans and tee look beyond fantastic on you, I have to say. With the wings and snakes, there's this ultra-cool visual contrast between the real world and the fantasy one. You look like you stepped out of a graphic novel. What did John think?"

When she'd emerged from the wagon in the outfit, John had gazed at her for a long, unsettling moment. He'd dressed by the shower, since it was easier to do so outside with his large frame, and he looked quite distracting in the jeans that creased in the right places and the dragon T-shirt that molded his powerful upper body.

His eyes had coursed over the baby doll tee. It provided a frame for her breasts in front, pushed up and displayed a little more prominently thanks to the bra garment. The hem of the shirt stopped at her hip bones, so his view of her lower body in the snug jeans was not hampered.

He'd backed her up against the side of the wagon and slid an arm around her waist, hand dipping into the jeans pocket to cup her buttock. Just like in the shower, he'd lifted her effortlessly against the solid wall behind her and given her another kiss that left her heart pounding and the snakes limp on her shoulders.

"He liked it."

Clara grinned. "Yeah, that dreamy look on your face told me that even before you said it. Men are great at making us feel pretty, aren't they?"

She thought of her impulsive admission to John that he made her feel beautiful. He'd done more than that, though. He'd opened her eyes to evaluating her appearance based on her own standards, not those of others. When she'd looked in the mirror, for the first time she'd noted the golden smoothness of her skin, how the red of her eyes *were* like rose petals. Her hair was thick and lustrous, adding to the gleam of the snakes' scales as they wove through it.

She was still amazed by her hands, the short nails and slim fingers, finally once again her own. Though the part of her that stayed on guard regretted losing the fight advantage the talons had given her, she would figure out something she could trade Gundar for one of his knives and compensate for that in a different way.

Medusa pulled herself out of weapons planning. She was in a safe place right now. She didn't have to plan for the next fight, though it seemed prudent to keep it in mind. She figured John Pierce would agree with her. Another thing they had in common.

"Will you tell me more about what they do during the Promenade?"

"Sure. We also do a quick, informal Circus school for the kids. Like we set up a small ground level trapeze unit and the trapeze artists demonstrate basics, putting people in harnesses so they can give them a try. Caleb will let them load up his shoulders with a dozen kids to prove his strength. The dwarves take them on mini-train rides down into a "mine shaft," one of Yvette's special illusions. We pass out candy and trinkets, like shiny cheap bracelets, balloons, fun things like that. It all usually runs for about a couple hours, though one night it went on until past midnight. There's an energy to it that feeds us. And speaking of feeding..."

With a quick grin, Clara stopped by a large open tent surrounded by the appetizing aroma of cooking food. "They're making an Italian sweet bread today. They bake it in these little braided lengths, perfect for carrying around as snacks. Marcellus says it's as good as manna, which is high praise from an angel, since the only food they can really taste *is* manna. Flag's not up yet for lunch, but let's see if we can grab a handful from Mary. She's the best cook in the known universe."

Clara introduced Medusa to Mary and the busy cooking crew, and snagged two fizzy drinks she called a Coca Cola to go with the braided sticks of bread. The dough, faintly sweet, practically melted on the tongue. Medusa had to agree that it was up to the standards of food for the angels.

Clara was watching her eat. Before Medusa could get self-conscious, Clara lifted her blouse, showing her a delicate jewel piercing the thin skin above her navel. "You should consider getting a tongue piercing. With your tongue forked like that, you could do a pair of sparkling gems. It would look like a set of dragon's eyes. Your whole look just screams for awesome accessories. I think that's why Charlie is so eager to get her hands on you for some of her costuming."

Medusa wiped her mouth with her napkin, touching her tongue thoughtfully with her fingertips. She'd always treated it as something to hide, unless it provided her an advantage over her enemies, but looking at the variety of jewels Clara wore so well had her thinking. What would John Pierce think of it? How would such an accoutrement feel, sliding over his skin...

As they took their leave of the cook house—apparently called that by all the Circus players, despite it being a large tent—Medusa tuned back in to find Clara had changed subjects again. The young woman was good at offering suggestions to mull upon without lingering long enough for them to hit uncomfortable terrain. She was liking Clara more and more by the minute.

"Initially, we all took turns cooking," Clara was saying. "Those of us who stay during the one-month off periods still do. That's so the cooking folks can vacation. However, we've gotten so big and busy, and doing so many shows, Yvette realized we had to hire a dedicated staff just to handle food so we didn't lose performance prep time foraging for ourselves."

While Medusa was listening, she was also occupied with the staff's reaction to her. Mostly friendly, speculative looks, and she was quietly thrilled with every face-to-face introduction. She was being treated the way any newcomer would be in a group where...she belonged. Her appearance made them curious, not repelled.

"You must have many acts that look different, like me," she ventured.

"Well, you saw the dragons yesterday. We also have a coven of witches who do a mock battle with the magicians. Then there are talking goats, a griffin, and the lizard boys who delight in blending with their surroundings so they can jump out at the girls and get them to squeal. There's also a lot of us who look 'normal' but are anything but, so they have a harder time blending in normal society than they first appear. We've barely covered a third of this place."

She smiled at Medusa. "Let me give you the full tour and, when your feet are aching, we'll head back to Charlie's and let you check out her outfits. She said she was going to be doing alterations most the morning so we could come by anytime. We also have centaurs, giants, a unicorn..."

"A unicorn?"

"Yeah." Clara grinned at her expression. "You know what those are? Well, I guess you do since you all have Pegasii and all that."

Medusa's brow creased. "Pegasii?"

"Winged horses? Pegasus? Wasn't sure if that was the proper plural."

"Oh, yes, we have those in our stories. I had not heard them called that."

"Hmm. Just goes to show even mythology can fall prey to grapevine distortion. What do you know about unicorns? Have you met one before?"

"No. I dreamed of one for a while, when I was younger. There was something special about her, something I could not explain. Then I stopped dreaming about her. I missed her, though I know it sounds peculiar to miss a dream."

Clara did a little spin, apparently just for the joy of doing it, sending her skirt wafting out from her in a colorful wave of movement. "Actually, a lot of things sound peculiar, but missing a dream doesn't sound that way at all. Let's go see Lianthe first. She doesn't talk human, but she has her own way of speaking."

Now that she'd voiced it, Medusa felt childish about her eagerness, so she focused on something more practical as Clara changed course and headed toward the lake. "What kind of security issues does Marcellus handle? Are there any here?"

"None to date. That's why we all like the in-between. But he likes to stay ready just in case. Out in the 'real world,' there are your usual troublemakers. Other magic-users who know who and what we are and want to cause problems. Like MyTech. Yvette also sort of inherited the Circus and so she runs into periodic conflicts with the Vampire Council. They've gotten new leadership lately that's more sympathetic to the Circus, so things are more copacetic with them these days. Thankfully."

Clara sighed. "On occasion we get a human who figures out our performers are the real deal. Then they get the brilliant idea to try and kidnap one of us. We have to watch out for Lianthe especially, in case someone wants his kid to have a special kind of pony and won't take no for an answer. Yvette's been offered all kinds of money for her. Even one time from a Russian mob boss. Think he never thought he'd meet someone scarier than himself, but now he knows better."

"I cannot believe anyone would think..."

"Yeah, like she's something to be bought and sold. I'm not even comfortable with treating animals everyone sees all the time like property. It seems wrong, like it denies they're souls like the rest of us. But we don't have that problem here." She pointed toward several kittens playing beneath the shade of a wagon and grinned at their antics as one fuzzed up and danced away from the others. The siblings pounced on her and started a new wrestling match.

"They're rescues we found at our last performance. You won't usually see any pregnant dogs or cats here. Yvette insists on getting all of them neutered. She claims it's the responsible thing to do, and it is." Clara smirked. "But we think she became particularly zealous about it after one of our pregnant cat rescues made her nest and gave birth in Yvette's fabulous shoe collection. After she shredded a bunch of them. You may have seen her, the calico with gold and gray tabby spots?"

Remembering the cat on top of her wagon, Medusa nodded. "I saw her this morning."

"She's a member of the Circus family now. We call her Ibee, which stands for Irony and Bitch, because we named her Irony and Yvette named her Bitch. The Irony part is because she's Yvette's favorite cat. Probably because after Yvette discovered her in her shredded shoe nest, the cat stared up at Yvette like, 'Yeah, what're you going to do about it?'"

Clara chuckled. "I got all that from Charlie, since Yvette would never admit to any of it."

The image of the intimidating female vampire being fond of a cat who'd destroyed her wardrobe was hard to reconcile. Yet Yvette seemed to have a serious moral code about protecting those who deserved protecting. It was a message Medusa was seeing echoed all around her at the Circus, so perhaps it wasn't surprising to hear Yvette had a fondness for a brave cat.

"Are you a performer?" she asked Clara. "You did not seem comfortable about using your gift."

"No, and I don't really use it, not directly. I'm a side show act on the midway. A fortune teller. Mostly I pick up on the clues I see in people and tell them things that make them laugh and feel good. It's rare that I open myself up to really delve into their heads and see what's going on. They don't want that any more than I want to do it."

As they moved away from another grouping of wagons and tents, Clara changed the subject, pointing down a grassy slope toward a distant open pavilion tent. "That's where the centaurs usually are, though I expect they're out for a run this morning. Unos is their leader. You'll know when they're back, because the ground will shake like from an earthquake. Subtle isn't in their vocabulary, but that comes in handy on performance night. You should see the kids' eyes get so big and round when they come thundering into the tent.

"*Rand.*" Clara nearly squealed the name, startling Medusa. Throwing a devilish twinkling look at her, Clara ran forward to where the enormous black wolf was lying beneath a shade tree. He cracked open his golden eye and heaved an exaggerated sigh as she dropped onto the ground beside him and gave him a hug, her arms not quite able to reach around his massive shoulders. "You give the best hugs. He's so furry. Come give him a hug, Medusa."

"Er..." She made a polite obeisance to the wolf as he eyed her. Since he was panting, she was looking at a formidable set of teeth. "I'll just say a courteous good morning."

"He's a big silly dog, is all." Clara laughed as Rand surged up and knocked her to her back. Then he pinned her, dropping into a prone position over her stomach and hips, eliciting an *oof*. Medusa noted that he'd been very careful in his wrestling, though, and no teeth were involved.

"Okay, okay, fatso. I give up."

Rand yawned hugely and gazed at a hawk flying overhead as if he couldn't hear her. "You can't blame me for hugging you. You're so huggable." Clara had one arm free and used it to scratch his side, making his back leg start to pedal. "See, I'm good for that."

He huffed in her face. "Ugh, wolf breath," she groaned. "Goddess, the raw meat diet. Why doesn't Cai brush your teeth?"

Probably because Cai valued all his fingers, Medusa surmised. But she did note the wolf seemed affable to the girl's teasing, and the gleam in his eye suggested he enjoyed her play.

"Okay, can't breathe. Up, help. Wheezing here. Marcellus will come if he thinks I'm being oxygen deprived. He might wait to pull you off me until I've turned the color of a blueberry, but he will come."

Rand got up and stretched, then gave her a chin-to-forehead sloppy lick that made her shriek with disgust. He bounded away behind a nearby wagon as Clara got to her feet, wiping her face with the hem of her shirt.

"Dog germs. Gross." But she was smiling. She glanced around them. "I'm surprised Cai's not nearby. Those two aren't usually far from one another. But sometimes Yvette needs Cai's help with vampire-related things. We perform in a lot of different vampire territories, which means she has to clear her passage with overlords."

Clara made a face. "Vampires are really uptight about territory boundaries. Her adherence to all the rules is part of her tentative truce with the Council. At least that's my understanding. Vampires can be very clique-y, not wanting to talk to humans about these things."

"It's the top-of-the-food-chain delusion." A shirtless, broad-shouldered male with a thick tangle of brown hair falling past his shoulder blades emerged from behind the wagon. He wore a ragged pair of jeans and nothing else, his feet bare. The silken pelt of hair on his wide chest was a gleaming dark chestnut color. As Medusa met his gaze, she started. Though his gaze was no longer bi-colored, both orbs a vivid blue with gold flecks, she was absolutely sure she was looking at the blue and gold-eyed wolf.

Pulling a crimson-colored packet from his pocket, he retrieved and unwrapped a small rectangle of some kind of food from it, popping it in his mouth. "Cinnamon Trident," he told Medusa, and extended the packet. "Want some?"

He shot Clara an amused look. "Since the lady did complain about my breath."

When he had shifted toward her with the offering, Medusa had stepped back from him out of instinct. She'd been told he was a shifter, but seeing the reality was more disturbing and reminded her of stories from her own time, where wolves with human eyes charged out of the Underworld to drag the helpless to a terrible death.

"It's gum," Clara said, taking two of the rectangles and handing her one. "You chew it, but don't swallow. It's for the flavor. It's not meant to be eaten."

Clara's steady gaze said she probably knew what Medusa was struggling with, but she was also sending her a palpable message to pull it together, as John Pierce might say.

Rand had dropped his hand and his gaze had shuttered. In another breath he'd likely turn away and leave.

Yesterday she'd met a blood drinker and felt a similar surge of alarm. Now as then, Medusa reminded herself of what people thought of her, mostly because of stories. She wouldn't call Rand safe, not exactly, but he wasn't a threat to her. Clara wouldn't have been so comfortable with him otherwise, would she?

He'd started to pivot when she found her voice. "Does it hurt?" She cleared the squeak out of her tone. "Changing forms."

Rand stopped and looked over his wide shoulder. Studying her a long moment, he at last turned to face her, easing her tension. She didn't want to treat someone like she'd been treated. She knew how it felt, after all.

"Sometimes. Shifting's easiest during the full moons, hardest during the dark moon, but I've been doing it so long now, I don't even think about it." He looked at the snakes. "What happens if one of them eats something big, like a rat? How do they get it through their digestive tract?"

She laughed as he pantomimed the visual of a giant lump being stuck inside the snake but outside her head. "They receive their main food from what I eat. The biggest thing they have ever caught and eaten themselves is a small lizard." She grimaced. "The sensation was horrifying."

He smiled, and she wondered if she'd put him more at ease, too. "Do they ever bite you?" he asked.

"They have, when they've been afraid. They don't mean to do it, though. It's just instinct. It's been a long time since they've done that." She thought of the Times Square portal. If John Pierce hadn't wrapped himself around her so securely, it would have been more recent.

"Yeah." He received the double meaning and his serious lips curved. She was forgiven. He extended his hand. "We didn't meet last night. Officially. Rand."

Though he was articulate, he had a slow way of speaking, and the words had a rumbling sound like a continuous low growl. He didn't seem comfortable speaking out loud, as if the sound startled him. Perhaps it was an initial transition thing, when he first turned from wolf to human. As Medusa took his hand, she noted the strong but gentle grip and scars along his wrist, overlaid by tattoos that looked like brands.

"What do those mean? If it is all right to ask."

"They're a warning. And a reassurance. The meaning is something between me and my... Between me and Cai."

"We're going to see Lianthe," Clara said. "Want to go?"

"Lianthe is not comfortable with me, even as human." Rand shook his head. "Too much history between horse species and wolves." Returning to the wagon which was apparently his, he opened a compartment in the back and retrieved a small sack. "Here's something she'll like. Don't say I gave it to you. She might spit it out. Or trample it."

"She won't," Clara insisted. Rand merely made a dubious noise and waved them on their way. When Medusa glanced over her shoulder a moment later, she saw the wolf under the tree again. Had he shifted merely to introduce himself to her? Even when the people she'd met had been busy with tasks, all had made a special effort to bid her a genuine welcome. Perhaps she could stay here indefinitely, as John had implied.

He'd seemed as reluctant to leave her island as she had, but maybe he would feel at home here, too. And this was a place with ample protection. He wouldn't have to stay with her just because he thought she wouldn't be safe without him. He claimed he felt no sense of obligation, that he desired to be with her, but to feel that the choice was pure and true? It was appealing and terrifying at once to her. She wondered if he felt the same way. Was that part of why he seemed as if he could have been content on her island forever?

They continued on their way. Medusa had the thrill of seeing the centaurs at a distance, their hooves kicking up a dust cloud behind them as they emerged from the distant forest and galloped by the far side of the lake. A few moments later she looked up in response to a series of piercing cries and saw the small dragons wheeling and dancing. Clara pointed to a nearby stand of trees and Medusa clutched her hand in involuntary reaction as she detected a pair of jeweled eyes, each as big as her fist.

"Jetana," Clara whispered. "Tragar, her mate, is likely off hunting. Best to make dragon parent introductions from a distance. They'll approach you if ever they want to say a direct hello."

"Is there a way to tell the difference between that and them coming to eat you?"

Clara chuckled. "It's a fine line. They've actually never harmed anyone in the Circus, but Gundar handles their performances and he advises us to treat them with a really high protocol kind of respect. Bowing before you address them, backing away when you've finished. They're really old-school about those kinds of things. Kind of like Yvette on steroids."

Following Clara's informative dialogue could be challenging as they hit terms Medusa didn't know, but thanks to her exposure to John Pierce, she'd become more accomplished at picking up context, so she was often only temporarily confused before she figured it out.

As they drew closer to the edge of the lake, a pair of women, one red-headed, one blonde, surfaced and waved at Clara. They both had blue-green eyes like the waters around Medusa's island.

"Hey Tawny, hey Gia. I'm just showing Medusa around."

"Welcome," they chorused, giving her friendly, curious looks. "You should come for a swim later," Gia said. "The day is perfect for one."

"We may do that. She has the day off until tomorrow. After that, you know Yvette. Leisure time will be a distant memory."

Tawny rolled her eyes in good-natured sympathy. "We've been practicing our act, but the nice thing about being in the water is she doesn't necessarily know when we're taking a break, especially since most vampires don't like to go into the water."

"You know she has her spies." Clara pointed skyward at the dragons. "They'll sell any of us out for her treats."

"Too true. We better get back to it." The two women turned and dove. Medusa gasped in delight as she saw their hips were covered with silver and pink lapped scales. The feathered fronds of their tails came out of the water as they propelled themselves back toward the center of the lake.

"Mermaids," Clara confirmed. "Isn't this the coolest place ever? You know, some of the first pictures I saw of you showed you with a snake's tail, but it was a lot like the size and shape of a mermaid's. I'll have to show you. You've inspired some awesome tattoo work. Not just John's, but that was inspired by something different, I think."

"You have seen his tattoo?"

"He had it upgraded here."

"I thought he said...he had it done many years ago."

"He did, as a teenager, the original basic design. But after he got involved with Maddock, a few months before he came to your island, he met with one of the two amazing tattoo artists we have here and said he wanted to update it."

Clara dropped her touch to squeeze Medusa's hand. Physical affection was so natural for her, and Medusa realized how much she was liking it, another woman, a potential friend, touching her without worry or fear. As Callidora had done, so often and spontaneously.

She closed her eyes, feeling her friend curled around her in the bed at night, the two of them innocently nestling together like baby rabbits.

The feeling hurt, as it often did to remember her and the other priestesses, but fortunately Clara distracted her. "I wish you could have been here to see him get it done. It took the tattoo artist a few hours, and the outlining part can be a little brutal, especially for a design that intricate. John Pierce just sat there, so still. It was mesmerizing, as if he was mentally following every movement of the needle gun, tattooing the design inside him at the same time it was being put on the outside."

Clara nudged her. "Watching him sit there shirtless and in a pair of jeans wasn't a hardship, either. I think all the women of the Circus strolled by a couple times. Even Yvette."

"Was he...with any of them then?"

Clara gave her a puzzled look. "Of course not. Why would you..."

She saw a flicker in the young clairvoyant's eyes, as if in a heartbeat she'd picked up a variety of things. Though it seemed as if she'd been ready to say something far different, Clara shook her head. "No. He wasn't with any of them."

Medusa shifted uncomfortably. She didn't want to pursue what the woman had been about to say. She expected it would be something about John Pierce's devotion to her long before they met. He was always very straightforward about those feelings, and asked her for nothing in return, but for reasons she couldn't explain, she didn't want to hear it echoed by others.

Or perhaps Clara was going to tell her he had been "with" women in that way he'd described. "Subs" and "sessions" and "clubs." She didn't really want to hear about that, either.

They moved through a thick stand of trees. Showing her sensitivity to Medusa's mood shift, Clara returned to the previous tone of their conversation. She pointed out a small family of gnomes and a cadre of dragonflies that turned out to be pixie fairies.

"During breaks in the performances, Yvette will send them out to fly among the guests. It's so fun to see them realize what they are. She had to do some serious negotiating with the Fae world to let them be here, but Chi-la, the pixie who's kind of in charge of the rest, really wanted to be here, so Queen Rhoswen and King Tabor finally allowed it."

When they emerged from the woods, they were at another grassy clearing, a set of hills that layered into one another and were dotted with more trees. As she stood in their shadow, a few feet from Clara, Medusa saw a female horse coming out of another grove some distance ahead of them. She was stepping delicately toward a small pond that looked like a silver mirror. When Clara raised her hand to get her attention and the creature turned in their direction, Medusa saw the sunlight glint off the spiral silver horn.

Rand had implied that a unicorn was connected enough to the horse species to have some of their historical fears of wolves. Yet the qualities a unicorn possessed were similar to those which made Rand so clearly not a wolf, even in wolf form. The magic to what they were was probably even further enhanced in this in-between world. She wondered what kind of auras Charlie saw when she looked at a wolf versus Rand, or a horse next to a unicorn.

There was a glow on the edges of everything here, or a vibration, that said this place wasn't exactly the "real world." She'd have to ask John if he felt it, saw it, the way she did, or if she, being be-spelled herself, felt it more strongly.

The unicorn was prancing toward Clara, snorting, one brown eye lit with a kaleidoscope of colors from the reflection of sunlight. As she turned more in Medusa's direction, Medusa put her hand to her mouth, shock coursing through her. This *was* the unicorn from her dream. She was sure of it. She knew those movements, the patterns of light pink pigment around the nostrils...

Ratqueen rammed her cheek, agitated. Earthson, too, was pressing against her windpipe as if he didn't want her to move toward the unicorn. Treebark slid straight up her face as if he was going to cover her eyes. She was getting a jumble of impressions from them and the other snakes, a warning, but it didn't make sense.

Moving Treebark out of her line of sight, she stepped out of the cover of the trees, absently trying to soothe the snakes while her full attention remained on the unicorn. Her knees were trembling. She was overwhelmed, amazed, and her hand had lifted of its own accord, stretching toward the dream that had helped her so much. First, during those initial lonely days in the temple when she was sure her family had left her there because they didn't want her. Later, after Ukrit. Even though she didn't have the dreams anymore then, she could remember and hold onto them as a reminder of when times had been better.

Lianthe had nearly reached Clara. Yet as those liquid brown eyes shifted, registering Medusa, the pink-tinged nostrils flared. A shrill whinny burst from the creature and Lianthe wheeled, so violently that Clara started backwards to avoid being knocked aside by one gleaming flank.

"What? Lianthe, what's the matter? What...*Medusa*."

Medusa fell to the ground, pain exploding inside her head. The snakes were hissing, jerking her this way and that as they struck the air, seeing things no one else could see, hallucinations coming out of the bright lights flashing in her mind. Their agitation intensified the pain, their agony as piercing as her own scream.

She was being pulled down a tunnel, into a pit, a place she was sure she didn't want to go. But it was too late, all of it happening too fast. Darkness enclosed her, and then the screams started.

She knew who was screaming. It was her, those wailing, pleading shrieks laden with memories she'd never wanted to recall again.

They swallowed her alive, a rat caught in a snake's maw. She was trapped between the world of life and death.

Darkness was the only end for her.

CHAPTER TWENTY

"Come, Medusa." The man's eyes gleamed red, red as her own. As she reached out to him despite the vehement protest in her mind, she saw she had claws. Her tongue, dry in her mouth, was forked. Her snakes were limp, heavy weights pulling against her scalp. When she looked down, she saw Ratqueen and Tunneltrap lying on her breast. Their eyes had that odd cloudy look that all dead animals had, even humans.

None of these things could be true. Her snakes could be neither alive nor dead, because this man had happened to her before her transformation. Yet her wings flapped helplessly on her back as if they were vestigial, no power to get her away from this memory.

"I want to talk to the loveliest priestess ever to serve Athena," he said smoothly, his own forked tongue flickering at her. When it slithered up the side of her face, it cut like a knife. She touched her cheek, feeling afraid as she saw blood on her fingers. "Won't you come sit with me in the temple, away from the others?" he wheedled, the conceited light in his eye saying he knew she couldn't refuse him.

"No." She was trying to back away, but her body paid her no heed. She was walking along with him in jerky frames of images, as if she was phasing in and out of the memory. Her lips were stretched in a smile that felt like an infected wound as she chattered to him about the temple routine. His red eyes watched her. Waiting.

~

Lianthe galloped back to Clara, almost as fast as she'd tried to retreat from Medusa. Clara, kneeling at Medusa's side, looked up at the unicorn. Though Lianthe could speak in images in Clara's mind, what was there was too agitated to comprehend. But Lianthe could understand her. "Go get JP. She belongs to him. And Yvette and Charlie. Anyone who can help."

Lianthe's eyes were rolling with distress. Clara put a hand on the white foreleg. She had no idea what had spooked the unicorn or had caused Medusa to collapse, but Lianthe was the one still standing, so one of the others could figure out the creature's distress and how it connected to this. "Go now. Please."

The horse charged away, golden mane and tail streaming. Clara tumbled back on her backside as Medusa abruptly opened her eyes and shoved up onto her feet. She moved as swiftly as a ninja warrior, sprinting back into the trees. The glimpse Clara had of her face showed the woman's eyes were vacant, her mouth stretched in fear. Like she was sleepwalking in a nightmare.

Clara ran after her, but the woman was far too swift. Looking up, she saw a pair of the young dragons and whistled, drawing their attention. As they swooped down, she pointed.

"Don't lose sight of her. Help me—oh Goddess."

Medusa ran straight into a tree, which knocked her backwards to the ground, blood blooming on her forehead. Clara pounced on her, holding the young woman's wrists as she thrashed. She gritted her teeth as she lost a grip on one of them and Medusa struck her in the face in her unconscious state. Fuck, she was strong. If the blow hadn't been glancing, Clara was terrifyingly aware the other woman could have caused her real damage. She yelped and started back as the snake that looked covered with rough gray bark shot out at her with a hiss, warning her back.

Clara wished she had some of the powers the others possessed, super strength or speed. Medusa could kill her in this state, that was obvious. She was even now trying to scramble back to her feet, despite being dazed by hitting the tree. The boundary to their camp wasn't far away and Medusa was swift. If she stepped outside it, her eyes would become lethal again.

Clara still wasn't used to calling him for help. But now she opened her mind. *Marcellus, help. I'm over at—*

He landed next to her with a gust of wind strong enough to blow her hair back and ripple her skirt across the ground. His dark eyes took in everything at a glance, though she was already babbling.

"I can't calm her. When you try to hold her, the snakes attack. Lianthe went to get JP and Charlie. We need to calm her without holding her down, and I don't know how to do it. Can you do it?"

He knelt next to Medusa, still trying to stagger to her feet. His face was always so stern and impassive. He didn't smile or laugh as often as Clara wanted him to do, but she knew compassion ran deep in him, connected to the Goddess Herself. Showing no fear of the dancing and striking snakes, he laid his hand on Medusa's heart, his other over her forehead, and he spoke in a language Clara didn't know. Slowly, she sank to her knees on the ground, and toppled to her side, Marcellus easing her down. The snakes went down with her, coiling in uneasy figure eights around her head. They watched the angel suspiciously, their tongues flickering.

Medusa was still twitching, her eyes moving rapidly under her lids. As she drew up into a protective fetal position, she started whimpering, tiny, half whispered pleas that tore Clara's heart out. There were no words, but it was as if she was being harmed, and pleading for it to stop.

From the harsh look around Marcellus's mouth, she thought that was a pretty good assessment. His expression also told her he couldn't pull Medusa out of wherever she was. Knowing she was in no outward physical danger was small comfort.

"Can you tell where she is?" she asked Marcellus.

He raised somber eyes to her. "In a very bad place. She needs JP."

"Take her to him. Go. I'll follow."

He touched Clara's face, his thumb passing over the mark Medusa's fist had left. It was a light gesture that tingled across her lips and straight down into her heart.

"You are always finding trouble," he said.

"Lucky I have the best guardian angel my student insurance plan can afford."

His lips twisted and he tsked. Scooping Medusa up, he shot back into the sky.

~

When Ukrit was done, he left her. Just left her, there by the statue. She stared up at Athena through eyes clotted with tears. Her clothes were in tatters. Her body hurt in a million terrible ways. She'd fought. Why had she fought? He was a god, wasn't he? Or fueled by the power of a god. So had she now incurred the wrath of both Athena and Poseidon?

She was in such pain she was weeping without a conscious decision to cry. She wanted that dream back, the dream of the unicorn. It eluded her, but she tried to create it from the other times she'd dreamed of the fantasy. They were on a beautiful island, with a waterfall, and goats, and blue sky. The unicorn would lay down when the afternoon heat came and Medusa would lie against her, listening to her breath. She would scratch the unicorn's forehead around the horn, because it was itchy there. She'd run her fingers through the silken mane and tail.

Sometimes, at a distance, she'd see a man walking along the beach, in strange, snug blue pants. He was tall and broad-shouldered, and she liked the look of him. Her unicorn would watch with her, and would nudge her, as if encouraging her to go see him. But there was something sad in the unicorn's gaze. Medusa was afraid if she walked toward the man, when she looked back, the unicorn would be gone forever.

But now she was. Medusa finally knew why the unicorn had left her dreams, never to return. The unicorn only bonded with the innocent, and Ukrit had ripped that bond to shreds, taking the dreams of the innocent from her forever...

~

JP was already headed out with Lianthe, him at a dead run, her at a fast clip, when he saw Marcellus winging down toward them, Medusa in his arms.

"Put her down here," Yvette said, clearing off one of the scattered picnic tables. A mat was unrolled on the surface by Charlie, who'd appeared with her bag of herbs and healing aids. "What happened?" John demanded.

Lianthe whickered unhappily and the vampire turned her gaze to her. Yvette's brow creased. "She's too agitated. Charlie?"

Charlie turned to the unicorn, but she wasn't the only one who knew all languages, and Marcellus could apparently decipher them quicker. "Medusa had a dream bond with Lianthe," he said brusquely. "Before she was raped and transformed."

"Damn it," Yvette swore.

"What?" John looked between them. He slid a hip onto the table so he could cradle Medusa's upper body in his arms. She calmed somewhat at his touch, but she was still twitching and making a terrible repetitive keening noise, like a wounded animal. "Someone fucking tell me something. What the hell is going on?"

Yvette answered him while the unicorn stood at her side, looking as miserable as if her horn had been taken. "In your world, unicorns are no longer safe. You know this. But they still draw spiritual nourishment from bonds with the pure. So rather than venturing out into reality, they dwell in places like this and bond through dreaming. When the girl they choose grows up and lies with a man, they disappear from her dreams, a fond memory."

Yvette paused, her lips tightening. "If ever the unicorn should encounter the woman again, whether in dream or reality, in that first moment of eye contact she will relive the memory of her lost innocence in a way that is enhanced threefold. For most, that is a lovely or at worst poignant experience, innocence giving way to mature love, a natural part of the life cycle, the transition to womanhood. It's a gift the unicorn can give to her, but over which the unicorn has no control." Yvette took a breath. "But if the first sex is violent, a violation…"

John had already guessed where the explanation was going. A fervent curse slipped from his lips. "So she's reliving it, three times as bad as it was. As if it wasn't bad enough."

"There is no waking her until it is done," Charlie said, grief in her countenance as she put her hand on Medusa's brow. "All that can be done is what you are doing, John. Stay with her. Keep holding her. Some part of her may absorb your presence. While it won't stop the dream, it may make it more bearable."

"What if it twists what we have, makes it part of the nightmare?"

Medusa made a sharper noise of pain, and he cradled her even more gently, while still trying to hold her closer. "It's all right," he murmured. "I'm here. *I'm here.* Please..." Fucking God, he'd never felt so helpless, even when she'd been pulled away from him in the portal transition. But her fingers caught his shirt, held on tight, and he put his forehead against hers. The snakes bobbed and weaved around his head, as if exhorting him to fix this. That didn't make him feel any better.

"No. What is between you..." As he lifted his head in response to her words, he saw Charlie was studying him, telling him she was looking at the pattern of lights that both he and Medusa were emitting. "It is pure and cannot be twisted. If it can break through and help, it will, but it will not harm."

The healer turned her attention to the unicorn and laid her hand on the gleaming white shoulder. "Lianthe wishes to tell you how very sorry she is. She did not know Medusa was here. The chances that she would meet one face-to-face with whom she'd bonded..."

"Are astronomical," Clara finished, putting another comforting palm on the other side of Lianthe's neck. "Because obviously a dream bond isn't limited by time. She had no reason to think Medusa would show up here, in this exact time and place. It's okay, Lianthe. It will be okay. John will take care of her. She has faith in John. She'll pull through it and be okay."

John took hollow reassurance from Clara's declaration. He wanted to ask her if she was using her clairvoyance or speaking from her heart, but the answer to that was on the young woman's distraught face.

When Medusa whimpered again, he felt as if his chest was being crushed by a cruel god. It wasn't far from the truth. He couldn't look at the unicorn right now. It wasn't because he blamed her. It was because of what she represented, a time before Medusa had to face all this shit. Something should have protected her. He should have been with her, now, then, always. What he could have done, he had no damn idea, but he had to be pissed at someone. Himself was his best choice. "Once she lives through the dream once, will it happen again?" he asked Charlie roughly.

Charlie paused, digesting whatever Lianthe communicated to her. "No. After the initial contact, there is no danger of it."

John took a breath. "So she could come and see Lianthe afterward?"

"Yes." Yvette studied Medusa's unconscious form, sympathy in the tight set of her mouth. "You think she would want to do so?"

"I know it. She remembered those dreams when things were at the roughest for her. They helped." Medusa would want him to say this, he knew. Would want him to help relieve the agony in the unicorn's eyes. Since he couldn't do a damn thing for Medusa except helplessly hold her, it was something.

Lianthe looked somewhat bolstered by that news, though Clara kept stroking her mane. "She says she'd like that," Charlie said.

"Take Medusa to my quarters," Yvette said brusquely, though she swept John with a look of approval. "Once there, everyone should clear out except Marcellus, who should please stay just outside until it is over, in case JP has need of anything. JP, my living space is yours as long as she needs it. You'll find it more comfortable, and the spells on it are strong and may also help pull her from her dreams sooner."

"If anyone can do that, it is you," Charlie told him, reaching out to put a small but reassuring hand on his forearm. "There are things that only love can heal."

"Okay." In a crisis, John was about action, not talk. As he lifted Medusa in his arms, his mind was already working on ways to bring her out of that fucking nightmare she shouldn't be having to endure again.

Sooner rather than later. Or it was going to destroy him as much as it could her.

Ukrit had come back. Oh Goddess, why had he come back? The first time, he'd left her there, bloody and broken, and that was the end of it. She'd never thought she'd consider that a blessing, but when he came back to do it all over again, she knew she'd choose the reality over this nightmare, which seemed endless.

And she couldn't move, she couldn't get away. She screamed at herself to fight, to resist, yet her body refused to do anything but lie limply, be his victim. Her tears and cries to *stop, please stop* were the only resistance she offered. She hated that worst of all. She hated the way his brutality made her his possession.

I do not belong to you. She knew who held her heart and soul, and she would not suffer Ukrit's trespass upon his territory any more than he would if he were here now. And oh Goddess, she wanted him here now. She shattered, splitting into pieces. She left that broken girl on the ground and stepped outside herself. She tore herself loose from the bindings of mind and soul, from her past and origins. She stood raw and exposed, a newborn created out of blood and necessity.

There were ceremonial blades embedded in the stone below the sculpture of Athena. She hadn't remembered them there before, but John had told her the story of the boy king and the sword in the stone. As Ukrit thrust into that poor girl, she ripped one free, never doubting her ability to do it, and plunged the blade into his back. Pulled it out, took a two-fisted hold on the hilt and began to swing it like an ax. To hack, to maim, to destroy and kill. Nothing had ever felt so good. Nothing would ever feel as good as taking life, exercising that ultimate power as a defiance against ever being weak, or the target of cruelty or ignorance.

But as she hacked and blood sprayed and flesh came loose, the scene changed. The temple vanished. She stood on her beach, sword in hand. Looking down at herself, she saw she was covered in blood. Pulling off the ruined tunic, she threw it from her and stood in the sunlight, breathing hard. She was home. It was okay. It was okay.

A movement caught her attention. The man, walking along the beach. He stopped, looked her way and raised a hand. As he came toward her, she retrieved the sword and stood ready to use it. When he was close enough, he looked at the sword.

"It worked," he said. "You freed yourself."

Fastening steady eyes on her, he shed his own clothes. As he pulled off the shirt that clung to his powerful upper body, he gave her an inviting look and walked into the waves, letting the surf wash over him. She saw a tattoo on his back, in brilliant colors of green, black and red. A tattoo of her face, the snakes curled around it in a way that looked fantastic and appealing, not monstrous. Yet her gaze was captured not so much by that as by the ripple of muscle along his back, the shift of his buttocks, the lengths of his muscled thighs. She saw marks upon him, scars of his battles.

He moved out waist deep and ducked under, coming back up to smooth wet-slick hair to his skull. As he turned to her, his gray eyes like a storm, like the bark of a tree, like the color of sand in the dawn light, met hers. Her body had responded when she looked at his. But when she looked into his eyes, deeper things responded to what she saw there. Her resolve trembled through her arm, through her grip.

She dropped the sword.

Walking into the waves, she went to him, where he already had his hand outstretched. Her claws were gone again. Now just her fingers closed around his. She was human. She didn't need the claws, because that girl cowering inside her soul, hiding behind the monster her fellow priestesses had created to defend her until she could stand on her own again, was standing. She was washing herself clean, and she was taking the hand of a man who understood all of it. Who would never hurt or betray her.

"Ukrit wasn't the first man to take your body," the man in the waves said. "I was. Wasn't I, snake-girl? Who did you give yourself to first? That's all that matters."

The question was vitally important. She could feel it, to the depths of her soul.

"You," she whispered. "John."

John Pierce was the man to whom she'd given herself, willingly. Who'd cherished such a gift the way it was meant to be cherished.

So she drew closer to him in the waves, twined her legs around his hips and framed his face between her two hands. She lost herself in the look in his eyes, swam there the same way they floated in the surf together. He waited on her to make the next move, though he could be demanding when she desired it. Needed it. She pressed trembling lips to his and made a noise when his arms circled her, his mouth opening beneath hers.

There was no pain anymore. She wasn't that broken girl. She was Medusa, on her island. When she kissed John, something swept through him, a release of tension so strong it seemed like joyous relief, as if she'd given him another gift, too priceless to be measured. He paused in the kiss, as if surprised by something, but then he smiled the smile of a sexy angel and kept kissing her, holding her close, bringing their bodies together. She could feel his sex brushing her thighs, and he was ready, as was she. She didn't have to let him go.

Adjusting her hips, he did the same and slid between the slick petals of her sex.

Dropping her head back, she moaned as he kissed her throat, her collar bone, the top of her breast. Her nipples were tight in the cool water, but he warmed them with his mouth as she spread her arms out to either side and floated. His powerful body was taking her on a slow build like the surf itself, rising up and up. His cock was thick, providing the right amount of friction, filling her, making her feel whole and connected to him in a way she knew wouldn't end when he broke the physical connection.

She arched, conveying her willingness to give him all of herself, her legs locked over his pumping buttocks. She savored the increase in his grip on her hips, more evidence of his male desire, and parted her lips, tasting the salt.

"Oh..." Her response was climbing even higher, with his. Levering herself back up in his arms, she wound her own around him, pressing her face against the side of his head.

"I'm here," he murmured. "I'm here, Medusa. I've been here since the first time I read your story. I would have arrived sooner if I could."

No. He'd come for Medusa, the woman she'd become, not the girl she'd been. That girl wouldn't have seen in him what she saw. What she felt. For all the pain, anger and rage, life unfolded as it unfolded. Sometimes, at the other end of strife and blood, pain and loss, there was this. Love. It made up for so much.

"Thank you," she whispered. "Please. Take me home. Take me deep inside yourself, and inside myself, where home can never be taken away."

He gripped her hair and captured her mouth in a kiss that went on and on, as their climax built and crested together. Eventually the kiss broke but their mouths were still together, his moving over her lips, the corner of her mouth and chin. Hers did the same to him as they cried out their mutual pleasure.

"Goddess, blessed Goddess. Thank you." It was the first time she'd given homage to Athena since she'd left the temple, but it was time. Athena wasn't a bland, apathetic statue in a temple with a faint, neutral smile on her face. No. She was the warrior, the huntress, the strong woman who stood for justice. She didn't smile. She bared her teeth in savage threat to her foes, she had a somber face full of compassion and terrible knowledge for those in pain. Her touch was a kind but rough-palmed brush of fingers against the forehead, a blessing that could not be taken away, no matter what challenge was faced.

The statue couldn't give Medusa anything, but the Goddess did. The strength to survive, to conquer. To love. That was the ultimate victory over Ukrit and any other in the world who tried to steal joy and leave only fear and darkness behind.

The ocean and island disappeared, but John did not. They were in a gray fog again, like when Maddock was bringing them to Lady Yvette's Circus. But the fog cleared, and she was lying in a bed that reminded her of thick strata of clouds on the horizon. There were beautiful hangings on the pavilion walls around the bed, tapestries in rich golds, reds and blues, showing giants marching, dragons breathing fire, unicorns prancing...

Unicorns. She saw those brilliant liquid kaleidoscope eyes again, the white horse wheeling, trying to run before...

Medusa snapped out of the dream as if she'd been shoved, as if she thought she might be sucked back to the beginning if she stayed. She was aware of the strong arms holding her loosening, helping her sit up. She was naked, faintly damp with perspiration and panting with sexual release, her heart still thumping. It was a peculiar mix of sensations, rolled into the nightmare that had evolved back into a dream. A wide palm was stroking her back. A familiar, wonderful hand.

"I thought I'd imagined it," she managed, her throat rusty as if she hadn't spoken in days.

"No. I wasn't sure it would work. Did it?"

She closed her eyes, remembering John's hands and mouth upon her, his cock stroking inside of her. He'd taken the nightmare and channeled it, spiraling it into something different.

"Yes. I think it did." Then she began to cry, and she realized that was why her throat was so thick. She'd been screaming, crying, sobbing. Oh, Goddess.

He moved her, stretched her back out on the bed, and put himself upon her, arms surrounding her, sheltering her from the storm of emotion. She slid her hands over his broad back, digging her nails into the tattoo, the significant words in its center. As she shifted her grip, she felt the scratches she'd put on him the first time he'd taken her body. She pressed her face into his chest, ironically finding more air for her lungs that way than if he'd given her more space.

"I'm here," he said. "I'm here."

His voice was hoarse, too. Lifting her head, she stared at him through her tears. His face was ravaged, as if he'd been through a battle with demons. Her demons. She placed her hands on his face as she had in the waves. "Thank you," she whispered. "I'm all right. I promise."

He pressed his forehead to hers, running his hands up and down her upper arms as a tremor went through his big body. "I knew you would be. I know you're strong. But seeing you suffer, and not being able to stop it? I'd rather endure anything but that."

"At the very beginning, before Klotho changed me, I thought I wouldn't survive," she whispered. "But the transformation, the eyes, the claws, the strength and speed of my wings, made me stronger. Made me believe I was protected." She started to shake. "The nightmare took that away. I was like this, but he still did it."

"No, nothing was taken away." He gripped her and stilled her trembling. "It wasn't real, Medusa."

"I know," she said, with a weary smile. "It changed. Things changed in the dream. Because of you. Because of me. Who I am now."

"A lot of things changed in the dream." He leaned down and pressed his lips lightly against hers. The tip of his tongue played along her lips, then her teeth, her tongue...

Her tongue. It was like his. And her fangs were gone. Her hand flew up between them to see, to touch and be sure. She bumped his chin, hard.

"Ow."

She laughed, she couldn't help it, and then she couldn't stop laughing. It wasn't that funny, but the surfeit of emotion chose to escape that way. He held her as she shook, cried and laughed, pressing her cheek against his chest and shoulder.

At length she became quiet, and he continued to hold her without speaking. Until she was ready to speak.

"Do you think the spell is losing its strength as time goes on?" she asked. "Or because we are in another place, far away from my time?"

"Maybe." He answered carefully. "Was there a moment in your

dream where you had to make a choice between being with me and... staying caught up in what was happening?"

"Yes." She met his gaze, suddenly understanding, though he finished his theory.

"You lost the claws when you trusted me enough to follow me into the portal," he said. "Maybe major turning points for you and me are breaking the ties of the spell. Piece by piece."

One aspect of that alarmed her. She could still feel her wings, but she swiftly put her hands to her head, searching for her snakes. They weren't moving.

"John...oh Goddess." The vision of them limp and dead flashed through her mind, but John caught her wrists, squeezing them in reassurance.

"They're fine. Yvette spelled them to unconsciousness until you woke again, because they were channeling your agitation from the nightmare. They were sensible enough not to hurt anyone, but we thought it was kinder to put them out. She can wake them up whenever you're ready."

As he helped her sit up again, she moved her fingers over their curious arrangement. They were coiled up and secured in some type of thin netting.

"Charlie's idea," he told her. "She said if you could talk them into staying like that when you want to go out around other humans, you could cover them with a hat or scarf."

It was a warm feeling, thinking of Charlie providing her snakes small nests and suggesting outings into John's world, as if no one had had any doubt that she would surface and be fine. She was fine. She was still shaking, and she desperately wanted to immerse herself in a clean body of water to scrub herself with soap and remove every vestige of the nightmare, but she was okay. She hadn't fled the dream. She'd walked out of it on her own two feet, so to speak, vibrating with the pleasure she and John had made, her lifeline back to the world.

"I'd like that. I want to go to Starbuck's."

He blinked. "What?"

"It was in the magazine you gave me. Many pretty, smiling people go to Starbuck's. And their coffees are delicious, the best in the world."

He chuckled. "Okay, yeah, Starbuck's has some good stuff, but keep in mind those pretty pictures are no different from the barkers in the marketplace. I know you said slaves went and bought things, but maybe you saw them when you were going somewhere with the priestesses?"

"Yes." She brightened. A mundane memory was a good tonic to help her level out, and she wondered if John realized that. "I remember seeing a man selling a woman several beautiful scarves. They appeared to be arguing, but the slave with us said they were just bartering. It was nothing to be alarmed about."

"Right. I bet every guy selling scarves in the marketplace says he has the most beautiful ones. And smiles the whole time, even if he has a bad rash that makes him want to snarl like a bear."

When she figured out the comparison, she dimpled. "I understand. But I still want to go to Starbuck's."

"We'll do it, as soon as we get some kind of word from Maddock on what the status is with MyTech and any other threats against you. Not until then. I won't risk you for a cup of overpriced coffee."

She was going to tease him about whether or not she was worth the risk if the coffee wasn't overpriced, but then another thought struck her.

"The unicorn." She sat straight up, remembering anew. "Is she okay? This didn't hurt her in any way, did it?"

"She's fine. Promise." John adjusted on the bed so he was behind her, his arms around her, cupping her breast and waist. His thighs framed her, legs long enough his feet brushed the floor on either side of hers. It was a secure feeling, and she sighed, settling back into his arms. It was okay. Everything was all right.

"I told her you'd want to see her," he said. "She was pretty broken up about what happened." Briefly, he explained what had triggered the nightmare, and how it wouldn't happen again.

"I need to tell her that it came back to the right place," she said, gazing up into his face. "I realized being with you truly was my first time, and then, we were in the waves. As euphoric as our first time was, this was as if we were both flying. I came to you in the ocean," she said, when a quizzical look crossed his face. "I wish you had been there, because it was beautiful."

"It was beautiful on this side as well," he said, nuzzling her throat. "Feeling your body respond to mine. At the beginning, fuck, you were struggling a bit, and I was afraid all I was doing was adding to it. I was going to give up, and then you got all still, lifted your hand and put it in mine..."

She turned in his arms and he adjusted her so she was straddling him, her knees pressing into the bed as she faced him. He framed her neck with his big hands. "It was..." He swallowed. "You came back to me."

She remembered the moment in the waves. "Yes. I knew I was not his. I am yours.""

Raw emotion flashed across his strong features. "There's nothing I'd like better," he said.

There was so much weight to their words. Feeling fragile, she looked around the room. "Where are we?"

"Lady Yvette's quarters. She wanted to make sure you had the maximum amount of comfort. Don't let that fool you. She's still scary."

"I know. But a scary woman can still be compassionate." She took a breath and drew herself up, laying her hands over his. "Just as a strong woman can face down her fear and turn a nightmare into a dream." When the right man stood at her back.

"Yeah, she can," John said, drawing her close again. "I had no doubt. Not now, not ever."

CHAPTER TWENTY-ONE

*S*he'd bathed, and in far greater comfort than she'd expected. She'd planned to take a shower at their wagon, but when John told Marcellus what she was needing, they were told to stay where they were. A big porcelain claw foot tub sometimes used as a prop for the clown act was brought to Yvette's quarters and filled with heated water. Medusa scrubbed herself thoroughly and then John lifted the washcloth and stroked her from head to toe, leaving her floating and semi-aroused. He also washed her hair, his fingers massaging her scalp and the snakes taking up residence on the tub sides to avoid the suds and full immersion as long as they could before he had to pour water over her head to rinse her.

After helping her, John told her to enjoy a soak in the tub. He would visit the outdoor shower at their wagon and then rejoin her.

Charlie had provided her a flowing dress with a halter back for her wings that was hanging up on a clothes rack in the corner. As she looked at it, Medusa could already imagine how the weightless fabric would float over her curves and swirl around her calves. John would like it, as would she.

It mystified her, the kindness relative strangers were showing to her. But while she laid back in the tub, letting the hot water permeate her muscles, she thought it over and understood it.

So many here were outcasts from normal society. Some had no choice in the matter because they were unable to blend, like Merc or

Charlie. Vampires could mix with humans, but they had to pretend to be human, so had obvious reasons for preferring supernatural company. Then there were those who simply did not feel connected to the mainstream consciousness, like Caleb. On first meeting him, she'd found the strongman exceptionally quiet. When he spoke, he had trouble forming words, perhaps some type of speech handicap. Clara had told her he was far more comfortable in an environment like this, where his reticence was accepted and no pressure was put upon him to talk more than he desired. He had a story, and she was sure it was an interesting one.

If she so chose, as long as Yvette was willing, she could learn all their stories. Become part of this family. They understood what being truly different meant, and depending on one another was the only way they'd not only survive, but find a quality of life worth embracing.

Once she dried off, she donned the dress and tidied up as much as possible to prepare to return to their own wagon. A short visit and hug from Clara was a welcome surprise, along with the young woman's invitation to join her tomorrow in the Circus's daily routine. A not-so-subtle way of helping Medusa feel less self-conscious about what had happened.

"Something crazy and dramatic happens here almost daily," Clara had told her with a wink as she took her leave. "Today was just your turn."

Medusa didn't want to overstay their welcome in Yvette's tent and truth, after Clara's visit, she was feeling almost...energized. She might crash soon and need a good, long nap, but for the moment she was still riding the high of defeating Ukrit once and for all. No more nightmares for her, damn it.

She decided to emerge from Yvette's lush pavilion and see if its owner was nearby so she could thank the vampire courteously for its use. She didn't have to look far—but she did have to duck.

"Heads up!" The bellow came from one of the "roustabouts", the workmen who helped with a variety of things, including the Circus show setup and breakdowns. He and a knot of other men appeared to have been playing a card game. Near where they were warily grouped, upended crates and strewn cards were spread out in a random crescent shape, as if the men had scattered in all directions when a...

The ball of flame whizzed by a few feet in front of her, that and the warning pressing her back into the tent entrance. A wave of heat from the opposite direction manifested into a temporary shield of blue energy as the ball hit it, then sprayed out into sparks.

The man behind the blue sparks was a handsome male scowling in a dangerous way. As the projectile came toward him, he'd thrown up an arm, producing the glowing blue defense that protected him from its impact. Now he said something caustic and returned fire, a spear of the same white-blue energy, like a lightning bolt.

She gasped as she saw Yvette brace for that impact, but instead of shielding herself as the man had done, the vampire sorceress caught the haft of the spear on a spin as she moved out of its path and turned toward it. Medusa saw a brief flash of red flame from her palms, as if she'd shielded herself from harm before clasping the magical weapon. It morphed in her hands, split into strands and swirled around her, turning into a whip of fire with serpent heads that snapped along the ground as she advanced on the male.

Medusa remembered John saying they'd been doing dress rehearsals tonight, and Yvette looked like it, in an astonishing outfit of thigh-high boots, a laced corset and snug sleek pants similar to what Gundar had been wearing the other night. The vampire wore the outfit so naturally, it could have been normal garb for her. But Medusa suspected this was not part of the dress rehearsal. Yvette's next words confirmed it.

"You owe me, Maddock," she said ominously. The whip popped. The sound was like a clap of thunder, similar to the thing John had called a gun when they were attacked on the island. When the whip snaked out and popped again within inches of Maddock's face, Medusa was surprised the scientist-wizard, as John often called him, didn't flinch. He also didn't throw up a shield this time. He sneered instead.

"Oh, bullshit. I've done you plenty of favors. What about the spell craft that surrounds half this camp?"

"You contributed here and there." Yvette sniffed. "But those workings were due primarily to my efforts. And Mikhael Roman's."

"Roman? That humorless fossil who refuses to accept science has anything to do with magic? I had the piece you were both missing. Your protections wouldn't be half as strong without my input."

"That fossil is mated now."

"No shit?" Maddock straightened, the hostility disappearing from his face. "I heard he'd hooked up with some half-succubus witch, but didn't know it had gotten that serious. Have they—ow, *fuck*."

He snarled as the whip snaked past his guard and wrapped his arm. Yvette did a quick jerk to loosen it, but as it fell away it left a ring of singed skin. The wizard hopped around, cursing and waving his forearm to cool its effect.

Yvette brought the serpent-head tails back into a coil in her hand. A blink later the whip was gone, the energy dissipated.

"There. Payment made. Though it would have been so much more satisfying on your bare ass. Or those beautiful naked shoulders and back."

"Yeah, dream on, Mistress Psycho. Son of a bitch, that hurt."

"Oh, don't be such a baby." Yvette scowled. "Charlie will put a poultice on it."

She strode across the ground to close the distance between them. Bemused, Medusa noticed the roustabouts returning to their card game, shaking their heads and chuckling, but otherwise undisturbed by the sudden battle or its equally quick conclusion.

Yvette clasped Maddock's wrist and lifted the arm to examine the mark. When he tried to pull one of her braids with his free hand, she slapped it away without even looking toward it. She tutted. "I've left worse on my servants. You're right, we wouldn't suit, even if you did butter your bread on the sub side. You're far too intolerant of pain."

"Thank God for small favors." He rolled his eyes. Despite the violent tone of a moment ago, the two now seemed affable. Medusa pushed warily away from the tent side, but remained where she was, watching. "So what was that with the whip?" Maddock asked the vampire. "That was a pretty bit of pyrotechnics."

"And heavily flavored with irony. I was seeking to emulate the flame whip wielded by the Balrog when he fought another meddling wizard."

Maddock snorted. "Woman, you're a closet geek. Where's JP? I've info he'll need and I'd like you to sit in on it."

"He's cleaning up. He'll be out soon enough, but there's someone else here you might want to meet." Yvette turned toward Medusa, showing she'd been aware of her presence all along.

"Medusa." Maddock brightened as soon as his gaze lighted upon her.

When he moved toward her, she finally had time to gain a physical impression of the man who'd brought John Pierce to her. He was tall like John, but not broad and wide. His whipcord leanness didn't suggest weakness, though. He emanated power on both the physical and magical side, suggesting he could have made the disagreement with Yvette far more acrimonious. Yvette was no fool, so Medusa concluded the vampire knew how powerful the wizard was, but also how far he'd restrain himself in the interest of fairly resolving a dispute. Especially if they were wary friends, as seemed to be the case.

The wizard's eyes were hazel, a mix of gray, green and gold. A black silken moustache and close-cropped beard followed his well-shaped jaw. His dark hair fell to his shoulders. He looked Persian to her, or from a country in that region. He wore the type of clothes John seemed to favor, jeans and short-sleeved shirts with pictures on the front, but from what John had told her of the Merlin character in the Arthurian tale, she liked the idea of a flowing cape and jeweled scepter better. The fluid way he moved suggested it would be a good look for him.

"Maddock," he said in introduction, extending a hand. Medusa was learning the gestures John and his kind favored for greetings, and was secretly proud of herself for not hesitating to take the hand and give it a healthy pump, which seemed to amuse Maddock. His hand was rough with calluses, which surprised her. As she'd told John Pierce, her experience with the demands of spell work were similar to what was required of an apothecary, mostly measuring and preparing ingredients.

"I am Medusa," she said courteously.

"Yeah, I know." He smiled, and it was a nice gesture, though it didn't detract from the sharpness of his eyes. He was studying her avidly, as if taking in every detail about her appearance. With faint alarm, she remembered what John had said about his capacity to ask endless questions. But such was the nature of a man of learning. When Klotho had met with scholars and philosophers, sometimes she and Callidora spied upon them during their prolonged discussions. His look of intense curiosity toward her reminded her of them.

"Thank you for making it possible for John Pierce to come to my island," she said.

"Well, the usual superheroes were all booked, so he was all we could scrape from the bottom of the barrel."

At her blank look, he grinned. "Sorry, you're still learning lingo, I know. Seriously, it was his will that did most of the work. I was just lucky enough to find someone crazy enough to believe my theories. Or crazy enough about the woman behind them to make that leap through the portals."

She blinked, warmed by the bald assessment. "It is still hard for me to believe he did that for someone he has never met."

"Most of us find our heart's desires in dreams and stories first, right?" He met her gaze. "The difference was, he's the exceptional kind of individual willing to jump into the story to meet them."

Maddock lifted her hand and examined it. "This is new. Your claws..."

"They are gone. As are my fangs. And my tongue is no longer transformed." She opened her mouth briefly to show him, since he looked as if he might pry her lips open to check before he recalled himself. "John Pierce can perhaps speak better to it, but he thinks..."

She wasn't sure how to proceed but Yvette, silently standing by and listening, helped. "He thinks it's a pivotal act of trust between her and him that's doing it. She lost the claws when she followed him through the portal. The teeth and tongue happened after an adventure today, but same issue. An act of trust occurred."

Medusa was grateful to Yvette for not going into the details and inclined her head to the vampire. Yvette blinked in acknowledgement. "Do you miss the fangs?" she asked.

"They did not serve the same purpose as yours," Medusa said. "Mine were intended, I think, merely for intimidation."

Standing next to Yvette, it seemed ludicrous to imply Medusa was intimidating. Her lethal gaze might strike terror in her foes because of what they knew it could do, but Yvette was purely terrifying. Medusa tried not to shift uncomfortably under the vampire and wizard's regard.

"That is not the question I asked," Yvette said. Maddock shot her a look, but Yvette's statement was neutral, not hostile. Medusa understood. The vampire was a literal kind of being.

"Oh, my apologies, my lady. You're right. I'm still deciding if I miss my claws and fangs. I'm glad in some ways, to be more 'normal,' but since I've arrived here, my definition of that has expanded. And I'm not sure if I want to be considered 'normal.'"

"Many here wish they could switch it on and off, the abilities they have. Not deny that part of themselves, but not always have to worry about concealing it in a world that doesn't understand them."

"I understand that greatly. I meant no offense," Medusa said courteously.

"No, you didn't. I think you meant it as a compliment to my Circus, and I appreciate it."

Charlie had arrived, evidently summoned by her mind-link with Yvette. Interestingly, Medusa noticed she hesitated before approaching Maddock, and executed her deferential head dip toward him before drawing close. "Lady Yvette said you had a wound that needed my tending?"

"She shouldn't have bothered you. It's less than nothing."

Medusa lifted her brows in Yvette's direction, as the vampire rolled her eyes.

"Still, perhaps I should look at it."

"All right. I might grab a plate of grub from those heaven-blessed ladies in the kitchen while we're waiting on JP. Want to join me? I'll buy you lunch."

Medusa became even more curious about the situation as Charlie flushed under Maddock's intent gaze. "The food is free."

"I know that. I was making a joke. You're spending too much time around Yvette. Let me reintroduce you to a sense of humor."

"Dry wit and sarcasm do not a sense of humor make," Yvette intoned. "Charlie, do not blush around this fool."

Which made Charlie blush worse and Maddock's eyes narrow on Yvette. Medusa thought it did unnecessarily draw attention to the healer's embarrassment, but she wasn't privy to their history and wasn't sure how to alleviate her discomfort.

"JP." Maddock saw John making his way toward them through the tents at nearly the same moment Medusa did. Fortunately, it broke the tension between Maddock and Yvette and drew attention away from Charlie.

Maddock looked pleased to see her champion. When John Pierce was close enough, the wizard clasped his hand warmly. For her part, Medusa was bemused to experience a surge of relief, as if a part of her had been missing until he returned. When she inhaled his damp, clean skin, Medusa wanted to slide closer to him and have him touching her in some way, but it seemed the inappropriate time to seek such contact. Fortunately, John Pierce didn't seem to think so. As soon as he released Maddock's hand, he shifted to her side, cupping his hand over her hip in a familiar way that encouraged her to lean against him.

Threading her hand around his waist, she shyly slid a finger in the belt loop of his jeans. He brushed a kiss over her forehead, and gave her a look that suggested he was pleased with her increasing the contact between them.

"You look like the tropics agreed with you," Maddock continued, though she saw him tracking the intimacy between them with those sharp eyes. "I'm in the lab working my ass off on formulas and spells, and you're out getting a tan."

John snorted, taking Medusa's other hand to link them in front of their bodies. "I assume you've met my lady Medusa."

"Yes. Despite Yvette trying to kill her with a shot of friendly fire."

"She was in no danger. The spell was tailored specifically to fry *your* sensitive parts."

John grinned. "Still have your usual way with females, I see."

Maddock chuckled, but then he sobered. "We need to talk. All of us." He included Yvette and Medusa in his gesture.

"We will go back into my tent," Yvette said. "Charlie will come with us so she can tend the hurt on your arm. Then you can take her back through the portal to the lunch you promised. To a restaurant where you have to pay for the meal," she added.

"But I love the cornbread the ladies make here," Maddock protested as Charlie mumbled something about him not having to put himself out for her.

"She likes Italian food," Yvette said, ignoring them both. "There is an excellent bistro within a few miles of your home, if I recall. Quiet, so it won't be too much of an overload for her sensitivities."

When Charlie would have said something else, Yvette looked in her direction. The healer subsided instantly. John had said a vampire could speak in a second marked servant's mind, and Medusa wondered what she'd said, because Charlie had two spots of color high in her cheeks. Whereas Maddock's expression suggested both conflict and desire.

She glanced up at John, but his slight headshake told her it was a topic for another time. Unfortunately, they had weightier issues to discuss.

Inside Yvette's tent, Maddock took a seat in a velvet and mahogany chair, indicating he'd been here often enough to be familiar with his surroundings.

John sat across from him and gestured Medusa onto a nearby stool. Yvette went to another velvet and intricately carved chair in a shadowed corner of the tent, which made her present for the conversation but left the focus for Maddock's explanation on John Pierce. Charlie knelt at Maddock's feet to treat his arm.

"MyTech's attempt to take Medusa on her home ground failed, fortunately." He grimaced at John Pierce. "As you suspected, it was another hacking attempt, rather than a genuine mastering of the entry and exit spells for the portal. I've not only doubled the fail safes on the accesses, but now have monitoring spells—trip wires if you will—to give us even more of a heads up if there's anything unusual happening at the ones we know about. And Lot is heading up another team working overtime to identify as many as possible beyond what we already know. We're taking nothing on assumption going forward. Time to get way more aggressive with these assholes."

Yvette and John Pierce made noises of approval at that and Maddock lifted a shoulder. "It was still my fuck-up, though, and I'm sorry for that. To both of you." He encompassed Medusa and John Pierce in his somber look.

"Yeah, enough with the excuses." John waved a hand. "I damn well expect you to be God. So don't make any more mistakes like a normal human and let me down."

As Maddock met John's deadpan gaze, his expression eased, his lips tugging in a near smile. "I'll keep that in mind."

He returned to the discussion. "My guess is MyTech realizes I've upped the game on the portals, so they're back to their strategy of trying to get at her from this side. My spies tell me they have the word out to every dark world spirit and lowlife human that can be bought to find her. They're watching a lot of my haunts, and comings and goings. At this point, they haven't thought of the Circus, so she should be safe with you."

"What is it they want from me?" Medusa asked.

"Your eyes," Maddock said bluntly. "They want to figure out how they work and weaponize them. Truth? MyTech isn't evil, not on its face. There are plenty of people who work in their rank and file labs who probably think they're on the verge of curing cancer. If you were willing to meet with their corporate recruiters for the paranormal, they'd probably set you up in some cushy, luxurious place that didn't look a thing like a prison. They'd give you a personal escort to Rodeo Drive and a fistful of credit cards to go shopping, whatever you wanted."

Since Charlie was still examining ointments from her case of medical remedies, he leaned forward, clasping his hands. "Until the day came that the tests they were running started to be more invasive and destructive to you. When you decided you were no longer into being their lab rat, things would turn a lot uglier. Your free will is a moot point to them. You just had the opportunity to see that faster than most, thanks to their attempt to steal you off your island."

"Why are you telling me this?"

"Because I'm not discounting that they might be considering a whole lot of ways to get to you and, if they do get access, they might try persuasion and bribery first. They'll tell you that I don't have your best interests at heart, that I'm just using you, or you'd be safer with a professional, high tech op like theirs with billions of dollars of resources. Rather than a fly-by-night wizard working out of his mom's basement. It's a really nice basement," he added, with a half-smile. "And she bakes."

"Great cakes," John agreed. "And blackberry cobbler."

Charlie was slathering something on Maddock's arm now, a pungent poultice. He glanced down at her bent head as she did it, and Medusa noted the flare of his nostrils as he inhaled the scent. She wondered if he was reacting to the poultice or the smell of Charlie's hair, though the wizard seemed a hundred percent present in their conversation.

Medusa glanced at Yvette. The vampire's expression was unreadable. Her legs were crossed, two fingernails of one hand tapping the armrest of her chair. Click, click. Click, click.

"Lady Yvette." Medusa drew her attention. "Do you think Maddock has my best interests at heart?"

If the vampire found the question unexpected, she didn't show it. Maddock said nothing, his expression dispassionate.

Lady Yvette studied the wizard, then looked toward Medusa. "I think men of magic and science often let their goals cloud their conscience. They rationalize that what they do is for the greater good, and so the ends will justify the means. They overlook that there is an energy in this world far more important than any scientific or magical advancement, and that energy is the collective soul of all life forms. Without a respect and love for it, a tender caring that comes so easily to one like Charlie because of her gifts, and so much harder for the rest of us, we can lose our souls in the pursuit of things that only *seem* more important than that."

Her gaze moved back to Maddock. "MyTech is one of those lost in the fog. Maddock...is not. His original vision, why John was sent to you, had to do with his romantic soul, his desire to right wrongs done to individual hearts, in order to help heal that collective energy. It is an ambitious and nebulous idea that most people think is hopelessly idealistic. I am one of those. But it does not mean I don't wish him to prove me wrong."

Surprise flashed across Maddock's face, followed by an emotion he quickly masked. He inclined his head to her. "Thank you, Lady Yvette."

In his serious expression, Medusa thought she glimpsed the range of capabilities that he possessed. They were far deeper, more convoluted and dark than his casual demeanor indicated. But beyond Yvette's opinion and Medusa's own impressions, she knew John Pierce trusted this male with her life. And she thought she now understood John's heart enough to realize his trust on that point was not so easily won.

"Very well," Medusa said to Maddock. "I trust my wellbeing to your care."

Maddock cleared his throat and looked toward John. "I'm starting to get why you like this girl so much."

"She's an incomparable woman," John said softly. "And I love her."

Medusa met his gaze. When he held out his hand, she came to him. She sank to her knees at his feet, leaving her hand knotted with his on his thigh as she looked up at him. "I told you the same in my dream, John Pierce," she whispered. "If you did not hear me say it with my lips, I said it with my heart."

His jaw flexed as he cupped her face and stroked her hair away from it. She saw those shadows come back into his eyes and wondered if he doubted her. Doubted that she knew her own mind, because of all those few choices he felt she had had. She opened her mouth, then closed it, knowing it was the wrong moment for the discussion.

"Our timing sucks," he murmured. "Let's remember this conversation when we're done here, okay?"

She agreed, and stayed where she was, shifting so she was leaning against John's legs and facing Maddock. "What is it you suggest we do for the foreseeable future?" she asked the wizard.

"Stay with the Circus," Maddock said, his expression suggesting John's admission had stirred him in some indefinable way. Medusa wondered if he knew his hand had fallen upon Charlie's shoulder, his fingers stroking her collarbone where her scooped neck top provided that access. She was certain Charlie was aware of it. "I hope making that a permanent residence will be a choice for you to discuss with Yvette in the future, rather than your only option, but for now it's your safest one."

Charlie finished tidying up her first aid kit and closed it. Maddock leaned forward to rest his elbow on his knee and feathered his knuckles along her cheek. "Thank you for the care," he said.

She nodded, a quick jerk, and returned to Yvette's side, kneeling at the vampire's booted feet. Maddock and Yvette's gazes met and Medusa sensed a current of tension pass between them.

"Do you have any theories as to why my body has altered twice since I have been here?" Medusa asked, hoping to head off another fire fight inside the confines of the tent. Glancing up at John Pierce, she saw he'd deciphered her intent and found it amusing. She would have pinched him, but Maddock answered her question.

"I believe JP's on the right path with that. Ukrit's attack created a deep wound in your soul." She saw sparks in Maddock's eyes like she saw in John's whenever the subject was raised. This was another man who felt nothing but abhorrence and cold anger toward what Ukrit had done to her.

"For a long time, you could rely on no one but yourself," Maddock continued. "Each time you take a pivotal step toward trusting John and trusting yourself, your feelings for him and about your path, I think it weakens the spell. It's also possible being here, so far from your time and world, could be a factor. If we're right about any of that, that's good news on several fronts."

His gaze shifted and held with John's. John made a noncommittal noise, as if discouraging him from going more in-depth into what he was implying. Maddock sighed and muttered something about stubbornness. "The really good news is, if the spell fully lifts at any point, MyTech has no reason to be interested in you any longer. Unless one of their kids needs a firsthand interview source for a report on ancient Greek history."

She blinked, and he waved away the attempt at humor. "If I can learn more about the specifics of the ritual, I could study it more closely. If you like."

She thought of when John Pierce had first suggested it, back on her island. She'd immediately been suspicious of the wizard's motives. Now she was surprised to see it was John who looked resistant to the idea, if the sudden tightness of his jaw and the look he pinned on Maddock were indicators. It didn't matter, though.

"I remember so little of it, I cannot help with that," she admitted.

"While I'm here today, I could use a technique called hypnotherapy to bring some of the memories to the forefront, if they're there to call," Maddock said. "I just need your willingness to try."

His words provoked hope, anxiety, and an unsettled weight on her stomach.

"Don't do that," John said sharply. "Don't guilt her."

Maddock shot him a look. "I assume she wants to know if the spell can be reversed."

"It's too soon." John said. "She just got dragged down into her memories and held prisoner there. You may not be taking her back to the actual event, but it's still too close to it. She's too fragile."

"Perhaps you should ask her what she thinks," Yvette interjected.

"Unless some kind of temporal rift has occurred in my tent and we are back in the time of Neanderthal cavemen."

John scowled. "I'm not overriding her wishes. I'm just trying to protect her."

"You are being a hardheaded male and protective Dom," Yvette said with deceptive agreeability. "But I want to hear her thoughts on her own state of mind."

"Like you can't be overprotective." Maddock glanced pointedly at Charlie. Yvette's predatory gaze locked with his.

"Do you really wish to discuss why I am so protective of what is mine and not yours, Mad Merlin?"

Maddock's expression shuttered, but his eyes glinted dangerously.

"I can do this." Medusa laid her hand on John's knee. "I must have whatever control over my fate I can. What happened earlier...I would have been far more fragile if you had not stepped into the nightmare and helped me fight my way out of it. You reminded me of my strength and my own will. I can do this. Please. Be with me on this."

"I'm with you on everything, snake-girl," he said, covering her fingers and clasping them firmly. "But if he starts being a bully, you just say the word and I'll knock him on his ass."

"Yeah, like that's ever going to happen," Maddock said.

"It would if you wouldn't use magic to protect your scrawny butt," John retorted.

Maddock ignored that. As he looked toward Charlie, his expression was hooded. "If you'll let me take you to lunch another day..."

"No," Medusa said. "I mean, yes, I am willing to try what you suggested. But may we do it after lunch? John Pierce and I can eat here while you and Charlie go...eat Italian food. When you return, I will be fed and well-rested. I feel like I need some time to get accustomed to the idea."

Charlie's cheeks had tinged that light pink again. While nothing about Yvette's expression had discernibly changed, Medusa sensed she'd earned a good mark in the vampire's book, not allowing Maddock to back away from his obvious feelings for the healer. Though Medusa was curious about how Charlie's service to the vampire would work if Maddock did openly pursue the relationship. It was clear if Maddock wanted a woman, he wasn't going to be kindly disposed to sharing her.

John Pierce rose, drawing her to her feet with him. "Sounds good," he said. "Because we have an errand to do at lunch."

She glanced up at him quizzically, but he offered her only an enigmatic wink and smile. There was still a tightness about his mouth that told her he wasn't entirely happy about her decision to work with Maddock, but he would support her in it. That was all that mattered.

Yvette spoke quietly to Charlie and then she rose. "If you need my quarters for your questions, you are welcome to use them after lunch. I will be with Gundar most of the afternoon, working with the other performers. Marcellus will be told what was said here, to keep him in the loop."

She pivoted and left them, something Medusa was beginning to realize characterized the vampire's communication. She said what she needed or wished to say, then absented herself from further human interaction. It made her think of what Clara had said about vampires being very "clique-y". She wondered how the vampire passed leisure time, or with whom she chose to spend her relaxed moments. Cai perhaps?

The portal Maddock suggested for exiting the Circus and taking Charlie to lunch was near the cook house, so the four of them walked toward it. The men were a few feet ahead, talking about other things, so Medusa slowed her steps, anticipating Charlie companionably matching her pace.

"So what's that about?" she asked in a low voice.

"What?" Charlie asked. She was clicking her middle finger and thumb nails together, a nervous twitch.

"You and Maddock?"

"I haven't known him very long. And he doesn't...he's never approached me that way. Not exactly."

"Is it because you're already spoken for? With Lady Yvette."

"No. Not like that. I mean, yes, Yvette takes me to her bed, but that's a vampire thing. They don't really bond with humans...like it is between you and John."

"So she'd be okay with you being with Maddock if you wanted to be?"

At Charlie's silence, Medusa bit her lip. She barely knew this woman, and Charlie barely knew her. Charlie was not Clara, who talked with such chatty girlish comfort, the way Callidora had. Dear

Callidora…maybe John was right. Maybe she didn't want to remember, to go back… It filled her with unease, as she thought about her friend.

"Oh, no. You don't have to be sorry." Charlie touched her arm, showing she'd picked up Medusa's distress. "I understand."

"I still apologize," Medusa said. "I know I'm being too forward. It's just been so long since I've been able to talk to other…women about things that matter to us. I mean, I'm sure John Pierce would have his theories if I ask him, but…"

"But men talk about feelings and relationships differently. Very minimalist. 'Yeah, he seems to like her.' Grunt." Charlie attempted a smile. "I hope I'm not that bad, but I'm just not good at this kind of talking."

"I do not believe that. Your touch and presence are so welcome and soothing."

"Oh, I didn't mean it quite like that. It's not about being socially awkward. It's…seeing the things I can see, I have to translate everything three times. Through the auras I see, through the words you say, and then there's the current."

"Current?"

Charlie's clouded eyes seemed to stare over Maddock's head as if she were focused on the sky, or some type of energy swirling above him. "There's a current that runs through everything. It's part of us, part of the earth, part of the universe. It has its place in every conversation, whether we know it or not, weaving us with other potential threads…so I have to put the three together. I can't take anything on face value, because I have to balance all the energy that flows toward me when someone is talking to me."

It sounded like a fragile mortal had been burdened with the omniscience of a goddess, something that would be continually overwhelming. Charlie seemed to channel it effectively for her healing role, though. Medusa considered the attraction between her and Maddock, the strong energy layers around the wizard.

"What happens when Maddock talks to you? Does he know all this?"

"He knows some of it. It gets…quieter, when he talks to me. In a certain way. Somewhat like Yvette, but different."

"Like when you were kneeling at his feet." Medusa studied the set of Maddock's shoulders, the tilt of his head as he spoke to John, his quick male smile. Yes, she could see it there. There was that similarity to the two men, the sexual Dominance, the protective nature, the single-mindedness when each man knew what he wanted from a woman.

She suspected he had ways to help cushion the effect of Charlie's form of communication, to simplify it with his own shielding. So what was keeping Maddock from reaching out?

It was likely the same thing that always held a person from committing to another when life was excessively complicated. Wasn't that the unresolved matter between her and John Pierce, one that kept raising its head? Though interestingly, when those moments reached a certain intensity, it didn't seem unresolved at all.

"Yes. It quiets when I treat him...as a Master." Charlie's voice dropped to a whisper and the petite woman seemed to draw in on herself, like she might narrow and disappear through a rift in the very air around her. "He touched me and...the colors, between our skin, it was..."

She stopped. In the healer's face, Medusa saw the same discomfort she might feel if she thought she were saying too much to a relative stranger.

"You honor me with your confidence," she said formally, touching the woman's arm. "It has been a long, long time since another woman has spoken to me of things of the heart. It is a gift, and I will not treat it carelessly."

Charlie's face cleared. "I know. You have spoken of your love for John, but it is still a new thing, isn't it? So many unknowns, so many things to explore. It's a wonderful feeling, but a frightening one, when so many things can go wrong. And he fears obligating your heart to him."

"Yes." Medusa walked silently for another few minutes. The cook house was ahead. "But John taught me, and I have learned myself, that often it's about taking one moment at a time. Today that moment is lunch. Italian lunch."

Charlie smiled at the phrasing, though her expression was shadowed. Hoping to help ease her tension, Medusa nudged her playfully. "Maybe he will kiss you. Or maybe you will kiss him. He looks like he needs you to kiss him."

"Oh, I..." Charlie spluttered. "I can't. I just couldn't."

At the young woman's genuine distress, Medusa immediately realized her mistake. Chagrined, she slid an arm around Charlie's narrow shoulders. "You do not have to. I did not mean to upset you. I was just doing girl talk, as Clara calls it. I am obviously not very good at it, either."

"No. It's not that." Charlie's deceptively blind eyes locked onto Medusa's face with fierce purpose. "I'll see things if I kiss him. Energy trails, intent, fate, a whole lot of possibilities that, with his life, are going to be scary and terrible, making me think I could lose him before I ever have him. I'd rather just have him at a distance. Where I can dream about him and never worry that that image will change in my head. That even if something destroyed him tomorrow, that part would stay the same, untainted. I don't even really want to go to lunch with him, but Yvette said I must."

Since the woman now seemed tense under the shelter of her arm, Medusa drew back, but she stopped and faced her, knowing Charlie could see the lights of her emotions, what she sincerely hoped would be true for the blind healer. "I do not want to cause you further distress, but I think you'll be glad you did go with him."

She couldn't see how Charlie refusing to be with Maddock when she so obviously wanted to be was better, no matter how short a time the relationship might work.

Maybe she needed to tell John Pierce something like that, to ease his doubts about her frame of mind. When merely seeing his quick smile filled her with a simple happiness, it had to mean something. Especially when that happiness seemed surrounded by an even easier feeling of *Yes, he's mine. I want that. Him.*

She'd disturbed Charlie enough with things that she couldn't even answer for herself. Tactfully, she changed the subject to ask her about some of the costumes she'd seen piled up in a corner of Yvette's large tent. She wasn't sure if the shift would work, but Charlie jumped on those questions with obvious relief.

They caught up to Maddock and John at the cook house. Maddock extended a hand to Charlie. "Ready to do this? You don't have to go if you don't want to. Don't join me for lunch because Yvette told you to do it. That would piss me off."

Medusa held her breath, since Charlie had said that was exactly why she was doing this. Now, though, the healer's face was as placid and readable as the face of a lake. She laid her hand in Maddock's.

"I like Italian food," she said.

"Don't let him stick you with the check, Charlie," John advised. "He's been known to do that. The old 'I left my wallet at home' ploy."

"I don't handle money," she said serenely. "So if that is the case, we will be washing many dishes."

CHAPTER TWENTY-TWO

*M*edusa shifted to John's side, brushing against him as they watched the two move away and abruptly vanish, smoothly as if they'd stepped through a door.

"Show off," John said. "Trying to impress a girl."

"I'm impressed," Medusa admitted, then smiled as he slid an arm around her and turned her so she was fully against his chest, his hand sliding down into her jeans pocket. His intent to tease her seemed to slide away as he studied her face. "You okay?" he asked.

"Yes, I am." She gazed up at him. "I like your face, John Pierce. I am glad it was the first thing I saw when I opened my eyes."

She wasn't sure if she meant when she came out of the nightmare, or if she meant the first time she looked upon him on the island, or if it had an even deeper meaning, but he seemed to absorb all possible nuances of it, because it made his eyes become an even deeper gray. There was a dark ring of black around the iris that made his eyes even more appealing, more capable of holding her caught in their spell. When he leaned down to kiss her, she leaned fully into it, a long moment where things became quiet, tender and yearning all at once.

He lifted his head and cleared his throat gruffly. "I need to feed you," he said.

They ordered food at the cook house, and John asked for it to be packed up to go. They were invited to join others seated around the tables, but when John indicated he was taking her on a picnic, they were treated to some teasing remarks and suggestive comments about the best place for a "private" picnic. The banter left Medusa chuckling and John rolling his eyes as they exited the tent.

"Circus people," he grumbled. "Minds in the gutter."

"You mean you're not planning to ravish me after lunch?"

"I didn't say that. I just meant there was no reason for them to point it out so blatantly. And who says I'm waiting until after?" He grinned at her.

As they moved beyond the tents and wagons, she realized where they were headed. "You're taking me to see Lianthe," she said, gladness filling her heart.

"Yes. Which is why I brought this." He produced a shiny red apple. "I assume there are some similarities between horses and unicorns. You okay with stopping on that knoll up there to eat first? I'm hungry enough to eat my own shoes and don't want to offend her with my stomach growling."

As they moved toward the picnic spot, she told him about her conversation with Charlie. "It seems sad to me," she said. "For so long, I couldn't reach out to anyone, because of the spell, and I was on an island by myself. They're standing side by side and it seems like there's even more distance between them than I experienced."

"Maddock is a complicated guy." John acknowledged. "He's like a monk—almost. Never known him to be with anyone. When I was going to dungeons where I could play with subs, he went with me a few times. He watched in this intense way, like he was creating scenes in his mind, but he wasn't a public player. Then there's the superstition thing."

"What superstition?" Medusa pushed away her unreasoning jealousy at the mention of the women he'd been with. He was with her now. Though in truth, she didn't know a great deal about his world's customs toward committing to one person. It certainly hadn't been the norm for men in her world. She wanted to ask him, but she quelled the insecurity, focusing instead on the story he was telling her.

"You remember I told you that we call him Mad Merlin, comparing him to the Merlin in the story I told you about King Arthur? In the legend, Merlin was eventually removed from Arthur's side by a sorceress named Nimue. There's a lot of different lore surrounding the character, even more than the stories about you." He split a bag of chips with her, giving her half. She liked the way they crunched, and their saltiness. "But she ends up using his magic against him to trap him."

Medusa frowned at the idea of the wizard trapped against his will. "What does that have to do with Charlie?"

"When she was a toddler, because of the gifts she displayed even then, Charlie's parents and her village were afraid of her. They put her in a sack, weighted it down and threw it in a lake."

"Oh Goddess." Her eyes widened. "How horrible."

"Yeah, people can suck." John shook his head. "Three hours later, she walked out of the lake, alive, water plants draped over her hair and body, wearing the burlap like a dress. Another family who lived in the hills took her in and no one ever bothered her again, at least not there. As time went on, they started calling her Lady of the Lake. Which is also what Nimue was sometimes called."

"Surely he doesn't think…"

"I don't know what he thinks. I just know he won't talk about her, and yet whenever he's around her, you can see that draw between them clear as what's between the sun and the moon. It's another reason Yvette wants to put his head through a wall most the time."

"How extraordinary."

"No, I think Yvette wants to put most of our human heads through a wall most days. Very ordinary reaction for her."

She chuckled. "But she acts in some ways as if she doesn't want him anywhere near Charlie."

"She has no patience for him being half-assed about it. She won't let him fuck with Charlie's head like that. It's probably pretty normal for someone like Maddock or Charlie to do the two steps forward three steps back thing because of all their other shit, but Yvette is way older than them."

"You did not do that," she said. "I have, but you haven't. From the time you set foot upon my island, you were sure. Even after you met me and found out who I really was, and how I was different from what you imagined."

He took her hand. "I told you my mom read your story to me. I didn't tell you that she did it because I mentioned to her that I was dreaming about a woman with snakes in her hair. She told me it sounded like Medusa, and bought a book about you. So it was me, and my dreams of you, that initiated her reading your story to me."

He slid a thumb across her wrist pulse, that almost unconscious caress he preferred that kept her connected and sexually aware of him at once. "Remember that I told you I dreamed of a man who called me by the name you chose for me, John Pierce?"

He stopped and faced her, gray eyes on her face. "Yeah, I remember."

"When we first met, I wasn't sure you were the same man. In the dreams, your face, it was not always clear. But I started having the dreams when I...became a woman. Started my courses. We walked along the beach, you touched my face. At times you spoke to me. Called me snake-girl."

She remembered how it had struck her to the core, the first time he'd called her that. She'd barely been able to speak for a few moments, and had almost flown off, ending their conversation. The similarities had been too unsettling. She took a breath. "As I became older, the dreams became more intimate. Things like we have done, started happening. Like you...commanding me, and me taking plea-sure in obeying your will. I dreamed of you binding me, scattering rose petals over my flesh, doing things that had me waking among the other girls...damp and shuddering."

He had shifted closer, expressions that were both unreadable and potent on his face. "Why didn't you tell me all that?" he said, low.

She looked down at her hands. "After Ukrit, like my dreams of Lianthe, you vanished for a while. Or if I dreamed of you...you became him. And I could not bear it. It was so frightening I think my mind, or the minds of my snakes, helped me, and always woke me up or changed the dream to something different. It was only several weeks before you arrived that I had started to have them again, without them becoming nightmares."

He touched her face, lifting her chin so she met his eyes. "I want you to look at me when you tell me things like that," he said, a note to his voice that made her quiver. She also saw his pain for her, the cold anger that Ukrit would infringe upon the dream. It made her remember how her anger at Ukrit for infringing on what she gave to John Pierce had helped shift a nightmare to a dream. Yet she had to tell him all of it.

She hesitated. "Also, after Ukrit...for a time, there were other reasons I didn't want the dream."

"Tell me," he said.

"I am afraid you will...misunderstand my intentions."

A grim smile touched his face. "I'm with you, however you need me. All that I require is your honesty."

"You require much more than that at times." She swallowed. "But I do not mind such demands."

"Glad to hear it. *Medusa*."

The note in his voice as he spoke her name told her he knew she was hedging. "When you dreamed of me," she said, "Did you not ever feel like your fate was being set for you in ways you resented?"

"Do you want me to answer for myself, or are you trying to tell me how you feel?" His voice slid into neutral, which hurt her stomach some, but he'd demanded honesty out of her. She would not be a coward.

"Both."

The hurt that flickered through his eyes dug jagged edges into her heart, but she steeled herself to hold his gaze without flinching.

"Okay." He pursed his lips. "No, I didn't see it that way. I thought of you the way a kid does when he imagines himself as a knight or a superhero in the midst of this big adventure. Then we grow up. Like I told you, I couldn't hold onto the superhero shit. But I held onto you. I've never left the fairy tale, in all its magical, bloody glory. I'm still all the way in it and wanting to be exactly where I am."

He withdrew his hand, though he caressed her fingers before he did it. "But that's why I asked if you wanted to return to your other life," he said steadily. "No matter how many things pointed me toward you, I ultimately chose that path. I want you to feel the same."

"And if I don't choose you, John Pierce? How is that fair? When you have risked all for me unconditionally, with no plans to compel me to stay at your side."

He stroked her face. "That's the risk everyone takes when they fall in love. Our story's just a little more dramatic than most."

She grasped his hand, taking it back to her heart. "I look into your eyes, and I see the dark paths you have walked. From the beginning, you understood the loneliness, the despair, because you have been there. You have stood in blood and wondered if there would ever be anything else."

"Because we can empathize with one another isn't enough." He set his jaw. "If you decide to be with me because I understand a lot of things you've experienced, because I helped you get off the island, because I made you laugh...that's still not enough."

"What will be enough?"

"You'll know it, and so will I." He swallowed, and she detected that vulnerability that could break a woman's heart when she saw it in a strong man's face. "I love you," he said quietly. "And I will always have your back. That won't change. But there's a part of me that's just like Yvette said. A caveman who wants to drag you off by your hair and say, you're mine, and that's the end of the discussion. But that's not love."

A pained smile touched his lips. "Well, okay, it can be an aspect of love, but one that sort of has to be kept in check. So there's something I need you to do. I know you care about me, and that you'll always have my back, too. As part of that, I need you to wait and be sure. To take the time to choose me, or not. We've barely met, and now we're in a whole new place. Nothing's guaranteed in life, but when and if you choose me, I want you to feel pretty good about it."

"I do."

"Yeah. But you asked me about whether or not I resented having fate make choices for me. Fate's been doing that all your life. In the form of your father, Ukrit, your powers and the spell that kept you isolated. We may seem in every way like we're fated to be together"— he locked eyes with her—"but this time, you tell Fate to fuck itself, and make your own choice. That's the only way I want you to come to me."

He took a breath. "I'll wait as long as you need to make that decision. Whatever that decision will be. I know you've been worrying about it, so if you want to do something for me, stop. Take that weight off your heart. Live your life and decide who you want to love. That's all I want from you."

She blinked back tears. Did he know his voice had become raw as he spoke, revealing the depths of his feelings, his understanding of what he had to lose, but also his willingness to face that if it became necessary? She'd told him she wanted to be in love with him, and that was true. She couldn't deny anything else he'd said, but she could offer him this.

"I am making choices every day." She looked down at their clasped hands and moved closer to him, laying her other hand on his chest and gazing up into his face. "And I want to be exactly where I am now, in this moment."

She'd never initiated a kiss with him like this. When she rose onto her toes to put her mouth on his, she felt the pleasure of it, of choosing him, even for this one act. He put both arms around her, as her own slid up around his neck. He took over the kiss fairly immediately, which she craved. He understood that, too, cupping her skull, her snakes winding around their shoulders as he delved deep, scraping her teeth, playing with her tongue, growling as she rubbed her body against his, against the evidence of his arousal.

He eased her back, reluctantly. "I am going to eat, woman, and then I'm going to ravish you. But I am eating first."

"That's your priority?" she teased him, pleased at his sexy smile that banished the seriousness between them. For now.

"I want the stamina to make you pay for tormenting me. Making you hoarse with three or four climaxes should do it."

With that thrilling and yet harrowing threat, he took her hand in a firm grip again. He guided her up a hill to a copse of trees, where they could spread out a blanket and have their repast beneath the shade of the thick branches. As they ate their sandwiches, he drew her attention to the centaurs in the distance. Greygirl moved ponderously among them, the dragon young flying above. Medusa held her breath when one of the adult dragons appeared and soared over her and John, headed for the herd. The centaurs stopped and formed a ring, heads lifted toward the dragon. One blew a horn.

"Tragar's eyesight isn't so keen, because he's blind in one eye. He has a good sense of smell, but centaurs smell enough like a mix of deer and horse that sometimes Tragar can confuse them with his dinner until he gets his claws into them. The horn and the circle alerts him."

The dragon bugled an acknowledgement and the centaurs dispersed into a wider pattern again. The dragon young ascended to play and circled their father. Medusa gasped in delight at the aerial acrobatics that ensued, Tragar dipping and spinning with them, helping them practice their dexterity.

"Have you ever met the dragons?" she asked.

"Not directly. They really are an ancient race. Most of them live in the Fae world now, and they're far more comfortable with Fae than humans. Yvette, Tragar and Jetana have a pretty unusual relationship. Tragar had a run-in with some of the Unseelie and he prefers this world to the Fae one. Eventually, though, I expect he'll make amends and go back, because the young will be safer living and growing up there."

Finished with his meal, John stretched back out on the ground and surveyed her with male pleasure. "So was it your whispered matchmaking with Charlie that nearly gave her a panic attack?"

Medusa felt alarm. "Did Maddock hear?"

"No. I don't think so. He was too busy trying to tell me his latest theory of what-the-fuck that I'm too dense to understand." He tugged her hair and did a playful form of boxing with Earthson, bumping his closed fist lightly against the snake's nose as the snake wove up and down, back and forth. "That is one weird little snake."

"He's the friendliest of all of them."

"Which is kind of unusual, since small guys tend to be more defensive."

"Perhaps he realizes because he is the smallest, he has less chance of success with aggression."

"Maybe. But sometimes it's the smallest cat that can puff up to the biggest, meanest size to scare everyone else off." He winked and picked up a finger-sized carrot, biting into it with a crisp snap. "So I heard from Clara that she came to see you after your bath this morning, before you walked into that firefight with Maddock and Yvette. What did you talk about?"

"She wanted to be sure I was all right. Said I could join her on the day's chores tomorrow if I wished. We're going to help Charlie fit costumes for the next performance, cook cornbread with the kitchen people and do laundry linens. There are so many ways to help here. You never have to be bored."

He smiled, leaving off his play with the snake to wind his hand around her hair. "No one's ever going to accuse you of ducking work."

"Why would I do that? Everyone is happier if the work is shared. It is done sooner and we have companionship and conversation while doing it."

"Not everyone feels that way. Glad you do. Now be quiet and come down here."

She obliged, despite the mild insult, because his heated mouth was waiting and she was still vibrating from the memory of it earlier. She relished the strength of his hands that pulled her close, roving down over her backside and thighs, up her sides to her shoulders. Easing her over his hips, he had her straddle him, her hands resting on his chest and hard abdomen. He cradled her there by bending his knees up behind her and clasping both her hands to let her rock against his grip. His gaze roved over her.

"Take off the dress."

The command shot pure need through her. She freed her hands to do it, and closed her eyes when his hands immediately captured her breasts, thumbs stroking slow over the nipples. Very slow. She had worn nothing under the dress, something he showed he'd noticed with his observation now, in a deceptively lazy, purring tone.

"That pretty embroidery concealed your nipples, but it was driving me crazy. I could tell from the nice way your breasts were quivering when you moved it was just you under this. But since Yvette made that Neanderthal comment, I figured I'd just prove the point if I groped you while we were in her tent with her and Maddock."

She smiled at that, but her breath was starting to shorten. He rocked her against his legs, forward, back. Her eyes stayed fixed on his strong features, his intent gray gaze.

"Touch yourself, Medusa. I want to watch."

She was self-conscious, until she thought of how she'd felt, watching him do the same under the waterfall. Cupping her breasts as his hands slid away, she emulated how he'd been touching her, because it had felt so good. Earthson doubled back and slid over her shoulder into her hair, leaving a tingle of sensation along her neck, because that was where John's hand had just been.

He clasped his hands on her waist and hips, flexing slightly, letting her feel his hold and strength as she obeyed him, arousing herself with her touch.

"Now put your hand between your legs. Stroke yourself. Make yourself feel it. I want you getting wet."

Down, down, under the unwavering supervision of his gaze. She found she was already on the way to complying with his directive.

"Show me how wet you are already."

When she lifted her damp fingertips, he guided them to his mouth, holding her wrist. He captured the other one, and drew her forward, holding her arms out to either side, her body canted over his as he nuzzled her breasts, idly licked a nipple, let her feel the edge of his teeth.

"Oh..." Her breath shuddered out, making her breasts quiver, this time with no clothing to impede his view. Easing her back, he bounced his hips beneath her so she felt like she was on a trotting horse. Which increased the wobbling motion of her bosom considerably. The mischievous look in his eyes, his unapologetic fascination with the movement, made her laugh in the midst of her arousal.

He grinned, but then his lips firmed, his eyes firing with a different light. "Stay still except for how I move you," he ordered.

Drawing her forward, he put his mouth to work on her breasts and nipples once more. He kept teasing her as she remained motionless, obeying his command until her need became too much to contain. She was making whimpering pleas in her throat, her eyes closed and body shuddering. Her sex was dampening his jeans and abdomen beneath her, her nipples aching points.

"I want inside you. Right now. Right here." Sliding his hand around to cup her buttock, he turned them in one lithe, strong movement, putting her beneath him. He opened his jeans and gripped himself, fitting the head of his cock in between the slick lips of her cunt. He stopped just inside that gateway, gaze fastened on her face, which she knew was taut with need.

"Do you want me inside you, Medusa?"

She nodded vehemently, fingers curling into his shirt. She couldn't explain why, but it increased her arousal all the more, him almost clothed and her completely naked, out here in the open, at his command.

As he eased in, inch by inch, her lips parted, tongue touching her dry mouth. His gaze fastened on it, a moment before he descended to cover it with his and thrust fully into her in the same move.

She whimpered, holding on as he pumped slow and sweet into her, every stroke like a lightning flash in her mind. Her muscles quivered, perspiration dewed on her skin, and she wanted more. She moved with him, giving as much pleasure as she was being given. She knew, because he whispered it to her.

"You're so generous, sweetheart. You're a gift. You've always been a gift."

Every time he spoke like that about her, he poured more healing balm on those deep wounds she'd never thought could be healed, until he'd come to her island. His hips slid in a sweet friction against her tender inner thighs, his cock so full inside her, his size stretching her in a way that felt good and intimidating at once. It made her tremble harder, being at his mercy, so vulnerable, yet cradled in his arms as if he'd protect her from the world.

"Ah..." The orgasm was rising, and he saw it in her face.

"Want to come for me?"

"Please...if you will."

"I want to see you go first." He punctuated that with several more well-timed thrusts, and she came apart, crying out, nails digging in and likely raking over those first talon marks she'd left on him.

He followed her over, pressing his face into her throat as he finished, his grunts of completion adding to her own aftershocks. They lay quietly for a few moments, breathing in rhythm with one another. She had her face against his hair, was lining small kisses along his temple as the arms she had crossed over his back allowed her to play in his hair with unsteady fingers.

"I'm happy," she said quietly. "You've given me that. Thank you."

"That's the gift you gave me," he corrected her.

They gave themselves a lovely quarter hour doze under a sunny sky with the breeze riffling over their perspiration-dampened skin. Then he drew her to her feet and helped her don her clothing with a tenderness that took away words. She hadn't felt any self-consciousness, doing what they were doing where the dragons could see or someone could stumble across them, but this natural area of the Circus seemed to be designed for those needing private time together. Wrapping his arms around her, John Pierce kissed the crown of her head and spoke against it.

"I'm glad you're here with me. What you said earlier to me in front of the others...you didn't have to say that for me to be whatever you need me to be, but it put an arrow right through my heart, in the right way."

"I meant it. I am new to love, John Pierce, but I cannot imagine that it is not what I am feeling."

"Then I'll consider it a blessing, no matter how long it lasts," he said.

She bit her lip. They'd said what they needed to say on that. But she did wonder again, when she *was* sure, how she would convince him of it. Did love have to have a prescribed amount of time to become real?

And was he that accepting of her making a different choice? For all his openness, she'd seen glimpses of a maelstrom of emotions in John Pierce, a storm he seemed to keep firmly locked down when he thought she needed that. She wanted to access those emotions. She wanted his passion, his lack of control, as much as she wanted the steady male that she did believe would be at her back whenever he needed her. That would honor her decision no matter what it was... while fighting to have it go his way.

She pursed her lips. Perhaps she was being contradictory and contrary, but wasn't part of making choices testing the ground for those choices and seeing what consequences or responses came of it?

He'd packed up their picnic and they were rising to continue their journey to Lianthe's meadow. She laid a hand on his arm. "Do you think it would be a good idea for me to engage with other males here?"

He was about to shoulder the tote holding the remains of their lunch, but at that, he stopped, straightened, and leveled a cool stare on her. "Say again?"

She quelled a flutter of nervousness and shifted her gaze to his throat. "According to my discussions with Clara, there are many men of your quality here... Dominant? And she says sometimes, in their leisure time, they like to engage in...sessions. Play parties? Here, at the Circus. Perhaps that is a good way to test my feelings, their uniqueness. You have said that you will be at my back always, John Pierce, but I have no wish to take advantage of your care and loyalty."

He closed the distance between them in one step. It was unsettling, how he didn't touch her, though there was barely a breath between them. After several charged moments, he spoke. "I've told you before," he said, low. "When you talk to me about things like this, I expect you to look me in the eye."

She lifted her lashes and swallowed an incoherent sound in her throat, evidence of a spike of reaction between arousal and hard need. She couldn't explain what she saw in his expression, but she knew everything in her responded to it.

"You want to experiment, snake-girl? Call someone else Master at the same time you're calling me that? You think that's what I was giving you permission to do?"

"No," she confessed, pulse beating hard in her throat. "But I needed to know...or I wanted you to know, this decision lies...between you and me. And...in my world, men were not often...exclusive, even after marriage."

"In my world, they are. Or damn well should be. And not just after marriage. The second they commit."

"Clara... She told me about your tattoo, about having it done here. I asked her if you were with any women...here. She would not answer; I think because she was worried about how I might feel."

"She also maybe didn't answer for the same reason I'm trying to give you breathing room. No one, Medusa. That was the point of having the tattoo redone. Soon as I knew you were real, not in my fucking head, and that Maddock had a way, a possibility, a slim chance of bringing me to you, there wasn't going to be anyone else. Not in session or out."

His gaze narrowed. "What is this, anyway?"

She lifted her chin, her fingers curling. "In your world, people are together until they are not. But when they are together, they are trying to be together, not continually suggesting they have...a way out. You have made me amply aware of my choices, John Pierce. If you honor my strength, my ability to make them, I need you to..."

She couldn't finish it, didn't know how, but at an easing of his jaw, the words, still stuck in her throat, fortunately found a voice from his.

"To stop being so damn courteous about it."

"Yes." She attempted a smile, though her knees were still quivering. And he saw it, his attention like a honed blade.

"Scared you a little bit there? In the right kind of way?" Now he touched her, framing her jaw with one large hand and drawing her up to her toes with that grip. "All right then. Here's the final word. You make your own choices, but be damn sure of them if they're not me.

Because I'm not going to let you go unless I'm a hundred and twenty percent convinced."

"Fair enough," she said, echoing a phrase she'd heard Gundar say.

"Christ," John muttered, and crushed his mouth to hers. He drew her against him, so she felt the full heat and weight of his body, the demand of it. It was as if he hadn't just taken her.

She'd wanted to access the emotions behind the wall, and she had, in a way that she wouldn't soon forget. The day was suddenly all the brighter for it.

He eased back, giving her a look of grudging amusement as if he'd figured that out. "Pretty pleased with yourself, aren't you?"

"And a little shaky."

"Good. Evens the score." He brushed back her hair, and gave Earthson a little playful flick. "Okay, enough of this shit. Want to go see Rainbow Pony?"

At her curious look, he chuckled, and took her hand. "I'll explain on the way. Probably best you *not* tell Lianthe I called her that."

They continued onward. As they walked, they transitioned to other, less intense topics. Thanks to what they had resolved, her concerns about her and John didn't interfere with her building anticipation as they reached the meadow.

She'd worried she'd feel an involuntary fear when seeing Lianthe, remembering what had happened the last time their eyes had met. But as the unicorn trotted out of the forest toward them, she felt nothing of the kind.

Instead, she stepped back into the dream she'd had as a girl, and those youthful impulses took over. She ran across the field, and the unicorn whinnied and trotted toward her, head bobbing with equine pleasure. When she reached her, Medusa felt a sudden shyness that kept her from touching the unicorn, but she curtsied to her, dropping to one knee. The shadow of the unicorn moved over her and Medusa closed her eyes as the velvety nose nuzzled her. Inhaling the unicorn's scent, it was as she'd remembered it from her dreams. Tears came, laced with regret and happiness, creating a moment she knew was all the more potent for containing both emotions.

As she looked up into Lianthe's beautiful eyes, she rose and received the honor of that velvet nose being pushed into her palm. Far more curious than overwhelmed, the snakes all slithered forward for a closer look.

She was about to call them back, but was surprised the unicorn tolerated them with no anxiety. Despite what Rand had said about wolves, Lianthe didn't seem to have the equine species' natural fear of snakes. She did snap at Tunneltrap when he became too enthusiastic about trying to twine in her mane and forelock, but it was the admonishment of an older matron, not a true attempt to bisect him, though he retreated hastily at the warning.

"I am sorry to have caused you distress," Medusa said to the unicorn. "I do not blame you for what happened. It ended up being a very nice dream in the end. I'm glad you came to me. I'm glad I had the kind of life then that you could use to nourish yourself."

Lianthe bowed her leg, a formal courtesy, and Medusa curtsied again in return. Then, because something about Lianthe seemed to encourage it, Medusa finally did what she'd done so often in her dreams. She put her arms around the unicorn's neck and hugged her tight, pressing her face into the muscled flesh. "Thank you," she whispered.

A living miracle. She'd been given a living miracle. How many times had she recalled Lianthe, something beautiful and unspoiled, while trying to endure the aftermath of Ukrit? Though she'd no longer visited Medusa's dreams, Lianthe had helped her more than she knew.

She thought Lianthe might have received those thoughts through the emotions Medusa was projecting, because the creature snorted and rubbed her face against Medusa's. When she looked in the unicorn's eyes again, she thought she'd also successfully removed any worries she'd had about causing Medusa unnecessary pain.

John approached, apple in hand. Lianthe took the gift with dignity but enjoyed the treat with a crunching eagerness that had Medusa and John exchanging a secret grin.

They stayed for a while, the two of them sitting on the bank of the lake while the unicorn drank and then grazed. When she laid down on her side, the look in her eyes beckoned Medusa, and she propped herself in a seated position against Lianthe's broad back, just as she'd done so often in her dreams, reading a book, or telling her about her girlhood dreams for a family, no matter that they'd had to be set aside when her father gave her to the temple. She'd been willing to serve

Athena and transfer that love to her, maybe because she hadn't been old enough yet to feel bittersweet regret for what might have been.

John remained by the lakeside, respecting their private time together, but as she looked toward him, she realized she had reached the age she did want to reach for her own dreams. And she had.

It was only when they were walking back toward the Circus camp that Medusa thought about what awaited her there. And when she did, she was glad she'd had that moment with Lianthe, the resolution with John, and his body joined with hers at lunch. She'd told Maddock she would submit to his idea of how to recall the details of the ritual her sisters had performed for her, but the closer the time was coming to do it, the more dread she felt.

She wanted to help, but as John had said, it had occurred within hours of her rape. She'd felt so filthy and beaten, so defeated in every way. It was impossible not to recall that when recalling the ritual details.

And...there was something...she flashed on Doris, an older priestess who'd told her—in a broken voice—to take what she needed from their stores before Medusa fled the temple. She heard the weeping of the other priestesses, and her throat got tight. It was too painful. She couldn't go back to that memory.

But she was stronger now, and it was in the past. That was what she told herself. By the time they reached the camp, though, she was gripping John's fingers more tightly. She tried to focus on the way the connection point swung between their bodies, but her calm demeanor drained away, becoming a thin veneer on her other feelings. She should have known John, intuitive as ever, wouldn't overlook her mood change.

Abruptly, he stopped and faced her. "You're not doing it," he said. "I'm going to tell Maddock to forget it."

"But he said it would help him understand how the spell works, how to remove it."

"Maybe. Or maybe he's just curious."

"I want to be helpful," she protested.

"Yeah, you are helpful. But I can say how helpful you'll be."

"Oh?" She mulled that over. "I see. In Athenian society, only a male family member could dictate what a woman did or did not do. A husband, or a blood relative."

He scowled. "That's not what I'm doing. I'm not trying to be one of those bastards who treated you like property or a second class citizen."

Her brow creased. "I am not sure what that means. Women were not citizens in my world. That was reserved to men, including male slaves who earned their freedom."

He sighed, taking both her hands. "I want to have the right to tell you no, because I don't want you to suffer through any more of that shit, but the truth is I don't have that right. No one does."

"Unless my service and submission is freely given," she said, recalling their earlier discussion. She tilted her head, giving him a speculative look. "Are you seeking my submission to your will in this, John Pierce?"

"And if I was?" An indefinable note entered his voice. She realized there was a line here. On this side of it was the way he used his Dominance to arouse her and drive their pleasure. If they stepped across, they were going to a deeper level with it. A level that had his gaze sharpening and sent a little quiver through her nerves.

"I have met no one in my life whom I trust as much with my well-being," she said. "If you tell me you forbid me to do this, I will honor you with my obedience."

"You have a way with words that can get me stirred up in a heartbeat," he said after a pregnant silence. She saw the truth of it in the kindled heat in his eyes. But then he sighed, a rueful expression crossing his face.

"Those words tempt me in all sorts of ways, but I know this is one decision I can't make, no matter what I want. You're right. This has to do with your future and determining your own path. I just wanted you to know—in a sort of overbearing way—if you decide you don't want to do it, I won't let him pressure you into it."

She gave him a tiny smile. "'Sort of' overbearing? It sounded completely so to me."

"Yeah, well, I'm a direct person." He made a grumbling noise and took her hand. "C'mon. Let's get this over with."

CHAPTER TWENTY-THREE

"Just focus on this." Maddock laid a crystal on the table before her. They were at one of the picnic tables they'd pulled under a tree some distance away from the noises of the camp. John thought being outside might help her, and it did. She'd turned to face Maddock, straddling the bench, and John had done the same behind her, his thighs on the outside of her hips, his hands resting on them. That helped, too.

"I need you to recall specifics of how you felt," Maddock instructed. "Keep looking at the crystal. Pick one or two things. What did the air in the ritual chamber smell like? Don't say it aloud. Just think about it."

Heat. Incense.

"Was there sound?"

Chanting. The priestesses were chanting, hands locked together.

"Focus on the sensory input. Let it take you there, but know we're here. Feel John's hand."

It clasped hers where it rested tensely on her thigh. Her fingers twitched beneath his grasp and he stroked her knuckles. "Right here."

"What is he?" Maddock's voice seemed to be getting farther away as she stared at the crystal and watched dancing lights within it.

"My protector. My champion." A light smile flirted over her lips as she remembered Clara calling him that.

But there was more, a special weight to Maddock's question, nudging her toward something else.

"Yeah. You know what it is." The wizard's voice was quiet but resolute. "Say it, and that word, his presence, that truth, anchors you here."

"Master. Sir."

John shifted, his arm sliding around her waist. "Right here, sweetheart," he repeated.

"Master..."

She opened her eyes and shuddered. She lay in the center of the circle of priestesses, and oh Goddess, she hurt. Her body was battered and torn, Ukrit's filth still staining her inside and out. Her split lip and cheek ached where he'd hit her for trying to bite him.

"You're still with us, Medusa. It's a memory. Breathe through it. This isn't like what happened before. You're not trapped. I can bring you back to us at any time."

She knew that. In that present time and place, Clara and Charlie were sitting across the picnic table from her. Their combined calming energy, as well as Charlie's healing skills, were intended to help monitor and manage her reactions. And John had made it ominously clear to Maddock he had final and irrevocable say on if and when she'd had enough and needed to be brought back to them.

But she was still afraid, and she didn't know why she was afraid. Klotho and all her sisters were in a circle around Medusa, holding hands, chanting, raising the energy they would need. Her heart rose up into her throat to choke her. Klotho's long brown hair was held back with a thin braided cord, her thin, blue-veined hands lifted, her eyes focused on the magic with which they were interacting. She'd had a sweet, thin mouth. She'd been stern, but kind. She'd been wise in the ways of knowing what she didn't know, quick to acknowledge her mistakes. Like her poor judgment about Ukrit.

"Klotho..." Tears clogged her throat and she looked toward her other friend, Callidora. She had dark hair, and dancing blue eyes, though they were serious now, suffering over Medusa's pain, angry at Ukrit.

She'd missed them so much. Goddess, it was terrible to hurt this much, the memory merging with the reality to become unbearable.

"Sssh...help us see the ritual, Medusa. Tell us how it went. It's a memory."

It didn't matter. Enough memories crowded together could become Tartarus while one still breathed. But she shifted her attention to what Klotho was saying.

She was exhorting Medusa to open herself up to them in all ways.

Show us the darkness in your heart, your soul, your mind. Release anger and betrayal. These are the weapons we will use to your benefit, sister. The magic that will protect you and keep those like him from having power over you again will come from yourself. From the spirit of Athena that lies within each of us. You are your greatest weapon, your greatest protection. You will become a fortress against the world.

Medusa threw back her head, her body contorting. She screamed at the pain as things changed, her back ripping open, something like the worst of poisons rushing through her blood. Her tongue split, blood filling her mouth.

"She's okay, it's okay..."

Someone was holding her, not letting her fall, which didn't make sense, as she was already lying on cold stone, but it helped her claw her way back to awareness. This was memory. Only memory. John was holding her. Her Master, the man who loved her, was holding her.

"No. I don't want to go forward. I can't."

"You can. You're already more than halfway there. You can do it. You're strong."

"I'm a monster. Please..."

"No, you're not. Damn it, Maddock, you bring her out *now*."

She was a monster. They didn't know. She was sliding down into an abyss, her fingers scraping on rock. There was a murmur of conversation, some kind of struggle happening, but it was too late anyway. The shadows were lifting, curtains she wanted to keep closed forever.

The metamorphosis had been painful, but it was also a release. Like a newborn bird breaking free of an egg, a slave throwing off chains, a babe fighting into the world from a dead mother's womb. Exhilaration filled her. Power. She could destroy the world if she wished. They'd given her a weapon. They'd made her into one.

She put her hands down on the stone and saw the claws scrape over it, leaving thin white marks. Something slithered over her shoulders, but it felt like the touch of a flame that did not burn. She turned her head and came face to face with a large white snake. It should have made her rear back, but it didn't. Her head was covered with snakes, her mind filled with their voices. She put her hands upon them and they wound over her forearms. She was the snake goddess. They'd made her into one. Pushing up off the stone, she stood up to embrace her sisters, to let them feel this power and pleasure. She would protect all of them. No one would ever try to hurt any of them again.

"No, no, *no*..."

Klotho hadn't known how it would manifest. She'd told Medusa that, hadn't she? The moment Medusa raised her deadly gaze, she caught Klotho and Callidora directly in its path. Callidora managed one short, cut-off shriek before the gray patina ran over her skin, locking her into a position of agonized fear.

Medusa stumbled forward. "*No. Callidora.*"

The others hadn't known what to do. Two pounced on her from behind, exhorting her to be still while they tried to put a blindfold on her. The snakes went berserk, striking, their rage and lack of comprehension fueling her own. They were trying to bind her. Why...what did it mean?

She spun around and three more died. It was Doris, the most elderly and practical of the temple, who at last understood what needed to be done.

"*Release her.*" The priestess's aged voice barked out the command. Though Medusa heard the horrified tremor in it, Doris had enough authority to cut through the panic. "Everyone, turn around and face outward from our circle. Do not look at her. Close your eyes. Do it now. Medusa, lower your gaze, my child. Do not look upon your sisters."

Medusa collapsed in the circle, numb, crying. She could not help but stare at five women who were now stone. It would not matter if she looked at the others, for they had their backs to her, shaking in fear, or crying from the same loss she was.

"No. Please. Doris. What have I done...I...help me..."

Doris's tone filled with indescribable sorrow. "Klotho would have done better to take your life, as you begged her to do. But now we must abide by what we have done."

"No. Undo it, please. Or kill me now..."

"It is black magic, and magic that draws upon your own soul, child.

There is no undoing it except from the mystery of your own self. And I will not take your life. There has been enough death here today."

"Please." She crawled across the circle, clung to Doris's robes and exhorted her for help. When Doris refused, she did the same to the others and felt her heart crack as some fled the chamber, too afraid of her to even bear her touch. "Please."

"Cease, child." Doris spoke in a terrible, harsh voice, the voice she used to chastise the younger acolytes. Later, Medusa would remember hearing the tears behind it. But now the priestess proved her bravery and her resolve to protect them all.

"What has manifested from inside you will make you feared. Ukrit will not pursue you, unless he is a fool. You are free of him. Take whatever food and supplies you think you will need from our stores. Head for the uninhabited islands and make yourself a life there. Goddess go with you, Medusa, and come to no more harm under Her care."

No. Medusa wanted to die. If they would not do it, she would. She would kill herself before Callidora and Klotho, let them know she had avenged the deaths she had wrought with her consent to this, with her foolishness. The gods had meant for her to go to Ukrit and, in her pride and fear, she'd defied them.

Wiping at her streaming eyes, she scrambled to her feet and stumbled over to the altar where the ritual knife for cutting herbs had been laid. It was consecrated. She would be ruining it, but she'd ruined everything else.

"No."

Doris's arms wrapped around her from behind, surprisingly strong, though the elderly priestess's voice broke with pain. "No, child. No. Take your ease. Listen to me. I will make it all right. Trust me."

She began chanting, a gentle singsong. It sounded merely like a healing lullaby she used in the infirmary, for Doris helped care for the sick. But then the words changed, became something more than song. Clouds invaded Medusa's mind. She struggled against them, but they promised peace from this raging pain.

"You will forget for a while," Doris said as she concluded the spell. Medusa slumped in her arms, barely conscious. Doris's voice started to drift away, but Medusa heard her final words. "It is what Klotho would want. She loved you as a daughter.

"Remember nothing of this moment, Medusa. Not until your heart is strong enough to bear it."

"3...2...1."

Medusa surfaced. She couldn't breathe, hunched over her knotted fists, pressed against her heart.

"JP..." Maddock's voice.

"Don't talk to me right now," John grated. "Just get the hell away. I told you this wasn't a good time to do this."

"Would there ever have been a good time for her to face something like that?"

"No. But not right after she'd re-experienced her rape would have been a fucking few steps better. You don't want to be here right now."

His rage was palpable, raw, and it stirred her own, though she had no target for it except herself. She would have preferred to experience the rape again. At least the only victim of that tragedy had been herself. She was weeping.

Now she knew why she never thought about the ritual, and, the few brief times she had, so many of the details had been cloaked by this fog. When she recalled Klotho, Callidora and the others, it was always well clear of the memory of that night. If she tried to think of them, then something would distract her, or...she would hear that lullaby in her mind and forget.

She'd killed her best friend and the woman who'd raised her. Doris was wrong. That knowledge could never be bearable. John couldn't possibly love her anymore after hearing that. No one could, especially herself.

Yet no one was pulling away from her. Charlie's hands were on her, stroking. Clara was murmuring something soothing. And John held her still, his arms strong and sure.

"They were my friends. My family."

"I know. I'm so sorry. It wasn't your fault. Klotho wouldn't have done it if she'd known. It was no one's fault but that bastard's."

So why did it feel even worse than when she'd purposely taken life, and she found that awful beyond description? She wanted a way to go back and undo it, not be what she'd become that day. She'd killed on the island, but the first lives she'd taken had been the people closest to her. And the spell had come from what lay in her own heart and soul.

"And the magic he used. Don't forget that, Medusa." She must have spoken aloud, because John answered her. "They made the magic out of what you were feeling that night *and* his magic. It's that combination that creates the darkness and rage you fight. But it's also where your courage and compassion come from, your will to fight that darkness. It's okay. It hurts to lose people you love. Just let it out."

"It's not okay. It can never be okay."

But the tragedy and miracle of life was that it could. Even after something like that, life could go on. She cried hard, holding onto his shirt front and wetting it. She cried until she made herself sick, and he held her hair and snakes away from her face as she vomited into the grass. After that, she rose, and made it several trembling steps before she fell to her knees and decided she didn't want to get up again.

John gathered her in his arms and carried her to a nearby tree, a beautiful oak with a graceful canopy, and a pattern in the bark that looked like a sorrowful, wizened face. She supposed that spirit had seen all sorts of tragedy. Hers was nothing special. Probably obscenely mundane.

As John sat down under the tree, holding her cradled in his lap, Charlie came to them and knelt. She began to put her hands on Medusa and Medusa knocked her touch away. When Charlie drew back, startled at the hiss, Medusa understood why. The snakes hadn't made that noise. She had.

"I do not want to feel better."

Her wrists were caught in one very strong hand as another clasped her chin, pulling up her face to meet a pair of implacable gray eyes. "Tough," John Pierce said. "Because I'm not going to let you punish yourself for this. Ukrit killed them, Medusa. Not you."

"It was my eyes. *Mine.* I...oh Goddess, why..."

"Sshh." He folded her in his arms as she began to weep again. He must have gestured to Charlie, for the healer's hands were on her once more, and a feeling of peace started to flow within her. In her current state, it initially felt like an invasion, a handful of daisies thrown on a field soaked in blood, but the petals did not stain. The flowers took root, and began to spread out over that field, nourished on the blood, changing it into something else.

"No..." she whispered.

"Your elder priestess knew what she was doing, Medusa," Charlie said, a disembodied voice at the perimeter of her consciousness. "While she cloaked your mind, she left your deepest consciousness aware of what had happened, so it could grieve, and come to grips with it. That darkness you feel, that rage, it was fed by some of it, but now you can lessen it with your awareness. Let the gateway open fully. You have been grieving this for a long time, so once that awareness settles in, you will be able to bear it. I promise. John Pierce is here with you. He will let you bear nothing alone."

Charlie's healing energy was filling her. Medusa drifted under those strong, female hands, while still cradled in John's powerful arms. She didn't want to feel better. She didn't. But as the tears fell and watered that field of daisies, they expanded even into the areas where they'd not yet covered. Years of daisies, growing up among the blood, symbols of time healing the wounds of grief.

And the pain lessened. Not in a way that negated the horror of it happening, or her fervent wish that it could be undone, but in the way that happened because life persevered. Time grew scars over wounds that seemed mortal when first inflicted.

The pressure on her heart eased as she relented and that part of her soul opened even further. She saw and felt the truth Charlie had. The undeserved gift Doris had given her was time for the heart and soul to handle the knowledge while the mind stayed in the dark.

Until now, when she faced it while held securely in the arms of one who understood, who loved her.

Because John Pierce did understand. She remembered how he'd told her about the family he'd had to kill, the pregnant woman. The four-year-old who'd died in his arms. And she'd suspected that for every terrible story he was telling her, there were more. He'd had to accept the blood he couldn't ever wash off his hands. In the dream she'd had of him, weeks before he arrived, she'd known it then.

The set of his mouth told her he preferred to be kind, yet the lines around it and his eyes said he had to be cruel and unyielding far more often, and it had taken its toll.

When she lifted her face from his chest, she saw the anguish in his expression. It was as if he'd suffered every moment of that terrible night with her, and maybe he had. He'd looked this way when she woke from the unfortunate incident with Lianthe. It was as Charlie said. He would let her bear nothing alone.

"It will get better," he said quietly. "You don't believe it right now, but it will."

She heard Charlie's dulcet voice murmuring something and then John had a warm washcloth he used on her face to clean the tears away. She would have done it herself, but as he cradled her in one arm and used his other hand to wipe her eyes and lips, her nose, she could only hold onto the front of his shirt and look at him, caring for her like a cherished babe. His feelings for her had not changed, unless one counted them intensifying. She was not alone in this.

She felt broken, yet also mended. She cleared a raspy throat. "Did Maddock get what he needed?"

"I don't give a fuck."

She pressed her forehead into his chest, loving him for his anger, but loving him even more for what she knew was beneath it. She waited him out and he sighed. "Yeah, he said he did."

"Can I... I'd like to hear what he thinks, if he has any new ideas." She wanted to be strong for John Pierce, show that she could handle this. She wanted him to look less anguished. "Is he still here?"

"I think he slunk behind one of the wagons," John said between his teeth. "Charlie, is he still here?"

"He is. I'll go and get him."

As the healer went to do that, Medusa struggled to sit up. Registering her need to be under her own power now, John didn't carry her, but he did support her as they moved slowly back to the picnic table. After he helped her sit down, he slid in next to her, keeping a bracing arm behind her so she was in the shelter of his body. Clara was sitting on the bench on the opposite side, studying Medusa with a troubled face.

"I wrote down most of the detail for Maddock," she said carefully. "He seemed to be making additional notes in the margins while you were recuperating, so I think it did trigger an idea or two for him."

"Yeah, probably a new way to turn someone else into a guinea pig for his fucking endless search for knowledge."

Clara pressed her lips together, wisely choosing not to address John's venomous comment. "Your snakes sort of got hypnotized too, but I don't think they were in the memory with you, because they were quiet through all of it. I'm so sorry," the young woman added, putting her hand over Medusa's. "So very sorry. I can't imagine how horrible that was. But they gave their lives to protect you, and I'm sure in whatever afterlife they ended up, they understood that you didn't know, that you didn't mean to harm them."

"Does that make it better?" Medusa said dully. She realized someone had brought a plate of cookies, and now the young woman nudged them toward her.

"Eat one or two of these. Walnut chocolate chip. Helps bring the blood sugar back up. Yes, I think so." Clara's eyes were serious. "Put yourself in their shoes. If you woke up in the afterlife, wouldn't it help to know that you'd been turned to stone by accident, not deliberately, by someone you considered a friend?"

"I think I'd just be angry to find myself dead, and blaming whoever put me there."

"That person would be Ukrit, wouldn't it?" Clara's expression didn't change, but her tone firmed, resonating with an unexpected core of steel. "They were trying to help you get away from him. I'm not saying you shouldn't feel terrible about it, but neither you nor any of them knew what was going to happen, so there was nothing you could have done to prevent it. And now that you've remembered, you can grieve their loss properly and find a way to heal your heart."

Sometimes it felt like her heart had been torn open so many times it would never heal again. John dipped his head and pressed his lips to her shoulder. He stayed in that position, offering comfort, his temple pressed against her cheek. She closed her eyes.

"Here come Maddock and Charlie." Clara squeezed her hand as John tensed beside her.

The wizard gave John a wary look which John returned with a bland one, though Medusa was sure Maddock saw the same simmering rage in his eyes she did. She laid her hand on John Pierce's thigh. "He is trying to help," she said. "Yes, I know it is also for his knowledge, but if it helps me, it is still help. And he is your very good friend who cares about you."

John's gaze slid over her face, his expression caught between anger and care. "Doesn't mean I don't want to beat his face into oatmeal."

But he sighed and relented, putting his arm around Medusa's waist again. "Sit down and tell us what genius thing you found out," he said in a cold voice, though the gaze he kept on Medusa's face was tender and protective, his arm still securely around her.

"Okay." Maddock took a seat and looked at Medusa. "I am sorry."

Everyone had their own demons and guilt to bear. She saw it in the depths of his eyes, the same way she saw it in John, and in herself. She inclined her head. Her voice was rough from crying, but she meant it when she spoke. "I know. There is nothing to forgive. What did you discover?"

He seemed surprised at her sincere response, but relieved to turn the topic toward a puzzle to solve. "Most of what I heard confirmed what I suspected. The spell is based primarily on what lies within you. There is some of Ukrit's black magic in it, but that was designed to lessen over time. Your priestess was one hell of a witch practitioner, especially when you think of how fast she had to put this together." He recalled himself at a warning noise from John Pierce. "But spells that use the darkest level of someone's soul often require a significant paradigm shift to get them to let go."

"The acts of trust," she said.

Maddock nodded. "I'm thinking the turning points that vanished the claws, fang and tongue were feeding off your own desires, strongly enough it broke that part of the spell work. And my guess is it's going in order of priority. The claws, fangs and tongue were the features you were more willing to let go than the others."

She put her hand on Ratqueen, coiled around her throat, the white snake's head resting on top of her breast. It made sense. Her wings had given her freedom and a lethal attack advantage, her eyes the biggest deterrent to her enemies. And the snakes...they'd been her companions, sharing her soul in a straightforward way. Would an act of trust make them vanish as if they'd never existed? Or worse, kill them outright? She thought of her dream again and felt cold. Earthson moved against her cheek.

"Do you think they'll stay if I truly want them to stay?"

"It's possible." At her look of distress, Maddock sighed. "So much of what I do, Medusa, is speculation. I walk along magical energy lines and try to figure out what they mean, how they work. Sometimes I'm right, sometimes I'm wrong. But in this case, I do hope I'm right. The down side is there is no immediate solution. It's up to you and time."

Her lips curved, a poignant and tired emotion gripping her, perhaps not entirely bad. "That sounds like the solution to most dilemmas."

"Yeah." He rubbed a hand over his face. "In the meantime, Yvette has reiterated you're welcome to stay here indefinitely, be part of the day-to-day routine. I'll...leave you to that."

He rose, for the first time appearing awkward and ill-at-ease. He glanced at John, who looked as unreadable as one of her stone statues. "I'll check back in with you, give you another update when I have more information on anything." His attention shifted back to Medusa. "And again, I'm sorry for how rough that was."

"You are trying to help," she repeated gently. "And it is appreciated. Thank you."

He turned away. Seeing Charlie's worried look, Medusa thought the healer was thinking what she was. The wizard might be as much in need of cosseting as she had been moments ago. Now that her head was clearing, Medusa realized how gaunt he had looked as he explained what he'd figured out. She also noticed the slump to his shoulders as he moved away. She wondered how much magical energy he gave to such efforts as what he had just done.

Medusa nudged John. "I think he might need you right now. Please, go to him? Clara and Charlie will be here with me."

From the flex of his jaw, she knew he'd seen what she saw, and it hadn't left him unaffected. "He's a pain in the ass is what he is," John Pierce grumbled. "Too many irons in the fire and trying to run the whole damn world." But he got up and squeezed her shoulder. "I'll be right back. I'm going to go punch him in his head."

She doubted that. She hoped. As he moved after Maddock and call to him to stop, the men paused at the side of one of the wagons. Medusa ate another cookie, letting it steady her nerves.

"Maybe you should tell her about Gundar's idea," Charlie suggested. She was sitting next to Clara, though her attention seemed to be on the two men, or, more likely, Maddock's state of mind.

"Is he okay?" Medusa asked.

"He is a very troubled soul at times." The healer's expression was sad. "He carries a great deal of responsibility on his shoulders. Some men, as they acquire power, they begin to take advantage of it, or feel entitled to it. Maddock...he worries about every decision he makes, yet he knows he cannot hesitate to make those decisions. I think it leads to many sleepless nights for him."

She shook her head and prompted Clara again. "Gundar's idea?"

"Okay." Clara studied Medusa's face, as if trying to decide if she was ready for that much of a shift. Medusa helped.

"It might be nice to have something else to think about for a few minutes."

"Yeah. I get that." The young woman folded her hands on the table. "Okay, well, here it is. Gundar came up with an idea for a new act. A flight sequence between a male and female performer, inspired by butterflies. He's actually had the idea for some time; we've just been lacking a female flyer. There's not a whole lot of rehearsal time needed. You could do it for this upcoming show if you're interested."

Medusa blinked. Waterlight coiled around her biceps and she reached up to stroke her head as Ratqueen dropped down along the other side of her face, extending to take the bite of cookie Charlie had broken off and left near her on the table's surface.

"Um...maybe. What kind of flying?"

"Nothing you don't already know how to do. It's basically the male butterfly chasing the female in a playful courtship way, so you'd just react to the male flyer however you needed to evade him. Up until the final close, where you come together in the air and drop in this dramatic plummet toward the ground. You'd separate at the last moment on a crescendo note."

Medusa glanced at John and Maddock. Some of the pressure in her chest eased as he reached out and clasped Maddock's shoulder, giving him a light shake. The sorcerer had his head down as if he were listening to John, but holding a weight greater than he could carry. In that moment, John almost looked older and wiser than the scientist-wizard, and maybe John's history had given him more experience in dealing with painful realities.

John pulled him into a masculine embrace. Then he pushed him away with a side head slap that Maddock dodged before shoving him back with affable annoyance. He was all right. They both were.

The men parted and John strode back toward her. The look in his eyes held her, such that she forgot about the cookie she was holding.

"It's kind of distracting, watching men like him walk, isn't it?" Clara observed. "You can't help but notice how it all works together so well, which makes you think of how they move at other times, for other activities."

Charlie choked on a chuckle. "Your timing can be so inappropriate," she chided.

"Oh, like you haven't noticed it with Maddock. And I'll bet you see it in a whole different range of shapes and colors. Probably with a big dose of pheromones thrown in. And I know every woman in the world wonders what Marcellus has on under that battle skirt and keeps hoping he'll give us all a glimpse. You notice he never bends over that much, and he flies away so fast there's no hope of catching a quick peek that way."

Medusa didn't want to laugh. She couldn't possibly, not after all that, but she had a field of daisies in her head, in her heart, and she felt her lips curve despite everything.

Life goes on. She noticed other things about John Pierce, other than his fine body and way of moving it. The lines around his eyes and taut mouth. He was still worried about her, and she wanted to ease that.

When he reached her side, Medusa took his hand. "Gundar wants me to join the Circus," she said.

He blinked and took a seat beside her as Charlie quietly excused herself, following the path Maddock had taken away from the camp.

Medusa had Clara fill John in on Gundar's idea. "No pressure," the young woman added. "She could do a run-through and see how it goes. If it pans out, great; if not, no worries."

"Who would the act be with?" John asked. There was a suspicious note to his voice Medusa couldn't fathom, until Clara lifted a self-conscious shoulder and shifted her feet.

"Merc. I know he seems difficult, but during performances and rehearsals, he's different. Very professional. Well, mostly professional. It is Merc."

John scowled. Medusa sipped her water. "This would be in front of an audience? Of humans?"

She knew that, of course. She just wanted to remind John Pierce that would be an additional safeguard against Merc's behavior.

"Yes," Clara responded. "I think they'd love it. Yvette said she could spell the snakes so they'd sleep. Or they can be part of it if you think they'd get a kick out of it."

"Waterlight loves to fly. The others can coil up under my hair, like they did on the island when I flew."

"Great. So they're already used to it, which works. Charlie has a costume in mind for the act. You'd be in a full black body stocking, and the headdress that would conceal the snakes is like a butterfly's antenna. They'd paint your wings. I think you'd be amazing."

"Sometimes, in the privacy of the temple, we would put on pageants and plays for one another, creating costumes out of odds and ends," Medusa said slowly. "It was fun."

Callidora had once dressed up like Scylla, complete with long teeth made from peeled sticks and tentacles made of cloth. She'd painted an extra set of eyes on her face and chased the other priestesses around with the spiraled appendages flapping. When she'd caught Medusa, she'd wrapped her arms and tentacles around her, pretending she was going to eat her.

Medusa blinked back tears, and John covered her hand with his own, giving her the reassuring pressure of his grip.

"This is a lot like that," Clara said. "I mean, I assume it is. It sounds similar."

Medusa shifted her gaze to John. He hadn't said anything, but she sensed an ominous mood from him. "John Pierce? What do you think?"

"Do you want to do it?"

"I think I do, yes." Like him, she'd seen how hard all the players worked. While Yvette wouldn't put any pressure on them to do more than manual labor, anything Medusa could do to convey her gratitude for the refuge at the Circus that wasn't outside the range of her abilities seemed little enough to ask.

Plus, any distraction would be welcome over the next few days, as she adjusted to Callidora and Klotho's death being a permanent part of her conscious memory.

Charlie returned as John was thinking. From her dissatisfied expression, Medusa suspected she hadn't been able to catch Maddock before he exited through the portal. Or maybe she had. She shook her head at Clara's quizzical look and Clara grimaced, giving her a little nudge, a friend's reassurance. Charlie managed a half-smile and sat down next to her.

"Okay." John looked toward Charlie, oblivious to the female byplay. "You tell Yvette several conditions. One, I'm present at every rehearsal, as well as someone else that bastard halfway answers to, like Marcellus or her. Preferably Marcellus, since he can fly, too. Two, he steps out of line, whoever his babysitter is pins his wings so I can have a fair shot at beating the shit out of him."

Charlie paused, obviously waiting for Yvette's response to that. Medusa found it fascinating, how a vampire could listen through a second mark's mind and respond to them that way. What would it be like to be in John Pierce's mind and he in hers? But sometimes it was like they already were. She thought of what had passed between them after lunch, when he was over her and their eyes had locked, his body moving inside hers, hers rising to him. She curled her hand in his, and earned a warm look from him.

"You'd have to get in line to deliver that beating," Charlie responded. "And you do not *tell* me anything, human."

Her gentle delivery and precise emphasis was so at odds with how Medusa was sure the vampire had said it, Medusa hid a smile as John's lips quirked.

His gaze returned to Medusa and, in it, she saw he was thinking of what she'd said to him earlier, about her obedience. Something tilted in her chest as he picked up the gauntlet, this time on his own, and made it clear he was exercising it. "Then you may do it," he said.

CHAPTER TWENTY-FOUR

The small town that would be hosting the latest performance of the Circus had a Starbuck's. When Medusa expressed her desire to go, John had serious reservations, based on what Maddock had said about everyone being on the lookout for her. However, once Charlie proposed and prepared Medusa's "disguise," he seemed to have fewer reservations and much amusement.

Medusa eyed herself in the mirror, and touched the downy thick hair on her face. She had a beard and moustache. She was the bearded lady, dressed in a silk black tunic and long jacket over teal leggings. A black rakish hat with teal feathers and rhinestones fully covered her snakes. Maddock's neutralizing contacts for visits outside the Circus boundaries had the added benefit of turning her red eyes a normal dark brown. Her wings were carefully wrapped against her upper torso and the cut of the coat concealed them.

"The town will expect the circus players to be out and taking advantage of the local businesses," Charlie said. "And every traditional circus has a bearded lady. All the players will have a residue of Yvette's magic on them, so your protection spell alone won't draw the attention of any magic users working for MyTech. She's spelled the snakes so they'll sleep soundly for about five hours. Plenty of time to get a mocha latte and people watch."

"A mocha what?" Medusa smiled at John's chuckle, but reached up under the hat and touched the sleeping snakes coiled in their netting.

Ratqueen had resisted the idea, channeling and representing the resentment of the others. It had taken extra coaxing for Medusa to talk her into it because, unless it was a case of immediate danger, she didn't impose her will on them.

Ratqueen's annoyance was understandable. During Medusa's rehearsals with Merc, it had become necessary to do the sleeping spell quite often, because none of the snakes liked him and would try to bite him whenever they had the chance. While the snakes were peaceful in their sleep, they were getting understandably restive at being put in the dormant state so frequently when they'd had no such necessity on the island.

We will figure it out, she'd "felt" at Ratqueen. *This is a big transition for us. We haven't figured out our permanent place yet. When we do, it will be easier. We're trying to protect you, protect all of us.*

Though a surge of guilt told her she didn't "have" to go to Starbuck's. This outing was a choice, and her snakes were once again being treated as a problem that had to be contained.

She thought of the disturbing dream again, all her snakes dead. No. She'd go back to the island and repel MyTech however was necessary before she'd let that happen. What had initially been seen as her curse had turned into her family.

John took her arm, drawing her out of her unsettling thoughts. He was staring at her in the mirror. Bending, he kissed her in an experimental way. His face twitched comically and he rubbed his lips and chin. "It's itchy."

"So no permanent beard for me?" she asked.

"Unless you like it," he teased.

"Well, I didn't think that a beard and moustache on a woman could look pretty," she admitted. "But Charlie has made it intriguingly...attractive."

"That's as much to do with her subject matter," he said gallantly.

"I agree," Charlie said with a smile. "It's very difficult to downplay your beauty, Medusa, but that's another reason I chose the costume I did. It and the glasses mask it somewhat, because another thing they will be looking for is a woman of extraordinary beauty."

"Beauty is not only in the eye of the beholder; it is inside the beholdee and shines outward."

Yvette had arrived in her usual silent way. She included them both in her next directives. "This is a small town, off the beaten path. We've been promoted as a typical circus. People don't know otherwise until they attend, so today you should be relatively safe moving around the town, especially with your disguise. But should you sense anything amiss—"

"We'll return here and you can send us back into the portal in a heartbeat," John said. He gripped Medusa's hand. "I won't take any risks with her. I did some training at one of the bases not far from here, so I know the area. Doesn't mean I'm any more comfortable with it, but she's insisting on Starbuck's."

"It's a universal addiction," Yvette said dryly, and met Medusa's gaze. "We must occasionally live so that those who would try to hamper our existence don't gain the upper hand on our hearts and souls."

The vampire stepped closer and reached beneath the hat to run a light finger along Tunneltrap's dark body. Though he was concealed by Medusa's black hair, the vampire had no trouble locating him and giving him the stroke without disturbing Medusa's silky ringlets. "They will be all right," she told Medusa. "Perhaps when you return you can spend the afternoon in the forest with them, letting them enjoy the trees and nature in the way intended, to thank them for their agreement for this."

"How did you know I was worried about them?"

"You have rather transparent features." The vampire's long nail slid along Medusa's cheek, an intriguing caress. When John shifted closer, Yvette tossed him an unreadable look.

"Think I will seduce her away from you, human male? I would be far more likely to seduce you both into my bed. I like variety."

She stepped back before John could respond, though Medusa wasn't sure he would have. He looked as if he knew the best way to deal with Yvette's challenges was to withhold comment. Medusa was imagining the two of them twined with the vampire in her large bed, her wickedly curved nails scraping over the scars on John's back. The scars Medusa had given him. Hers. She found John's hand. Yvette noted it, a glint in her eyes.

"Ah, young love. It has so much room to grow and learn." Moving to Charlie, she tunneled her fingers through the dressmaker's long hair and took a firm grip, drawing her head back as she shifted behind her.

Charlie leaned against the vampire and offered her throat without hesitation. Medusa held her breath at the sensual picture as Yvette didn't immediately take the invitation. Instead, she cupped the young woman's breast and stroked the nipple to tautness beneath her thin dress.

"Don't be late returning. Performers are required to be back on premises two hours before show time."

Yvette was speaking to them both, forcing Medusa to pull her attention back to her. John was giving Yvette a barely masked exasperated look. Yet consciously or not, he had shifted into an almost mirror position behind Medusa, and had evidence pressed against her that he wasn't entirely unaffected by the erotic sight of the two women.

Yvette studied Medusa as she slid her fangs slowly along Charlie's carotid. Charlie lifted her hand to touch Yvette's, but at an admonishing noise from the vampire, she dropped it back to her side, giving her Mistress full access to whatever she desired. "Do you feel ready for the performance tonight, Medusa?" Yvette asked. "Any stage fright?"

"No," Medusa managed. Fortunately, it was true. As she and Merc had practiced the flight sequences in the main tent, or Big Top as they called it, she'd become more comfortable with what was expected. It was just flying. Choreographing aerial maneuvers had been surprisingly enjoyable, and Merc had seemed dedicated to helping her do her best.

Despite her snakes' reaction to him, she couldn't point to anything the part-incubus had done that could be called inappropriate. She stayed on guard with him because of the way he looked at her, but she wasn't sure if he could control that. As she'd learned the timing of her banking and turns, he'd more than once been there to steady her so she didn't hit a center pole or crash into other props or the tent walls. The slide of his hands along her body had been intimate, no mistaking it, but the male was an incubus. Clara had told her there were certain things he couldn't turn off. Not yet.

"Most sex demons don't have long lives," she'd told Medusa. "A lot of them get destroyed by Dark or Light Guardians who are in charge of watching out over nonhuman interactions with the human world. That's because the older sex demons get, the more they lose touch with whatever humanity they have. A fully mature incubus might gorge himself on the life energy of a whole village in a single night and leave nothing but husks. Not because they need that much food, but because once they start, they're like addicts. They don't stop. 'Eating' becomes everything."

She tuned back in to the present, aware of John watching her. Yvette was also, while continuing to play with Charlie's quivering body. Medusa smiled brightly. "Truly, I'm ready. I'm looking forward to it. When variety happened on the island, that usually meant bad things. Someone trying to attack me, a need to hide or fight for my life. Here, something different happening is a good thing."

"Unless it's the Big Top coming down because someone didn't set a center pole correctly, or one of the clowns misses his cue because he decided to get drunk before the show," Yvette said. She straightened, keeping her hand on Charlie's shoulder to hold her in place. "But I expect that's still better than fighting for your life. Enjoy your outing. I plan to take my meal from Charlie and enjoy her charms." The vampire curled a lock of the dressmaker's long red-gold hair around her fingers. "You may stay and watch."

"We have a mocha latte waiting," John said firmly, ignoring Yvette's chuckle as he tugged Medusa out of the tent. Medusa glanced over her shoulder, mesmerized as Yvette dipped her head and bit into Charlie's shoulder without any other foreplay. Yet Charlie's expression was one of bliss, her eyes half closed, lips parted. An arousing plea broke from between them as Yvette slipped a hand inside the waistband of her skirt to massage between her legs while she drank her meal.

The pressure of John's grip drew Medusa fully outside the tent. He let the flap fall back into place as they moved away. While he seemed as if he wanted them away from the heady stimulation, he had his arm around her, his hand molded over her hip, his fingertips kneading the top of her buttock in an urgent way she recognized. Pressing closer to him, she slipped her hand inside the opening of his button down shirt to caress his chest, the rough curling hairs there. When he glanced down at her, she saw the same desire in his expression that she was sure was in her own.

Quickening his pace, he ducked into one of the storage tents, populated by crates and a series of mirrors leaning against them. With a firm hold on her hand, he positioned her before one of the mirrors and then clasped her waist, standing behind her to meet her gaze in the reflection.

Bending, he kissed her throat as Yvette had Charlie's. When he used his teeth, a bolt of sensation went through Medusa. His capable hands slid over her hips and abdomen and up to caress her breasts.

"You wanted to stay and watch," he said.

"So did you," she answered, breathless.

"Yeah. Vampires are dangerous that way. You can get caught in that net they spin and never find your way out. But all I want right now is you."

She purred, laying her head back on his shoulder, and drew in a breath as his hand slid into her leggings, down into her panties, and stroked between her legs as Yvette had done to Charlie. "I want you wet for me, not just her," he growled, shifting his other hand to her throat, clasping right below the silken hairs of the beard Charlie had made so realistic. Yet it was still her beneath all of it, responding to the things he did to her so easily.

"I am," she promised. She struggled against his hold, not because she wanted away, but because it did something to her, feeling his strength pitted against hers, overwhelming her, taking her...

The climax was short but intense, shuddering through her as he watched her in the mirror, her parted lips and glazed eyes. He kept stroking her through the aftershocks. "My beautiful snake-girl," he said. "Mine."

"Yes." She turned weakly in his arms, and he let her. Curling her fingers in his shirt, she swept her lashes down. "I want to do that for you."

She was pressed against his abdomen, so she could feel his erection. His gaze burned into hers. She'd never done that for him, though she'd tasted him that once on the island. She vividly remembered how he'd reacted to that brief touch and, now that she'd seen how he reacted to her volatile response when his lips and tongue were all over her sex, she wanted to see if he reacted with the same near-violent pleasure.

He seemed to be weighing whether or not to allow her to serve him that way. She sank to her knees, her fingers hooking into his belt, and looked up at him, lips parted and eyes conveying how much she wanted to pleasure her Master.

He muttered a quiet oath and put his hand to his belt, unbuckling it with that clinking sound that tingled through her nerves. "Do a good job and I'll buy you a chocolate muffin to go with the latte."

His voice was gruff and she hid a smile behind the bright heat of her desire. When she knelt and wrapped her hand around his base, she relished the steel heat of him, the taste, the tensing of his muscles as she slid down his length with lips, tongue, the wet heat of her mouth, determined to give him the same pleasure he gave her.

Muffin or no muffin.

She followed her own desires and instincts, as well as his firm guidance to learn the way of it, and discovered she loved the way he reacted, the contraction of his thigh muscles under her forearms, the way he thrust himself into her mouth, the fervent words he said to her as he came closer to his release. It was a carnal version of the rapture she'd felt at Athena's feet; the hint of what service could mean in a sexual context. It had teased her adolescent mind then, and came to fruition now. When she raised her lashes, his eyes were like gray fire. She somehow knew that him seeing her look up with a pleasure-filled gaze, while her mouth was stretched by his thrusting cock, was what sent him catapulting off that ledge.

She fought to swallow him down, not spill a single drop of the salty, thick liquid of his seed. His groans sent shivers of pleasure through her body, amazing her when it provoked her own quickly recovering response. She wanted him again.

She wondered at that, trembling as he slowly slid from her mouth and tucked himself back into his jeans, refastening them before moving to a crate to sit down. When she shifted so she was still kneeling at his feet, all without rising, that heat kindled in his eyes anew.

He lifted her up onto his lap, making her straddle him. Her legs curved around his hips as he wrapped his arms around her and pressed his face into her breasts and throat. When he spread kisses over both, she dropped her head back. Her breath caught in her throat as he sealed the heated moisture of his mouth over her left nipple through her clothes. He paid equal, thorough attention to the right.

At last he lifted his head and caressed her face with one large hand. His expression was so enraptured by her, she couldn't deny how it spoke to her own heart. It was not just her body he held in his hands.

"Did you ever imagine this?" she asked. "Me being in your world? Doing things with you like you might do with another woman here? Have coffee?"

"No," he said. "I didn't let myself get that far. I started with just getting to you, to the island. I figured anything else after that would be frosting on the cake." He chuckled against her breast. "And you're already a hell of a cake."

She stroked his short hair, the curve of his solid skull, and smiled, pleased at what she was sure was a compliment. "My island was your sanctuary, wasn't it? From your life before."

"No." He lifted his head. "That was you. Still is."

She pressed her face against his, closing her eyes. When he cupped her buttocks through the thin leggings and moved her against the fly of his jeans in a slow, pleasurable rub, she savored the feeling as he did. It didn't matter that he'd just released. He wanted to feel that contact still, and so did she.

"Is it wrong that I wanted to watch them?" she asked. "Yvette and Charlie? Is it dangerous in the way Merc is dangerous?"

"No. If we stay here for any length of time, my guess is you'll get the opportunity again. A lot of the players are into the Dom/sub stuff. Like you already heard"—he gave her a look full of erotic heat, recalling that potent conversation—"when they're not getting ready for a performance, they'll have play parties and set up some of the same equipment they use for performances for different purpose." He sighed. "It's just a lot of this stuff is new to you. I want to give it to you in bite-sized pieces but hell, I'm only human. Watching two beautiful women like Yvette and Charlie go at it, I could completely forget about slow and bite-sized and take you right there in front of them, devour you whole."

She didn't think that sounded bad at all. She framed his face in both hands, bemused as always by the slimness of her fingers against his masculine features, the differences between them that seemed to mesh so well together. "I want to be devoured by you sometimes," she admitted. "Get lost and never find my way back."

"Same goes." Lifting her off of him, he rose, towering over her. As he did, he blew on one of the hat feathers. Despite the casual gesture, his eyes were intent and heated on hers. He wanted more. So did she.

"Then no mocha latte." She made the abrupt decision with full enthusiasm. Who needed coffee, even if it was the most wonderful coffee in the world, according to John Pierce's magazine? This moment was still far better.

Stepping back from him, she removed the hat, pulling the pins free from her hair. "*Salia Motana.*"

It was the trigger phrase Yvette had given her to remove the spell on the snakes. As she felt them slowly start to rouse, she pulled the other pins from the netting, letting them roll free and her hair loosen to spill down her back. She shrugged out of the coat and unlaced the tunic so she could draw it over her head. When Charlie had bound the wings, she'd done so with wide, stretchy strips of cloth she'd wrapped around Medusa's torso above and below her breasts. Taking her shoes and leggings off, Medusa stood before him in black silk panties and the upper body wrap.

"Will my Master free me so I can fly?" she asked.

His eyes glittered in the darkness. Stepping close to her, he fingered the edge of the wrap. "I would have taken you out for coffee," he said.

"I know that. I'd rather you take me. Several times. I want to come to the performance tonight with my body well-used and marked by your attentions. Please, Master."

His gaze snapped to hers. "You're getting real good at asking me for what you want, sweetheart. In a very pretty way. I like that."

Tunneltrap slid groggily over her shoulder and rested his head on the section of wrap above her breast. John captured her nipple below it and shaped it to a peak with stroking fingers as she swayed on her feet, her eyes half closing.

"I'll free you after I take you. Don't want you trying to fly away from me."

She caught her lip in her teeth as he paid similar attention to the other nipple. Her toes curled into the floor of the tent, a worn smooth wooden platform.

"Call me that again," he demanded.

"Master," she whispered. His mouth was hard, his eyes like concentrated lightning upon her. Though she'd just given him a release, his cock was already starting to press against his jeans again. He caressed her face.

Charlie had given her an ointment to remove the beard and moustache adhesive. John had pocketed it with the soft cloth she'd recommended using so it wouldn't cause abrasions on Medusa's face. He drew them out now and began to take off the facial hair with careful, gentle hands. "I want to see you as you are."

He could. He did. He'd done that from the beginning, and it hadn't been a matter of seeing her beneath the features other considered monstrous. He'd accepted those as part of her. Thanks to that, he'd opened her eyes to the realization that she considered them part of her, too. She recalled her earlier thoughts about her snakes. It worried her an act of trust, something good and positive, might take them from her, dissolve them to nothingness like her forked tongue or talons.

"Hey..." He'd finished and was stroking her face with his fingertips. "Where'd you go?"

"I'm afraid of losing them." She lifted her arms and, responding to her feelings, the five snakes came forth, overlapping her arms. She turned her face toward Ratqueen, closing her eyes as the snake bumped her face. "This is frightening for them, too, John. Help us know it will be all right."

"That's my job. And it will be all right." He caught her chin in thumb and forefinger to hold her gaze. "I know it. They know it. Trust your Master."

Even though unease still trickled through her breast, when he bent and kissed her, that and his words helped. He wrapped his fingers around her raised forearms, allowing the snakes to slide over his knuckles and glide around his wrists, binding him to her.

The kiss was slow and deep, his tongue twisting around to play with hers, his lips teasing, teeth pressing against her flesh. She swayed, and he put his arm around her back, hand dropping to smooth over her backside.

"That outfit you're wearing tonight. Does it show any skin?"

"Not much. It's formfitting, but not overly revealing, so Merc... won't be overly agitated."

His lip curled, but he forbore comment and began to unwrap the strips of cloth. The snakes slid away to her shoulders again as he turned her, once, twice, three times. She closed her eyes, dipping her head at the dizziness while her wings stretched out, full and free again.

Drawing her over to the crates, he pressed her down so her breasts pressed against the rough slats of the one on top. He ran his hands over her wings. Bending to tease them with lips and fingers, he explored and found where they were most responsive; at the joining point with her body, and along the thin membranes between the bones. He dropped to his knees, kissing his way down her spine, hands cupping and kneading her buttocks, pushing her up on her toes, making her feel the strain in her thighs.

"John."

"Master," he said against her flesh. "Right now, that's what you call me."

"Master." She hitched over the last syllable, because he'd wet a finger and was tracing it along the rim between her buttocks, setting off a cascade of feeling that rippled through her sex, making her dampen anew.

He bit one cheek, and she gasped at the cutting pressure of his teeth. As he rose, he gave the curve a healthy smack, making it wobble. The sting of his bite and impact of his hand shot a glorious spiral through her once again.

"Sometimes, when a submissive soul is afraid of something, it helps if her Master reminds her he's in charge of her wellbeing. That she doesn't have to worry so much. Stay where you are." He moved into the recesses of the tent and came back with a handful of slim wooden sticks that he slapped against his hand, showing they were flexible.

"A birching usually helps with that, and I think these will do the trick. The marks it leaves will remind you."

He wasn't asking her opinion on it. That deep part of her that responded to the unconditional demand for service, the right kind of service, rose to the top, taking her voice until he summoned it from her.

"Say, 'Yes Master.'"

"Yes, Master. Thank you." She added that last spontaneously, and it seemed to please him. He ran a hand over her backside, massaging, pinching, giving her an occasional slap that made her jump. When he hit her with that handful of slim rods, the slapping noise made her jump too. The resulting sting was dispersed over both buttocks, so it hadn't hurt, not much, but she quickly realized he was warming her up as he did it a few more times.

As he increased the weight of the blows, he slowed down. Each impact sang through her nerve endings and had time to spread like the warmth of the sun before he did it again. It hurt, but it was also arousing her.

She didn't keep count, lost in the sensation. When he paused, running his hands over her burning, stinging flesh, she had tears in her eyes. But she wasn't thinking of her worries anymore.

The snakes were arranged on the crate around her head and shoulders. They were caught up in the usual lethargy they experienced when she became aroused, though Ratqueen's head rested on the top of her hand.

"What do you want, Medusa?"

"You," she whispered. "Inside me. Please."

That marvelous belt sound and the tick of a zipper. When he put his hands to her hips, he slid into her wetness as easily as she might have dived into the pool at her waterfall. She groaned at his size, how her tender flesh had to stretch to accommodate him.

"Yeah, you got me big as a piling there. When you call me Master, it's like a trigger. I want to fuck you right then and there. So keep that in mind if we're ever in a Starbuck's."

She was too aroused to giggle, but she felt the frisson of amusement in among the pleasure. She gasped as he began to pump into her slow. He slid his hands over her wings, her back, and curved his hand over her nape, holding her down as he increased the power of his thrusts. "Goddess...Master..."

"You feel so fucking good. Love your cunt, and love you. Love you..."

She closed her eyes as he drew them both to that quivering, shimmering edge. "Please..."

"Going with me. Going over that same cliff. Right...fucking... now..."

They both came as he'd demanded, him keeping her high on her toes as he slammed his hips against her backside, her making moans of pleasure as the climax rippled through her in continuous waves, tightening and loosening everything at once.

When he slowed, he wrapped both arms around her, holding her wings folded against her body and all of her inside the span of his arms.

"Christ, you're going to kill me. And I'll die with a smile on my face." But his hand dropped, smoothing over her buttock. It was sore, but she didn't mind the feeling. "You liked that," he said.

It was a statement, not a question, and she wasn't sure if that was okay. "Yes. I felt how you liked it, as well."

"Yeah. There are a million ways I want to have you, and it seems like we're only getting started."

She liked the sound of that. She liked it a lot.

CHAPTER TWENTY-FIVE

The Big Top was full, nearly a thousand parents and children. Clara told her a thousand was a small crowd for most circuses, but Yvette considered that the optimal house size. Gundar had offered Medusa a complicated explanation involving supply and demand and marketing strategies that mostly went over her head, but the end result was they usually had sellout crowds. Through ticket and novelty sales, that number provided enough of a "take" per show to make the "nut", the Circus's operating expenses, and a profit besides.

The practical side of the business was Gundar and Yvette's responsibility. After hearing all that went into it, and getting slightly lost with all the unfamiliar terminology that even the translation spell couldn't completely decipher, Medusa was glad her only job, at least for tonight, was her performance with Merc. Fortunately, it left plenty of time for watching.

As Medusa stood hidden behind the curtain at one of the troupe entrances to the rings they called a "back door," she was as dazzled by the show as anyone in the stands. She couldn't imagine any child attending tonight who wouldn't be planning to join a circus after seeing it.

The show had started with a dramatic encounter between Lianthe and Tragar, the male dragon. Lianthe had stood next to Medusa, letting her rest against her side, until the unicorn was cued and came cantering out to a wave of oohs and aahs from the house. The reaction escalated into gasps as Tragar emerged from the other end of the tent with a dynamic flap of his wings and a bugling call.

The unicorn and dragon performed a mock fight that would look very real to anyone who hadn't seen the rehearsal. Yet Lianthe dissipated the intensity when she later pranced up to the dragon with an olive branch. Tragar shot fire perilously close to her as she skittered out of harm's way. The audience laughed harder when she came back carrying a raw steak in a basket decorated with flowers. The dragon's heart was won and a truce declared. At the conclusion of the act, Tragar was coiled around Lianthe, his large head resting upon the unicorn's back, her touching her muzzle to his brow.

After that, the centaurs burst upon the scene, doing their ring tossing and flame jumping. The three male performers rakishly flirted with their audience. Medusa hadn't had a chance to get to know them the way she had others in the Circus, but John had told her the centaurs were very tribal and treated most non-centaurs as outsiders.

"You think I'm protective?" He'd rolled his eyes. "Have you yet seen a centaur female or one of their young?"

When she shook her head, he'd grimaced. "You won't, until they're absolutely sure of you. If you ever stumble upon one of them in the forest by accident—which even that would be a miracle, because they have natural concealment abilities that would eclipse even Maddock's magic—promise me you'll lower your eyes and back away as fast as you can. A centaur male will kill a stranger for being within a stone's throw of his family and ask questions later."

She'd promised, though she couldn't wait for the chance to someday see a centaur foal. As she stood in the shadows, watching the performers and the reactions of the crowd, she realized she was near humans again, many of them, and it wasn't frightening. She was excited.

She'd expected to have some trepidation about this, and suspected Merc had a backup act ready in case she'd rabbited. But as she watched the children's eyes light up, heard their laughter and calls to the players, saw the parents smiling and sometimes with equal looks of wonder on their faces, she felt no fear. Just amazement and gratitude that she was here, able to do this.

That was the magic of the Circus, wasn't it? Gundar had explained it well when she'd sat and watched him do his metal working one afternoon. As he hammered and turned the steel, creating his knives and swords, he'd talked about why the Circus was a sanctuary to so many.

"When people attend a show, they can straddle a line. Tell themselves it isn't real to keep them in their comfort zone, but believe it is real during the performance to give that part of them that wishes it was real a chance to get out, stretch its wings."

The Big Top went fully dark, a spotlight highlighting the huge black wolf standing center ring. Medusa knew glitter had been added to Rand's coat to augment its gleam beneath the lights. It intensified the gold and blue stare of his bi-colored eyes. Rand stalked along the edge of the audience, the spotlight following him. Parents tried to keep their children from reaching over the rail to rub his fur, but inevitably one slipped past a mother's guard.

When the little girl's palm slid along the line of his spine, he merely kept moving forward. As if a string holding them back had snapped, the children instantly crowded against the rail along his path. He trotted along the perimeter, staying close enough their hands could pass over his coat, one after the other. Medusa was delighted by the expressions on their faces, the excitement as they turned to their parents, palms up to show the coating of glitter, likely another reason it had been used.

The air was punctuated by a shrill whistle. Rand stopped and wheeled, ears pricked. Another spotlight hit the center ring and, a breath later, a giant purple shoe with green laces landed there with a thump.

He bounded away toward it, leaping a strategically placed group of crates to highlight the power and flexibility of his muscular body. As he landed on the shoe, a cacophony of noise and protests happened behind the back door curtains. A clown wearing only one purple and green shoe emerged, shaking his finger and trying to persuade Rand to give it back. The lights went up and a small army of the clowns came pouring forth to back him up.

A hilarious skit ensued where the wolf kept trying to chase them out of the ring and away from the shoe.

Feeling a movement to her left, Medusa glanced up to see Cai at her shoulder. A light smile was on his serious lips. While he had that predatory stillness that told her she shouldn't be anything less than careful and respectful around him, he often seemed more approachable than Yvette, perhaps because he was a younger vampire. She hadn't confirmed that; it was just a feeling.

"Rand loves the kids," he told her in a low voice. "We don't get the chance to be who we are in their world often. The Vampire Council wasn't on board until they came to one performance. After that, I think they all wanted to join the Circus, too. Yvette has created a magical world here."

Hearing the note of regret in his voice, she asked, "Why does that make you sad?"

He glanced at her. "Because eventually it'll be destroyed. It's what happens to things this good. There's my cue."

The clowns had scattered, and Rand had settled down to chew on the oversized shoe he'd successfully retained. Because Cai moved with vampire speed, it looked as if he'd suddenly appeared behind the wolf. The lights dimmed again, leaving two spotlights on the pair of central players.

Seeing the vampire, a growl started in Rand's throat, a rumble that grew to be heard in every corner of the large tent. Cai dropped to his heels, fingers templed on the ground, a predator's crouch. The crowd gasped as he bared fangs that lengthened to lethal curving points that pricked his chin. He looked as wild and untamed as Rand. He was also admittedly an erotic fantasy, the widow's peak of his dark hair increasing the intensity of his sculpted face and deep set eyes. His costume was a black silk shirt and snug trousers over silver tipped boots. A pair of silver chain link bracelets glittered on either wrist. His eyes glowed crimson.

Then they both leaped.

She'd seen them practice, and she still gasped, making Waterlight jump, coiled on her brow beneath the antenna headdress. Seeing a vampire and a werewolf wrestle was like watching a pair of gladiators fighting to the death. Though they were doing this for show, it wasn't the first time she'd wondered what issues the two of them worked out during these battles. A couple times during practice Cai had come away bleeding after having to pin Rand, hold him in a choke hold until he settled. A rage roused in the male when he was in his beast mode. But based on what she'd heard in Cai's voice when he spoke of the

Circus not lasting, she wondered if that rage had its complement in the vampire's own demons.

"One of them needs to get it over with and rip the other one's head off," Merc murmured at her side.

She met his eyes; she always did, and it was always an effort, because she was predisposed not to meet a Dominant's eyes. She hadn't recognized that in herself until John made her more cognizant of it. She could almost tell who was Dominant by whose gaze she had trouble meeting. Yvette, Gundar, Marcellus, Cai... Oddly enough, sometimes even Rand, for all that he was Cai's servant.

There were many vanilla troupe members, as John called them, but as he'd said, there were quite a few who had embraced the human BDSM world because they were of a Dominant or submissive orientation themselves, regardless of species. Merc was hard to classify. She sometimes thought he was a Dominant, but there was something about him that wasn't.

Perhaps it was the lack of control she felt in his core, a foe he was fighting daily. He lost or won that fight too unpredictably to determine which way the final war would go. She saw that knowledge in Yvette and Marcellus's eyes when they looked upon him. It gave Medusa a cold shiver, because it would be one or both of them that would step in if the war was decisively lost. She could relate to that too well. Maybe that was why she tolerated Merc, far more than she should, in John's opinion.

"They love each other too much. Even though they drive each other crazy," she added.

"Think so?" Merc studied the vampire and wolf shifter. "I don't see it."

Because he didn't really understand love. She wondered if he ever would. Thinking of what she was exploring and discovering with John, she believed that was an even greater tragedy than Merc having to be put down at Yvette and Marcellus's hands. "Yes," she said. "It's obvious. Watch. See, where Rand starts to lose control, and his beast takes over, Cai balances him. He takes that control from him, holds it, cares for him."

"That's just the vampire thing about owning his servant."

"Yes, maybe. And no." She thought of how John had reacted to her calling him Master. "It's a give and take, I think."

"Looks like he's pinning him hard enough to bruise ribs," Merc said dubiously.

"Well, he is a wolf shifter, and an exceptionally strong one. Yvette says that's because his third mark enhances the wolf's already super-natural strength. He's not stronger than Cai, but he doesn't make it easy. He's a very good fighter, whether in wolf or human form. He could rule a pack of his own, but he chooses to be with Cai." Something else Clara had told her. While the clairvoyant shied away from telling people their future, she was an intense student of relationships and behavior, a necessity she said contributed to her "fortune telling" skills.

Medusa had watched Cai and Rand spar when Rand was in human form, and she'd found it very...fascinating. The two powerful males, usually dressed in nothing more than the clinging type of garment they called workout shorts, grappling in ways that not only spoke of their fighting skills, but their carnal knowledge of one another.

It fascinated her enough that John had reaped the benefits when she found him and ravished him in their wagon, to his amusement and pleasure.

"Vampires sometimes don't leave much choice about that shit," Merc said flatly.

She suspected that comment, and its barely concealed bitter edge, was directed more toward Yvette than Cai. A sidelong glance showed her Merc's jaw was in a belligerent set. Sometimes he reminded her of an angry adolescent, frustrated by not being grown up enough, yet feeling so many things that grown-ups could feel and not knowing how to manage those emotions and impulses.

Don't humanize him. Not ever. John had admonished her about that several times, and he was emphatic enough about it that she heeded him. Though she wondered if he might give her another of those fascinating spankings or "birchings" if she made him believe she wasn't mindful enough of the warning.

Her cheeks warmed at the memory, and she put that away. She and John might disagree about her empathy toward Merc, but on one thing they were in full accord. It was best never to have any sexual thoughts around the incubus, since he could pick up even a trace of human arousal. According to others and her own instincts of self-preservation, he didn't react well to that.

"You ready for our part?" he said, those unnerving eyes trained on her. "We're up next."

"Yes, I'm ready." She looked at her wings, enchanted by how Charlie and her talented army of assistants had transformed them into a Monarch butterfly pattern. Merc's were a dark purple with gold highlights. The purple would shimmer under the stage lights. While she wore the black bodysuit, his outfit complemented it. Charlie had designed it to be similar to what the acrobats wore. A sleeveless black vest loosely laced over his chest, and pants that clung like a second skin to his muscular backside, thighs and groin. His hair was brushed to a gleam on his bared shoulders.

Purely from a female perspective, Medusa couldn't argue with Charlie's decision to not cover it with an antenna headdress like her own. But when she saw Merc noticing her evaluation, she hastily looked away. Harmless appreciation of the appeal of any of the Circus players was as natural as breathing, but with Merc, one had to curb such instincts.

She wasn't expecting to see John Pierce, since Marcellus had him on security detail, but she was very glad when she saw him approach from the shadows. She closed her eyes to inhale his scent as his arms slid around her and he did his now usual and very welcome press of lips along her throat. Merc shifted several feet away, either to give them the courtesy of some privacy or, more likely, to give John a wider berth, based on the men's distaste for one another.

"Doing all right?"

She clasped her hands over John's. "Yes. And you?"

"Better for having seen you. Your eyes are dancing like stars. They're going to love you. You should think about doing the Promenade."

"Oh. Well...maybe." Standing back here or performing far above their heads was one thing. But to walk close to a crowd, within touching distance? She thought of Rand and the little girl touching him. In their minds, he was a large, furry dog. She was something for which they had no context. But there were plenty of beings in the Circus as different as her.

"What if MyTech hears about me?"

"We're here for three days, and you're only doing the first night's performance. They don't allow any phones or recording devices in the tent. By the time word gets out you're here, you're back in the portal, and they have to predict where the Circus goes next. It's covered. You don't have to worry about that."

He touched her face, his gaze passing with pleasure over her butterfly wings and the form-fitting dark costume she wore. "No pressure on any of it. Just have fun with this."

John turned his attention to Merc, his expression neutral instead of outwardly hostile for once. "Take care of my girl up there."

"Yeah." Merc showed a flash of surprise at John's straightforward request, but shrugged. "She's got it down. Even showed me some new moves."

"She's good about that." John stroked the shell of her ear. "All the snakes still zzz'ing?"

"Earthson is snoring," she said. "Despite being the smallest, he's good at making his presence known the most vehemently."

"Well, you barely come up to my chest, and you pack a powerful punch." John's eyes gleamed and he brushed a kiss over her lips. "Knock 'em dead, butterfly. You've got nothing to worry about."

At a gesture from Caleb, positioned across from them behind another screen, John gave her one last nudge and moved away to see what help he needed. The Circus's strongman headed up the prop team that made sure everything was in place for each act. She saw the rings being set up in the shadows that would be lit on fire before she and Merc twisted through them. Lifting her gaze, she located the piece of equipment that would create a sheet of water like a waterfall, sparkling with the lights. It would also douse any sparks their costumes might catch after they passed through the fire rings.

Cai and Rand had relinquished the stage to the aerial silk and trapeze performers. Her heart lifted right along with the audience's as she watched their graceful movements and the twisting, soaring conclusion act. It was a good segue to their routine.

Yvette stepped into center ring. She wore a silk top hat, a black corset and snug latex pants. Her ropes of dark hair fell to her waist and were sparkling with silver glitter. Her boots went to her thighs. She was an erotic fantasy to the adults, a glittering character for the children. When she spoke, her fangs caught the lights, deliberately elongated. Medusa shivered, remembering them penetrating Charlie's throat, a display that had compelled new erotic territory for her and John in the tent of mirrors.

"You have seen our human performers fly on the trapeze and weave themselves in the silks," Yvette said. "Now you will see a pair of butterflies bring silken wings and acrobatics together, in a way you won't see anywhere else, because we are the Circus. The things you see here touch upon the dreams we all have of what life can be like...if we just free our imaginations."

Her voice could charm and seduce. Medusa thought if she recited the alphabet, the audience would pay rapt attention. Even the members of the troupe seemed to pause to absorb the hypnotizing tones. She caught a glimpse of Gundar, standing beside the waterfall feature. His gaze was on his Mistress. While Medusa didn't doubt his devotion to the vampire, she was startled by the bald emotion revealed in his expression. He loved her.

Did Yvette know? How would that even work? Gundar was a clear Dominant. Though he served Yvette's blood needs as one of her second mark servants, and obviously shared pleasures with her as Charlie did, there had to be key differences to their relationship. Sometimes it felt as if the whole troupe was a book of stories waiting to be read.

She took a breath, shifting her focus to the here and now as Yvette withdrew and the first strains of the music Merc had chosen for their performance started. The classical piece would evolve into what he'd called a Latin number, a tango. To help Medusa better understand what that was, Clara had showed her the dance with one of the trapeze artists. Medusa remembered Marcellus watching, a slight set to his jaw as the trapeze artist moved her in the provocative movements, Clara laughing.

Another mystery. She'd never seen the two share even a kiss, yet the sexual energy between Clara and Marcellus was thick enough to cut with a knife. John's phrase, when she'd asked him about it.

After the Latin part, there would be heavy metal rock for the more antagonistic part of their flight. From there it would rein back to a romantic denouement, a resolution. The act had been choreographed to convey excitement, danger and romance.

There'd been some concern about Merc's handling of the male-pursuit-of-female theme, but after reviewing the idea in detail with

John and Merc, and speaking to Merc at length, Yvette had indicated that the sexual tension element was low key enough, and Merc was showing enough self-restraint in rehearsals, that they could risk it with the current safeguards in place. Namely that it was being done under the close supervision of her or Marcellus, and tonight it would be in full public view.

John had been less placated. In fact, originally, some of his deepest follow-up concerns about her doing this lay with what he'd just reassured her about, MyTech's search for her. But in the aftermath of remembering Klotho and Callidora's deaths, as well as that of her other sisters, Medusa had struggled with a few dark days, despite Charlie's healing touch. The worst moments came during idleness, when her chores were done and John was busy with his own. He'd therefore become more amenable to her performing when he'd seen how the rehearsals provided her a necessary distraction. As such, he and Merc had reached a wary accord, which he'd demonstrated just now by telling the male to look after her.

However, as the lights darkened and she backed out into the spotlight with precise, delicate steps, Merc matching her gait with a deliberate stalk, she realized something that none of them might have recognized until now. She'd already seen how the first acts—those whose rehearsals she'd witnessed—could transform into something far more substantial and magical when lights, music and an audience was involved. The audience might not only pick up on the sexual component to the piece she and Merc were about to perform, but feed it with their own subtle reactions. Which in turn could make it more vibrant, powerful and *real* for the two of them.

She wanted to believe she was imagining it, but she thought she saw a gleam in Merc's eyes, as if he'd anticipated that all along.

It's a performance, she told herself, holding his gaze. He moved forward, a quick lunge, and she left the ground in a short hop, her wings fluttering. That part hadn't been choreographed. She'd reacted to the look in his gaze, and now his lips curved, the tip of a fang showing.

She admonished herself to follow the choreography. She told herself what Yvette had said to her, several times. She hadn't understood the context until this moment.

Don't feed a wild animal.

She and Merc circled one another, and he put out a hand. She shook her head. When he tried to grab her, she spun gracefully beneath the mock attempt and flew behind him, settling in a half kneel as he turned and studied her, considering his options.

He did a somersault, followed by a pattern of elaborate twisting movements all around her, the dance of the male butterfly to impress the female. She changed positions several times to watch him and let the spotlight hit her spread wings.

He landed and stalked toward her again. She mimicked his movements, the somersault and the twist, proving she could do it as well. Mocking him, challenging him. He left the ground and they started to spiral upward together, their movements becoming more complex. As the Latin tango beat took over from the classical score, they moved forward, back, up and down, wings brushing, hands clasping and then releasing with the façade of reluctance. His eyes were burning into hers, and she moistened her lips, betraying a shift in her feelings from fantasy to reality.

"You like to submit, Medusa," he muttered as he hovered close to her. "Your body hungers for it. You like a male to prove he can catch you. So let me prove it to you. Try to elude me, knowing you'll fail."

Abruptly, Medusa wasn't thinking of the impact on the show, or the reaction of the audience. That kindling light in Merc's eyes was a warning sign both Charlie and Clara had told her about. Maybe he'd honestly thought he could maintain control, but the live environment was triggering his incubus instincts, the deeper, far more violent nature he harbored.

If she kept her wits about her, she could handle it. She wouldn't let the past rise up and try to choke her. She wouldn't let this remind her of how Ukrit had used violence to subdue her, to take. As Merc would, if he could catch her.

She already knew showing fear was the wrong decision. Instead, she improvised, modifying one of the things they'd practiced to dive under him, catch his leg and twist him off balance. It gave her a head start. Right on time, the heavy metal started up with a clashing of symbols and primal drum beat.

She was vaguely aware of the audience's applause and gasps as she navigated around poles and banked sharply against the sides of the tent. As she shot through the fiery hoops and waterfall, drops sprayed out over the rows of upturned faces. He caught her several times, spinning in the air with her, but she always twisted free. And somewhere along the way, she figured out what she needed to do.

She started to laugh, to tease him. Doubling back, she caressed his chest as she brushed past him, evading his grip again. She pulled the aerial silk loose from where it had been tied off and spun around him with it, tangling his legs and one of his arms. She draped it over his face, sliding her fingertips down to his lips as she hovered close, her wings beating to hold her aloft. As his gaze gleamed and fangs bared, she did a full flip and dove straight toward the ground as if she'd lost her balance, and was falling, falling, falling...

A collective cry exploded, but he caught her at what seemed like a scant few feet from the ground. This was what they'd practiced, but as he set her on her feet, she felt his tension. She knelt, her wings spread out over her back, one hand clasping the silk as he held the other end twisted around his arm. He was staring at her, breathing hard. His wings were fully spread, the purple gleaming like the light coating of perspiration on his muscled arms. The music ended.

The thunderous applause was enough to vibrate the tent, yet self-preservation kept her focus on her partner. Lifting her gaze to Merc's, she let her lips curve, even though her stomach had turned into a mass of nerves. Yes, he liked control as John Pierce did. She could see that in the way he stared at her, kneeling at his feet. But unlike John, there was something that had control of Merc, something that might forever endanger anyone he wanted to call his own. The hunger of it was in his face, the quiver of his body. She wasn't sure if he could move without hurting her, and wondered if that was why he remained locked in place, motionless. He confirmed it with a stiffly worded command.

"Go. Move slowly."

She rose and curtsied to the crowd before she daintily walked toward the shadows. She was all too aware of the force of heat she felt behind her, and knew Merc had not taken his eyes off her, like a wolf watching prey.

She was halfway across the ring when the lights were turned off. She thought she heard a hiss from Gundar.

"Fuck, don't kill the lights. He—"

Merc was on her in a heartbeat, with hard hands far too powerful to throw off. A fang punctured her throat as her head was yanked back. She bit back a scream, but then Merc was gone. John had her. She heard the sickening thud of a fist hitting flesh as she was pulled behind the curtains. She smelled Yvette's scent with John's, but then it was just John, holding her at his side as the lights went up. Merc was gone and Yvette was in the center ring, announcing the next act as if nothing had happened. The benefit of having players who could move faster than the human eye could follow.

She thought she'd felt the brush of another set of wings during the struggle. Looking down, she saw a dark green feather caught in the threads of her black costume. It told her Marcellus had been involved in pulling Merc off of her and taking him away.

Her heart was hammering against her rib cage. John held her close, and was pressing a square of cloth to the shallow puncture in her throat. "You okay?" he asked, his voice angry, but not with her.

"Yes. I think this just triggered...whatever his problem was."

"You think? Christ, I knew it was a bad idea."

"I wanted to do it," she said softly. "And the audience loved it."

"Yeah. Right up to the point where he would have drained your life energy in front of their eyes. Just...don't talk for a few moments. I want to strangle you as much as I want to hold you."

She much preferred him to do the latter, so she remained still, glad for the comfort of his arms. And for his next unexpected comment.

"You were amazing. I've never seen flying like that. You ran circles around him. He wasn't expecting that. You followed his lead in rehearsals."

"He is the veteran performer. But when I sensed he was losing control, I thought I should not be predictable. I've depended on my flying ability for my life plenty of times."

"It showed." John sighed. "When I saw what was happening, I wanted the snakes to be awake, to keep him away from you. I almost shouted out their trigger word myself."

Remembering the look in Merc's eyes, she shook her head. "Caught in whatever he fights inside himself, he would have hurt them."

"Maybe. I feel for the guy in some ways, but at the same time I want to rip his goddamn wings off, just like Yvette's always threatening to do. You sure you okay?"

"Yes." She conveyed it by holding John as tightly as he was holding her. Yes, Merc posed a threat to her, but they were surrounded by friends.

Friends. She thought of them all as friends. It was a comforting revelation. And standing there with John, realizing how surprisingly *not* rattled she was, she realized something else.

Whether it was naïve or not, when John was nearby, she was beginning to have faith in happy endings.

CHAPTER TWENTY-SIX

*J*ohn would have been gratified by her confidence, but he was dealing with more than just his tension. Before Medusa's act, Marcellus had given him the okay to watch it, the others covering his security area assignment. Yvette had stood at John's side, so he knew she'd become aware of the shift in Merc at the same moment he had.

"Fuck. He said he could handle doing this with a partner," she grumbled.

She'd latched onto John's arm as he started forward. "Marcellus and I will interfere if needed," she said firmly. "I've already made him aware of the problem and he can be here in a blink. We don't interrupt the performance as long as things are under control."

And they had been, John grudgingly admitted. Yvette's lips had curved in a rare look of admiration at Medusa's aerial maneuvers, the way she soothed Merc's predator instincts while inspiring secret dark longings in the adult audience members.

Maybe what had him out of sorts was Yvette's observation at that key moment. "She's magnificent. She'll serve any Master or Mistress worth serving, JP. Even if circumstances take you out of her life, she will always have a place here. And we have plenty of Doms who would be pleased to help her continue to explore her needs and desires."

Circumstances. Like her deciding, despite her stated love for him, that she had barely had a chance to live her life, let alone explore relationships? He remembered the day she'd confronted him at their picnic, calling him on that bullshit. He was blowing smoke up his own ass. He had only one reaction to her choosing someone else.

Over his dead body.

When it was just the two of them tonight, he'd let her know again how incredible her performance had been. And then redden her pretty ass to communicate how much of a scare she'd given him. She'd admitted she wanted him to go deeper into her submissive instincts and her wish was his own. Especially if it could get this need to kill someone out of his gut.

Lady Yvette had said she didn't have to join the Promenade. So had John. But the children's delight with each of the acts, their lack of revulsion or fear, the energy they created, made her want to do it. So when it drew close to time for the Promenade, Medusa donned the outfit Charlie had provided her. Despite how busy the dressmaker was throughout the performance, adjusting and pinning, smoothing and tweaking costumes with her assistants, she'd been enchanted to have Medusa come looking for hers.

"Have fun," the young woman said, pressing the costume into her hands. "I don't have time to ensure the exact fitting, but if something is hanging loose, run back in here and I can do a temporary fix."

The flesh-colored sparkling garment with thin straps and a low back to accommodate her wings had fit her like a second skin from neck to ankles, making Medusa wonder what Charlie would call an exact fit. The bodysuit was comfortable and pretty, its sequins flashing as she turned in a circle under the backstage lights.

John was working one of the exit points, but when he saw her, his eyes drank in the way she looked. He gestured, a wordless command to have her turn and show him the garment from every angle. Since he couldn't leave his post, she came to him.

"Got to love a circus," he murmured. He lifted his gaze to her face, to her hair, which she'd brushed out so it swirled in silken waves around the now-awake snakes. They were weaving through the tresses, this time in curiosity, not agitation, trying to follow all the activity going on behind the scenes. "So you're going to do it, snake-girl?"

"I think so. I'd like to try." She'd been a nightmare, a monster for so long. The thought made her stomach flip flop, but John kissed her with firm, heated lips, centering her.

"Like I said, the kids are going to love you."

A trio of dwarves were passing by. As if picking up on her hesitation, or maybe John had thrown him a significant look, Dom-to-Dom, Gundar stopped and gave her his sexy smile, tossing back a lock of his thick, handsome mane of hair. He was in a green velvet doublet with gold trim, matching hose and shiny black boots. "Coming with us, Medusa?"

He extended a broad hand, and she let hers be clasped. His hand might be smaller, but his grip was as strong as John's. When he tugged her along in their wake, she tossed one last look over her shoulder at John. She wondered if this sudden wave of nerves was what Clara had called stage fright. John Pierce winked and pinched her buttock with the benefit of his long arm, making her yelp and narrow her gaze at him, a distraction that took her out under the lights.

She was moving forward with a parade of other players. Some of those things Clara had described were already happening. Caleb had four small children balanced on his shoulders and one on his raised leg as their parents surrounded him, perhaps concerned about any of them falling. Medusa had seen his lightning-quick reflexes; plus, he had the balance of an anvil. None of them would come to harm.

The laconic Marcellus was a particular surprise, but even from her time and place in the world she knew the reputation of angels. If he would unbend for anyone else other than Clara, it would be children. He was in the center ring, Yvette correctly understanding he would be so popular it would be best to let the children come to him in controlled groups from the beginning, rather than have him in the Promenade.

As the serious angel knelt among them, the children were touching and petting his wings, talking to him in animated, childish voices. Their innocent enthusiasm made Medusa smile, even as her stomach clutched anew, the result of imagining herself in the same situation.

What was she thinking? She was no angel. Gundar had released her hand, leaving her presumably at ease strolling among the ranks of other players. Instead she was giving serious thought to bolting out the nearest back door, especially when a piercing shriek made her heart jump.

"She has snakes in her hair!"

Usually her anxiety would communicate itself to her snakes, but they surprised her. Ratqueen sent *her* a wave of reassurance, reinforced by the other four, helping her to look toward that high-pitched voice rather than retreating in haste.

It belonged to a young boy. He was pointing at her, and hanging over the side of the rail. He gestured at her wildly. "Please, please, please come over here. Pleeease!"

Other children around him took up the cry. She tried to move that way, but her feet were stuck as if she'd turned them to stone herself. The din around her became a muted roar. She didn't see children or an assembled crowd. She saw a montage of horrified looks as she turned every child to stone, no matter Yvette's protective spells. She couldn't do this. She couldn't.

An arm slid around her waist, a broad chest against her shoulder blades. John dipped his head and kissed her temple. "I'm right here, sweetheart. I'm with you."

She took a steadying breath, gripping his hand on her hip bone with tight fingers. Somehow her feet were moving again. Maybe because he'd given her a little nudge, but she wasn't balking anymore. As she drew close to the short wall that separated the seats from the rings, she saw the boy's mother was holding him about the waist too, presumably so he wouldn't fling himself at her.

"Hey, little man." John inserted himself partly between her and the boy, as well as the other children suddenly crowding around to see her better. She could understand why Marcellus had known he would excel at security. "She might let you touch the snakes, but everyone has to calm down so they don't get startled. She's a little new to this, too, and she's shy. Can you settle down for me?"

It was miraculous, how his slightly stern, firm tone worked. It worked on her all the time, in an entirely different way. The wry thought bolstered her courage. The children in this section became mouse quiet, all wide, staring eyes as she drew closer. It had been so long since she'd been near a child, been able to look at one without fear of causing harm... A tight achy feeling in her throat warned her it was best not to think about those things right now. John's hand gripped her own, another reassuring pressure.

She drew on memories prior to her island, far more positive ones, before Ukrit. Well-to-do female children had sometimes been brought to the temple to meet with the priestesses for instruction before they participated in public rituals. Klotho often had her and Callidora talk to such visitors because they related so well to the young ones...probably because they'd not been much older than children themselves.

"Hello," she ventured, and smiled, jumping only a little when a chorus of "Hellos" rebounded back. John grinned at her. "Um, this is Ratqueen," she said, reaching up and inviting the large white snake to extend herself to rest on the top of Medusa's hand. "She's in charge of all the rest."

"What are the others' names?"

"Does it hurt when they tug on you, like someone pulling your hair?"

"Have they ever bitten you?"

She had to smile at the second question, since it paraphrased John's own when he'd met her. Gaining more confidence, she answered their questions. Ratqueen was the first to indulge their desire to touch, accepting a variety of single fingertip touches and a few brave strokes. The other snakes came down soon after that, Treebark typically being the most cautious, staying at her throat and allowing the occasional finger touch but mostly peering at the children from the cover of her hair.

The children were oohing and ahhing as she bent so they could feel where the snakes' bodies seamlessly attached to her skull. They watched every move the snakes made with avid appreciation as the animals coiled around both of Medusa's arms and overlapped one another.

When Earthson lifted his body, trying to investigate the sparkles in one little girl's tiara, she put out her finger and drew back with a giggle when he flicked his tongue against it.

"That's their way of smelling you," John told her. "But it's also a very special thing that usually only works when a snake is with a

person and that person says it's okay. Snakes are like any wild creatures. They're best observed and respected from a distance. Right?"

The children nodded vigorously and dutifully parroted the things
they'd been told about respecting wildlife. All except one boy, too
currently enthralled with Ratqueen's decision to wrap around his small
wrist to say anything. Medusa noticed his mother looked fascinated
but wary, too. "Are they defanged?" she asked over her son's head.

As Medusa puzzled over the word, Ratqueen deciphered it, with a
great deal of indignation. Medusa sent her a soothing thought and
answered the woman's question. "No. But they will not bite the
children."

"Are they poisonous?"

"Only two of them have venom, but it is usually used to incapacitate prey, not to bite."

"How is that possible?" One father drew his child back from closer
proximity with the snakes. "How do they know the difference?"

Medusa considered the answer. John's world had a different view of
reality from hers, and even hers had trouble believing some of the
things she now knew to be true about magic. Then she thought about
what Gundar had said. People from the mundane world believed any
answer was part of "the act," not a truth that would challenge their
understanding of reality.

"I think in the wild, they wouldn't," she said slowly. "If they saw
something as a threat, they'd use the poison to be sure they were
protecting themselves as much as needed. But they are connected to
me. We share minds, so they use the information they find in my head
to help guide them. And I am able to do the same. Their language is
more feeling than words, but those feelings are usually clear."

More necks were craning, people trying to get closer. John
gestured to her to move down into the three ring area. The Promenade had finished, and many audience members were headed that way
or grouped in the stands around troupe members like herself who'd
become an informal focus. The Promenade was morphing into a
gregarious social event.

John's firm hand was on her elbow, keeping her close to his side as
he eased her into the left hand ring. It allowed more people access to
her, for now they were gathered in a circle around her. Yet he stayed at
her shoulder, her back, sheltering her. She noticed that several addi-

tional security team members had approached, a similar set up to those casually flanking other popular members of the troupe, to help with crowd control if needed.

Surprisingly, she found she was starting to relax. The children's eyes were bright and shining, their smiles and curiosity infectious.

"The ticket price is twenty-five dollars and a child," Yvette had told her, earlier in the week. *"No adult is allowed to come without a child. It puts them in the right mindset to see what we have to offer."*

Medusa could see the reasoning, watching adults pulled from ruminations of "how it's done" by the tug of a young hand, a happy exclamation to go here, go there, look at that—and be immersed in the fantasy.

A half-dozen children had been placed in the coveted grandstand area, because they were all in wheelchairs. One of them approached her, pushed by a woman who must be his mother. The boy was twisted in such a contorted way Medusa realized his spine was deformed, his head at a permanently cocked angle, his shoulders hunched under his ears.

"I'm Vinnie. When I get old enough, I'm going to join the Circus," he informed her as she stopped in front of his chair. "I'll be the snake charming hunchback."

"We need one of those," Medusa said, without missing a beat. "Lady Yvette would love to have you." As she knelt in front of him, she sent a silent request to her snakes. His smile would have made angels weep as all five of them slithered onto his arms, his lap and around his shoulders. Medusa leaned forward to rest her elbows on his chair, to give them as much range as they needed. He touched all of them and asked a million questions. The children who had moved with her clustered around the boy and her, but showed a kind sensitivity, not crowding against his chair. As they overcame their shyness about the boy's differences, they threw in questions of their own, and she saw the boy brighten as much from being treated as part of the group as having the chance to touch her snakes.

Vinnie reached out and touched her face. "Why are you crying?"

"It's been a long time since people looked at me and liked me for who I am," she said simply. "I'd forgotten how nice it feels."

"There's nothing better," he said, the full knowledge of it in his blue eyes as he slanted a meaningful glance around him at the other kids. "I think you're the coolest person I've ever met." His gaze slid behind her and up. "Is that your boyfriend?"

She didn't have to look, because John was a warm heat flanking her. She wasn't familiar with the term the boy used, but she picked up the gist of it. She expected it didn't mean the same thing as Master, but it was in a similar category. She wasn't sure if Vinnie would understand the implications of Master.

"Yes," she said. John gripped her shoulder, a warm acknowledgement.

"Does he like you for who you are?" His eyes slid over the snakes and her wings.

"Yes."

The boy's lips pursed. "My mom's like that. She loves me *and* gets me. There's nothing better than that, either. You looked awesome flying. Do you take people for rides, like he does?"

She turned to see Marcellus returning from a flight around the tent. He wore a harness much like she'd rigged for John when they visited the topmost peak of her island, so the children he took around the tent could feel like they were flying in the tandem set up. He seemed like he had quite a few more waiting for the opportunity, so her gaze shifted to Merc.

He was hanging upside down like a bat from one of the clown props and rocking back and forth. She noticed he had a similar harness on him, so he could offer the same flying option if requested. It was probably the odd energy around him that kept children clustering around Marcellus and giving him a wider berth. She wondered if that made him feel like she and Vinnie did, isolated from a group.

Don't humanize him. She heard John's warning again. But Clara had said Merc would give rides to the kids, so Yvette did trust him for that.

"He's set up for carrying someone. Would you like to go with him?" At the boy's nod, she smiled. "Hold on a minute. We'll see if we can't arrange a flying demonstration."

Merc's eyes fixed on her like a hawk on a mouse as she gestured to him. She ignored it, as well as the wave of pheromones that preceded him as he strode in their direction. She could tell it touched all the adults around them, because of the nervous shifts from the women, their eye rolls toward one another, and the visible concern of the men.

It echoed John's, voiced perhaps a little more emphatically in her
ear now.

"If he touches you, I will take his arm off at the shoulder," he
muttered.

"It's fine. He's fine. He just lost control. He's okay now." She could
tell, because his eyes didn't have that odd silver glow to them, and the
energy around him was... Calm wasn't the right word, but during
rehearsals, she had learned to tell when he was on a more even keel.
That awareness was how she'd so quickly detected it when he wasn't
tonight.

She wasn't sure if she could say the same for her Master, but he
seemed to rein back his desire to do violence, perhaps thinking of the
impact on the children.

"Merc, can you give Vinnie a flight?" she asked quickly as he
approached, just in case John changed his mind about that.

"Oh, I don't know." The mother had missed the thread of the
conversation between her son and Medusa until now. "His spine, I'm
not sure..."

"I'll be fine, Mom. He has a harness, and it's a short flight."

"Merc can take him on a flight without harm," Medusa assured
them. He was more than strong enough. And as Merc's gaze shifted to
the boy, she saw an intriguing softening there, which became more
apparent at the cries of *me, too, me, too* the children around Vinnie
started to voice. Merc gave them an indulgent smile that changed his
face, making him look almost approachable.

"Let me take care of Vinnie first and then we'll see," he said.

John helped lift Vinnie with his mother's help and strapped him
into the tandem set up. He was the right one to help with that,
because with Vinnie's twisted body, some adjustments needed to be
made to support joints and torso in places where they weren't
normally located. He secured some additional rope from nearby
rigging and made that happen. Merc stood patiently, supporting
Vinnie and talking to the boy, explaining some of the mechanics of
flying and his adventures in flight that had the other children pressing
forward asking more questions.

It was like seeing a whole different person emerge from the dark
quagmire of Merc's usual personality. With the children, he was
patient and verbal, putting parents more at ease with the odd energy

vibrating off of him...as long as he didn't look at them directly. She was helping John, Merc and Vinnie as needed, yet whenever Merc met her gaze, she would fumble or stammer in a way that had John giving her an unreadable look and making her blush.

It's not my fault, it's how he is, she wanted to defend herself. But Merc's knowing, small smile didn't help matters.

John stepped back, drawing Medusa with him with a firm hand to her elbow.

"You're all set."

Medusa touched the mother's arm reassuringly. "He'll be safe. Merc will take very good care of him."

"Not too safe." Merc grinned down at Vinnie. "Else it wouldn't be fun."

He launched them into the air. Though Medusa wouldn't have suggested it if she hadn't been sure that Yvette trusted him for this, she still felt her heart leap in her throat as he shot toward the top of the tent and did a spiral maneuver. Vinnie's arms were out like wings, spinning with him, and they heard his whoop of joy. Glancing at the mother, Medusa saw her eyes glisten.

"I wish they allowed camera phones in here," she said. "I would love to video this for his father."

"The expression on his face will tell the whole story," John assured her. "And you'll tell him all about it."

"I know you probably can't tell me, but how do the wings work?" Vinnie's mother asked. "I've thought of all sorts of mechanical possibilities, but there's no evidence of it anywhere, and he just moves...as if the wings are part of him."

"He's part angel," Medusa said matter-of-factly. "That's all you need to know."

The mother continued to watch her son's flight, though her lips twisted. "He may be part angel, but with that stare of his, he's also part something that is so *not* angel."

"Yeah, we're neutering him with a pair of pliers," John said under his breath. "Right after this show."

Medusa glanced at him. He still had his hand on her elbow and was stroking it, but there was a possessiveness to the grip creating little butterflies in her stomach. She leaned against him to experience more body contact. She had no problem using Merc's overabundance of pheromones to enjoy the man she wanted to desire. Even if he looked like a brooding thundercloud.

When Merc came in for a landing, Vinnie's expression was just as John had described. A sun could not have beamed more brightly. Medusa thought of her time on her island. Yes, she had been cursed and isolated, but, thanks to her sisters, she'd had the physical capability to learn how to take care of and defend herself. Vinnie faced a life entirely dependent on others to care for him. She couldn't imagine how one adjusted one's thinking to make that a life worth living. But the smile on his face said he had the ability to do just that.

John unstrapped the boy and helped ease him back into his chair. Medusa smiled at him, but then her attention was pulled away by the other children who wanted to fly, too. She waved a fond good-bye to Vinnie when his mother backed him out of the crowd.

Gundar approached from the center ring and motioned to John to get his attention. "If Merc and Medusa have it all under control over there," he called, "I need another pair of hands in the back."

John Pierce looked between her and Merc, his expression saying he wasn't going anywhere. But before he could tell Gundar that, Medusa spoke. "I'll be fine," she assured John. Lifting onto her toes, she spoke into his ear, pleased when he bent and wrapped an arm around her waist to help her with that.

"He's all right now. I promise. And we're surrounded by plenty of Circus people. I don't want him to believe I am afraid of him and using you as a shield."

John frowned, probably because he knew she was right. "Are you afraid of him?"

"No. I have you, as close as the nearest thought." She smiled at him. "Thank you for helping me do this. I'm so happy I did."

John's set jaw eased. "You look almost as happy as Vinnie," he agreed. "You belong among people." His expression became more intent. "Remember what I said about you calling me if you need me?"

She did, her skin warming under his look. He bent so his cheek was against hers. "I don't think I heard you."

"Yes, Master. I remember."

He hadn't asked her to call him that, but something in his voice, his expression, brought it out of her. And truth, that exchange reinforced a lot of things for her, including that she was capable of facing down the Mercs of the world.

John's gaze flickered in that appealing way that happened when she touched his Dom side so directly. "All right. Don't forget."

She watched him stride off, and suppressed a small smile when he tossed a look to Merc that said the incubus's mortality might be in question. In typical male fashion, the response was a curled lip and a sneer. Then Merc turned his attention to her.

"We doing this?" he asked, gesturing to the next waiting child.

"Yes. Certainly."

Though she expected Merc could buckle each child into the tandem arrangement, it moved more quickly if she helped. So for the next ten riders, she moved into the shadow of his body and felt his fingers whisper over hers as he guided her on the buckles. Once, his head bent over hers and she felt his breath along her nape, which sent a startling tightening to her loins.

It was his effect on women, she knew that, but it had her thinking of the differences between the two men. Merc was not as broadly muscular as John, but he was still all muscle. The way his hair fell over his brow, the intensity of his eyes, had her wetting her lips and shifting nervously. She didn't want to recall it, but she did, that moment in the air when he'd told her he could sense her submission like a drug. It made her imagine herself in some of the same positions she'd experienced with John, only with Merc.

During a brief pause where he had to adjust the harness and the children were standing back, waiting, she was close enough to him he could speak in her ear.

"If we were alone, I'd tie you up in this harness. Hold you down and pleasure you until you screamed. I'd make you my slave in all ways and you'd beg for more. You'd never want any clothes on your body so that I could touch you however, whenever I wanted."

She swayed, closing her eyes. John had said that part of her, the one that wanted to surrender and be bound in ways that were only just now becoming clear in her mind, was intrinsic to who and what she was. But it felt wrong, like this. No matter that she was sure the magical energy Merc commanded as an incubus was fueling her confused response, it felt as if her body was betraying John.

She pushed away from him, giving him a hostile look. "Eating is a necessity for survival. When there is food, you eat. It does not mean you prefer the food put before you."

"Your scent says otherwise," he said.

"That is the hunger of the body. Feeding my heart and soul is something different, and you have no interest in that. Thus, I have no interest in you."

She'd hit a mark there, she saw with mixed satisfaction. She had no desire to hurt anyone, not ever again, but he was being an asshole, as Clara might say. He might not be able to help it, but it didn't make it any less true.

Thankfully, she saw the signal from Yvette that the show was winding up. She told the disappointed remaining children to be sure to come to a future show. She found herself hopeful that she would be able to participate.

The decision that she would not appear in more than this one show until MyTech was handled was sound. She understood that, but she liked what she'd felt here tonight. And logically, if they were in this town for three days, those who came on the subsequent two nights would expect to see the acts they were told about by their friends and neighbors.

It was foolish to put that consideration over her personal safety, but John was right. She loved this energy, she loved the way she felt as she performed. She loved the children.

She put her hand down, against her stomach. Having her own children was a dream that had disappeared when she'd been given to the temple of Athena. Her opinion about or desire for a family had never been considered, but now she was in a position to wonder, wasn't she? Was she still fertile? John and she had lain together multiple times. Would she conceive with him? Was that something he would welcome? She'd given it no thought at all up until this second. If it was a possibility...

Her cheeks warmed and that fluttery feeling increased. She would love to carry his child. She would love to have a family and a life with him, particularly in a world like his, where people married for love and were partners, not one owning the other. At least not that way.

She remembered his reaction to her calling him Master and closed her eyes, letting that entirely welcome shiver take her. That was a form of belonging to another that she didn't mind in the least, because with John it seemed entirely based on her willingness to belong to him, to let him take ownership; not having it taken from her.

Merc disappeared as the children dispersed and people started filing out of the Big Top. This was what Clara had called the "blow off" period, when patrons exiting the show would be engaged by criers on the midway to indulge more concessions, novelties and sideshows like Clara's fortune telling.

Though she wanted to check out some of those things herself, Medusa first went looking for John Pierce. He'd been called outside, perhaps to help with the shepherding of people outside the Circus boundaries. She didn't want to interrupt him for long. Just touch his arm and make contact, see his eyes turn to her with the look that said he knew she was his. Perhaps she could win a kiss from his generous mouth and dispel any doubts he might still harbor about their future together. She'd been having less and less of those with every passing day.

As she approached, she realized he was talking to a woman. Medusa slowed, thinking he was providing the woman directions from the Circus or other information, but as she watched them, she thought that was not the case. This woman knew John. Since he'd said they were not far from a place where he'd done some covert ops training, it was possible he'd see someone he knew here. But as she continued watching, that didn't make her feel better.

The woman was canted toward him in an intimate way, and she was talking earnestly. Her hands were moving, her eyes riveted to his face. Fortunately, Medusa could read nothing in his expression but kind attentiveness. However, though she told herself to stay away, she drew closer, where she could overhear more of the conversation.

She saw a child nearby being entertained by one of the dwarves' sleight-of-hand tricks, and surmised from the similarity in appearance that she was the woman's daughter. The woman nodded to John, body language suggesting she was concluding her conversation. And then Medusa heard a snippet of the dialogue.

"Master—I mean, John, it's good to see you."

Medusa was jolted to the core, not just by the term, but the tone. The woman's voice held a hundred emotions, as did her eyes. John may have let this woman go, but she hadn't wanted to be let go. And she was lovely, in a sweet, gentle way that complemented John in so many ways Medusa lost count of them in her head even on this first, brief glimpse.

She knew logically she wasn't the first to call him by that honorific that aroused him so greatly. But it still hurt to hear and see it firsthand.

Here she was, dreaming about home and family, children, but how could John truly find that with her in a place like the Circus? Yes, this was home to many of the performers, a place they loved, but John was normal. He wouldn't be here if he wasn't protecting and looking after her. He could have an easy life, with the white stone home she'd imagined in the middle of a simple community, loved by this woman or someone like her. Served by her, because she obviously had the same qualities Medusa did in that regard. It was all over this female, through and through.

Yes, he'd sworn his devotion to her and, as little as an hour ago, she'd believed it, she thought with her whole heart. But the way it felt right now, as if the ground was falling out from under her, made her understand why John had had concerns about her commitment. Though John had thought about her for so many years, and she'd dreamed of him, they'd only known each other for a short time. What if after a certain amount of time, he regretted his declarations of devotion?

She was being an idiot, she knew she was. She knew it. But she couldn't look away as John spoke to the woman with warmth and gave her a hug that pierced Medusa's heart. It wasn't lingering or sexual, but the placement of his hands, low on her hips and around her shoulder blades, said he knew her body.

She felt something she hadn't felt since they'd walked through the portal into the Circus. That dark rage, simmering, looking for an excuse to break free. It was likely a good thing she was within the Circus's boundaries; else she might have been tempted to turn the woman to stone before she could kneel before John. Medusa sensed the woman wanted to do just that, so overwhelmingly her knees were probably trembling with the effort not to commit the act in such inappropriately public surroundings.

Medusa pivoted and returned to the Big Top, seeking refuge in an aisle lined on either sides with crates, ready to be repacked with the show's paraphernalia. She moved to the end of the corridor, massaging her temples and then Waterlight as the snake curved over her knuckles. "It's all right," Medusa said. "I'm okay."

A crawling sensation on the back of her neck followed by an immediate sense of warning from her snakes told her that might not be the case.

Turning, she saw Merc sitting on top of the crates. Watching her.

CHAPTER TWENTY-SEVEN

They were out of anyone's sight here, yes, but she could hear the roustabouts not far away, already starting to remove some of the scaffolding from the final acts, their voices punctuated by pipes being thrown down into a pile. One scream would bring them here. *Do not show fear.*

"It's easy to make things work on a deserted island, isn't it?" he observed. He'd braced one of his legs against the opposite tower of crates. "Not so easy even in an in-between place like this, where you can see how people will fit together like puzzle pieces. Not with just one other piece, but lots of other pieces, depending on what they need."

She pressed her lips together and strode with purpose back up the aisle, stopping before his braced leg. He'd changed into a pair of jeans and nothing else, his upper body showing a tapestry of tattooed symbols that enhanced the eye-catching appeal of his muscled upper torso. She kept her eyes on the exit beyond his leg, her goal to reach it and be rid of him.

He put the other leg up behind her, caging her between them unless she wanted to duck beneath.

"You're looking a little green there, snake-girl," he said.

"Don't call me that," she snapped, and Ratqueen hissed at him for good measure.

He closed the distance between his legs, his knees brushing her breasts and just beneath her shoulder blades. "It's hard for one person to meet all your needs. No reason you should have to settle for that. You were on that island a while. Why not sample what else is out there? John knows. That's why he dislikes me so much. Because I'm a possibility."

"You're a troublemaker," she said bluntly, and felt an annoying swirl in her belly at his smile, far too sexy and dangerous.

"I am that. But I can only make trouble where there's an opening for it."

"I suggest you go off somewhere and meet your own needs, Merc, and stop being...you."

She shoved his leg out of her way, ignoring his chuckle. She took a little too much satisfaction in hearing Earthson strike at him in passing, but then she gasped, yanked to a halt.

In a blink, he was off the crates and had seized Earthson just behind his head. Merc had his other hand up, and she felt an emanation of dizzying magic from his palm that disoriented and held the other snakes at bay.

Her primary concern was Earthson, though. She knew the strength in Merc's hand. He could crush his spine. The snake was helpless, trying to wriggle free.

"Let him go," she said sharply. Merc's eyes glittered with anger.

"He struck at me."

"On my behalf. Because you were being a bastard."

"You mocked me and he acted off your disrespect," Merc retorted. "You may think of me what you will, but I will not tolerate mockery. Do you think I'm so harmless?"

He was far from harmless, but she would not be cowed.

"You hurt him in any way, and I will rip one of your wings off. You'll fly in circles for the rest of your life." When the strength of Merc's grip increased, she curled back a lip. "Yvette told me how to remove the spell on my gaze if I need it. With one word, I will be able to turn you to stone."

"Yet won't that turn him to stone as well, the part I'm holding? Is your pride so great you'll risk his life?"

"My pride?" The wording puzzled her, but he clarified.

"I want evidence of your humility. An apology. And I want you to kneel before me. You will feel the full weight of what mindless pleasure I can inflict upon you with nothing more than a look or touch. I can take you places in your submission that John can only dream about." He cocked his head. "Kneel, put your lips on my foot, and find out where the consequences of your actions will take you."

"My thoughts exactly."

The cold voice came from the opening beyond the crates. Relief flooded Medusa as Yvette materialized there, her eyes like shards of glass. "Let the snake go, Merc. Let her go."

His eyes glinted dangerously, but after several heartbeats, he released the snake and took a deceptively lazy stance, though Medusa sensed some disquiet behind the insolent expression. She slid out of the way, moving behind Yvette and cupping Earthson in her hand, stroking his abused throat. She should probably just go away, not witness whatever Yvette was about to do to him, but curiosity had her lingering.

"You seek out ways to cause trouble, Merc. Do you truly wish to be banished from our company?" Lady Yvette put a fist on her hip, her long braids sliding over the point of her shoulder.

"I am here at your pleasure, my lady," he responded in a flat tone. "And for your pleasure, if you are ever brave enough to take it."

Medusa drew in a breath. Taunting Yvette seemed the height of folly.

"You offer me a soulless whore's pleasure. Based only on what you will be paid."

His lip curled, his eyes firing. "You should not debase what you have not experienced."

"I don't have to experience a drug to know it will be a moment's ecstasy only, followed by sorrow and a longing that will never be met, no matter how much of that drug I take. Perhaps you should turn that mirror on yourself. Enough of this. I will not allow your unhappiness to infect this Circus."

The female vampire moved into the incubus's immediate space, their gazes inches apart with Yvette wearing tall stilettos. Medusa shifted nervously. She hadn't wanted to cause trouble, and the air was ripe with violence. She was aware of a pregnant silence in main tent area hidden behind the crates, as if those who couldn't see them knew a fight was brewing.

But then the tension broke. Merc stepped back a pace and gave her a stiff bow. "I will leave your sight, my lady, since you find it so offensive."

He pivoted but was brought to a sudden halt by Yvette's sharp voice. "I believe I told you to kiss my feet. You will do so and then take your leave."

He turned and stared at her. Menace coated him like a poison, from rigid jaw and gleaming eyes to bared sharp teeth.

Yvette didn't move. That energy Medusa had felt from her from the beginning built now, surrounding the three of them. She trembled, responding to it as John had told her was instinctive for one of her nature to do. If that command had been leveled at her, and John had reinforced it with his consent, telling her it was his desire to see her lips press the top of Yvette's fine, arched foot, her knees would already have been on the floor.

Though Merc had a different nature, Medusa sensed a yearning in him, as if some part of him hungered to do as Yvette commanded. But in a heartbeat, those emotions vanished, caught in an ugly maelstrom of dense energy that multiplied the fearsome things she saw in his face. The temperature around them dropped, and she thought she detected an actual tremor through the ground beneath her feet.

All those things compelled her to step to Yvette's side. The phrase to awaken her snakes was not the only spell breaker Yvette had given her. Proving that Medusa had earned the vampire's trust, Yvette had also provided her the words needed to remove the neutralized effect of her eyes, should she have justified need for the weapon.

Yvette was powerful, yes, but what was coming off the incubus was even more so. Medusa realized the only thing stronger than Merc was probably Marcellus, and Marcellus wasn't here right now. She would not let Yvette be harmed.

Yvette's gaze flickered, acknowledging her presence, but she didn't take her eyes off Merc.

He moved toward the two women. One step, two steps. Medusa's lips parted to speak the words, a cold knot forming in her stomach. But before she could utter the phrase, Merc dropped to a knee before Yvette.

He did it with an insolent flourish of his wings and muscular arm, like a courtier flipping his cape. He bent from that position to her foot, and put his mouth to it.

Yvette suffered his touch for one long moment, staring down at the curve of his back, the symbols tattooed upon it. Then she kicked him in the face with the other boot, sending him tumbling backwards and slamming into the crates. The force of the impact knocked over four towers of them, sending them tumbling and revealing a knot of gaping roustabouts in the left side ring.

Medusa gasped. He was on his feet in an instant, though he should have had broken limbs with the force Yvette had used. But he was part angel, and Clara had said Marcellus was almost invincible.

They could bleed, though. Merc wiped some off his lip, baring his teeth at Yvette. "My lady, I trust you are now content to have me out of your sight?"

"Eminently so."

He took flight. As soon as he was gone, Yvette's shoulders lifted as if she'd sighed.

"I appreciate your assistance, young one. However foolish it might have been for you to step into the middle of that fight. He has enough angel blood he could have killed me with little effort."

"Which is why I am here," Marcellus said, stepping out from the shadows. "You taunt him too much, Lady Yvette."

"It isn't taunting. It is teaching. And I would not have called you into a fight I started, my lord."

"No, you wouldn't have. But this Circus cannot be leaderless." His serious lips didn't curve, but there was respect in his eyes. "Clara is very fond of you. She thinks of you as a beloved aunt."

Yvette snorted. "Auntie Yvette. Merc is in a tough spot, Marcellus. You and I both know this. He has nowhere to go. If he leaves our sanctuary, a Light Guardian is waiting to dispatch him for his crimes."

"Still, it is dangerous to assume self-preservation always trumps his darker side. He might be looking for a way to take away all choices. Suicide through violence gives him final release from all his failings."

Yvette turned and met the angel's gaze, her own thoughtful. "I hope we are only speaking of Merc's state of mind, my lord. I am not the only one precious to Clara. She waits only for you to realize it, though patience is not her strongest quality. I expect she will continue to try and force your hand, Goddess bless her."

A muscle jumped in Marcellus's jaw. "She is a foolish girl."

"No. She is a woman, and one in love with you."

He made a dismissive motion, his expression suggesting he would not tolerate the subject further. Respecting it, Yvette gave him a slight bow. "My thanks again for your assistance, my lord. If you do not mind, I would speak to Medusa alone."

He left them, headed in the same direction as Merc. Medusa wondered how that conversation was going to go, since she had no doubt Marcellus would be having a serious discussion with Merc about his temperament. She wondered if it would do any good or if Yvette was right. Medusa uncomfortably remembered times where she halfway hoped one of her attacker's arrows would find her and send her into oblivion.

"I am sorry for whatever part I caused in that, my lady," she said.

"You have no reason to be sorry. You did not invite him to antagonize you."

"But I spoke unkindly to him. Earthson struck at him as a result of my temper." She stroked the snake, who was in a spiral on her shoulder.

"He provoked first. But that isn't why you are still here with me now. You have other issues to resolve."

"My lady?"

Yvette raised her voice. "Your snake-girl seems to think you would be better off with a fully human submissive in the nice picket fence world that knows nothing of any of this."

"Is that so?" John was standing beside several stacks of still standing crates. Medusa had been so focused on Yvette she hadn't seen his arrival.

His tone sent a shiver through her, and the expression he leveled on her now hadn't been on his face when he looked at that other woman. Her gladness about that warred with her worry that the words Yvette had spoken were truth. But how had the vampire known Medusa's feelings? The vampire seemed to have not only eyes and ears everywhere, but ways of plumbing people's feelings in a very unsettling way.

"Be mindful of whom you talk to, John." Yvette looked at Medusa. "I appreciate your willingness to come to my defense. I respect bravery and loyalty. It will not be forgotten."

When the vampire took her leave, John snagged Medusa's wrist and drew her over to another alcove of crates, away from the eyes of those working in the main tent. She found herself bracketed against the crates by two long arms that were far more welcome than Merc's legs.

"So you saw me with Susan. What's going through your head?"

It sounded so much better on his lips than Merc's. She realized the incubus's mocking use of the endearment was what had launched her unwise challenge to him. Seeing John Pierce with the other woman had made her think of a time when she might not be with him, when she couldn't hear him call her snake-girl. Yet if he would truly be happier, she couldn't stand in his way. He was her protector, yes, but she was not helpless, not even in this world that wasn't her own.

"I have been so focused on my own choices, and I have never questioned yours," she said slowly. "You spoke of this, how our understanding of one another's lives, empathy, is not enough to create a permanent bond. Am I penance, reward or escape? Are you so sure I am love?"

His brow creased. "Wait just a minute—"

She raised a hand. "You rescued me. You came to me, brought me to a place where my life can have more possibilities. You have helped me see I have as many choices as I am willing and brave enough to grasp. There is no reason you must stay with me now. I no longer need you to...serve me. You deserve an easier life. A happier life."

He pursed his lips and crossed his arms over his broad chest. Though the posture was more casual, she didn't miss the set of his jaw, the muscle tic in it. "Easier doesn't mean better or happier, Medusa. There were a lot of women I enjoyed before I met Maddock, but none made it through to my heart. He helped me realize the dream I'd always had of you could become a reality. But it wasn't until I landed on your island and met you I knew that it could become better than that dream times a thousand. I told you all of that. It's still true, in every way."

She closed her eyes as he leaned in and brushed his lips against her temple. "So stop this shit," he said softly.

She put her palms down against the crates, clasping the slats so she wouldn't reach for him. "But the way she looked at you..."

"She has a thing for a strong-handed Master, because she hasn't found the right one for her," he said with a touch of impatience. "We had a good thing, but she was well in my past when I started on the path that led me to you."

"She called you Master." It burst out of her in such a spiked ball of anger, she made Earthson start and hiss, looking around for another foe to fight.

He stared down at her, then his lips curved. As she nervously began to lift her hands to push him away, he shook his head. "Leave them where they are."

He ran a thumb over her lips, which parted at his touch, then tested the elevated pulse in her throat with another stroke there. "So responsive," he murmured. A shadow crossed his gaze and he straightened. "When I was watching you fly with Merc tonight, Yvette said something to me. 'Medusa will serve any Master or Mistress worth serving.' She meant it as a comfort, suggesting you would be cared for here, even if I wasn't your ultimate choice."

The shock of the words took away any voice she had to respond. For three blinks. Then she found them. As well as an overflowing cup of anger.

"Yvette should realize that I am not Charlie," she said hotly. "And so should you. I thought you weren't Merc, but perhaps I was wrong about that."

If she'd suddenly sprouted an extra pair of wings, she could not have startled him more. She saw the surprise in his eyes, followed by a flash of dangerous annoyance. Good.

"He thinks he is just as suited to meeting my needs as you, because he only sees the desires of the body."

"Medusa—"

"No." She pushed past him so she was on the outside of the aisle of crates, so she could leave when she was damn good and ready, as Clara might say. He didn't stop her, but his hand curled around her forearm as if he thought she was about to take off. She had plenty to say first, though.

"Yes, I might serve any Master or Mistress worth serving. I obeyed and served the senior priestesses of the temple. I served Athena, my Goddess. I will give my loyalty and service in that capacity because yes, that is who I am. Loving a Master is different."

She could feel the heat in her face, and realized her hands were clenched. "I may be younger than you by a significant amount of years, but I am not so indiscriminate in my choices. You chide me for forgetting what you have told me of your desires, but you have forgotten things I have said to you as well. So let me remind you."

His expression flickered, perhaps because she couldn't keep the hurt out of her voice. "You came for me. You understood my hurts, my needs. You have fought and lost in your life, John Pierce. You have stumbled and made mistakes that give you nightmares. You were willing to give up your life and serve me in an unexpected way only a Master understands."

She remembered those moments of branding possession, him taking her body so decisively it felt as if he'd taken her soul and heart at the same time. *Mine. No one else's.*

She hadn't known how to respond to that then, but she did now. This required a different kind of courage than what Yvette had just commended, but it was courage nonetheless. Stepping back up to him, she put her hands on his shoulders and neck and went onto her toes. "Mine," she whispered, staring into his eyes. "No one else's. Until you ask to be set free, John Pierce. You serve me, do you not?"

The fire in his serious eyes kindled into a different kind of heat. But then it was banked, replaced by another emotion. Chagrin. "I apologize," he said quietly, resting his hands on her hips. "You're right. But I think I just made my point, didn't I? Doesn't matter who called me Master before; not if I've found the one I want to call me Master forever."

She opened her mouth, closed it. His expression reflected a combination of amusement, exasperation, and some deeper emotions, ones that they shared enough to bring things back together now.

"Just as that solitude I had on my island may not have given me many options to explore," she said. "But it did provide ample time to think about the qualities I would most desire in a man. You fit most of them, John Pierce."

"Most of them, hmm?"

She sniffed. "There is always room for improvement."

"Not for you. I like you just fine the way you are. Head to toe, heart and soul. And your beautiful, clever mind, which just put me right in my place."

She had enough woman's pride not to reveal he'd done the same.

But she placed his palm over her heart. "It is right here. And you have rested there for quite some time."

His gaze softened and he shifted both hands to her shoulders. He considered her for a long, thorough moment.

"So that's it, then," he said at last. It was almost as if he was speaking to himself. He met her eyes, though, tying her into his one-sided conversation. "We're done second guessing ourselves and ignoring what we want so much for fear it's not real."

She let out a relieved breath. "That is my wish as well. And—"

His kiss took her under and left her knees weak, but his urgency that robbed her of further words said she wasn't the only one affected. She curled her hands in his shirt, holding on, kissing him just as passionately, her body pressed as close to his as was possible without merging into one being. And that didn't sound like a bad fate to her, either.

Lifting his head after a blissful length of time, he pinned her with that penetrating stare once more. "Glad we got that settled. Though I think I should reinforce it some, preferably in a way that will give you trouble walking. I don't want you to ever worry again when you see me with another woman."

"And I will endeavor in my surrender to your demands to convince you that you never need worry about me around the likes of Merc."

"Or Gundar, or Marcellus, or Maddock, or any other male."

She smiled, then let out a startled gasp as he claimed her mouth again. This time he took over, clamping a bruising hand on her buttock and lifting her up to pin her against the crates. "You better brace yourself for the consequences of pissing me off, sweetheart," he muttered against her mouth. "Penance, my ass. Comparing me to Merc?"

He was holding his body solidly against hers, letting her feel his need to imprint the conclusion of their conversation on her right here and now. Her body yielded as she drew him closer, locking her legs around him. She wanted the same thing, to purge that woman's voice from her mind, to make sure she was the only one imprinted upon his soul, from now forward.

The call of another voice was distant, irritating, but when he lifted his head, she realized it was Marcellus, probably looking for John to help with whatever security tasks were left for the night. He bit back a curse.

"I'll take it on account," he promised her in a rough voice she loved.

"All right." She was breathless as he eased her down to the ground.

He held her tightly for an extra moment before reluctantly leading her out of the Big Top and the forest of crates and onto the midway again. The crowds were thinning out. "You stay out of dark corners unless you're with me," he ordered. His expression eased and he stroked a lock of hair from her face. "I love you, snake-girl."

"I love you, too." It was easy to say it after all, even more so when the smile he gave her lit up her heart brighter than the flood lighting in the parking lot.

"See you in a bit. I expect they just need some help with traffic flow in the parking lot."

She watched him stride away. Other women watched him with a feminine pleasure she fully understood, but this time, instead of feeling the unpleasant bite of jealousy, she embraced something far better.

He was all hers, and she was his. It was a wonderful, complete feeling. In this moment, standing on a circus midway under a crescent moon, she was perhaps closer to happiness than she'd been since her earliest days in Athena's temple.

Passing a fingertip over her lips, she savored the lingering tingle that John's mouth had left on hers. Tonight, they would be back inside the portal. Perhaps they'd take a blanket out into one of the meadows and lay under the stars to make love. Sleep there and be woken by the sunrise, the sounds of dragons and hawks, the thunder of centaur hooves.

As she circled around to the back entrance of the Big Top, she smiled. She'd find Charlie and return this outfit to her, then help her however would be most needed. It would make the time go even faster until she could be in his arms again.

She felt a twinge of guilt at using Charlie as an example to prove her point to John. Charlie's heart seemed to be halfway into Maddock's keeping, but she served Yvette, suggesting service drove her more than personal preferences. Yet Medusa hadn't known the woman long enough to understand what drove her. She would tell

John the same later. She didn't want him to think she had a bad opinion of the dressmaker. Though John being John, he probably knew she'd made the careless remark in the heat of her anger.

She thought of John's promise of future retribution and what that could mean. Erotic longing passed through her every limb, reflected in her increased heartbeat.

It was obscene to have all that she was feeling interrupted by a cold shot of fear. The feeling was a premonition, instincts honed by years of fighting for her survival. Unfortunately, it happened only a blink before hard hands closed on her and jerked her out of sight.

The roustabouts coming and going out of the back doors of the Big Top never saw her disappear.

She was pulled behind a storage trailer. As she opened her mouth to scream, a gag was shoved in her mouth and a bag yanked over her head. The bag was cinched tightly around her neck, a frightening restriction of air as her snakes were contained. Rope was wrapped around her torso swiftly, disabling her wings. Then she was tossed in the back of a vehicle.

The rough hands never left her, taking away any opportunity to fight. Ratqueen was hissing and Treebark was striking at the burlap covering them, his muscular body hitting her jaw and face.

Her assailants flipped her and bound her wrists and ankles, connecting them to one another so she was toppled on her side, which increased her terrifying helplessness.

The vehicle jerked into motion, the exhaust choking her before the door was slammed.

"Soon as we're outside the Circus boundaries, those eyes go live, boys," a dispassionate voice said. It was harsh, like a crow's call. "About fifteen seconds from now. Take care of it."

"Hope T's right, that they regenerate." This voice was thin and sharp, like nettles that passed over the skin in a seemingly harmless way but left fiery pain in their wake.

"You ever know him to be wrong about anything? Shut up and do it."

Before she could feel more than a blink of abject panic—she

wasn't sure if that was good or bad—pain exploded in her eye sockets. Through the agony, the gag the only thing that kept her from biting through her tongue, she smelled the sickening odor of her burning flesh.

She was too strong, too not-mortal. She didn't pass out from the unbelievable extremes of pain. Instead, every layer of her being reacted in rage, in fear, in denial that this was happening. Something was once again being forced upon her that she didn't want. She screamed like a feral animal from the pain and fear.

They'd used some type of hot iron to put out her eyes through the fabric of the hood. As she gasped for air, the taut cord bit into her neck. The burlap smelled like rotten fruit.

John, help. Help. She wished fervently they could share thoughts as Yvette and Charlie did. But John would sense her distress. She believed that. And Yvette had taken her blood. There had to be something to that. She pushed down the terror that she was being taken somewhere she didn't know, and she wouldn't know how to get back to the Circus even if she escaped. *Help. Oh Goddess, help...*

Whether it was an answer or not, the inability to control her emotions didn't put the snakes in a mindless panic as it had in the past. Instead, as she fought for calm, she felt something remarkable. They were consciously sharing her pain, trying to pull it away from her as much as they could. They were helping her clear her mind, a recognition that she was their best chance for escape.

She tried to calm her breath, the crazed galloping of her heart. Oh Goddess, her eyes hurt. She wanted to put her hands up to them as if it would help, as if it would remove this horrible burning sensation.

Focus, Medusa. Focus.

"Wish we could just chop off these damn snakes," one of them said. She could hear the typical human fear of serpents in his voice, no matter that they'd contained her snakes. She logged that as a possible advantage, one man's fear. She telegraphed the test to Ratqueen and the brave albino responded, striking against the burlap near the source of that voice. She heard him jump back and curse.

"Fuck, her fangs came through. Did you see that? Can we double bag her?"

"She'll suffocate," Crow's Voice said. "Stop being such a pussy."

"Then let's kill the damn things."

Up until John, she'd only had herself to depend upon on the island. She couldn't let pain dull her wits. She might have powerful allies now, but those allies would have to find her first. She had to take care of herself until then. She was no longer the fearful maiden she'd once been. But them not realizing that might be another advantage.

Weeping piteously wouldn't be difficult, considering she was in agony. The irony was that she resisted the idea because it twisted her pride to make them think she was weak and afraid, even if she was faking it. Well, the weak part. She *was* afraid, but she was also angry, and she wanted to lead with the anger. But that might not serve her well here.

Men were men, and they often erred on the side of thinking a woman was weak, especially if her behavior supported it. Sharp Man's words stabbed her with a deeper fear, adding to her genuine tears of anxiety. *Please not my snakes. Leave them alone.*

Her expected weakness got some results, at least on that. "She's done fighting for now. Leave her be," the gruff voice said curtly. "And we don't know how the snakes are connected to her other abilities. Except for neutralizing the eyes, we're supposed to bring her to the containment chamber as is."

Bide our time, she thought silently to her five serpents. *Do not attack. Play asleep. We wait for our advantage. Or help to come. Or both.*

She could feel Ratqueen's seething anger, and loved the female for it. It would settle the others, keep them from being fear-aggressive. They were far more effective when they were battle-aggressive. More patient and calculating, just like her.

When the time came, these men would regret laying hands on her. If she could not overwhelm them, she would die trying. She'd die with the vicious pleasure of knowing when John, Marcellus and Lady Yvette caught up with them, they would wish they'd met death at her hands, rather than theirs.

Brave thoughts. She held onto them, refusing to let panic rise, refusing to let the girl Ukrit had raped resurrect herself and make her catatonic with fear. But her body was shaking, and the mantra she'd used when men came to her island to attack her was going at top speed through her mind.

Never again. *Never* again.

CHAPTER TWENTY-EIGHT

*J*ohn was supervising the exit of cars from the parking lot, but when he came to a dead stop and Yvette appeared at his side a moment later, he knew she'd been hit by the same abrupt wrongness that had speared his gut.

"Where is she?" he demanded.

"They have taken her, John. I've summoned Maddock. His intel was obviously incorrect. Someone tipped them off that she was with the Circus, and somehow they tracked us here far more swiftly than we'd anticipated." Her tight voice held her fury about that and he wouldn't envy whoever had provided that tip. Though he would be happy to stand on the sidelines and cheer on whatever horrible torture she had planned for them.

Anger worked better for him than the cold ball of fear in his gut. "How long ago?" he said in a flat voice, falling into step beside her as she led him out of the parking lot and toward the tents. He glanced up at a rush of wings and saw Marcellus and Merc had joined them. As the incubus met his gaze, the rage exploded.

"John." Yvette's protest fell on deaf ears as he seized the incubus by the throat and slammed him against a trailer so hard the metal dented. Merc used the propulsion of his wings to shove away from it and toss John, landing him on his ass in the dirt. Fuck, the asshole was strong. He didn't give a shit. He was up and ready to attack again, but Marcellus stepped in front of him, stopping his forward charge. Merc stood behind him, quivering, killing energy sparking off him, his eyes gone a weird and chilling silver color.

"It was not him, John Pierce," Marcellus said quietly. "You may trust me on this. He might kill Medusa with his hunger, but he would never betray her to MyTech."

"He's right," Yvette said, coming to John's side and dusting the dirt off his backside and shoulders matter-of-factly. She shot him a reprimanding look. "I need the covert ops agent right now, not the man in love and losing his fucking mind over what's happening to his woman. If you can't provide that—"

"You got it," John snapped. "And you didn't answer my question. How long?"

"A matter of minutes. It is likely they know nothing about the blood I took from her. I can track her whereabouts."

As long as they didn't pass into an interdimensional place because they'd finally learned what Maddock knew. He pushed away that sick possibility.

"Once we determine where she is, we can plan an extraction," Merc added. John gave him a hard look.

"Did you think my name stood for Mercury?" the half-breed sneered. Marcellus lifted a hand.

"Lose the attitude, Merc. JP, he is a good ally for this kind of work."

"Good enough," John said, but he shifted toe-to-toe with the incubus, staring into the unblinking eyes that were back to their usual color. "I know you're a messed up motherfucker, but that woman is my heart and soul. Got it? None of your bullshit."

"Got it," Merc said succinctly. He flashed fangs, his eyes glinting with a sudden coldness. "Marcellus is correct, John Pierce. I may not be good at many things, but I am very good at this."

John nodded. When Maddock had come to visit him the second time, he'd brought John back some of the weapons he normally had at hand in the "real world." As they headed for Yvette's tent to plan strategy, he peeled off from the group long enough to pull the guns from his trailer.

The world never stayed peaceful, did it? He refused to let himself linger, to inhale Medusa's scent or touch the small collection of clothes she'd gathered since she'd been here. He would have her back soon. He could smell the real thing.

However, seeing the set of ribbons he'd first given her on the dresser clamped a vise around his chest. Balling them up, he tucked them in his jeans pocket. Every knight had to have his lady's favor, right? Maddock would appreciate that, with his Arthurian obsessions.

As he came out of the tent, Charlie and Clara were there. Clara hugged him and, though he wasn't much for touchy-feely stuff when in mission mode, the wave of good feeling that always emanated off her like a perfume did help steady him, and he took it as the asset it was.

"I can't see her future, but that's not a bad thing, JP. That means nothing is yet set such that it can't be changed. And Marcellus...if you have him by your side, everything will be all right. I've never known that not to be true. He doesn't usually get involved in human matters —angel codes and all that—but this is different. She was taken on his watch."

He understood that. Giving Clara a look, and touching a silent Charlie on the shoulder, he strode away. The two women watched him until he was out of earshot, then Charlie spoke.

"You didn't tell him the whole truth. You didn't tell him how you felt her pain. She's been badly wounded."

"Wounds can be healed."

"Some wounds can be healed." But Charlie took her hand. "I'm going to go to my tent and rest up. When they bring her back, she'll need all the energy I have."

When. Clara thanked the healer mentally for her optimism and prayed she'd be right. Not just for Medusa. A death was never a loss of one. For how short a time they'd actually known one another, JP's bond to his "snake-girl" was extraordinarily strong. It would be a blow that could topple the powerful male.

Speaking of powerful male... Marcellus landed next to her without a word. Clara had not expected to see him before he left. Yet when she opened her mouth to ask him what she could do to help, what he needed, the words died in her throat, because he stepped close to her and cupped her face in his large hand. His eyes were dark as night from corner to corner, which often made them hard to read, but she saw things in them right now that made her heart stop.

He curved a hand around her nape and drew her to him, bending his head to put his mouth on hers. Oh...Goddess. She gripped his considerable biceps tightly, making a small noise in his mouth as he penetrated deeply with tongue, teeth and the demanding pressure of his lips. She swayed and folded into his body, melding every curve to his.

He'd worn the jeans and placket shirt of the security team earlier tonight, covering his wings with illusion, but now he was back in his typical Legion garb. A sword strapped to his back, the short red belted half-tunic, and nothing else. Praises to the Goddess gleamed in iridescent bronze lettering against his tanned skin. His dark green wings reflected the glow of the energy coming from them, since they tended to charge with magic before he went into battle.

"Try to stay out of trouble while I'm away," he said against her lips. "Gundar and Cai will be in charge but they will have their hands full. No one will be watching after you."

"Who'll watch after you?" she asked.

"You do. No matter where I am. Your prayers are as inscribed on my heart as these praises are on my skin. You are my guardian angel."

He gave her the rarest and most wondrous gift he'd ever given her. A smile. Then he was gone.

She knew angels were supposedly invincible, but he was with her because he wasn't, because he bore scars that prevented him from fighting with the Prime Legion, the warrior arm of the angelic host. So though she thought MyTech didn't have a chance against her people, she knew nothing was certain when it came to armed conflict. She didn't want him to lose any more battles, of any kind.

No matter how unrealistic that was, it was the way love worked. A person just wanted those she loved to be bathed in rainbows and sunshine every day, never knowing fear or cares. Even if, ironically, the trials were what made them into what you loved.

She started adding to those prayers written on his heart and headed toward Charlie's tent. While there was plenty left to be done to batten down the Big Top for the night, tonight there were bigger priorities. She would curl around the young woman and add whatever energy she could to her rest. Just in case Charlie needed more than her usual reservoir.

Thinking about that, Clara increased her pace. There also might be other ways the two of them could combine their gifts to reach out and help Medusa. Whatever would help Medusa would also help Marcellus, John, Yvette and Merc. And Clara knew, even if Marcellus had been teasing her about being his guardian angel, one thing about that was true.

She would protect him however she could.

The homeless man shuffled in their direction, pausing to check out a box left next to a trash can, emptying it out and muttering to himself. John tried not to grind his teeth in impatience as the grungy individual moved into the paid parking lot and wove between cars, disappearing behind a brace of SUVs.

Maddock materialized inside the black van with tinted windows. His pungent disguise melted away, leaving him sitting in the second seat in his jeans and T-shirt, his eyes sharp and hard.

"They're there. I overheard a couple of them talking. T got there about thirty minutes ago." Maddock spat out the name. "Otherwise known as Dr. Tyrone Oswald. MyTech's personal Dr. Frankenstein."

They were parked in a spot across from a collection of warehouses, part of the industrial district of the larger city which was about twenty miles from the small town where the Circus had performed. Through the corridor provided by the warehouses, John could see a small vertical strip of the one where Yvette sensed Medusa was being held. Maddock had counseled parking this far away so they wouldn't trip off any magical or human sentries they had while he confirmed her mental GPS.

"Once we head in that direction, that will happen soon enough. But the shields they have in place are breakable. They obviously still don't have anyone on staff with a better grasp of magical workings than me." He said it without ego, underlined by his next words. "Goddess help us if they ever do. Anyway, once we get close enough, I should be able to split those protections open and give you a window to get inside and retrieve her."

John checked that the safety on his nine mil was off before he holstered it under his arm. He checked his combat knives and verified the scabbards were oiled well enough to release the knives quickly. He knew they were, but neither agent nor soldier questioned his prep rituals. More often than not, they could save his life or others. He had an assault rifle propped between his knees.

He told himself to focus on this the way he did any op, because getting his mind fogged up by who was in danger, who they were going in there to get, wouldn't help her. But underneath the ritual and cold calculation, he was a fucking lava pit of rage, just waiting for the chance to erupt. He thought of her on her island, a million different images. The first time he'd heard her laugh, watched her swim, or felt her curled up against him on top of the highest peak. Her wariness, her longing to trust, to simply be, had been so obvious to him from the beginning. He was all kinds of pissed off that anyone thought they had the right to take that from her, especially after everything else she'd endured. This shit had to stop.

He understood her conflict between losing her snakes, who'd become so bonded to her, and desiring a life that wasn't all about defending herself against those too fascinated with who and what she was.

"JP." Yvette drew him out of his head. "You are clear on our objective?"

"Get her out with minimal damage and loss of life, get her home."

"Firestorms cause questions. I have a whole Circus to protect." She met his gaze. "That said, I trust your training to tell you when lethal force cannot be avoided. I want to bring all of us home."

A moment of silence ensued, disrupted by an obtrusive crackle of paper. Glancing toward the rear seat, he saw Merc was eating a package of Lance Nekot cookies. Marcellus, sitting next to him, was staring at the half-breed angel with the impassive look that could mean he was meditating. Or thinking about driving one of his wickedly sharp and exceedingly long daggers through Merc's ear.

"Well, most of you," Yvette said under her breath.

Looking up, Merc noticed their regard, and extended the package with a bland look. "Anyone want one? I brought several packs."

Despite the seriousness of the situation, John felt a loosening in his gut, his lips tipping up. Even Yvette's dark expression transformed to exasperated amusement.

"Idiot," she said. "Let's go."

Full darkness had fallen, so John and Maddock left the vehicle, slipping through the cover the other cars provided. Yvette used her vampire speed to get to the first rendezvous point ahead of them. The winged pair disappeared aloft, the plan being for them to provide air support and whatever intel their vantage point could provide as the extraction progressed.

John was the forward point of the spear that would be thrown once Maddock dismantled the protections. Maddock was armed only with his magic, but John suspected it was as effective as any hardware he was carrying. He hadn't seen him use it in a combat situation, however.

"So have you ever been part of an op like this?" John asked the wizard.

"No, but I've seen a lot of action films." Maddock crouched behind a Dumpster with him. Yvette appeared at John's elbow.

"Asshole," John murmured without rancor.

"Yeah, the asshole that might just save your ass." Maddock propped his head against the Dumpster and closed his eyes. Drawing in a breath, he spread his hands out loosely on his knees as if he were centering himself for a meditation. He wasn't the Zen type, but JP guessed it was indicative of the effort Maddock was about to expend. "Once we leave this cover, I'll break the protections. You two just keep moving forward. Don't worry about me."

"Wasn't planning on it," Yvette commented. Maddock made a rude gesture at her, but it was absent-minded, his focus obviously still internal.

"I'll cover you in whatever way is needed," he added to John.

"Sure you can keep up?" JP asked.

The wizard's teeth flashed in the darkness. "I'll do my best. Just for the record, Lot was pissed he couldn't come. He said having to secure other portal perimeters against MyTech is cutting him out of all the fun."

"Yeah." However, as John looked at the light filtering through the warehouse's upper windows, his humor died away. He wished Lot was here, too. He would have felt better having the SEAL watch his six with that assault rifle.

Christ, John didn't know how she was doing or what she was enduring. He was going to lose his fucking mind.

Maddock put a firm hand on his shoulder. "Hey. We're getting her back, JP."

"Yeah. Goddamn right." He hefted the assault rifle and got ready to move. *Just please God, let her be in one piece.*

~

"I'd intended to do this in more controlled conditions, but this way we get what we want much faster, and it will be better for you, too. I fear our time is very limited."

This man, the one obviously in charge, had arrived about a half hour ago. His voice was smooth and accented, his words broken into crisp syllables. He sounded calm and kind, which was what made him more frightening to her than the others. There was a detachment to his kindness, as if everything being done to her was an unavoidable necessity, and nothing she could say or do would convince him otherwise.

She still had the bag on her head, but they'd removed the other bindings and strapped her down to a cold metal table.

Now he gripped her arm. She fought down the panic as he inflicted a sharp pain upon it. She was helpless to whatever they wanted to do to her. The sharp thing was still in her arm, and he put something over it, something sticky to hold it in place. "You see?" he said, pleased. "If you give me what I want willingly, it increases the power of the gift. You probably know that, don't you? Most women do."

"What...do you want?" Suddenly, her head was swimming and felt so heavy. Her snakes were sinking down, their coiled bodies piling up on either side of her head. When the rope loosened and the head covering was pulled away, they thumped limply onto the table surface. *No.* She wanted to gather them up and cradle their insensate bodies in her arms.

She felt a suffocating moment of fear, thinking they were dead, but then she realized she could still feel their hearts beating in time with her own. They were alive. Whatever thing he'd just done to make her feel so dizzy and confused, teetering on the edge of sleep, had affected them even more quickly. She struggled to stay conscious, terrifyingly aware she was losing that battle. She couldn't tell where she was. It was a large room, the ceiling far above with crisscrossed metal beams and high rectangular windows lining the upper walls. There was an acrid smell to the place, as if animals had inhabited and abandoned it long ago.

The man continued speaking in that nightmarishly reasonable voice.

"The spell that turns people to stone manifests through your eyes, but it is driven by a part of your brain. That's where the coding for the ritual is based, and I can lift out that programming and inject that programming into other brains. A set of protective goggles for those soldiers, and some lucky general will have a small army of men who can turn their foes to stone."

"You want to use it to hurt others." She didn't understand everything he was explaining, but that was clear enough.

"You have hurt others. You know it is often justified. It does not have to be your concern. A beautiful woman should not be involved in such matters. I can take it all away. You can go back to before Ukrit came into your life, and I can change that timeline so he never does. Even better, you will have no memory of anything that was ever done to harm you. Or that you did to harm others. How would you like that? To see your sisters alive again? All of them."

His tone became more soothing, and there was a clicking noise, a slight discomfort as he seemed to adjust the sharp thing. "There we go. Just imagine it. Seeing your sisters..."

Her vision swam. She tried to keep her eyes open. Her eyes were open, weren't they? But she was no longer in that large room with the smell of disuse.

She was in the temple.

She knew this had to be a trap, but how could it seem so real? She swayed on her feet. The priestesses were all there, beckoning to her, smiling. It was morning prayer time, which happened right before breakfast. Callidora's eyes were dancing as if she had some particularly good gossip to share with her.

Oh Goddess. She didn't feel it... That oppressive weight of memory, of something beyond her awareness or recollection, but something she knew was bad. Had been bad. But it had never happened. Bad things happened to other people, not her.

The feel of it, of never having experienced whatever it was she couldn't remember, swept her with ebullience. How could she have not realized how heavy that weight had been? The pieces of her fragmented mind twirled together like dancers at a festival. She was laughing, squeezing Callidora's hand, seeing Klotho's admonishing but fond look for both of them. Her friends. Her family. Her life, before it was all taken away. She could have it back.

"Yes, you can. All I need is that."

She looked toward the smiling, pleasant-faced bald man. He was standing at the entrance to the temple, on the steps. He had eyes like a raptor and a strong body. He was gesturing to her hair. Putting her hands up into her thick tresses, she felt five braids. He wanted her hair?

He shook his head, pointed again. Lifting the braids, she saw she had several ribbons twined around them. "Just those," he said. "A favor from a pretty girl. And you can have everything else and never lose it again. Ever."

She fingered the ribbons. Priestesses gathered around her, young ones who had been here not much longer than she had. They giggled at the man's attention as he smiled in such a charming, intriguing way.

But two others were pulling on her hands as if they wanted to take her away from him. They were her friends, her sisters, but different from the other priestesses. One appeared to be blind. The other wore bangles on her wrists and a pretty gauzy skirt that flowed around her ankles, like a traveling gypsy. She liked their differences. They wanted her to come play.

"You can't go play, you can't have any of this, unless I can have the ribbons. It's the price, you see. For happiness. Just those ribbons, freely given."

Something was missing here. Something niggling at her. Pulling the ribbons free, she held them in both hands, tangling them over her fingers, twining them over her wrists. The man had taken a step closer. His smile had not wavered. He smelled good, like open fields and baked bread.

"It's festival day," he reminded her. "The day you sing to the city people, eat sweets and dance. Let me have the ribbons, pretty girl, and you can dance for the rest of your life. No cares, no fears, no worry. Only laughter and dancing and happiness."

Yvette made short work of the two guards on the western side of the warehouse. Maddock muttered something about her being a show-off, and breached the double doors with a quick flash fireball that knocked out another two inside the threshold.

As they moved swiftly down an echoing corridor, the concrete floor recorded the slap of their hurried feet. Yvette moved past them, a blast of air. Three men rounded the corner ahead. John dropped to a knee to take aim and make a lower target, but Yvette was already there. She knocked one's head into the wall, swept the leg of another and punched the third in the face hard enough he crumpled where he stood.

"Why am I here?" John complained to Maddock.

"You're here to get the girl." Maddock said grimly. "Don't worry. Save your energy. You'll likely need it. This battle isn't going to be won with brute strength."

There weren't many places to hide a captive, especially one who had to be kept sedated. They found her quickly, if the six guarding a hallway that led to a far more substantial door were any indication. The warehouse had apparently once had a refrigeration area.

This time Yvette used John's help. As she took on four, he met the other two, using the butt of his gun to take one down, but the other had to be dispatched with the combat knife, no help for it.

They progressed to the door, and Maddock took care of it, ripping it off its hinges with barely a pause and a wave of energy that felt like being on the sidelines of a storm surge. It reminded JP exactly why he liked the guy so much.

Yvette went in high, he went in low, but the muscle had been focused outside. It was a temporary lab, populated by two techs and a man in a suit.

John snarled his rage at the sight of Medusa and her snakes, all of them lying far too still on a table. She was hooked up to blinking machines and surrounded by a variety of medical equipment. The man in the suit was between him and her, not a safe place to be, but he pivoted toward them with a calm look on his face that warned John to lead with his wizard and vampire sorceress, not his emotions. Yvette and Maddock, in accord, spread out to flank the man, John standing at ready for whatever opportunity they provided.

"Tyrone, get the fuck away from her," Maddock said with a calmness that held the fury of compressed hellfire.

"Considerable reinforcements have arrived." Yvette spoke in a low voice to JP, her expression tightening at some communication she was receiving within. "Merc and Marcellus need help to keep casualties to a minimum."

"Go to it," Maddock said shortly, showing he'd heard her as well. "We've got this."

She was gone in a blink. "Marcellus and Merc could kill all of them where they stand," Maddock said. "Believe me, it's tempting."

John understood that all too well. He wasn't above putting the three in front of them into early graves. There was something wrong with Medusa's face. He couldn't tell if blood was on it, or something else, but he had to get to her. Now. The techs weren't fighters. They were looking from him and Maddock to Tyrone, showing their nervousness. He could scatter them like birds with one stream of gunfire.

The man in the suit spoke, his voice grating with a patronizing mildness. "Maddock. Concede defeat on this one. Walk away. You lost this pawn."

"It's not a fucking chess game, you British ass. She doesn't belong to you. To anyone, unless it's this guy right here. And that's just because she wants to belong to him. You try to keep her, he's going to end you."

John leveled the assault rifle at him and Tyrone's lip curled in derision. "Such weapons mean nothing to you and me, Maddock. You know that."

"Yeah, but it gave me a moment to re-charge my batteries."

John had been within the blast zone of IEDs. Recognizing the swelling of energy preceding the big boom, he dropped and rolled away from Maddock without being told.

As that force exploded from Maddock, Tyrone was ready for him, shielded against the onslaught, and hurling his own back against him. It was the firestorm Yvette had feared, but at least not producing fallout a forensic lab could trace.

Ducking a fiery hail of projectiles lethal as bullets, John was gripped by terror, but not for himself. Then he realized there was some kind of force field over Medusa, protecting her. The techs had scampered for cover.

He didn't know who was providing the force field. If it was Tyrone's it could knock him out if he tried to clear it. He rolled and then crouched at Maddock's side, debating whether to just rush it and take the chance. Maddock was a little busy to answer questions. Or so he thought.

"Get in there," Maddock snarled. "Put your hands on her and I'll take you the rest of the way into her mind. You have to talk her out of what he's doing to her. He's excising a part of her brain. Consider it a magical lobotomy. If he gets her past a certain threshold, she'll give up what he wants and she stays a happy vegetable the rest of her life."

A crash jerked John's attention to the upper windows. Three guys rappelled down, armed to the teeth the same way he was. He sprayed them with the assault rifle, sending a mental apology to Yvette for abandoning the low profile idea.

He got those three, but more were coming in. Fuck, they had to be special ops, because they were as well armed as he was and they weren't hesitating under fire. But almost as soon as they landed, two of those were yanked off their feet and casually tossed into walls, where they bounced off like a kid's stuffed animal and collapsed.

Merc slowed to a speed that could be detected by human sight and did a somersault, giving JP a quick salute. "Yvette and Marcellus have the perimeter," he called out. "I'm your muscle for whatever Maddock can't do while you handle your shit. Just get it done so we can get out of here."

He didn't need to be told twice. Dashing forward to Medusa's side, John set aside the rifle and put his hands on her face. As he looked at her, it felt like a lightning bolt went through his chest. Tears of fury clogged his throat. "Christ..."

They'd burned out her beautiful eyes, leaving charred sockets. The remains of viscous fluids still stained her cheeks. What the fuck?

He was going to murder that fucking British prick. For a second, even what Maddock had told him to do was swallowed by the rage, the desire to charge right into the fray between the two wizards. But everything wavered like a TV losing signal. He swayed on his feet.

"Hold onto her with both hands," Maddock bellowed. Another explosion of light made him and Tyrone disappear. John didn't know if that detonation came from without or within. But he held tight to Medusa. He wasn't letting go. He wasn't...

Medusa loosened the ribbons from her hand and began to offer them to the nice man.

"No. Those are mine."

She frowned. From the shadows of the statue of Athena, a man shuffled forward. A hideous-looking man, cloaked in foul clothes, hunched over. A beggar. The priestesses cared for beggars. Ostensibly, because they could be gods in disguise, but humans in such need also deserved compassion and care. Perhaps he was hurt and needed tending.

While the nice man wanted the ribbons, he was well-to-do. Surely he wouldn't deny charity to a beggar.

"I will buy him clothes and give him a place in my household," he assured her. "He will value that more. Give me the ribbons and I will give him the care he needs."

"Those are mine."

She gasped. The beggar morphed into someone else. Someone tall and straight, who made her afraid. He stepped forward, his hand out, his cold eyes pinning her in place.

"They are mine. You are mine. You must trust me. Come with me."

"No." As she started to back toward the nice man, darkness gathered around the man who'd been a beggar. He'd turned into someone she feared. Though she couldn't remember why she feared him, words came to her lips she didn't understand. "I can't go with you. You'll hurt me. I'm not yours. I was never yours."

The darkness loomed up over him like a waiting monster. "Look into my eyes, Medusa. See the truth."

"Do not look into his eyes," the nice man said sharply. "You know what happens when you look at someone."

She heard the distant wailing of female voices and recoiled from the shadows that closed in around her, as if the sun had disappeared in full daylight. "The truth is fearful and painful," the nice man scoffed.

"Why would you wish that on her? Why do you wish to cause her pain, to take from her?"

"I have no desire to take from her," the man who frightened her responded. "Only to give to her. And I would never cause her pain. But I know she is strong enough to endure pain, to face truth, because she is strong enough to love."

The nice man tried to step in front of Ukrit. She knew his name now, and it filled her with loathing, but that voice...she knew that voice. It didn't remind her of Ukrit.

"Everything you are belongs to you, Medusa," Ukrit with the non-Ukrit voice said. "It is yours, to give or take. I am yours too. Do not let anyone take any of it away. You promised yourself you'd never let anyone take what you did not willingly wish to give."

"She willingly wishes to give me the ribbons," the nice man pointed out.

"She has not decided. It is her choice. Look into my eyes, Medusa. Don't be afraid."

She didn't want to look in his eyes. She never wanted to look in his eyes again. Even as a statue in her garden, she never looked into his eyes. Because she had, when he'd raped her, and it was like looking into the soul of all evil. "No," she whimpered.

"Don't look with your eyes," he said. "Look with your heart."

The nice man was struggling to block her view, to stand in front of the other man. She saw a white snake slither between her feet, followed by two black ones. One rested around her throat, a slim collar with a light flickering tongue. She started as another, its skin rough like tree bark, coiled around her calf.

Ukrit couldn't move either, or was choosing not to move. Yet he was there, suddenly closer as if she'd summoned him, as if she wanted him closer. But that wasn't possible, was it?

She slowly, slowly lifted her lids, fighting the part of her that screamed at her not to do it, not to face the pain and shadows. She wanted to be a girl who ran through the temple hallways with her friends forever, who would never know pain or fear. Who had not killed her friends and family. Who had listened to an elderly woman before she turned her grandson to stone.

But if she did that, she would also never know love. She hadn't realized that before, but she did now. Love that grew out of suffering and hard-earned wisdom was the strongest kind there was. And the worthiest of treasuring.

She met Ukrit's eyes, but she did not find Ukrit there. She swallowed. "John Pierce."

"Trust me. Trust me now and always."

Her trembling hand was out, the ribbons draped over her wrist. He clasped her palm, holding the slips of satin between them. She jumped at a howl that exploded around her, the wolves descending. Darkness swelled into a cavern and swallowed them, but John pulled her close, wrapping his arms around her. His muscles bunched into steel to stave off the darkness and howling. It was as if she were in the center of a storm created by a battle between two elements.

She did not realize how true that was.

She was with him. Even though she appeared unconscious still, JP could feel that connection and held onto it as tightly as he was holding onto her. He had about a second to assess the situation, which was a second more than he'd had in other firefights, so he considered it a blessing.

They were back in the warehouse, in the middle of a maelstrom of magical energy. Maddock and Tyrone looked like they were in a tug of war. Tyrone had his arms raised, his feet braced apart as if he was holding himself against a strong wind at the same time he was about to fly. Maddock was a contrast, his arms at his sides, his body rigid as if he were channeling all energy toward his objective, which John deduced was holding Tyrone's magic away from where John held Medusa. All the energy surrounding Tyrone was green. What was around Maddock was blue, and spikes of either color were trying to penetrate the wall of the other, making the battle lines unpredictable.

One deep breath, a flutter of her hair, and she'd be touched by Tyrone's shit-green magic again.

Fuck with that. Pulling all the leads and the IV free, JP scooped her up and charged away from the table, toward Maddock. The blue energy swallowed them like the welcome touch of the ocean.

"Keep going," Maddock snarled. "Get her out of here."

John hoped their reinforcements had handled any threats, because he exited the lab and pounded up the corridor outside the lab with both hands occupied, the assault rifle bouncing in a bruising rhythm against his back.

Good fortune—and good allies—were with him. He saw no one on his way out the door, and a whistle when he emerged drew him toward the alley rendezvous point.

Marcellus had collected a pile of bodies in that narrow opening between warehouses. He appeared to be keeping watch over them in case any roused from their sudden and decisive state of unconscious-ness and various states of injury. Merc was nowhere to be seen, but John guessed he was running point to keep an eye out for anyone they'd missed.

Yvette was squatting against the wall near Marcellus, her gray and gold eyes trained on the alley entranceway like she was a leopard about to strike. She was tapping the flat of a dagger against her thigh, and it looked sharp enough to puncture someone's kidney with minimal effort. When JP appeared, she sheathed it and straightened, her attention fixating on the precious bundle in his arms.

"Alive," John said shortly. "But in bad shape. Can you take her back inside the protection of the portal?" he asked Marcellus. "You can get her there faster than anyone. I need to provide backup for Maddock."

"I'll join you," Yvette said. "Merc can help us. He's right." She directed that to Marcellus. "Taking her away removes their main reason to stick around."

"Merc can take her just as quickly," Marcellus pointed out.

"No." Yvette shook her head before John could voice his own protest. "You are everything I want with me in a fight, but her safety is most important. Even in this circumstance, we cannot trust Merc alone with what he can too easily see as prey. The temptation could be more than he can resist."

Marcellus bit back an irritated response, but Yvette cinched it with one more observation. "Do you want Merc in the camp with Clara, Charlie and the others, and neither you nor I there, the only two who can stand against him? Though I've no doubt Cai, Rand and Gundar would die trying."

His jaw set and he reached for Medusa.

"No." Medusa mumbled it, coiling her arms tighter around John. "Don't leave."

Her voice was the sweetest thing he'd ever heard, even thick with drugs that he hoped were keeping her from feeling pain.

"I have to help Maddock, sweetheart," he told her. "I'll be right behind you. Marcellus will get you back home."

"Home is with you."

He couldn't have asked for more than that. Even Marcellus's stern mouth eased at the simple declaration.

"I want you out of harm's way," John said to her gruffly. "I need you to obey me, snake-girl."

While he sensed a brief hesitation, other priorities apparently overrode her submissive tendencies. She merely tried to hold onto him more tightly. He was loathe to peel her off forcibly, especially since he didn't know her condition, beyond the horror of her eyes, but a breath later, the decision was made for him.

Marcellus's expression changed in a blink. Yvette bellowed "*Run,*" and then made that command unnecessary. Seizing John by the collar, she tossed him and Medusa bodily toward the open back end of the alleyway. John bit back a curse, tucking and rolling as best he could while holding a nearly unconscious woman.

He was hit from behind by a solid wall of muscle, and then the percussion of the explosion lifted and flung them again. He had a sudden and very unpleasant flashback to an op where he'd ended up in a building when it exploded. He curled himself tighter around Medusa as a blast of heat hit and rolled over them.

He was pretty sure they were about to die. At least in this case he had the woman he loved in his arms. If there was no avoiding death, there was no better way to go than that. But he was pissed that she wasn't going to get the chance to experience better things in this life.

Fortunately, they didn't die. When the danger seemed to have passed and he could raise his head, he figured out why he was still alive. Marcellus was lifting his considerable weight off John and Medusa. As he did, he was shaking out his wings, dislodging several feathers that were on fire. Once detached, they settled to the asphalt and burned down to cinders. Leaning down, the angel helped Yvette up, where she was braced between the Dumpster and the wall of the adjacent warehouse. John noticed the Dumpster had her handprint in it, where she'd kept it from rolling over top of all of them.

Her clothes were torn and she was bleeding, but not enough to incapacitate her. Wounds wouldn't kill a vampire, though they could weaken her. While John knew she could get blood from Charlie or Gundar to help with that, and the wounds were even now closing before his eyes, the vampire and angel had worked together to save his and Medusa's lives. A debt he wouldn't be forgetting anytime soon. And he'd thank them, as soon as he could hear his voice over the ringing in his own ears.

For now, he assessed what had happened. The warehouse that had held Medusa was a pile of fiery rubble. A hard feeling of loss seized his chest, but it quickly loosened as a smoke-stained and bleeding Maddock trudged toward them. Behind him, the fire was dying out as if it was being quenched by invisible hoses. Since Maddock was leaving a visible energy trail of that blue light, it wasn't an inaccurate description.

"Did I not suggest we should avoid excess attention?" Yvette said in a deceptively sweet voice while she inflicted murder on him with her gaze.

"Shit happens, babe," Maddock said wearily. When he stumbled a few feet before reaching them, she was there to catch him, sliding his arm over her shoulders to support his weight.

"You are no fun to torment when you aren't at your best," she said irritably. "I'll tear you a new one when you're back on your feet."

"Just need a nap. And one of Charlie's massages. Maybe some of Mary's cornbread. Christ." Maddock looked at John. "You two okay?"

"Me, yeah. Her, not sure. Her eyes..."

"They should be all right. They'll regenerate. That's why Tyrone did it. To take them out of commission temporarily until he could accomplish what he wanted to accomplish. Taking the part of her brain that controlled them. He failed."

The wizard flashed a dangerous if tired smile. "That was thanks to your will and hers. Let's get the hell out of here. And no," he added to Yvette. "Tyrone probably isn't dead. He's too wily not to have left himself an exit strategy. But he's out of our hair for now."

His gaze went back to Medusa, slipping in and out of consciousness in John's arms, though her own remained banded around him. "If I'm right, and it looks like I am, she won't be of interest to him any longer."

John looked down at her. So distracted by the atrocity that had been committed to her eyes, he'd completely missed what had Marcellus and Yvette's attention now. As Merc landed next to them, he noticed it right away.

"Hey, where are her snakes? And her wings?"

Her snakes. Her beloved snakes. Oh Christ. Not a sign of them. Only thick, blood-matted hair. Though he hadn't had the bond with them that she had, he'd been fast becoming attached to them, and he was forever, fiercely grateful for their loyalty and care for her. They deserved better than to be atomized, as if their existence didn't matter.

"Let's get her back through the portal. We'll worry about all that then." Maddock looked toward Marcellus. "I think it's best Medusa stay with John. Her mind is in a fragile state and his connection was what pulled her back. Go on ahead and tell Charlie what to expect. The rest of us are basically pain management and recharging. And one through and through."

Yvette stiffened and stopped him, putting her hand on his abdomen. "Where?"

"Not me. Him." He nodded to Merc. "Tyrone got one shard of energy through my shield. Would have taken out a couple major organs, but Merc stepped in between. Went through his thigh."

Merc glanced down at the wound. "I plugged it with a bit of cloth. It's fine until we get there. Painful, but pain means little to my kind." He flashed fangs. "Or quite a bit, depending on the pleasure involved. Very little can kill me."

"One of life's little annoyances, since so many people want to do so," Yvette said dryly.

Despite Merc's offhand comment, John could tell Maddock had some concerns about the long term effects of not treating a wound created by the magic, and he saw signs of Merc's discomfort, in the slight stiffness of his body and a flexing muscle in his jaw. Marcellus saw it as well.

"Ride with them," he instructed the incubus. "It is best not to exert yourself with flight. Do not defy me on this."

For once the incubus didn't mouth off, which was worrisome in itself. Marcellus went aloft, disappearing from view in less than a blink. As John carried Medusa, Merc and Yvette supported Maddock on either side. They used whatever cover they could to head back to the SUV unseen. Maddock mumbled something about providing a light shielding that would hide them from casual eyes, so John was relieved when they were in the vehicle with its darkened windows and the wizard didn't have to expend any other energy. From Yvette's tight expression, he expected she would agree with him.

Law enforcement and fire trucks arrived on scene as they were driving out of the industrial district. The unpopulated area and Maddock quenching the fire before it could start cresting rooftops had provided them the extra minutes to get clear. With Merc at the wheel, they took side streets and passed unnoticed by the incoming army of red and blue lights.

Maddock put his head back on the seat. "I'm going to pass out now," he mumbled to Yvette. "Wake me when we get there. Don't dump me out on the side of the road as a joke. It wasn't funny last time."

"It was, a little." She stroked his hair back from his face. "You are fine, wizard. You did well."

"Not well enough. Can't ever seem to convince them they're doing it the wrong way. If I could do that, *then* I'd be something special. Someone who deserves someone like Charlie."

Yvette and JP exchanged a glance as the wizard let go of consciousness, his breath evening out. Then JP left him to Yvette's care as Medusa shifted in his arms, a whimper escaping her lips.

She was in pain, and all he wanted was to take that pain away. Since she kept moving her head as if the lights were hurting her eyes, Yvette opened a sterile bandage from the first aid kit to wrap around them. Maddock hadn't said how long the regeneration process would take, damn it. Soulless fuckers had burned out her eyes. Teardrops like blood seeped from beneath the bandage. John used another cloth Yvette handed him to keep that wiped away.

"How are you doing?" he asked quietly, when he could tell she was conscious again. They had the whole back seat, her stretched out upon it, her upper body cradled in his arms. Yvette and Maddock were in the second seat.

"Okay." Her voice was little more than a whisper, but he could find no fault with her grip. She'd switched it at some point to his shirt. Even without her claws, she hung on like a baby eagle.

Her "okay" was a lie, but the branding and subsequent shock had to have some kind of cauterizing or numbing effect; otherwise she would have been screaming in agony.

"Ratqueen, it's okay," she said softly. "We're all right."

He met Yvette's gaze as the vampire looked over her shoulder at him. The concern in her face was reflected on his own. He felt Medusa's brow and it was hot. Too hot. Maybe a fever delirium. Damn it.

At least he'd be able to tell her the snakes hadn't been taken from her by force. He'd seen them when she'd been strapped to the table. The snakes had been unconscious but alive, in limp loops, figure eights and S-shapes around her on the table.

"You're going to be all right, too," he said to her, gathering her even closer, dipping his head over hers. "I promise."

They'd come to grips with it earlier in the night, in that confrontation in the Big Top. But now, fuck it all, he didn't care about choice anymore, hers or his. He loved her and could no more face letting her go than ripping his own heart from his chest. She was just going to have to deal with that, and him, for the rest of their lives.

CHAPTER TWENTY-NINE

For the next week, Medusa was in and out of consciousness. She walked on her island, she ran with the temple priestesses through the gardens, she made love to John Pierce in a field where a unicorn played. In hindsight, she would decide that Charlie had some very good herbal pain remedies. Not a single shadow followed her into her dreams. The down side was, during the times she surfaced, she couldn't form a single word to ask a question about those traumas. Every time she tried, a sense of wellbeing would steal over her, dreams would beckon, and she'd be off sleeping again.

When she was awake, she usually sensed John near, another vital healing element. On the rare times he wasn't, someone would be there to reassure her of his presence as soon as they realized she was awake. "He's helping Gundar." "He's getting you dinner." Usually it was Charlie or Clara who told her that, for they took turns nursing her.

Because of the peculiar floating sensation of days and nights, she suspected they were back in the Circus's preferred in-between portal place, where she'd first seen Lianthe running across the fields. It was a beautiful spot, a protected spot. Had they finished the remaining two days of performances in the quaint small town with a Starbuck's, or had Yvette had to fold, end it early? She hoped not.

Then she remembered the crisp voice, the smell of her own burning flesh, and came surging up out of the dream, panting.

"Easy. It's okay. Take it easy." She clung to John's soothing rumble.

"Charlie said when she started cutting back on her healing mojo you might deal with some unpleasant flashbacks. But it's a memory, nothing more. The past. You're safe now."

She blinked. "My eyes are...blurry."

"But you can see?" His voice reflected his pleasure with that, reassuring her.

She nodded, then she recoiled, shutting her eyes tightly. "Oh Goddess. I looked at you. John..." Her hands were out, seeking, making sure he was still flesh.

"I'm here. It's okay. Remember? Yvette spelled them. They can't hurt anyone within the Circus boundaries."

"Oh. Yes." Her heart leveled out some from its frantic pounding. Opening her eyes, she clutched his hand, then lifted her other to his face, tracing his features she could make out, despite them being fuzzy on the edges. Or literally fuzzy. A smile touched her lips at the stubble on his jaw. "Is it nighttime?"

"It is. And I missed a shave yesterday. Had to help with a breakdown. You and I have been staying safely inside the portal while the rest of the troupe goes out to do their shows, but when they pack up to move on there's always work to do. I've been shouldering a double load to earn our keep, what with you lazing around in bed all day."

His teasing tone was belied by the faint tremor of his hand as he stroked her head, then he tunneled his fingers into her hair, cupping her skull to hold her against him. "I never want to feel that way again," he said fervently. "Having you taken from me and not being able to get to you right away was the worst kind of hell."

"I prefer not to experience that again myself." She held him in return, pressing her lips into the juncture between his shoulder and throat. She loved his smell, a mixture of clean sweat from his exertions and his normal identifying scent. She loved the feel of his arms, his body, familiar and yet always so excitingly new.

She felt surprisingly well enough to notice that, to want him, whether or not that was yet advisable. She was also mostly pain free. It was as if she'd taken a long nap and now she was awake, ready to do anything.

But as she regained her wits, something intruded on her exhilaration. She became aware of other things. Or rather, the absence of other things.

Her wings were gone. And so were... Her hands left John and flew up to her hair, searching through the locks. "John, where are they? Are they...no. This doesn't make sense. I can hear them, John. Please..."

Please don't tell me they're dead and I'm hearing their voices from an afterlife. Don't take them from me.

"I'm glad you asked. So are they. You know what an insecure lot they are. Especially that runt, Earthson." The warmth in his voice flooded her with relief. "Want to hear a story?"

He reminded her of the nights they'd spent on the island, his deep voice taking her into worlds familiar and different, with Wesley and the Dread Pirate Roberts, or a team of oil drillers who journeyed into the stars to destroy an asteroid. Or a young wizard who faced down the evil Voldemort.

"Yes," she said. But she reached out. "Please. I want...will you hold me while you tell me? In your lap?"

"Are you okay for that?" His concern for her fragility touched her to the extent she almost couldn't speak. Her large, wonderful champion. He was as he'd always been, but in this moment, what that was hit her even more deeply.

"Yes."

He slid his arms under her back and legs, and drew her from the bed, bringing the blanket with her as he settled her into the cradle of his arms. She sighed and put her head on his chest. "Tell me about my snakes."

"They disappeared after you handed me the ribbons. Do you remember that? When I came back to our reality, so to speak, they were just gone," he said. "I thought what you did. I was sure they were lost to us, and I couldn't imagine how I was going to tell you that. And, truth, it hurt me deep inside, too. They took care of you for so long. It didn't seem fair."

He took a breath. "You were still talking to them. That worried us, and we thought maybe you were delirious from pain, but I should have known you were too practical for that." His lips pulled against her temple in a smile. "A few hours after we got back here and Charlie was tending you, Rifkin, the snake charmer, came to Yvette's quarters. That's where we are. You'd think she'd make an infirmary, but she says until we came along, injuries were few and far between."

"I can imagine she said it in an appropriately accusing tone, as if the disruption is all our fault."

"Better not let her know she's that predictable." He chuckled. "Anyhow, so there he's standing, looking all apologetic and like he'll wet himself if Yvette looks at him cross-eyed. She said he's still pretty new."

She traced his smile. His lips firmed under her touch, and he kissed her hand, holding her by the wrist. She'd been dreaming about his touch for the past few days. Feeling the reality was even better.

"He smiles this shy smile and extends his basket. He doesn't speak great English, but he manages to explain that pretty soon after he'd returned from doing that night's performance, he'd heard his snakes making a ruckus. So he opens up the basket where he keeps them for transport. Five new snakes are in the basket. He was able to charm his snakes out, and left the other five, but he sought out Yvette immediately. Everyone is supposed to let her know right away if something unusual happens that might be an indication her protection fields are being messed with."

"But it was my snakes." She closed her eyes, reaching out with her mind to feel and locate them. They were outside. Slithering through the grass, coiled up on top of a barrel, sunning on rocks. At her mental touch, though, they were on the move, headed toward her.

"Yeah." When she opened her eyes, John gestured to a basket lying on its side, kept stable in a nest of pillows. "They've been coming and going as they please, which they seem to enjoy immensely, but they come back here to sleep and watch over you with me. They seem to like the basket, so that's why we've kept it in here."

He shifted her back over to the mattress as Ratqueen slithered under a fold of the tent and headed straight for her. The others came in from other directions. She felt a palpable relief as they made it up onto the bed and swarmed over her. Ratqueen coiled around her upper arm while Earthson moved to his usual position at her collarbone. Tunneltrap and Treebark deposited themselves in her lap. Waterlight moved right to her head, forming a crown and weaving through her tresses as if she was stroking Medusa the way John stroked her hair. "Look how long you all are," she marveled. For the first time she was seeing them from head to tail.

"Remember the African Medusa I told you about?" John said.

"Charlie said she's working on a pouch for you. You can be just like that Medusa, carrying them around with you whenever they don't want to be left behind."

"I'm glad I can still talk to them, but I'm so happy they're free to roam as they wish, and live a normal life." She paused.

Now that her first concern, the snakes, were resolved, she was hit by the second. Losing her wings was a hard blow, she had to admit, since they'd been vital to her freedom and defending herself. But she realized something else that eased that sting. As long as her eyes were be-spelled by Yvette's protection or Maddock's contacts, it meant she could now walk among humans as unremarkably as anyone.

"Did the change with my snakes and the loss of my wings happen because of what Maddock and you thought?" she asked slowly, digesting the staggering thought.

"We think so. I don't know how much you remember, but you took the ultimate step of faith. The spell broke." John touched her chin, drawing her gaze. "All the way. I told you your eyes were still neutralized to calm you down, but the truth is, there's nothing to neutralize. Your eyes are normal again."

It took a second for his words to register, and when they did, she could hear the thud of her heart, hammering against her chest. Her fingers clutched the sheets.

"They are...harmless?"

"Except for the solid punch to the gut I feel every time you look at me the way you're looking at me now. Yeah."

It was done. Over. She was...fully human. Normal. The spell was lifted. It was hard to comprehend, because all that had driven it, all the consequences related to it—Ukrit, her sisters, her life on the island, her life in the temple—were still just as present in her mind and memories.

"Your eyes are green," he said, after a few minutes, as if he realized she needed time to gather her whirling thoughts. "Like the sea on an overcast day, as Klotho said."

Rising, he went to a vanity and returned with a large hand mirror. "Yvette doesn't keep mirrors in here, because her image doesn't reflect, but Clara brought it, figuring you'd want to see."

She did, but not yet. She held the mirror face down on her thigh. Earthson used it as a platform to form a loop with his body that followed the inside circumference of the porcelain decorative surface. Her mind darted in a hundred directions.

"But MyTech and Dr. Tyrone..."

"He's so over it," Maddock said cheerfully. John had the tent flap pinned open to allow them access to the comfortable afternoon breeze, but Maddock paused, waiting until they acknowledged him before he entered. Medusa saw he was in a different kind of outfit today, a softer pair of trousers that she remembered were called slacks, and a white button-down shirt. It was what men of this time wore for more formal occasions, and she wondered what occasion that was. John was giving him a once-over with the same question on his face.

"Grant crap," Maddock explained. "Yvette had this crazy idea of letting me meet with the head of research associated with the Vampire Council. Lord Brian is keenly interested in what I've been figuring out on portals. Apparently it intersects some stuff he's doing with the Fae world." Maddock shook his head. "Before the Circus, I didn't think fairies existed except as a Disney merchandising opportunity."

"Bullshit," John said mildly. "You believe in everything."

"Yeah. Even happy endings. Because this one is looking promising." Maddock crossed the tent in one long-legged stride and took Medusa's other hand, giving it a light squeeze before withdrawing, since Treebark was looking less than welcoming.

"That one still isn't sure about me," the wizard noted.

"Smart snake. What were you saying about Tyrone?" John asked.

"Oh, yeah. You're clear of him, too, Medusa. You probably don't remember, but the first time you woke and your eyes were fully healed, I sent him an Instagram picture and a big fat thank you. If it hadn't been for his attempt to pull that coding from your brain, it might have taken you much longer to reverse the spell. You okay with it so far?"

She lifted a shoulder. "It is...odd, to be so defenseless."

"That's the last thing you are." Maddock pulled up a chair. "The coding he wanted is no longer there, but elements important to you are, like your warrior instincts. I also expect these snakes will stay bonded to you, and you'll always have a particular ability to call serpent spirits to you if needed. A handy talent, particularly if you need a venomous viper on your side. Oh, I forgot. Yvette already likes you."

"You two should get a room," John advised. "The sexual tension is overwhelming the rest of us."

Maddock snorted. "She booby-trapped the portal this morning. Didn't tell me she'd changed the formula. Damn near fried my nuts when I stepped across."

"She's probably just trying to keep you on your toes. And—hey. Sweetheart."

Medusa had started to cry, and John's attention snapped back to her. "Oh Christ, I'm sorry. We've known this for a few days. I wasn't even thinking about how it would feel to know all of a sudden... I'm an idiot. Scram, Maddock."

She wasn't sure if the wizard heeded him, but she thought she felt his hand pass kindly over her hair before he retreated, leaving her in John's care. "It's okay," John said quietly, pulling her back on his lap and rocking her. Tunneltrap and Treebark tumbled to the mattress, but the other three came with her. "It's a good thing, right?"

It was. A very good thing. A wonderful thing. Yet it was a loss, too. She couldn't explain it, this sudden transition, not to what she was before, because that girl was gone, but something different and unknown. Something that wouldn't be defined by how she had to protect herself, but by how she wanted to live. And she had several worlds to choose from. The decisions had quickly become overwhelming.

"You don't have to decide anything right away," he said, reading her mind so easily as he always did. "You're welcome here as long as you want. Well, as long as we work to earn our keep." He pressed a smile against her forehead. "You can just enjoy the journey, figuring it all out. I can't wait to see everything you decide to explore, because you take such pleasure in life and the people around you. I'll be with you wherever you want to go, as long as you want me there."

She nodded against his chest. "That is what I want, too. You."

She closed her eyes once more, and shuddered at the weight of all of it. Or perhaps the lifting of that weight. He stayed silent for a little while, then spoke, his breath stirring her hair.

"Hey, did you know it's a full moon soon?"

She shook her head.

"Didn't you promise me you'd dance for me sometime?" He tilted her head back to meet his eyes. "I like that idea," he said, gaze roving over her face. "But then, I like the idea of doing anything with you. Maybe tonight we'll just start with a stroll and see where your strength is at. We can go anywhere. To see a unicorn, buy Starbuck's coffee... One day there's this little place in the Caribbean Sea I want to show you. It might remind you of your island. It's mine. Ours. You can go anywhere, Medusa."

"With you," she confirmed, hiccupping over a sob.

"Just try to get rid of me." His gaze upon her intensified. "We had that discussion, remember? I won't forget the sharp side of your tongue anytime soon. You convinced me. If I don't doubt my love for you, it's pretty patronizing of me to say you don't know your own mind. Just because I want you to feel that way so badly, doesn't mean it's not true. That night, I think we both had something to learn about believing in dreams coming true."

She was too overwhelmed to smile, but she felt it, deep in her heart. She wanted to see the world with him. Almost as much as she wanted to remain here, quiet in his arms.

She could do both, thanks to him. And thanks to her own courage, which his love had helped her find, enough to love him back.

She no longer needed a gaze of stone to protect herself. Just a heart open to his love.

EPILOGUE

*N*o claws or wings. No snakes, though they were not far, hunting and exploring the woods around the silver-green meadow she'd chosen as the perfect spot to dance for John Pierce.

She'd come here alone first, so she stood in the moonlight, a priestess taking slow, measured breaths. Only now there was no temple. It was just her and the Goddess. She would dance for Her, and for the pleasure of her Master. She served them both.

"Marcellus said you wanted..."

His voice trailed off as he arrived at the clearing. Turning on the ball of her bare foot, she faced him. The tunic was sheer silk, molded to her body, belted at the waist with a beaded chain that pressed cool metal and sparkling crystals against her bared hip bones, because the garment was open along the sides. She'd brushed her hair until it was thick and shining, falling to her backside. Clara had introduced her to henna tattoos, so she'd decorated her ankles and feet with a delicate design the young woman had helped her apply.

She knew she would be considered beautiful to anyone with eyes. But she wanted to *be* beautiful to the one set of eyes that saw her within, more deeply than any other.

Healing from what had happened at the hands of MyTech, and adapting to her restored human form, were slow processes. But she was gradually gaining ground over that darkness and rage she'd carried for so long. The fathomless rivers of loss and regret in her soul were carrying them away, but she hoped those waters would create greater wisdom, to help her with the choices she made today and tomorrow.

"Yes. I want," she said.

On the island, she had written poetic descriptions of her life there. In her isolation, she'd come to realize words had a magic of their own. The simple description of a breathtaking sunset or an innocently sleeping rabbit connected to things with far deeper meanings. So now she spoke that layered language to him.

"I want to wake with you every sunrise, John Pierce. And go to bed together once the sun sets. I want to watch you laugh, and smile. I want to close my eyes to hear your voice, because when I do that, it is as if what I see and enjoy with my eyes becomes a touch on my skin. Your touch. I want to swim with you again, because I like how water leaves beads like jewels on your flesh. I want to watch the fine way your body moves, and feel the softness of your hair, the roughness of your jaw, under my hand."

She drew a breath and took a step toward him. He was watching her without moving, but as he was adjusting to the surprise of her appearance and starting to understand her mood, she could feel an energy vibrating off of him, intensifying.

"Do you remember, when Vinnie said his mother 'gets' him?" she asked. "Can you tell me what that means?"

John's gray eyes were silver in the moonlight. "It means she understands him, why he acts the way he acts, who he really is, what he wants and needs."

Warmth filled her. "That's what I thought. Which means you 'get' me."

"Glad to hear it, snake-girl." His voice was husky, heavy with emotions that interlocked with her own.

"I want something else, John Pierce."

"Whatever it is, you'll have it. Just tell me what it is."

He knew as well as she did some things could not be had just by wanting. But hearing his determination to provide anything within his power to give, swept longing and joy through her, such that her next words came out as a near whisper.

"I want to lay upon the earth with you, feel its heat and life, and create life of our own."

It took a moment for her meaning to register with him. As her mind caught up with her heart's impulsive declaration, she wondered if she should have said it.

Then his eyes filled with his response, a pool of mixed emotions. The same feelings she had about it. Terror, pleasure, certainty. Desire. Those emotions would be shared, an accord. *Yes.* He wanted to give her a child.

He took a step toward her. His lips pressed together, the muscle flexing in his jaw underlining all that she saw in his gaze. "Dance for me," he said.

She spread her arms to either side and knelt, bowing her head to him. First, she listened. To all the creatures singing, to the leaves and grasses moved by the wind, to the sounds of the night that mixed together and became the music. Crossing her arms over her chest as she listened, she began to tap the rhythm out against her body. She wasn't surprised that the cadence she found matched the song she wanted to sing for her dance. Energy flow was like that. She'd known it instinctively as a young acolyte, but now she had the pleasure of recognizing that astonishing truth as a woman.

Lifting her head, she met his eyes and began to sing. Melodic notes poured from her lips and out into the meadow and wood, coaxing birds to speak from their nighttime roosts, and other chirping insects to join in the composition.

She had started to learn his language, so that one day she would no longer need the translation spell, and she'd learned this song in that language. She'd first heard it on Clara's music player. Clara had said the song was called "I Need You." The words, which spoke of a lover's need for another like the need for mercy or water, and about finding freedom in his arms, were words that spoke truly of her own feelings for John Pierce.

Rising, she started to dance at last, turning, twisting, her arms moving in graceful syncopation with her body. She dipped her head back, her hair flowing out around her, the fabric of her gown rippling with the movement. She'd bathed in a soapy froth that Charlie had given her which left her skin with a lustrous sheen. She wanted to be touched. The movements of her body told him so, because he was coming closer.

He was looking at her in a way that made her believe he would always look at her like this, no matter if she had a forked tongue and clawed hands, or if she was old and wizened, a crone preparing to face the end the Fates had designed for her. She felt the same about him. He could become craggy or thin with age, and her heart would still pound at his smile, at a look from his penetrating gaze. She would still kneel at his feet, call him Master, and surrender her will to him, for he would always cherish that gift, and her.

She concluded her song as he came into her self-imposed dance circle, but she continued to use the music of nature around them to guide her rhythm. She stepped lightly as a deer, bounding and twirling, her hair and clothing whispering against his body as she drew closer. Putting his hands to her waist, he lifted her higher, joining in the dance, delighting her. She continued around him, only she took his hands, seeking his support for another lift. And another. She lifted her arms to the sky, arching back, trusting his strength to hold her.

When he lowered her this time, she looped her arms around his neck, interested in another form of dancing. She brought her lips to his, shifting her hands to cup his face.

Her lips parted from the coaxing of his as he took over the kiss. He let her feet touch down so they rested on the top of his work shoes, but banded his arm more securely around her waist, keeping her close to prolong the kiss and make it an even deeper exploration.

When she tugged at his shirt, he obliged, stripping it off an instant before he had his arms around her again, holding her against his heated, muscled flesh. Since her dress was open on the sides, his palms found the skin exposed at her hip and thigh, her rib cage and the curve of her breast. A release of the belt, a shrug of her shoulders, and the garment slipped away so she stood naked against him, accessible to him however he desired her. He was her Master to serve.

She whispered that to him and saw the lust build in his gaze. She knew the things that pleased him, as he knew so many that pleased her. He took her down to the ground, laying her on her discarded clothing as gently as a bird he held in his palm, but his dangerous strength, the intent in his eye, incited an appealing shiver.

"Arms over your head, priestess," he murmured, transforming that shiver into an arrow of sensation to her core. When she complied, he explored her body with mouth and hands, suckling her nipples, tracing her breasts with his tongue, the curve of her stomach and hips, her navel. He rubbed his rough jaw against her hips, making her squirm, but when he kissed a line over her mound and feathered his breath over her clit and labia, she breathed out on a moan.

"Yeah, that's right. Let me hear you as I give you pleasure," he demanded in that growl she loved. "I want to know what I'm doing to you."

He left her little choice as he put his clever tongue and mouth to work between her legs. She was gasping, crying out, then ultimately shrieking her release as he pushed her all the way there and kept her going, turning her body into one vibrating, taut string of need.

"More," he demanded, turning her over on her stomach and starting the process over, this time by caging her between his braced arms and knees as he bent and went after her sensitive nape with his teeth, his breath, his lips and tongue again. His hands cupped her breasts, and played with her nipples against the friction of the lush grasses. Her hips lifted, brushing against his erection beneath his jeans, teasing, taunting, begging.

She thought he might take her from behind, but instead he brushed an almost tender kiss over one buttock and moved back.

"Be still," he ordered softly. He stood over her, and she heard him removing the rest of his clothes. When he knelt and guided her over onto her back again, he was beautifully uncovered by anything but her hungry gaze. Yet as he shifted, twisting his upper body to push his shoes and pile of clothes out of their way, another feeling eclipsed desire. Or maybe it was all part of the same.

She turned onto her hip and rose to her knees to be closer to him. His eyes darkened in comprehension as she put her hand on his broad shoulder and shifted partially behind him to lay her palm over the tattoo on his back. Leaning in, she pressed her lips to it, the words she now knew to be true on several levels.

Medusa's Heart. Because he carried her heart with him, and because he *was* her heart.

When she lifted her head and moved in front of him again, he slid his arms around her. Even on his knees, he displayed his formidable strength, cupping her buttock with one hand to steady her descent as he used the hold of both arms to lay her down on her back. He ran his hand down her side, to her thigh, drawing it up over his hip, but then he stopped. He stared down at her, his gaze like a glittering silver stream.

"You've been able to turn men to stone," he said, low. "But when I came into this meadow and saw you in the moonlight, I felt like I couldn't move. And what you said…" A fierce expression crossed his face. "For all that I thought I knew my feelings for you before we met, there's a whole set of rooms inside my heart I never imagined, that you've opened since then. I'll go anywhere with you. Take any journey we need to take together. Good or bad."

The portent in his words reminded her that there were many things ahead of them, many decisions to be made. There would be challenges, and very likely some of those challenges would strain the bond between them. But she knew hardship. She knew all about surviving against difficult odds. A relationship was as fragile and resilient as a life. How it was lived all depended on the will, and she couldn't help but believe that their wills combined would make it unforgettable. They would also be formidable opponents against anything that threatened it.

"I feel the same," she whispered. "And I want to feel you release inside of me, Master."

His lips curved, eyes lighting. "So I should shut up with the serious talk and get down to it? How about I make sure you go right over that cliff again with me?"

In answer to his teasing, she tightened her arms around his neck, a mute plea to close the distance between them, and take her lips with his own once more. She gave everything to him, her body arching, legs folding into a taut hold over his backside.

He broke the kiss, but only to give them both what they wished. Holding his weight with one arm, he guided himself into her and then sank into her slick folds all the way to the hilt, wrenching a primal cry from her throat.

Her internal muscles clutched his thick length so that he groaned in answer and kissed her more fiercely, tunneling his fingers through her hair to grip and tug.

She never stopped wanting him, but his ability to command her libido with just a few words was astonishing, a miracle. Or perhaps it was just that she'd wanted someone like him for so long, her body had a surfeit of desire to offer.

As he began to thrust, he kept his gaze locked on hers. She saw the brilliant shift as animal instinct took over. As her own climax built, it caught up to his, so when the orgasm ripped through him, she went over at the same time, just as he'd demanded.

The release turned his features rigid, but in the right way. Not stone, no. He was containing a reaction that was anything but stone. It was the eruption of a volcano, the power of a summer storm, the force of life itself, and he swept her along with him, his grunts and her moans a pleasurable music added to the night.

In the way of such things, they drifted back to earth in a fog of satisfied desire, hearts beating slower and breath evening out. At length, he shifted off of her and turned them so she was held in his arms, and they could both look at the night sky. The grass and her robe were soft beneath their pleasure-dampened skin. Locks of her hair fluttered across her cheek and his chest, carried there by the evening breeze.

"You all right, snake-girl?"

In more ways than she knew how to express. She tightened her arm across his abdomen in response, but then she thought of her earlier words to him.

"What I said earlier... I do not know if I will conceive," she said shyly. "But Charlie said there doesn't seem to be anything inhibiting that. She said maybe the spell kept it from happening and now..."

"If it happens, I'll cherish our child as I cherish you," he said, tipping up her face to meet her eyes. "If it doesn't happen, I'll still love you more every day."

"As I will you, Master. You have my love and my service, just as the Goddess does."

"Good to hear." He paused. "Because there's something that traditionally comes before the whole kid thing. Marriage."

Medusa's breath caught as that look came back to his expression, as if he were looking at the whole world, though he was only looking at her.

"You're going to marry me," he added, as if he wanted to be sure she was clear on what he was asking. Or demanding.

She closed her eyes, joy sliding through her. He was sure of her, as she was sure of him. "I am yours to command, Master." She cracked an eyelid. "On most things."

"Hmm. Just like a woman, to qualify." He sobered, touching her face. "No doubts?"

She shook her head and smiled. Lifting her eyes to the sky, she looped her arms around his neck, holding him close. "I will never again doubt what love can make possible, John Pierce. It brought me you."

~

WANT MORE? You just met Cai and Rand from the Vampire Queen series. The first book, Vampire Queen's Servant, is a **FREE** full length novel. Read it today!

His blood. His soul. His body. Hers for the asking...

Jacob, an alpha male and former vampire hunter, will protect a woman without thought. Submitting to her is a different matter. However, Lady Lyssa needs him. A thousand-year-old vampire queen, she is besieged by enemies, and haunted by past losses. Jacob may be the only soul she can trust.

In the vampire world, a human belongs to his Master or Mistress in every way. All choices belong to the vampire. But when love is involved, ownership becomes a tricky thing...

CLICK HERE TO READ FREE
VAMPIRE QUEEN'S SERVANT or at
https://dl.bookfunnel.com/qnv6il2rce

Reading this in print format? Use the BookFunnel link or look for it at your favorite vendor! (Not free at Nook, but BookFunnel link can provide Nook format.)

ABOUT THE AUTHOR

Having penned over fifty acclaimed BDSM contemporary and paranormal titles, which includes six award-winning series, *Joey W. Hill* has been awarded the RT Book Reviews Career Achievement Award for Erotic Romance. A submissive herself, Hill brings authenticity to her intensely emotional love stories.

She is grateful for the support of a wonderful and enthusiastic readership, which allows her to live on her beloved Carolina coast with her even more beloved husband and menagerie of animals.

- On the Web: https://storywitch.com
- Twitter: https://twitter.com/JoeyWHill
- Facebook: https://facebook.com/JoeyWHillAuthor
- Facebook Fan Forum: https://facebook.com/groups/ JWHMembersOnly
- MeWe: https://mewe.com/i/joeywhill
- GoodReads: https://www.goodreads.com/author/show/ 103359.Joey_W_Hill
- BookBub: https://bookbub.com/authors/joey-w-hill
- Amazon: https://amazon.com/Joey-W-Hill/e/B001JSCIW0

ALSO BY JOEY W. HILL

Arcane Shot Series

Arcane Shot

Arcane Madame

Arcane Chaos

Arcane Knight

Daughters of Arianne Series

A Mermaid's Kiss

A Witch's Beauty

A Mermaid's Ransom

Knights of the Board Room Series

Board Resolution

Controlled Response

Honor Bound

Afterlife

Hostile Takeover

Willing Sacrifice

Soul Rest

Knight Nostalgia *(Anthology)*

Mistresses of the Board Room Series

At Her Command

At Her Service

At Her Call

At Her Pleasure

Nature of Desire Series

Holding the Cards

Natural Law

Ice Queen

Mirror of My Soul

Mistress of Redemption

Rough Canvas

Branded Sanctuary

Divine Solace

Worth The Wait

Truly Helpless

In His Arms

Ignition Sequence

Naughty Bits Series

Naughty Bits

Naughty Wishes

Vampire Queen Series

Vampire Queen's Servant

Mark of the Vampire Queen

Vampire's Claim

Beloved Vampire

Vampire Mistress *(VQS: Club Atlantis)*

Vampire Trinity *(VQS: Club Atlantis)*

Vampire Instinct

Bound by the Vampire Queen

Taken by a Vampire

The Scientific Method

Nightfall

Elusive Hero

Night's Templar

Vampire's Soul

Vampire's Embrace

Vampire Master *(VQS: Club Atlantis)*

Vampire Guardian *(VQS: Club Atlantis)*

Vampire's Choice

www.ingramcontent.com/pod-product-compliance
Lightning Source LLC
Chambersburg PA
CBHW051935020726
47501CB00001B/138